I0634476

Terra Mythica

A LitRPG Adventure
Volume One
Volume Two
By Fobywoby, aka John Stax

Shadow Light Press

Contents

We Hope You Enjoy This Story

To stay up-to-date with our latest releases, sign up for our mailing list at ShadowLightPress.com

"Don't believe what your eyes are telling you.
All they show is limitation.
Look with your understanding.
Find out what you already know and you will see the way to fly."
—— *Richard Bach*

Volume One

In Shadow and Light

Shadow Light Press

Prologue

Darkness of a Different Kind

D arkness fell.

It wasn't the usual darkness that came with the end of day, carrying a hint of warmth, however faint. Nor was it the darkness of midnight, wrapped in silent peace, disturbed only by the occasional rustle of leaves in the cold wind. It wasn't the comforting darkness found moments before sleep, safe and warm in your bed, for that darkness holds the promise of a new day and new light.

No, this was a void, an emptiness found only in lost places and forgotten times. Heavy and oppressive, it seeped into the soul, turning every heartbeat into a thunderous echo.

And this darkness belonged to one man.

Henry stood silent and still on the plush grass encircling Castle Roandia, the fortress looming like a shadow against the dark veil he summoned to shroud the kingdom. The chill of the coming siege crept into his bones. His thoughts wandered to a time when his hands knew the smooth stroke of quills instead of the cold weight of swords, when his nights were bathed in the flickering glow of candlelight and not the blood drawn from hate and torment.

Osira had often been beside him then, her laughter a faint melody now swallowed by that same void. The memory of her smile tugged at his heart, drawing him deeper into the past—to the day they first met, to the life they shared before... all of this.

But the present surged back into focus, a cold wind cutting through his reverie. His eyes, once filled with dreams of knowledge, now held the darkness that flickered around his body, the twilight cloak licking at the air as he concentrated on the siege ahead. The time for reflection was over—now, only war remained.

His army waited in silence behind him, tension rising off of them like heatwaves in the cold air, a lull before the coming storm. He could almost taste the answering fear as it poured forth from the battlements before him.

Were they afraid of the battle to come, or of him? Was this truly what he had become? He pushed the thought from his mind. There was no room for it now. He had to focus.

Torches lined the stone walls of the castle and fought to shine through the inky waves of eldritch power. Occasionally, a piece of light would find its way to cast the faintest glint upon the Roandian soldiers' armor.

Inside the castle, hidden in a secret chamber within the king's quarters, lay the beautiful Osira. Her thick black hair splayed out across a makeshift cot as her entire body sweat in exhaustion. The chambermaids that attended her had never delivered a baby before.

Though in a few moments, that would change.

This fact was not what was troubling Osira.

She clung tightly to the emerald crystal that hung from her neck and tried to focus through the pain. The crystal glowed gently through the gaps in her fingers. Her tears were not from the pain or coursing adrenalin. Nor were they for her own life.

These concerns were pushed far from her mind by the single, dominating demand she made.

"Protect my children."

The crystal hummed in understanding.

In the corner of the room, a small dust of light that called itself Pik chimed anxiously.

"I know, but what can we do about it? We can't take on the whole cursed army ourselves," Bertrude complained, his voice a blend of frustration and helplessness as he cleaned his unusually large, pointed ears with a silver letter opener he had "found." His stout half-goblin frame was taut with tension, every muscle coiled as if ready to spring. The dim light caught on his mottled greenish-brown skin, highlighting its rough texture. Unruly chestnut hair tumbled into his sharp, angular face, partially obscuring the vivid emerald of his eyes, which glinted with a fierce, watchful intensity.

Pik chimed sharply.

"Alright, alright, no need to get nasty," Bertrude sighed. "I don't want to leave her either. But we have our orders."

Pik's green glow dimmed slightly as he let out a low whizz.

"I know, old friend."

When midnight found them, the air was damp and thick. If not for the cursed darkness filling the sky, the moonlight might have struggled past the impending storm clouds and cast a solemn light across the two armies.

"Steady!" The king, resplendent in Roandian blue steel, paced the battlements.

He barked orders and profanities to the Masters of War.

The Master of Archers repeated his orders, shouting his own curses and critiques at his men, adjusting their armor and their aim. Memories of his younger days as a simple farmer, before the war changed him, flickered in his mind. The Master of Swords followed suit, slamming his gauntlets on the back of a slightly slouched swordsman, nearly knocking him over. He remembered his own training, the harsh discipline that had shaped him into the warrior he was today.

The soldier did not cry out, but saluted as he rejoined the ranks. This was a familiar thing, the only comfort they had, and the familiarity of it helped the soldiers stand their guard.

The king strode across the ramparts with more confidence than he felt, each step a battle against the gnawing fear in his gut. "If you move before I command, the creatures below will be the least of your worries!" His voice echoed in the night.

He stared down at the darkness below, trying to pierce it with his mind. He did not see Henry so much as he sensed his presence. And with that, Henry sensed him. The blade of the king's sword glowed faintly as the crystal embedded in the hilt hummed.

"We could spare these men," the king whispered into the night.

"And spare the fun?" A silent whisper came back.

Suddenly the clouds were ripped by a blinding flash of light and the dull pound of thunder. Streaks of white tore at the sky and then vanished, consumed by the dark curse above. Thunder rolled like stone giants in the distance and rain crashed down upon both men and undead alike.

The minions of darkness marched, and the earth trembled beneath their iron-clad feet. Their march quickened to a trot and then surged into a full run. The ground pounded in unison with the hearts of the defending soldiers. Arms trembled, not only from fear or exhaustion, but from the quaking earth beneath them. They had stood there, poised and ready, since the first whispers of night crept across the horizon. The once vibrant energy of anticipation had long faded, replaced by a bone-deep weariness and the relentless grip of dread.

"Steady, damn you! Steady!"

An infinity passed in a moment.

"Fire!"

Arrows mixed with the night sky and found their marks along the ground. Blood of all shades spat across the grass from the injured creatures. Cries of pain turned to vicious howls as the army of terror surged forward faster.

"Lightning Acid, ready!"

His orders were repeated in shouts across the length of the crenelated walls. Men with glass vats of glowing liquid moved gingerly to the edge, careful not to spill a drop.

"Release!"

As the undead creatures reached the base of the castle and clawed, the glowing green death poured over their heads. Shrieking hisses filled the night air as the alchemical solution quickly ate through the nearest invading forces.

Clouds of arrows filled the sky and fell with the rain upon the encroaching undead. The undead creatures wore little protection from arrows and appeared to hold no regard for their own wellbeing. As they fell, more climbed over their still bodies and fought through the falling acid and steel. Not a single answer of arrows came in return, only the vicious howling of undead beasts and gnashing of teeth.

Minutes became hours, became lifetimes.

Horns blared out from across the undead army, and more creatures surged forward, an unending torrent clawing their way past their fallen brethren.

They piled up the wall and a few of the foul creatures made it to the parapets. Lightning flashed again and seared the sky for a moment before being eaten once more by darkness.

The men upon the battlements poured down vat after vat of alchemical acid, followed by enormous stone boulders, crushing the undead creatures below and causing them to collapse upon themselves—all in a vain attempt to stem the tide.

The battlefield seemed to pulse and surge in sync with Henry's own heart. He allowed the darkness to lift for a moment, granting the candles and moonlight a breath of freedom. In that moment, the horde of creatures became clearly visible to the Roandians, the horrific sight piercing them to their core.

When ropes and claws failed to get his undead successfully over the battlements, an alternative approach had to be used.

Henry admired his handiwork as his army surged past him and battered themselves against the castle walls. Grotesque half-faces, patchwork figures, amalgamations of bone and steel... the sight was more horrifying than death itself.

Henry felt the waves of fear roil off the castle and smiled a bitter, wicked smile.

He welcomed the fear, drawing it in with each slow breath as it seeped into his core, intertwining with his aether like a dark current, quietly fueling his power.

"Goodbye," he sent a thought to the king.

He grasped the black crystal upon his neck. Holding it to the night sky, he cried out. All the pain and hate that filled him flooded the crystal and it lit with a black void of energy that enveloped all that touched it. Lightning crackled in the sky.

It struck the ground not fifty paces from him. Then it struck again before cascading in a searing line through his soldiers, ripping skeletal figures in half.

Sacrifices must be made, he thought, and urged the ripples of lightning towards the castle.

When it met the castle walls, not even the king himself could hold it back. The wall beneath the king staved in like brittle clay beneath a mallet and he was swallowed by an avalanche of stone and steel.

The undead army poured in.

Henry pulled out his User Interface stone, a rough, silver device barely larger than his palm. Its edges were jagged and the mismatched pieces of metal hinted at its hasty assembly. The runes carved into its surface flickered weakly, some already fading.

He took a deep breath and activated the stone. Instantly, his HUD flickered to life, but it was far from functional. The screen shook violently, and garbled symbols and fragmented words replaced the usual clear text.

Henry squinted, trying to decipher the jumbled messages. It was as if the universe itself resisted the integration; the world pushing back. He tried to navigate through the chaotic interface, but each tap only resulted in more distortion. His health, aether pool, and quest log were lost in a sea of glitches.

He sighed and closed the HUD with a frustrated swipe. "Great," he muttered. "Just what I needed."

I'll have to let the support team know about this, he thought, pocketing the stone. For now, there were more pressing matters.

Cries of a different sort came from the hidden chamber where Osira lay.

"He's beautiful," a chambermaid said softly, placing the first child in Osira's trembling arms.

Osira smiled weakly, tears of joy mingling with the sweat on her face, but her relief was short-lived as another wave of pain seized her.

"The other one is coming," the chambermaid said, her hands moving swiftly. "Keep pushing, my lady. One more to go."

Exhausted, Osira summoned the strength to bear down once more, the room filled with tense anticipation, punctuated by the cries of the firstborn.

Finally, a second, stronger cry echoed through the chamber as the twin was born. The midwife quickly cleaned and wrapped the baby, placing him gently beside his brother in Osira's arms.

Pik wisped anxiously.

"Praise Eileithyia," the maid whispered.

"I'm not crying. Just got something in my eye," Bertrude protested, rubbing furiously at his face with a sodden sleeve. The motion only acted to smear dirt across his eyes and cheeks.

The roar of undead crept closer.

Osira soothed the babies, whispering, "Hello, Alexander. Hello, Greyson," her voice trembling with a mixture of relief and resolve. She took a moment to embrace them, inhaling their scent, feeling the gentle rise and fall of their breaths. Some moments last longer than others, and she willed this one to stretch as long as the gods would allow. In that fleeting eternity, she held them forever, feeling the rapid beats of their tiny hearts against her chest.

Alexander, with strikingly bright gray eyes, stared up at her with a calm, curious gaze, his tiny hand reaching out to clutch her finger with surprising strength. Greyson, with darker, stormy gray eyes, squirmed restlessly, his small cries louder and more demanding.

There was no sadness to be felt, only a deep and unending love. She marveled at their differences, the quiet strength of the first and the fiery spirit of the second. Tears slipped down her cheeks, but she smiled, savoring the warmth of their tiny bodies and the soft cooing and cries they made.

But like all moments, this one too had to end.

"Fetch Harkenwell from the hall."

Her words were certain and martial.

A chambermaid darted from view and returned moments later with the king's guardsman, a tall, tanned figure. Though Hark and Osira were roughly the same age, his scars and ivory hair made him seem older, his youth stolen by years of war and strained magic.

"It's time, Hark. We need to move fast now." She whispered an enchantment, and the babies fell asleep.

He nodded and drew a pouch from his leather satchel.

"Are you sure we can trust these two?" He asked Osira, nodding towards Bertrude and Pik. If they were offended, they said nothing. The scrape of claws and howls of hate continued to grow nearer.

"I trust Bertie and Pik with my life," she said. Bertrude flushed at the pet name.

This seemed enough for Hark. He knelt beside Bertrude and handed him the pouch, pausing before letting go.

"Use this when you are outside of the kingdom and beyond the Trackers. The boys must survive. If either of them dies, so do you." The last statement was not a threat, but a warning. If they died, so would they all.

Hark allowed himself a glance at the newborn boys sleeping in their mother's arms and instantly regretted it. Emotion swelled in his throat, but he shoved it down, steeling himself for what was to come.

Pik hummed.

Osira wrapped them in warm cotton blankets and handed them to Bertie.

"Now go! And don't stop for anything or anyone," Osira said as she sat straight in her bed and forced an air of command to her voice.

A small servants' entrance opened and closed and Bertie, Pik and the children were gone.

Only then did she allow herself to feel the loss, sobbing in deep, gasping breaths.

Henry let hold of the darkness relax across the night sky and the moon burst through in all its wonder. The rain was fading then and had waned to little more than a trickle, leaving the stars visible and bright. But their light came with little hope or joy.

Men, unlike undead, grow tired and hungry and Henry relied upon this fact. It only took a few hours of battle within the castle walls before most of the remnant soldiers had either died or surrendered to him.

Henry walked along the halls of the castle, slightly peeved that the king's sword and Shard were lost beneath the rubble. He knew his creatures would find it, eventually.

Bodies lay lifeless at his feet, and he took solace as he made a mental count. This would raise quite the army for him when he had time to summon their remains.

Two skeletal figures walked behind him. He called them Death Knights, for each was worth a dozen enemy soldiers. And each was the product of a month's conjuring.

His Black Shard warmed upon his neck, telling him that another was close.

His lesser minions raced ahead of him, crashing into walls and breaking open doors, leaving a cacophony of wreckage in their wake.

A blue light exploded from the king's chambers and several undead flew out the door and fell into crumpled heaps.

Henry smiled darkly and walked closer, urging his Death Knights ahead of him. They entered the room and flew out in a burst of light. Two months of work, lost.

"Hark, I thought I'd find you here!" Henry called down the hall.

Another burst of blue light streamed from the room and bent itself toward Henry's voice.

"Temper, temper. Let's not be too hasty. I just want to chat, for old times' sake."

"What happened to you, Henry? It's not too late to stop this," Hark called out.

Yes, it was.

Rage dug into Henry's chest. He clung to his heart and felt the cold crystal. He let it numb him, and his feelings faded. "Where is she?"

"You're too late. She's gone," Hark replied from around the corner, his tone casual, almost bored. "She left the moment she knew you were coming."

The words struck Henry like a blow, and for a moment, he faltered, his shoulders sagging under the weight of despair. He had fought through the hordes, driven by a single purpose—to find her. Now, that purpose was hollow, slipping through his fingers like quicksilver.

I need to talk to her... to reach her somehow.

He had believed—no, he had hoped, desperately—that if he could just speak with her here...

Hark's voice softened, a rare tenderness creeping into his flat tone. "Stop this, Henry. Please, I don't want to hurt you."

A cold, deadly calm took hold, and his fists clenched as anger simmered beneath his skin. "Too late," he murmured, his voice low, carrying the weight of a thousand unspoken words. "Let's not pretend to be friends, Hark. Orisa isn't here to see us play nice. But not all is lost, I suppose. At least she won't witness what I'm about to do to you."

Hark's eyes narrowed, his softness vanishing as quickly as it had appeared. "As you wish."

With a flick of his wrist, Hark sent a bolt of searing energy toward the door. Henry moved like a shadow, diving beneath the burning light, his body a blur of motion. In a fluid movement, he hurled a beam of black energy into the chamber, its darkness cutting through the air like a blade, and he rushed in behind it.

Hark had only a moment to deflect, or he would have been baked beneath its dark-fire heat.

In answer, he sent blue beams of energy to slash out at Henry.

Henry parried them with ease and sent the broken beams flying off in every direction. Chairs burst into flame as the blue light splashed against them. The king's bed collapsed. The stone ceiling ruptured, strips of itself flinging down.

Torrent after torrent shot from the dueling men. Black and blue energy swirled around the room, drawing into a vortex of chaos.

The darkness crept closer and closer to Hark. Lashes of black velvet licked at his face, leaving lines of red flesh. Henry smiled and pressed forward.

"Tyr, hear me. I need your strength." Hark cried out. He whispered a Word of Power, summoning a protection field around him.

Henry laughed, his voice a tortured rasp, "Your gods can't help you now."

The darkness grew closer and Hark bent onto a knee, pouring his entire essence into his concentration. But it wasn't enough.

Rage and tainted joy covered Henry's face. Black ink spilled from his very skin. He laughed as he gave himself to the darkness. He would need to surrender to it if he was going to make the killing blow.

Hark felt the end coming closer.

And then green light filled the room.

"Enough!" Osira shouted, as pulses of brilliant green shot from her outstretched hands.

In that moment, Henry lost focus, his concentration broken by her sudden appearance. Wild black tendrils of energy, barely contained, swung madly around him.

"Osira?"

Time slowed.

It had been nine months since Henry had seen her. Golden robes wrapped around her body, covering all but her arms and face. Her cheeks were flushed, and eyes shined bright from tears.

He reached out to her with his mind, but was immediately rebuffed.

What are you hiding? He thought to her.

She fought to keep up a screen against his intrusions. Something was different, but what was it? With a surge of effort, he pierced her mind for the barest moment.

The answer came with a flood of emotion that nearly knocked Henry to the floor.

"A child?" Henry called out.

He tried to stop the current of energy he had unleashed, but he couldn't.

Once he had given himself over to the darkness, there was no way back.

Hate turned to fear as the tendrils poured out from him.

Hark charged forward in that moment, gripping Henry by the neck and using his focus to hold him.

Henry tried to scream, tried to tell Osira to run, but nothing came out—Hark's grip was too tight.

"Hark, stop!" Osira shouted.

Hark did not stop. The fate of the kingdoms was in his very hands in that moment. The countless deaths that could be prevented... he had no choice but to squeeze tighter.

Green light flashed out and crashed into Harks side, knocking him to the floor.

The vortex grew unchecked.

"Stop this, Henry!"

"Run!" He screamed, choking through his strained neck. But it was too late.

Shards of darkness encased the room, the walls pulled in and the ceiling gave way.

Henry focused everything he had left within him on the crystal. It would not obey. In an irrevocable act of desperation, he slammed the black jewel as hard as he could upon the stone floor, willing it gone with every part of his mind. He could feel it crack. It was a deep, guttural feeling. Like suddenly forgetting something important and knowing you have forgotten it.

There was a scream. And then silence.

The black vortex calmed and then faded from the room.

There was no sound now. He frantically looked around, searching for any sign of her. Dust and blood fogged his vision. His heart met his throat when he saw her.

Her hand lay still, jutting out from under a stone slab. He rushed to her, but he knew it was too late. He grasped her hand in his and prayed to Hades, but there was no pulse and Hades did not respond.

He looked around, his mind numb, senses dulled.

Hark was nowhere to be found.

The night became silent. And a new darkness found the room.

This last darkness was not one of magic and power, but of hope lost and a shattered soul.

Horns and drums sounded behind them as the half-goblin and pixie raced as fast as their will would take them.

"They've found us!" cried Bert. "And they are coming!"

Doom, doom, doom - with each beat of the drum, the earth shook beneath them.

Pik whzed fiercely.

"No!" said Bert. "There's no chance we can take them. We have to hide."

Another shrill horn-call bleated into the night sky, the stomp of hooves and the clank of steel close behind it.

"There! Under that."

Bert and the twins, with Pik in tow, dashed to a large felled tree; its slightly hollowed carcass providing a small canopy of cover against the moonlight. They tucked their bodies as close as they could against the rough bark. Pik dimmed himself into the darkness. Alexander and Greyson were blissfully silent, still asleep either because of or despite the rhythm of the run, Bert could not say.

They waited for a year in that single, agonizing moment. A rustle of bushes sounded just feet away, sending a shiver down Bert's spine. He fought several urges within him then - the burning impulse to look, the desperate need to flee. But his wits told him to stay steady and still.

The sound of hoofs drew nearer until they were right behind them. His heart throbbed in his chest and he covered his mouth to muffle his breathing. In the moonlight, he could see the faint shadows of a horsed figure standing above and behind them. It moved closer and Bert could just make out the horse's bit as it flashed in the light.

This was no normal horse. A stench filled the air. Rotting flesh mixed with fresh blood and dirt.

Even more terrifying than the sight and smell was what was not present. There was no sound. No breathing from either the horse or its rider.

The creature moved closer still. When it passed the tree it stopped. Its head tilted from side to side as if trying to peer through the darkness.

A thick, feral fear took hold of Bert, and he clenched his hands on the bag Hark had given him. He knew that if he used it now, they would be tracked, and the boys' safety couldn't be assured.

His breath caught in his lungs, and it became terribly real to him how easily he could escape certain death if only he used it now. His hands were frozen, fixed between the two urges. He fought against his fear with all the might and courage of his goblin ancestors. He wasn't sure it would be enough, but he clung to that hope.

At that moment the creature turned its head sharply to the side. In the distance a blue flash of light shot into the sky followed by the red flicker of flames.

Horns blew again, and the creature kicked hard at its horse, taking off at a full gallop.

The moment it was out of earshot, Bert took off with babies in arm and Pik beside. They didn't know what caused the flame in the distance, but whatever it was, they would not waste the gift it gave them.

They raced on until they safely cleared the kingdom's limits and were outside of the Tracker's abilities.

"We are far enough." Bert emptied the contents of the bag on the ground in front of them. A silver dust spread itself along the dirt and hummed anxiously, awaiting their next words. "A rush of wind, a flash of light, far away and lost from sight," he chanted the incantation; just as Osira had made him practice.

And with that they were gone.

Far away and lost from sight.

Henry activated his heads-up-display and selected [Log Out]. A timer counted down from ten and he was safely exported back to reality. Unjacking his VR set, he took a breath to gather himself and get oriented in his surroundings. His HUD faded, replaced by the familiar interface of the real world. His heart pounded as he wiped the sweat from his face.

Session Complete
    Duration: 7 hours 12 minutes Standard Time.
    Time Dilation at 42-1.
    In-Game Duration: 12 Days 14 hours, 24 minutes.

"Clock, check. Grey walls, check. Bed, check. Window, check." His eyes and equilibrium took a moment to reset, and he assisted them by noting familiar objects around the room. He shook his head, trying to focus as the intense emotions of the game faded, becoming no stronger than the remnants of a dream.

The simulations were getting more and more real each time he jacked in. And if he was being honest with himself, he was getting more into the mind-mapping experience. He didn't mind being studied by the integrated AI of the gaming system. He was used to this interaction. What caught him off guard were the intricacies and depth this game went through to analyze him, learn from him, and even predict him.

While inside, it didn't feel like a game. If someone had told him it wasn't real, he would have dismissed them as crazy. But now... he couldn't understand how he had ever thought otherwise.

When he had first signed up for the trial group, the agency told him that there might be side effects, but this was on a whole different level. He had never given much interest to VR gaming, and the horrible media coverage made him even less inclined. "What effect does this have on young minds?" he recalled a newscaster asking pointedly. He didn't really buy into all the worry. But still, he didn't like them. They were unreal. They were distractions. They were... his only means of making a living, if you could call it that.

Since the war, and then the famine, times were tough. A man took work where he could get it.

He leaned back in his bed and stared up into the darkness of his downtown studio flat. Ubiquitous city sounds filled the room and helped him to orient himself further.

The image of Osira lingered vividly in his mind. "Queen Osira," he chuckled to himself, the title tinged with bittersweet nostalgia.

His heart ached as he opened her profile in his Grid Interface. He wanted to call her but he knew how that conversation would go - the same as it had for months now. He hesitated, his gaze fixed on her picture. They hadn't really spoken much since... well, since the game and all that had come with it. It was as if she didn't know him anymore. With a heavy sigh, he closed the profile.

His neighbor's heliport clanked in preparation for a landing, and the sirens along the street were momentarily drowned out by the electric whoosh-whoosh of single passenger propeller blades slowing.

He needed to eat. He needed to relieve himself. He needed... he needed to get back into the game.

Henry had been playing for the past seven hours, real-world time, without a break. He wasn't hungry; hadn't been hungry in a long time. He would make a note of that for the testers. He addressed his physical concerns first, checking his messages while preparing a meal ration. Advertisement after advertisement flashed across his viewfield. A notification lit small in the corner of his vision.

"1 New Message... From: Citywide Health."

"I'm calling for Henry Williams to confirm his appointment for this Tuesday at 8AM. Please call, message back or..." Henry deleted it and swiped the notification from his view. He forced himself to eat half the ration. His stomach flexed in protest, and he felt the familiar shivers ride along his nerves.

He fumbled for his pills and downed two with a glass of water.

He placed the sleek, metallic helmet back on his head and jacked the VR cord into his cerebral adapter. A large blue pop-up notification appeared in his viewfield.

System Connected
        Sunday, March 9th, 2232, 10:17 PM
        Session 247, Game Beta Test Code Name: Terra Mythica
        Initialize Session?
        Accept | Reject

He paused for a moment.

"She had a child... a child?"

He shook his head and punched [Accept].

Chapter 1
Jason's "Choices"

S ystem Initializing...

With a deep breath, Jason closed his eyes and felt the tingling sensation as his mind connected to the world of Terra Mythica. A flood of black pixels engulfed him, but through it, he could see a stream of text moving across his vision. He raised his hands, and they materialized in front of him, flickering with old, low-resolution pixels. As he waved them around, he couldn't help but smile at the nostalgia. This must have been an intentional effect they put in.

Analyzing DNA...

His anxiety spiked. *Doing what now? Shit. What if the system can tell that I'm not him? Will it call the cops? What if I get thrown out before I even start?*

The pixels shimmered and twined, conjuring a mirror out of nothing. As he approached, his reflection began to form, but the face staring back wasn't his own. It was Alex, his twin brother. Though others struggled to tell them apart, he perceived the subtle differences as vividly as a painter sees hues in a sunrise. The familiar features gazed back at him, a sharp pang of regret twisting in his chest.

Synching... Attempt 1..2..3..4..5..6...

He could feel his heart hammering in his throat. His digital heart? Each second an eternity.

He reached out, fingertips grazing the cold, reflective surface of the mirror. There was a moment of resistance before his fingers slipped through, not entirely solid. The mirror image flickered, wavering like a candle flame. When it smoothed, the face look back was replaced with his own, his stormy grey eyes gazing back at him.

Jason's breath trembled, misting the pixelated air with each exhale. Barely nineteen, his body was lean from missed meals but honed by constant motion. His dark hair fell in untamed strands around his eyes.

Synching...Attempt 20..21...

Deep breaths. Come on, come on, come on.

Compatibility error...

His muscles froze and he couldn't breathe. *That can't be good.* Sweat beaded on his forehead.

Deviance at .37%...

· *What does that even mean?* His mind raced through possibilities.

Can the system detect my real identity? If I log out now, would it know it was me? Do these things even have GPS tracking?

Fatal Error...

Jason's stomach dropped. This was it. He was caught.

Diagnosing... error.... Error...

A stream of unintelligible symbols flash rapidly across his view field, too fast for him to read.

Error...

"Shit. Exit. Close. Logout! No, no, no."

He tried to reach up and remove the device manually from his head, but his hands grasped at nothing. His physical body wouldn't respond. Desperately, he moved his virtual hands instead.

Suddenly, the world went completely black. No screen. No text. And worst of all, no logout option.

Jason yelped as the next words appeared.

System override successful... User accepted.

Jason gasped for air, his chest heaving as he released the breath he didn't realize he had been holding. A wave of relief crashed over him, but it was quickly swallowed by a nagging sense of apprehension. The system had begrudgingly accepted him, but what did that mean? "System Override? How? Who?" He couldn't shake the feeling of unease.

Welcome Traveler

The screen repeated, this time with a gentle chime.

Memories of the events that had led him to this moment flooded his mind, causing a pang of grief to crash over him. He fought to suppress it, knowing that he couldn't let his emotions get the best of him. There were feelings he would have to confront eventually, but not now. Not yet. Right now, he had to push through and pull this off.

The text vanished as a blinding light engulfed him, pulling him away from the sterile digital world of the initialization phase. His senses were overwhelmed all at once. The light was so intense he had to squeeze his eyes shut, his head spinning with the sudden shift.

Opening his eyes, Jason found himself standing in the dimly lit room, the air thick with an ancient, musty scent. A single pedestal stood in the center, bathed in an eerie glow, with a book resting upon it. Each step echoed in the silence.

His fingers brushed the cover of the book, sending a ripple of energy through his body. He opened it, and as he did, shimmering lines of magical script began to etch themselves across the page. The next notifications weren't bold, like the last.

Traveler's Handbook

A dazzling show of lights erupted from the book, wrapping around Jason in a luminous cocoon before fading and leaving a warm, comforting weight in his hands.

"What the...?" He yelped.

Please be patient while your Handbook calibrates to your soul.
Don't Panic

In filigree script the words formed in light upon the page, and then quickly vanished.

Soulbound
A running record of your existence. All that you have learned, all that you know, and all that you are.

Jason flipped through the pages, marveling at the sections labeled for maps, quests, status effects, attributes, and a page that displayed a figure resembling himself, down to the last detail of what he was wearing. Most of the pages were blank, however, waiting to be filled with the story of his journey.

Another burst of light enveloped him, binding the book to his very soul. He experimented, willing the book to disappear, and it did, vanishing from his hands only to reappear in his mind. He could call forth parts of it without opening the physical book, like a blank map that flashed into his consciousness.

A system notification chimed, acknowledging his understanding of the book.

You have successfully attuned to the Traveler's Handbook.

You have learned more about yourself.

Gain +1 to Spirit Constitution.

As the notification faded, the room around Jason transformed. The walls peeled back, revealing a vast, otherworldly hallway that stretched beyond sight. Before him stood an endless row of ornate doors, each one unique, adorned with intricate engravings.

Jason faced the row of doors, each more elaborate than the last—gateways to the realms of Terra Mythica, where the only certainty was uncertainty. These weren't leading to honeymoon suites; they were portals to lands beyond imagination, where the odds of finding a mint on the pillow were slim to none.

He hesitated, his gaze drifting over the intricate carvings and glowing inscriptions. The doors demanded attention, every detail screaming, "Look at me! I'm the portal to untold wonders and probably a few unspeakable horrors." He wasn't just admiring craftsmanship; he was staring down the handiwork of gods.

A soft glow pulsed from the doors, warming the cool air around him as if they sensed his presence—or maybe they were just impatient for his decision. Each light was a whisper, a dare, but those whispers were trapped behind locks—big, ugly things that clearly stated, "Not today, buddy." These were the boundaries of Terra Mythica, and they weren't letting just anyone in.

But Jason wasn't just anyone. One door would open. In his pocket, he held an invitation—golden, shimmering, and addressed to... well, not him, technically. The weight of it pressed against him, a constant reminder that he was trespassing in a destiny meant for someone else.

First in the array of doors was Asgard, with a door forged from shimmering metal, engraved with scenes of mythical creatures and majestic halls.

Then came Avalon, with a door of polished wood and emerald inlays, with carvings of knights, fair maidens, and ancient trees, exuding an aura of timeless magic and serene tranquility.

And the Celestial Court, with a door of jade and gold, carved with dragons and phoenixes, surrounded by a halo of divine energy.

They continued as far as Jason could see, each sealed tight. All except one.

Finally he had found it, the door to Mount Olympus. It was a grand door of white marble and shimmering gold, adorned with scenes of gods and goddesses in majestic poses, surrounded by celestial clouds and lightning bolts, standing upon the vastness of a mountain so grand it touched the heavens. The effect was mesmerizing, and he found his eyes drawn to the door with an inexorable pull that none of the others had. And just as he had hoped, and feared, the door to Mount Olympus stood unbarred, a glow emanating from it, brighter than the others, inviting him forward.

You have been accepted on scholarship into the tutorial of Mount Olympus University.

This is a four-year tutorial.

After completion, other realms will unlock.

Please provide your access codes.

Access codes? Jason's mind raced back to the acceptance letter he had received, recalling the strange mental phrase inscribed on it. He remembered memorizing its strangeness and without further hesitation, he spoke the phrase.

"Ducks shake hands when no one is listening to Shakespeare," he said softly.

Nothing happened. He recalled that he needed to envision it, not just say it. It was a mental phrase after all. He pictured a duck shaking hands with another duck, Shakespeare in the background being totally ignored. There was a loud click! The door to Mount Olympus glowed brightly, opening before him. He stepped through, the light engulfing him in a brilliant flash.

On the other side, Jason was greeted by a shimmering interface displaying a list of character options, each one pulsating softly. As he examined them, he noticed something uncanny: each race had his face, but with different levels of muscle and form.

First was the Centaur, his own face atop a powerful, equine body, muscles rippling under a glossy coat. Then came the sturdy Satyr, with his face on a more compact, muscular form, legs ending in hooves. The imposing

Cyclops appeared next, his own features with a single, intense eye and a body built like a tank. Other mythic options followed, all variations of himself.

Jason tried to select the Centaur, but nothing happened. Confused, he moved on to the Elf, a lithe version of himself with pointed ears, then the Dragonborn, a more muscular and scaled rendition, but each attempt was met with a frustrating buzzer sound.

"Why can't I pick a race?" he muttered.

A prompt appeared as a cold, mechanical voice echoed through the void, sending a chill down Jason's spine.

Initiating Player Assessment to determine race and starting attributes.

Please stand by.

The chamber around him shimmered and morphed, the sterile walls dissolving into towering shelves of ancient tomes. Each book was bound in cracked leather and adorned with gold leaf, relics of eras long past. The scent of aged parchment and dust filled the air, a testament to the room's long-forgotten wisdom. At its center stood a grand, oaken table, bearing a curious wooden device. It was intricate, constructed of dark wood with a hundred blocks, each etched with a unique symbol.

A large wooden board stood beside the table, its surface smooth and polished. Six empty slots, in the shape of the wooden blocks, sat below it.

As he approached, an elegant script materialized, shimmering with a magical glow.

"I am not alive, but I grow; I don't have lungs, but I need air; I don't have a mouth, but I can drown. What am I?"

Jason frowned, his fingers tapping on the table in a rhythm that matched his racing thoughts. *How do I answer?* The walls of the chamber pulsed, subtly at first, then with increasing insistence. The shelves of ancient tomes pressed inward, the wall moving closer and closer.

"How do I answer?" he asked aloud, his voice trembling.

His eyes darted over the blocks. He found one depicting flames and smoke.

"There! It's fire."

He placed the block into the first slot, and a soft click resonated through the chamber. The walls paused momentarily, then resumed their ominous advance.

The board shimmered again, presenting a new challenge:

"I am taken from the earth, placed in a wooden case where I am never truly free. I am used every day, and with each use, a part of me dies, yet I serve until nothing remains. What am I?"

His mind raced. What could it be? The walls inched closer, the air growing thin. "Lead!" he exclaimed, choosing a block with the shape of a pencil etched in.

Another soft click. The board shimmered once more.

"I'm light as a feather, yet the strongest man cannot hold me for long. What am I?"

Jason's patience wavered. Frustration grew.

What is this trial? What is the point of this?

He felt suffocated as the walls came ever closer.

Memories of his foster parents came unbeckoned - the warmth of their kitchen, the comforting aroma of freshly baked treats. Baking had always been his solace, a ritual demanding precision and patience. He recalled their gentle guidance, anchoring him in the present, curbing his tendency to either shut down or explode. Alex had been the calm one, the steady force in the storm. But Jason, he was always the storm itself.

Jason remembered a time when they let him help. He couldn't have been older than seven and he'd accidentally poured salt instead of sugar into the banana bread. Food was scarce since the War. He was on the verge of crying, shouting, or throwing the pan in frustration.

"If you ever feel lost and overwhelmed," they had told him, "or have an urge to run or react, just stop for a moment. Take a deep breath and make a cup of tea. Then, tackle the problem one piece at a time."

Remarkably, they ate that cake, salty as it was. It tasted terrible, but in that moment they carved out a slice of happiness together. A tear traced its way down his face. He hadn't thought of that moment in years.

He closed his eyes, drawing in a deep breath. He didn't have any ingredients for tea, so the breath would have to do.

And then he saw it - a picture of someone breathing on one of the blocks. The answer to the riddle.

"Breath!" He took the corresponding block and placed it in the third slot with a click.

"I can do this. Alex would tell me not to give up."

With renewed determination, he scanned the blocks. The board shimmered again:

"What has keys but can't open locks, space but no room, and you can enter but not go outside?"

He hesitated, the walls now brushing his shoulders. Then, clarity struck. Easy.

"A keyboard." He slotted the block into the fourth slot.

He channeled the same patience and care he used in baking into solving the puzzle.

The next riddle appeared:

"I can fly without wings. I can cry without eyes. Wherever I go, darkness resides. What am I?"

Jason's heart pounded. Shadows twisted around him. Sweat dripped from his brow.

"A cloud!" He realized. As he placed the block, the device glowed, the symbols aligning perfectly.

No new riddle arrived.

He watched, breath held, but the walls continued their relentless advance. Anger surged through him—there were six slots, but only five riddles. He clenched his fists as the walls pressed closer. Desperation clawed at his mind, urging him to panic, but he forced himself to stay calm. He scanned the remaining blocks and his eyes fell on a blank one.

It didn't make sense. Only five riddles had been provided. The walls were nearly upon him now, squeezing the air from the room. With a mixture of frustration and determination, he grabbed the blank piece and placed it in the last slot.

The walls halted their advance, and the sound of grinding stone filled the room as a door at the far end creaked open. The door beckoned him to the next trial.

Wisdom, Intelligence, and Luck Calibrated
    Initiating Strength, Dexterity and Constitution Assessment

The world around him shifted into an abyss of shadows.

A panel in the middle of space opened slowly, a blinding light pouring out and cutting through the void. From the panel, a white rabbit emerged. It seemed innocent enough, a fluffy bundle with a twitching nose, but Jason sensed the sinister truth.

If there was one thing that Jason knew from old movies is that that was no bunny. That was a death machine masquerading in a cloak of cuteness.

The bunny halted, its crimson eyes boring into Jason. In a heartbeat, it became a blur of fangs and claws, hurtling toward him. He threw himself aside, the creature's teeth snapping inches from his neck. He hit the ground with a crunch, cracking black tile beneath him.

Scrambling to his feet, Jason's heart hammered. The bunny turned with eerie precision, its eyes alight with malice. It sprang at him again, and he lashed out, his boot connecting and sending the bunny skidding across the floor. But it twisted in mid-air, landing gracefully, its furry fury undiminished. It dove at him again, this time tearing a chunk from his leg and knocking him to the floor.

Blood trickled from the gash in his leg, but there was no time for pain. Jason grabbed a shard of shattered tile, clutching it like a makeshift dagger. The bunny's claws raked his arm, leaving deep, burning wounds. He gritted his teeth, the taste of iron mingling with fear.

He stood and they circled each other, a deadly dance of predator and prey. Jason was obviously the prey. His breath came in ragged gasps, his vision swimming. The bunny's relentless assault was taking its toll, but surrender wasn't an option.

With a last, desperate surge, Jason tackled the creature, pinning it beneath him. It thrashed and snapped, but he held fast, leveraging his weight to keep it down. Raising the tile high, he drove it into the bunny's chest. It screeched, a nightmarish sound that reverberated off the walls.

Blood sprayed as he stabbed again and again, driven by sheer survival instinct. At last, it fell still, its death throes echoing in the silence.

Jason slumped beside the lifeless form, his body a canvas of pain and blood. A prompt appeared.

Congratulations!

You have defeated the Bronze One Rank monster, Wittle White Bunny Wabbit.

He staggered to his feet, dragging himself toward the door. But just as he reached for the handle, a chilling noise stopped him in his tracks—a low, guttural growl. He turned, dread coiling in his gut.

The bunny's corpse twitched, spasmed, then convulsed violently. Its fur began to rot away, revealing patches of decayed flesh and exposed bone. Eyes that had once held malevolent cunning now glowed with an eerie, unholy light. The creature reanimated, its claws sharper, its fangs longer, and a foul stench of decay filling the air.

A Zombunny?

Jason's blood ran cold. The zombunny lunged at him with renewed ferocity, an undead nightmare given life. He barely dodged out of the way. The creature's claws swiped at him, catching his side and tearing through flesh.

Pain flared, but adrenaline surged. Jason swung with all his might, catching the zombunny across the face. It howled, a sound of pure torment and rage. But the zombunny didn't relent.

Jason tripped backward, his breath ragged, his body trembling. As he pulled himself to his feet, a grim determination settled in his bones. If he could conquer this horror, he was ready for anything this twisted world had in store.

Looking up, Jason saw the creature was gone, hidden in one of the many shadows of the room. Determined to end this nightmare, he stood, eyes scanning the room for any sign of the zombunny. But the chamber was silent. There was no sign of the creature anywhere.

A chill ran down his spine. His instincts screamed at him to move, but he couldn't see the threat. Then, a soft, sinister rustle came from above. He looked up to find the zombunny flying towards his face, its undead form descending like a harbinger of doom. Before he could react, its claws and fangs met their mark.

You Have Died
> You Have Respawned

The monster had vanished and Jason was alone again, fully healed, staring at a blue screen with white writing.

Assessment Complete
> You qualify to choose from the following races: Human.
>
> Attributes and race are based on performance and current assessment of mental and physical tolerances:
> > Strength: 9
> > Dexterity: 11
> > Intelligence: 12
> > Wisdom: 12
> > Constitution: 8
> > Charisma: 8
> > Luck: 10
>
> Achievement Unlocked - Entirely Average
> Congratulations, you are entirely average.
> Your total attributes earned combined are 70, averaging 10 per attribute (the earth average).
> Plus 5% chance you will be overlooked while in a crowd.

"Well, that's stupid," he muttered. "Not much of a choice, then." He selected human, feeling a surge of energy and light as the system processed his "choice".

Character Creation Complete.

Please stand by while you are transported to Terra Mythica.

As Jason waited for the Terra Mythica loading sequence to finalize, he couldn't help but marvel at how far technology had come. During the Great War, an AI virus had spread through everything connected to the internet, leading to the largest technological purge in human history. To stop the virus, humanity had destroyed everything operating on binary code—computers, flash drives, and even old DVDs, just in case the virus had infiltrated them.

Print media, vinyl records, cassette tapes, and surviving VHS cassettes were all that remained. For fifty years, computers were banned. Technology only made a comeback with the advent of Excelsior Tech, introducing a new system impervious to malicious AI. The Internet had been replaced by the Grid, accessible only through Excelsior technology. And all the old VHSs were uploaded.

Jason compared the sleek prompts and immersive attributes of Terra Mythica to the old movies he'd watched on VHS. He didn't have video games, but some movies had shown technology at its pre-war height. He remembered one where two teens created a living, breathing woman using a computer. Another depicted a kid almost starting a global thermonuclear war by playing tic-tac-toe with an AI. And then there was the historic recounting of people getting zapped into game machines to fight as digital gladiators.

He thought back to the times he and his twin brother would watch the holodiscs together. They must have seen the masterpiece Double Dragon a hundred times. Now, here he was, immersed in a virtual reality that finally caught up with the incredible technology of the 1980s and 90s.

Chapter 2
Tickets to Olympus

The surrounding light intensified, blinding him again before finally easing. When it did, the room was gone.

Jason's vision blurred as the game-world materialized around him. He found himself in the luxurious cabin of a massive ship, the gentle creak of wood and the rhythmic hum of distant engines filling the air.

The plush leather seats were a deep, rich burgundy, their smooth surfaces inviting and luxurious. Dark wood paneling adorned the walls, polished to a gleaming finish that reflected the soft, ambient light from ornate brass sconces. Delicate scrollwork and intricate carvings decorated the trim, adding a touch of classical elegance to the space. A small table, also made of dark wood and inlaid with a fine mosaic, sat between the seats, completing the sophisticated ambiance.

Outside the porthole, the vast ocean stretched endlessly, its surface rippling with a silvery sheen under the light of an unseen sun. The ship sailed through the mist, which clung to the vessel like a shroud, hiding the horizon from view. The water lapped gently against the hull, a soothing contrast to the thrill of anticipation coursing through Jason's veins. As the ship sliced through the mist, a massive mountain began to emerge in the distance, rising from the far shore like a monolithic sentinel. The peak thrust into the heavens, its jagged slopes veiled in clouds that swirled with diffused radiance, weaving a living tapestry of shadow and light.

Jason's breath caught in his throat as he recognized it: Mount Olympus. Even from this distance, he could make out the glittering spires and grand colonnades of Mount Olympus University, nestled high on the mountain's slopes, with its enormous marble pillars and intricate friezes. It was all breathtakingly real, yet he knew it was an illusion. The sky above the mountain was brushed with hues of orange and pink as the sun hung low, casting long shadows across the landscape.

His awe was tinged with disbelief. It was like stepping into a fantasy painting. Every detail was meticulously crafted, from the ornate carvings on the cabin's wooden paneling to the shimmering water outside. As the ship glided through the digital sea, Jason couldn't help but feel a surge of adrenaline mixed with nervousness. This was just the beginning of his journey, and there was no turning back now.

Jason let out a slow breath, trying to steady his pounding heart. This was the moment he had been waiting for—the chance to start over in Terra Mythica, a virtual world where he could leave behind the mistakes and regrets of his past. But first, he had to survive Olympus University, the Tutorial. He flexed his fingers, fascinated by how real they felt. The texture of his skin, the tiny lines and creases, all seemed impossibly detailed.

The ship plunged through a patch of thick mist, the world outside momentarily swallowed by a dark fog. The sudden transition was disorienting. Then, just as abruptly, the mist parted, revealing a new expanse of the mesmerizing landscape. His vision shimmered, and he blinked hard, trying to clear his sight.

"First time, huh?" A woman, no older than twenty, was seated by the sliding door of the cabin, her attention absorbed in a holographic tablet. She glanced up briefly, pushing her glasses up the bridge of her nose.

How long had she been sitting there?

"Is it that obvious?" he managed, his voice dry and cracking.

She offered a faint, knowing smile. "I'm Alice. As in Wonderland. This place is something, right?" she said, gesturing to the view outside.

Jason took a moment to study her. She had an almost otherworldly quality, with porcelain skin and piercing blue eyes. Her blonde hair was tied into a neat bun with a silver pin that glinted softly in the light. She wore a simple yet elegant dress made of finely woven linen, its classic folds draping gracefully over her slender frame. The fabric, plain and unadorned, made her blend into the background, yet there was an undeniable elegance to her presence that was impossible to ignore.

The room fell into a silence. Jason wasn't sure if it was an awkward silence or if it was just a regular silence that he felt awkward about. He shifted uncomfortably, glancing around the cabin for something to focus on.

Alice broke the silence, her voice softer this time. "Want to see something cool?"

Jason nodded, grateful for the distraction. "Sure."

Alice leaned forward, her eyes gleaming. "Watch this." With a few subtle gestures and an incantation, the scene outside flickered. For a brief moment, part of the porthole vanished, revealing a matrix of strange swirling symbols and unfinished textures, all moving around and within thousands of glowing circles. The opening quickly collapsed, and the view of the distant mountain appeared again.

"Totally fake," she explained, her voice gaining a touch of excitement. "Right now, we're being calibrated and prepared. This is like the game's loading screen."

Jason's curiosity was piqued. He could feel the detail and craftsmanship of the world around him, and now he understood why it was so captivating. "That's... really impressive."

Alice leaned back, her reserved demeanor softening. "The calibration process is fascinating. They're syncing our minds to the game world. It takes time, but they designed it to feel engaging. It's why everything feels so real. And don't worry, it only glitches and horribly mutilates someone every once in a while." Her eyes sparkled with a touch of dark humor.

Jason felt the blood drain from his face as a wave of nausea churned in his stomach. His expression must have betrayed his horror because Alice's smile faltered, and she quickly looked away, her cheeks flushing with embarrassment. The silence that followed was definitely an awkward one.

"What's your name?" she asked.

Jason tried not to show his moment of panic. A prompt appeared.

New Quest

A Rose By Any Other Name

You have been asked for your name. I know it may seem an insurmountable task, but I believe in you. As this is a new account, you may choose a new name.

Notice: You are currently on a scholarship. Well done! You must have studied very hard and impressed the High Council during your application trials.

Your scholarship includes a full ride to Year One of the Four Year Tutorial: Mount Olympus University. Choosing a new name will not alter your acceptance credentials, which will be viewable to all university faculty.

Objective: Choose a name.

Reward: A name.

Failure: I will choose one for you.

Warning: This name will be publicly available and displayed to all on your Friends List, World Standings, and Message Boards.

Jason stared at the prompt for longer than he meant to. Alice waited patiently, knowing the telltale sign of someone reading a prompt.

He couldn't use his regular handle. What could it be? He recalled an old card game. He chose the first name he could think of. "Jace." [Select]

Quest Update

Congratulations! You have chosen the name: Jace.

I never doubted you for a second. May this be the start of something great.

"It's Jace," he said.

"Oh, like Jason. I like it," she replied.

Jason palmed his forehead and grimaced.

Can't believe I didn't make that connection. Way to go, Jason. Get it together, man.

A faint knock echoed through the compartment door, which slid open to reveal a man in a crisp, navy blue uniform adorned with brass buttons and gold piping. His cap, also navy, bore a polished badge that gleamed under the compartment's soft lighting. The ticket collector stepped forward, his posture rigid and professional. "Tickets, please," he requested, extending a hand gloved in white.

Jace patted his pockets, a frown deepening across his forehead. "I don't think I have one," he murmured, a hint of panic threading through his voice.

Alice leaned in close and whispered, "Check your inventory."

How do I check my inventory? As if in response to his unspoken question, a translucent menu materialized before him, displaying a neatly categorized grid of items. Only two icons were visible: a silvery metallic stone and a golden ticket adorned with the Excelsior Tech emblem.

With a sigh of relief, Jace selected the ticket. It materialized in his hand, and he handed it to the ticket collector, who scanned it with a practiced motion before moving on to Alice.

Once the collector was out of earshot, Jace turned to Alice, curiosity gleaming in his eyes. "Was he a non-player character?"

Alice nodded, her expression thoughtful. "They're called Citizens. Players are called Travelers. It's hard to tell the difference sometimes."

Jace leaned out of his seat, poking his head through the compartment door to catch another glimpse of the collector.

The vividness of it all was overwhelming. He hadn't expected Terra Mythica to feel so... real. He'd heard stories—how immersive the place was, how people sometimes got lost here, unable to tell where the game ended and reality began. Rumors claimed that the longer you stayed, the more this world replaced the one outside, turning life into a distant dream. But those were just conspiracy theories, the kind of talk you'd hear from people too far gone to make it back to reality. No one had ever proven it. Just whispers from the fringes, from those who'd already decided there was nothing left for them outside.

Jace could see why. If you had nothing to go back to, this place could easily become your everything.

"They really blur the lines," he said, watching the inspector disappear into another cabin.

Just as he started to pull back, he noticed a young woman heading quickly in his direction. Their eyes met—hers sharp with intent, his startled by the sudden connection.

Quickly, he ducked back into his seat and slid the door shut behind him. No sooner had he done so than the door clicked and slid open again with a soft whoosh, revealing the same young woman who had just caught his eye.

She practically bounced in, a whirlwind of energy and color. She was striking, with olive skin that radiated warmth and deep, expressive eyes that carried a quiet depth. A cascade of dark, curly hair framed her angular features, and she wore a vibrant ensemble of bold colors and eclectic patterns that seemed to mirror her lively personality.

"Mind if I join you? Great." She didn't wait for a response, plopping down next to Jace with a dramatic sigh. "You haven't seen a man run by, have you? Tall, thin. Brown hair. Sort of handsome in a 'Huckleberry Fin" kind of way. Or maybe in a 'I'll probably hate myself in the morning' kind of way." She flashed a mischievous grin. "You know the type."

Alice's subtle reaction was immediate. Her shoulders tensed slightly, and she shifted uncomfortably in her seat, her eyes narrowing just a fraction as she observed the new arrival. She glanced at Jace, then back at the newcomer.

Jace, caught off guard by the sudden entrance and the whirlwind of words, blinked and shook his head. "Uh, no, I haven't seen anyone like that."

The girl leaned back, crossing her long legs with a fluid grace. "Figures. Probably took a wrong turn somewhere. I'm Ell, by the way." She extended a hand to Jace, her confidence radiating.

He shook her hand, still processing her vibrant presence. "I'm Jaso.. Jace. This is Alice."

Jace, not Jason. I need to start thinking of myself as Jace to avoid any further slip-ups. He chided himself.

Alice offered a polite nod. "Nice to meet you, Ell," she said, her tone reserved.

"I'm sure," Ell replied, her attention immediately shifting to the window in the door. She peered through it furtively, as if expecting the man she described to appear at any moment.

Jace watched Ell with a mixture of curiosity and bemusement. "So, what are you running from?" he asked, trying to lighten the mood.

Ell turned to him, her eyes sparkling. "Just a little misunderstanding. You know how it is." She waved a hand dismissively, though her eyes kept darting back to the door. "Anyway, this place is wild, isn't it?"

Jace wasn't sure what she meant. Alice frowned.

Chapter 3
Very Old, New Friends

The door burst open again, and a man stumbled in, breathless and grinning. His eyes sparkled with a mischievous glint, and his tousled hair and slightly disheveled appearance only added to his roguish look. He wore a faded leather jacket over a casual shirt, paired with well-worn jeans and boots that hinted at a love for adventure and a disregard for rules.

"What did you do this time?" Ell asked as he shut the door behind him. "Shhhh."

"Don't 'shhhh' me, Dex. I was minding my own business when you slipped me this, I assume, stolen ring and told me to 'run and hide'. I'm not four anymore, Dex; I only play hide and seek when I'm feeling naughty."

Dex flopped into the seat across from Jace, his grin widening. He leaned back, a picture of casual defiance, and glanced around the cabin before settling his gaze on Jace and Alice. "Well, first off, I'm truly offended. The ring was hardly stolen. More of a parting gift from a very old, new friend. But she had stolen something from me first..."

"And what was that?"

"My heart." He dramatically clasped his chest with both hands. "And a kiss. Which I didn't really mind. Her husband, on the other hand... I mean honestly, how was I to know she was a royal?"

Ell shook her head. "Dex, you're going to get yourself killed one of these days. And then captured, and killed again and again until you have no choice but to leave Terra Mythica behind."

Dex shrugged, the grin never leaving his face. "What's life without a little risk? Besides, now, it's with someone who appreciates fine jewelry. Like me." He winked.

Jace watched the interaction, intrigued by their dynamic. He could see how Ell's initial wariness melted away in Dex's presence, replaced by a familiar camaraderie. Alice, on the other hand, remained tense, her eyes focused on her tablet as she pretended not to listen.

"How rude of me. Dex, this is Jace and Alice. Jace and Alice, this is Dex."

"Howdy," Dex said, tipping an imaginary hat. "So, what's the deal with you two? Friends? Lovers? Enemies? All three?" He raised an eyebrow.

Alice blushed furiously. Ell slapped Dex's arm. "Now don't scare the little ones, Dex. They're my new friends."

Dex looked at her appraisingly. "Well, first time here, then?" He changed his question, eyes sparkling with a smile.

"It's all of our first times here, Dex," Ell replied.

"I meant in Terra Mythica. Of course, it's all of our first times at the great M.O.U."

Dex waited, but everyone just stared at him.

"Mount Olympus University."

"Yeah, first time. Just getting used to everything." Jace nodded.

"Not my first," Alice interjected, her blush fading as she regained her composure. She offered a polite nod, her gaze lingering on Dex as if trying to decipher him. "Nice to meet you, Dex," she said, her tone reserved but not unfriendly.

"Well, you're in for quite the voyage. Just stick with us, and you'll be fine." He shot a playful glance at Alice. "And if you ever find yourself in a jam, just remember - it's all part of the adventure."

"So, how do you two know each other?" Jace asked.

"Oh, how don't we? Ow!" Dex was immediately kicked in the leg by Ell.

"Dex and I go way back to Mythos High."

That tracks, Jace thought.

He had heard of it. It was one of those fancy prep schools for rich kids that were all but guaranteed to get into whichever Terra Mythica university they chose.

"Not sure how I got in, to be honest," Dex said as he leaned back and spread his arms expansively, nodding appreciatively at the ship's cabin.

Jace followed his gaze as Dex took in the opulence of his surroundings. He had seen a cabin like this in a picture somewhere, a relic of a bygone era brought to life with magic and science.

Ell rolled her eyes but smiled. "Dex, you're impossible. You know exactly why you got in. What I'm not sure about is how you managed to actually graduate. You were nearly expelled, what, a half-dozen times? I swear, they probably graduated you just so they didn't have to deal with you for another year."

"It's all because of my natural charm. Some might go so far as to say that I have a sort of animal magnetism," Dex said, winking at Alice. Ell jabbed him again for this.

Dex shrugged, unbothered. "Now, I'm hoping to get a specialized class in the first year."

Jace's blank expression must have said it all because Ell jumped in. "Oh, you don't know about class specializations? Where did you come from, under a rock?"

He felt a twinge of defensiveness. "I've heard of classes, but specializations?"

Dex leaned forward, his eyes gleaming with excitement. "Ignore her. She was raised with a silver spoon stuck up her little..."

Dex yelped as Ell kicked him hard. "Will you stop that? Anyway, you unlock specializations when you rank up your base Class Title. Most people get them during their last few years at M.O.U. through achievements. If they don't, they still get at least one novice-tier specialization when they graduate."

Dex leaned back against the plush, burgundy upholstery of the ship's cabin, a glint of mischief dancing in his green eyes. The gentle rocking of the ship on the waves created a soothing backdrop as he explained. "Think of it like this," he said, his voice low but animated.

"You have your basic class or titles: Mage, Fighter, Cleric, Rogue. They're technically called Class Titles, but people use Class or Title interchangeably to mean the same thing. They're not just roles; they're reflections of what you've accomplished. Your actions shape them, not the other way around."

He took a swig from a canteen before tucking it back into his jacket, the flickering gaslight casting shadows across his face. "Now, the real magic happens with specializations. Take a Rogue, for instance. Focus on sneaking and poisons, and you might become an Assassin. But, say you're more into picking pockets? You could become a Thief, nimble-fingered and sly. Or if you're the kind who loves disarming traps and unlocking doors, you might end up a Trap Finder, or Treasure Hunter."

"Specializations enhance your skills and grant unique abilities. Sure, you might lose a bit of variety, but you gain powerful focuses. Like this one guy I heard about. He went on a rat-killing spree, clearing out basements for months. The System awarded him the title 'Rat Slayer.' And when he took it to the extreme, killing thousands of rats with just a pointy stick, wearing nothing but his heart-covered underwear, he became the 'Hobo Stick Master.' As he was the first to receive it, he got some pretty cool bonuses too."

Ell shook her head. "Sounds glamorous."

"I think so. That's the beauty of it. Every title tells a story. Your story."

"Some stories are better not to tell." She quipped.

The cabin's ambiance was filled with the warm, rich scent of leather and the distant creak of the ship. "Your first title isn't everything. It's just the System's way of nudging you towards something to hone your skills on. The real prestige comes with the specialization titles, which are all about your achievements."

The cabin fell into a comfortable silence, the flickering gaslights casting a warm glow over the group. Outside, the ocean rolled gently beneath the ship, the mist parting occasionally to reveal the distant mountain, crowned with clouds, as the ship carried them onward.

Ell nodded enthusiastically. "Dex here is aiming for Rakish Vagabond or something weird like that. As for me, I'm keeping my options open until the right opportunity presents itself. I want to make sure I have the best chances of min-maxing."

"Min-whating?" Jace asked.

Alice looked up as if about to speak but then said nothing, her expression thoughtful.

Ell stood up, her excitement palpable.

"Here she goes," Dex said, rolling his eyes. "It's not every day someone knows less than her about an academic subject. Once you get her started, man... wake me when she's done." He leaned back, eyes glazing over as he seemed to disappear into his own thoughts.

Ell sighed, but her smile remained. She glanced to the side, and a prompt appeared in the middle of the room, illuminating their faces with a soft glow.

"Oh, wow! I initiated a quest prompt."

New Quest

Maybe You'll Learn Something

Your new friends have decided to help you overcome your woeful ignorance of game mechanics. Traveler Ell has nominated herself to teach you the basics that any beginning player should have known before they started.

Objective: Get a passing familiarity with the fundamentals.

Reward: Knowledge is its own reward. Still need more? How about a +1 to Game Mechanics Lore?

Failure: You will stay just as uninformed as you are right now.

Warning: Prepare for an info dump!

Accept | Reject

Jace shook his head and mentally selected [Accept].

"Wait," Jace said, "how did you start a quest? Isn't that something the System usually handles?"

"I can only share what I've heard; there isn't an official explanation for this one. But one of my teachers once said that in Terra Mythica, the System isn't just a set of rules or some overseer. It's more like a living, breathing part of the world—an effect, not a cause. It adapts to each Traveler, shaping their experience based on factors we don't fully understand. Excelsior keeps the System's secrets close to the chest."

Jace had heard all kinds of complaints about the System—how it could be biased, cruel, too friendly, too robotic, too personal. The opinions were all over the place, but one thing was clear: the System interacted differently with everyone.

"Quests, like the one I just kicked off, are less about some grand mission handed down from above and more about what you're doing in the moment. They can come from anyone—Citizens, gods, even other Travelers. The rewards? All over the map. Sometimes, the System itself throws in a quest with a prize. It could be gold, experience, or just the satisfaction of getting the job done."

"Experience—EXP—is not just some number the System hands out either. You earn it, bit by bit, with every challenge you take on. From what I've heard, the System doesn't as much award experience as it tries its best to calculate it based on your growth."

The way she described it, the System felt like it was always there, lurking in the background, guiding Travelers and pushing them to keep up with the strange, ever-changing world of Terra Mythica.

"How does that tie in with specializations?" Jace asked.

"Alright, let's break it down. As Dex said, specializations are like... advanced titles. They help you focus your skills and become exceptional in specific areas. For example, a Shadow Mage blends stealth and dark magic, perfect for sneaking and casting powerful illusions."

A magical display appeared in the middle of the cabin, showing diagrams and pictures as Ell spoke.

"There are hundreds, maybe even thousands, of specializations. Everyone has their own particular way of getting things done. You can aim for whatever class you want, but it's best to find out which you have the most affinity for first and go for that, with a bit of min-maxing."

"Min-maxing is when you focus your abilities and skills for your class and don't waste time and energy on areas you don't need. But you have to be careful, or you'll wind up super unbalanced. Imagine a genius with a brain so big he doesn't have the strength to lift it. That would be all points into Intelligence and none into Strength."

"Dex is naturally more agile and is going for a rogue specialization. So, he is going to want to focus on upping his Dexterity." She paused. "You do know how attribute stats work, right?"

"Of course." Jace nodded unconvincingly.

"Okay, the basic stats are Strength, Intelligence, Dexterity, Charisma, Constitution, Wisdom, Luck, and Karmic Balance. I like to think of it like dancing with someone."

Alice shook her head and focused even more intently on her tablet.

Ell slid next to Jace, her fingers walking across his shoulder. He tried to swallow and take a deep breath simultaneously, causing him to choke on air. She leaned closer, her voice dropping to a conspiratorial whisper.

"Think of it like this: Strength is your ability to lift her or move her without spraining something. Intelligence is your ability to read her body language, sensing her desires and responding in kind. Dexterity is all about the grace and precision, making every movement count. Charisma? That's your ability to charm someone into dancing with you. Constitution measures your stamina, how long you can keep the dance going before you need to take a break. Wisdom is knowing when to be slow and when to intensify the pace, what type of moves go with what type of song. Luck is whether there is the right dance partner around in the first place. And Karmic Balance? That's the measure of how genuine you are. Sort of like a cosmic scale of how much of a douche you are."

She quickly stood back up and took a little bow.

"Welcome to the game, newbie. You'll catch on."

Quest Update

Congratulations, You've Learned Something

You've been upgraded from Bungling Buffoon to Incompetent Nincompoop.

+1 to Game Mechanics and Lore.

Keep this up and you'll be a novice in no time.

Dex's eyes refocused, as if arriving back from somewhere far away. "You done with your lecture, Ell? We should be pulling up shortly. Why are you blushing, Jace?"

Chapter 4
Twist and Shout

B efore Jace could answer, an announcement crackled through the overhead speakers, "Final announcement. Passengers, please strap in. The ship is about to commence a rapid ascent before arriving at its final destination."

Jace's eyes darted around, noticing the seatbelts tucked discreetly beside each seat for the first time.

Ascent? Final announcement? What happened to the first one?

The ship shuddered, and Jace felt a deep rumble resonate through the wooden floor beneath his feet. He looked out the window just in time to see the massive wings of the ship begin to unfurl, their intricate sails billowing out like the wings of a mythical bird. The sails were woven with threads of shimmering light, catching the sun as they spread wide, a majestic silhouette against the deep blue of the ocean below.

With a sudden, graceful motion, the ship began to rise. The giant wings flapped slowly, powerfully, propelling the vessel upwards. The resistance of the water lessened as the ship climbed higher and higher, leaving the waves behind. The transition from sea to sky was seamless, the ship ascending with a majesty that took Jace's breath away.

As the ship soared, Jace felt the sensation of weightlessness. He glanced out the window again, watching in awe as the world fell away beneath them. The ocean's surface became a distant mirror, reflecting the ship's shadow as it climbed steadily into the heavens.

The ship continued its ascent, leaving the last remnants of the ocean behind as they glided over rolling hills. Jace watched the landscape unfold beneath them—a patchwork of forests, mountains, and rivers, all shrinking as the ship soared higher. The transition from sea to open sky was both exhilarating and surreal.

Jace barely registered the beauty of the scene before the ship jolted forward with terrifying ferocity. The sudden acceleration pinned him against the back of his seat, and then, without warning, the ship shot upwards, transitioning into a steep, nearly vertical ascent. His stomach lurched as gravity seemed to double its pull on him. The seatbelts, so inconspicuously hidden moments ago, now flapped wildly about.

The cabin transformed into a chaotic maelstrom. The ship slowed suddenly and then lost altitude, lifting them from their seats and sending them into the air. Jace flailed desperately, hands grasping at nothing but empty space. The ship surged forward and up again, twisting and turning as if it had come alive with a mind of its own.

Jace's vision blurred, the world a swirl of motion and sound. The ship looped in a full circle, his body weightless for a heart-stopping moment before being slammed back down by the relentless force.

Dex managed to grasp a seatbelt, and with a quick motion, helped Ell stabilize herself.

Through the pandemonium, Jace caught sight of Alice. She was suspended in mid-air, her long hair having come undone, whipping around her face. Her eyes were wide with fear, arms reaching out desperately. He could see her lips moving, perhaps calling his name, but the roar of the winds drowned out all other sounds.

Alice's body twisted in the air, her fingers brushing against the seats, failing to find purchase. With a sickening thud, Jace and Alice collided, eyes wide and faces inches apart, the impact knocking the wind out of them both.

The ship continued its frenzied climb, the walls and ceiling blurring together as it spiraled. Every lurch, every twist sent waves of panic through them. Jace's muscles burned from the strain of trying to control his own body, to find some stability in the madness.

The air was filled with the blare of straining engines. Jace tightened his grip on Alice, using his knees to push against the wall, shielding her from the worst of the impacts and pressure.

Finally, the ship began to level out, the pressure easing as gravity resumed its hold. Each in turn slowly regained their footing, nursing bruises and shaking off the disorientation. Jace and Alice untangled themselves, breathless and shaken. When they looked at each other, a blush crept up Alice's cheeks, mirrored by the flush on Jace's face.

The clouds parted like a theater curtain, revealing a dreamscape of rolling skies and endless horizons. Hills and trees emerged, seemingly adrift on an island of mist, floating in the vastness beyond.

The ship slowed, and Jace's heart pounded in sync with the rhythmic hum of the engines.

"Approaching Mount Olympus Sky Dock. Passengers prepare to disembark. We know you have many options for your travel needs, and we appreciate you choosing Olympian Airways. Have a fine stay, and we hope to see you again soon."

The ship glided into the docking platform with a soft shudder. Jace clung to the wall of the compartment, his vision swimming as the dizziness from the ascent ebbed away. A sharp hiss announced the release of the ship's air pressure, and the doors parted with a smooth whoosh, revealing a platform teeming with life.

High, vaulted ceilings stretched above, adorned with intricate mosaics that depicted epic battles and legendary figures. A colossal relief spelled out "Mt. Olympus Sky Dock" in elegant ancient Greek lettering, beside which a stone phoenix stood guard, its eyes glinting with golden fire.

Jace stepped off the ship, the void yawning beneath the narrow bridge that stretched toward the platform, a thin thread between worlds. He tread carefully, the abyss below hinting at a fall that felt as if it would stretch into eternity. As his foot met solid ground, the air crackled with energy—vivid, almost tangible—swirling around him like a storm of unseen colors, teasing his senses awake.

The air was rich with the mingling scents of exotic foods from vendor carts, their bright canopies flapping in a gentle breeze. Excited conversations and bursts of laughter reverberated off the mosaic walls, creating a symphony of student life.

Dex, Ell, and Alice were immediately swept up in the crowd, leaving Jace to his own devices. Dex already bantering with a group of students who seemed equally mischievous. Alice vanished into thin air. Jace felt a pang of isolation.

He drifted through the crowd, the vibrant colors of the dock pulsing around him. His eyes landed on a quaint shop with a sign that read "Bits and

Bobs," where strange but familiar wares spilled from its shelves in a chaotic display. As he stepped inside, a clerk greeted him with a smile that barely moved as he spoke.

"Looking for something specific?" the clerk asked.

"Just browsing."

Scrolls glowing faintly with embedded enchantments were neatly stacked beside trinkets that hummed softly, pulsating with unseen energy. Jace's attention was drawn to a wooden drawer filled with small orbs, each no bigger than a marble. He picked one up, its surface swirling with colors that seemed to shift and dance, drawing him in. He felt a gentle warmth emanate from it, as if it held a tiny piece of the sun.

The orb began to hover slightly above his palm, spinning faster and faster until it projected a constellation of stars around him, each one twinkling with a magical brilliance. Lines formed between the brightest stars, morphing into the image of a giant eagle. The eagle let out a piercing caw and dove toward him. Jace stumbled back and quickly placed the orb back into the drawer.

"Aquila. The eagle of Zeus. Carrier of his thunderbolts," the shopkeeper said, his voice carrying a hint of amusement.

Jace nodded, cringing with embarrassment, and continued to browse.

Keychains hung from a rotating display, each one enchanted with a tiny charm. He picked up a keychain adorned with a miniature dragon, its eyes gleaming like rubies. As he held it, the dragon came to life, curling around his finger and letting out a tiny, playful roar before returning to its inanimate form.

Next to the keychains, a rack of enchanted pens beckoned. He picked one up, its sleek surface cool to the touch. As he scribbled on a piece of parchment, the pen transformed his writing into beautiful calligraphy, the ink shimmering with a metallic sheen.

He moved towards a stand of postcards, each one depicting a scene from a different fantastical realm. He picked up a card showing a serene, moonlit lake. As he held it, the image shimmered and moved, the water rippling under a soft breeze.

He spotted a peculiar book bound in dark, supple leather. The cover bore intricate, glowing runes that pulsed in a slow, rhythmic pattern. As he opened it, the pages came alive, unfurling like a blooming flower. Each page revealed a different scene, vivid and animated, depicting ancient myths and fantastical landscapes. He watched in awe as a tiny dragon, no larger than a thimble, leapt from the book and fluttered around his head, its wings shimmering with iridescent scales.

Jace wanted to inquire about the price of the book but abruptly realized that he didn't have any money.

Maybe the system generates some sort of welcome kit or starter money.

Checking his pockets, he found them empty, save for a smooth silver stone. He pulled it out and looked it over curiously. A small faint tag appeared above it.

Item

    User Interface Stone

    Rarity: Mythical.

    Soulbound.

    For more information and functionality, please complete the calibration process.

There was no other description.

When did I get this?

"I see you like that book?" the man said, smile widening slightly. "I'll give you a good deal."

Jace pulled out his empty pockets and shrugged. The shopkeep's eyes sharpened, but he still did not frown. "A trade, then, perhaps?" He nodded toward the silver stone. Jace thought it over for a long moment, realizing that he had no idea the value of things here.

Chapter 5
New Friends

"**M**aybe another time," Jace said, already worrying about how he'd handle his basic expenses in Terra Mythica. Would he need to get a job? What exactly did the scholarship cover?

He was quickly pulled from his thoughts as a loud voice boomed through the station, summoning all new students. Jace reluctantly left the book, shop, and now frowning shopkeeper, and joined the gathering crowd, waiting for further instructions.

Jace was surrounded by a dizzying array of students and passersby, each one more unique than the last. Elves with shimmering hair that seemed to catch the light in a thousand different hues, dwarves with intricately braided beards and robust frames, and humans from every imaginable background. There were beings with dragon-like scales peeking out from their collars, others with the hooves and horns of satyrs, and even a few with the stoic, towering presence of Vikings.

"First time here, huh?" a voice said behind him. Jace turned to see a tall young man with pointed ears, tanned skin, and a confident smirk beside four others, their immaculate, tailored clothes stark against the casual attire of the crowd. One of them, a thin boy with pale skin, glanced around nervously, his demeanor a sharp contrast with the others' bravado.

"I keep getting asked that," Jace replied, striving to sound casual despite the knot of tension forming in his stomach. A fiery sensation surged within him as his fight-or-flight instinct kicked in, reacting to an unknown threat.

"Name's Marcus." He extended a hand and shook Jace's, his gaze sharp and assessing. "Welcome to Olympus." His attire was a flamboyant display of wealth and status, befitting a man accustomed to luxury. He wore a doublet of rich velvet in deep burgundy, embroidered with a golden thread that traced intricate patterns of vines and leaves. He wore a single ruddy bronze ring on his left hand with plain design, the only thing slightly less lavish about him. Around his neck hung a chain of polished emeralds and diamonds, glinting in the soft glow of the room.

"Thanks. I'm Jace."

"Well, Jace," Marcus said, leaning in just enough to invade his space, his smirk widening. "Word of advice: watch who you hang out with. Some people here are more trouble than they're worth." His gaze flicked to Dex, who was laughing loudly with a group nearby.

"I'll keep that in mind," Jace replied, keeping his tone even. Blending in was essential, and getting tangled in school politics was the quickest way to fail at it.

Marcus's smile twisted into something more sinister. "Don't get caught on the wrong side of the dock. This place has its own way of sorting the riff from the raff."

"I don't think that means what you think..." Jace started, but before he could finish, Ell and Dex strolled up beside him, cutting off the exchange.

"Hey, Jace!" Dex called, his grin broadening as he spotted Marcus. "Making new friends already?"

Marcus's eyes narrowed at Dex. "Wouldn't want our new guy to get in over his head. I'm just giving him some friendly advice."

Ell stepped forward, her gaze icy. "Oh Marcus, I wouldn't take anything from you without a shot of penicillin and some anti-itch cream."

Marcus's smirk returned, but his eyes gleamed with a dangerous light. "Real cute. We'll see how long that lasts." He turned to walk away.

"Thinks he's real tough ever since Mythos High," Dex said, just loud enough for Marcus to hear. Marcus looked back, a shadow of malice in his eyes. "But the scared little boy isn't even man enough to fight his own battles," Dex continued.

"Why don't you shut your mouth, Dex," Marcus spat, stepping back toward them. His friends, sensing the tension, flanked him, ready for a confrontation. All but the pale boy who stayed back.

Dex didn't back down. "Or what, Marcus? Gonna run crying to mommy and daddy?"

Something snapped in Marcus, and without warning, he lunged at Dex with a blur of ferocity, shoving him with brutal force. Dex, quick on his feet, narrowly avoided being sent over the edge of the dock platform, his arms windmilling to regain balance. Jace stepped forward, hands raised in a gesture of peace. "Hey, let's just talk this out. Two stupids don't make a smart." But before he could say more, Marcus's friends closed ranks around their leader, forming a wall of muscle and menace that cut off any chance of diplomacy.

Marcus advanced on Dex, a predatory glint in his eyes, his intentions unmistakably lethal.

"Keep him back, Gregor," Marcus called to the hulking brute that blocked Jace's path. "Stay out of it, newbie. This doesn't concern you." He turned back to his prey. "You're gonna pay, Dex. You're going to pay for everything." Venom dripped from his words.

Dex swung at Marcus, but Marcus deflected the blow with a swift, practiced ease. He moved with an unnatural speed, his fist connecting with Dex's jaw in a sickening crunch. Dex crumpled to the ground. Marcus was relentless, kicking him viciously in the ribs as Dex gasped for breath.

Not my fight, not my problem. Just stay under the radar, stay out of trouble, Jace reminded himself, but the thought was already slipping through his fingers like sand.

Marcus leaned in, his breath hot and heavy with aggression, and yanked Dex closer to the edge of the platform, forcing his head over the brink. Dex flailed in panic, his movements wild and desperate, but Marcus's grip was unyielding. With a last-ditch effort, Dex spat in Marcus's eyes, startling him just enough to wrench himself free and stumble away from the brink.

But his escape was short-lived. One of Marcus's goons was already there, a hulking shadow looming, and with ruthless efficiency, he seized Dex, locking him in place like a steel vice. Marcus's grin widened—a predator savoring the helplessness of his prey—as he sent his fist into Dex's gut with brutal force.

"Just log out," Marcus sneered. "Pain too much? Hmm? Just log out and it'll all be over. Log out and don't come back." He punctuated the words with a knee, each blow delivered with surgical precision, designed to hurt, to break. He pushed him back, forcing him closer to the edge of the dock.

"Knock it off, Marcus," Ell snapped, stepping forward, but her path was quickly blocked by another of Marcus's friends—a wiry figure with a sharp, angular face, his eyes cold and gleaming with a cruel delight.

"Out of my way," she snarled, her voice low and dangerous.

"No can do, girly," he sneered, shoving a thick hand against her shoulder.

With a quick, sharp movement, she drove her knee into his groin. The man grunted, his face contorting in pain, but he didn't go down.

Instead, he grabbed her, pulling her back with a practiced strength that betrayed years of experience. These weren't just bullies—they were trained.

Jace caught a flicker of something in Marcus's eyes—a cold, twisted gleam that sent a chill through him. He'd seen it before, back in the real world. The longer he stared into those eyes, the more it felt like reality itself was slipping, making his tiny room above the bar seem like the dream and this moment—the brutality, the raw, merciless intent—the truth.

Guilt stabbed at him, sharp and unrelenting. Those eyes were built to inflict pain, to take a sick pleasure in it. They were the eyes of someone who relished in suffering, like that neighbor who used to tear the legs off spiders just to watch them squirm. The same kind of eyes that had taken everything from him.

Ell struggled to reach Dex but wouldn't make it before he was sent off the edge.

Something snapped inside him in that moment, like a taut wire finally breaking under pressure. He wasn't that powerless kid anymore. He could do something about it now.

And he would.

Jace's vision narrowed, the world reducing to a tunnel with Marcus and Dex at its end. He ducked under Gregor's arm, shoving his way through the wall of flesh.

As Jace broke through, he hurled himself at Marcus, slamming into him and knocking him to the ground near the edge of the dock. They grappled, Jace landing a few punches, but Marcus's ring flared with heat, searing Jace's skin.

With a savage grin, Marcus grabbed Jace by the collar and slammed him hard onto the edge of the platform. "You think you can stop me, runt? You're nothing."

Marcus raised his fist and pounded into Jace's stomach, the ring now glowing with a blinding, lethal red. His smile was gone, replaced by a terrible scowl. His eyes, lifeless orbs. Panic surged through Jace. This wasn't just a schoolboy fight. Marcus meant to kill him.

The sound of waves crashing against the cliffs below was deafening, a chilling reminder of the deadly drop just inches away. Jace's vision blurred as he struggled. Marcus, gripping him tightly, pushed his head over the edge, the abyss below seeming to pull him in.

Jace's mind raced, searching for an escape, any way to stop the impending disaster. He heard Dex's ragged breaths, felt the crushing weight of Marcus's grip tightening around him, and then, just as the world teetered on the edge—

A prompt appeared.

Word of Power Available
    Description: Unknown
    Would you like to activate Word of Power?
    Accept | Reject

The prompt showed a glitched message with indecipherable text where the ability description should have been.

Jace mentally selected [Accept] without hesitating.

Chapter 6
How to Successfully Stay Under the Radar

A word—a word that felt ancient and dangerous, from a dream he had no right to remember—burst from Jace's lips. The air crackled with energy as pain coursed through his body, threatening to tear him apart. He screamed, his voice raw and desperate.

A deafening crack split the air. Marcus's grip slackened, his eyes widening in shock.

Time fractured. Reality twisted as Jace felt an unseen force pulling at his very core. Everything around him froze, suspended in a crystalline stasis. His vision blurred, and an immense power surged through him, draining his essence with a ferocity that left him trembling.

System Error
Cannot comply with code instruction, insufficient resources. Attempting to pull from ambient aether.

The system error flashed before his eyes, a glitch in the very fabric of reality. Then, everything went black.

When his vision cleared, he was in the middle of a desert, under a high, full moon that cast an eerie light over the vast expanse of sand. The cold wind whipped across the dunes, chilling him to the bone. A shimmering mist moved through the air, glowing faintly in the moonlight.

Ruins of an ancient civilization sprawled out around him, their broken columns and crumbling walls a stark contrast to the smooth dunes. The remnants of a once-grand archway stood tall, partially buried in the sand. Its faint markings were worn away by time.

The frigid air bit into his skin. He turned at the sound of a low growl, eyes widening as monstrous creatures emerged from the shadows. Their eyes glowed with predatory hunger, their grotesque forms a nightmarish blend of sinew and shadow, with elongated limbs and razor-sharp teeth.

Panic surged through him, but his body was too weak to move, his aether completely depleted. The creatures closed in, their snarls growing louder, their hunger palpable.

Move! Get up. I need to move!

The first creature, a hulking beast with eyes like burning coals, lunged at him, its smile wide, teeth bared to devour him. Jace's mind raced, but his body remained frozen, helpless. He closed his eyes as tight as he could.

System Error Detected
Traveler outside of Permitted Realm. Elevating issue.

The world hit pause, drifting into a fog. Beasts froze mid-leap, as if a director had yelled, "Cut!" on a horror set. Reality rippled, shimmering like a cosmic pond disturbed by a pebble. Out of the distortion stepped a kid, maybe thirteen, with the air of a monarch and a grin that knew all the universe's little jokes.

Jace groaned, sitting up. His body ached, head spinning. "What the...?" He looked around, bewildered. His thoughts felt like gossamer in the wind. The last thing he remembered was the desert, the creatures, the crushing hopelessness. "Am I dead?"

The kid's grin widened, eyes twinkling with ancient knowledge. "Guess again."

Jace blinked, rubbing his eyes. "A glitch?" He scanned the frozen scene.

"Bingo."

"And who are you?"

The boy shrugged. "Names vary. Your kind calls me the AI, others the Primordial or the Infinite. But I prefer Jack."

Jace struggled to his feet, trying to wrap his head around it.

"Look, you weren't supposed to end up in the desert realm," Jack said. "Not yet. That's way above your level and technically it shouldn't have been possible with your User Interface Stone."

"So you... saved me?"

"Fixed a mistake," the boy corrected, mildly annoyed. "You ended up where you shouldn't have. That's on me. Didn't expect you to try and break the universe. But now you've got my attention and it won't happen again."

"Well, that's... reassuring," Jace said. "So, what's next?"

The boy's smirk grew, warning in his eyes. "Send you back. Just try not to screw up... too much."

Jace met the kid's gaze, the weight of his words sinking in. This wasn't just a casual encounter. The universe's fixer-upper had taken a personal interest in him. Did it know who he really was?

The boy turned to leave, the ripples of reality fading around him. He glanced back. "Don't make me regret saving your skin, kid."

In an instant, the desert dissolved. Jace was yanked back, finding himself in the station, watching Marcus from ten feet away. Time resumed its relentless march. The world continuing its chaotic dance.

Jace staggered back, collapsing to the ground, gasping for breath. Marcus's fist struck the air where Jace's head had been, the force of the blow causing a ripple of displaced energy.

Marcus glared, confusion mingling with fury. "What the hell just happened?" he growled.

The man restraining Ell suddenly released her, his eyes catching something that made him hesitate. Without a word, he slipped away, melting into the crowd.

Jace lay on the ground, struggling to piece together the fragments of what had occurred.

"Enough!" the word boomed over them, ending the fight instantly. Two senior students, their university badges gleaming, appeared from nowhere. One was a tall, red-haired woman, thin, her gentle demeanor hiding the tension in her eyes. The other, a muscular young man with an air of authority, stepped forward.

"I'm Rain and this is Sairie. Faculty Aides. What's going on here?" His tone was sharp, cutting through them like a knife.

Marcus stepped back, smoothing his clothes and forcing a smug smile. "Just welcoming the new guy. No harm done."

Rain's eyes swept over the group, finally settling on Dex, who struggled to catch his breath. "You okay?"

Dex nodded, pain and anger flickering in his eyes. "Yeah, I'm fine. Luckily, that pussy hits like a girl. No offense, Ell." He grimaced as he stood.

Ell shot him a sharp glare but held her tongue. For now, it seemed that Rain and Sairie hadn't noticed her participation in the fight.

Sairie stepped forward, her expression softening as she reached into her pocket and pulled out an amber stone. It glowed with a warm, healing light as she held it over Dex. The light enveloped him, and with a sickening crunch his ribs popped into place. Dex gasped, the pain fading as the stone worked its magic.

Jace tried to speak but his voice would not comply. He started to panic. He could move his lips, but nothing would come out.

Sairie finished with Dex and turned to Jace, the stone's light mending his bruises and burns.

Jace stared at the ground, his mind a whirlwind. Despite the healing, he could barely move. His entire body ached, every muscle protesting with each attempt. The Word had drained his essence, leaving his aether utterly depleted. Sairie struggled to channel energy back into him but found little success. Her brow furrowed as she rummaged through a small bag, finally holding out a vial filled with shimmering blue liquid.

"Drink this," her eyes searched his face as if looking for answers.

Jace took the potion, hesitating for a moment before downing it in one gulp. A warm surge of energy spread through him, revitalizing his aether reserves almost instantly. Slowly, his voice started to come back to him, and he thanked her with a deep rasp. He felt better, physically at least, but something inside him had shifted. It was like trying to fit into old clothes that weren't quite right anymore.

The healer's gaze lingered on him, her expression a mix of concern and curiosity. Jace forced a weak smile, but her searching look made him uneasy. What was the power I had used? And what was the glitch? He wondered. His head throbbed as he tried to remember it.

After the healing, Rain's attention shifted back to the group, his expression hardening. "This isn't a playground, and you are not children, though you are certainly acting like them. Unauthorized duels are strictly prohibited and can result in immediate expulsion." He paused, letting the gravity of his words sink in. "You three are to report to the Archmage's office immediately after the Welcoming Ceremony."

Quest Alert
>   Report to the Archmage
>   See him immediately after the Welcoming Ceremony.
>   Mandatory: This quest cannot be rejected.

Marcus's friends, who had been smirking, suddenly looked nervous. A crowd of onlookers, silent and wide-eyed, watched as the combatants hung their heads. The red-haired girl's gentle touch starkly contrasted with the stern reprimand of her companion. The tension in the air was palpable, and the students knew they were in serious trouble.

Marcus's confident facade wavered for a moment, but he quickly regained his composure. "It won't happen again," he said, though the edge in his voice hinted at lingering defiance.

The senior man's gaze remained unyielding. "See that it doesn't. The Archmage will decide your fates. And believe me, he's not as forgiving as we are."

Marcus's smile faltered slightly, but he maintained his composure. "Of course," he said smoothly, casting a sidelong glance at Jace and Dex.

As Marcus and his entourage moved on, the pale boy glanced back at Jace with a sinister smile. There was something unsettling about him, something Jace couldn't quite put his finger on.

Dex seemed to have regained his carefree attitude. He clapped Jace on the shoulder, using his other hand to flip off Marcus as he walked away. "Don't let that Malfoy-wannabe get to you. He thinks he owns this place," Dex smiled and waved innocently as Marcus shot a glance back at him.

Ell nodded, her expression serious. "Partly because he does. Or at least, his father does."

Jace forced an uneasy smile. This is not how you stay under the radar.

Chapter 7
Giant Swamp Pigeons

T he groups stood huddled near the massive barn-sized exit of the station, herded like sheep but each clinging to their own anticipation, nerves, and curiosity. Their guide, a woman with deep brown eyes and an expression that brooked no nonsense, took her place at the front. She wore authority like a second skin, her long violet dress embroidered with a shimmering gold phoenix that seemed to flicker and shift with each graceful movement. A gleaming golden belt cinched her waist, and a large ruby hung low on her chest, catching the light, flaring with fiery brilliance. The way she carried herself made it clear: you did not cross her.

Demi, they would learn later, wasn't just a senior student. She was the kind of upperclassman whose name echoed through whispered conversations and dorm-room warnings. Beside her stood two men in simple tunics, one a deep blue, the other a dark green, their outfits belted at the waist with silver cords. Their presence was far less commanding, more like silent shadows flanking a queen.

When Demi finally spoke, her voice wasn't loud—yet it carried, amplified in a way that silenced all other sounds. "Welcome to Mount Olympus University. I'm Demi, and I'll be your guide. Stay together. We've got a bit of a trek ahead, and you'll want to conserve your stamina."

Without waiting for questions or hesitation, she led them outside. The mountain path stretched before them, steep and winding, carved through the dense landscape. Jace felt the pull in his legs immediately, muscles protesting the incline, but he gritted his teeth and followed. Thirty minutes passed in near silence, the quiet only broken by the occasional murmur of conversation and the relentless hum of nature.

The air grew thicker, the path narrowing as the landscape shifted. Ancient stone ruins whispered of past ages, draped in creeping vines and moss, while the treetops seemed to close in, casting long shadows that danced with each step. The sky above darkened as they ascended, the climb pulling them into a higher, stranger place.

Demi stood at the edge of the boundary, her posture relaxed, yet there was a palpable tension in the air. She gestured for the students to pass, her voice steady and authoritative. "Inside the line, everyone. Stick close."

Jace's eyes were drawn to a faint glow up ahead. A barrier. It hovered in the air, a shimmering prismatic wall that buzzed with energy, drawing closer with every step. The very air crackled, thick with magic, as they neared. One by one, the students hesitated, stepping through with a mix of awe and trepidation. The barrier resisted for a moment, pushing against them like a hand pressed to their chest before it gave way, allowing them to pass.

Jace felt it—the tingle of magic as it brushed over his skin, the taste of metal on his tongue. He staggered, a brief dizziness taking him before it passed, leaving him breathless. On the other side, Demi waited, eyes sharp as she watched them gather. "That, what you just passed through, is the Fourth Zone barrier," she explained, her tone more teacher than guide now. "It repels the largest and most dangerous monsters. Think of these zones as nets, filtering out progressively dangerous monsters. The deeper we go, the tighter the net. But don't get comfortable. Smaller creatures can still slip through, and they will."

The new students shifted hesitantly, eyes darting from her to the dense forest. Jace felt a shiver ripple through him as he crossed the invisible threshold. The air changed—metallic, thick, a moment of vertigo that made his head swim before his senses snapped back.

In her hand, she held a pulsing amethyst, glowing with a soft purple hue. "This," she continued, raising it for them to see, "is a Ward Shard. Minor version of the Great Heart Shard protecting the university itself. Out here, you're vulnerable without one. Though they are far from foolproof. Stay within the barrier or in a zone your rank can handle. Otherwise…" Her eyes drifted meaningfully to the trees, dark and looming. "Well, let's just say, they'd pick your bones clean."

With a whispered incantation, her lips barely brushing the surface of the Ward Stone, the shard's light flickered, then faded, sinking into the folds of her dress. The sunlight, already feeble beneath the dense canopy, seemed to vanish entirely, plunging the world into a sudden, bone-deep chill.

A distant rumble. The ground trembled, leaves rustling unnaturally. Jace's heart skipped as the roars echoed, growing louder with every passing moment. He could feel the primal energy pulsing through the air.

"Here they come," Demi murmured, her gaze locking onto the shadows ahead.

The creature emerged—a towering bird, its body encased in metallic feathers that gleamed like polished steel. Its eyes, glowing crimson, fixed on them with malevolent intelligence. The beak, long and jagged, looked sharp enough to split stone.

It screeched, the sound piercing the silence, its wings spreading wide to cast a menacing shadow over the group. With a predatory lunge, it surged toward Demi, claws outstretched.

She didn't flinch. "Overgrown swamp pigeon," she muttered with a smirk, sidestepping the charge with effortless grace.

"Technically, it's a Stymphalian Bird," she said, her voice calm and instructional even as the beast screeched and slashed at her. "Nasty things. People-eaters. And their feathers? Sharp as blades." She ducked as one of those very feathers shot toward her, the projectile clanging harmlessly against the invisible barrier that shielded the students.

The ruby on her chest began to glow, rising slightly from her body before a flash of light revealed a sword, the blade shimmering with an ethereal silver sheen. Intricate runes danced along the edge, pulsing with power.

The bird lunged again. This time, Demi met it head-on. Her sword sang through the air, striking the beast with precision. Sparks flew as metal met magic, the clash ringing out like thunder.

"The Metal Star System ranks creatures and items by their power," she explained mid-combat, her voice even, as if she were lecturing in a classroom. "Bronze is your weakest. Gold? Well, if you see a Gold-ranked anything, run. Fast."

A student, wide-eyed, shouted from the back, "What rank are you?"

She ignored the question, her focus sharp as she deflected another series of deadly feathers. Her muscles tensed, her form hardening like marble. When the bird's talons slashed across her arm, they left only faint scratches, quickly vanishing as her body healed.

"Your Inspect skill will show you the ranks," she continued, unfazed. "But be careful—fighting above your rank can be fatal."

The bird screeched, recovering from the blow, and launched itself at her again. This time, Demi spoke an incantation, her voice low and resonant. Flames erupted from her outstretched hand, a blazing torrent of ruby fire that engulfed the creature. Its metallic feathers warped and melted under the searing heat, its agonized screeches filling the air.

The firestorm subsided, leaving the bird charred and motionless on the ground. Demi exhaled softly, her sword gleaming in the fading light.

"To answer your question," she finally said, turning to the student, "I'm Silver One. Two Words of Power at the Rank One. Final year at M.O.U."

With a swift, elegant motion, she decapitated the creature, its head rolling to the forest floor. Jace's Inspect skill flickered to life, the familiar text scrolling before his eyes.

Creature Inspection Success
    Stymphalian Bird: Bronze 5
    Strengths: Metallic feathers, toxic dung, flock hunter.
    Weaknesses: Unknown.

The forest fell silent, save for the hushed murmurs of the students. But the silence was short-lived. From the shadows, more birds emerged—two, then four, their eyes burning with fury. The screeching began again, louder, more piercing than before. Jace clamped his hands over his ears, wincing as the noise battered against him.

Demi, her breath steady despite the strain, retreated toward the boundary. The birds slammed into the barrier, their beaks and claws scratching furiously against it, but they couldn't break through.

With a graceful bow, Demi turned to the group. "Lesson one," she said, her voice carrying over the chaotic noise, "know when to fight... and when to run."

She spun on her heel and began hiking up the hill, the students trailing behind her, too stunned to do anything but follow.

Chapter 8
Calibrate Good Times

An hour passed, and the pace slowed, students panting and sweating.

Couldn't they have put in an elevator or something? Jace thought, frustration bubbling up.

"How much further?" asked a stout dwarf, wiping his brow.

"Not too far now," Demi replied, her voice carrying an edge of determination.

"Zone two includes a lot of the surrounding areas—cabins, homes, farms, and so on. This is where most of the locals live. There are monsters there too, but they're lower tier, rarely exceeding Bronze Two Stars. It's a place where newer Travelers and Terra Mythica Citizens can get accustomed to dealing with threats without constantly dying."

"And then there's zone one, the inner campus. That's where you're safe from everything except your own stupidity. The magic protections are strongest there, ensuring that even the most novice of students can study and train without constant fear of attack."

Jace exchanged glances with Dex and Ell, who walked beside him. Dex seemed unfazed by the climb, while Ell looked equally determined despite the strain.

"Seen Alice around?" Jace scanned the group but saw no sign of her.

"Not since the ship," Dex replied.

As they continued, Jace took in the diverse array of students. A short, graceful woman with lavender eyes and delicate wings folded against her back caught his eye. Nearby, a young man with horns and a mischievous smile chatted animatedly with a group of centaurs. The diversity was astonishing, making Jace feel both a part of something extraordinary and incredibly small. Surprisingly, though, amidst the array of magical creatures, most were entirely human.

As they continued their walk, Jace couldn't help but notice the sheer number of humans in their group. He turned to Dex, curiosity getting the better of him. "Hey, Dex, why are there so many humans here? I mean, I know there are a lot of different races in Terra Mythica, but I thought more people would choose something more... magical."

Dex chuckled and shrugged. "It's all part of the System, man. The System analyzes you, tries to predict what would cause the least amount of mental difficulties, the least amount of shock to your system. Some people are just wired differently, you know? Everyone gets offered the races the System thinks they'll handle best. And if it's not sure, it errs on the side of caution and offers human."

Jace nodded, thinking it over. "Makes sense, I guess."

His his device was originally set up for someone else, after all. Maybe human was the best the System could do with the conflicting DNA.

Dex glanced at him, a thoughtful expression on his face. "I've heard stories from my dad—back in the early days, people could choose all sorts of races, but then their minds started rejecting them. Like, they couldn't handle the change and started pushing back. It caused a lot of problems, so the System adapted. No one really knows how it decides, but I think it built in some extra safety measures."

"Is that why you're human too?" Jace asked, curious.

"Whoo, speak for yourself." He reached up, pulling back a tuft of his messy hair to reveal a slight peak to his ear, barely noticeable unless you knew to look for it. "One-tenth elf."

Jace raised an eyebrow. "One-tenth?"

Before Dex could answer, Ell, who had been walking just ahead of them, turned around with a playful smirk. "Is he showing off his ears again? Dex, you had elf as an option and you chose one-tenth? Such a waste."

Dex grinned, unbothered by the jab. "And lose some of my rugged charm? No, thank you. One-tenth is just enough to have that sort of elven flavor. And it's not like you went with another race."

Ell's eyes sparkled mischievously. "And what makes you think I haven't? Hmmm? Are you so sure?"

Dex stopped dead in his tracks, staring at her. Jace and Ell kept walking until Dex hurried to catch up, his curiosity piqued. "Wait, you got a human variant race? Which one?" He peered at her closely, searching for any telltale signs.

Ell just gave him a mysterious smile. "Wouldn't you like to know?"

For the next several minutes, Dex pestered her with questions, trying to get her to reveal her race. Jace watched the exchange with amusement, eventually deciding that Ell was likely just messing with Dex. Still, a small part of him wondered if there was more to her than met the eye.

Demi led them through a dense thicket that opened onto a plateau. "Here we are," she said, waving them forward.

They were greeted by the sight of ancient ruins. Up close, the grand vision of Olympus University dissolved into disappointment and confusion. The once-majestic structure looked like a decaying relic. Marble columns lay in shattered heaps, their intricate carvings worn and weathered by time.

The grand arches that should have framed a gateway to knowledge and power now sagged under the weight of years, their beauty marred by cracks and missing pieces. What remained of the statues and stones were eroded beyond recognition, mere shadows of their former glory. The stone pathways were overgrown with weeds and moss, hinting at long years of neglect.

Jace's heart sank. This hardly seemed like a place deserving of the title of the top tutorial university in Terra Mythica. The awe and excitement he had felt moments before were replaced by a gnawing sense of disillusionment. How could this be the renowned Mount Olympus University?

The other students apparently shared his sentiment, their faces reflecting a mix of confusion and disappointment. Whispers of disbelief and frustration filled the air as they took in the dilapidated state of the ruins. Some kicked at the stones in frustration, while others exchanged worried glances, wondering if they had made a mistake.

Jace glanced at Ell, who looked equally bewildered. "This can't be it," she muttered, her voice tinged with disbelief. "There must be some kind of mistake."

Dex tried to lighten the mood with a forced grin. "Maybe the budget's been tight. Can't judge a book by its cover, or a school by its lack of a roof, huh?"

The reality of the situation weighed heavily on all of them. The grandeur and magic they had anticipated seemed to have vanished, replaced by the stark reality of the crumbling ruins.

Demi seemed to notice the mood shift and addressed the group. "Not what you thought it would be? Well, too bad! You are free to turn back now if you so choose. If you wish to proceed, you must follow my lead exactly. Watch closely."

She then held up a silver User Interface stone, its surface gleaming under the dim light. "Activate your stones," she instructed. The students followed suit, their stones emitting a soft, silvery glow.

Jace took the stone from his pocket and felt a mental pull. He stopped resisting and allowed a trickle of his own energy to flow into it. The stone hummed in response.

"Now, mimic my movements," Demi continued, her tone serious. She performed an intricate sequence: stepping left, then right, tapping the stone twice, closing one eye, walking backward, waving it in a figure eight in the air, and turning three times. Finally, she closed her eyes, counted to ten, and opened them again.

The students mimicked her, albeit awkwardly. Half of them bumped into the others, their movements disjointed and hesitant. The seniors visibly tried not to laugh. Jace hesitated, feeling a flush of self-consciousness, but then followed suit. Left, right, tap the stone twice, close one eye, walk backward, figure eight, turn three times, close both eyes, open them.

Demi's laughter bubbled up as Jace heard the frustrated murmurs from his fellow first years. When he finished the sequence and opened his eyes, nothing had changed. Demi watched, her eyes sparkling with a playful glint, and a soft giggle escaped her lips.

"I was just messing with you," she said, her voice light with amusement. She waved the stone with a casual flick of her wrist. "This is all it takes to let you in." She murmured a phrase into the silver stone, then gave it a casual flick. The stone glowed softly, and a moment later, all the students' stones lit up in unison. "Access granted."

The silver stone in his hand now glowed brilliantly before it dissolved into a fine dust that latched onto his skin, seeping into his pores. He felt a surge of energy flood through him and heard gasps from the crowd as they experienced the same. A powerful force burst from his skin as a light erupted from his eyes, making him feel more alive than ever before.

As the energy settled down into a soft glow inside of him, a notification appeared, glowing with a white light on a faint blue screen.

Calibration Process Complete

You have completed the calibration and full immersion process. Welcome to Terra Mythica.

Current Realm Access Permission: Tutorial, Mount Olympus University, Terra Mythica.

Complete the tutorial and Realm Quests to unlock additional features and Realms.

For a full list of System commands, please select Help.

For System interface and HUD controls, select Display.

For all other inquiries, please see your User Manual.

Jace tried to look away, but the prompt followed his gaze, blurring the background. This one was different—more real, more solid—since the calibration process had finished. He'd need to explore the [User Interface] options in more detail later, when he had some time alone.

How do you close this thing? The prompt vanished instantly. *Okay, still mental commands. Nice.*

The mental commands felt different now, more intuitive. He didn't need to think the words, just feel what he wanted, and it happened.

The ancient ruins shimmered and shifted before Jace's eyes, transforming from decayed remnants into a breathtaking spectacle of magic. It must have been some sort of illusion magic, because now the stone columns rose tall and pristine, as if freshly carved from the finest marble.

The crumbling pathways and broken sculptures reversed their decay, each piece returning to its rightful place with a soft, ethereal glow. And now the air hummed with an ancient power, filling Jace with awe and reverence.

Still chuckling at her own prank, Demi grinned as the students marveled at the now majestic-looking campus.

There were a few continued mutterings in response to her practical joke, but mostly everyone was preoccupied with the options of the now unlocked interface.

The group moved forward, the path now clear and defined. Intricate carvings on the columns depicted epic battles, and symbols etched into the pathways glowed faintly with residual magic. The ruins morphed into a magnificent Grecian structure, glowing with golden light.

Majestic statues of gods and heroes appeared, standing in solemn guard. The marble gleamed, reflecting the late afternoon sky. Runes on the stone columns pulsed with energy, casting a magical aura over the scene. Fountains sprang to life, crystal-clear waters cascading down in harmony. Lush gardens bloomed in verdant colors. The structures grew around them, forming a sprawling temple complex.

Ell's eyes sparkled with wonder. "This is incredible," she whispered.

Dex was speechless. Another gasp went through the crowd as the sky dimmed behind a total eclipse, casting a hush over the scene. Then, an explosion of color lit up the sky, dazzling fire and magic arcing above the temple. Brilliant bursts of red and gold showered down like molten stars, illuminating the ancient marble and intricate reliefs. The temple pulsed with vibrant energy, its towering columns glowing in the beginnings of twilight.

A series of rapid-fire explosions followed, each more spectacular than the last. Blue, green, and violet streaks of light twisted and danced, forming magical symbols that hovered before dissolving into glittering sparks. Smoke of different colors billowed from strategic points, blending hues into a mesmerizing tapestry, catching the fireworks' light.

The show reached a crescendo. A giant phoenix made of golden fire soared above the temple, its wings spreading wide, shimmering with colors. It swooped and dived before disintegrating into a thousand glittering fragments. The grand finale began with the sky erupting into a symphony of light and color. Silver comets shot upwards, leaving trails of sparkling stardust, while enormous blooms of multicolored light blossomed and faded. As the last sparks faded, the crowd erupted into applause.

Jace stood spellbound. The campus spread out before them, a blend of nature and ancient architecture. Towers and spires reached towards the sky, connected by stone bridges over misty valleys. Jace took a deep breath, feeling the crisp air. The eclipse passed, and the world was again basked in the warm light of the sun.

"Alright, let's keep moving," Demi urged. The path leveled out, making the walk less strenuous. They passed through groves of ancient trees, their branches forming natural archways. Questions and conversations filled the air as the students relaxed. Jace overheard discussions about classes, the best places to eat on campus, and rumors of hidden secrets.

As they neared the main gates, the path widened. Large marble pillars flanked the entrance, each carved with intricate designs depicting scenes from myth and legend.

"Welcome to Olympus University," Demi announced as they stepped through the gates. "This is where your journey truly begins. The climb may be difficult, but the adventure is worth it."

Ell nudged Jace, her eyes wide with excitement. Jace smiled in return.

Chapter 9
Did you just say "gulp"?

J ace and the rest of the "newbies", as Ell called them, were guided through the expansive grounds of M.O.U. by senior students. They meandered through lush gardens, passed under stone archways, and strolled by bubbling fountains. Statues of Greek gods and heroes stood sentinel along the paths, each one a masterpiece radiating power. Jace could have sworn one statue adjusted its gaze as they walked by. The sunlight, freed from the eclipse, filtered through the leaves of ancient olive trees, casting dappled shadows on the marble paths. As sunset approached, the air was rich and filled with the scent of blooming flowers and the distant hum of magic.

The main lecture hall was a colossal structure with towering columns. Massive bronze doors swung open to reveal a vast ceiling painted with murals of legendary battles and chandeliers of crystal.

The students filed into the hall, finding seats on polished wooden benches facing a large raised platform. The walls were lined with bookshelves filled with ancient tomes, and the air carried the faint scent of parchment and old leather. Jace sat with Ell and Dex, his eyes wide with amazement.

The hall buzzed with excited murmurs that quickly hushed as a figure stepped onto the platform. The man was tall and imposing, with a stern expression, green eyes, and neat black hair. He wore a flowing robe of deep blue, embroidered with silver runes that glowed faintly.

"Welcome, new students," his voice resonating through the grand hall. "My name is Archmage Theon Laviette and I am honored to welcome you to Mount Olympus University - a beacon of knowledge and magic. Here, you will be challenged, tested, and, if worthy, become part of a legacy that spans millennia."

He raised his hand, and a shimmering projection of the cosmos, stars, and swirling galaxies whooshed above them. The hall fell silent, eyes wide with wonder. "Before the beginning, there was the Infinite Potential, the Great Prismata, and the Eternal Void. Each was bound to the other in an endless struggle.

Then the First Word was spoken, a light in the eternal darkness. And thus the first Affinity was born. As the light shone through the burgeoning universe, it struck the Great Prismata, a prismatic force of endless endurance.

The First Word's boundless light fractured into eternity, separated by the Prismata. The fragments became life, magic, and the many Words of Power we use today. The force was so great that Prismata itself was shattered, scattering its shards across all reality, creating time, space, and energy. This union created the universe as we know it today, and thus the Eternal Void was defeated, and our story began."

Theon gestured to a table where six glowing crystals lay. "The Words of Power are the breath of the universe, each a thread in the tapestry of existence. From mundane words spoken in everyday life to transcendent, world-altering ranks, each carries a unique affinity, shaped by the caster's alignment and Shard."

He picked up a sapphire crystal, its blue light reflecting in his eyes. "Our Prismata Shards focus and amplify our mana, allowing us to channel Words of Power with precision. By the end of your first year, you will be expected to reach your Second Star in at least one Affinity and gain proficiency with your attuned Shard. This Shard will be your magical anchor, a lifelong companion."

The students exchanged glances, whispers of excitement and anxiety flitting through the hall. Theon's eyes softened as he continued, "Your time here isn't just about learning magic or gaining power. It's about discovering who you are, forging bonds that will last a lifetime, and understanding the true nature of power and responsibility. Your journey here will be shaped by the choices you make along the way."

Theon continued, "Now, let me introduce the High Council Professors."

A towering centaur rose, his presence both imposing and magnetic, muscles rippling under his skin with every movement. "Professor Orion Blackwood, Master of Affinities." Orion surveyed the students with a slight bow, his sharp, calculating eyes glinting beneath a furrowed brow, the click of his hooves echoing in the hall.

He then gestured to an elderly man with a long, flowing beard and eyes that twinkled with curiosity, his robes whispering with every movement. "Professor Dranice Thorne, Master of Games." Dranice's hands moved with a subtle grace.

Beside Dranice stood a petite woman with a gaze that seemed to pierce through reality, her presence a strange blend of serenity and disquiet. "Professor Tanner Frost, Master of Shards." Tanner's intense eyes and the way she held herself spoke volumes, as if she were both a gentle breeze and a brewing storm.

Finally, a burly cyclops stepped forward, his single eye gleaming with determination, his skin rough like ancient stone. "Professor Brutus Ironclad, Master of Artifacts and Alchemy."

"Now, Society Presidents, step forward."

A group of twelve Senior students, their robes adorned with various gods' emblems, moved to the front and faced the new arrivals. Theon's eyes scanned the crowd.

"You will be assigned to a Society aligning with your chosen deity and natural affinities. For instance," he said, pointing to a student with an owl emblem, "the Society of Athena for wisdom and strategy." Another student, with a spear and shield emblem, "the Society of Ares for strength and combat." And a third, with wings on their robe, "the Society of Hermes for speed and cunning."

Theon's gaze swept over the students once more. "After tonight, you will eat with your Society, you will practice with your society, and you will compete alongside your society in the Winter Olympian Games, occurring at the end of each year, showcasing the progress of the best and brightest of each society.

Theon's gaze grew sharp, his voice carrying an unyielding authority. "Our mission here is more than mere education. We are the keepers of order, the defenders against the encroaching darkness. Each of you carries a piece of that responsibility."

He paused, his words hanging heavy in the air. "Some of you come from illustrious academies and noble upbringings, while others hail from humble beginnings. No matter your origin, I expect greatness from each of you."

His eyes bore into Jace's for a brief, intense moment, a silent challenge, before he swept his gaze over the assembly.

"With that, I wish you a very warm welcome. May you die and be reborn in the fiery crucible of your hero's journey."

As Theon stepped down, applause erupted.

Jace leaned toward Dex. "The what of the what?"

Dex just shrugged.

As the applause died down, the grand hall was transformed, tables laden with an opulent feast appearing by magic. Platters overflowed with roasted meats, vibrant vegetables, breads, and stews under the soft glow of enchanted chandeliers.

Jace filled his plate and took a bite, but to his surprise, the flavors were disappointingly bland. The roast lacked seasoning, the vegetables were insipid, and even the fruits seemed devoid of their natural sweetness. It was as if the feast was a mere illusion, promising more than it could deliver.

Ell, sitting beside him, marveled at their surroundings. "This place is incredible, isn't it? The grandeur, the magic... It's like a dream."

Dex, seated across the table, scoffed. "With all the money poured into this place, you'd think they could afford a little salt. But hey, food is food." He took another bite, grimacing slightly but continuing to eat.

Once the meal was finished, the next transformation was just as swift. The hall was cleared with a wave of Theon's hand, the tables vanishing as quickly as they had appeared. The students were ushered outside into the courtyard, the cool night air a welcome contrast to the warmth of the hall.

Under a canopy of stars, Jace glanced around at his fellow students, feeling a mix of anticipation and uncertainty. The journey had only just begun, and already the path ahead seemed as mysterious as the night sky above.

Senior students distributed maps that outlined the sprawling campus.

As Jace accepted his, a system notification appeared.

Item Acquired
    Basic Map of Mount Olympus University
    Would you like to transcribe to Traveler's Handbook?
    Yes | No

Jace chose to accept. The handbook materialized before him, hovering in mid-air. Beside it, the map sprang forth. Suddenly, in a flash of light, the map ignited, bursting into flames. Jace instinctively jumped back.

For a moment, the pages remained blank, and worry creased his brow. But then, the handbook gently floated down, settling into his hands. As he watched, intricate lines began to trace themselves across the map page, forming a detailed illustration.

The entire campus unfolded before him, far larger and more complex than he had imagined. It was a sprawling labyrinth of buildings, pathways, and layers upon layers of structure. There were numerous stores and facilities stretching out in every direction. The depth and intricacy of the map revealed a vast, multi-level university, teeming with hidden corners and secrets yet to be discovered.

"Where are our dorms?" Jace asked, scanning the intricate map.

The campus sprawled before him, divided into twelve distinct sections, each dedicated to a different Society aligned with the gods of Olympus. Every section boasted its own dormitories and lecture halls, forming a vibrant mosaic of academic life. At the heart of the campus lay a vast courtyard, anchored by the imposing Grand Hall and a bustling communal mess hall.

A winding path meandered through the landscape, leading to Hero's Shrine, a place steeped in legend, and the Olympus Promenade, a lively hub teeming with eclectic shops and eateries. To the east, an expansive area marked only as "The Games" hinted at epic competitions and grand spectacles waiting to unfold.

Jace noted a few prominent sections on the map: Zeus' Hall, dominating the skyline with its towering structures gleaming with a golden hue, symbolized the king of the gods. Nearby, Athena's Domain stood sleek and elegant, with architecture that reflected wisdom and strategic prowess, featuring numerous libraries and study halls. Further on, Poseidon's Quarter was located near a serene artificial lake, its buildings adorned with intricate water motifs and aquatic gardens. The campus seemed like a realm of myths brought to life, each corner brimming with the essence of its divine patron.

Ell shook her head, a knowing smile playing on her lips. "Oh, we aren't going to the dorms. We need to go to the Oracle Trial, where we get invited into a Society."

Jace's stomach lurched. The Oracle Trial? Already?

"But before that, we have a date with Archmage Theon," Dex added.

Quest Update
    Report to the Archmage
    See him immediately after the welcoming ceremony.
    Mandatory: This quest cannot be rejected.
    That means now.

A glowing line appeared on the map, directing them to the executive section of the campus and the Archmage's office. As Jace looked up, he saw Dex receiving the same notification.

    "Gulp," he whispered.

    "Did you just say 'gulp'?" Jace asked.

    "Yes, yes I did."

Chapter 10
Asking a Pegasus Not to Fly

The architecture grew increasingly elaborate as they neared the faculty offices. Gold and silver filigree adorned the doorways. The atmosphere shifted to a hushed reverence, a solemn acknowledgment of the power within the Archmage's office.

Massive double doors, intricately carved with scenes of cosmic phenomena and magical rites, loomed before them. They swung open silently at their approach, revealing a vast, high-ceilinged office. Shelves lined the walls, brimming with ancient tomes and glowing artifacts that hummed with untold power.

A satyr, legs crossed as he read a thick, dusty tome, barely glanced up. His desk, polished to a sheen, bore a plaque reading "Assistant to the Archmage."

"You can wait here," the satyr said, his voice gruff but not unkind. "The Archmage is finishing with someone. I am the Assistant Archmage."

Dex looked down at the plaque. "Says here, Assistant TO the Archmage."

"Same difference." The satyr said dismissively. They both sat, deciding not to push it.

Marcus stormed out, a sneer twisting his lips before disappearing down the hall.

"Dude, what's that guy's problem?" Jace asked.

Dex sighed, frustration tinging his voice. "Believe it or not, we were friends back at Mythos High."

Before Jace could press further, the "assistant" looked up. "You can go in now."

At the center of the room, behind a massive oak desk, sat the Arch-mage. He regarded Jace and Dex with a mixture of curiosity and intensity.

"Jace, Dex, step forward," he commanded. "I'm assuming you are smart enough to know why you're here," he began, his tone brooking no nonsense.

Dex jumped in, "We were only trying to—"

The Archmage raised a hand, silencing him. "Dex, I know your history. Your high school principal warned me about you."

Dex's face flushed. "He started it. We just—"

"Marcus is a known provocateur, this is true," the Archmage cut in, leaning forward. "But that does not excuse your actions. This is a place of learn-ing, of discipline. You must rise above petty squabbles. I have over five-thousand students to manage and a staff of four-hundred with enough bickering and problems to last me a lifetime. Please don't make me deal with yours."

Jace felt a surge of defiance, but forced himself to stay calm.

Don't cause any more trouble. Jace reminded himself. Stay under the radar.

"We understand, sir. It won't happen again."

The Archmage studied him for a long moment before nodding. "See that it doesn't. Now, I must officially ask if either of you wishes to elevate this conflict to Council Arbitration?"

Dex and Jace exchanged glances before shaking their heads. "No, sir," Jace said firmly.

"Good. Arbitration involves a lot of paperwork and headaches, and expulsion would be on the table for all three of you. Since this is a first infraction and no one wishes to escalate the issue, I will simply issue a formal reprimand to all involved. A second infraction will not be dealt with so lightly."

Before they could protest, he added with finality, "That will be all."

As they turned to leave, the Archmage spoke again. "Jace, hold back a minute. I have something to discuss with you in private."

With a concerned glance at Jace, Dex left the room, leaving him alone with the Archmage.

Theon opened a drawer and produced a small tin, its metal gleaming softly in the dim light. "Care for one?" he asked, holding out a small, or-ange-filled cookie, its delicate surface glistening with a thin layer of sugar that sparkled in the room's muted glow.

"No, thank you."

With a shrug, he bit into the cookie, a slow smile spreading as the tangy citrus filled his senses. "Suit yourself. These are a favorite of mine, straight from the Western Isles. They say the oranges there are kissed by the sun goddess herself during the harvest festival, when the air is so thick with the scent of blossoms it feels like you could drown in it. Quite the experience."

Jace nodded, his eyes roaming the room, taking in the artifacts and relics that lined the shelves. A particular piece - a small, intricately carved box—caught his attention, pulsing with faint, golden etchings. The lines moved subtly, connecting to form a cryptic poem, each line replaced by the next as he read.

"In Shadow and Light
Destiny calls
Beyond the Veil
To Face the Darkness
As the Phoenix Falls
For the Fate of All
In Infinite Eternal"

"Intriguing, is it not?" Theon's voice pulled Jace back to the present. "It's is a relic from the last great Convergence, said to contain lost memories of a long-forgotten past."

Jace leaned closer curiously. "Have you ever tried to open it?"

Theon's smile was enigmatic, his eyes glinting in the box's strange light. "I have, many times. It seems to require a magical key or a specific incantation. But, alas, some mysteries are better left undisturbed. After all, not everything that glitters is gold, as they say."

Jace frowned, sensing layers of meaning beneath his words. As their conversation continued, an uneasy feeling needled at him - a sense that the Archmage was studying him, weighing each response. There was an undercurrent here, something subtle and elusive.

The Archmage's expression softened, a hint of a smile playing on his lips. In that moment, he seemed more like an old man than the formidable figure he had been just a moment before. "Much like that box, we all have our secrets, Jace." He paused, his gaze piercing. Jace nodded slowly.

"Secrets that may be wise to keep, at least for now. There are things about you, Jace, things you do not know yourself."

Jace shifted in his chair, the leather creaking under his weight. Theon's words carried a veiled warning, one that settled uncomfortably in his stomach. "You are here by means of a scholarship. A scholarship based on tests that I personally oversaw and approved with the support of the High Council. My reputation is, to that degree, tied to your success. When your second-year entrance exams come, I expect you will excel. You know the scholarship must be renewed by exam each year?"

"Yes, I'm familiar," Jace lied, trying to maintain his composure.

"Good. I'll be keeping a close eye on you. Stay out of trouble and don't draw any undue attention to yourself."

"I'll do my best." Jace meant it.

Still, something tugged at him, beyond the veiled threats and the unsaid words. There was something else, something familiar in the Theon's eyes. It was a wild thought, but he had to ask. "Sir, are you a Traveler?"

His smile widened slightly, a glint of amusement in his eyes. "What makes you ask that?"

Jace hesitated, trying to articulate the feeling that had been gnawing at him. "It's... something I can't quite put my finger on. Travelers and Citizens, they have a different feel. It's strange. Maybe I'm reading too much into it."

The old man nodded thoughtfully. "It's true. And it is a rare perception, indeed. Have you studied your Traveler's Handbook much?"

Jace shook his head.

"Well, I suggest you do. It may offer some interesting perspectives. But yes, I am a Traveler. And I may tell you my story, but not today. What I will tell you is that it took me nearly three hundred years in Terra Mythica to achieve the title of Archmage and find any degree of acceptance among the Citizens. I am the only Traveler on official faculty, beyond an assistant. My senior staff know me and have worked with me for many years. But most here, including many of the Citizens, do not know my true origin, and I would prefer it to remain that way. Much as I am sure there are things about yourself you would prefer to remain secret."

Jace nodded, feeling the weight of his words.

Theon leaned forward, his gaze sharp and penetrating. "One more thing," he said, his voice dropping to a conspiratorial whisper. "During your fight with Marcus, something unusual happened, didn't it?"

Jace's heart pounded. He felt the memory surge, a flicker of something ancient and powerful. "I... I spoke a Word of Power. I didn't know where it came from or how, but I did."

Theon nodded slowly, his expression grave. "Words of power are not merely learned or memorized. They are discovered, often in moments of great need. A teacher may guide you, but the true understanding comes from within. Some say that words find their Speaker, choosing those who have seen or felt their very essence."

"As a Speaker, you start as a Bronze One when you learn your first Word of Power. You'll gain your second star when you improve your use of that word beyond mere reactionary skill."

"Words have two different ranks that show your Affinity with them: Scope and Proficiency. Simple Words replace simple actions but can be very effective when mastered. Like this," He extended his hand and whispered a guttural sound. It wasn't a word Jace had ever heard, if you could even call it a word. It was more of a feeling and an image put into vibration and wind, its force palpable to all who could hear it.

"More advanced Words create wider-reaching effects and can handle more difficult tasks," he said, motioning with his hand, twisting the vary air around him, before he dismissed the currents of power. "As you master Words, you gain insight into new ranks, unlocking new domains of magic. To rank up requires rigorous training and Breath or Aether cultivation."

Jace's mind swirled with confusion and fragments of the moment when he used his Word, as he tried to digest the information he was being told. "Do you remember the word you used?" Theon asked, his tone gentle yet insistent.

Jace tried to recall, but the effort made his head throb. "No," he admitted, frustration edging his voice. "I can't remember."

"Be cautious," Theon warned. "Using a Word of Power without sufficient Breath can deplete you. Different Words require different amounts of

Aether to use. Speaking a Word you do not understand can rob you of your ability to speak even at all. Push too far, and the consequences can be dire." He paused, letting the weight of silence hang in the air. "Jace, it tears at the soul, and fractures the mind. Many have gone mad for less."

Jace felt a chill settle over him. "Don't seek the Word out," the Archmage continued. "It will come to you when you are ready to speak it again. Build your strength.

Learn to manage your Breath. You won't reach the sky by jumping, but by building a tower."

Beginning with an advanced Word might seem exciting, but it is a double-edged sword. You will have to train even harder and push past your limits. We are limited by the depth of our Aether. One must grow one's lungs, so to speak."

His voice regained its pleasant, official tone. "Now, you better get going. The Oracle Trial should be starting soon. You will want to find out which Society you belong to."

The Archmage, traces of the old man vanished, now wore an air of polite formality, his gaze brooking no nonsense. He gave a curt nod, signaling the end of their meeting. Jace turned and walked out, his mind racing. As the heavy doors closed behind him, he glanced at Dex, who was waiting in the hallway.

"What did he say?" Dex asked, his curiosity barely contained.

"To keep out of trouble."

"Just that? Might as well ask a pegasus not to fly."

Jace hoped Dex was wrong, but knew this would be harder than he had thought.

Quest Update

Report to the Archmage.

Quest Complete.

You survived an encounter with the Archmage and didn't get expelled. Go you

Reward: You get to keep living a lie. Not being expelled, maimed, or dragged into the abyss is reward enough.

Chapter 11
Thirteen Banners

Jace and Dex stepped outside, joining the stream of freshmen flowing through the campus grounds. As they walked, Ell appeared beside them, seemingly out of nowhere.

"Still here, huh?" Ell said with a smirk, directing her comment at Dex. "I swear, Dex, I'm going to start a pool on how many times you can dodge getting kicked out of here before you earn your fourth star."

Dex laughed. "I'm a master of survival, Ell."

Ell grabbed Dex's arm as a surge of the crowd pushed them ahead. Jace struggled to keep up, weaving through the mass of students.

"We'll catch up with you later!" Ell called out over her shoulder as they were swept further in the current of the crowd.

Jace slowed his pace, glancing around. He looked for Alice, but she was still nowhere to be found.

The courtyard plaza was a tapestry of colors and textures, blending smooth marble tiles with rough cobblestones, all illuminated by glowing amber orbs set high in ornate lamps. The fountain at its center was a glittering spectacle, with streams of water arcing gracefully into the air and cascading down in an endless, mesmerizing cycle. Moonlight filtered through the droplets, making them shimmer like precious jewels.

But the true marvel of this fountain wasn't its size or intricate design but the statue at its heart; a magnificent sculpture of Aphrodite, carved from pure white marble. The goddess of love stood poised, leaning forward with a seductive grace, her bare breasts exposed as she washed her hair. The water flowed over her smooth, flawless form, accentuating every curve and adding a touch of ethereal beauty to her already captivating presence.

The chatter of students mixed with the gentle rustle of leaves in the breeze. Aphrodite's mischievous eyes seemed to tease the viewer with an enigmatic allure that hinted at secrets only the most daring could uncover.

As Jace looked around, he caught the eye of a woman in the distance staring in his direction. Her long, wavy hair shimmered like spun gold, and her piercing blue eyes locked onto his. She smiled, a fleeting but radiant smile that made his heart skip a beat. He tried to wave subtly, and she giggled. He could swear it sounded like wind chimes in the distance. She made a follow-me gesture with her hands. Jace couldn't believe it. He looked around quickly to make sure she was actually gesturing to him. But when he turned back, she was gone, leaving him momentarily breathless and confused.

"Nymphs, my man," a deep, masculine voice said. Jace turned, but no one was speaking to him.

"Down here," the voice insisted. Jace looked down to see a short gnome standing beside him, wearing a tall blue hat adorned with silver beads. Jace took a step back, grateful he hadn't accidentally stepped on the small figure.

The gnome grinned, revealing a set of perfectly white teeth. "Nearly impossible to catch, those nymphs. Nearly. But I'm still hopeful."

Jace blinked, trying to process what he was seeing. "Who—?"

"The name's Thistle, Society of Ares," the gnome interrupted, extending a hand.

Jace hesitantly took it, a thought striking him. "Hey, I don't mean to be rude, but are you..." He let the sentence hang for a few uncomfortable seconds, then leaned in to whisper, "real?"

Thistle laughed heartily. "You mean, do I have to take a piss when I log out? Yeah. But I'd be careful about tossing that word around. Better to use Traveler for players and Citizen for the locals. Rumor has it the AI doesn't like the real/not-real distinction. Besides, what's real, really? It's all subjective, my man."

Jace shrugged and nodded to his point. "Oh, sorry. I'll keep that in mind," Jace said.

"Don't sweat it. I made the same mistake a bunch of times in my first year. It's my second year here, but I had some... complications come up out of game last year and didn't get to advance. So, I'm taking the first year again."

Jace nodded, "I'm Jace."

"I know. It's on your name tag."

Jace looked down, startled, but saw nothing. Thistle chuckled.

"Not that type of name tag. Only the faculty can see it. I can see it because I'm one of the Faculty Aides, assigned to help the noobs." He reached out and tapped something in the air in front of Jace's chest. "Says on your profile you're here on scholarship. Gotta say, don't see too many of you around. Golden ticket winner, huh? Must have been pretty impressive on your entrance exams. Never seen a full ride before."

Jace nodded slowly, still somewhat dazed by the encounter with the nymph, when trumpets blared.

"Oh, it's about to start." Thistle looked forward.

The students gathered around the fountain. Advancing toward the centerpiece was the same girl in the purple dress who had introduced them to the grounds. Was it Demi? Jace was going to need to keep a log or something of everyone's name.

She stepped into the middle of the fountain's flowing waters, instantly drenching her from head to toe and making her dress cling to her body. She kept her face focused, seeming not to notice the effect she was having on much of the crowd. This time her voice was quiet as she leaned in to Aphrodite's ear and whispered something, like a lovers secret.

The marble figure shifted and relaxed. Aphrodite's stone lips curved into a teasing smile, and she gracefully stepped aside. The once-brimming fountain transformed as the water spiraled into a vortex, creating a mesmerizing whirlpool. Jace leaned forward, trying to get a better view, while Thistle grumbled beside him about never getting to see this part. "Be a gnome, they said. It'll be epic, they said."

"Want to get on my shoulders?" Jace offered, seeing Thistle's struggle.

Thistle hesitated, but then nodded. Jace hoisted the gnome onto his shoulders.

They watched as the vortex formed stone steps, spiraling down into the darkness below. Demi gestured for everyone to follow her, and the group began their descent.

As they walked down the winding staircase, small reliefs on the walls came alive. Thistle pointed out various figures, explaining in a hushed voice.

"These are some of the academy's alumni. Legends and heroes who once walked these halls," he said. Jace marveled at the moving reliefs, some depicting epic battles, others showing tender moments of love. One carving even showed a couple locked in a passionate embrace, their figures moving entwined.

At the bottom of the stairs, they stepped into a dimly lit hall, its shadows softened by the warm glow of amber lights that flickered gently, casting dancing patterns on the walls. The air was still and laden with the mingled scents of incense and old stone, carrying a hint of something ancient and powerful. Thirteen massive banners lined the walls, each bearing the symbol of an Olympian god, and fluttering gently, as if stirred by an unseen breeze. The hall was a tapestry of colors, each banner with a group of people standing beneath it, their attire coordinated to represent their chosen deity.

To the left, the vibrant blues of Poseidon flowed like the ocean, the students beneath it adorned in sea-green and deep blue robes, their hair decorated with shells or pearls. Next to them, the rich golds of Apollo gleamed, students in golden-yellow attire radiating warmth and confidence, their faces illuminated by an inner light.

Further along, the dark reds of Ares dominated their section, the students exuding strength and intensity, their red and black garb making them seem ready for battle. Beside them, the earthy greens and browns of Demeter's followers gave a sense of calm and growth, their simple, natural clothes reflecting a deep connection to the earth.

In the center of the hall, the white and silver of Zeus shone brightly, students standing tall and proud, their white robes flowing like storm clouds. Adjacent to them, the shimmering silvers and blues of Artemis gathered, students looking serene and focused, their attire reflecting the moonlit forests.

Nearby, the passionate reds and pinks of Aphrodite sparkled, the students' elegant clothes and accessories enhancing their natural allure.

Then there was a banner for the combined Society of Dionysus and Hestia. Its members dressed in a motley of oranges and browns, their section giving off a sense of home and hearth, juxtaposed with wine and revelry. Hermes' area buzzed with energy, students in green and yellow, their eyes bright with mischief and curiosity. The students of Hephaestus stood solidly in their section, their deep reds and bronzes reflecting a sense of craftsmanship and strength.

Finally, the deep blues and whites of Athena's followers glowed with wisdom and strategy, the students beneath the banner wearing robes that seemed to shimmer with intelligence.

Each banner had its own crowd, animated with anticipation and camaraderie. The only exception was a single banner off to the edge of the hall. It was shrouded in shadow, its fabric tattered and old, hanging limp as if forgotten by time. Jace wouldn't have noticed it except for the wide berth the rest of the students gave it when walking by. He squinted, trying to make out its details, but the amber light barely reached it. A chill ran down his spine, a sense of foreboding settling over him.

Before he could ask Thistle about it, Demi's voice rang out, calling everyone to attention.

At the far end of the hall stood a massive, ornate archway. Demi, her dress now somehow dry and pristine, reached into her robes and pulled out a glowing Ruby Shard. She placed it into a slot on the archway, causing it to hum with energy. Light burst out from the archway, runes glowing across every inch of its surface. The air seemed to inhale sharply, then popped as a shimmering event horizon of black waves formed within the arch.

"This is where you will face the Oracle," Demi called out. "Here, the gods will observe you, seeing you for who you truly are. Remember, your family, fortune, and reputation mean nothing here. You will be stripped bare before the Oracle. Perform well, and you will receive an invitation from a god or gods to join their Society. May the gods grant you favor."

Jace felt a knot tighten in his stomach as he listened. He wiped his sweaty palms on his robes, stealing glances at the other students, who seemed far more confident. The weight of his past and the expectations of his future bore down on him, making it hard to breathe. He leaned over to Thistle, whispering, "Has anyone ever not received an invitation before?"

Thistle shrugged nonchalantly. "Not that I've ever heard of, but hey, there's a first time for everything," he said, giving Jace a playful nudge. "You'll be fine. Everyone's nervous about their Oracle Trial."

Jace stood among the five hundred freshmen, feeling the weight of the moment pressing down on him. Thistle had mentioned this was a small batch for the year, yet the room buzzed with anticipation.

This was going to take some time, but once it got moving, it was surprisingly fast. Students would go up, enter the Trial and then reappear a moment after, the entire process happening in mere seconds. One by one, names were called. He watched as a girl stepped out, tears streaming down her face, and declared her alignment with Apollo, her voice trembling yet strong.

Each student came out with a different expression - some looked confused, others joyful or resolute. Some wiped tears from their faces. As they exited, they announced their name and the Society they had accepted, receiving applause from the crowd. None cheered louder than those Chosen by the same deity.

Jace watched, his heart pounding, as the unchosen group grew smaller, knowing it would soon be his turn.

"Maximus Taximus, Master of wit and speed. Chosen by Hermes." Applause followed, mingled with murmurs of admiration.

Then it was a young man. His wild curly hair and sparkling eyes exuded an infectious energy. His robes were flamboyant and colorful.

Hearing the different students introduce themselves, Jace noticed that many had chosen both a first and last name. He hadn't realized that was an option and briefly wondered if he should have done the same. But having only one name wasn't unusual; plenty of students did. It was a bit like being a single-named celebrity.

As if on cue, the next student introduced himself with just one name, making Jace feel more confident in his choice.

"Hey guys! It's Drake," he announced, flashing a huge boyish grin to the crowd. "Chosen of Dionysus. Let's party!"

The room erupted into applause, cheers, and laughter, the energy instantly lifting as Drake's infectious enthusiasm spread through the crowd.

It continued on like that for some time. People that were chosen by the same god found each other, naturally forming groups.

"Alice Candor." Demi called, the name hanging in the air. "Alice Candor." Silence. Eyes darted around. Footsteps echoed down the stairs. Candor appeared, breathless. "Here!" She steadied herself, approaching the glowing arch.

She hesitated, then stepped through. Light enveloped her, a burst of energy and sound. Emerging moments later, she seemed different.

"Alice Candor, Chosen of Harpocrates, god of silence and secrets. Under the banner of the Society of Athena."

The Society of Athena burst into applause.

Thistle leaned over. "The Societies represent the Olympian Gods. Each of the other gods has a place within the Society of an Olympian." Jace noticed that the Societies were broken into internal divisions with a small flag for each. The section Alice joined was more conservative in dress and demeanor.

When it was Marcus's turn to go, he walked with a smug grin, emerging with a blinding flash of white lightning across the arch's event horizon. He said only one word, "Zeus." The crowd broke into an uproar of applause while Marcus went to join the other followers of Zeus.

"What's the big deal?" Jace asked quietly.

Thistle whistled softly. "One of the Big Three. Super rare match. Those three are picky," he said, stretching the last word for emphasis. "Sometimes they'll go years without choosing anyone. Getting picked by a Big Three is huge. And the stat bonuses are supposedly incredible."

"Stat bonuses?" Jace asked, confused.

"Yeah, each god gives different bonuses and penalties to stats, abilities, and unique boons. The bigger the god, the more powerful and focused the boon. But that doesn't mean there aren't drawbacks. There can be. Especially if you pick a god that doesn't really benefit your desired class title. Or worse, one that protests your Shard element. Try being an Amber Shard healer and a follower of Ares. Bad match, and expect your heals to be super nerfed. But a thief and Hermes? Now, that's a perfect fit."

Jace realized he really should have studied more before diving in. He had thought he could just pick it up along the way. Now, he was discovering he was woefully unprepared. He was sure that Alex would have had this all planned out. He didn't even know what class he was going to be.

Dex went next, his mischievous grin never wavering. He emerged aligned with Hermes, the god of thieves and trickery. Ell followed, aligning with Athena, the goddess of wisdom and strategy.

The most accepting Societies appeared to be Ares, Athena, Apollo, Hermes, and Artemis. There were others, but their groups were noticeably smaller. Then there were the followers of Zeus and those of Poseidon. Jace thought back to his few years of high school. He sort of got the Jocks and the popular kids vibe from them. If this place had a homecoming, the king and queens would definitely be from one of those groups.

Startled from his reverie, he heard them repeat his name. "Jace. Please come forward."

Thistle nudged him. "That's you, bud." He gave Jace a gentle push forward.

The archway loomed above him. As he approached, the air grew thick with a palpable energy, the kind that made the hair on the back of his neck stand on end. He swallowed hard; the sound echoing in the sudden quiet. His footsteps felt heavy, each step resonating in the silent hall as if the ground itself were amplifying his presence.

The archway hummed with a low, almost hypnotic vibration, drawing him closer. Jace felt a strange mix of fear and fascination, his senses heightened to an almost painful degree. The dark light glowed intensely, casting long, ominous shadows that made it appear as though it were the mouth of some great, ancient beast.

New Quest

The Oracle's Trial

You are about to embark upon the Oracle's Trial, a test that will determine your alignment with one of the many gods. The gods are watching, evaluating your every move. Convince at least one of them to offer you their favor. No pressure.

Objective: Complete the Oracle's Trial and earn the favor of a god.

Reward: Become the Chosen of a Deity, granting access to a Society.

Failure: Fail to gain the favor of a god. Gain title - Godless and Alone and receive -500 to Reputation with all University students, faculty and alumni. Try not to think about it too much.

Warning: The choices you make here will impact your path forward. Once you accept an invitation, you cannot un-accept it without severe consequence. Good thing you are totally prepared for this and know the pros and cons of each path... oh wait.

Accept | Reject

"You got this." He whispered to himself and chose [ACCEPT].

Jace took a deep breath and stepped through the archway.

Chapter 12
Oracle's Trial

For a brief moment, Jason felt weightless, as if suspended between worlds. The air thickened and crackled with energy, a tingling sensation spreading over his skin. The world around him shifted.

When he opened his eyes, he found himself in a dark, empty chamber. "Hello?" His voice echoed across ancient, distant walls.

He squinted, trying to see anything in the darkness.

"Interesting," a soft voice drifted across the void.

Gradually, the room warmed and brightened. Jason felt a presence behind him and turned slowly to see a woman emerging from the shadows. She was draped in flowing robes that shimmered. Her fiery red hair cascaded down her back, framing a face that was both stern and amused.

"Are you the Oracle?" he asked.

She nodded, moving towards him with an otherworldly grace. Her piercing blue eyes glinting with secrets she would never tell.

"Jason," she said, her voice a melodic whisper that echoed through the chamber. "You are brave to stand before me."

Jason swallowed hard, unable to tear his gaze away from her. "I-uh," he stammered, feeling exposed under her scrutinizing eyes. "You know who I am?"

She circled him slowly. "I know much about you, Jason. More than you do, perhaps. I see fear, grief, and regret. So much regret. You carry a burden and a dream not your own."

Jason's heart ached as memories of Alex flooded his mind.

"What are you holding on to so tightly, Jason?"

She vanished, her words stretching into the now complete darkness.

As the echo of his name faded, the darkness parted, revealing a scene hauntingly familiar. Jason found himself back in the cramped, run-down apartment he had shared with his twin brother, Alex. He breathed in the smell mildew and rust, the dim light from a single flickering bulb casting long shadows on the peeling wallpaper. It was as though the past had come alive to confront him.

Jason's breath caught as he saw Alex sitting at the small kitchen table, hunched over his study materials. Despite the grim surroundings, Alex's eyes were filled with hope and determination. The sight was almost unbearable. Alex must have just gotten back from his shift at Albert's Hardware store.

Jason watched the scene unfold as his past-self stormed into the apartment, slamming the door behind him. The sound echoed loudly in the confined space, but Alex didn't flinch. He remained focused on his textbooks, unwavering in his resolve.

"Do you even hear me?" Past Jason shouted, his face flushed with anger. "Why are you always studying? It's pointless. We're never getting out of here."

Alex looked up, his eyes calm but resolute. "Jason, we have to believe in something better. We can't let this place define us."

Jason scoffed, running a hand through his hair in frustration. "Believe in what? Dreams? They don't pay the rent. We do. And barely."

Alex's gaze hardened. "This scholarship is my way out. Our way out. I'm going to make something of myself, and then I'm coming back to help this town."

Jason sneered. "You're delusional. No one cares about us. They see us as trash, and that's all we'll ever be."

Alex stood up, his chair scraping against the worn linoleum floor. "That's where you're wrong. It's not just shit and more shit all the way down. You know better than that. The good doesn't cancel out the bad, but the bad doesn't get rid of the good either."

Jason's shoulders slumped. "Why do you care so much about this town? What's the point?"

"Because it's the right thing to do," Alex replied, his voice unwavering. "They're good people. They didn't kill our foster parents. And they didn't put us back in that place. A drunk driver did that. And hating everyone isn't going to bring them back. Besides, someone has to take care of my little brother."

"You are literally five minutes older than me," Jason scowled, though his mood was slightly lighter.

"Jason, they would have wanted us to pull ourselves out. And there are good people here. Lost souls without a chance. But if we were successful, if we made something of ourselves in Terra Mythica, we could do something about it. Maybe, just maybe we could help. Even if only a little. I want to build something better. I know it's a long shot, but fuck, I gotta have hope."

Jason shook his head, tears of frustration brimming in his eyes. "And what about me? What am I supposed to do?"

"First, don't be such a little brat." Alex smiled as Jason flipped him off. "Second, join me. Study, work hard. We can both get out of here. Together. Double dragon."

Jason turned away, his voice barely a whisper. "I can't."

Alex sighed, looking at his brother with a mixture of sadness and determination. "You're not alone, bro. We can do this."

They hugged, Jason crying silently against Alex's shoulder. Alex whispered, "I miss them too."

The world went dark again.

When the light returned, two years had passed.

The seedy alleyway was dimly lit, shadows clinging to the walls like dark secrets. The world was cold and damp, making Jason's skin prickle with unease. The leader of a local gang, Rin, stepped forward, a hulking figure with a scar running down his cheek and a perpetual sneer. His eyes, cold and calculating, matched the sinister grin that never quite reached them.

"Come on, kid. You want to square things or not?"

He glanced around, noting the other faces lurking in the shadows. Their eyes followed his every move.

"Your brother has all the keys and codes for the hardware store. We just need you to get in and turn off the security. Tonight. Eight o'clock. We'll all be waiting. Don't mess this up, kid. Do it, and we'll be good."

The alleyway seemed to close in around him, the darkness deepening as Jason nodded, a reluctant agreement escaping his lips.

Jason had no intention of ever working with them, but he needed the money when times were rough. The money he and his brother made often wasn't enough, so Jason secretly paid some of their bills without him knowing. Now they were offering to wipe his debt clean if he joined them. Just one job.

That night, as the clock ticked towards eight, Jason found himself unable to go through with it. He couldn't betray his brother like that. He didn't show up to the store and instead wandered the streets aimlessly until he heard the wail of sirens in the distance.

When Jason finally made it home, he found Alex sitting at their worn kitchen table, a rare smile lighting up his face.

"No, please, not again," Jason whispered as he watched the events unfold. He stood, like a ghost in the corner, helpless as the scene played out.

"Jason," Alex called out, his voice brimming with excitement. He held up a crumpled envelope with trembling hands. "I did it! I got accepted."

Jason paused in the doorway, the weight of his guilt momentarily lifting. "Accepted? You mean—"

"Yeah," Alex interrupted, his grin widening. "The scholarship. The kit just arrived." His eyes sparkled with a mixture of relief and hope, emotions that had been scarce since their foster parents' deaths.

In the center of the table sat a sleek, silver helmet, smooth and featureless, with no buttons or visible seams. Alex ran his fingers over its polished surface, his excitement palpable.

"This is it, Jason," he said, his voice trembling with anticipation. "I can finally see a way out of this mess."

Jason managed a smile, feeling a lump form in his throat as he took in his brother's joy. "That's incredible!" This could change everything for them.

Alex's eyes lit up. "We just missed the enrollment. The next enrollment period isn't for another week and a half, and I haven't gotten the official access codes yet but... I want to try it out. Maybe there are some in-game manuals I can start on."

Jason was just as excited as him.

Alex wasted no time, positioning the helmet over his head. As soon as it touched his scalp, a soft hum filled the room and then vanished. Alex's eyes fluttered shut, his body relaxing into the chair. His breathing slowed, and for a moment, he looked serene, as if he were drifting into a deep sleep.

Jason watched, a mix of awe and trepidation coursing through him. Then, without warning, the door was violently kicked open, slamming against the wall with a deafening crash. Jason's heart leaped into his throat. "Bro!" he yelled, but Alex was already immersed in the game. Desperation surged through Jason as he ripped the helmet from Alex's head.

Alex screamed, his eyes snapping open, unfocused and glassy. For a split second, there was an odd, distant look in his eyes, as if a part of him was still elsewhere. He shook his head, trying to clear the fog, and blinked rapidly to focus on the surrounding chaos.

The gang leader, flanked by his men, stormed into the cramped apartment. Their faces were masks of rage, their eyes dark with anger. The leader's scarred face twisted into a sneer as he looked back and forth between the brothers. "Double trouble. Which of you is Jason and which is Alex?"

Without even a glance between them, they both answered, "I'm Jason."

"Real fucking cute. We just have to beat the shit out of both of you," he spat, grabbing Jason by the collar and yanking him forward.

Jason barely had time to react before the first blow landed, a sharp punch to his gut that left him gasping for air. Another punch followed, then another, each one more brutal than the last. The pain was immediate and overwhelming, radiating through his body with every strike.

"Stop it!" Alex's voice cut through the haze of pain. He lunged at Rin, trying to pull him off Jason. "Leave him alone!"

One of Rin's thugs, a wiry man with a snake tattoo winding up his neck, backhanded Alex, sending him sprawling to the floor. Alex scrambled back up, blood trickling from his lip, his eyes blazing with protective fury. "Jason, get out of here!"

"Hey, look what we've got here?" another thug said, grabbing the VR kit.

"Put that thing back, Kyle. For fuck's sake. You don't mess with Excelsior's tech," growled a hulking brute with muscles straining against his shirt.

Rin added, "Yeah, my uncle tried to steal one once. Spent the rest of his life eating through a straw. Shit will fry your brains."

The brute dropped it to the floor. He stomped on it, bending the sleek metal inward.

Alex pushed himself up again, eyes fierce with unyielding determination. "Now's your chance, Alex! Run!"

Jason tried to stand to fight, but his legs buckled under the relentless assault. He watched in horror as the gang turned their attention to Alex, their fists and feet a blur of violence. Alex fought back with everything he had, but he was outnumbered and overpowered.

"No! Stop!" Jason screamed, his voice cracking with desperation. He reached out, his fingers brushing against Alex's outstretched hand before another blow knocked him back.

Alex's cries of pain echoed through the apartment, each one tearing at Jason's heart. The gang's leader kicked Alex in the ribs, the sickening crunch of bone audible even over the chaos. Blood splattered across the linoleum floor, mingling with the dirt and grime.

"Leave him alone!" Jason's voice was a raw, anguished plea, but the gang showed no mercy.

Alex's movements grew weaker, his attempts to protect Jason faltering as the beating continued. The light in his eyes dimmed, replaced by a haunting emptiness. With one final, brutal kick to the head, Alex's body went limp, collapsing in a heap.

The gang leader wiped the blood from his knuckles, a satisfied smirk on his face. "That's what happens when you mess with us," he growled, casting a disdainful glance at Jason and starting toward him.

A loud boom shot through the room as a buckshot burst into the fridge. In the doorway stood their neighbor and owner of Albert's Hardware Goods. He was wearing a bathrobe, with a shotgun, slippers and disheveled chestnut hair. "I don't know who the fuck you are, but you have until the count of 'one' to get the fuck out of here. I won't ask again."

He fired another shot just above their heads. "One."

The gang retreated, their footsteps echoing in the silence that followed. Jason crawled to his brother's side, his vision blurred by tears. He cradled Alex's head in his lap, his hands shaking.

"Alex, no," he whispered, his voice choked with grief. "Please, don't leave me. I'm sorry. I'm so sorry."

Albert took in the gruesome sight and immediately called the police. It would take forty-five minutes before they arrived. Another ten before Alex would be taken to the ER.

The room closed in around Jason; the walls pressing in, suffocating him. The smell of blood and sweat was overwhelming, mingling with a bitter taste that filled his mouth.

The darkness enveloped him once more.

Jason now stood watching himself stand numbly in the harsh sterility of the hospital, as the fluorescent lights buzzed overhead, casting a cold glow on the floor. The rhythmic beeping of monitors mingled with distant announcements from the nurses' station created a symphony of clinical sounds.

He stood at the threshold of a hospital room, his heart heavy. Inside, his brother lay motionless, a tangle of tubes and wires connecting him to life-support machines. His pale face was a stark contrast to the vibrant person he once knew, eyes closed in an unending sleep, the gentle rise and fall of his chest the only indication of life.

A doctor approached, clipboard in hand, his expression a blend of sympathy and resignation. "Your brother's condition is... beyond what we can manage here," he said, hesitating. "The Stasis System will keep him alive, but without advanced tech intervention... he will never wake up." The advanced treatment would cost 800,000 credits.

Jason recalled the holos of the sky turning a sickly orange after the Great War, the air heavy with the acrid smell of burning cities. The relentless famine that followed eroded communities, leaving behind only husks of what once were thriving towns.

The war had been far worse than anyone could have imagined, nearly wiping away the 20 billion people on Earth. Famine struck next, devastating the survivors. Many good-hearted individuals poured their fortunes into relief efforts, but when that proved insufficient, governments turned to the largest industries and tycoons, taxing them heavily with massive fines and penalties.

At first, the tycoons managed to survive and adapt, but soon even their resources were depleted. Businesses collapsed, poverty swept the globe, and life deteriorated for everyone. The wealthiest, with their remaining fortunes reduced to mere pittance, went into hiding, trying to preserve what little they had left for their families.

Crippling taxes had turned even the wealthiest families into paupers. Innovation had ground to a halt. And forty years went by in silence.

Then, the game appeared. Twenty years ago, John Rearden, a gas station worker, invented and founded Excelsior Deep Dive VR, a technology light-years ahead of anything seen before. He quickly became one of the last wealthy men on the planet, building an empire from the ashes. He started buying land, factories, and farms. They got into production again and the quality of life started to improve, subtly. It wasn't much, but it was something.

The most powerful players in the game became highly sought after, earning substantial sums for their crafting and raiding skills. In-game gold could be exchanged for real-world currency, offering a potential lifeline. There were no taxes in the game, and it became so important that real-world finances started to tie in. In the game, anyone could make a career, join a powerful guild, or become a successful artisan. The game functioned on a 42-to-1 time dilation, greatly increasing the quality of life for those who could afford access. The time dilation meant that a month's work in-game could fit into a day. And above that, it was the only place where people could live truly well.

However, people still needed to keep the real world functioning, and there were a limited number of tickets each year to join the game. Rumors spread that with enough money and influence, one could bypass the line, as many of the wealthiest had done. The rest needed to compete for scholarships or wait for the annual lottery.

People worked hard every year to earn acceptance into the game and a scholarship to one of the Tutorial Universities. Many had tried for nearly 20 years without success.

He gazed at his brother, determination hardening his resolve. If the game held the key to saving him, then into the game he would go, ready to face whatever challenges lay ahead to secure the future they both deserved. Getting in could change their lives forever.

The scene shifted to another memory. He was back in their apartment, alone. Days had passed since the attack. The gang hadn't returned. Jason assumed they were lying low, biding their time. But the damage was done. After the police left, the silence in the apartment was almost deafening. Part of him wanted Rin and his goons to come back to finish the job. Another part couldn't stomach the thought of leaving the place where he had grown up with Alex.

He sat there for days, the weight of loss pressing down on him. With no food, he survived by drinking from the dirty tap, the metallic taste of the water a bitter reminder of his helplessness.

Rent was due in a week. He had nothing. The loneliness was suffocating, each second stretching into an eternity. His mind was a whirlwind of grief and guilt.

A few days later, a knock at the door tugged Jason from his stupor. It was Albert. He stood there, a worn-out look on his face, offering Jason a place to stay. He didn't try to soothe Jason or apologize for the loss or his inability to help cover the needed medical treatment. Jason knew Albert was barely surviving on the store's meager earnings, just as trapped as the rest of them. The whole town probably didn't have enough between them to even cover the equipment needed for the operation.

Jason barely registered Albert's words. He shook his head, declining the offer. As Albert turned to leave, he handed Jason a roll of bills. "Your brother didn't pick up his last paycheck. I've added something for you." With that, he left without another word, the creak of the door closing behind him echoing in the silent room.

A few more days passed in a blur of sorrow. Then, another knock at the door. This time, it was a deliveryman, holding an envelope. Jason stared at it, uncomprehending, until the man handed it over. "Sign here," he said, his voice just another sound in the uneasy silence. Jason scrawled his name and took the envelope and returned to his bed.

He held the envelope with trembling hands. The letter inside bore the emblem of Excelsior, an intricate design that shimmered subtly in the light. He unfolded the paper.

"Dear Mr. Rolander,

Congratulations on your acceptance into Mount Olympus University.

By now, you should have received your state-of-the-art, latest edition VR kit. This kit is yours to keep and will not be reissued in case of loss or damage.

We hope you have had a chance to explore the entrance hall and get accustomed to the controls.

We thank you again for applying and were very impressed with your entrance exam results.

A world of magic and wonder awaits you.

Please find a slip inside. It has your code for entrance.

Memorize it. It will provide you with official access to Terra Mythica and Mount Olympus University."

Jason's eyes flicked to the strange slip of paper enclosed. It felt metallic to the touch. Written in neat, precise handwriting was the mental code he needed to gain entry. He read it aloud to himself, committing it to memory.

"Ducks shake hands when no one is listening to Shakespeare."

He repeated the phrase under his breath, over and over, until it was etched into his mind. This was his key, his passage to a new life—a life where his brother could be saved, and where they could both find a future worth living.

Jason headed to the local hardware store, borrowing some tools from Albert. He didn't explain why he needed them, and Albert didn't ask. With a day loan ticket in hand, he gathered a small mallet, precision screwdrivers, and clamps, knowing his hands were skilled but unfamiliar with this advanced tech.

Back in his dingy apartment bedroom, Jason carefully inspected the dented helmet. He worked methodically, easing it back into shape. Hours later, it still bore signs of damage, but he hoped it would be enough.

He remembered what Rin had said about it frying people's brains. What have I got to lose? Jason thought as he put on the helmet.

The world around him transitioned into darkness. For a moment, he feared it was broken. Then, his hands started to form in front of him, illuminated against the void.

A prompt appeared.

Welcome, Alex.

Jason quickly took the helmet off, his heart pounding. It felt like he had just seen a ghost. That night, he cried harder than he had ever cried before.

The next morning, he made a decision. If this was going to work, if he was going to use his brother's scholarship, Jason knew he needed to get out of town, far away from any trace of Rin or even Albert. Somewhere he could live in private. What he was about to do was not only highly illegal, but highly dangerous. And if anyone found out he would probably be whisked off to one of those black sites. Or something. Honestly, he had no idea what would happen if anyone found out. But he knew it wouldn't be good.

He took the money Albert had given him and purchased a one-way ticket to an obscure destination, several hours away by Excelsior Rail. Using a fake name, he hoped to bury his past and forge a new beginning.

The rail ride was long and uncomfortable, but it gave him time to think. As they passed through towns and cities, the signs of collapse were everywhere: shuttered businesses, abandoned factories, streets empty except for the occasional scavenger. With unemployment at nearly 80% worldwide, most production had ceased, and the economy had crumbled. People were starving, and desperation hung in the air like a toxic fog.

When the bullet train finally stopped, Jason stepped off into an unfamiliar town. He wandered its streets, seeking a place where he could lay low. Eventually, he found a dingy bar with a "Help Wanted" sign. The owner, a burly man with a thick beard and a perpetually furrowed brow, looked him up and down.

"Can't pay you," the owner said gruffly. "But the job comes with a room and a meal a day."

Jason nodded, relief washing over him. "Deal."

The owner extended a hand. "Name's Teddy."

"John," Jason lied, shaking Teddy's hand firmly.

"Let's get you a meal. Consider it an advance on tomorrow's work."

Teddy led him to a small, dimly lit room above the bar. It smelled of stale beer and cigarettes, a far cry from home, but it was a place to hide and try to forget. Jason threw himself into the work, taking any odd task that Teddy needed done—cleaning tables, washing dishes, unloading deliveries.

Jason worked harder, the physical labor a welcome distraction.

Days came and went, and he got into a routine. He would work the night shift, cleaning after everyone left. He would have a late breakfast and then eat the uneaten leftovers, when there were any.

He kept a countdown until the day of the official orientation at Mount Olympus University.

When the time finally arrived, it was just after his shift, and he sat alone in his room. He stared at the helmet, its faint inner light pulsing steadily.

"This was your dream, Alex," Jason murmured, his voice barely above a whisper. He reached out, his fingers brushing against the cool surface of the helmet. "I'll make you proud."

Jason steadied his breath and slipped the helmet over his head.

Tuesday, April 21st, 2251, 12:03 AM.
Initializing...

The surrounding darkness lifted, and the scene dissolved into a bright, blinding light. When it faded, Jason was back in the chamber, standing before the Oracle.

His vision blurred with tears. He no longer cared about the risks he was taking, about the borrowed identity, or the potential consequences. Let them find out. Let them take everything. He just wanted the memories to stop, but they kept coming, relentless and unforgiving.

"Do you see now?" the Oracle's voice echoed in the void, raspy and resonant. "You carry the weight of your brother's dreams. But do you truly understand the burden you bear?"

Before Jason could respond there was another voice, darker and more sinister. "Interesting," it intoned.

The shadows beside the Oracle twisted and writhed, coalescing into the form of a dark, imposing figure. His silhouette exuded an aura of quiet menace, the very air around him seeming to chill. Muscles rippled beneath his obsidian-black robes, each movement as precise and deliberate as a predator stalking its prey. His face was a mask of stern resolve, carved from the very essence of darkness, revealing nothing of the thoughts that churned behind those cold, calculating eyes. Every sound muted, every movement stilled.

His gaze was piercing, two burning embers in the shadows, devoid of warmth or mercy. The weight of his presence pressed down on the room. The atmosphere grew heavier, the shadows around him deepening, as if they were drawn to the gravity of his presence. The figure's aura was one of unyielding authority, a stark contrast to the curious light of the Oracle.

"Oh?" The female voice asked. "Could he befit your domain? You are ever so... prudent with your invitations."

"Perhaps," the dark figure mused, his tone filled with a dangerous curiosity. "Perhaps."

The dark presence loomed closer. "You think you can handle this burden?" it hissed. "You think you are worthy?"

Jason stood tall, his heart filled with a newfound resolve and fury at all the personal intrusions. This was just a game. And fuck them if they thought they could put him in his place. Fuck them for making it so damn hard to climb to success. He would do it just to spite them.

"I know I'm worthy," he said firmly. "And I won't let you or anything stand in my way."

Jason thought he almost caught the remnants of a smile on the shadowy face as it vanished from the room.

"And the rest of you?" The Oracle spoke, looking off into the middle distance of the dark. "He could be a worthy choice for many of you."

She paused, as if listening to someone speak, and nodded somberly. "I see. Very well then."

She turned back to Jason. Her look was soft, and her eyes hid something more. Sympathy? Hope?

"The choice is yours, Jason. Good luck."

With that she vanished, leaving Jason alone with a short prompt in his view.

Quest Update
    The Oracle's Trial
    You have received the favor of a god. I knew you had it in you.
    You have been invited to follow the following deities - Hades.
    You have no other invitations.
    Would you like to align with - Hades?
    Accept | Reject

Jason started at the prompt for a long moment. "What the...?"

Chapter 13
The Fields Below

J ace stumbled out of the chamber, his vision still blurred by the intensity of
the experience. The hall buzzed with a mix of whispers and murmurs. Every
gaze felt like a needle piercing his skin, a sharp reminder of the weight of his
revelation.

"Jace," a voice broke through the haze, snapping him back to reality. It
was Demi. Her expression was unreadable, a mask of calm amidst the storm of
reactions. "State your name and the god who chose you."

Jace hesitated. The lingering chill of the dark presence from the trial
clung to him, its cold eyes seeming to watch from the shadows. He drew in a
long breath, steadying himself. "Uh, Jace. Society of Hades."

A hush fell over the crowd. The weight of a thousand unspoken words
pressed down on him, making it hard to breathe. Their silent whispers were
drops of dismay, lost in an ocean of shocked surprise. Then, from the back, a
single voice shattered the stillness. "Hell yeah! That's my boy!" Dex cheered, his
voice a defiant note in the symphony of shock. He clapped loudly, a broad grin
spreading across his face.

The applause that rose was scattered and hesitant. The once tattered
and shadowed banner of Hades suddenly flashed to life in a green fire, revealing
a pristine banner as large as those of Zeus and Poseidon but as black as the void.
It loomed behind him, an imposing presence. Jace walked over to stand beneath
it, feeling a mix of relief and isolation.

The rest of the night passed in a surreal blur as the remaining freshmen
were chosen. Jace couldn't tell who was chosen for what, the names and faces
blending into a haze.

And then it was over.

As the groups were shuffled off to their respective dorms, Dex called
out over her shoulder. "Hey, there's a Society orientation tonight for each of us.

We should definitely meet up after!" His words were swallowed by the crowd as they merged into the throng of students, leaving Jace alone with his map and the weight of his new destiny.

Jace thought it was strange to have an orientation so late; it must be nearing midnight. His vision was already a little blurry from tiredness.

He wandered the campus in a daze. Sometimes it felt good to be alone for a moment—to think, to gather himself from what he had felt. But everywhere he went, he felt watched, judged. Whispers trailed in his wake, eyes lingering a fraction too long.

As he turned a corner, he bumped into someone, nearly knocking them over. "Watch it," he snapped, the words out before he could stop himself. The startled student, a girl with wide eyes and a stack of books, looked up at him in surprise.

"Sorry," she mumbled, stepping back.

Jace's face flushed with shame. "No, I'm sorry. That was rude. I was just, somewhere else."

She nodded, offering a small smile before hurrying away.

Man, was I always this grumpy? He thought.

His tiredness gnawed at him, prompting him to look for his dorm. Where was he going to sleep? Where even was the Hades Society? He opened his Traveler's Handbook and flipped to the map. A new section of the map appeared, a line drawn from his current location to his destination.

He glanced down at the parchment, the inked lines and symbols guiding him toward the section marked Hades' Fields Below, situated adjacent to the catacombs of the Campus. The path led him through the grandiose halls of Mount Olympus University, past bustling common areas and ornate courtyards, until he stood before an ancient, weathered door marked with the symbol of his Society, a two-pronged scepter entwined with spectral flames.

Taking a deep breath, Jace pushed on the door. It resisted him so he shoved harder, feeling immediately fatigued by the exertion.

Was I always this weak? He wondered.

At last, the door gave way and opened, its hinges groaning in protest. The sound reverberated through the dimly lit passage beyond. He stepped inside; the door groaned shut behind him. He fumbled with the map, its inked lines faintly glowing, guiding him down a narrow staircase. Each step creaked ominously underfoot, the air growing colder and mustier the deeper he descended.

Cobwebs brushed against his face, their sticky threads clinging to his skin. He swept them aside with a grimace, feeling the cold grit of ancient dust. The walls, rough under his fingertips, were worn and cracked with age. Faint glimmers of ancient runes peeked through layers of grime, their light pulsing faintly as if breathing.

A flicker of light caught his eye. He turned, noticing a faint, ethereal glow emanating from a hidden alcove. Stepping closer, he pushed aside the heavy, dust-covered curtain that concealed it.

The alcove opened into a small, hidden grotto, bathed in a soft, otherworldly light. Vines adorned with glowing flowers draped from the ceiling, their petals shimmering with an inner radiance. A small, clear pool of water reflected the enchanting scene, creating a magical atmosphere. It was a stark contrast to the rest of the dreary dorm.

Jace marveled at the beauty hidden within the darkness. Exploring further, he realized just how ancient and forgotten the Below was. The labyrinthine passages twisted and turned, often leading to dead ends or areas that seemed to have no purpose. It was easy to get lost without a map. The only light came from occasional cracks in the ceiling or faint luminescence.

He followed the map to what was once a grand hall, now a mess of crumbling stone and tangled vines. The mess hall was vast, filled with long-abandoned tables and benches. It was easy to imagine the lively gatherings that might have once taken place here, but now it was silent, haunted by echoes of the past.

The map led him further down to a room called "The Shrine of Hades". The room grew more somber with a gothic aesthetic. As he approached, he felt a chill in the air, a palpable sense of foreboding settling in his bones.

The shrine was tucked away in a secluded grove, ancient trees with gnarled branches forming a natural archway overhead. The air was thick with the scent of damp earth and decay, every breath carrying a hint of old death. Jason hesitated at the threshold, feeling the weight of the place settle on his shoulders like a shroud.

Inside, shelves stood filled with decaying books, their spines cracked and pages yellowed with age. Jason ran his fingers along the spines, feeling the brittle leather. One book fell to the floor and immediately disintegrated into a cloud of dust.

At the heart of the room, an ornate book rested atop a pedestal, its cover embossed with ancient symbols. Unlike everything else, it looked pristine, untouched by time. He reached out and opened it. As he did, an interface materialized before his eyes, text shimmering in the air above the pages.

"Welcome, Chosen One. To access the Society Control Function, please activate your President's Token."

He checked his inventory. Nothing there.

Flipping through the pages, he read more about the Society President's role. The President was the sole representative of the deity to their Society, responsible for overseeing quests and building up the Society's influence. The position came with considerable perks, funded through fees for services. He would have to explore this more thoroughly later, but for now, exhaustion was catching up with him.

The map guided him to another set of stairs, leading down even further. He needed to find somewhere to sleep before delving deeper into the mysteries of this place.

Jason froze as he heard something move in the distance, the sound echoing through the eerie silence. His heart jumped, and he called out impulsively, "Hello?"

Great, he thought, I'm like every idiot in a horror film. Tell them exactly where you are so they can find you easier.

Jace had grown up in a world where the Techno Purge wiped out most digital content, leaving only the classics - VHS tapes, records, cassettes, books, anything that wasn't ones and zeros. New art was scarce, and distribution was a lost cause. For a long while, it was a dark age of entertainment.

The old media wore down over the years, and not everything survived. But what did survive became a refuge in those bleak days. It wasn't until Excelior Tech came along with the Grid that the world started seeing anything new.

Yet, the classics remained, and Jace knew them all. The old library, where movies, shows, and music were uploaded onto holodiscs, was his and his brother's sanctuary.

Jace knew one thing for sure - in a horror film, you never start shouting. Rookie mistake, he thought.

He stood utterly still, listening intently. Nothing. He strained to hear any sign of movement, any indication that he wasn't alone. Could have just been the cave settling in, he reasoned, though he wasn't even sure if that was a thing caves did.

The hairs on the back of his neck stood on end, and he remained on high alert, every sense heightened, as he slowly continued down the stairs.

He reminded himself that the campus was protected by magic. "Safe from everything except your own stupidity," Demi had said.

Finally, he reached the bottom, the passage opening into a small, dimly lit chamber. His dorm. Or what was supposed to be his dorm. The room was terrible, a far cry from the luxurious quarters he had imagined when first arriving to M.O.U. The walls were damp and cold, the ceiling low and suffocating. An old bed sat in the corner, its frame creaking as he tested its weight. The mattress was lumpy and worn, but it was something.

The mattress sagged under his weight, but he was too tired to care. He and Alex had lived in worse. Water dripped somewhere in the distance. As he lay there, staring up at the cracked ceiling, he couldn't help but wonder what other secrets the Below held.

The Archmage's words hung over Jace like a shroud. He pulled out his Traveler's Handbook, the leather cover worn and frayed. Flipping through its pages, he stopped at the entry for Words of Power. There, next to the word he had spoken during his fight with Marcus, was a dark smudge, the ink gray and fading as if it had been erased from existence. The page it was written upon was burned around the edges.

Jace traced his finger over the mark, the Archmage's warning echoing in his mind: "Using a word of power without sufficient Breath can deplete you. It can rob you of your ability to speak." What had he unleashed? And at what price?

"It tears at the soul and fractures the mind. Many have gone mad for less."

He turned to his Character Sheet, reading over his status, before passing out. The debuffs explained his severe exhaustion, weakness, and maybe even a bit of his mood.

Character Sheet

    Name: Jace

    Class Title: Classless

    Rank: None

    Society: Chosen of Hades - Current Members: 1

    Debuffs:

    • Cranky: You need a wittle nap.

    -1 to all stats until condition remedied.

    • Classless:

    You've got no class, kid.

    -1 to all stats until condition remedied.

    -2 to Wisdom and Intelligence.

    Attributes:

    • Strength: 9 (Currently: 7)

    • Dexterity: 11 (Currently: 9)

    • Intelligence: 12 (Currently: 9)

    • Wisdom: 11 (Currently: 8)

    • Constitution: 8 (Currently: 6)

    • Charisma: 9 (Currently: 7)

    • Luck: 10 (Currently: 8)

    • Karmic Balance: 0

    • Affinity Shards: None

    • Word of Power: None available at this time.

    Gain Hades' favor or explore Terra Mythica to unlock hidden features.

    Congratulations!

    As the only member of Society of Hades you are automatically assigned as Society President.

    Error: You do not meet the minimum requirements to be the President of a Society. Ritual Component Missing: President's Token.

    Gain required components to unlock title and privileges.

Chapter 14
Debuffs

When Jace stepped into the mess hall for breakfast the next day, he found Dex and Ell already deep in conversation, their voices carrying a morbid, conspiratorial edge. Alice sat nearby, engrossed in a book titled "Ancient Artifacts and Artificers, Volume Four by Lester Wanderbelt." The hall buzzed with activity. Satyrs with mischievous grins darted between tables, centaurs with their proud, muscular forms stood in clusters, and dryads with skin that shimmered with an ethereal glow floated gracefully past. Elves with sharp, angular features conversed animatedly, while cyclopes loomed large over their meals, and minotaurs cautiously avoided scraping their horns against the ceiling beams.

"I don't know," Dex said, his eyes narrowing. "He looks way too excited to be here. Like, first day at clown school excited."

"Trust me, he's not one of them," Ell said.

Dex's lips twisted into a sly grin as he scanned the room. "Alright, what about that guy over there?"

"Lottery winner," Ell said without missing a beat. "You really are terrible at this. Now, check out Mr. Monocle by the buffet. If he didn't arrive in a gold-plated helicopter, I'll eat my hat."

"You don't have a hat." Dex said.

"Alright, then I'll buy a hat and then eat it."

Jace strolled up, eyebrows raised. "What are you two scheming about now?"

Alice, without looking up from her book, interjected dryly, "They're playing 'Spot the Bribe.'"

Dex shrugged, mischief twinkling in his eyes. "Not that we mind. We didn't bribe anyone. But our parents? They have a knack for nudging the universe in their favor."

Ell jabbed him in the ribs. "Dex, stop being tacky. Our parents just... set us up for Mythica since birth. My mom's in PR at Excelsior. And his dad is..."

"A royal pain," Dex cut in. "We're not exactly loaded... just not exactly broke either."

Ell rolled her eyes. "Shut it, Dex. Our parents' money isn't ours. And from what I can tell, you're two wrong turns from being cut off from your family."

Dex's cheeks flushed. "Hey, I just can't dance to their stuffy tune. It's not my fault they're more into social climbing than backing my dreams."

Alice finally looked up, her gaze sharp. "They did get you here, didn't they?"

Dex and Ell shifted uncomfortably.

"Well, then, maybe show a bit more gratitude to the family footing your bills," Alice said, blushing as she went back to her book.

They all exchanged glances before continuing the conversation. Sure, Dex and Ell had a touch of privilege, but they weren't the spoiled brats one might expect. Most students here came from wealthy or influential families—children of politicians, investors, and, as he realized now, upper execs at Excelsior. Then there were those who got in on merit, like Alex, and the few who won their spots through the annual lottery.

Alice, noticing Jace's disheveled appearance, wrinkled her nose and decided to change the topic. "Did they not have showers in your dorm?" she teased. "You kinda reek."

"I don't want to talk about it." Jace said.

"You look like you've been crawling through a cemetery." Dex made crawling motions in midair.

"It's likely causing a status effect," Alice said. "Actually, take a look and tell us. For science."

Jace pulled out his Traveler's Handbook, fumbling with its worn cover.

Debuff

    Stinky

-1 to Charisma and +10% to all costs when bartering until debuff removed.

"Great," Jace muttered, "just what I needed."

Dex laughed, clapping Jace on the back making a small puff of dust explode into the air. "Hey, at least now you know. Might want to hit the showers. Maybe a change of clothes."

"Maybe burn them," Ell suggested.

Jace gave a rueful smile. "Noted."

Dex's eyes lit up with excitement. "Can we talk about what happened last night? Chosen of Hades? Dude, that was epic!" he exclaimed. "The way you came out of that trial, all badass and mysterious."

Jace forced a smile. "Why was everyone freaking out? It's not like I'm the first person to get Hades, right?"

Ell and Dex exchanged a glance. Alice looked up from her book.

"Am I the first to choose Hades?" Jace asked.

Dex shrugged. "Honestly, no clue, man. I just know that there aren't any others on campus. And when you came out, the arch went crazy. Black and green light shot out across the room. It was like something out of the Poltergeist. This is uncharted territory, my friend."

"Do you have any weird powers yet?" Alice asked.

"Um, not that I know of. Most of my character sheet is just numbers or blank spots," he pulled out his Traveler's Handbook and flipped to the Character Sheet.

"You know you can set that to digital, right? The book. You don't need to pull it out each time," Alice explained, a hint of amusement in her voice.

With Alice's guidance, Jace navigated the menu and showed him how to change the setting. "There, now you'll be able to see your notifications, map, etc. You can always switch it back."

Following her instructions, Jace watched as the interface changed to a digital display.

He toggled the setting, watching the book shimmer into a holographic prompt. After a moment, he switched it back to the book. There was something about the weight and feel of it in his hands that felt grounding. But it was good to know he could switch back and forth when needed.

He opened his Traveler's Handbook and flipped through blank pages. "Quest Log," he thought. The lines on the map vanished, replaced by a list of quests.

A Rose By Any Other Name — Complete
    Learn Something — Complete
    The Oracle's Trial — Complete
    Get Some Class — Active

Jace selected a quest marked "Active" and the words shifted.

Active Quest
    Get Some Class
    Speak with Hades in the Underworld and go through the Class Challenges to get awarded a Class Title.
    Reward: Variable.
    Failure: I don't need no help. Wander the world classless until you stumble upon one, doing everything on your own like the strong independent adventurer that you are.

Jace shared his quest with them.

"Dude, did you piss off the System or something? It's pretty snarky."

"It's not like for everyone?" Jace asked.

They all shake their heads.

Dex reads it again. "Your quest has you going directly to Hades? The rest of us just get to speak with our Society President. That's insane," Dex said, his eyes wide with disbelief.

"Yeah, I guess I kind of am my Society President, seeing as it's only me," Jace replied.

The words hung in the air, leaving Dex, Ell, and Alice staring at him. "What the hell, man? That's epic. Do you have any idea of the perks that come with being a Society President? And the amount of ladies you're going to have knocking at your door," Dex said, a mischievous grin spreading across his face.

Both Ell and Alice punched Dex simultaneously. "Seriously, Dex?" Ell chided, shaking her head.

Jace managed a wry smile. "Not like I can do much with it, though. I need something called a President's Token to gain access."

"Probably just a quest reward or something," Alice said, her voice carrying a note of encouragement that warmed him more than he cared to admit.

Ell grinned. "Who knows? Maybe we'll all benefit from having a President in our midst."

The conversation drifted off, each lost in their own thoughts. Jace contemplated the possibilities. Perhaps he could turn his new status into an opportunity, a way to secure enough credits for his brother.

A booming voice pulled him back to the present. "My boy, I knew you would make it!" A large stout man with one giant eye in the center of his forehead clapped Jace on the back with enough force to make him cough and nearly choke on his egg sandwich. "After what we saw in your scholarship trials, I knew you were a prime candidate." He spoke with a thick Scottish accent. A young woman with brown hair and an assessing look stood beside the cyclops, nodding along and taking notes in a book.

"And on your first day you get chosen by Hades." The cyclops' expression soured. "Well, I guess it had to be one of the Big Three for you, eh?"

"You know me," Jace said, hoping to strike the right balance between familiarity and nonchalance.

"Quite the understatement, my lad," the cyclops said, turning to the young woman beside him. "Did you know this man right here passed the entrance exam without dying once? And that dragon egg? I still can't get over what you did with it! I'd never seen anything like it…" He trailed off, lost in reminiscence. His assistant nudged him gently, snapping him back to the present. "Oh, this is Molly, my assistant."

When she spoke, her words seemed to not match her lips. "Follower of Hecate, Society of Hermes. Communion with the Dead." She bowed subtly to Jace.

The Master of Artifacts coughed. "I'll expect great things for you at the Winter Games. I'll be keeping my eye on you." He gave Jace a mock menacing look before breaking into a wide grin and walking away.

"Wow, you definitely made an impression during your entrance exam," Alice said, looking up from her book for the first time since he sat down. "And with the Master of Artifacts, no less. He's difficult to impress."

Jace tried to maintain a pleasant expression while he inwardly cringed. "Yup, I'm pretty impressive."

He hadn't realized the extent of what he had gotten into. He thought the tests were written or just an application form or something. But now, as he looked around, he noticed many of the teachers seemed to recognize him—or rather, recognize Alex.

You really put a lot into this, didn't you bro? He thought.

Chapter 15
Zero Divided by Zero, Carry the Zero

One teacher, a stern-looking centaur with a mane of silver hair, kept shooting Jace furtive glances, whispering to the Archmage before twisting his face like he'd just sucked on a lemon.

Ell sidled up, her voice gentle but laced with concern. "Since you're meeting Hades later today, maybe you want to change?"

Jace blinked, caught off guard. "New clothes? Shopping in-game? Totally uncharted territory."

"I thought the rugged, first-day, adventurer look was working, but..." Ell's voice trailed off, her eyes critically assessing his ensemble.

"Where do I even..."

"Check your Inventory tab," she suggested, her tone almost casual.

Jace toggled to digital, thought *inventory*, and a grid materialized before his eyes, displaying what he was wearing in each slot along with a picture of his digital self. "Is that really what I look like right now?" he muttered, dismayed. All slots were empty except for two.

Inventory
> Starting Robe: Common. Status: worn and dirty.
> Old Shoes: Common. Status: Falling apart.
> Don't know where you are going, but I think I know where you have been. Is that dirt or...?

That's rough, he thought, staring at his avatar.

Jace glanced around, suddenly hyper-aware of his tattered attire. Everyone else wore robes, dresses, and clothes in a variety of vibrant colors, draped elegantly across their forms. Sandals were common, but some sported footwear that resembled tennis shoes.

How had he not noticed this before? Was he usually this unobservant?

Hesitant due to his empty pockets and lack of funds, Jace wondered if he was even supposed to pay for breakfast. He didn't see any cashiers around and had no clue how the system worked here.

Alice, noticing his unease, stepped in to save him. "You're on a scholarship, right? Have you gotten your university bank notes yet?"

Jace shook his head.

"Oh..." Ell checked her clock. "We have time. Come on, guys, we need to get our personal newbie here squared away before classes start."

Using the map, they navigated through the labyrinthine halls to the Treasurer's Hall and Disbursements Office.

They rushed him through the dimly lit corridors to a faculty office. The room was filled with the musty scent of old parchment and ink. Behind a cluttered desk sat an ogre, Madam Crunch, as indicated by her nameplate and plaque. Her huge brown-green eyes narrowed as they approached.

Jace didn't remember ogres being part of Greek myth. Come to think of it, he had seen several races that were from other pantheons. He'd have to ask about that later.

"Can I help you?" she asked, her voice like a rusty hinge.

Dex stepped forward, attempting his most charming smile, but it only deepened her scowl. "Hello, Mrs. Crunch. Might I just say that you look lovely this fine morning."

"It's Madam Crunch," she snarled.

Dex did something between a grimace and a flinch. "I tried." He backed away.

"Charisma check failed," Ell whispered, taking his place. "This is Jace. He's on a scholarship and needs his account checked."

Madam Crunch's expression softened slightly as she tapped her keyboard with gnarled fingers. Her eyes widened a bit, surprised. "According to your records, you have a full scholarship. Don't see these too often. And you have been given the maximum allowance. Would you like to know your current balance?"

"Yes!" Jace realized he was shouting. "I mean, yes," he said more calmly. She wrote it down on a piece of paper and slid it over to him.

It read, "five hundred gold".

Dex and Ell looked at it, nodding somberly. "We can work with that," Ell said. "We'll have to be frugal."

"What does that come out to in real money?" Jace asked.

They both looked at each other, a little perplexed, before Ell spoke up. "I mean, it IS real money. What happens in Terra Mythica is just as important as outside. Often more important. But if you mean the exchange rate to out-of-game currency, ten copper is equivalent to about a credit out of game. But, in-game, ten copper buys you lunch at a food cart or local mart, while fifty copper gets you a night in a seedier hotel."

"When have you been eating at food carts and staying in seedy hotels?" Dex asked, surprised.

"Wouldn't you like to know?" She winked. "The conversion from one metal to the next is ten to one. So, ten copper is one bronze. A bronze converts to one credit out of game. Ten bronze is one silver. And ten silver is a gold. There are higher denominations, of course."

"The trick to University Bank notes," Ell continued, "is that they can only be spent at the University. Which should cover just about everything you need while here."

Jace's hopes of exchanging the gold for out-of-game credits were dashed. Still, he tucked the idea away for a rainy day. Maybe someone would trade. But how could he do it without attracting suspicion?

"So, five-hundred gold," Jace did some mental math, but it was slow coming. "That comes out to..."

He thought for a while before looking around helplessly.

"Don't worry about mental math right now. Our stats are all pretty nerfed until we get a class. Plus, you have some heavy penalties until you get cleaned up."

"Why aren't you and Dex feeling it as bad?" Jace asked, a mix of curiosity and frustration in his voice.

Ell and Dex exchanged grins, the kind that suggested they had a secret. Ell leaned in, her eyes sparkling with mischief. "We knew the nerf was coming.

You build your stats up at Mythos, but it all resets after graduation. Sure, you get a lot of practice and familiarity, but everyone starts with their base stats when they hit U. Unless," she added, with a dramatic pause, "you have some magic items that help balance things out." She pointed to her earrings. "Plus two to Intelligence."

Dex wiggled his foot, showing off a sleek shoe. "Plus one to Dexterity. I don't dress like this just to look good, you know."

Jace's face twisted in realization. "So, I have the equivalent of fifty-thousand credits?"

Ell nodded, her expression serious. "Exactly. Which means we have to be on a tight budget for the semester. Nothing too needless. That resets, right?" She looked at Madam Crunch, who nodded curtly.

Madam Crunch, clearly done with their banter, interjected, "How many notes would you like?"

Dex, ever the quick one, answered, "Fifty."

Jace nodded, and Madam Crunch retrieved fifty blank notes from a locked drawer, handing them over with a stern warning. "Don't lose these. There is a ten copper fee for each lost note that you want canceled."

The notes were thick, decorated with intricate designs of mythical creatures and enchanted symbols. They were blank, with a space for Jace to write an amount.

"These are only usable at university shops," Ell explained. "Which is fine, because that's all we'll have time for today. For outside shopping, you'll need to earn some bronze, silver, or gold through quests or profession tasks."

Dex pulled out a dagger from seemingly nowhere, causing Jace to jump. "Did you have that the whole time?" Jace blurted.

Dex grinned. "Always be prepared, my friend. Now, let me show you how these work. Just a little prick of blood." He nicked Jace's finger with the dagger. "Think of a number," he instructed. Jace did, and watched as the note transformed, now showing five copper written across the center. "This will pull the funds directly from your account."

Jace now had to balance two budgets. At least his out-of-game budget was simple: zero divided by zero, carry the zero. Even with his nerfed Intelligence, he could manage that math.

"Okay, good. That's five-hundred gold per year. Plus your tuition, which isn't cheap. Meals are automatically deducted from your account with the school. You'll need to pass a new exam to keep the scholarship next year. But you shouldn't have any trouble with that. Do well, and you should keep seeing that gold flowing. It'll be tight, but we can work with five-hundred."

For the first time in his life, Jace had any money to speak of. He would need to be careful how he spent it.

Dex's grin broadened. "You know what this means?"

"Shopping!" Dex and Ell chorused, their enthusiasm infectious.

Jace felt a knot of anxiety tightening in his stomach, but a small part of him couldn't help but feel a spark of excitement. Alice shook her head, an odd mix of amusement and resignation in her eyes.

Chapter 16
Directly Stones

The shopping district was a labyrinth of opulent storefronts, each vying for attention with gilded signs and ornate displays. The smell of fresh flowers and coffee filled the air, along with the subtle hum of enchantment. Cobblestone paths wound through the marketplace with an elegance that suggested both history and wealth. Here, students with money to spare moved about with practiced ease, their robes and attire reflecting a rank of luxury that was both beautiful and bizarre. As Jace looked, students seemed to shift in and out of existence, like walking through a hazy mirage, only to appear somewhere entirely different.

"Let's see. Ah, there it is." Ell made a beeline for a stand in the center of the plaza. A sign hung above it, reading "Directly."

A case sat below the sign, brimming with green glowing stones inscribed with runes, each one emitting a soft, bluish light. Jace eyed it skeptically.

"Shouldn't that say 'Directory'?" Jace asked.

"Why would it say that? It's a Directly." Ell picked up a stone and held it in front of her. "You just picture what you need," she explained. "Then start walking, and the shops will find you." She closed her eyes, and the stone glowed brighter. She then latched arms with Jace, Dex and Alice, and strode confidently forward.

The storefronts seemed to shift and shimmer, adjusting their positions to guide them toward their desired destination. It was a whirlwind of motion and lights and then they stopped. Jace thought he was going to be sick. That -1 to Constitution was terrible.

When he could gather himself, he discovered they were now standing in front of a line of stores that hadn't been there before. Etched names adorned the shop fronts, each sign morphing between ancient Greek and their English translations.

Would someone with a different native language see a different sign? He wondered.

As they moved through the winding paths, Jace couldn't help but be captivated by the shops they passed. Shields and armor glinted in the windows of Athena's Armory, each piece radiating strength and protection. Just beyond, Hermes' Haberdashery displayed enchanted hats and cloaks that shifted colors and whispered secrets to their would-be wearers.

Ell tugged him forward, giving him an overview of the shops he would need to visit first. At The Papyrus Scroll, shelves lined with ancient texts and mystical scrolls, their covers alive with shifting symbols. Next, Apollo's Apparel dazzled with robes and tunics in every conceivable color and fabric, each more luxurious than the last.

Hephaestus' Forge caught his eye with sparks flying as magical weapons were crafted by unseen hands. Nearby, Artemis' Arrows showcased bows and arrows with intricate designs and enchantments that pulsed with power.

The scent of freshly baked goods drew him to Dionysus' Delicacies, where a bakery displayed an array of enchanted sweets and pastries. Finally, they passed Hestia's Hearth, a cozy shop filled with home goods and charms that exuded a warm, inviting glow.

Dex and Ell treated the shopping spree like a game, their laughter and banter echoing through the rooms. They moved with the certainty of seasoned veterans, piling their arms with robes, shoes, and various other items. Jace, on the other hand, approached each transaction with caution, carefully selecting only what he needed.

Each shop was a marvel. One specialized in enchanted garments that shimmered with hidden runes, another in rare potions whose vibrant colors danced within their glass containers.

Dex and Ell made sure to do all the haggling for him, as his current debuff could cost him greatly.

The first thing they purchased was a Waist Satchel that looked suspiciously like a fanny pack. "You'll need to upgrade later, but this will do for now," Ell said.

He looked it over closely, and a notification appeared.

Item

>Waist Satchel

Description: Minor Pocket Dimension. Capable of holding up to 200 lbs. and 20 item slots. Refer to individual item descriptions to determine how many slots they require.

Caution: Overfilling the satchel may have undesirable consequences.

Definitely not a fanny pack.

They went on to pick up "the essentials", storing each in Jace's new "satchel".

Ell included a Cleansing Stone in her assortment of tools. It was a blue marble stone adorned with intricate, shimmering inscriptions. Without a word, she activated it and tossed it at Jace. As soon as he caught it, a burst of water erupted around him, practically tearing the dirt from his body. He had to grip his robes tightly to keep them from being swept away, the stone's magic unable to distinguish which parts of his robes were cloth and which were dirt. Jace didn't blame the magic, he couldn't really tell either.

They bought new robes, sandals, paper, and a list of items Alice deemed necessary.

The robes, lined with black accents and intricate designs, matched his deity. Finding the robes with Hades' symbols wasn't easy. They had to go to the back of the shop and ask the shopkeeper, who looked at them as if they were pulling a prank. "No one has bought one of these in many years," he muttered, disappearing into the back room and returning with a dusty box. "And no returns."

Everyone had specific color accents and symbols to represent their patron god. It wasn't exactly a uniform but more like personalized touches that showed their allegiance.

"You don't need to go crazy with it," Dex advised as they browsed through the selections. "Some of the Zeus boys do, but they're super into themselves. You want something understated, but still acknowledging your god. It's a balance between personal style and patronage. Don't want them thinking you're trying to hide your affiliation, but also, don't go prancing around all, 'look at me, look at me.'"

They ended up choosing a series of dark-colored robes with rich golden and black accent sashes, each laced with the symbols of Hades: a scepter and keys, snakes, a horn of plenty, white leaves, an owl, and a chariot. "We've got them all." The shopkeeper said. "Can't say I've had much use for them." They mostly opted for the scepter and keys. "Less is more," Dex commented, and Ell agreed. Could always buy more later, after he made some money in game.

Jace felt a mixture of pride and apprehension as he donned the robes, the weight of his new identity settling on his shoulders. These were the nicest things that he had ever owned and he enjoyed it, despite the fact that they were all virtual.

As they left the shop, he couldn't help but notice the curious and wary glances from other students, their eyes flicking to the symbols on his robes.

"Oh, before we forget. Here!" Ell popped up in front of Jace, her eyes sparkling with excitement. "Dex and I got you something. Consider it a welcome gift."

She handed him a cloth tote bag with "Spellbound - Scrolls & Tomes" written across it in elegant, swirling letters. Jace took the bag, feeling a mix of curiosity and gratitude.

"Thanks," he said, pulling out a book from the tote. The cover was brightly colored, featuring an animated character waving a wand. The title read: "The Verse for the Informed: A Primer on Game Mechanics. Ages 3 and Up."

Jace chuckled, flipping through the pages. "Ages three and up, huh? You think I need to start that basic?"

Alice grinned. "Hey, don't knock it until you've tried it. This book is actually really helpful. It breaks down all the game mechanics in a simple, easy-to-understand way. Plus, it's kinda fun."

Alice pointed to a section in the book. "Check this part out - explains how to rank up your skills and what to look out for. And this," she flipped a few pages, "shows you how to maximize your EXP gains. And here, it talks about the basics of Societies."

Jace nodded, appreciating their thoughtfulness. "Thanks, guys. This will definitely come in handy. I'll make time to read it soon."

They stared at him for a moment. "Read it?" Dex said. "My man, you don't need to 'read it'. Give it a quick INSPECT."

Jace did.

Item

The Verse for the Uninformed: A Primer on Universal Mechanics

A brightly colored tome designed to simplify the complexities of the Terra Mythica. Topics include such things as basic game mechanics, skill ranking, EXP usage, and other fundamentals.

Would you like to activate this book?

Yes | No

Jace chose yes. A flash of light erupted from the book, bathing him in a blinding glow. He squinted against the brightness, a sudden headache splitting through his temples, only to vanish as quickly as it came. Then a notification appeared.

You have used Skill: Absorb Knowledge

You might not read too good, but now you can skip the reading and go straight to knowing. Increase ABSORB KNOWLEDGE to improve retention from absorbed books and tackle higher-ranked subjects.

Item Consumed

The Verse for the Uninformed: A Primer on Universal Mechanics.

Ages 3 and up. Good on you for absorbing a fairly advanced tome, from your point of view.

Skill Increase

Absorb Knowledge +1

Universal Lore +1

Congratulations! You know some stuff.

Chapter 17
But Wait, There's More

J ace blinked, the information settling into his mind as if he had spent hours studying. He felt a rush of understanding, the mechanics and nuances of the game world now clear in his head.

"Whoa," he said, looking up at Dex and Ell. "That was... intense."

Alice grinned. "Told you it was helpful."

Ell glanced at Jace and said, "Now that you are sorted, Dex and I have to run some personal errands real quick. You'll be fine, right?"

Jace nodded.

"One second." Ell disappeared, returning a minute later with another Directly stone. She passed it to Jace. "Here. Meet us at the entrance in fifteen minutes. Just think 'entrance' and start walking." Without another word, Ell and Dex slipped away into the street. Alice chose this time to go buy some personal items, leaving Jace to his lonesome.

Jace wandered through the elegant streets, his eyes drifting from one opulent storefront to another. The elaborate displays were a feast for the senses, all glitz and charm. It was the kind of place where even the air felt expensive.

He opened his book to the map tab. The small location dot flickered and glitched. "You are here. Calibrating. You are here. Never mind, you are nowhere," the dot jumped erratically from one place to another before vanishing, clearly unable to function properly in the dense spatial magic of the shopping district. "Perfect," he muttered, tucking the book away. "Just what I need - a map with commitment issues."

His mind raced with a whirlwind of emotions, each one fighting for dominance. Thoughts of Alex, Hades, and a looming sense of unknown danger clashed and tangled in his mind. There were countless ways this could all go terribly wrong. The solitude haunted him. A thousand questions burned in his mind.

Lost in thought, he absently fiddled with his Directly Stone. His fingers traced the smooth surface, the motion grounding him as his mind churned. In this world of elites and secrets, Jace felt like a mere pawn in a game he didn't fully understand. And he hated feeling like a pawn.

Gradually, the bustling crowd and vibrant shop windows around him began to fade, but Jace didn't notice at first. It was subtle, like the slow dimming of lights before the main act of a show. When he finally looked up, the bright, opulent district had transformed into something darker. The colors were muted, the air colder, and the sense of wealth and luxury had been replaced by an unsettling stillness. It was as if the lively shopping district had slipped away, to be replaced by its shadow.

The once bustling street now lay eerily empty. No shoppers, no shops - only a single dark building looming ahead. It stood alone, a solitary spire twisting into the sky.

The building was tall and narrow, its facade made of ancient, weathered stone that seemed to absorb light rather than reflect it. Ivy clung to the walls like dark veins, and the windows were small, set high above the ground, their glass panes thick with grime. A wooden sign, illegible and precariously attached, swayed above the door, creaking softly in the whispering breeze. He felt inexplicably drawn to it, even as his instincts urged him to run. As if something was waiting... for him.

The door itself was heavy, constructed of dark, weathered wood reinforced with iron bands. The knocker was a grotesque face, twisted in a perpetual grimace, its eyes following Jace as he approached. The face looked like a tortured soul, a once-noble dryad with hollow eyes and a mouth frozen in a silent scream, as if eternally trapped in its metallic prison. The air around the building was thick with the scent of old, damp wood and something else - something ancient and indefinable.

Feeling a strange pull, Jace reached out but before he could touch the handle, the door creaked open. Groaning wood echoed through the silence as he entered. Shelves sagged under the weight of peculiar artifacts. Ancient tomes with cracked spines, odd trinkets glimmering in the low light, and jars filled with substances he couldn't identify lined the walls.

The dim glow from lanterns cast shadows that danced across the room, giving life to the inanimate objects. The room, like the street outside, was silent except for his footsteps.

"Hello?" Jace called out. "Anyone here?"

The wind echoed outside as if in response.

He made his way toward what he felt must be the back of the shop, passing shelves cluttered with a bizarre assortment of items. Delicate glass vials filled with strange, shimmering liquids and tarnished trinkets. A brass sundial, intricate and arcane, sat among them, its surface etched with runes that glowed faintly. Though it made little sense, as there was no sun present in the room, a shadow moved across the sundial. It lacked hours or traditional markings of time, instead displaying strange symbols. As Jace leaned closer, the shadow line moved, flickering between two images - one, a skeletal figure with a scythe, hanging upside down, and the other, a white skull wreathed in flames.

Next to the sundial, on a mostly empty shelf, sat a lone white ring.

The ring was exquisite, crafted from a bone-like metal in the design of a raven wrapping its wings around itself. Each feather was intricately detailed, glinting in the dim light. The head of the raven was turned to the side, its eye a deep, blood-red ruby that seemed to pulse with its own inner light.

Jace wasn't into jewelry much in real life, but something about this ring captivated him. The craftsmanship was astonishing; every feather meticulously carved, the raven's body crafted with perfect symmetry.

The ruby eye caught the light. Jace reached out, his fingers brushing against the cool metal. The moment he touched it, a shiver ran down his spine, and he knew this was no ordinary piece of jewelry.

He picked it up, feeling its weight in his hand. The raven seemed almost alive, the ruby eye watching him, judging him. Jace slipped it onto his finger, the metal cool against his skin. The ring fit perfectly, as if it had been made for him.

A voice startled Jace from his reverie. "Ah, you've found your way to my humble establishment," it said. Jace quickly removed the ring and set it back on the shelf. The voice belonged to the shopkeeper, a gaunt figure whose face was etched with lines of experience and calculation. His thin lips curled into a smile that never quite reached his eyes.

"This shop houses items from all over the world," the shopkeeper continued, his voice laced with a cruel sense of humor. "Artifacts of immense power and significance, each with a story to tell."

Jace's eyes fell back to the ring, and he couldn't help but ask, "What about this ring?" He tried to sound casual.

"Oh, that ring?" The shopkeeper raised an eyebrow. "I thought I had lost that one. Haven't seen it in a while. It had lost hope of finding the right buyer." He spoke as if the ring were alive, capable of feelings and desires. "Funny that you would want that ring."

"Is it magic?" Jace asked.

"It is, though, exactly what type of magic, I cannot say. Some have called it a key, others a tool, and some have even called it a weapon. It was said to have been pulled from the River Styx." Jace remembered the Styx as part of the Underworld. Perhaps that was why it felt like it was calling out to him. Jace picked it up again.

"Well, if it fits my deity, then I should probably get it," Jace said, trying to justify his desire. "How much is it?"

The shopkeeper laughed, a sound devoid of warmth. "Pricing? I don't accept University money. Pah, little rich kids cannot afford my shop. But you, you seem like you just might be able to."

Jace's hope deflated. "I don't have any gold," he admitted.

"Oh boy, I don't accept gold either," the shopkeeper replied, his eyes glinting with amusement. "Only trades."

Jace frowned, considering the implications. "What kind of a trade?"

The shopkeeper's smile widened. "Hmm, given the value of this ring, how about a favor? Not now, but sometime in the future. I promise it will be something you can easily give and will only be of equivalent value to the ring."

Jace thought long and hard, weighing the potential risks and rewards. The ring felt right, like a piece of his destiny, but a favor for this enigmatic shopkeeper? It was a gamble.

"You have my word," the shopkeeper said, sensing Jace's hesitation. "Nothing beyond the value of the ring and nothing that you cannot easily give."

Just as Jace felt like the man was about to say, "but wait, there's more," a prompt appeared.

Tinker's Pact

You are being offered a Blood Pact by a mysterious old shopkeeper. He has presented you with a deal that seems too good to pass up:

A magic ring of unknown type, rank, and power. In exchange, you agree to grant him one favor in the future of equal value and within your power to give.

Go ahead. Make a vaguely worded deal with a complete stranger. What could possibly go wrong?

Accept | Reject

This is probably a terrible idea, Jace thought, but the warmth spread, tingling at his fingertips.

Jace stared at the ring, its surface shimmering with an otherworldly glow, casting fleeting patterns across the shop walls. He felt a delicate warmth radiating from the it, an elusive power just out of reach. It thread through his thoughts, beckoning him.

"I'm really not sure that I should..." Jace began.

"I'll throw in a free wooden ring box."

"Deal."

And like that, a bargain was made.

The shopkeeper's movements were quick, almost too quick. Before Jace could even flinch, a needle pricked his finger. Blood welled up, and in the blink of an eye, the shopkeeper had done the same to himself. Their blood mingled, and a flash of light sparked between them, accompanied by a sudden, bone-chilling gust of air. The shop fell silent, the kind of silence that clings to your skin.

The shopkeeper's smile widened, revealing teeth that seemed a bit too long. He reached beneath the counter, producing a box made of wood stained a deep, blood-red. With a deliberate slowness, he handed the box to Jace. The moment Jace slipped the ring onto his finger, he felt it - a subtle hum of magic thrumming beneath his skin like a heartbeat out of sync.

Jace got an immediate feeling of regret.

"Good luck," the shopkeeper said with a smile, though his voice carried a tone of condolence.

Jace emerged from the shop, his mind in a fog. How long had he been inside? As he walked, he checked over his recent notifications.

Congratulations, I guess.

> You have made your first Blood Pact.
> Really diving in headfirst, aren't you?
> Status Update
> You have impressed a being of great power.
> Update: Attribute Change
> +1 to Charisma.
> -1 to Karmic Balance.

Was his lowered Wisdom affecting his choices? He had to get his Classless Debuff removed.

Checking the time, he realized he was already late. He grabbed the Directly Stone and thought, "Entrance," as he jogged forward.

In moments, he found himself standing by Dex and Ell. "What took you so long?" Ell asked. "Eh, no time, we're going to be late," she added quickly. "We gotta get to our first class. It's Affinities with Professor Orion. All four of us have it, and Alice went ahead to make sure we had good seats. It's over by the stables on the east side of the campus."

Jace, Dex, and Ell walked quickly together, the cool breeze ruffling their robes. Dex glanced at Jace, curiosity etched on his face. "Where were you, man? You look like you've seen a ghost."

Jace hesitated, then shrugged. "Just exploring," he said, his voice distant. "Got a bit lost in thought."

Dex raised an eyebrow but let it slide. "Alright, keep your secrets."

They walked in companionable silence. The scent of hay and the sound of horses neighing grew stronger as they approached the stables.

Chapter 18
Apples and Affinities

The students sat on stone benches arranged in a sweeping semicircle. Before them, a vast stone floor stretched out, smooth and cool under the shade of a grand oak tree that burst from the ground, its roots intertwining with the stone in a harmonious embrace. In the near distance, the gentle swoosh of waves lapping against the shore of a quiet lake could almost be heard. This setting, just off to the side of the stable sections of the campus, was a tribute to the Society of Poseidon, the Earth-Shaker and Lord of Horses.

Open paths meandered away from the assembly area, leading deeper into the verdant expanse, surrounded by the gentle neighs and whinnies of the nearby equine. The students chatted idly, their conversations a low hum, as they waited for the class to begin. Jace, Dex, and Ell arrived just in time, sliding onto the front bench beside Alice.

A hush fell as a centaur approached. Professor Orion Blackwood, Master of Affinities, stepped forward, his powerful legs grounding him with a strength that mirrored the oak tree beside him. He surveyed the students with a keen, evaluating gaze, the rustling leaves amplifying the tense silence.

The students leaned forward in their seats, their anticipation palpable. Orion's presence dominated the space, his mane flowing like a living part of the natural world. A dark leather satchel crossed his broad chest, and his bare torso revealed a physique of power and grace, muscles rippling under tanned skin. His emerald eyes glinted with ancient wisdom, and silver-streaked hair cascaded down, merging with his equine form.

The students' eyes were glued to Orion, who seemed unaware of the captivated silence.

Blackwood reached into his satchel and grabbed an apple, taking a bite with a loud crunch. He surveyed the group with calm intensity.

Dex leaned over to Jace, whispering dryly, "Is this where he tells us the apple symbolizes knowledge?"

Without warning, Blackwood lobbed the apple straight at Dex's face. It sailed through the air and struck him square on the cheek with a soft thud. Dex blinked, eyes wide, a startled yelp escaping his lips. The students gasped, then broke into laughter, only to fall silent as Blackwood raised his hand. Rubbing his face, Dex glared at the apple rolling away, a smear of juice glistening on his cheek.

"Hey, what was that for?" Dex blurted out, but the centaur ignored him completely. Jace and Ell exchanged amused glances, visibly struggling to stifle their laughter as Dex glared daggers at them.

"Affinities... Words..." he began, his gaze piercing as it swept across the students. "To be a Speaker in a world of silence is no minor thing." The wind rustled through the grass, filling the silence between his sentences. "How does one measure a Speaker?" Orion asked, his voice challenging.

Two people raised their hands - Alice and a satyr. The satyr had curly, auburn hair that framed her face, her bright, curious eyes wide and eager. Small horns peeked through her curls, and a light dusting of freckles danced across her nose.

"Yes, Miss... let's see." He squinted, examining a prompt only he could see. "Miss Snugglebutter. Honestly, that's the name you chose when you came here? Is this some kind of joke to you?" His surprise was evident, and his reaction was immediate.

She flushed a bright pink. "I... I didn't know it would be permanent. My friends said it would be funny if..."

"Never mind that," he interrupted, clearly regretting his initial reaction. His tone softened. "I apologize, Miss... Butter. Now, you were saying, how do we measure a Speaker?"

She gathered her courage. "There are six tiers of Speaker, each with six Stars of Proficiency and six Scopes of Influence."

"That is correct. Very well done, Miss...," he drifted off, choosing not to say her name again.

"We have Tier, Proficiency, and Scope. Learning your first Word grants you the title of Speaker, having heard but a fragment of the universe's ancient song. Tiers start at Bronze and work their way up through Silver, Gold, and eventually to higher levels, such as Celesteal and Divinium. Each new Affinity you gain advances you to the next level. A Bronze Speaker knows one Word, while a Silver knows two. Following so far?"

The students nodded and made quiet noises of affirmation. He reached into his satchel and pulled out another apple. This time, he didn't take a bite but moved it through his hands as he spoke. The class watching it closely.

"And then there are the Proficiency rankings, or the Star System. As one's proficiency increases, they are awarded stars to symbolize that growth. Who can tell me what each star indicates?"

The group was silent. He waited, allowing the pause to stretch just a moment longer than was comfortable.

With a sudden burst of motion, Blackwood chucked the apple at a dragonborn man. Jace couldn't help but wonder how he got that race option when all Jace had was human. The students gasped again, not having learned their lesson from before. Some were startled by the throw, others by the result.

The apple didn't hit its mark. Instead, it stopped a few feet from the dragonborn's head and exploded in a burst of heat and light, spraying sticky apple pieces across the students. Apple chunks landed on Jace and Alice. The dragonborn looked as surprised as everyone else, blinking in confusion and wiping apple bit off his scales.

The centaur continued with a smile. "The first Star marks you as a reactive user of your Word, like Master Armon, here. His affinity only works on a stimulus-response basis. Apple heads toward you, and your power activates. We call people at this rank Novice Reactionaires."

Orion's eyes sparkled with the memory of countless adventures. "The next rank is that of Apprentice Perceptor. Your Affinity entwines with your senses and emotions. Abilities are activated by physical and emotional sensations, rather than logic. Perhaps the touch of a familiar object, the tune of a loved song, the memory of a kiss."

He plucked a falling leaf from the air, holding it aloft. "A Three-Star, the Logician Adept, commands their Words with purpose, shaping reality with thought and calculation. Imagine, if you will, bending this leaf with a mere mental command." He blew and let the leave drift away.

Orion's voice grew softer. "At your fourth Star, you become a Master Artisan. Your Affinity flows through you as naturally as breath, an extension of your very being. This is the stage of the artist, the swordsman beyond all others, the prodigy. Sculpting your power with the grace of a poet crafting verse."

He stepped closer, leaning in. "At Bronze Five, your Affinity surpasses the material realm and touches something... more. As an Astral Sage, you Speak with the very essence of your soul."

"Great King Aegius is a Gold Five-Star Speaker. He commands three different Affinities, each at the Astral Sage Rank. He wields power that shapes kingdoms. A noble thing to aspire to, though many will never even reach Bronze One due to their inherent Aether limitations."

He paused, letting the gravity of his next words sink in. "And then there is the Sixth Star, that of the Divine Champion. A Speaker of the Sixth Star, even with only a single Affinity, would be ranked among the demigods of the world. But these are so rare as to be barely worth mentioning, if not as a warning." Orion's voice dropped to a conspiratorial whisper. "The gods do not often like competition."

"Now," he straightened, his voice returning to normal. "Stars and titles like Logician or Artisan mark your proficiency. Metals show your number of Affinities. You could say that your journey is a tapestry woven of Metal and Stars."

He raised his hands, the sunlight catching the glint in his eyes.

Orion extended his hand, palm facing the ground. ""I am a Silver Star Logician. Meaning, I have two Affinities, their combined proficiency at the third Rank. The ability gap between Silver One and Silver Two is nearly the same between three ranks at Bronze." He stomped a hoof into the ground, and instantly, the earth responded, forming a large, intricate sculpture of a tree rising from the soil. The students watched in amazement as the tiny tree swayed slightly, as if blown by an unseen wind, before collapsing back into the earth. "My first Affinity is Earth."

He closed his eyes. A profound silence enveloped the area, muting all sounds of the forest. The rustling leaves, the chirping birds, even the distant sea breeze - everything fell silent. The students looked around, their mouths opening and closing as they tried to speak, but no sound emerged. The air seemed thick, as if it absorbed their voices.

The only sound that came was his voice. "My second is Silence." Orion's eyes opened, and with a slight gesture, he moved the silence around. Suddenly, Alice could speak again. "This is incredible," she said, her voice the only sound in the eerie quiet.

Orion moved the silence once again, allowing everyone to hear and speak except for Jace. Jace felt his very Aether being suppressed, as if an invisible weight pressed down on his soul, silencing not just his voice but his very essence. He released the silence, and the normal sounds of the forest resumed. The students exhaled collectively, the sudden return of noise almost overwhelming.

"Consider the Scopes of Influence. There are six. And please, I hope you're taking notes. I won't be repeating this, so don't come crying to me later. We're almost done, and then you can get back to your existential crises or whatever it is you get up to between classes."

"Let's take Fire as an example Affinity. There are six Scopes of Influence. First, we have Internal Effects - this means you can heat your own body, maybe even auto-immolation."

"Setting yourself on fire," Alice whispered to Dex, Ell, and Jace.

"Next are Touch Effects, where you can ignite anything you touch," Orion continued. "Then there's Distance Effects, allowing you to shoot flames from afar. Moving up, we have Aura Effects, where you influence everything within a certain radius around you, creating an aura of fire or granting fire immunity to allies."

"Then we have Domain Effects, where you control entire regions, like turning a forest into a blazing inferno or affecting all who can see or hear you. Finally, the top tier: World Effects, where you can alter the very fabric of existence itself.

"When you gain an Affinity, you'll start unlocking abilities tied to that Affinity. Each ability will have its own influence and power."

"Ranking up Tier, Scope, and Proficiency becomes harder as you advance, each level requiring about ten times the experience as the last. As you gain more power and learn to tap into the deeper meaning of your Affinities, you will need to deepen your well of Aether, increasing your ability to breathe power into your Words."

The field was silent. Orion's gaze hardened, emphasizing his next words. "Now, how does one unlock their first Affinity, you might ask?" He let the question hang in the air, a silent challenge. "By being thrust into life. I'll need a volunteer." He looked around. No one met his gaze this time.

"Jace," Orion called out at last.

Chapter 19
Small Steps

J ace hesitated, feeling the weight of everyone's eyes on him. Professor Blackwood waved towards a nondescript wooden shed that seemed to melt into
the sprawling field. Jace hadn't seen it there before. "There are things, even here
at the University, which live amongst us, hidden in plain sight. This shed, for
example, leads into an underground cavern that few would dare open."

The centaur handed Jace a key, its cold metal biting into his palm like
an overenthusiastic handshake. "Good luck," he whispered.

Jace turned it over, feeling the gravity of what was to come. The old
hinges groaned as he forced the latch open, the sound like a reluctant ghost.

He paused and looked around. Blackwood gestured for him to move
forward. He stepped inside, feeling the earth soft and yielding beneath his feet.
From the shadows, a tiny creature stepped forward. At first, it was just a flicker
of movement against the backdrop of darkness. Jace squinted, his eyes straining
to make sense of it. The creature moved again, more confidently this time,
stepping into a sliver of light that pierced the gloom.

It was small, no taller than two inches, with goblin-like features and
sharp, glinting eyes. Its skin was a mottled green, its movements quick and
jittery. The soft rustle of its tiny feet against the floor seemed magnified in the
stillness of the shed.

A chill ran down Jace's spine as more creatures began to appear, their
eyes reflecting the dim light. They filled the shed, a small army of goblin-like
beings. Each one was as tiny and menacing as the first, their presence both
fascinating and terrifying.

Nervous chuckles rippled through the group of students behind Jace,
tension settling over them. Blackwood walked over to the door, a knowing
smile playing on his lips. "Meet the brownies," he said, his tone dripping with
irritating smugness. "We have an arrangement with their king."

The student's amusement quickly turned to shock as the brownies launched their attack. They swarmed over Jace's feet, knocking him off balance. He stumbled, barely managing to stay upright as other students began to back away, trying to flee the onslaught. The centaur's voice boomed, "No running away, now. What fun would that be?" Stone walls shot up around them, trapping everyone inside the courtyard.

Chaos descended.

The brownies, surprisingly strong and agile, darted between the students, tripping them with tiny ropes and jabbing at their legs with sharpened sticks. "Ouch!" "Get off me!" echoed through the night as they tried to fend off the relentless little monsters.

Professor Orion Blackwood's laughter boomed above the fray. "Don't go easy on them! They're tough little things."

Jace ducked and weaved, dodging a barrage of tiny arrows. A group of brownies roped his ankle, yanking him off balance. He hit the ground hard, the creatures swarming over him, their tiny hands pulling at his clothes and hair.

"Get off me!" Jace shouted, swatting at the brownies. They were everywhere, like ants at a picnic. Ropes tightened around his legs and arms, binding him to the ground. Each sting of their tiny weapons sent jolts of pain through him.

Nearby, Ell stood amidst the chaos, her eyes closed in concentration. A faint glow surrounded her, and with a sudden thrust of her hand, an invisible force sent the brownies flying. "I did it!" she squealed. The brownies tumbled through the air, landing in a heap several feet away. Ell had unlocked her first Affinity.

Dex wasn't faring as well. He swung wildly at the brownies, but they were too quick. Tripping over their ropes, he fell face-first into the dirt. "This is not what I signed up for!" he yelped, spitting out grass and glaring at the tiny tormentors.

Alice, usually the picture of composure, was flustered, her movements erratic as she tried to fend off the tiny attackers. "Is it just me, or are they multiplying?" she shrieked, batting at a persistent brownie clinging to her hair.

A tall student with glasses fell to the floor. "Get these things off me!" he shouted, flailing as the brownies climbed up his legs.

A girl with bright red hair conjured a small flame in her hand, trying to scare off the brownies. "Stay back!" she warned, but the creatures seemed more annoyed than frightened, advancing on her with renewed vigor.

As the battle raged on, some students showed their magical abilities. Sparks flew, waves of energy erupted, and elemental forces burst from their hands. About a quarter of the students had unlocked their powers, pushing the brownies back with their newfound abilities.

Frustration boiled inside Jace as he fought against the brownies. He watched in awe as his classmates unleashed their powers, each one discovering something new about themselves in the heat of battle. Just as he felt the battle was hopeless, Blackwood's voice cut through the chaos.

"Enough!" he bellowed, and the brownies froze in place, their tiny eyes darting around nervously. He stepped forward, surveying the scene with a satisfied grin. "Terrible. Just terrible."

He looked around. Some brownies had their heads bowed in shame. "Not you, little ones. You did great. Thank you for your service, as usual." The brownies immediately smiled as one and retreated in an orderly fashion back to the shed. The field, moments ago a battleground, was now eerily quiet.

Blackwood clapped his hands, the sharp sound bringing the students to attention. His demeanor was once again rigid and formal. Some students were still catching their breath, others nursing minor bruises and scrapes.

Jace, still struggling against the ropes, freed himself and stood up, brushing dirt off his clothes.

"Some of you might think my methods are heavy-handed, but do you really expect gentleness when facing the Dark One's minions?" Blackwood asked.

"The who?" Jace asked, breaking the tension with his confusion.

The professor sighed deeply. "For eons, the Twelve Great Kingdoms of Terra Mythica flourished. From the scorching deserts and tumultuous seas to the towering mountain realms and fertile river lands beyond. But there is a thirteenth, ruled by a disciple of the Eternal Void, a malevolent force waging an unending war on all that breathes and grows. He is known only as the Dark One. Over the past millennia, the Thirteenth Kingdom has gradually gained ground, casting its shadow over far too much of our world."

Blackwood reached into a pouch and pulled out an ancient scroll. With a flick of his wrist, he tossed it into the air. The scroll unfurled, revealing a grand map of Terra Mythica, vibrant with the colors of its kingdoms but marred by a creeping darkness. The map seemed almost alive, its edges curling and twitching. An intricate dial upon it shifted, showing the relentless march of time. Darkness surged and retreated, beaten back again and again, until nearly eight centuries ago. The birth of the Thirteenth Kingdom saw it consume one of the Twelve, obliterating the grassy lands of the Kingdom of Roandia.

"This is not merely a clash of armies. It is the Infinite Potential against the Eternal End. Mount Olympus University was founded to prepare you, the next generation, to face this peril, to fight back against the encroaching shadow. Should the Thirteenth Kingdom prevail, light will turn to dark, beginnings to ends, and life to an endless void."

The students exchanged uneasy glances, the weight of Blackwood's words sinking in like stones in a pond.

"Alright," he said, his tone serious and leaving no room for questions. The scroll rolled itself back up before returning to his pouch. "Some of you have unlocked your first Affinities. Stay back after class so we can discuss them. The rest of you, I expect to see progress in a week's time, and if you haven't unlocked something by then, it's only going to get more painful... for you."

As the class dispersed, those who had unlocked their Affinities clustered near Blackwood, their expressions a mix of pride and curiosity. The open field, now a chaotic landscape littered with tiny ropes and scattered projectiles, bore witness to their first real test of abilities.

Just as they thought the ordeal was over, a shrill cry shattered the uneasy calm. Jace whipped around to see Dex, still tangled in ropes, being dragged unceremoniously across the ground by a few very determined brownies. "A little help here?" Dex shouted, his face a display of unbridled annoyance.

Ell sighed dramatically but couldn't hide her smile. "How will you learn if I we do everything for you?" she asked, her voice teasing.

Dex scowled as he was slowly dragged across the field toward the lake.

"Think we should help him?" Jace asked, glancing at the others.

"I think he's got this," Alice said, her tone light but her eyes watching Dex closely.

Professor Blackwood, who had been observing the scene with a mixture of indifferent amusement, finally turned back to his students.

"I hate you guys," Dex muttered as he was dragged further away.

They laughed, but eventually helped Dex. Charging at the brownies and shouting, they scared the creatures away and quickly untied him.

Ell stayed behind with the others who had unlocked an Affinity, while Jace and the rest of the gang made their way out of the field. Alice, brushing herself off, sauntered up to Jace.

"You know," she said, a twinkle in her eye, "I didn't think our first lessons would be quite so... hands-on."

Jace nodded, a grin spreading across his face. "Welcome to the academy, where survival of the fittest is taken literally."

Alice's eyes sparkled with excitement. "And where even the cute things are out to get you?"

Jace smirked. "Who knew death by brownie was on the curriculum?"

Alice rolled her eyes but couldn't suppress a smile. "Seriously, though, it's kinda thrilling, isn't it?"

Jace tilted his head, considering. "Yeah, if by thrilling you mean slightly terrifying. Death by a thousand tiny little pokes."

The tension from the class melted away as they walked. Behind them, Dex, finally fully untangled, shot a look at the retreating brownies. "Next time, I'm bringing bug spray," he muttered.

Jace shook his head. The academy was a madhouse, no doubt about it, but it was their madhouse.

Chapter 20
Ah, Rats

After the Affinities class, his next scheduled step was to visit Hades. The rest of them headed to their respective Societies. Here, they would gain their first class titles and party roles.

Jace opened his map using the digital display. It created a mini-map in the top right corner of his HUD.

There was a tiny mark on the map labeled [Active Quest]. Looking closer, two options appeared. The one marked [Fast Travel] was grayed out. The other, [Navigate] was selectable. Jason chose his only real option, [Navigate], and immediately his location on the map started to glow. This time, it knew exactly where Jace was and a dotted line sprang from his position, winding down the path to the Entrance of the Underworld.

The air grew cold and restless as he walked beside the wall of a cliff face. The light faded in the late afternoon, darkness enveloping him. The cliff face was overgrown with moss and branches, the foliage clinging desperately to the rocky surface.

An alert flared before his eyes, casting an eerie glow on the path ahead.

You Entering Protective Zone Two.

As he continued to follow the map, another notification appeared.

You Entering Protective Zone Three.

Warning: Your rank does not meet the recommended minimum requirements for entry to this level. Proceed at your own risk.

Why did they put the entrance to the Underworld so far from the Campus proper? Jace thought about it and decided that the question answered itself. *Right, who wants to be that close to death?*

The trees grew gnarled and twisted, their branches clawing at the sky. Thick clouds loomed overhead. The dense canopy blocked out what little light remained, casting deep shadows over the ground.

Jace squared his shoulders and pressed on, each step echoing the quiet determination thrumming in his chest. The forest seemed to close in around him, silence broken only by the occasional rustle of leaves and the distant snap of twigs. He could feel unseen eyes tracking his every movement, the sensation prickling the back of his neck. Every sound set his nerves on edge, a reminder of the lurking dangers.

The path wound deeper into the heart of the forest, the air growing colder, as if the very essence of the Underworld was seeping through the earth to greet him.

A loud ding rang through Jace's mind, nearly causing him to jump out of his body.

New Area Discovered
    Path of Echoes has been added to your map.
    Status Effects:
    • Reduced Visibility
    • All Sound Reduced by 25%

The forest whispered ancient words in the language of rustling leaves and creaking moans. Distant growls reverberated through the trees, muffled by oppressive magic. Jace treaded carefully, knowing this place was alive with threats. Squinting into the shadows, he strained to pierce the inky blackness, but the darkness seemed to shift and mock his efforts. Shapes moved within, blending seamlessly with the gloom, creating an ever-present sense of dread.

He was pretty sure he should turn back.

A chill enveloped him as he advanced, ignoring his instincts. Trees loomed like ancient sentinels, their twisted branches clawing at the sky. The scent of damp earth and decaying leaves filled the air. Jace's heartbeat quickened, matching the rhythm of his cautious steps.

He continued forward, senses heightened, every rustle and murmur amplifying the tension. The shadows pulsed with life, and Jace knew he wasn't alone in the dark.

A faint sniffling sound pricked Jace's ears. From the oppressive shadows emerged a grotesque abomination, a rat-like beast lumbering into view. Matted fur, slick with grime, coated its hunched back. Malevolent red eyes glowed above yellowed fangs that jutted from a slavering maw. Pus-filled sores oozed a rancid liquid, mingling with the stench of decay. Its long, worm-like tail lashed the ground, kicking up dirt and debris.

Jace's heart pounded like a war drum as he faced the monstrosity unarmed. Staring down at this nightmare, a cold sweat slicked his brow. Dread coiled in his stomach, heavy and nauseating.

It' just a game. It's just... a... game. He reminded himself.

With a ferocious snarl, the giant rat launched itself at Jace, razor-sharp claws slashing through the air. He stood his ground, trying to steel himself. But as the beast closed in, panic surged through him. He turned to run, tripping over a root, his dexterity betraying him.

The rat was upon him in an instant, claws raking across his chest. Jace gasped in pain, rolling to the side as the beast's fangs snapped inches from his face. Scrambling to his feet, heart pounding, he searched frantically for a weapon. His eyes landed on a fallen branch, jagged and sturdy, lying a few feet away.

Combat Log

     Greater Plague Rat deals 15 Damage with Glancing Gash.

     Health: 25/40

     Status: Moderate Injuries, -1 to Stamina

Jace lunged for the branch, gripping it tightly just as the beast charged again. He swung with all his might, the branch connecting with a sickening crunch against the creature's skull. It reeled back, a guttural scream ripping through the air.

But the rat was far from deterred. It shook its head, blood and black ichor dripping from the wound, and launched itself at Jace again, this time knocking him to the ground. The creature's onslaught was relentless, its fury ripping claws and disgusting mouth fueled by primal instincts and a hunger for blood. Each swipe of its claws sent Jace sprawling to the ground, his limbs flailing as he desperately tried to fend off the assault.

Greater Plague Rat deals 15 Slashing Damage.
   You are Poisoned and Bleeding
   Health: 10/40
   Status: Severe Injuries, -4 to Stamina

He pushed himself back, crawling away from the beast. His eyes darted frantically, searching for any escape. Dizzy from the stamina drain, a sudden, searing pain shot through his hand. His silver raven ring burned fiercely. With a yelp, he yanked his hand back, the pain instantly subsiding. "What the hell?" he whispered through clenched teeth.

The ring tugged his hand sideways, guiding him toward a vine. His gaze followed its length, realizing it led to the top of a cliff. Perched precariously above were loose rocks, teetering on the edge. The beast's snarls grew louder, and with a sudden, gut-wrenching lunge, it charged at him. Jace fell prone, hands scrambling for the vine in a desperate bid for survival.

Clutching the thick vine, he used it to shield his face from the beast, its dripping maw inches away. The vine tightened, pulling taut against the rock face. Over the creature's deafening growls, Jace heard the ominous rumble of shifting stone. A cascade of rocks tumbled down, each impact reverberating through the ground.

Jace rolled away just as a series of massive stones crashed down, smashing the rat's head with a sickening crack. The relentless downpour of debris continued, a thunderous roar drowning out the beast's final, muffled squeals. Rocks piled high, burying the monstrous rat under a suffocating mountain of earth and stone. Jace lay on the ground, breathless and bleeding.

His heart hammered in his chest as he stared at the pile of rubble. Adrenaline surged through his veins, the realization of his narrow escape washing over him like a tidal wave.

Enemy Defeated: Greater Plague Rat
    Rank Difference: 2 ranks above yours
    EXP Gained: 500 + Rank Disparity Modifier
    Total Experience Gained: 750

He didn't know why, but he laughed. He had survived. Looking at his ring with newfound appreciation, he asked aloud, "Did you know that was going to happen?" as if expecting an answer. For a brief moment, the gemstone eye caught the light, glinting mysteriously.

Health: 5/40

"Wait, why am I losing health?" Jace pulled up his status effects.

Status Effect: Poisoned
    Status Effect: Bleeding
    Health Loss: -15 over 10 seconds until cured.

"Shit."

You Have Died

Chapter 21
Will They, Won't They

C ongratulations

You have died for the first time in Terra Mythica proper. As this is your first death, no penalties have been applied. This one is on the house - but don't expect any more freebies.

Respawn Point Has Been Forcibly Changed by Deity

New Respawn Point: Entrance to the Underworld

Jace stood before a large, gray office building, its stark facade looming like a monolith against the sky.

He paused, reflecting. He had just respawned in the game after dying for the first time. This felt different from his experience in Character Creation. Something was off, an unsettling feeling lingering like a half-remembered dream. The memory of his body lying in bed above Teddy's bar was foggy -fragmented. He felt tired and stiff.

Shaking his head to clear his thoughts, he approached the building. An old, rusting plaque on the door read, "Death and Co. - An Underworld Corporation."

"This must be the place," he muttered.

He pushed open the door and stepped inside. It was like entering a time warp back to a dreary 1990s office. The walls were a dull beige, the carpet a drab gray, and the faint hum of fluorescent lights added to the oppressive atmosphere.

As he walked toward the reception desk, a ghostly woman with a beehive hairstyle and cat-eye glasses looked up from her bulbous computer monitor. "Do you have an appointment?" she asked, her voice as flat as her expression. He scanned the maze of cubicles, the air filled with the musty scent of old paper and stale coffee.

Before Jace could answer, a tall, awkward specter of a man with large teeth and thick glasses stumbled into view. His suit was a size too large, and his tie was slightly askew. "Ah, you must be Jace! I'm Jerald, but friends call me Jerry."

From a nearby cubicle, a voice called out, "You don't have any friends, Jerald!"

"Oh, Clive, such a joker," Jerald replied, his smile strained as he turned back to Jace. "I'll take it from here, Barbara. The boss is expecting him. Let's get you started, shall we?"

Barbara rolled her eyes and returned to her typing. Jerald motioned for Jace to follow him. "We kinda have a thing going on, me and Barb. A sort of will they, won't they office romance. You know how it goes." He nudged Jace with an elbow and a wink.

As they navigated the labyrinth of cubicles, Jerald pointed out various desks. "That's Brenda's desk over there. We had quite the celebration for her 277th birthday last week. And over there is Karen's area. Best to avoid that section. She's, um, particular about her space."

Jace nodded, trying to take it all in. The office felt surreal, a strange blend of mundane bureaucracy and otherworldly eeriness.

Jerald continued his enthusiastic tour, gesturing wildly as they moved through the office lit by flickering fluorescent lights, one bulb dead and casting a long shadow. The ceiling tiles, once white, were now yellowed with age.

"You know, Hades gets a bad rap," Jerald said. "People see him as the god of the dead, but his role's way more complex. He's the guy keeping the balance between life and death, making sure everything stays in order. Without him - it'd be chaos everywhere, undead nibbling on your little toes at night. It's pretty fascinating if you think about it."

Jace listened intently, curious about anything that could give him insight into the deity and Jace's potential class. Plus, he had to admit that Jerald's passion for his work was infectious.

"The Underworld isn't just some pit where souls go to rot," Jerald said, his tone tinted with disdain. "It's a realm of transition, a place of balance. You think respawning just happens? Guess again. Our department handles that admin. We're the ones making sure souls find their proper place. It's not about punishment or reward - it's about keeping the cosmic scales from tipping over. Without us, everything goes to hell in a handbasket."

They passed by a series of cubicles where ghostly employees were busy at work, filing paperwork and processing scrolls. "These folks," Jerald continued, "are part of that process. Every soul that enters the Underworld is accounted for, their deeds weighed, and their destinies assigned. It's meticulous work, but it's crucial."

Jace glanced around, noticing the ghostly figures moving with purpose. "So, it's like a giant supernatural sorting system?"

Jerald chuckled. "In a way, yes. But it's more than administration. It's a mission. We all work hard to go above and beyond to help Hades do his job. Because, after all, you can't spell 'extraordinary' without that little 'extra'."

Jace tried not to visibly cringe.

Jerald seemed not to notice or mind. "Hades ensures that life can continue by managing the cycle of death. Without him, the living world would be overrun by the restless undead, and possessed. Every life and every death is part of a greater tapestry, and Hades weaves it all together."

Jerald paused by an imposing desk, cluttered with scrolls and papers. "You'll find this fascinating, I know I do," he said, unfurling a thick scroll to reveal an intricate map of the Underworld. "Here's Tartarus," he continued, pointing to a spot on the map. "That's where you've got your murderers, tyrants, and people that say 'stay sleazy' with finger guns." He shuddered.

"Over on this side, you have your Elysian Fields, sort of a retirement community for heroes. It's honestly a hoot down there. Just the other week, at bingo..." He noticed the look on Jace's face and decided to change course. "Anywho, there's a whole lot more." He moved his hand along the map, shifting it to zoom in on different areas.

"Some souls hang around for eternity, while others take their chances with reincarnation," Jerald said, smiling broadly. "It's quite the ecosystem we've got going on here."

"Do you handle all of the souls on the planet?" Jace asked.

"Oh no, that would be a disaster," Jerald replied with a chuckle. "We only handle those who seek our assistance, those who follow the Olympians."

"And what about the others?"

"They have their own pantheons, like followers of Osiris. We simply redirect them to the proper realm through an inter-domain exchange system."

"What about people who don't follow any deity?"

Jerald's expression turned somber, and he shrugged. "Those poor souls are left to figure it out for themselves. Most of them do. Some don't. Not really my department."

Jerald closed the scroll, and they continued walking through the rows of cubicles. When they reached the elevator, Jerald pressed the down button with a flourish. "Now, we're heading to the Underworld Proper."

The elevator arrived with a ding, and they stepped inside. The doors closed, and "The Girl from Ipanema" played as they descended, floor after floor. Jerald nodded his head to the rhythm.

"This place isn't what I expected," Jace admitted, partly to distract himself from his thoughts. He wasn't sure why, but he felt more and more nervous as they descended.

Jerald beamed. "Oh, it's wonderful, isn't it? We like to think of it less like a job, more like a family."

Jace winced at the sentiment but kept quiet.

After a very long while, the elevator doors opened, revealing a vast, dark cavern. "Here we are! Your final destination, as it were." Jerald paused with a suppressed grin. "Oh, just a little bit of Underworld humor. Right then, off you pop."

The atmosphere pressed down with the scent of damp earth, accompanied by the faint sound of running water in the distance. Jerald led Jace through a series of passages that opened onto the shore of a river, where a hooded figure waited silently at the prow of a long, black boat.

Jerald handed Jace a coin. It was gold with smooth, angular edges, and it bore the face of an old man with deep, sunken eyes. "You'll need that as payment to cross. Just hand it to the ferryman. Don't drop it now; the last person who lost their travel coin waited a very long time in here."

Jace nodded, clutching the coin tightly as he stepped into the boat. The ferryman held out his hand, and Jace placed the coin in his palm. Silent and foreboding, the ferryman began to row them across the dark, still waters.

"How do I get back out of here?" Jace called as the boat drifted away.

"Sorry, can't hear you. Also, I wouldn't be too loud in here. There are sleeping things here that even I don't know about." Jerald shrugged off a brief shiver and waved before turning and heading back to the elevator. Jace could swear he was dancing a little as he walked.

The waters were black, and every once in a while, a glowing mist swirled through them. He could hear whispers of screams in the distance, or maybe it was just the wind. Jagged rocks loomed overhead, casting long shadows, and occasional growls echoed through the darkness. Every so often, a hand would claw up from the water, and the ferryman would strike it back with his oar with practiced ease.

"So, how are the benefits here? Must be pretty good, right?" The stifling silence made Jace nervous, prompting him to speak quietly to fill the void. "I knew a truck driver once. He said it was decent when he had the work. Long hours, but at least it's peaceful."

The ferryman remained mute, his face hidden in the shadows. "The quiet type, huh? I get that. I'm known as the strong and silent type myself."

He paused for a moment. "You know, I never got your name. Can't keep calling you Ferryman forever. Mine's Jace." He reached out a hand, but the darkness under the hood stared back at him. Jace could only imagine a blank expression hidden there. Awkwardly, he pulled his hand back. "I think I'll call you Joe."

Nothing of note occurred during the rest of the ride, except for a prompt announcing a new skill gained.

Skill Gained

    Darkvision - Rank 1

    You've been squinting a lot. Here, have a skill.

    You now can squint a little less when trying to see things in the dark.

After what felt like an eternity, they reached a small, decrepit dock. "Thanks for the lift, Joe," Jace said, as the ferryman expertly guided the boat alongside the dock and silently gestured for him to disembark.

Jace stepped cautiously onto the wooden planks that creaked ominously under his weight. The ferryman remained silent, watching as Jace made his way onto solid ground. Jace looked back to find the ferry had already set off again, quickly disappearing into the darkness. He hummed and murmured to himself in the dark, "...hmm hmm hmm hmm, the girl from Ipanema hmm-hmm-hmm-hmm."

"Damn it, I'm going to have that stuck in my head all day."

Chapter 22
That Little Extra

Jace stood at the mouth of three diverging paths, each leading into the impenetrable darkness of the Underworld. "Yup, this is just perfect," he muttered, his voice swallowed by the thick silence. He inhaled the stale air deeply.

As he debated which path to take, a flicker of green light caught his eye. It hovered in the air before him, bobbing gently like a curious firefly. "Hey there, little guy," Jace said, squinting at the light. The light pulsed softly in response. "Are you lost too? Because I sure am."

The green light floated closer, its glow casting an eerie shadow against the jagged walls. It moved up and down, then side to side, as if trying to communicate. Jace watched it intently. "Are you trying to help me?" he ventured.

The light bobbed up and down in what seemed like a nod. It circled around his head once, casting shifting shadows, then darted a few feet down one of the paths before pausing, as if waiting for him.

Jace took a tentative step forward. "Alright, I'll follow you. Just don't lead me to my death," he said with a weak smile. The light responded with another gentle pulse and started moving slowly down the path, ensuring Jace could keep up.

With a final glance at the other two paths, Jace steadied himself and followed the green light into the unknown. Each step echoed softly in the cavern, the light's glow offering a small, reassuring beacon in the darkness.

The light danced ahead, bouncing off the walls like a playful spirit. Jace followed, doing his best to keep up in the twisting passages. The air grew warmer with each step, sweat beading on his forehead despite the cool stone surrounding him. Shadows twisted and danced along the rough stone walls, their shapes playing tricks on his mind.

The path wound deeper into the earth; the heat intensifying. The green light wove through the labyrinth with ease, but Jace struggled to keep pace, his breath ragged in the thickening air. Faces carved into the tunnel walls leered at him from the shadows, their expressions of eternal torment, moaning ancient words that sent shivers down his spine.

The ground beneath his feet quaked, forcing him to an abrupt halt as a yawning chasm appeared before him. Pebbles scattered and plunged into the depths below, swallowed by the abyss. Spinning around, he found the light had disappeared.

Ahead, the cavern widened into a grand chamber, illuminated by erratic, flickering flames. The ceiling soared, a canopy of stone stretching into the underworld's perpetual twilight. Jace's breath caught as he beheld Hades' palace at the far end, a fortress of pure obsidian. Its walls gleamed with a sinister sheen, the flickering firelight dancing across their smooth, dark surface like malevolent spirits.

Drawing closer, the palace's imposing presence grew with towering columns of black marble. Each was etched with intricate depictions of the Underworld's somber history, tales of sorrow and torment immortalized in stone. Colossal spires rose from the palace, their tips lost in the cavern's upper darkness, reaching futilely for a sky that did not exist.

Massive iron doors guarded the entrance, adorned with writhing serpents and grotesque scenes of eternal damnation. The doors seemed almost alive, pulsing with a dark energy. The air around the palace vibrated with a low hum, a sound that seemed to resonate deep within Jace's bones. He approached, every step weighed down by the dark majesty of Hades' domain.

As he approached, the iron doors creaked open with a groan, revealing a grand hall lit by flickering torches.

At the far end of the hall, seated at a desk of blackened bone, was Hades himself. The god's eyes gleamed with an unearthly light as he regarded Jace with a mixture of curiosity and amusement. His presence was palpable, a force that seemed to bend the very air around him.

Hades leaned back in his chair, his muscular frame barely contained by the dark, flowing robes. His face was rugged, with dark eyes and a smirk that exuded authority. Cerberus, the three-headed dog, played in the distance, but upon noticing Jace, the massive creature bounded over.

"Whoa, easy there," Jace said, steadying himself. He watched as the giant creature rushed towards him. Well, this is it. Jace said to himself, accepting his imminent demise.

Hades chuckled and called Cerberus back, who stopped just short of crushing Jace beneath one of his massive paws. Hades pet Cerberus and pulled a large steak from his desk drawer. "He's the best boy," Hades said, tossing the steak, which Cerberus caught with one head while the other two barked happily.

"Lights," Hades commanded. Ghouls in the corner turned a knob, and the flames in the room brightened, casting a brighter glow over the atrium. "That's better. Now we can see what we're doing."

Looking up, Jace noticed the false sky outside through a glass ceiling. His steps echoed through the grand chamber as he approached. The dark splendor of Hades' palace seemed to swallow him whole, its obsidian walls and skull-adorned throne casting a foreboding aura. The god of the Underworld, perched regally on his throne, noticed Jace's hesitation. With a casual wave, a chair emerged from the shadows.

"Sit, Jace. Let's talk," Hades said, his voice smooth yet laden with power.

Jace sat, feeling the cool, unyielding surface of the chair through his clothes. Hades reached for a silver platter on a nearby table. "Scone? My wife makes the best pomegranate scones. Simply to die for," he offered, extending one towards Jace.

Jace blinked, momentarily caught off guard by the unexpected gesture. "Uh, no thanks."

"Suit yourself," Hades replied, biting into a scone with pleasure. "Straight to business, then. It's been a while since I've had a Chosen. I'm sure you have a lot of questions. You're probably wondering why I picked you," he said, leaning back with a raised eyebrow. "Well, tough cookies. I'm not going to spell it all out for you. It's a quest - one of those 'the journey will take you where you need to go' type things. You hero types should know that by now. But since you are my Chosen, I'll answer any other questions you have, within reason."

Jace's mind raced, trying to focus. He decided to start with something practical. "How do I take full advantage of my role as the President of the Society?"

Hades nodded, a sly smile playing on his lips. "Ah, the token." He rummaged through a drawer and produced a small, intricately carved medallion. "This will get you access." He held it out but did not hand it to Jace. "As the President of my Society, you are representing me, in a way. Muff it up and you'll have Tartarus to pay." He handed him the coin without further ceremony.

"The Society gains EXP much in the same way that you do, through overcoming challenges and consolidating its gains. You'll need to complete Society-related tasks and win favor for me among Travelers and Citizens alike. If we ever have more Chosen or people in the Society, you would oversee them. Some gods are unhappy with their current Olympian Banner representative."

Jace gave him a questioning look.

"There are the Thirteen Major Olympian Gods, of course, each represented by one of the Thirteen Banners or Societies. Zeus, Hera, Poseidon, Demeter, Athena, Apollo, Artemis, Ares, Aphrodite, Hephaestus, Hermes, a shared society with Hestia and Dionysus, and of course, yours truly. Sometimes, the last one is forgotten as I don't technically live up top. But these are only the major gods. Many others exist, and they all need a place. So, they form clubs or sects within one of the main Societies. Take Hecate, for example. She'd fit better under me, though Hermes is a decent fellow. She oversees the realms of magic, secrets, and crossroads—a domain quite intertwined with mine. I've been out of the game for a while though, and she needed somewhere to go."

Hades paused, studying Jace. "But let's not get ahead of ourselves. You need to prove yourself before you start recruiting. Walk before you run. Glide before you fly. And all that."

"For starters, we need to get you an official Profession. And we'll need to unlock that pesky Affinity of yours. You seem to have used it and scared it away." Hades flipped through an ancient tome, its pages yellowed with age. "Been a long time since I've done this. Let's see here," he muttered.

"Profession? Like a job?" Jace asked, puzzled. It wasn't included in the primer knowledge.

"Yes, yes. Your Speaker Rank improves with practice and mastery of your Affinities. Professions are more subtle, like business contracts. Instead of EXP, they earn you a different kind of power—gold and influence."

Jace's ears perked up. This was what he needed. To save Alex, he'd need gold and lots of it. The idea of craving power felt strange to him. His past had taught him to survive on grit, not wealth or influence.

"A person might be a Bronze Speaker with an Affinity for stealth. Depending on how they use it, they might earn the Class Title of Rogue and gain special boons from on high. Between you and me, I think titles are sort of arbitrary, gifted by the Infinite based on your actions, affinities, and inclinations. But a Profession is something you earn from your peers and employers. Sometimes they align, sometimes they don't.

A Profession is a pact in the here and now, between us. Occasionally, a Profession can sway the Infinite, earning you a new Class Title. Sing well, and people might start to call you a Bard. If enough people do, the Infinite takes notice."

Hades stood and stepped into a side room. Peeking in, Jace saw him rummage through a pile of ancient artifacts and books, finally pulling out an old TV and something that looked remarkably like a dusty VHS tape. Jace had seen one once in an old holodisc. Hades popped it in, and the screen flickered to life with a grainy video. An awkward though peppy host introduced himself. It was Jerry!

"Welcome to the Office of Hades!" Jerry began. "As the Chosen, you have access to various Underworld Professions. Our job is to help souls find their rightful place, keep the undead from wreaking havoc, and deal with demonic pests. You'll start as an assistant or floater, getting a feel for the roles. Now, you're not working directly for Thanatos or as a harbinger of Death, but there may be times when you'll be asked to handle tasks for other Underworld deities. Think of it as a sort of inter-divisional work exchange.

The video cuts to scenes of the bustling Underworld offices. Jerry leaned on a reception desk next to a slightly younger Barbara.

"Soul jobs fit into standard difficulty ranks, Bronze One through Divine Six. Bronze One involves run-of-the-mill tasks: souls stuck in the wrong place, souls unable to move on. Bronze Three is for demon-possessed and cursed souls - more dangerous, but nothing a Bronze Three Speaker can't handle. Silver, Gold, and higher ranks deal with powerful curses, demon possessions, and evil specters. Eerie, dark, evil, bleh." He made a sour face.

The video panned out to reveal the sprawling Underworld offices. Jerry pushed a cart of papers from desk to desk, pausing as if suddenly aware of the camera. "And don't be afraid to go above and beyond. After all, you can't spell extraordinary without that little extra." He held an awkward smile at the screen for a few seconds too long, then glanced around and asked, "Is it off?"

Hades clicked off the TV and leaned back in his chair, his piercing gaze fixed on Jace.

Profession Available

Hades' Little Helper - Novice Rank

Complete Hades' Little Helper tasks to gain rewards in the form of influence and gold. As well as Society EXP.

Accept | Reject

Jace accepted the profession.

He shifted awkwardly for a moment, then decided to finally ask, "Sir... uh, your godliness... I'm sorry, I have no idea what to call you."

"Hades is fine," he said, a slight crinkle forming around his eyes.

"Hades," Jace began, fidgeting before asking, "something has been bothering me. Everyone here seems to know a lot about old Earth. Like, I've only seen TVs like that in old holodiscs. How do you have that... down here?"

"Since the Tethering—" Hades started.

"Tethering?"

Hades shook his head, an exasperated sigh escaping his lips. "Furies, boy! Do they teach you nothing up top? Oh, what should I expect with the state of things?

The Tethering was the event, many years ago, when our worlds became linked and the first Travelers began to appear in Terra Mythica.

When it occurred, the first thing the Infinite, or the System as your people prefer, accessed was your holodiscs and data archives. It is there we learned of your 'Techno-Purge' and the 'War.' "We, too, have struggled with a war for many millennia, between the Infinite and the Endless End."

Hades continued, "It is also where we learned of your culture. For nearly eight hundred years in Terra Mythica, you have been studied, much as your people have studied us. Unfortunately, or fortunately, your culture has intertwined with ours in ways that are difficult to quantify. Perhaps even gods are not immune."

Hades leaned back, a wry smile playing on his lips. "You know, at first, the Infinite thought it would be a great idea to make things cozy for you. Make it feel like home. We saw your media and figured it was a decent blueprint of your culture. So, we went all in, as you say, trying to replicate it. We even provided you with your User Interface Stones to ease the transition. Sure, the first few models weren't that great, but over the years we worked alongside your scientists and refined them."

He chuckled, shaking his head. "But then we realized - too late, mind you - that your fiction is often just that. Fiction. But the damage was done, and your world had permeated ours in ways beyond calculation, sparking considerable chaos. Not everyone welcomed these changes or the impact on our culture, on our very way of life."

Hades paused, letting the gravity of his words settle. "Eventually, we hit a sort of balance, an equilibrium between our traditions and yours. There are people here who don't even know that they are named after your heroes and popular figures of the past."

Jace nodded thoughtfully, the silence between them deepening as he processed the information. Hades, apparently satisfied that the topic was concluded, moved on to his next item on the agenda.

"Now, for your first Affinity. I can see that you've used a Word already, but it seems to have tucked itself away inside you. There's some soul damage - a bit of scuffing around the edges. Nothing we can't deal with. We'll need to coax that out of you."

"Um, with all due respect, the Archmage suggested that I shouldn't try to force it. Just let it come naturally," Jace said.

"By the Titans, boy. I'm Hades. And I'm not having my Chosen walking around without an Affinity!"

Hades' presence expanded in an instant, his towering figure looming over Jace. Dark tendrils of black flame stretched out from his body like tentacles, emanating a palpable sense of power and danger. Fear welled up within Jace, but he fought with all his might to stand his ground as Hades revealed the tiniest sliver of his true aura. Just as quickly as it had emerged, the aura dissipated. Hades appeared relaxed once again, though a subtle air of menace still surrounded him.

"So, we have two options here. The first would be to get you a second Word. The alternative is to unlock the one you already have. Acquiring another

Word would advance you to Silver. While I expect nothing less eventually, jumping to Silver without practicing your first Affinity could tear your soul apart, a fate from which not even I could restore you. No, it's better to try our hand at the one you already possess. That way, you've got a fifty-fifty chance of keeping your sanity."

Jace tried to protest but found himself unable to speak.

"Now, the quickest way to coax an Affinity out of hiding is brute force. Well, actually, that's not entirely accurate, but it's the best we can do without sending you on some epic quest of self-discovery. Beggars can't be choosers."

He flitted through a few books, his fingers tracing ancient symbols, before suddenly exclaiming, "Aha, here we are. We might actually be able to handle two birds with one stone. Based on your Oracle Trial and your current...situation, shall we call it? Hmmm."

A list of options materialized before Jace, each glowing with a faint, ethereal light. Dozens of class options flickered past. Hades shook his head at all of them. "Death Knight? Dark Reaper? No, no...let's see. Shouldn't get too far ahead of ourselves. Let's try some of the basic classes."

With a snap of his fingers, the world around them dissolved into a swirl of colors. In an instant, they reappeared in a grand coliseum, its towering walls stretching toward the sky. The stands, carved from gleaming marble, were empty, yet the air buzzed with an almost palpable anticipation, as if the spirits of countless past spectators still lingered, eager to witness the unfolding drama.

Jace blinked, taking in the vast arena. The sand underfoot was soft yet firm, marked by the scars of previous combat. Overhead, the sky was a brilliant azure, with a few wisps of clouds drifting lazily across it. The scent of the sea, carried by a gentle breeze, mingled with the faint aroma of distant pine forests.

"Okay, Chosen," Hades' tone was both challenging and amused, a hint of a smirk playing at the corners of his mouth. "Let's test you out."

In an instant, Jace found himself clad in heavy armor, a massive sword in hand.

Chapter 23
Since When Did a Little Death Hurt Anyone?

"Let's see how you'd do as a fighter." Hades gestured toward a shadowy form in the distance.

The beast erupted from the shadows, a grotesque marvel of sinew and bone. Muscles coiled like serpents under its dark, leathery hide, and jagged spikes jutted out in chaotic rows, like shattered fangs. Its eyes blazed with an ancient, malevolent fury. The creature was a monstrosity, towering and formidable, with claws like scythes and venom-dripping fangs. It looked like someone had bred a dragon with a rhinoceros.

Jace felt the armor lock around him, a prison of metal that seemed to constrict with every breath. There was no time to adjust; the beast charged, its roar a shockwave that reverberated through his very bones.

His first swing was desperate, the sword slicing through the air with a hollow whoosh. The beast moved with terrifying speed, its claws raking across his armor as if it were paper. Jace stumbled, the weight of the armor dragging him down, each movement a herculean effort. He gasped for air, his lungs burning, as the creature's jaws clamped around his torso. The last thing he saw was the triumphant glow in those feral eyes, before darkness engulfed him.

Hades stood beside the mangled remnants of his body, watching with a bored expression. "Well, that didn't go too well."

In a blink, the scene reset. Jace was alive again, standing in the same spot.

"What was that thing?" Jace asked breathlessly.

"A house pet from Tartarus," Hades mused. Jace thought he saw a spark of mischief dancing in his gaze. "But I believe we can find something more suitable for you."

With another snap of his fingers, Jace's heavy armor vanished, replaced by lightweight leather gear. A bow materialized in his hand, and a quiver full of arrows settled across his back.

"This is more your style, perhaps," Hades said.

Jace's eyes widened at the change, and the sudden realization that he would have to go again. This time, the beast was different—a flying creature with a wingspan twice the length of Jace's entire body screeched in the sky. Its beady eyes locked onto Jace as it dove straight at him.

Jace gripped the bow awkwardly, his fingers fumbling as he tried to notch an arrow. His grip was all wrong, and the string twanged noisily as he released, the arrow flying off to the left, nowhere near its intended target. He fell to the side as the creature swiped at him, just missing his leather-armored chest. His cheeks burned in embarrassment, but there was no time to dwell on it.

With a quick, unsteady movement, he grabbed another arrow from the quiver. His hands were trembling. He attempted to steady his breathing, but his heart pounded like a drum in his chest. As he pulled back the string, his footing slipped on the loose dirt, sending him sprawling backward. In his fall, his fingers released the string, and the arrow flew haphazardly. It struck the stadium wall and ricocheted wildly.

Determined, he scrambled to his feet, grabbing the last arrow. The creature screeched and launched itself at him again. His movements were frantic, desperation clear in his eyes. This time, he tried to find a solid stance, but his legs felt like jelly. Drawing the bowstring back, he aimed shakily at the creature. As he let the arrow fly, he stumbled once more, his balance off. Miraculously, the arrow arched through the air and, by some stroke of luck, grazed the creature's wing. Jace stared in disbelief as the creature faltered in the air.

"Yeah!" he cheered as the creature crashed to the ground. He looked over at Hades with a smug grin. "Not too bad for a—"

Hades only smiled and nodded his head back in the direction of the beast.

Jace turned just in time to see a beak rocketing towards his face before everything went dark again.

He reappeared in the same spot as before. "Ah! Stop doing that!"

"I'd give that a two out of ten," Hades commented dryly, shaking his head. "What about a rogue?"

The coliseum shifted, the ground beneath Jace's feet trembling as the arena transformed. Before him, a complex obstacle course appeared, filled with twisting pathways, tall walls to climb, and treacherous pits to navigate. It seemed manageable at first glance. "The goal," Hades said, "is to make it through the obstacle course and retrieve the artifact at the end."

Jace surveyed the scene and nodded. "That doesn't look too hard," he muttered.

Hades smirked, raising an eyebrow. "Oh, really?" With a snap of his fingers, the scene changed dramatically. Flames erupted from the ground, roaring to life and turning the course into a fiery inferno. The heat was intense, and the once simple obstacles now gleamed with shard blades and spikes.

"Better get going!" Hades shouted over the cacophony of crackling flames.

Jace's heart pounded as he stood at the edge of the fiery maze, his eyes wide with trepidation.

Teach me to open my mouth.

"Okay, Jace, you got this. Just a bunch of fire and... death... everywhere. No big deal," he muttered to himself, shaking his hands out. He forced a grin, psyching himself up. "Piece of cake."

With a final nod, he leapt into action, sprinting forward with determination. His confidence lasted all of two seconds before a wall of fire erupted right in front of him. "Oh, come on!" he yelled, flailing as the flames engulfed him. The searing pain was immediate as his skin roasted. The agony overwhelmed his senses, and in an instant, everything went black. Consumed by nothingness, he had no time to even register his failure.

Moments later, Jace reappeared at the starting line, his body restored. He glanced around, a mix of confusion and frustration etched on his face. "Will you stop that? Dying hurts, you know!" Suddenly, his eyes widened with realization. "Oh no, my EXP!" He frantically opened his character sheet, bracing for the worst. To his surprise, his EXP count was unchanged.

"No respawn fees in here," Hades explained with a wave of his hand. "Technically, you're already sort of dead. Anyone here gets the Dead Status while in this realm. Perks of being my Chosen."

Jace could hardly call the ability to die over and over again in the Underworld a "perk."

"But the System said..." Jace started.

"The System said... the System said." Hades mocked. "Listen, Chosen, when you are under the direct purview of the 'System,' as you call it, you are correct. Death comes with quite a cost. Loss of aether, items, and potentially, something far more dear. But even the Infinite does not micromanage. And this," Hades waved his hand expansively, "this is my domain. Now, let's try again," he said, motioning to the fiery doom-maze.

Jace's heart slowed as he focused. "Can't really die. Yeah, okay. Since when did a little death hurt anyone?" He recalled a martial arts movie he had once watched with his brother. "Pain is just pain. It won't kill you," he repeated the words, calming his mind. Hades watched with keen interest.

The intense heat licked at his skin as Jace dashed into the maze, keeping low to avoid the flames. Sweat poured down his face, stinging his eyes. The roar of the flames and the distant rumble of shifting walls filled his ears. The path twisted and turned unpredictably, forcing him to rely on his instincts to navigate the labyrinth.

As he rounded a corner, a jet of fire erupted from the wall, narrowly missing him. The heat singed his hair, prompting him to quicken his pace. His mind raced, trying to anticipate the next trap. Each step was a gamble.

He leapt over a chasm, barely making it to the other side. The flames behind him roared louder, as if angered by his escape. His lungs burned with every breath, the air thick with smoke. But he pushed on, driven by the desire to prove himself.

Ahead, he saw the faint glow of the artifact, a small, shimmering object radiating an otherworldly light. Jace grinned in triumph, but his victory was short-lived. A wall of fire erupted in front of him, blocking his path.

He skidded to a halt, eyes wide with panic. There was no way around it. The flames were too high to jump over and too wide to dodge. He was trapped.

"Think, Jace, think!" he muttered, his mind racing. He glanced around, searching for anything that could help him. His eyes fell on his ring. He touched it and felt a cool energy emanating from it in a faint glow. He focused on it, and a prompt appeared.

Ring of the White Raven has requested access to your Aether Pool.
    Accept | Reject

Jace hesitated for a moment before choosing [Accept]. Instantly, a powerful pull seized his mind, tugging at his essence like the exhaustion of a marathon compressed into a heartbeat. His aether surged into the ring, slowly at first, then faster and faster. A cool aura enveloped him, forming a protective barrier against the encroaching flames.

You Have Gained a Temporary Buff
    Fire Resistant
    Stay cool, Ponyboy.

Where was the System coming up with these references? Jace was pretty sure that one wasn't even right.

He sprinted forward, ducking and weaving through the inferno. The ring's power gave him just enough protection to push through the worst of the heat. The exertion took its toll, his stamina waning as the mana draw drained his strength. His legs felt heavy, his breath labored, but he pushed on.

Halfway through the fire, he felt the heat pressing on him again, the ring's energy fading. His muscles ached, and his vision blurred. He needed to push through before the protection ran out completely. The artifact was in sight. Just one final stretch, one small jump between him and it.

Jace gathered his remaining strength, took a deep breath, and leapt. But the aether drain hit at the wrong moment, sapping the last of his energy.

Aether Pool Critically Low
   Insufficient Resources to Maintain Resistance

The ring's glow flickered out, leaving Jace in sudden darkness. Mid-jump, his legs gave out, sending him stumbling as the flames surged, the barrier failing. "Fuck!" he cried, engulfed by searing pain until darkness claimed him.

Jace reappeared at the starting line, panting and frustrated. Hades stood beside him, eyes fixed on the ring with a glint of reserved curiosity.

"Where did you get that?"

Jace glanced at the ring, then back at Hades. "I bought it," he replied, defensiveness creeping into his voice unbidden.

Hades smiled knowingly. "Is that what you think?"

Jace frowned. "Wait, what do you mean?"

Hades remained silent, his expression unreadable.

"Come on! You can't just say stuff like that and not explain," Jace said, shaking his head in frustration. *Why is nothing ever straightforward here?* he thought.

Hades shifted topics smoothly. "Enough of the maze. Let's see. How about Mage? You do look a little... home-schooled, after all."

In an instant, the fiery maze dissolved, replaced by an intricate ritual chamber. Arcane symbols glowed ominously on the floor, and strange, ancient markings lined the walls. Jace stood in the center, holding a staff in one hand and an old leather book in the other.

"This one should be simple. Just read the book and chant the spells correctly," Hades instructed, a smirk playing at the corners of his mouth.

Jace glanced at the staff, then at the glowing symbols. Cautiously, he began reading the incantation, trying to sound confident. At least it was in English. "By the power of the arcane, I—"

Suddenly, the symbols flared to life, and the staff buzzed in his hands. The magic spiraled, the energy crackling wildly around him and sending a gust of wind around the room. The chamber trembled as the chaotic magic swirled, growing stronger and more erratic.

"I... summon you, the essence of night and light... and er..." He could barely see through the wind, the pages of his book fluttering in his hand. A sudden gust caused him to drop the book, its pages flying out and joining the spiraling vortex.

"Wait, wait, no!" Jace's voice cracked as he tried to regain control, but the spells twisted and tangled. The magical energy lashed out, striking the walls and floor, creating a cascading clash of sparks.

"Stop, stop, STOP!" Jace shouted, waving the staff around desperately, but it only made things worse. The energy engulfed him, wrapping around his body like a serpent. His eyes widened in horror as the magic pulled him apart, piece by piece.

He screamed as his body disintegrated rapidly. His mind was a whirl of panic and pain until, mercifully, darkness took him.

Jace reappeared, gasping for breath, his body whole once again but his mind reeling from the experience. "Nope, nope!" he yelled. "Definitely not a Mage."

Hades chuckled, shaking his head. "Not your forte, I see. Let's try something else, shall we?"

"Can I at least have a minute?" Jace asked, his voice tinged with desperation.

Hades seemed to consider it for a moment before saying, "I don't think so."

Without warning, Jace found himself in the midst of a battlefield. Explosions thundered around him, the cries of the wounded piercing the air. He was wearing an old medic's outfit from the third world war. The acrid smell of smoke and blood filled his nostrils, and his heart raced with the intensity of the chaos. A bodiless voice echoed around him, "Let's try cleric on for size."

Jace's eyes darted across the battlefield, taking in the carnage. He saw a soldier with a severed arm, blood gushing from the wound, and a female medic, her leg crushed under rubble, her face contorted in pain. The sergeant, his face set in grim determination, tossed Jace a healing spell scroll. "Use it wisely," he barked, his voice carrying the weight of command and urgency.

It was a test. He had to choose.

Jace knelt beside the medic, her eyes wide with pain and fear. She tried to reach for him with her uninjured hand, but her strength was fading fast. He glanced at the soldier, whose eyes were filled with pleading and agony. The spell was only meant for one. The weight of the decision bore down on Jace, a knot of anxiety tightening in his chest. "This isn't fair. Neither of you should die," he whispered, feeling the cold tendrils of fear creeping up his spine.

Then, something shifted in his senses, like an answer to his plea, a thought that had been just out of reach, a dream that had faded away. He latched onto the perception. A faint glow appeared around them both and around the sergeant. The sergeant's glow was strong and vibrant. Both the medic's and the soldier's lights were dim and flickering like dying embers.

He had an idea. A crazy idea. He felt his own life force, reaching out to each of them. He focused on both, attempting to connect them, to bind them temporarily, perhaps tricking the spell into counting them all as one. He had no idea if it would work, but he had to try.

The scroll glowed in his hands, and he channeled the energy through himself, directing it towards both the medic and the soldier. The spell resisted at first, the magic intended for one fighting against the division. But Jace's determination and sheer force of will pushed it beyond its limits, pouring his life force into the spell. He felt his energy draining rapidly, the life force ebbing away as he pushed harder, binding their fates together.

A soft, radiant light enveloped them, knitting their wounds with an otherworldly grace. The soldier's severed arm regenerated, the medic's crushed leg mended, and the agony in their eyes gave way to profound relief and gratitude. Jace, however, felt his strength ebbing away. His vision blurred, and his limbs grew heavy.

He collapsed, energy spent, a sense of triumph mingling with the encroaching darkness.

He tried to halt the spell, but it defied him, accelerating its drain on his life force. His final thought lingered on the lives he had saved, the emotional victory offering a fleeting moment of satisfaction.

This is just a game. Why does it feel so real? he wondered.

Jace reappeared beside Hades, panting heavily, exhaustion evident on his face. His body trembled from the exertion, a lingering effect even after his regeneration.

"Well," Hades mused, a glimmer in his eyes, "that's something we can work with."

Chapter 24
Classy

A system notification appeared.

Congratulations, Traveler!

    The System has recognized your impressive knack for resilience and good ol' stick-to-itiveness. While you may not excel in many areas, your ability to take a beating is truly commendable. Hey, everyone has their talents!

    To acknowledge your unwavering tenacity, the System is offering you a choice of one of four initial Class Titles. Choose wisely, and remember, it's not just about surviving; it's about surviving with style!

    Base Class Titles Available:
- Fighter
- Mage
- Rogue
- Cleric

Choose your path and let the good times roll!

He stared at the list. The option of Cleric was underlined and glowed faintly.

    Jace thought it over.

    Nothing else seemed to fit. *Maybe Rogue...*

    Jace sighed, feeling a twinge of disappointment. The idea of unleashing massive fireballs or hacking through goblins with a greatsword had its appeal, but then he remembered the coliseum and how quickly he had been turned into a smear on the floor. "Yeah, okay, maybe not," he muttered.

Quest Complete: Get Some Class
    Congratulations! You have accepted the Class Title: Cleric
    Rewards:
    • 200 EXP
    • Class Title: Cleric
    • Item: Simple Cleric's Rod
    Bonus Reward:
    • Word of Power Unlocked: Soul Affinity (One Star)
    You're a Speaker, Jace.

A surge of energy coursed through Jace, the dark power of his released Affinity merging with his essence. His body glowed faintly as he felt the transformation take hold.

    Jace's body erupted in a swirl of dark, spiraling energy, like a thousand shards of broken glass catching the dim light. For a fleeting moment, he felt weightless, suspended in midair before being gently set back down. He stood there, a strange sensation simmering beneath his skin, every cell buzzing with energy. A grin spread across his face as the feeling intensified, and a brilliant light expanded from within before vanishing entirely, leaving him blinking in surprise. He checked his notifications.

Ding!
    Rank Up
    You have gained the rank: Bronze One, Novice Reactionaire.
    You now meet the minimum requirements to attend the bi-annual Star Ceremony and receive your first Bronze Star.
    Status Update:
    • Classless (Debuff) Removed

Attribute Points Changed:

• Intelligence: +1

• Wisdom: +2

Total EXP: 950

EXP Capacity: 950/950

Warning: You have reached the limit of your maximum stored EXP. Please spend EXP or increase capacity. Any EXP gained over the threshold will be reduced by 90%.

Time to level up or face the wrath of wasted potential!

Alright, more brains and wisdom. That's good. He felt a surge of mental clarity, ideas connecting faster and more smoothly than before.

As he looked over his character sheet, knowledge from the primer flooded his mind, soaking into him like water into a dry sponge.

Turns out the System's effects were not to be underestimated. An increase to Intelligence or Wisdom or Strength really meant just that—an increase. The room seemed slightly brighter, more vivid, and the colors and details crisper. He suspected that was his improved Intelligence.

Analyzing the overall impact, Jace realized his mental faculties had received a significant boost.

But all in all, he felt he had made some decent progress, especially now that the Classless Debuff was removed. He shifted from foot to foot, trying to take in all of the changes he was feeling.

"I gained the 'Soul' Affinity."

Hades mouthed a silent praise to the Fates, his eyes sparkling for a moment before returning to his usual inscrutable demeanor.

"Ah, 'Soul'. Very well."

Jace raised an eyebrow. "So, that's good then?"

Hades chuckled. "That will depend on you. It is... hopeful. Promising even. But whether it is good or an entirely wasted opportunity is up to you."

"Do a lot of people have this Affinity?" Jace asked.

"Unfortunately, it's not that simple, kid. No two Words are ever truly the same. When you say soul, it means something different to you than it does to me. You see, possessing the Word grants an Affinity. But Affinities are just that—affinities. They aren't powers in themselves. They're inclinations, a natural sort of affection and understanding for a domain, and they manifest very differently in each individual."

Jace nodded slowly. "So, it's like a head start?"

"Exactly like a head start. Possessing the Word 'Run' doesn't give you all the practice required to run a marathon. But it might speed up the process. Words must be used; abilities must be cultivated and grown. As you do so, you'll feel the Word move through you, creating pathways for your Aether, or Breath, to flow.

But I'm afraid there's no—what did your people used to say?—no 'get rich quick scheme' or 'miracle pill' for this. Even now, you should feel some abilities working their way through you, fighting to determine your new aether channels. But it is you that will have to put in the work."

Jace nodded. That was the first thing in this world that really made sense. As Uncle Albert used to say, "you don't get nothin' without work." He wasn't really their uncle, of course. Just a neighbor Alex and him started calling that for some reason when they were kids. Jace couldn't quite recall why.

"With practice, you'll eventually progress from Reactionaire to Perceptor," Hades continued. "That said, no one can predict precisely what abilities will be gained as a Speaker cultivates their Word."

Jace grinned, feeling a strange mix of excitement and dread. "So, what you're saying is, even you have no clue what strange things I'll be able to do?"

Hades shook his head. "Don't get too casual with me, Chosen. You forget precisely how much of your puny little life rests between my forefinger and thumb." He put heavy emphasis on the last words, but he did not release his aura.

"I'm kidding." Jace quickly backpedaled and forced a nervous laugh.

Desperate to change the subject, Jace latched onto something he had seen in his notifications.

"It says my EXP has reached its maximum capacity. What does that mean?" Jace asked. He guessed the authors of the Primer didn't think that info was chapter one material.

"This is something your Society President would know, so take notes. You'll need to pass it on when we start accepting new followers.

EXP is gained through completing quests, besting challenges, and exploring Terra Mythica. It fills up a store of energy within you, but there's a limit to how much can be stored. When you reach that limit, you need to consolidate it, and direct it into your abilities, skills, and attributes.

Think of it like this—you gain experience by diving into chaos, you gain wisdom by reflection upon that experience. It's a cycle—face challenges, step back to learn, then dive back in."

"Do I need to meditate or something?" Jace asked, recalling something his brother had mentioned during his studies. Jace wished he had paid more attention when his brother talked about Terra Mythica. All those countless hours of study and preparation would have really come in handy right about now.

"Not necessarily. Spending EXP is like using a Word—the process is different for everyone. Some people record their experiences in books, becoming Inscriptionists. As they climb in rank, their writings begin to grant others a touch of experience or theoretical knowledge in addition to helping the author consolidate their gains. Others take leisurely walks, staying present and letting their gains fortify naturally. Then there are those who are more methodical, systematic in their approach. Some even share their experiences with an audience, providing minor buffs to the listeners. You'll find what works best for you.

Understanding your growth is a personal journey. There are tomes and scrolls that delve into these topics, but no authoritarian approach works unless it simply encourages you to look.

Any great philosopher can be judged by whether their teachings have made it easier or more difficult to observe the world in which we live and the magic upon which it stands. There are laws of nature and truths in this universe. But even the presence of a law does not relieve you from your duty to observe it for yourself. A teacher can guide you, ask the right questions, and help you train your skills and mind. But you must do the looking and the seeing. You are the adventurer in your own story, after all."

Jace tried to ask more, but Hades raised a hand, with a soft chuckle. "You've got me monologuing like an old professor of rhetoric. There's only so much I can tell you, Jace. Some things you simply have to discover for yourself."

Sensing the shift in tone, Jace knew he wouldn't get any more free information out of Hades. They shared a moment of comfortable silence as Jace scrutinized the changes to his stats.

Chapter 25
Character Sheet

C haracter Sheet

Name: Jace
Speaker Rank: Bronze One Star, Novice Reactionaire
Class Title: Cleric
EXP CAPACITY BAR: 950/950

Attributes
- Strength: 10
- Dexterity: 12
- Intelligence: 13
- Wisdom: 14
- Constitution: 10
- Charisma: 9

Skills

• Dark Vision (Novice): Improved ability to see in darkness with limited clarity.

• Knowledge Absorption (Apprentice): Enhances the retention and comprehension of absorbed knowledge.

• Universal Lore (Apprentice): Increases understanding of game mechanics and world lore.

• Minor Resistance to Death (Novice): You are good at dying. So much so that you have built up a natural immunity to it. Keep it up to increase your resilience. Take 5% less damage from necrotic, evil, and shadow-based attacks.

Words of Power / Affinities: Soul – Bronze One, Novice Reactionaire

Unlocked Abilities and Effects

• Soul Survivor (Internal, Passive): Your soul is resilient. You have Spoken a Word of Power far beyond your ability and lived to tell the tale. You are defying the course of natural selection. +10% increased resistance to all soul damage.

Aether Cost: None

• Soul Mend (Touch): You have gained some passing insight into how the soul can heal the body.

Aether Cost: Moderate

• Soul Tether (Distance, Sight): You can perceive and influence the connectivity between souls, allowing you to transfer minor limited effects between two entities.

Aether Cost: High

• Soul Sense (Distance, Sight): Increased perception of emotions in others and wandering spirits.

Aether Cost: Low

Chapter 26
A Little Push

"Now, we need to get you attuned to a Shard. Can't have my Chosen walking around Shardless. Follow me." Hades started walking outside, and Cerberus let out a soft whine. "I'll be back, boy. And with a treat." This seemed to pacify him.

Jace remembered Alice mentioning that a Speaker's first Shard usually came from their Society, which kept a collection for the newcomers. He hoped this process would be straightforward because he was growing tired of the Underworld's perpetual gloom. He knew he would need to build up stamina to endure this kind of dreariness.

Walking alongside Hades, Jace couldn't help but note the god's casual stride, like a man taking a stroll down a garden path. Jagged stones and ancient pathways twisted and turned, lined with luminescent fungi and misplaced shadows.

"So, how does it work? Do I just pick one?" Jace asked.

"Just pick one? Furies, what am I going to do with you, kid? No, you don't 'just pick one.' Shards are no minor thing. They're integral to the socioeconomics of Terra Mythica and will serve as your lifelong companion."

Jace was really wishing he had something he could use to simply absorb on all of this. He wasn't looking forward to another info dump. As they walked, Hades spoke, his deep, resonant voice echoing through the darkness, each word carrying the weight of the centuries.

"I'll keep it simple," Hades said, as if in answer to Jace's thoughts. "Shards choose their Speaker, never the other way around. They have to resonate with the very core of your being, reacting to your thoughts and feelings—often before you even realize you're having them. While not technically alive, a Shard embodies a perfect harmonic of life. It vibrates at the same frequency as its Speaker. Got it?"

Jace did not.

"Eh, not enough time. Don't worry about it. Your Shard will find you. That's all you need to know."

"You said it was tied in with economics?" Jace asked, interested in anything that could point him in the right direction for acquiring gold.

"Socioeconomics. Money and society," Hades began, gesticulating casually. "The gods do not directly rule the inhabitants of Terra. Mythians must rule themselves. We are just custodians of vital offices, core functions that keep the fabric of reality intact. We each have a Society or Following to help us in our duty, but ruling? That's your kind's gig."

Jace glanced around, unsure where they were headed, but he didn't want to interrupt Hades.

"And how that ruling structure works ties closely with your Shard. A Shard doesn't guarantee a position in society, but it does tend to foreshadow one."

Hades continued, "There are six Shards—Sapphire, Amethyst, Ruby, Amber, Moonstone, and Emerald.

Sapphires tend to be your scholars and scientists, striving for invention and unraveling the mysteries of the universe.

Amethysts lean toward protection magic and the finding of lost things of the past. They are keepers of memory and great admirers of wisdom.

Once, long ago, the Sapphires and Amethysts worked together to ward away the Void, keeping it at bay. But now, there is no love lost between them.

Emeralds are known to be keen observers and powerful allies, becoming masters of persuasion; they're also often silver-tongued politicians.

Rubies are your fighters, the royal guard types. None are better when brute force is required.

Ambers prefer a natural life, often living outside structured societies, roaming the plains and seas.

And then there are the Moonstones, known for their secrecy and knack for moving behind the shadows. When you want something done without any noise, you give it to a Moonstone."

As they walked, they neared a cliff edge, the path precarious and narrow.

"The universe is governed by two great powers: Chaos and Order," Hades continued. "Life, the Infinite Potential, strives to instill order into the

Void, while the Eternal End is bent only on the Chaos that ends in silence. You'll find beings on both sides of that coin, and their Affinities will differ greatly."

Jace thought about this. It was a big decision, and he felt woefully unprepared for it. "How will I know I've found the right one?"

The sound of rocks falling echoed down a very long way as the surrounding air crackled with latent energy, making Jace's skin prickle.

"You'll know," Hades said, eyes gleaming with a sinister light. "Attuning to your first Shard comes naturally to most, though some do require a little push."

Hades paused, placing a firm hand on Jace's shoulder. "Good luck," he said, then shoved.

The ground vanished beneath Jace's feet. His scream was swallowed by the void as he plummeted into the abyss. The initial freefall was a terrifying blur, his stomach lurching as he tumbled through darkness. Suddenly, the fall twisted into a brutal, bone-jarring descent. Sharp rocks and jagged outcroppings tore at his clothes and skin, each impact sending jolts of pain through his body.

He crashed into a wall, his shoulder absorbing the brunt of the blow, before being flung into another harsh turn. His head slammed against something hard, stars exploding in his vision. Blood trickled down his face as the tunnel walls shimmered with streaks of phosphorescent minerals.

Finally, he was spat out onto a rough, uneven floor. Jace lay there, battered and bruised. Every part of him ached, a symphony of pain making his vision swim. He forced himself to his feet, wincing with every movement. His legs felt like they were made of lead, but he could still walk. Barely.

He found himself in a wide cavern filled with a kaleidoscope of colors shining from crystals of every hue, transforming it into a mesmerizing sea of light.

Jace took a tentative step forward, the crystalline light reflecting off jagged walls in a mesmerizing display. The air was cool, carrying a faint, sweet scent reminiscent of honeysuckle. The distant trickle of water calmed his racing heart. The sheer beauty surrounding him stood in stark contrast to the darkness and danger he had left behind.

As he ventured deeper, the paths diverged in countless directions, splitting and merging in a labyrinthine pattern, each bathed in different hues. One glowed with a soft, inviting blue; another shimmered with a fiery red. Yet, an inexplicable pull drew him towards the darkest path, where light and shadow intertwined in a delicate dance. The light was neither harsh nor dim, but perfectly balanced.

He walked for some time until the path eventually opened to a crystalline lake. At its center stood a small island, crowned by a single tree with leaves that glowed a soft, golden light, swaying gently despite the stillness.

Searching for a way across, his eyes fell upon a narrow path of floating stones, barely wide enough for one person. The stones stretched from the shore to the island, their surfaces worn smooth by water and time.

Determined, he set foot on the first stone, each step cautious yet steady. The water below shimmered with a light, casting rippling reflections on the cavern ceiling. Reaching the end, he found a cluster of shards in all different colors strewn around the tree. Tentatively, Jace reached out to touch a vibrant green crystal. As his fingers brushed its surface, it erupted in a verdant blaze of magical flame, searing his hand.

You Have Taken 20 Damage

He recoiled in pain, stumbling back into another cluster of gems. Each one he touched detonated in a burst of light and energy.

You Have Died In The Underworld

The notification appeared just as he found himself sliding down the cliff face again, landing back in the cavern.

"Shit." He was all the way back at the start.

"At least there are no penalties for death here," he muttered, flexing his sore hand. "But the pain still sucks."

Jace ventured through the cavern again, this time careful not to touch anything. He navigated the maze of gemstones with caution. He crossed the lake again and passed the clusters of stones.

Then he saw it—a gem nestled among the crystals near a cave wall. Its surface shimmered like liquid silver, swirling with deep, obsidian hues. As he approached, the gem seemed to sense his presence. It trembled, then convulsed violently. Jace's heart pounded in his chest. The gem ripped itself from the wall with a deafening crack, rocketing toward him with a fierce, almost malevolent energy. He reached out instinctively, his fingers closing around it with a loud clap. A violent surge of power exploded through him, sending shockwaves up his arm and nearly knocking him off his feet.

Moonstone Shard is Attempting to Attunement
Accept | Reject

The moment that Jace chose to accept, the Moonstone shattered into a thousand pieces, each transforming into a tiny drop of silver and black. The drops clung to his skin, slithering up his arm like a swarm of living ink. Suddenly, a searing pain pierced his chest, digging into his heart. The liquid fire spread through his veins, covering his skin in a shimmering layer before vanishing, leaving behind a faint, glowing mark like a tattoo over across his chest. He felt its presence inside him, a steady pulse of power.

His mind buzzed with newfound clarity, the cavern's colors now sharper, more vivid. He could hear the hums of the other Shards. The pain dulled, replaced by a sense of unity with the Shards magic. The surrounding crystals pulsed in a synchronized rhythm, as if acknowledging his attunement and welcoming him into their world.

Concentrating, he summoned the Shard, watching as it materialized in his hand. The moonstone glowed with a mesmerizing radiance, surrounded by swirling tendrils of ethereal darkness. It felt both foreign and familiar, an extension of himself yet entirely distinct.

Checking his status he found that he had been fully healed.

"Cool." He whispered.

Jace moved through the cavern, with the path ahead illuminated by the Shard's glow. Each step felt lighter, more sure.

That was, until the ground vanished beneath him again.

One moment, he was walking on solid soil, the next, he was plummeting. "Oh, for the love of—" His yell echoed off the cavern walls, bouncing back to him in a mocking chorus. The world spun, and his Shard glowed, a last wink of reassurance before the darkness swallowed him whole.

He landed with a bewildered thump beside Hades, back in the office of his grand palace. The god's expression was inscrutable, a faint smile playing at the corners of his lips. Dusting himself off, Jace looked around, dazed but unhurt.

"How the Furies did I get here?" Jace wondered aloud, frustration evident. Jace also wondered why he had said furies. He had never said that before.

"We are in the Underworld," Hades said with a shrug, as if that was answer enough. Straightening, Hades' expression turned stony again.

"Now, for your first quest," he said, pulling out a massive tome from his desk. The book thudded heavily as he opened it, flipping through the pages until he found what he was looking for.

"Enough," Jace said flatly.

Hades paused to consider him.

"Enough throwing me off cliffs and tossing me to dragons. Enough laughing as you get me killed again and again."

Hades put on a concerned face, but Jace could tell he was holding back a smile.

"Fine, fine. No more tricks, Jace."

Jace stared at him for a long moment before nodding.

"You have a quest for me?" He said, feeling slightly awkward after his outburst.

"If you are ready. I don't want to rush you." Hades said as if handling a grumpy child.

"I'm fine."

"If you're sure," Hades said, turning back to the tome and running a finger across the page. "There's a woman in the wilderness, a three-hour walk east of the campus. She was supposed to arrive more than six weeks ago," Hades explained.

Jace frowned. "So, she is still alive? But isn't her surviving a good thing?"

"Not when it's like this, no," Hades replied, his tone grave. "Look here," he pointed to an entry. "It clearly states she died six weeks ago. But where is her soul? If she hadn't died, it wouldn't be my concern. But she did, and so it is. And, as Fate would have it, what is my concern is your concern, Chosen."

Hades continued, his voice slipping into a lecturing tone. "With you Travelers, death just means a trip to me. My staff sends you back to your most recent respawn spot. Sometimes we take ranks, experience, and other resources to balance the cost of the trip. Pretty cut and dry. For Citizens, it's different. When they die, their souls are weighed, their fate determined, and their energy directed. Maybe they're reincarnated, or maybe they move back into the cosmic void to help create new things."

He tapped the entry in the tome with urgency. "But this soul, right here, has been lost for six weeks without showing up. Missed her departure. And the longer a soul remains unweighed and unrouted, the more chaotic things get. Trust me, you don't want to see what happens when the natural order is disrupted."

Jace nodded.

"So," Hades said, closing the book with a heavy thud, "your quest is to get out there, figure out what's keeping this woman 'alive', and fix it."

Quest Chain Received

Profession Quest: Hades' Little Helper

I ain't 'fraid of no ghosts...

There is the soul of a woman in the wilderness east of the campus that was supposed to move on six weeks ago, but something is keeping her there. You must figure out what is causing this anomaly and set things right.

Reward: 500 Society EXP, 50 Silver

Failure: Impending doom

Bonus Objective: Give it that little extra

Bonus Reward: Variable

Accept | Reject

Rejecting this quest is possible, but it would start things on a rather bad foot. Do you really want to be known as the ungrateful little... well, you get the idea.

Jace wondered exactly how much influence Hades had over the quest prompts or if it was all System.

He quickly chose [Accept].

"Now get out there and bring me back that soul. Do well, and I might have something special for you." Suddenly, Hades' figure grew larger, towering over Jace, his eyes glowing with fiery light. His voice deepened, echoing through the room like rolling thunder. "But fail this quest, and you will suffer the endless pain and torment of the fires of the Underworld!"

Jace's heart pounded in his chest, the weight of Hades' words pressing down on him like a giant hand. Just as he felt the terror take hold, Hades' form shrank back to normal, and he burst out laughing.

"I'm just joshing ya," Hades said with a quick grin. "Relax, kid. Now get out there and enjoy the adventure. Kids these days..."

Jace exhaled, the tension in his shoulders fading slowly. Hades' ability to switch between terrifying and casual was unsettling. Despite his intimidating presence, Jace couldn't help but feel that Hades had a bit of a dad vibe.

"Oh, before I forget, hand me your wrist," Hades instructed. Jace hesitated, but complied. Hades pulled a medallion from his robes, shining with intricate silver. He pressed the medallion to Jace's wrist. It burned like acid, causing Jace to grit his teeth, but when he looked, it had transformed into a silver tattoo, glinting in the firelight.

"When you see Charon—"

"Who?" Jace asked, confused.

"You know, the guy who just paddled you across the River Styx. Charon."

"Oh, him. I didn't know his name. More of a Joe, if you ask me," Jace said.

Hades raised an eyebrow. "Anyway, show him this medallion. As long as you're my Chosen, he'll give you free passage. Think of it like frequent flyer miles or a bus pass. It'll also act to shroud your aura," Hades explained. "Stop any busybodies from getting too nosy about your... unique situation."

Status Effect - Permanent Boon Gain
    Title: Mostly Dead
    You exist in a state of perpetual limbo between life and death, distinct from the Undead. This condition accompanies you wherever you go. Attempts

to [Scan] or [Identify] you will result in confusion, as readings fluctuate between signs of life and death, revealing no further data.

Effects:

• Condition: Cannot be [Scanned] or [Identified].

• Condition: Eerie; -1 to Charisma.

Your secrets are safe with Hades.

"Great," Jace said flatly. "If lose any more Charisma, I'm going to start scaring people."

Chapter 27
A Throne of Leaves

Jace's steps faltered as he retraced his path from the Underworld, his mind consumed by recent events. The route the wisp had led him before now seemed like a distant memory, and without its guidance, he found himself lost in the maze of corridors. The darkness pressed in around him, a living, breathing entity seeking to consume his very soul. Whispers slithered through the air, carrying half-formed words that made his skin crawl and his sanity waver. Whether he pressed on or turned back, both choices filled him with dread.

A flicker of light appeared before him, bobbing in the air and beckoning him forward. "Oh, thank the Fates. It's you." He followed the green light, winding through the twisting paths, guided away from the route he had been on.

As he trailed the wisp, Jace couldn't shake the feeling that the Underworld itself was watching him, unseen eyes following his every move. The wisp guided him through narrow passages and around sharp corners; the path grew more convoluted with each step. Despite the complexity of the route, the wisp never hesitated, always knowing exactly where to go.

The tunnels gradually grew colder until his breath formed visible puffs in the air. He pulled his dark tunic closer.

"Where are we going?" Jace asked. "This doesn't feel right."

But he was committed now, with no way back. Small bits of ice formed around the edges of the path.

Finally, the wisp stopped at the entrance to a hidden grotto, a secret you'd never find unless you knew where to look.

A warm light hummed from the grotto as billows of fog drifted out, obscuring everything. The wisp hovered for a moment before vanishing, leaving Jace alone in the glowing chamber. He took a cautious step forward, his eyes scanning the room through the white haze.

As the fog lifted slightly, it revealed a mist that cloaked the high ceiling, creating the illusion of a swirling, tempestuous sky. Tiny flakes of snow drifted down, blanketing the floor in a soft, shimmering layer.

In the center of the grotto, a pool of deep blue water glowed with an ethereal light, its surface shimmering as steam rose from it like a hot spring. Jace's eyes were drawn to the figure standing in the middle of the pool, her form bathed in the radiant glow. She was a vision of beauty and danger, her dark tresses cascading down her back like liquid silk, framing her perfectly sculpted features.

Jace froze in place, unable to decide if he should back away or move closer. The foggy glow from the pool seemed to intensify, casting a mesmerizing light on her skin.

"Don't be shy," she said, her voice smooth and inviting, a rich melody that sent a thrill through Jace. He stood frozen, his feet rooted to the spot.

"Come here," she commanded softly. As if drawn by an invisible force, his body moved of its own accord. He approached cautiously, taking in every detail of her form. The pool's glow pulsed as he drew nearer, resonating with an ancient power.

"There's a good boy," she said, her full lips curving in a way that made his heart skip a beat. "Hand me my robe, would you? It's just there."

Jace noticed the white robe draped over a nearby rock. He hesitated, the weight of the moment pressing down on him, then picked it up and approached her. She stood, water streaming off her skin, her naked body a vision for the gods. Looking away with every ounce of will left to him, Jace handed her the robe. Their fingers brushed, and his face flushed, a shiver running down his spine as if the very fabric of her robe held a touch of destiny.

"Thank you," she said, her eyes locking onto his with an intensity that spoke of eons. "You've been brave to come this far. Now, let's see if you can go a little further."

She slipped the robe on, the thin fabric barely covering her. "My name is Persephone."

"Uh, I'm Jace," he stammered, his thoughts slightly clearer now that she had put on the robe.

Snowflakes gently drifted toward them, but seemed to dance and just barely miss her each time.

"Oh, I know who you are. I hear you'll be doing some work for my husband," she said with a playful lilt, her voice as warm as a flower basking in the sun. "He's been so very busy lately. It seems demon possessions are on the rise once again. He's always juggling so much, so I'm glad he's finally accepted another Chosen. You'll do your best to lighten his burden, won't you?"

Jace nodded, his words caught in his throat.

"He's told you about your part in all of this, I assume? About that thing on your finger? About your past, Jason Rolander?"

Her use of Jason's real name snapped him out of his daze. "What? Do I know you? Are you a Traveler?"

She laughed, a sound like delicate wind chimes. "No, dear child. But I know you."

"How?"

She seemed not to hear him as she roamed to a small alcove in the wall. As she walked, the earth rose, and plants bloomed in vibrant greens, blues, and reds, weaving together to form a large, plush chair before her. No, not a chair. To call it a chair would be like calling the sky big or a snow-capped mountain quaint. It was a throne of leaves and life amidst the snow.

Jace shivered again.

"Oh, the cold? My mother's doing. She seems to think she's being funny," Persephone said, a touch of exasperation in her voice. "I missed her birthday, and she has her ways of letting me know when I've displeased her."

Jace's eyes widened. "Your mother can influence the Underworld?"

Persephone shook her head, a wistful look in her eyes. "When Hades is paying attention, no. He has absolute domain here. But, I don't mind so much. You do miss the seasons while away."

A moment of silence passed between them, filled with the echo of dripping water and the soft rustle of newborn leaves.

"I love my husband dearly, but he sometimes forgets that I straddle two worlds. There are matters from my other life that need attention from time to time," she said with a soft, wistful smile, her voice as smooth as silk. Then, as if a thought had just struck her, she said, "Say, you wouldn't mind helping me with a task or two, here and there, would you?"

She tilted her head slightly, the casual gesture belying the hidden weight of her words, her eyes twinkling somewhere between mischief and sincerity.

"Oh, don't worry," she continued with a reassuring smile. "It won't be too difficult. Just an errand, every now and again."

Why do people keep saying that? Jace was starting to get concerned about how the Citizens of Mythica measured difficulty.

He was about to agree when he felt a sharp pain in his hand. Looking down, he saw a thin line of blood trickling from a pinprick on his finger. He scrutinized the jeweled eye of the ring.

Did you just bite me? he wondered.

A cold breeze swept through him, prompting him to look up. For a fleeting moment, he thought he saw a shadow of worry—or perhaps a scowl—cross her face. But as swiftly as it appeared, it vanished, her expression returning to one of serene dominance.

Jace hesitated. Deep down, he knew that whatever task this woman had in mind would not be easy or safe, and he didn't like the idea of keeping secrets from Hades—endless torment being on the table and all. Yet, he couldn't bring himself to flatly refuse her. Was he not allowed to do some light questing on the side?

He wanted to agree to everything she said, to bow at her feet, to worship her. Her charisma must be through the roof. He felt drunk, his senses overwhelmed by her presence.

Could the game really affect me this much? The thought unsettled him deeply.

It's all a game. He reminded himself. However, the sentiment felt more and more like empty words.

"It depends on the task," he managed, the words feeling heavy and foreign in his mouth.

She smiled as if he had just passed a secret test. "Nothing too out of your way," she said, reaching out a hand towards him. Jace accepted it, and she pulled him close to her until they were mere inches apart, her scent intoxicating.

Jace tore his gaze away, swallowing hard, his throat dry, unable to find his voice.

"Help me, and it'll be worth your while. I know many truths, Jason—dark, terrible truths, but also wonderful ones, the kind your heart desperately yearns to know. Agree to help me, and I will share some of that truth with you."

He nodded slowly, his eyes locking on hers. "Yes." Was the only word he said.

He immediately felt a surge of dread, like he had just failed a test of wisdom and willpower.

Her smile widened as she let go of Jace's hand, leaning back and resuming her luxuriant air. The room began to warm, and the snow slipped away like a forgotten dream, melting into the earth. From it, plants grew with the life and energy of Persephone's smile.

"Thank you," she said.

Hidden Quest
    Persephone's Errand
    You have agreed to undertake an unknown task in the future.
    Rewards: Variable
    Consequences of Failure: Variable

Suddenly, a loud crunch echoed as stones hit the floor in the distance, the sound bouncing off the walls of the cave. Her eyes became fierce and alive all at once, jolting Jace out of his trance-like state.

"You need to go," she said. "Now."

Jace's heart lurched in his chest.

"Pik," she called. The bouncing green light that had aided him before reappeared, bobbing eagerly. "Take him to safety. Avoid the main routes. You know what to do." Pik hummed in assent.

Jace turned to see the green wisp swirling around his head before heading to the entrance of the grotto. It waited there, bobbing anxiously.

He hurried down the path behind Pik, glancing back only once to see that Persephone and the grotto had vanished. The path was narrow and winding, with shadows dancing at the fringes of his vision.

After what felt like an eternity, spectral lanterns flickered in the distance, guiding Jace toward the riverbank. As he got closer, the hooded and imposing silhouette of Charon, the boatman, emerged from the gloom, standing tall and silent as the night. Pik hummed briefly before vanishing.

Charon turned slowly, his movements deliberate and unnerving. Despite the hood obscuring his face, Jace could feel the weight of his gaze.

Without a word, Charon gestured toward the boat.

"Let's get outta here, Joe," Jace said, showing his medallion tattoo as he stepped forward. The cold, damp air enveloped him like a shroud, and the still water reflected the spectral lanterns. They set off, gliding into the abyss, the sound of the oar dipping into the water the only break in the silence.

Chapter 28
The Shrining

B y nightfall, Jace returned to The Fields Below, his footsteps heavy as he descended the stairs to his dorm, each step marking the relentless grind of the day. Fatigue was etched deep into his bones, and he longed for the refuge of sleep. Using Dark Vision, he could make out the grim details of his surroundings. The walls, perhaps once vibrant, were now a filthy brown, choked with layers of grime that buried any hint of their former glory. The cracked marble floor spread out like a battlefield after the war, strewn with debris and discarded remnants, the detritus of a forgotten age.

He sighed, knowing another sleepless night awaited him, haunted by debuffs.

As he fumbled in his pocket, his fingers brushed against the unfamiliar weight of the Society President's Token. Smooth and cool, it offered an unexpected comfort. He traced the intricate insignia with his thumb. Upgrades to this dismal space would be his first order of business, a faint glimmer of hope in the midst of exhaustion.

With a flick of his thoughts, Jace activated his mini-map. His eyes locked onto his destination: "The Shrine of Hades." An invisible force seemed to guide him as a faint path materialized, winding through dark byways to the secluded underground grove. Ancient trees, their gnarled branches clawing at the ceiling, cast eerie shadows on the soft, molded floor beneath his feet. In the heart of the grove, the shrine loomed, its stone walls alive with intricate carvings. Jace approached with measured steps, the token humming eagerly as he got closer.

Inside the shrine, the atmosphere shifted with his improved vision. The once dull gray walls now glowed with hidden hues. Layers of neglect couldn't obscure the history and majesty that filled the small room. The book at the shrine's core beckoned.

Jace took the token from his pocket, turning it about in the light to watch it gleam.

How do I activate this thing? he wondered.

He reached out to touch the book, and a circle appeared on the thick cover, perfectly matching the size and shape of the token. As coin met leather, a surge of energy rippled through the air. The book sprang to life, its pages rustling and glowing with otherworldly light as they absorbed the token's power.

Chain Quest Unlocked: Reawaken the Fields Below

Phase One: Complete.

Reward: 200 Society Points for the Society of Hades

New Objective: Spread the influence of the Society of Hades. Discover and complete hidden quests to gain more Society Points. Spend these points at any Society Interface throughout The Fields Below.

Map Upgrade

Your map of The Fields Below has been upgraded to display all currently available areas and their statuses.

New Features Unlocked: Explore the Map Details for additional functionalities and insights.

The pages shimmered, revealing a hidden grid with a dizzying array of options. The interface looked like a mad scientist's blueprint, full of upgrades and enhancements, each one demanding its own price in Society Points.

Jace's eyes widened at the possibilities. The grid showcased a buffet of choices: upgrades for the dorms, library, and bathrooms, and even the option to hire spirit staff for various chores. Defensive measures were also on the menu, but those were grayed out, teasing him with their unattainability and higher requirements. Whole sections of the menu were locked, labeled "Prerequisites Not Met."

"Let's see what 200 points can do around here." He selected a list labeled "Basics."

"Okay, now we're talking," Jace muttered.

Sleeping Quarters Upgrades:
    • Current Status: Disgusting Beyond Belief
    o Upgrade to Serviced and Working: 100 points
    o Upgrade to Comfortable and Cozy: 200 points
    o Upgrade to Luxurious and Enchanted: 500 points

    Library Enhancements:
    • Current Status: Dusty and Neglected
    o Upgrade to Organized and Stocked: 150 points
    o Upgrade to Mystically Enhanced: 300 points

    Bathroom Improvements:
    • Current Status: Disgusting Beyond Belief
    o Upgrade to Serviced and Working: 50 points
    o Upgrade to Pristine and Enchanted: 150 points

    Spirit Staff:
    • Current Status: None
    o Basic Cleaning Spirits: 500 points
    o Maintenance Spirits: 750 points
    o Guardian Spirits: 2000 points (currently unavailable)

Jace glanced at his point total—200. Barely enough to yank his living conditions out of the medieval dungeon category. The bathrooms and sleeping quarters were a biohazard nightmare, each proudly earning the title "Disgusting Beyond Belief". The thought of not risking tetanus every time he brushed his teeth was just too good to pass up.

"Time to class up the joint," he muttered, selecting both upgrades. As his points drained away, the grid on the page shimmered, a digital nod of approval.

He hurried over to the sleeping quarters, eager to see the results.

A soft hum resonated through the walls. A shimmering light enveloped the room, casting a glow that pulsed with life. A counter appeared in the air.

Time to Upgrade Complete: 4:59

Jace watched in awe as the room transformed before his eyes. The grimy, decrepit facilities shimmered and shifted, touched by invisible hands. The air filled with a soft, melodic chime, a sound resonating with the magic infusing the space.

The sleeping quarters, once little more than squalid bunks, began to morph. The old, rusted frames dissolved into a fine mist, replaced by elegant, wrought-iron beds with intricate designs that seemed to dance in the soft light. The bedding transformed from musty rags to cotton sheets of deep, midnight blue, embroidered with silver constellations that twinkled softly.

The walls smoothed and brightened, taking on a pearlescent sheen that reflected the magical light. Mysterious runes appeared briefly, shimmering before fading into the smooth surface, leaving behind a faint aura of enchantment. Subtle lighting fixtures materialized, floating gently along the ceiling, casting a warm and welcoming glow.

As Jace marveled at the changes, he had to dodge a stray pillow that zipped past his head, trailing a faint sparkle. Books flew from nowhere, their pages fluttering as they settled onto newly formed shelves. He ducked as a particularly heavy tome zoomed over his shoulder, finding its place with a soft thud.

The floor, previously littered with debris, became a polished mosaic of enchanted tiles, each one depicting a different scene from mythical tales. The tiles shifted and changed, telling stories as Jace walked across them. He had to leap out of the way as a cluster of tiles sped toward him, clicking into place with a harmonious chime.

New storage units appeared beside each bed—beautifully carved wooden cabinets with intricate inlays that glowed with a faint light. Drawers opened and closed themselves, arranging items with meticulous care. Above the beds, shelves of dark mahogany floated into place.

In the corner of the room, where there had once been a pile of broken furniture, now stood a small seating area; a round table crafted from gleaming crystal, surrounded by chairs upholstered in rich, velvety fabric that changed color with the light. Jace sidestepped quickly as a chair floated by, settling into place around the table.

The dorm's communal area underwent a similar transformation. The old, broken-down sofas dissolved into the air, replaced by comfortable seating made of plush materials that would mold perfectly to the shape of anyone who sat down.

The bathroom facilities, once the epitome of neglect, now sparkled with cleanliness and subtle magic. The tiles on the walls and floor gleamed with a radiant light, the sinks and showers now were white and clean; the water was now running clear and warm.

As the counter ticked down the final seconds, Jace marveled at the transformation while dodging a vase that floated past, trailing a stream of flowers that arranged themselves perfectly within it. At this point, he was sure the repair magic was actually trying to hit him with things.

Additionally, the dorm now held a remote interface to the Society Upgrade Features. Checking them, he looked over some of the more advanced upgrades available, each promising additional benefits and comforts—private quarters with ensuite bathrooms, personal study desks with advanced holographic interfaces displaying arcane knowledge, and even a communal kitchen area where ingredients prepared themselves under the guidance of an enchanted cookbook.

He had a newfound goal of getting this place as ranked up as possible.

Jace stepped into the newly transformed bathroom, a sense of awe still lingering from the recent upgrade. The tiles glowed softly under his feet, and the air was filled with a faint, fresh scent, a far cry from the musty odor that had previously plagued the space.

He turned on the shower, watching as the water cascaded in a perfect, steady stream. The water's temperature adjusted instantly to his preference; a luxuriously warm embrace. He undressed and stepped in, closing his eyes as the hot water poured over him, washing away layers of grime and tension that had accumulated over far too long. The warmth seeped into his muscles, melting away the fatigue and stress. For the first time in ages, he felt truly clean, the magical water leaving his skin feeling rejuvenated and refreshed.

He took his time, savoring the sensation of cleanliness and the rare moment of peace. Jace couldn't help but smile, the hot shower working its magic on both body and soul. If this was only Rank 1, he couldn't imagine what it would be like fully upgraded.

Stepping out, Jace grabbed a fluffy towel from the rack, savoring its warmth. He made his way to the bedroom, where the bed awaited with fresh linens, practically begging him to dive in. But first, he accessed his inventory and selected a pair of pajama pants from their recent shopping spree. A puff of magic enveloped him, fading to reveal the pajama bottoms snugly in place. He couldn't help but admire the subtle patterns woven into the fabric, tiny constellations that shimmered in the room's soft light.

Curiosity piqued -Jace explored the upgrades to his map. The map now displayed the labyrinthine expanse of the Fields Below in much finer detail. It spiraled in many odd directions, some leading to dead ends and others to hidden passages only visible if you doubled back at just the right moment or walked at a strange angle. He decided to take some time to explore this place in depth.

The map revealed direct connections to several new locations: the mortuary, the campus graveyard (seriously, who thought that was a good idea?), and a series of chambers with cheerful names like "The Silent Vault," and "The Whispering Crypt."

Some areas were now accessible, while others remained locked off. One particularly intriguing route was labeled "Forgotten Path," a hidden passage leading directly to the Underworld, now marked as available. That was going to come in handy.

An additional feature caught his eye. It displayed the number of people currently in the Fields Below. Curious, he selected it.

The Fields Below
       Current Occupants: 2

The world seemed to freeze around him. His breath hitched, and a cold sweat slicked his skin. A faint noise moved through the silence, a sinister rattle that seemed to come from everywhere and nowhere. His heart pounded, a frantic drumbeat in his ears as he strained to listen. He wasn't alone.

Chapter 29
Shadow

Jace rose slowly, the oppressive silence hanging over him like a sodden cloak. The rustling sound came again, sharper this time, tightening his frayed nerves. He followed the noise, each step a cautious dance on the cold stone floor. The trail led him to an old storage room, and with a creak that shattered the stillness, he pushed the door open, bracing himself for whatever lay beyond. He summoned his Shard to his hand, its glow cutting through the darkness.

"Hello?" he whispered.

The rustling emanated from the far corner, a sound that echoed in the quiet. Jace edged closer, his eyes adjusting to the dim light. There, huddled among old crates and tattered blankets, was a girl. Her wide, wary eyes caught the faint light, reflecting it like a cat's. She was thin, her clothes ragged, and she clutched a crust of bread as if it were the most precious thing in the world.

She seemed to be about his age, though the haunted look in her eyes made her appear older. Around her neck was a collar of ruddy brass.

Curiosity piqued and his heart finally steadied, Jace's intense expression softened into a concerned smile. "Are you the shadow I've been seeing around this place?" he asked gently, crouching to her level.

The girl didn't respond immediately. She watched him with a mix of fear and defiance, her grip on the bread tightening. She nodded slowly. It was a snack he had left out the day before.

"I'm Jace," he said, his voice as soothing as he could make it. "I live here too. You don't have to be afraid."

Her eyes softened just a fraction, but she remained silent. She had deep green eyes and long jet-black hair. Her frame was slight and almost fragile beneath layers of ragged cloth.

"How long have you been down here?" he asked.

She shrugged, the movement barely perceptible.

"Can you speak?"

She shook her head.

"Okay, that's alright. Are you alone?"

She nodded again, a slight tremor in her movement.

Jace felt a pang of empathy. He remembered the days when he, too, had been alone and desperate, living on the streets with Alex after his foster parents' accident.

"Well, you're not alone anymore," he said firmly.

She looked at him, her eyes revealing both hope and mistrust. Jace's Spirit Sense picked up on her fear and concern, but there was something more—something deep and vast, as wide as the ocean, that he couldn't quite name.

"Do you know your name?" Jace asked softly.

She shook her head, the motion small and hesitant.

Jace's heart ached for her. "Alright then. Well, we have to call you something. How about, just for now, I'll call you... Shadow. Does that sound okay?"

Her lips curved into a tentative smile, and she nodded.

For a while, they sat in silence, the light of his Moonstone casting shifting silhouettes on the walls. Jace glanced at the crust of bread in her hands. Activating his inventory, he pulled out a bag of dried fruit he had been saving for a snack.

Despite her disheveled appearance, there was an undeniable grace in her movements, a subtle elegance.

"Here," he said, extending it toward her.

She eyed the bag warily before snatching it with a quick, darting motion. She opened the bag and took a piece, biting into it with visible relief. Jace watched her, feeling a mix of sorrow and determination.

"We don't have to stay here," he said softly. "There's a way out of the Below. I can help you."

Shadow's eyes snapped open, filled with fear. She shook her head vehemently, clutching the bag tightly.

"Okay, okay," Jace said quickly, holding up his hands. "We don't have to go anywhere. There's no rush."

He watched as she relaxed slightly, though the tension didn't completely leave her body. Jace sighed, feeling the weight of her unspoken fears.

"You're safe here," he said gently. "I don't know what else might be living down here, but I promise I won't force you to leave."

Shadow looked at him, her eyes searching his face for any sign of deceit. Finding none, she nodded slowly.

One step at a time, Jace thought.

Jace resolved to bring her food whenever he could, giving her time to grow comfortable with him before attempting to move her out of the Below.

"Do you need somewhere to sleep? I just got the dorm upgraded, and it's not bad," Jace offered.

She suddenly became very excited, her eyes sparkling with anticipation. She stood and began moving about. Jace couldn't tell if she was happy or needed to use the restroom, but then she made a "come on" motion with her hand.

Jace stood and stepped forward cautiously. She then took his hand and dashed from the room, dragging him along behind her.

They ran through the winding corridors, their footsteps echoing in the vast emptiness. Cobwebs clung to the corners, and the walls were covered in a patina of decay, a testament to the long-forgotten history of the Below. Room after room they passed, each more dilapidated than the last, the air thick with the scent of age and neglect. The sound of their breathing and the soft patter of their footsteps were the only things breaking the eerie silence.

She moved with a grace that was both wild and controlled, like a dancer leading a partner through an intricate routine. He felt the warmth of her hand in his, a stark contrast to the chill that permeated the air around them.

Finally, they stopped at a heavy, ancient door. Jace saw a plaque and blew off the dust. It read:

The Whispering Crypt.

A sense of unease washed over Jace. Was she bringing him closer to this place to hide his body? He shook his head, trying to dispel the morbid thoughts.

"Why are we here?" he asked.

She simply smiled and opened the door, revealing a sight that left Jace in awe.

Inside was an incredible crypt, unlike any he had ever seen—not that he had ever seen one outside of a holodisc. This wasn't a usual crypt, suffocating and small, with tiny corridors. This place was massive, the ceiling stretching several stories high, painted with a stunning night sky, dominated by a huge, glowing moon. Enchanted stars bathed the room in a gentle, magical light.

Wisps of energy floated about, radiating an ethereal glow. The ground was plush with green grass, and vines covered nearly everything. The place looked like a hidden forest, untouched by time. At the center of this secret haven stood an impossible tree, its leaves large, thick, and green.

Energy floated in gusts of green and white mist, swirling and dancing through the air. The crypt felt alive, brimming with an ethereal essence that hummed softly, almost like a heartbeat. Jace felt the energy swirl around him, catching the moonlight. It was an odd sensation, like standing in the middle of an electrical storm.

It was so strange to see and feel and smell so much life in a place meant for the dead. Jace was starting to understand how this place might have gotten the name - The Fields Below. Were there more places like this?

Jace looked closely at bit of glimmering mist.

Identify Skill Used - Success

Spirit Essence

In places of high concentration of the dead, traces of extra energy can sometimes be found—remnants of souls that have transitioned peacefully.

She smiled brightly, watching Jace's expression.

"How did you know this place was here?" he asked.

She pulled him into the room, her excitement palpable. She slipped off her worn shoes and wiggled her toes in the grass, a look of pure joy on her face. Then she led him around the back and into another section, where she climbed a stone lattice. At the top, she gestured for him to follow. He did, eyes wide with a sense of wonder.

At the top, Jace discovered her hideaway. A cot woven from leaves lay amidst a scatter of assorted goods, each item a puzzle piece hinting at her past. A chipped teacup, a broken silver comb, a worn-out book with pages missing—tokens of a life abandoned.

She sat down and patted the space beside her, inviting him to join. He hesitated for a moment, then settled next to her. Together, they gazed up at the moon, its light casting a gentle, magical glow over them. They sat there for a while, wrapped in the tranquility of the moment.

Jace felt a peace he hadn't known in years. The warmth of her presence, the moon's soft glow, and the rustling leaves created a symphony of stillness and connection. He turned to her, a hint of a smile on his lips.

"Not your typical crypt, is it?" he said, trying to lighten the mood.

She looked at him with a raised eyebrow and a smirk, her eyes twinkling as if to say, You think?

For the first time in a long while, Jace felt like he belonged somewhere. The moonlight painted their faces, and in that shared silence, the world outside seemed to fade away.

He turned to her, his voice barely above a whisper. "It's beautiful."

She nodded, her eyes reflecting the soft light.

They sat there, side by side, in companionable silence, two souls finding friendship and solace in the most unlikely of places.

Sometime later, Jace returned to his dorm, ready to unwind before bed.

Remembering Hades' suggestion to practice spending his EXP, he felt a spark of inspiration. Why not give it a try?

He sat on the edge of his bed, the firmness of the mattress grounding him. The faint constellations on his sheets mirrored those on his pajamas, making him wonder if there were sub-settings for everything or if it was just a random quirk.

Earlier that day, he'd been mulling over his options and he had decided to try his hand at Inscription.

Settling cross-legged on the floor, Jace placed a new leather-bound journal in his lap and pulled a magical self-refilling quill out of his inventory. As he began to write, the ink flowed with difficulty at first but gradually became smoother with each word.

Sometime later, a notification blinked in his peripheral vision.

Skill Gained: Inscription

You Have Unlocked a Profession

Inscriptionist

Would you like to adopt this profession? Note: While the profession is not required to use the Inscription skill, it is essential for unlocking special abilities and bonuses exclusive to those who take on this role.

This will replace your current profession.

Accept | Reject

Jace considered the option for a moment before choosing [Reject].

He wasn't even sure if this would be the best way to cultivate his aether and spend his EXP, let alone if he wanted to change his profession.

As he wrote, Jace felt the EXP bar gradually emptying, channels of aether weaving their way through his body like a network of glowing streams. Each pulse of energy was a tiny river, carving new paths through the landscape of his being, seeking out and smoothing over the rough edges within. The sensation was both soothing and invigorating, as if the very essence of the universe was flowing through him, renewing and enhancing every fiber of his existence.

The ink on the page seemed to shimmer with the energy he channeled, each word a conduit for the aether that permeated his being. His body thrummed with the power, every stroke of the pen aligning his internal currents, forging stronger connections, and opening new pathways. The aether found its way to his core, spiraling inward like a delicate dance, touching upon hidden reserves and kindling latent potential.

He felt his attributes shifting, each one subtly improving. Strengthened by the aether, his mind became sharper, his reflexes quicker, and his body tougher. The very act of inscribing his thoughts and experiences seemed to crystallize the knowledge within him, embedding it into his soul.

Ignoring the notifications blinking at the edge of his vision, Jace remained focused on his writing. The events since entering Terra Mythica flowed onto the pages—the classes, the people, the mishaps in the Underworld, and Shadow.

It felt as if he were being sculpted from within.

Finally, as the last word dried on the page, Jace leaned back, feeling a profound sense of accomplishment and peace. The constellations on his sheets twinkled softly as he closed the journal, his hand aching but his spirit rejuvenated. With a sigh of relief and exhaustion, Jace climbed back into bed.

Just before drifting off, opened his status screen to look over the gains.

Attributes Improvements
All standard attributes: +1

Skill Rank Ups
Dark Vision:
• Rank increased to Apprentice.
• You can now see in complete darkness with improved clarity.
• Perception debuff from darkness is halved.

Knowledge Absorption:
• Rank increased to Apprentice.
• Your ability to learn has significantly improved. Good job, brainiac!

Lore - Universal Mechanics:
• Rank increased.
• You now have a deeper understanding of the game mechanics and world lore.
• Congratulations, you've been promoted from Incompetent Nincompoop to Bumbling Noob.

With the increase of his Lore Skill, he noticed more information was available about skills overall.

Skill Ranks

Skills, like Affinities, have six ranks. Each requires ten times more practice than the previous tier to rank up.

Skill Tiers:

- One Star: Novice
- Two Stars: Apprentice
- Three Stars: Adept
- Four Stars: Expert
- Five Stars: Legend
- Six Stars: Myth

Chapter 30
Midnight Meeting

J ace rolled out of bed the next day, relishing the rare pleasure of waking up without any debuffs. The dining hall was buzzing with energy, a vibrant symphony of student chatter and laughter. Most people clustered with their Societies, but as the sole member of the Society of Hades, Jace didn't have an assigned table.

He piled his plate with some mystery meat, steaming vegetables, and fresh-baked bread before claiming a small table tucked away in the corner. As he started to eat, Dex, Ell, Alice, and their gnome friend, Thistle, sauntered in, trays laden with food. Dex's Hermes robes flowed like liquid, Ell's Athena robes shimmered subtly, Alice's Harpocrates robes balanced elegance and practicality, and Thistle's Ares robes were a rugged black.

Thistle pulled a high chair out of his inventory and plopped down, his look daring anyone to comment. Jace raised an eyebrow but kept his thoughts to himself. He knew Thistle was probably teased enough and understood what it felt like to be the butt of a joke.

"Rebel without a table," Dex quipped.

"Aren't you guys gonna get in trouble for slumming it with me instead of your Societies?" Jace asked.

Alice snorted. "This isn't high school, Jace. We sit where we want."

They settled in, diving into their meals. The first bites hit their tongues like a bland ambush.

"What's up with this food?" Jace grimaced, pushing his plate away.

Thistle sighed, his fork clattering on his now-empty plate. "Just choke it down. The debuffs for skipping meals are brutal. Rumor has it that Terra Mythica's got this weird thing about toning down sensations to keep us from avoiding fights because of combat pain. Supposedly, the higher your perception though, the more intense the sensations."

"Even those with high perception say the food at the University barely has any flavor," Alice added.

The group shared a collective sigh, pecking at their lunches with new-found resignation.

"So, Jace, how'd your Class Title quest go?" Ell asked.

"I survived-ish," Jace said, keeping his tone nonchalant.

"Mine was pretty standard," she said, "Temple of Athena, met the Society President, tried out a few skills, and boom, first Title: Tactician. Fighter with a strategy twist."

Dex leaned in, eyes sparkling. "Rogue. First title. Called it."

Jace smirked. "No surprise there."

He turned to Thistle, who was contemplatively chewing on a piece of bread. "And you, Thistle?"

"Got my Class Title last year," Thistle replied with a shrug. "Fighter."

Dex raised an eyebrow. "A gnome fighter?"

"Tank focused," Thistle said nonchalantly.

Ell shifted her gaze to Alice, engrossed in a book. "What about you, Alice?"

"We just going to let Thistle's tank class go by without comment?" Dex asked, eyes wide.

The others shrugged.

Alice answered Ell without looking up. "Arcanist. Ancient magics and all that jazz."

"And you, Jace?" Ell's tone was casual.

"Cleric," Jace replied, leaning back in his chair with a half-smile.

"Guess you'll be the one who'll be patching us up when things go south," Ell said.

"Interesting. A common title, like mine," Dex mused, rubbing his chin like a faux philosopher. "I thought you'd be something more dramatic, like Dark Destroyer or Fang Knight."

Alice rolled her eyes. "A base class is a good starting point. The bonuses are well-documented, which can't be said for the rare and unique ones. The obvious effects are on our character sheets, but there are hidden stats too. Titles can even mess with those."

Dex and Ell shared a knowing look. "It's actually kind of freaky how little we know about the System and Terra Mythica," Dex whispered, leaning in like he was about to spill government secrets. "Everything we know, we had to figure out in-game and pass along. There's so much unexplored.

And John Rearden, the creator? Total enigma. Went from zero to billionaire, buying up everything. I mean, props to the guy—he's a legend. But no one's seen him in years."

"Legend? More like a power-hungry megalomaniac. Too much power for one man, if you ask me," Ell scoffed.

Dex leaned forward, eyes narrowing. "Come on, at least he's trying."

"Trying? The guy's a corporate vulture," Ell shot back. "First chance he got, he swooped in on the failing economy and bought up everything."

"Yeah, to try and improve it," Dex countered.

"Fat lot of good that did. Buy up everything, build some farms, then vanish? Real philanthropist."

Silence fell, thick with old arguments and unspoken tension. Jace and Thistle shifted uncomfortably while Alice focused on her book. The debate over Rearden was as familiar to them as breathing.

Jace couldn't tell if Terra Mythica was a blessing or a curse. What he did know was that it had become the lifeline in a world plagued by shortages and despair. The massive time dilation offered a strange kind of relief, a respite from the endless struggle to survive. Inside Mythica, the near-coma state meant people could stretch their food supplies further. For those with a Stasis Chamber, it meant surviving years in a world otherwise teetering on the brink.

For now, Jace decided to leave the question of right and wrong, and who should wield the power, to others.

"Maybe he's just living in Terra Mythica, enjoying his creation," Alice suggested, shrugging.

Ell frowned, her eyebrows knitting together. "Maybe. But it's weird. That's all I'm saying. He made it fully immersive, unlike anything else. The old VR tech can't even touch Terra Mythica. The data needed to run a small town in-game is probably more than anything we've ever seen."

"And the tech is still super top secret," Dex added, finding some common ground with Ell. "No one's cracked it or hacked the Device. You just put it on and bam, you're in the Myth. No ports, no charging—it's like magic."

"The security is insane. Locked to the first user with a DNA scan. The System AI is integrated into the very nerve fibers of the world," Ell said, leaning in. "Remember the political debates about it on the holos when we were kids?

Access to Terra Mythica and your Device is a Protected Human Right. The government can't take it away unless you're a felon. And even then, there are activists trying to repeal that."

Jace wasn't one for conspiracy theories, but he couldn't deny there were a lot of strange things about the whole situation.

Dex nodded. "If someone steals a VR kit, it's even worse. They face life imprisonment at best. And buying headsets from Excelsior doesn't guarantee compatibility. Some people just can't connect, no matter what."

Jace's stomach didn't feel well.

Ell laughed. "We're basically guinea pigs with swords and magic. Could be worse."

Jace shook his head, his mouth suddenly dry. "I knew the consequences of theft were bad, but not that bad."

Alice reached out, giving his arm a reassuring squeeze. "Don't look so worried, Jace. The good news is, once you're invited and prove compatible, you're in for life."

That was the problem. Jace wasn't invited. Alex was.

"Unless you piss off the System," Dex quipped with a smirk.

Alice rolled her eyes. "Those are just rumors. No one has any firm evidence of anyone being booted or banned, no matter how terrible they are. The game expects other Travelers to handle it."

"But why is it such a big deal? Why so many laws?" Jace asked.

Alice sighed, glancing around as if to ensure no one else was listening. "I have no idea. But I do know Excelsior Tech has its hands in everything now. They own parts of almost every major company in the world."

Ell spoke next. "My parents work for Excelsior. Even they don't know anything that's not public knowledge. Other than the fact that it's all very hush-hush. They don't even know where the Devices are made."

"Alice, how did you get your kit?" Jace asked.

Alice smiled, though it didn't reach her eyes. "Lottery."

There was a long, heavy pause while they all chewed their tasteless food.

"Hey, you guys unlocked your first affinities yet? I know Ell did back in Affinities class," Dex said, trying to smoothly change the topic. He winced theatrically and shifted in his seat. "Little demons. I'm still sore in places I can't mention in polite company."

Each nodded, sharing knowing glances.

"Well, spill the beans. What did you all get?" Ell prompted, curiosity sparking in her eyes.

Before Jace could answer, Dex jumped in, his eyes alight like a kid on Christmas morning. "Actually, hold that thought. I've got a better idea." He grinned, mischief dancing in his expression. "Yes... a much better idea. I need to prepare some things, but meet me tonight after classes. At the Fountain of Aphrodite."

Ell raised an eyebrow, suspicion and amusement mixing on her face. "Dex, I know that look. You're about to do something really stupid, aren't you?"

Dex's grin widened. "No, Ell, we're about to do something really stupid. Just meet me at midnight." With that, he took off.

Ell and Thistle exchanged quick goodbyes with Alice and Jace before heading to their next classes.

A notification blinked in Jace's vision. It was his [Hades' Little Helper] quest. He selected it, and nothing seemed to change. "Yeah, yeah. I'll get to you," he muttered, swiping it away.

He opened his map and saw a marker in an area he'd never been to before—Zone Three. Way out of his rank.

"What's up, Jace?" Alice asked, noticing his furrowed brow.

"It's this quest I have from Hades. It's in Zone Three."

Alice's eyes lit up. "You need a Ward Stone. Like Demi used on the way up the mountain. It's the only way to get around in higher-tier Zones. Unless you have a high-rank party."

"How do I get one of those?" Jace asked, intrigued but clueless.

Alice grinned, her excitement palpable. "Actually, it's pretty simple. I'll show you. I've been studying them for a quest from my deity. But it'll take a few days—they require some time to craft properly."

"You'd do that?" he asked, surprised.

"Of course, we're all in this together. Plus, it helps me rank up my skill. But you'll have to cover the ingredients. No free rides, even in Mythica."

She stood up and put her book away, brushing off her robes. "Come on, Jace. Now's as good a time as any to get your Ward Stone started."

Alice led Jace through the winding paths of Mount Olympus University, navigating the sprawling campus until they reached the heart of the crafting district - Hephaestus Foundry. This area was a bustling maze of workshops, each one alive with activity. Sparks flew from anvils as red-hot metal was pounded into shape, cauldrons bubbled with mysterious concoctions, and the heady scent of exotic herbs and minerals filled the air.

The buildings themselves were striking. Marble columns supported glass domes that glittered in the sunlight, creating an almost surreal contrast. Artisans of all kinds labored diligently, producing everything from intricate jewelry to massive, enchanted weapons.

Alice guided Jace to a small, nondescript workshop tucked between two grander buildings.

"Here we are," Alice said, nudging the door open with a creaky protest from the hinges. The inside was a treasure trove of magical components. Shelves lined the walls, crammed with glowing crystals, ancient tomes, and jars of rare ingredients. A large workbench dominated the center of the room, cluttered with tools and half-finished projects.

"This place is the real deal," she said. "You can find anything here, if you know what you're looking for."

Jace glanced around, taking in the organized chaos.

"And the best part? Everything here has a story. See that jar of dragon's blood? Rumor has it the dragon it came from is still looking for it."

Alice's smile widened, her eyes gleaming with the joy of sharing a piece of her world. "This is where we'll make your protection crystal. First, we need to gather the right materials. Follow me."

She led him to a set of shelves, picking out various items: a sliver of amethyst, a vial of phoenix tears, and a sprig of nightshade.

"Got it. Now what?" Jace asked, eyebrow raised.

"Now, we combine them," Alice said, her excitement barely contained. She placed the materials on the workbench, hands moving like a maestro's, weaving intricate patterns in the air as she chanted softly. The items began to glow, their energies merging into a single, brilliant light.

Jace watched, mouth slightly agape, as the light coalesced into a small, shimmering purple crystal.

"And now, we wait two nights. It has to bathe under the moon. Lucky for us, we've got a perfect one for the next few nights."

Alice picked up the crystal and headed up a spiraling staircase to a roofless platform. There, dozens of different crystals lay in gleaming materials, each presumably needing moon or sunlight. She gingerly placed theirs in a holder and wrote a tag with Jace's name on it, tearing the tag in half and handing one piece to him.

"Bring this in two days, and they'll let you pick it up."

Alice carefully held out the crystal to him. "Once it's done cooking, this will let you enter Zone Three safely. But it won't fend off higher-level monsters in Zone Four. We'll need better crafting and materials for that."

Jace smirked. "Thanks, Alice. You're a real lifesaver."

Alice grinned back.

Jace checked out his notifications.

Crafting Process Initiated:

- Objective: Create a Ward Stone
- Materials Required:
o Sliver of Amethyst
o Vial of Phoenix Tears
o Sprig of Nightshade

Skill Gained: Artificer, Novice Rank
- Description: You have learned the basics of crafting magical items.

- Benefits:
o Improved efficiency in preparing materials.
o Better success rate in crafting basic magical items.
o Access to novice-level crafting recipes.

The rest of the day blurred into a routine of lectures and training. Basic classes like Rune Etching, Combat Strategy, Alchemy, and Mythical History consumed their hours, each session a whirlwind of information and practice. As the sun dipped below the horizon, the students trickled out of their classrooms, the anticipation of the evening's meeting growing with each step.

Night enveloped the campus, casting a serene, shadowy blanket over everything. They converged at the Statue of Aphrodite, their faces softly illuminated by the silvery moonlight. The moon hung high, casting an ethereal glow over the statue, highlighting the delicate features and flowing robes of the goddess. Shadows danced around them, adding a mysterious ambiance to the scene. An eerie quiet settled in, broken only by their hushed whispers. The fountain lay still, the water shut off, leaving Aphrodite standing in a mirror-like pool, her reflection shimmering softly under the moon's watchful eye.

A voice sliced through the quiet, nearly causing their hearts to leap from their chests.

"What's the midnight rendezvous for?" Dex's voice was casual, almost too casual, as he stepped from the shadows.

"Furies, Dex!" Alice exclaimed, clutching her chest. "You trying to give us heart attacks?"

Dex grinned, a wicked gleam in his eyes. He waggled his eyebrows mischievously. "Now, are we gonna stand around here all night, or are you coming with me?"

Ell narrowed her eyes. "Lead the way, oh great master of surprises."

With a mock bow and a flourish, Dex turned and strode off into the night, Alice, Jace, Ell, and Thistle trailing behind him.

Dex was practically skipping with excitement.

"Where are we going?" Alice asked, struggling to keep up.

Dex turned, his grin practically Cheshire Cat-like. "Shhh, trust me. You're gonna love it."

Ell rolled her eyes. "This better not be like the last time you had an idea, Dex."

Dex shot her a wink. "Oh, ye of little faith. This is gonna be epic."

As they crossed the courtyard, they ran into Marcus and his cronies. Marcus, with his ever-present sneer and swagger, flanked by his usual entourage. But Jace's eyes were drawn to the pale boy walking beside Marcus. The boy's eyes locked onto Jace's with an intense, unblinking stare that sent a shiver down his spine.

"Hey, look who it is," Marcus called out, his voice dripping with disdain. "The lone wolf of the Society of Hades. How's life in the dark, Jace?"

Jace didn't bother to respond, but he couldn't tear his eyes away from the pale boy. There was something off about him, something deeply unsettling.

"Cat got your tongue?" Marcus taunted, his cronies snickering. The pale boy remained silent, his gaze never wavering.

The pale boy's eyes felt as if they bore into Jace's soul, and for a moment, Jace thought he saw something flicker behind them—something dark and sinister.

Dex stepped in, smirking. "Marcus, what are you doing out so late? Shouldn't you be in front of your bathroom mirror, practicing that sneer?"

Marcus's smirk faltered. "Mind your own business, Bishop."

Dex almost lunged at him, but Ell's gentle hand on his shoulder stopped him.

Ell chimed in, her voice dripping with sarcasm. "Having daddy problems again, Marky? Wanna bring the real world into this? Honestly, if you spent as much time studying as you do sneering, you might actually pass a class."

Marcus's cronies snickered, but this time at his expense. Marcus glared at them until they fell silent.

"We'll see who's laughing," Marcus growled, turning on his heel. His pale companion lingered, his unsettling gaze fixed on Jace before following Marcus.

As they walked away, Dex clapped Jace on the back. "Well, that was fun. Now, about that idea..."

"What's the deal with you two, anyway? There's definitely a backstory there," Jace said, raising an eyebrow.

"Long story," Dex forced a smile. "Now, if you'll just follow me..."

Jace stopped and pulled Dex to the side. "Is that your name? Bishop?" he whispered.

Dex cringed. "Yeah."

"Wait, wait, wait," Jace stammered. "Your dad's Terry Bishop? As in, Mr. Stasis Pod?"

"Yeah," Dex shrugged.

"That would make you..."

"Listen, I prefer to leave that outside."

Jace's mind did a triple axel. Terry Bishop, the mastermind behind the Stasis Pod—the tech that lets people live full-time in Terra Mythica—was Dex's father? The same tech hospitals around the world used. The same tech keeping Alex alive.

"But, it's…"

"Please," Dex said, something in his eyes telling Jace this was important. Jace nodded and left it at that.

With a final glance back, they continued on their path with Dex in the lead.

"That guy's creepy," Jace said, changing gears. "Keeps giving me this death glare."

"Marcus? Yeah, he's a monster. Probably pulls the wings off ladybugs," Dex replied.

"No, I mean one of his goons. The thin one, really gives me the creeps."

"Which one?" Ell asked.

"You know, the really thin, pale guy."

They all shrugged. "I try not to pay attention to his goons of the week," Dex said before urging them forward. "Come on. We don't have all night."

As they rounded the corner, Jace glanced back to see Marcus and his "friends" had vanished into the shadows. Turning his attention forward, Jace finally saw where Dex had been leading them, and it did not disappoint.

Chapter 31
The Thundergnome

The moon hung high, its light slicing through the night like a blade, casting a glow on the massive dome of gold and glass ahead. The structure was a fever dream brought to life—an enormous coliseum of sand, glistening under the shimmering dome, a gigantic half-filled snow globe of golden grains. Stadium seating spiraled around the perimeter in a mesmerizing yet disordered dance, rising halfway up the immense structure, as if conjured by a mad architect with a flair for the dramatic. The moonlight painted the glass dome in a ghostly silver.

Dex, with the flair of a seasoned showman, spread his arms wide. "Behold, the Combat Chamber! Or as I like to call it, the Thunderdome... with bleachers. Citizens and Travelers can duke it out here without, you know, the whole dying bit."

They approached a large door marked "Faculty Only."

Thistle crossed his arms, eyebrows raised. "Really, Dex? I've seen this before. The professors put on a demo every year. It's impressive, sure, but we'll see it live at the end of the week. Did you seriously drag me out of bed for this?"

Dex, undeterred, flashed a roguish grin. "Sure, it's boring if we're just looking. But where's your sense of adventure, my vertically challenged friend? Watch and learn." With a flourish, he produced a peculiar gadget from his inventory, a cross between a key and a screwdriver. He crouched by the door, his fingers dancing over the lock with finesse, each click and clink echoing through the silent night.

Thistle crossed his arms. "Even if you could crack that, which you can't, you need a Faculty Token to activate it. More advanced than your toy, I'm sure."

Dex winked. "Oh, my sweet, sweet Thistle. Do you think I keep you around just to make me look tall? You were a Faculty Aid during Orientation, right? If I were a betting man—and I am—I'd bet you haven't turned in your Token. I know I wouldn't have, the perks are too sweet."

Thistle looked sheepish but shot back, "Okay, wannabe Houdini, what's your point?"

"What kind of perks?" Jace asked.

Dex glanced back while his hands continued to work. "Quite a suite. Faculty and aides get instant success on scans and identifies around campus. Including character names, usernames, and stat blocks!"

"That's amazing... and really creepy," Alice said.

"I have trouble remembering people's names. It's useful." Thistle shrugged.

"Thistle, Thistle, Thistle. No judgment here. I've been known to carry a few things I'm not supposed to myself. I'm proud of you. But right now, you're in the unique position of being someone I need help from." Dex gave him a wink.

"I'm not risking my butt so you can play rogue. Grow up, Dex. We have classes tomorrow." He turned to leave.

Dex stopped fiddling with the lock and called out to Thistle. "What will it take?"

There was a long pause as Thistle studied him. "I want your plus to dexterity shoes."

Dex grimaced and thought it over. He was just about to agree when Thistle added, "And, you can't refer to my height for a month. Or else, I get to ride around on your shoulders for the rest of the semester."

"You can't be serious!" Dex said. Ell and Alice stifled laughs.

"Sounds fair," Jace added.

"That's outrageous. I mean, there are going to be so many opportunities... Oh, fine. Deal," Dex said with a huff.

Thistle nodded, and they shook hands. "Okay, it's a deal. But you won't be able to get in so it really doesn't—"

The lock clicked and the door swung open.

Dex smiled broadly as Thistle sighed in exasperation.

"Oh, I had that thing cracked ages ago." He stood and waved them in with a bow. "Alons-y."

Thistle rolled his eyes. "You know, sometimes I wonder if you actually have a plan or if you just wing it and hope for the best."

Dex laughed, stepping through the door. "A bit of both, my vertical... virtually perfect friend." Dex choked out, swerving off from a collision.

"Oh, this is going to be so worth it," Thistle said, walking in.

Stepping inside, they found themselves in a control room brimming with an intricate array of dials, pulleys, and levers—more fitting for a steam engine than a mythical world. Sleek, silver pods, reminiscent of oversized Devices and User Interface stones, lined the walls of the room, standing almost monolithic.

Dex moved towards the control panel, fingers dancing over the buttons and dials like a maestro. "You see," he said, pulling a lever with a dramatic flourish, "this was a joint project between Travelers and Citizens. My dad had a hand in building it."

"How?" Alice breathed, her eyes wide with wonder.

Dex shrugged, a casual smirk on his face. "Just a bit of earth tech and a whole lot of weird. Welcome to the wild side, folks."

Thistle rolled his eyes and slid a coin into a slot, true to his promise. The dials whirred to life. The sand within the dome glowed like molten gold, the grains shifting and swirling as if animated by some unseen force.

"Keep rolling your eyes, and they'll get stuck like that," Ell said, flashing Thistle a playful smile.

Through a window, they could glimpse the activity within the chamber. A large bowl in the center of the room provided an overview of everything else.

"Just looks like a lot of sand," Jace said.

"It's technically gold. Well, gold dust," Dex explained, his eyes gleaming with excitement. "The magic adjusts the chemical structure, rearranging atoms and reconfiguring elements until it forms a whole new world. Think of it as a high-tech, magical alchemy show."

"Aren't we going to get in trouble for using it?" Alice asked, her voice tinged with concern.

"Oh, don't be such a worrywart. You can't get in trouble if you don't get caught. Besides, where's your sense of adventure?" Dex hit a few dials, and a countdown timer appeared, starting from fifteen minutes. "There, that should give us enough time to get ready before the fun starts. Plus, no one's coming here until the annual presentation match, and that's not for days."

Ell grinned. "It's kinda cool."

"This is a terrible idea," Thistle said, crossing his arms.

"Surprisingly, I think I'm with Thistle on this one, guys," Jace said, hesitating. The last thing he needed was to cause any trouble for himself.

"I don't know. It could be fun," Alice chimed in.

Jace met Alice's eyes, which sparkled with unexpected mischief, and decided. "Alright, let's make it a quick match. Just to test our powers, then we're out. Technically, this is part of the facilities, and we have a chaperone in Thistle, our personal Faculty Aid."

"That's the spirit, Jace. It's not wrong if you have a loosely assembled excuse," Dex said, choking back a fake tear. "He takes after me. Oh, they grow up so quickly, don't they, Ell?"

"I'm not sure that's a good thing," Ell replied.

They each stepped into one of the sleek, silver pods, the doors closing with a soft hiss. Jace felt the interior hum with energy, the air thick with anticipation. Within moments, a rush hit as his surroundings blurred and shifted in a spiraling vortex of lights. When the lights settled, Jace opened his eyes and found himself standing inside the dome.

The glass walls from the inside were silvery and impenetrable, offering no visibility of the outside world. Jace looked down to discover his clothes had changed. He noticed that the rest of theirs had too; their usual outfits were gone, replaced by full combat tunics of their Society. Each tunic was adorned with a jewel on the shoulder indicating their Shard: Emerald for Dex, Sapphire for Alice, Amethyst for Ell, Ruby for Thistle, and Moonstone for Jace.

"Wow," Jace said, mesmerized by his own transformation. He wore sleek, pitch-black armor adorned with shimmering silver accents that traced intricate patterns along the sleeves and chest. He caught a glimpse of the silver sigil on his back in the dome's reflection—a fleeting image of a majestic white raven spreading its wings, feathers gleaming against the dark backdrop.

Dex was clad in flowing, light-colored robes with subtle azure highlights, a loose hood framing his features. Intricate swirls adorned the fabric, hinting at swift, graceful movements. He appeared like a breeze, given form, embodying the essence of an agile swordsman.

Alice admired herself in a form-fitting, black combat suit that highlighted her short but athletic build. The material blended matte and glossy black with indigo, interwoven with silver threads creating elegant, lethal patterns. Her Sapphire Shard gleamed on her shoulder, and she looked fierce and formidable, a stark contrast to her usual conservative attire.

Ell stood tall in her Amethyst combat gear, exuding an intimidating presence. Her armor featured a striking mix of black and violet, adorned with sharp, angular designs that seemed to pulse with energy.

Thistle wore a tunic of deep crimson and dark gold, crafted for durability and strength, with hardened plates at crucial junctures. His Ruby Shard glinted on his shoulder, and his attire possessed an organic essence, as though forged from living materials, which accentuated his lithe form.

"How'd we get all dressed up?" Jace asked.

"Technically, we didn't. Our bodies are still back in the preparation room," Dex said.

"How does that work?" Alice asked, still marveling at her new look.

"It's all about syncing up with Terra Mythica," Dex explained. "Our minds control these avatars, while the magic handles the rest. It's like our mind, body, and soul are sharing an apartment, you know?"

"This is going to be good," Thistle muttered.

Ignoring him, Dex continued, "They're connected but can operate independently. These pods let us jump in, transferring our consciousness into avatars made from the same golden dust as everything else here. Honestly, it's way above my pay grade."

"So all our magic is here because it's part of our minds and souls?" Alice asked.

"Beats me," Dex replied, hopping from foot to foot and kicking up golden mist. "Couldn't care less. Now, come on, let's see what this place can really do!"

Above them, the glass dome stood like a silent guardian, its crystalline surface reflecting the moon's light into a thousand fragmented beams, casting a mosaic of luminescence across the dunes below.

Up close, Jace understood what Dex had been trying to say—it wasn't sand at all. It was a kind of golden dust, shimmering at the slightest touch, suspended somewhere between liquid and solid. Each fine particle glittered with its own light, tiny motes drifting into the air with every breath.

As the countdown reached ten minutes, the dome sprang to life, soaring into the air and swirling around them in a whirlwind of chaos. Inside, the dust coalesced into a golden vortex. Then, in an instant, it settled and vanished, revealing a lush, tropical jungle in its place. The transformation was seamless, leaving not a speck of gold behind.

They now stood in the heart of a vibrant tropical forest. Towering trees with broad, emerald leaves formed a dense canopy overhead, filtering the sunlight into a mosaic of gold and green. Vines twisted around the trunks, adorned with bright, exotic flowers. Jace breathed deeply, savoring the scent of blooming flora and the sound of distant waterfalls as they mingled with the chirps and calls of unseen creatures. The last vestiges of the moon and night had vanished, replaced by a late afternoon sky illuminated by a magical orange sun.

"You know, if I were the chosen of Zeus, I think I'd call this place..." Thistle grinned wide, his eyes gleaming in awe. "The Thundergnome."

They all groaned at the same time at the pun.

Jace checked his inventory. His items were still there and available to him.

The clock ticked down.

9 Minutes and 32 Seconds Until Battle Commencement

"Okay, I've set it to have us fighting test dummies," Dex said. "Should be a cakewalk. But let's form a party so we can see each other's stats and abilities as we go." He reached out his hand, and a silver stone appeared—the User Interface Stones Jace thought had been destroyed during calibration.

Alice and Ell did the same, their stones shimmering into existence.

"How did you...?" Jace began.

"Just will it out. It's still inside you, like your Shard. It's always there. Where do you think your Interface comes from?" Dex grinned.

Jace focused, and the silver stone materialized in his hand. A notification popped up.

Traveler Dex has formed a party.

You have been invited to join Dex's party.

Accept | Reject

Note: Current visibility settings will allow all party members to view your active status effects, Affinities, skills, and attributes. Visibility settings are determined by the party leader upon formation. If you do not wish to display this information, please reject and request changes before joining.

Jace accepted, and a flood of data hit him instantly. Blue prompts filled his vision, blocking out the world.

"Hide! Close! Dim!" he shouted.

The prompts vanished.

"Sorry about that, should have warned you," Dex said, smirking. "Set your prompts to Important Only and View All Others Later."

Jace did as suggested.

"Alright, team, we've got a few minutes before the attackers show up. Wanna show off your skills?" Dex prompted.

Alice stepped forward, nervous but eager. She raised her hand, and a sapphire light enveloped her. Before her, a large tome materialized, floating within reach. The book looked ancient, its cover shifting and shimmering like it was alive. She flipped it open, revealing mostly blank pages with intricate runes along the edges.

"I gained an Affinity for hidden knowledge," Alice said. "My Word of Power is Secrets."

She began to chant softly, her fingers tracing the glowing runes. The air around her shimmered, and two spells inscribed themselves onto the pages of her tome: one for detection and the other for concealment.

Jace noticed a small blinking notification icon appear. He selected it.

Part Member Alice Candor Has Revealed the Following Information
    Word of Power: Secrets.

Abilities:

• Summon Tome of Secrets: Collect hidden knowledge to unlock spells and special abilities. Current secrets revealed: 2.

Aether Cost: None.

• Spells Available -

o Arcane Detection: Reveals hidden or magical objects and entities within a radius. Five-minute preparation.

Aether Cost: Moderate.

o Veil of Shadows: Conceals the caster and allies from sight, blending them into the environment. Requires continued casting to maintain.

Aether Cost: Moderate.

Current Boons:

• Enhanced Knowledge Gathering: Bonus to Investigation, History, and Arcane Studies.

• Intelligence Boost: Increased intelligence attribute.

Alice's sapphire shard glowed softly, surrounding her with an ethereal aura. "I can summon this tome and read spells from it. It's mostly blank now, but as I level up, I'll be able to add more spells. I have to find them first, though."

Dex nodded. "Nice, Alice. That's really cool. Slow, but really cool. Who's next?"

Ell stepped up next, her Amethyst Shard glowing with a deep, regal purple. She grinned.

With a touch on his arm, she conjured a shimmering force shield around Dex, causing him to jump back startled. "Relax, it doesn't hurt you, dummy. It's a Force Shield. Right now, it's at Touch Scope, so I have to be in contact. It'll give a glowing protective barrier that cuts most damage by half."

Dex stepped closer, and she activated the shield again. He tested it with a jab at his own arm. "I feel pretty," he said, watching purple sparks glisten where he touched.

Ell continued, her eyes now taking on an eerie glow. "And then there's this. I call it the Pathfinder's Sight. It highlights the easiest path between me and wherever I want to go. I think I can share it with you..." A golden trail appeared, zigzagging through imaginary obstacles before vanishing.

"The third ability is harder to show. Basically, I can spot weaknesses."

Jace opened the prompt.

Party Member Ell Has Revealed the Following Information

Word of Power: Strategy

Abilities:

• Force Shield: Touch-activated, reduces incoming physical damage by 50%.

Aether Cost: Variable depending upon damage.

• Pathfinder's Sight: Highlights the easiest path to a destination and helps predict potential dangers.

Aether Cost: Negligible.

• Spot Weaknesses: 50% boost to detecting opponent weaknesses and reduces EXP cost for perception-based abilities.

Aether Cost: None.

Current Boons:

• Survival: Enhanced survival skills, increasing resilience and adaptability in various environments.

• Insight: Improved ability to understand and anticipate enemy tactics, granting a strategic advantage in combat.

• Perceptiveness: Heightened senses, allowing for quicker detection of hidden threats and opportunities.

Dex clapped. "Impressive, Ell. Now, my turn."

He stepped into the spotlight, twirling his rapier with a flourish. "Word of Power: Dance." He winked at Alice, who scoffed playfully. "Watch closely, folks."

In an instant, a slender rapier appeared in his hands. With fluid grace, he began to move, each step and strike part of an intricate, deadly ballet. His rapier became an extension of his body, slicing through the air with pinpoint accuracy. The movements were mesmerizing, each flourish was a blend of lethal precision and effortless elegance.

Party Member Dex Has Revealed the Following Information
Word of Power: Dance

Abilities:
• Dancing Sword: Conjure a magically imbued rapier. Master a fluid, graceful combat style with increased agility and precision. +5% chance to bypass all defenses, +25% attack speed, +15% critical hit chance.
Aether Cost: Negligible.

• Evasive Waltz: Enhance your ability to dodge attacks with swift, nimble movements. +30% evasion rate, +20% movement speed.
Aether Cost: None.

Current Boons:
• Agility Boost: Increases overall agility, enhancing speed and reaction time.
• Evasion Mastery: Enhances ability to dodge and avoid attacks.
• Puckish Charm: Increases chances of getting out of trouble.

Dex finished his display with a dramatic bow.

"That last one has to be a System joke," Ell quipped.

"Thistle, you're up," Dex said.

Thistle rubbed the back of his neck sheepishly. "You know how I had to end early last year because of some real-world stuff? Well, I just got my Affinity, and I'm not entirely sure how to use it yet."

Dex clapped his hands together. "Just give it a shot. We're all learning here. No judgment, right, gang?"

Everyone nodded in agreement.

Thistle activated his Affinity. "I've only got one thing figured out so far."

He held out his arms, and the transformation began. Muscles bulged and expanded rapidly as he grew taller and broader. His arms lengthened, bulging with new strength, and his legs thickened, grounding him like tree trunks. His hands, once nimble and quick, swelled to the size of pizzas, fingers transforming into powerful digits.

His shoulders broadened, straining his clothes to the limit. His neck thickened, and his face took on rugged, chiseled features. With a deep, resonant rumble, his voice dropped several octaves, echoing like a bass drum.

"What do you think?" Thistle asked, towering over the others.

Dex grinned, eyes wide with approval. "You dirty rat bastard," he laughed. "Oh, you made me promise... but... you knew."

Thistle laughed, a booming sound. "Can't mention my height or you know the consequences," he chided.

"My man, this is epic," Dex said.

"Gnome tank. I get it now," Jace said.

The others nodded in agreement, equally impressed.

Thistle beamed with pride and took a tentative step forward, but his newfound size proved challenging. He tripped, his massive body crashing into the sand with a loud thump. The others scrambled to get out of the way as he reverted back to his gnome form, looking sheepish as he dusted himself off.

"I haven't quite gotten the controls worked out," he admitted, his voice back to its usual tone.

"No kidding," Dex said with a smirk.

Party Member Thistle Has Revealed the Following Information
  Word of Power: Size

  Abilities:
  • Gigantify: Enter Giant Form, temporarily transform into a half-giant, significantly increasing size and strength. +100% Strength, +150% Defense.

Aether Cost: Moderate.

Current Boons:
• Strength Surge: Increases overall strength, enhancing physical power while in Giant Form.
• Resilience Boost: Improves durability and resistance to physical damage while in Giant Form.
• Intimidation Factor: Increases presence, making enemies more likely to hesitate or flee while in Giant Form.

The countdown timer reached the final ten seconds until battle commencement.

"Well, Jace, you'll just have to show us what you've got in action. Contestants, we are out of time," Dex announced.

"Here we go," Jace said, steeling himself.

"Dex, what happens if we die?" Alice asked, her voice tinged with worry.

"Hardly possible. I set it to the lowest setting," Dex replied confidently.

"But if we do?"

"It's set to Beginner Mode. So, if we get seriously injured or our hit points drop below 50%, we instantly return to our bodies and these avatars turn back into dust."

That made Jace feel slightly better, but only slightly.

As the timer reached zero, they looked up, then clutched their ears in pain as a loud, high-pitched sound pierced through them, sending them into agony. The sound disappeared as quickly as it came, replaced by a prompt flashing in front of each of their eyes.

System Error

"What is happening, Dex?" Ell demanded.

System Adjusting For Error
- Modified Instructions Accepted
- Damage Reduction: Disabled
- Pain Reduction: Disabled
- Damage Transference: Enabled
- DEATHMATCH: Enabled

The sky darkened to a starless night, and a sense of foreboding crept into every shadow. The green banner overhead turned a menacing red as a chill settled over the arena.

Monsters began to materialize in the distance, their forms twisted and terrifying. Undead spiders with rotting exoskeletons and eerie green eyes skittered towards them. From the distant darkness, a colossal figure loomed, a mountainous form blocking out the low-hanging moon. Its bulbous head was grotesque and towering, eight eyes glowing with a sickly green. It moved with an unsettling, predatory grace, each step sending tremors through the ground.

"Did the Chamber just create a mountain? Please tell me you told it to create a mountain, Dex," Ell said.

Alice spoke quietly, "That's no mountain."

"This is the easiest setting?" Jace asked, wide-eyed.

Dex shrugged, his face pale. "I never said I really knew how to set this thing up."

Chapter 32
Fanged and the Furious

The group huddled together, their breaths forming ghostly plumes in the now frigid air. Jace's hands trembled as he summoned his cleric rod, the Moonstone Shard in his other hand glinting ominously in the pale light. Dex spun his rapier, the silver blade slicing through the darkness as he shifted his stance. Alice's eyes were wide, but she held firm, her Shard glowing against her determined expression. Ell pulled a sword from her inventory, the amethyst Shard transforming into a heavy necklace around her neck. Behind them, Thistle's form grew towering and sturdy.

For a heartbeat, time stood still.

Then, the silence was ripped apart by a sudden rustle in the underbrush. From the shadows, a monstrous undead spider scuttled forth, nearly half their height, its cracked and decayed exoskeleton reflecting a sickly gleam. Eight eyes, glowing with malevolent light, fixed on the group. With a screech that pierced the night, it lunged forward, a hideous blur of speed and malice.

Dex was the first to react. His rapier flashed as he darted toward the spider. "I've got it!" he shouted. His blade struck the spider's thick exoskeleton with a sharp, metallic ting, but it merely glanced off, leaving only a shallow scratch.

Jace raised his cleric rod, channeling energy through the Moonstone and striking with a determined thrust. Alice focused her Shard, sending bursts of blue energy at the creature, but the spider shrugged them off with ease.

"The joints!" Ell shouted. "Go for the joints," her assessment magic revealing the spider's weak points with a faint violet glow. She stepped forward, her sword gleaming with the power of her Shard, and struck at the spider's thin, whip-cord tendons between its legs and body. Dex followed suit, his blade finding purchase in the vulnerable spots. The creature hissed in pain. Thistle, now a towering giant, moved to the rear, ready to defend against any threat.

The spider screeched, its frantic movements creating a cacophony of horror. It lunged at Dex, its fangs aimed for his throat. Dex parried just barely, his face a mask of concentration.

A glancing claw swiped at Ell, tearing into her arm. She grunted against the pain but kept up her attack.

Jace cast Soul Mend, reaching out and touching Ell, his energy knitting together the minor wounds of his friends. Alice, gathering all her strength, unleashed a concentrated blast of sapphire light that struck the spider directly in its eyes. The creature reeled back, its screeches reaching a fever pitch as it thrashed in pain.

Jace's voice cut through the chaos. "Hit it again, now!" he shouted. Ell's heart pounded, a mix of fear and determination, as she channeled her Shard's power. With precise, fluid movements, she lunged at the spider, her sword guided by the pulsing light of her amethyst Shard.

The spider, now a frenzied blur of legs and fangs, fought back with savage desperation. Its exoskeleton cracked and splintered under the relentless assault, dark ichor spilling onto the ground. Thistle, with a roar that echoed through the forest, brought his massive fists down on the creature, shattering its body in a final, earth-shaking blow.

Thistle shrank back to his normal size, a sheepish smile tugging at his lips. "Can only hold it for a little bit before I gotta recharge."

The silence that followed was deafening, broken only by the ragged breaths of the Travelers. They stood among the remains of the spider, the air thick with the stench of decay and the faint, lingering glow of their Shards. Breathing heavily, adrenaline still coursing through their veins, their smiles were thin and fleeting—victory was a transient thing in this hellish forest.

Then, a sound like bamboo rainmakers filled the air. They stood frozen, trying to process the noise—a sound few had ever heard. It was the eerie clatter of a thousand skeletal legs racing forward, echoing through the forest like a macabre symphony.

From the shadows, the horror emerged—a swarm of undead spiders, pouring forth like a black tide. Their green eyes glowed with rage, casting a sickly light over the forest floor.

"Run!" Jace's voice sliced through the growing dread, sharp and urgent.

The group turned and fled, their feet pounding against the damp forest floor. Dense foliage seemed to close in around them, vines and branches clawing at their clothes and skin as they sprinted through the underbrush. The air was thick with the sound of skittering legs and snapping twigs as the swarm pursued.

Ell led the way through the dense forest. "Keep moving! Don't look back!" she shouted. Dex was close behind, his rapier flashing and slicing through the overgrown foliage.

Of course, everyone looked back. A mass of legs and eyes surged toward them.

"It's just a game, it's just a game," Dex panted, his voice a shaky mantra as he ran. He didn't seem convinced, and truthfully, neither was anyone else.

"We need to find somewhere to hide!" Jace yelled, his voice strained and hoarse.

Ell quickly scanned their surroundings, her eyes landing on a dense thicket. "This way!" she called, activating her Pathfinder ability. A shimmering path appeared, cutting through the underbrush. The group followed, their breaths ragged, the sound of the spider swarm too close for comfort.

In the distance, a monstrous silhouette loomed, shrouded by the night. Its deafening roar sent shivers down Jace's spine, igniting a frenzy among the swarm of spiders below.

A spider leapt from the shadows, its fangs sinking into Alice's leg, causing her to stumble and scream, the sound of agony piercing the chaotic night. Jace reacted instinctively, barreling into the spider and knocking it back. Thistle quickly transformed back into his massive form and belly-flopped onto the creature with all his weight, stunning it just long enough for them to escape.

Jace felt the strain on his Aether, the healing sapping his energy. Each step became heavier, each breath more labored. He cast another quick Soul Mend at Thistle, who was bleeding from his encounter with the spider, a shard of its exoskeleton lodged in his chest.

"Keep moving!" Jace shouted, casting Soul Mend as fast as he could. Healing energy surged through his hands and into Alice's torn flesh. It wouldn't heal completely, but it was enough to keep her on her feet, though she limped noticeably. They couldn't afford to stop. Not now. Holding her hand as they ran to keep the link, he focused, trying to finish the heal, feeling his aether draining fast, nearly sucking him dry before he cut it off. The wound still refused to fully close.

The giant silhouette in the distance grew gradually closer, the ground shaking with each thudding step. Jace's heart raced as he struggled to keep up with his companions, his cleric rod emitting a dim glow from the last of his energy.

The spiders kept up their ferocious attacks, not trying to kill but to maim, as if they were simply playing with their food. They'd burst from the darkness just long enough to slash and then vanish again, their long legs whipping out with sharpened bones, striking with deadly precision and a sick sense of humor.

Jace cried out in pain as one of the creatures cut into his side, blood gushing from the wound. He pushed it off fiercely, but his movements grew sluggish and weak as the blood drained.

If not for his Minor Resistance to Death, he was sure it would have been fatal. As it was, the pain was near unbearable, adrenaline the only thing keeping him standing. He had never felt pain quite like this, not in Terra Mythica. Not since the night Alex went to the hospital. Icons flashed in his view, alerting him to notifications, which he ignored with a flick of his mind. He healed himself enough to keep going, draining the tiny amount of aether he had regained.

Alice, her leg still injured and stained with blood, hobbled beside Ell. Her sapphire blasts grew weaker with each passing moment. "I can't keep this up," she gasped, her face twisted with agony.

Thistle, bleeding from multiple wounds, had a piece of exoskeleton from the spider he had crushed still lodged in his chest. He was struggling to keep up, so Dex hefted him onto his shoulder. "Never mention this," Dex grunted, pushing forward with determination.

Each step felt heavier, the air thick with fear and desperation. The group moved as one, driven by sheer survival instinct. Every breath was a battle, every heartbeat a countdown to the next attack.

Behind them, the monstrous creature's roar echoed, a chilling reminder that these undead spiders were not the only nightmare lurking.

Ell's sword flashed in the dim light, slicing through thick webs and fending off the scuttling spiders with fierce determination.

"Just a bit further! We can make it!" Ell said.

Jace's vision blurred as he cast another Soul Mend the moment his Aether could handle it, this time targeting Thistle. It wasn't enough to do much more than dislodge the white sliver from Thistle's chest and breathe some life back into his eyes, but Jace could see that Thistle was recovering, aided by his own abilities. Jace's aether was depleted again, and he knew he was running on borrowed time.

Suddenly, a clearing appeared ahead, the dense forest opening up to a small rocky outcrop. Pale moonlight illuminated the jagged edges of the rocks, casting shadows over the group as they stumbled forward.

"There! Head for the rocks!" Ell yelled, her voice cracking with exhaustion.

The group scrambled towards the rocky outcrop, their bodies battered and bleeding. Reaching the base of the rocks, Jace collapsed against a large boulder, his breath coming in ragged gasps. The spiders followed closely behind.

Jace swung his cleric rod desperately, using it more as a bat than a focus, striking the nearest spider to keep it at bay. "Climb!" he shouted, his voice hoarse.

They scrambled up the rock face with desperate effort, helping each other over the rough surface. Fear fueled their frantic climb, the relentless spiders driving them upward. As they neared the top, a small cave came into view, illuminated by Ell's guiding power.

One by one, they clambered into the cave. Thistle, summoning the last of his aether and strength, shifted into his massive form. With a determined grunt, he hammered the cave wall and ceiling by the entrance, each blow causing the rock to tremble under the force of his rage.

The others retreated further inside, their eyes wide with fear and confusion.

"Thistle, what are you doing?" Alice called out, panic sharpening her voice. But he ignored her, his focus unyielding.

Outside, the spiders were climbing the rock face, their skittering legs growing louder, echoing like a thousand nails on a chalkboard. Thistle struck again, his fists colliding with the stone in a powerful rhythm. The entrance began to crumble and shake, loose rocks cascading down.

"Get out of there!" Ell shouted, her voice breaking with urgency.

Thistle screamed in a feral fury, a raw rebellion against the world as he struck again. His voice carried the weight of all his pain and anger, echoing through the cave like a thunderclap. Despite the obvious aether drain, he held his massive form, every muscle trembling with the effort.

His roar was a primal cry, filled with defiance and desperation. His eyes burned with intensity, the rage and sorrow in his heart driving him to protect his friends at any cost.

Dex sprang forward in a blur, diving toward Thistle just as the first spiders came into view. The sight of their glowing eyes and gnashing fangs sent a jolt of terror through him. The rumble grew into a deafening roar as the rocks fell all at once, piling up in booms of stone and dust.

"No!" Jace shouted, his voice lost in the chaos. He watched helplessly as the cave entrance collapsed, stone after stone crashing down, sealing them in darkness.

The air was thick with dust, choking their every breath. Coughing and gasping, they struggled to regain their bearings. The silence that followed was oppressive, broken only by the distant sound of stone falling and the occasional screech of the spiders outside. Ell and Jace illuminated their Shards, the dim glow reflecting off the dust and casting everything in a hazy blur.

Jace, his heart pounding, made himself focus. He forced his recovering aether into his Spirit Sense and peered through the haze. The effort left him dizzy, the energy drain nearly too much to bear.

"No," Ell whispered, her voice trembling, eyes wide with fear.

As the dust finally began to settle and the cloud of smoke dissipated, faint shapes emerged. Dex was dragging Thistle toward them, both alive but battered and bruised. The relief was palpable, cutting through the lingering dread.

"Oh, hey guys," Dex said, attempting a weak smile despite the pain. "What's up?"

Ell let out a sob of relief, tears streaming down her cheeks. She rushed to Dex, her fists pounding weakly against his shoulder. "Don't you ever do that again, you good-for-nothing idiot!"

Dex quickly set Thistle down and wrapped Ell in a tight hug. Neither spoke for a long while, their emotions too raw for words.

They huddled together inside the dark cave, faces pale and drawn with pain and exhaustion. For now, they were safe from the relentless creatures of the forest.

The sound of bones scratching against stone outside echoed, a grim reminder of the danger that awaited them. Jace leaned against the cave wall, his breath still coming in heavy gasps. Beyond, the spiders scrabbled relentlessly, their sharp legs skittering across the ground with an insatiable hunger. He could feel their desperation, their relentless desire to capture and consume.

The group's weary eyes met in the dim light, a silent acknowledgment of the fragile safety they had found. The cave, though a temporary refuge, felt like a sanctuary in the heart of the nightmare they were living.

Chapter 33

Not a Particularly Good Plan

They rested inside the cave, the only light coming from their glowing Shards. The eerie luminescence cast long shadows on the cave walls, highlighting the full extent of their injuries. Blood and dirt smeared their clothes, and the weight of their ordeal hung heavily in the air. Jace pressed his back against the cool cave wall, finding surprising comfort amidst the chaos of his thoughts. "Rest now," he whispered, barely able to speak through the aether drain.

Twenty minutes passed in tense silence as they regained their energy. They had survived this far, and as long as their Shards still glowed, they had a fighting chance. Jace's injuries seemed to heal themselves as his aether recovered, an interesting phenomenon. He didn't need to focus on it; his Mend ability activating on its own.

Soul Mend Has Gained a New Aspect

(Internal, Passive)

A small portion of your aether is now dedicated to personal healing, providing a constant, passive restoration. This ongoing aether expenditure reduces the total cost for all self-mending by 50%.

Having recovered somewhat, Jace summoned all the aether he could muster and began to heal the worst injuries first. Alice lay before him, her body trembling as poison seeped through her veins from the spider's bite. He placed his hands near her wound and, though she flinched in pain, he didn't pull back, knowing that the closer his hands were to the injury, the stronger the Mend would be.

Channeling his energy into a powerful Soul Mend, the light from his cleric rod flared brilliantly on the ground beside him, casting a silver glow. The rod was bent and battered, barely useful, but he kept it near, feeling it gave him a slight boost in efficiency, even though no notifications confirmed it. The poison wasn't completely eradicated, but the bleeding stopped, and some color returned to her pale cheeks.

Next, Jace turned to Dex, whose side was torn and bloody. His hands trembled from exhaustion, but he pressed on, placing his hands near the wound and using Soul Mend. The torn flesh knitted together under his touch, leaving only a faint scar. Dex winced, then sighed in relief, nodding his thanks to Jace.

Ell, though bloodied, bore no serious wounds and declined further healing, preferring to conserve Jace's strength. She stood watch at the back of the cave, her sword ready, eyes scanning the darkness behind them.

Thistle, drained from the battle and in his effort to collapse the cave entrance, sat slumped against the wall, awake but disoriented. Jace approached him last, placing a hand on his shoulder. He used Soul Tether to transfer a small but vital amount of aether to Thistle, revitalizing him enough to keep him conscious and alert. Thistle's main issue was aether exhaustion, having pushed past his limits. Jace knew that feeling all too well from his first day and wouldn't wish it on anyone. Unfortunately, they didn't have any potions, so Thistle would need time to recover fully.

"We can't stay here," Jace said, trying to regain his spent aether.

"We need a plan," Ell replied, her voice low but steady. "We can't outrun them."

Dex's voice cut through the gloom, tinged with a sort of logical resignation. "I don't mean to sound crazy here, but why don't we just log out?"

"Have you tried?" Ell asked. "The option has been disabled since that thing showed up. Already checked."

"Okay, then why don't we just let it kill us? We'll wind up back with our bodies and should be able to log out then. Worst case, we respawn and lose some EXP."

It made sense. It was a logical suggestion. But something felt off, and everyone sensed it. Jace was the first to voice their shared unease.

"There's something wrong with the system. Did you see those glitches?" he asked tentatively.

The group exchanged uneasy glances, each recalling the strange anomalies they'd noticed.

"I've never even heard of anything like that. The system glitching? It's crazy," Alice said, shaking her head in disbelief.

"I have. I've been seeing them since I arrived," Jace admitted, a deep, guttural dread filling him. What if he was causing all of this? What if their actual lives were in danger because of him and his stupid plan? What if the system knew he wasn't supposed to be here... that he was the wrong brother?

"I'm not sure what will happen if we die," Jace continued, his tone more somber. "Maybe nothing, maybe a respawn. Or maybe we're one of those cases the conspiracy theorists talk about."

"You mean people going insane inside the game? There's zero evidence of that," Ell retorted, clearly skeptical.

Thistle, having regained enough strength to speak, drew all eyes to him with a rasping breath. "My uncle did," he said slowly, each word a struggle. "Don't know for sure."

They sat in patient silence, waiting as he worked out the sentences through the aether drain. "He was fine, and then one day, he wasn't. Kept complaining of a glitch, but no one believed him. The last time he logged out... he wasn't the same. Never spoke again. Just sort of sits there, you know. And we never found out why."

His words settled over them like a storm cloud. "I was young when it happened. My parents say me and him used to be close, but I don't remember too much. I just remember everything changing after that. My parents got a big check from Excelsior, we moved into a nicer neighborhood. Never spoke of it again. They pretend it didn't happen. I'm not even supposed to talk about it."

He paused, his breath ragged. "But it's how I got into M.O.U. They gave us access for the whole family, free Devices, University of our choice. I was the only one that wanted in... it's crazy, but I think there might be some part of him still here somewhere. I don't know."

The cave was silent for a long moment. Jace, Alice, and Ell exchanged looks, the gravity of Thistle's story sinking in.

"That's terrible, Thistle," Ell said softly, her voice filled with sympathy. "And even I have to admit that it sounds pretty fishy. But it doesn't necessarily mean the system caused it."

"No, but it doesn't mean we're safe either," Jace interjected. "Our best bet is to heal up and figure a way out of this. Dex, does the match end on a timer?"

"It was supposed to," Dex replied, looking disheartened. "But this is uncharted territory. Guys, I'm... I'm really sorry."

"We know, Dex. But we'll have time to be sorry later," Jace said. "Right now, we need to figure this out. What do we know about this place?" He had been in bad situations before.

Stay calm. Breathe deep. Gather resources. He repeated his foster parents' words in his mind.

"We know that big thing is probably the boss monster," Ell said. "I'd bet that when it dies, this thing is over."

"Okay, that's as good a guess as any. What are our resources?" Jace asked.

They quickly listed everything they had on them, but nothing seemed useful for the situation.

"I actually have a theory," Jace began, the idea solidifying as he spoke. "It's a long shot, but hear me out. You know how Ell can spot a weakness?"

They nodded.

"Well, when we fought that first spider, I could tell something was off. It didn't have a soul, per se—just a husk. And there was something inside it that didn't belong, something tethered to pure hate. It's hard to explain, but it felt... tangible. If I can somehow attack that connection, I might be able to cut off whatever's controlling them. I know it sounds nuts, but I just have this gut feeling I can do it."

"You want to cut the connection between that big guy and whoever's pulling the strings? Just a quick little snip-snip?" Dex asked, eyebrows raised.

"That's the plan," Jace replied.

"And here I thought I was the one full of terrible ideas."

"It's a plan. I didn't say it was a particularly good plan, but it's the best I've got. Ell, can you see if there's a way out through the cave?" Jace asked, turning to her.

Ell's eyes went white for a moment, then returned to normal. "I think so. It's faint."

"Alright," Jace said. "Alice, Thistle, Dex, you stay here. Ell and I will go."

Dex protested, and Alice insisted she would be fine. However, Jace could see she was in no condition to walk. The bleeding had stopped, but despite his desperate attempts to heal her, the venom surged through her leg without relenting. The pain was etched on her face, her eyes a silent cry.

"No, there's no reason to risk everyone, and I'm not even sure this will work. I'm just going to test it on a straggler. Ell can help me get out there and find one. Then either way, I'll come back and we'll regroup."

"And if you get caught?" Alice asked, worry etched in her voice.

"We find out what happens when someone dies." Jace smiled weakly.

"Okay, but take this." Dex handed him a small locket with a glowing glass top from his inventory, its light illuminating the dim cave with crystalline brilliance. "It's a one-off. If you're in trouble, break it. It'll create a massive burst of light for five seconds. Enough time to call for help. I didn't use it earlier because it would blind us just as much as them. Thistle will keep a lookout."

"I don't need it," Jace protested, but Dex insisted.

"Just take it. Don't use it unless you have to, but if you do..."

"Alright, Dex." Jace accepted it with a nod of appreciation.

Jace cast a few more Mends, his hands glowing softly as he worked to heal his friends. Once satisfied they were as well as possible, and his aether mostly recovered, he turned to Ell. With a curt nod, she motioned for him to follow, leading him deeper into the cave.

As they moved, Jace's Dark Vision leveled up, sharpening his sight in the dim light. The cave, mercifully quiet, led them through winding paths and eventually out to a small cliff face draped in thick green vines. Vines twisted and writhed like serpents, their leaves glistening with moisture. It was like a scene from a jungle nightmare, the vibrant green stark against the shadowy backdrop.

"We have to be quick. And quiet," Ell whispered, her voice barely more than a breath.

Ell went first, descending the vines with slow, deliberate movements. Jace followed, his heart pounding in his chest. The vines were slick under his fingers, making the descent treacherous. Once on the ground, they moved in slow, deliberate silence as they navigated the shadowy labyrinth of trees.

Every rustle and crackle of leaves set their nerves on edge, the jungle alive with unseen threats. Jace's enhanced vision picked up the glint of hidden eyes and the subtle movement of creatures lurking just beyond their path. Tension hung heavy, every step a precarious dance on the edge between survival and disaster.

They left the cave behind, venturing deeper into the tangled undergrowth. Ell moved with a purpose, her keen sense of direction guiding them through the foliage. Jace followed, his senses on high alert. The darkness was suffocating, the heavy scent of decay and rot growing with each step.

The deeper they went, the more the jungle seemed to come alive. Shadows danced at the edges of his vision, and he could almost hear the whispers of unseen creatures. It was as if the jungle itself was watching, waiting. Jace's mind raced, the tension mounting with every step.

Finally, they spotted it: a lone spider, separated from the horde. Its cracked exoskeleton glinted in the dappled moonlight filtering through the canopy. It moved slowly, its movements jerky and unnatural, as if controlled by some unseen force.

"It's a Bronze Three," Ell said after scanning it.

"Good as any to try," Jace replied, his voice steady despite the fear gnawing at his insides.

They crouched out of sight, the creature looming nearby. Beside him, Ell's hand closed around his, her grip a silent reassurance that they faced this together.

The beast's twisted head turned towards them, and Jace could feel its evil energy pulsing through the air. He closed his eyes and steadied himself..

Gathering all his Aether, Jace tapped into his Soul Sense, reaching out to connect with the creature's essence. He forced as much Aether into the ability as he could, trying to peer deeply into the creature. The moment their minds touched, he recoiled in disgust at the darkness and malice that consumed it. It was unlike anything he had ever encountered before.

As he sensed it, the beast sensed him. With a deafening screech, the undead beast lunged at them, its razor-sharp claws just missing Jace's face. He struggled to maintain his connection as he stumbled back. Ell, seizing the moment, slammed her sword into a joint, causing the creature to hiss in pain. She focused on distracting it, giving Jace the precious time he needed.

Drawing on every ounce of power within him, Jace poured more Aether into his Aura Sense. He feared he was wrong, that what he had seen before was just a trick of the mind. Then he saw it—a faint connection, a point between the demon, or whatever it was, that was using the skeleton as a puppet. Jace focused on it and, with all his power, pushed. Nothing happened.

Ell fought valiantly, but it wasn't going well, the creature pushing her back.

"Any time now, Jace." It must have just looked like Jace was staring at it as she fought.

"Trying," he said.

He pushed harder on it. Still nothing. Then, with a moment of clarity, he relaxed and used Soul Tether to connect himself with it. In that moment, he could feel the beast and all of its feelings—hunger and pain.

Ell was just an annoying noise in a quiet night, a pest to be killed. The creature must have sensed the intrusion because it wheeled on Jace, ignoring Ell's attacks.

"Uh, Jace..."

The creature lunged at him. Jace's focus sharpened, and the world seemed to slow. For a brief, intense moment, he became the connection. He was the spider, feeling its alien thoughts and primal instincts. In that instant, he severed the bond. The connection between the beast's undead body and the demon shattered.

As the twisted energy dissipated, the beast collapsed onto him with a heavy thud, pinning Jace to the ground.

"I'm okay," Jace gasped, struggling beneath the heavy corpse.

Ell hurried over and helped him shove the beast off. It took nearly all their strength to move it. Jace got to his feet, a single tear escaping despite his efforts to hide it. He sighed, wiping sweat and dirt from his face.

They stood for a moment, catching their breath. Jace used the moment to inspect his most recent notification.

Affinity: Soul

Ability Unlocked: Soul Severance

• You have gained a deeper insight into the connection between the soul and the body, enabling you to detect and remove incursions that do not belong. This ability allows you to sever the connection between a foreign entity and its host body. Increase this ability for reduced aether cost and increased effectiveness.

Aether Cost: Severe

Soul Sense has Gained a New Aspect

• You have gained an enhanced perception of souls and their connections. You can now see and feel from the perspective of the connected entity, with a chance to glean potentially value insights and memories.

"You did it, Jace," Ell said, a huge grin spreading across her face, her eyes filling with hope.

Jace smiled back, but his expression quickly darkened. "It was strange, Ell. Really strange. I felt it. Like I was a part of it, like it was me. And I sensed the demon too. But there was something else. Something darker. Ell, these things aren't just in the Chamber. They're possessed."

Ell's searched his eyes before turning to look around, the silence suddenly more menacing. "We need to get out of here," she said, her voice slicing through the tension. "Let's get back to the cave."

Jace nodded, his mind still reeling from the encounter.

As they approached the cave, an unsettling silence enveloped them. Each step felt heavier, the weight of dread pressing down on their shoulders. The usual jungle sounds had faded away, replaced by an eerie stillness that set their nerves on edge.

Then they heard it: the distant, horrifying screams of their friends. Jace and Ell exchanged a grim look, their pace quickening. Their hearts pounded in unison, each beat echoing their growing fear.

They skidded to a halt, concealed in the shadows. Before them lay the entrance to the cave, alive with movement. Hundreds of spiders, their bodies grotesque and menacing, swarmed in and out of the dark maw.

Terror surged through them as they watched, helpless, while three forms wrapped in gray webs were carried out by the monstrous arachnids. The cocooned sight was sickening.

Jace and Ell locked eyes, a silent understanding passing between them. They would go after their friends, and they would do everything they could, even if it killed them.

Chapter 34
A Deadly Game

As they trailed the eight-legged undead, they did their best to stay hidden in the shadows. The creatures no longer seemed to be actively searching for them, and with Ell's Pathfinder ability leading the way, they skillfully avoided any large groups. The winding path eventually led them to a ghastly clearing, where bodies hung like macabre decorations from twisted tree branches.

Their friends dangled limply above, swaying slightly in the putrid breeze. In the center of the clearing, a massive skeletal spider loomed, its bony limbs stretching outward. The air was thick with moisture, and the unnerving sound of rustling leaves.

The spider, a king among its kin, was an immense figure of deathly stillness. Its skeletal frame was adorned with dark, oozing ichor that dripped from its mandibles. The air seemed to hold its breath, and the monstrous spider's presence filled them with a primal dread. It sat motionless, almost as if it was aware of their presence, patiently waiting for them to make a move.

Jace's heart pounded in his chest. "We have to get them down," Jace whispered, his voice barely audible.

Ell nodded, her gaze never leaving the monstrous spider.

It twitched, and the slight movement was enough to send a shiver down their spines. It was as if the beast could sense their fear, feeding off it, growing stronger with each passing second of their hesitation.

"First, we need a plan. Rushing in blindly will just get us killed," she said. Ell's sharp eyes scanned the clearing, searching for any advantage. "I can't even get a read on its rank. It must be at least Gold. How long do you need to sever the connection?"

"It was hard enough with a Bronze Rank, but that thing? I don't even know if it's possible. And when I start juicing up my Soul Sense, it can see me. It's like we're linked. Then, game over."

"Alright, we split up. You hide where you can see it. I'll distract it," Ell said, trying to sound confident. "Just like we did before."

"Yeah, except this time it's like fighting a mountain," Jace replied grimly. "Okay, what will the signal be?"

Ell narrowed her eyes, surveying the clearing. Activating one of her abilities, she tried to see its weaknesses. Not much data came back, but then she saw a faint glow. "Its eyes... Jace, give me the locket."

He pulled it from his inventory and handed it to her, keeping his hand over it to suppress the light.

"I'm going to blind it. At least temporarily. That'll be the signal."

"So, you plan to alert every creature in the forest to where you are, and get close enough to flash bomb it? I don't know how good of a distraction you'll make if you're dead," Jace said.

"We need to draw its attention and stall it from finding you. This is our best shot, Jace," she said firmly. "You just wait for my signal, and then get to work."

They shared a knowing look and a nod.

"I know I came up with it but... this plan is insane," Ell said, her heart racing.

"Yup," Jace said.

"And Jace, try not to die," she said with a faint smile.

"No promises," he replied.

With a final glance at each other, they split up—Ell moving to one side while Jace took the other. Each step was calculated, their breathing shallow, as the tension grew suffocating.

Jace looked back to find Ell had already disappeared into the shadows. He was alone now. He could see the monstrous beast in the distant clearing.

Don't die, he thought. Definitely no promises.

Jace pushed deeper into the forest, skirting the edge of a clearing. He spotted a tree with thick foliage and scrambled up, each branch groaning under his weight, the bark rough and unyielding against his hands. He hoped the dense leaves would offer some concealment from the beasts lurking below.

From his perch, he could see the scene more clearly. He forced himself to breathe slowly, calming his racing thoughts. The forest felt like a living entity, watching his every move, waiting for him to slip.

Peering through the thick foliage, his eyes widened. His friends hung cocooned in webs, suspended high in the air like grotesque chandeliers. Below them, the giant skeletal spider sat, its bony limbs twitching as it toyed with the web strands. Their bodies jerked and swayed, puppets in a macabre marionette show. The monstrous creature reveled in its power and cruelty.

Jace couldn't see Ell, but he knew she would reach her position and give the signal. The plan depended on her, and he trusted her to come through. Hidden among the dense foliage, he strained to hear any sign of her.

Suddenly, the silence shattered. A rock flew out of nowhere, striking one of the smaller spiders dead on. The creature screeched, a high-pitched wail echoing through the forest. The sound was chilling, a signal of pain and anger that cut through the night.

The effect was immediate. The boss spider's many eyes swiveled toward the noise, its attention fully captured. Jace felt the ground tremble with each step as the massive creature began to move, its body a shadow in the darkness. The wait was unbearable, every nerve in Jace's body on edge as he watched the monstrous spider shift its focus.

As it grew closer, its maw opened wide, an abyss that could swallow a tree whole—a nightmare given form, hunting for Ell among the shadows. Jace's heart pounded, adrenaline surging as the monstrous beast moved nearer to her, each moment a slow beat in the deadly dance.

He waited. And waited. And...

Suddenly, an intense flash of light burst from a tree directly in front of the spider, illuminating the forest with a blinding brilliance. Jace shielded his eyes as the searing light cut through the darkness, the forest alive with stark shadows and sharp contrasts, every detail etched in harsh relief. For a moment, everything stood still, the world frozen in the aftermath of the explosive light. Then, just as quickly, the darkness enveloped the world again.

The creature recoiled, disoriented, slashing wildly at the trees and toppling them like mere twigs. It screeched, a bone-chilling sound, as a swarm of smaller spiders surged toward the source of the light. The monstrous creature lashed out blindly, its once-methodical hunt now a frenzied rampage.

"Alright, showtime," Jace muttered, taking a deep breath as he activated his Soul Sense. Immediately, he knew something was wrong. The spider's soul was a spiraling vortex, like a black hole. He felt himself being sucked into it, overwhelmed by endless hate and a desire to end it all.

There was no mere thread to an unseen puppeteer. No demon pulling the strings. Just a sea of pain and loss whirling within, like ink and fire. But the soul inside did not belong to the creature, of that Jace could be sure. The mind controlling it was a force unlike any he had encountered, save for the rare moments when Hades let a sliver of his aura slip through. This was similar but twisted, darker, and infinitely more menacing.

He focused on the endless current of burning ink connecting the spider to its malevolent master. It sensed the intrusion and resisted, but couldn't pinpoint the source. It wheeled in his direction, still blind from the flash. Shouts erupted from the trees behind it—Ell, making noise. She was going to get herself killed.

Jace couldn't think about that now. He had to concentrate. The beast turned back to the sound while flashes of amethyst light shot into the air, and the smaller spiders swarmed toward it.

Jace finally found it—the link between the corpse and the soul. This one was different—solid, tight, like a noose around the beast's neck. He zeroed in, feeling the bind. With a determined breath, Jace mentally reached out, straining against the viscous energy that held the creature captive. The world around him blurred, his vision fading into the murky depths of the creature's mind.

The darkness swirled around him, a malevolent vortex. He stood in that abyss, a lone, glowing light against waves of darkness. Black vines coiled around his arms and neck, resisting his intrusion, tightening with an incredible force. Every move he made met with a violent pushback, the knot of darkness thick and unyielding, threatening to engulf him entirely.

Each breath a struggle. The connection point came into focus, soldered in its hate and despair. With a deep breath, he reached out and pulled with all his might.

A thought slithered through Jace's mind, alien and unwelcome. I can feel you, poking around where you don't belong.

The inky blackness retaliated, tearing into him with vicious force. Tendrils of darkness clawed at him, each touch a searing pain, but Jace held on, refusing to surrender. The air crackled with the clash of forces in the void, a deadly game of shadow and light.

Jace felt, more than saw, the spider's resistance growing fiercer, its movements erratic and aggressive. It lashed out, tearing through the underbrush in a frenzy. His heart pounded as he struggled to maintain focus. Sweat dripped down his face, his vision blurring as he pushed his limits.

Where are you hiding? the dark presence whispered in his mind, its voice oily and invasive.

"Come on, you've got this," Jace muttered to himself, a thin thread of hope snaking through his mind.

The beast's eyes swiveled wildly, hunting for the source of the incursion into its soul. Jace focused every ounce of his willpower on the connection point, picturing the dark energy splitting like a rusted chain. He activated Soul Severance, the mental image of a blade slicing through the black tendrils. With a final, desperate push, he felt the connection falter, shaking as if on the verge of breaking.

Jace felt a sudden, unnerving shift, his vision fracturing into a kaleidoscope of images. For a heartbeat, he saw through the many eyes of the spider, its awareness merging with his own. The monstrous creature moved with a swift, mechanical precision, turning its gaze toward him. Jace's blood ran cold as he watched himself in the tree, countless eyes locking onto his position.

Ah, there you are, the thought dripped with a strange glee.

Then, with the force of a tidal wave, Jace was thrown back into his own mind, his Soul Sense shattered. His heart raced, the echo of the beast's gaze lingering, its predatory focus burned into his consciousness.

And then he heard it: the strangest sound he'd ever encountered. A voice, more like wind moving through bone than speech, intoned from the creature's mouth, "It has been a long time since I have felt such magic from another. A long time, indeed."

Jace's body froze as he listened.

"I see you, Chosen of Hades. Do not worry, you can come out. I will not hurt you. I only want to talk."

In an instant, with a speed that belied its massive size, the monstrous spider's legs shot out and snatched Jace into the air. He was tossed high like a ragdoll, only to be caught again in a cruel game of cat and mouse. Smaller spiders, each nearly as large as Jace, swarmed along the giant's bony limbs, leaping toward him. They swiftly encased him in a cocoon of sticky webbing, binding his arms tightly to his sides, leaving only his head exposed.

A long thread dangled him upside down, suspending him face-to-face with the beast's enormous, unblinking eyes.

"Let me go!" he shouted, thrashing against the webbing that held him tight, his aether reserves dangerously low.

"Oh, and where would be the fun in that?" the spider purred, its voice a slick, oily caress. "It is ever so rare that I get to converse with my prey. Rarer still that they possess this particular Word of Power. Soul, isn't it?"

Jace could almost see a twisted smile behind the creature's dripping mandibles. He fought to keep his resolve, but the presence of the spider was overwhelming, a crushing weight on his mind.

Breathe deep. Take a moment. Gather resources, he mentally repeated to himself.

"Goblin got your tongue, Little Thing? Too scared to speak? They really don't make heroes like they used to," the spider bellowed, its voice echoing through the forest like a death knell.

Jace glanced at his friends, each of them ensnared in the web, their bodies unmoving. Only Ell was still free, hidden somewhere in the forest.

Stay hidden, he wished. Stay safe.

"Don't worry, Little Thing. Your friends aren't dead... yet," the spider hissed, relishing the words. "Just paralyzed. Waiting for the full collection. Waiting for me to have this little chat with you."

He forced himself to slow his racing heart. What do I have? What do I know? What are my resources?

Right now, all he had was the briefest breaths of time—time to gather his aether, time to distract the creature so that Ell could come up with a plan. Time, and the slightest, dimming shard of hope.

"Why are you here?" Jace asked, his voice steady despite the fear and exhaustion eating away at his will.

"Ah, that is the question, isn't it?" The spider's voice oozed. "Let's play a game. I'll answer a question for each that you answer. The moment one of us cannot, the game is over. Hmm?"

It paused, savoring the moment, not really expecting an answer.

"I am here to end Theon and his mindless followers. They should have been here when I was summoned... but alas, no sign of him or his professors," it spat the last word. "But all is not lost. I have you," it said, its eyes glinting.

"Who are you?" Jace asked, struggling to keep his voice steady.

"Ah ah ah, not your turn," the creature hissed, a note of mockery in its voice. "My question first. Judging by your garb, you are a Chosen of Hades," it growled with palpable disdain. "But what does Hades want with a new Chosen? Why you?"

"That's two questions," Jace replied.

"Fine!" It shifted, sending a gust of wind that made Jace sway. "Why did Hades choose you?"

Jace found the question puzzling, its relevance escaping him. He considered his answer carefully, wary of any traps hidden in the question.

"He chose me to help rebuild his Society," Jace said, hoping it was enough.

"Lies!" the spider hissed, drawing closer, its breath hot and foul. "Liessss... He chose you to get to me. But he can't. It's far too late for that." The beast laughed, a chilling sound that seemed to echo from another world. "Hades has never cared for the Societies. He only desires one thing. One thing that I have and he does not. But, perhaps, you don't know... interesting, Little Thing. Kept in the dark. Ah... I see."

"It's my turn. How did you get in here? The grounds are protected from things like you."

"Ah, it thinks," the spider said, looking at Jace with a twisted amusement. "The grounds are protected from beasts entering, yes... but not from things already here."

"What do you mean?" Jace asked.

"My turn," it hissed.

Jace's aether was slowly recovering, but he needed more time. More time for Ell... He heard a scream pierce the air.

The beast's smile widened. "Oh, you weren't counting on her, were you?"

A body wrapped in webbing was dragged by a group of smaller spiders. It was Ell. Her form was strung up alongside the others.

"Now, tell me, Little Thing, how did you come by your Word?" the spider asked, its tone mocking.

Jace's mind raced. He honestly didn't know, but he couldn't just say that. He needed to keep the beast talking -buy time for his aether to replenish. If he could just get enough, he might have a chance to sever the connection.

"My parents died when I was very young. Then my foster parents died. Then my brother..." Jace felt a sudden swell of emotion. He hadn't spoken of this to anyone. Alex had always been his anchor, his confidant. But since Alex was hurt, he'd kept everything bottled up.

He blinked away a tear, forcing himself to stay focused. "The Word came to me in those moments. Each loss carved it deeper into my soul."

The spider's eyes gleamed with interest, its focus entirely on him now. Jace could feel his aether building, a slow but steady trickle. Just a little more time...

"Such delicious pain," the spider purred, rubbing its fangs together in pleasure. "Yes, great loss could explain it. Hmmm. But still... I don't think that's all. No, there's more hidden there, behind the loss."

"I don't care what you think!" Jace spat back, his anger flaring.

In that moment, he concentrated and forced his growing aether into Soul Sense and Soul Severance.

Immediately, he was back in the beast's mind, black waves lapping against his knees. The cold was biting now, and he stood as the only light, casting reflections on the inky waters around him.

A voice moved through his mind, terrible and unwelcome. It laughed. *You think you can use this type of magic against me? The Soul Affinity does not belong to you alone.*

The sea grew turbulent, and waves crashed against him, pulling him under and sucking him downwards. He pushed with all his might, forcing himself deeper into the creature's essence.

Little Thing, open a connection and it goes both ways... You asked me a question before... I think I shall answer you. 'Who am I?' You want to know... How about I show you!

It was a battle of wills, and Jace was quickly overwhelmed. Yet, the shared nature of their Words of Power created an unexpected resonance. Their differing understandings of the Soul clashed, manifesting as distinct, vibrant energies.

The beast's darkness wasn't merely an absence of light, but an all-consuming void. Images of desolation and despair flooded Jace's mind—an abyss so deep it swallowed hope itself. This was a darkness that whispered of finality, where even the memory of light dared not tread.

Then Jace was hit with a flood of deep, abiding sadness, visceral and endless.

So much pain, Jace thought.

Pain? Oh, you naive Little Thing. Pain is just the beginning. Hades took everything from me! Everything. They all did.

Flashes of color and death, and lights. Green lights. Amethyst lights.

Theon is blind to the truth. Ask him, Chosen of Hades. Ask him about his past. This world is dripping with deceit. Pain? They will know pain.

I'm not afraid of you! Kill me. I'll simply respawn. He screamed in his mind.

Oh! Are you so sure, Chosen of Hades? Is that the lie they've been feeding you? Blind devotion to your god, John Rearden? Hmm? The worst of them all, more rotten than the rest. Because he knew... he knew and he said nothing!

In the chaos, Jace sensed the tether binding the entity to the undead form. He struck at it with his Soul Severance, but it held firm. His aether was too weak, too depleted.

A single spiked claw moved slowly towards his still-dangling body. Without hesitation, it began to sink into his chest. "Shall we test your theory?" the creature hissed.

The claw pressed deeper, and Jace screamed in agony.

"Or perhaps," the beast continued, "I should show you how a Soul is truly severed. Rip you apart and let my minions feast on your remains while you watch, my venom coursing through your beating heart. The demons are so very hungry, confined to these rotting bodies. But before I let you die, let's see what secrets you hold. Maybe you can still serve your King. Show me everything!"

With that, a torrent of energy burst into Jace's mind, wrenching it open.

Images flashed before his eyes: places he had never seen, faces unfamiliar yet hauntingly known. He couldn't tell if he was glimpsing into the mind and memories of the darkness or if the darkness was delving into his own.

Suddenly, he was there. A woman cried, then fought with fierce passion and love. An ancient darkness, as old and deep as time. A green light. A face with long ears, both familiar and strange. A flash of light. Then the burst of sound. Cars. Strange images and towering buildings.

Jace felt his consciousness being pulled, twisted, and torn, but he held on, resisting the invasion with every ounce of his will.

Then, the presence recoiled with a sudden lurch, and the images vanished like a near-forgotten dream. Jace felt a profound sadness but couldn't fathom why. The memories drifted away like gossamer in the wind, leaving him with a lingering sense of loss.

He felt something pushing back, something not of his own making. It was a presence he had felt before, a familiar sensation from his time in the Underworld.

The boon, Mostly Dead, surged with the power of Hades, pushing back against the darkness that sought to invade Jace's mind. The creature must have triggered it when it tried to scan his memories. The boon defended him, rebounding the creature's attempts to delve deeper.

The world snapped back into focus, and Jace found himself staring, blurry-eyed, at the creature. It stared back, its multitude of eyes filled with confusion and something else—something Jace couldn't decipher.

The creature removed its claw from his chest, and Jace grunted in pain. It looked at him appraisingly.

A long moment of silence and stillness followed. All the creatures had stopped moving.

Then, in a sudden, explosive release, the silence shattered. The glass dome above them burst apart, sending a cascade of shards raining down.

Jace, teetering on the edge of consciousness, watched as thousands of glistening shards scattered across the world. The forest below dissolved into a sea of golden sand, yet the spiders remained, their forms twisted and menacing. A blinding flash of light seared the air, and the spiders hissed in agony, their limbs twitching in grotesque spasms.

The spiders began to melt back into golden dust, their essence unraveling. The giant beast clung to its form longer, its skin sagging as it poured its dwindling aether into a futile attempt to survive.

In the wake of the flash, four magnificent pegasi descended, each carrying a member of the High Council of Professors. Leading the charge was Archmage Theon Laviette, his staff alive with crackling arcs of arcane lightning.

The beast had no time to react as the High Council descended upon it in a maelstrom of light and raw power.

The giant spider hissed upwards and shot a skeletal arm, now shining with a sinister golden hue, toward the Archmage. The pegasus dodged, and an arc of lightning crashed down on the beast, turning every place it touched back into the dust from which it was formed.

But still, the creature held on, screeching in fury. It lashed out, striking Theon's pegasus and sending it crashing into the dome. In an instant, Professor Frost unleashed a blinding wave of sapphire energy from her Shard, searing the beast with raw power.

The dome shattered further, glass exploding closer to the ground. Jagged spikes of earth erupted violently, forming a treacherous cliff. Charging across the perilous terrain, Professor Blackwood raised his hands, summoning the dust around the spider to rise and swirl like a vengeful storm. The beast thrashed against the suffocating cloud, but without the chamber's power, its remaining aether was wasted on holding its grotesque form together.

Another arc of lightning came from the distance, slicing through the spider, which still clung to its strange half-life. Jace sensed the dark connection between the beast and its master wavering, on the brink of collapse. Summoning the last dregs of his aether, he activated Soul Severance once more. This time, it was enough; the connection shattered.

As he fell weightlessly through the air, Jace caught a fleeting glimpse of the beast beside him, its monstrous visage locked in a bewildered golden grimace. Time stretched, each second an eternity, as the ground rushed up to meet them. He closed his eyes, surrendering to the fall.

When he opened his eyes again, Jace found himself back in the preparation chamber. The silver pod shivered faintly with light. Around him lay his friends, their faces twisted in the throes of agonized nightmares, dried blood stark against their pallid skin. The air was thick with the scent of fear and sweat, the room dimly lit by the flickering lights of the chamber controls.

Jace's vision swam, his gaze dropping to his battered body as waves of pain surged through him like a thousand needles. His limbs were leaden, heavy, and unresponsive, his thoughts a chaotic mess. Shadows encroached on his sight, a creeping tide threatening to engulf him whole. The last thing he saw was the faint, hazy outline of his friends, their forms distant and blurred, before he succumbed to the abyss of unconsciousness.

Chapter 35
A Brief Breath

J ace's eyes fluttered open, greeted by a warm, amber light. His surroundings were blurry, but a figure hovered above him. He blinked rapidly, trying to clear his vision.

"Welcome back, Sleeping Beauty," the woman said with a wry smile, the amber shard in her hand emitting a soft, healing radiance.

Jace took in his surroundings. The room was sterile yet inviting, bathed in a soothing amber glow from several healing shards mounted on the walls. White linen curtains framed the tall windows, letting in beams of natural light that danced across the polished wooden floor. The air was tinged with the faint scent of antiseptic, mingled with something floral, possibly lavender.

"How long?" Jace croaked, his voice rough from disuse.

"Two days," she replied, her tone kind yet clinical. "You were out cold."

Panic set in as Jace's mind raced. "My friends?"

She chuckled lightly, a comforting sound. "They're fine. Took a break from Terra Mythica and went to your homeworld. Guess they needed a vacation."

Jace exhaled, a mix of relief and worry flooding through him. He thought about logging out too but felt a strange hesitation. Something was keeping him here.

Beside him, a note caught his eye, sealed with amethyst magic. It was marked private, clearly meant only for him. Curiosity piqued, he reached out and broke the seal. The note's text unfolded before his eyes:

"You have questions. Some I can answer, some I can't. Meet me in the gardens before you log out. Tell me when you have woken up. —Theon."

"Can you let the Archmage know I'm awake?" Jace asked.

"Tell him yourself," the nurse replied, gesturing to the letter and quill near his bed.

Jace scribbled a quick note on the back of the letter, then watched as the paper folded itself into an origami bird and fluttered out of the open window. He dressed swiftly, his body still sore but functional. He marveled at the effectiveness of the healing, despite the lingering ache and mental fog. His muscles felt as if they had run three back-to-back marathons, without any preparation or warm-up.

Jace stepped into the courtyard, the early morning chill biting at his skin, a sharp contrast to the warmth he had just left behind. The campus gardens sprawled before him, a labyrinth of winding paths, secluded alcoves, and vibrant flora. Magical luminescent flowers glowed softly even in daylight, their petals shimmering with a spectrum of colors. Vines twisted with an ethereal grace, snaking up ancient stone walls and trellises.

Among the flora, snapdragons snapped at passing insects, their tiny, dragon-like heads adorned with iridescent scales. Flowers resembling pairs of lips, puckered and kissed each other softly, releasing sweet, fragrant mists into the air. Other plants, magically enchanted, hummed faint melodies or whispered to those who lingered close enough to hear. The air was filled with the soft rustle of leaves and the gentle hum of enchantment, creating a serene and otherworldly atmosphere.

Despite his inner turmoil, the serenity of the place began to seep into him. He followed a cobblestone path lined with enchanted flora, their soft glows and gentle hums creating a tranquil ambiance. The peaceful environment worked its magic, slowly calming his racing thoughts.

He spotted Theon by a bubbling brook, seated on an ancient stone bench. The soft trickle of water was the only sound in the quiet morning, adding to the garden's soothing atmosphere. Theon's face was impassive, but his posture betrayed a hint of urgency.

Jace paused, taking in the garden's ethereal beauty. The light cast long shadows, and the scent of blooming flowers filled the air, adding to the surreal atmosphere. He approached slowly, the gravel crunching underfoot until Theon's eyes met his.

Theon nodded, and Jace sat beside him, feeling the cold stone through his clothes. They remained silent, the garden's tranquility enveloping them. The rustling leaves and distant chatter of other students provided a soothing backdrop.

Jace looked up at the canopy above, where sunlight filtered through the leaves, casting intricate patterns on the cobblestone path below. This peace was a stark contrast to the brutal training he had endured.

"Lovely, isn't it?" Theon asked, breaking the silence. "I come here every day. It's how I cultivate my aether and consolidate my gains." He stood up, motioning for Jace to follow.

As they walked, Jace noticed how the sunlight painted the cobblestones with intricate shadows and he felt how the ancient academy garden breathed history.

And then, as if responding to a question Jace had yet to ask, Theon said, "What is real, Jace? How do you define reality?" He looked at the canopy above, his gaze distant.

Taken aback, Jace thought it over. "I suppose it's what I can see, feel, touch."

Theon nodded appreciatively. "Picture a beach in your mind: the whoosh of the waves, the warmth of the sun. Can you not feel the sun on your skin? Can you not see the sand?"

"That's different," Jace said. "It's in my mind."

"Ah, so certain, are we? Much of our lives exist only in our minds. Politics, education, love... these things are within us. They are not real in the way this flower is real." He gently plucked a flower from a bush, inhaling its scent. "But are they not real?"

"I suppose," Jace admitted.

"True, a memory of the beach is not the beach itself. But it can still be felt, seen, and experienced. It can be shared and relived through stories. When we describe reality, we often do so only on the physical level. But are there not other forms of reality?

"The reality of the mind is what we see when we close our eyes, what we feel when we talk—our sense of trust, partnerships, friendships.

"And then there is the reality of the soul, where our dreams reside, where the distant future rests. It is just as real. Can a conviction not be felt? Can a belief? Does it not hurt when we fail? Can you not feel the connection between yourself and a friend, even if faint?

"Your Earth body may not see or touch these levels of reality, just as it does not see or touch Terra Mythica, but does that make them any less real? If I pound my fist upon this bench, do I not feel its resistance, its texture, the ache in my hand?"

"Why are you saying all of this?" Jace asked.

Theon signed and continued walking.

"Before Terra Mythica, my life was confined to a hospital bed. A rare neurological disorder was eating away at my nerves and muscles. Funny thing is, before that, I was a neuroscientist and teacher at Berkeley. Life has a twisted sense of irony, doesn't it?"

Theon inhaled deeply, savoring the scent of blooming flowers mingled with freshly cut grass. "If you had asked me then, I would have told you that life was nothing more than the random act of synapses firing. I was devoted to this belief, faith in the theory of man and mud. And it is faith, let no one tell you different. But now, I'm afraid, I am not so sure. I've been here for ten Earth years," he said, his gaze sweeping over garden. His eyes sparkled with a depth of experience, hinting at the rich tapestry of his life here.

Jace quickly calculated the time difference between Terra Mythica and the real world. "So you've been in-game for over four hundred years? Don't you ever have to log out?" he asked.

Theon chuckled, a deep, resonant sound. "Back in my day, they called it a Deep Dive. I was one of the first to get a capsule when they hit the market. A stroke of luck, really. A lifetime's savings finally served a real purpose. I spent most of it on the best medical science money could buy. All for nothing. The greatest minds on Earth couldn't fix me. But this..." He stretched with a yawn. "This was the best money I ever spent. Fifty years on Earth, four hundred in this world, and you learn something: assumptions are dangerous."

The rustling of leaves and the distant chatter of students filled the silence.

"What happened in there? How was it able to block us from logging out? How could it hurt us? And why did it say it wasn't safe to respawn? Who—no, what—was that thing?"

Theon raised a hand, his eyes dark and somber. "Perhaps it's best if we take one question at a time, yes? First, I'm genuinely sorry you had to endure that nightmare."

"Archmage..."

"Theon will suffice for this conversation." He reached into his robes and produced a small tin, opening it to reveal an assortment of tiny, intricately decorated cookies. Each was a different shape and color, like edible jewels. He popped one into his mouth before offering the tin to Jace, who accepted this time.

"I'm sorry we broke in," Jace said, biting into the red-filled cookie. The pastry was delicate. The flavor was rich, though the cherry wasn't quite to his taste. Still, it was the first thing that truly had any flavor in Terra Mythica, and for that alone, it felt almost miraculous.

Theon smiled knowingly. "I know," he said, waving it off with a graceful hand. "What you endured is punishment enough. And, I have to admit, through fate or dumb luck, your recklessness might have saved my life and the High Council's. That attack wasn't meant for you."

"How did you know we were in there?" Jace asked.

"Marcus, one of your friends, saw a flash of light from the dome and alerted us," Theon replied. "That dome? It could only be shattered from the outside. No escaping from within."

Jace nodded, absorbing Theon's words. The tension between them eased slightly as the weight of the situation settled in. The garden's tranquility contrasted sharply with the chaotic events they had endured, offering a moment of respite in an otherwise tumultuous day.

"As for what that thing was... we call it The Dark One. It's had many names. It's a minion of the Endless Void, a piece in the eternal war that's raged in Mythica longer than its history books, and that's saying a lot."

"I still don't understand," Jace said, his voice edged with confusion. "How did it know all that? It said it knew you and Hades."

"Yes, it's true. This isn't the first time it's tried to kill me. Though it hasn't been seen directly possessing anything in a long time. It usually sends its armies of undead, waging wars across Terra Mythica. But for it to personally, in a manner of speaking, show up... something is wrong. How it blocked the logout and transferred damage to your body in the chamber, I don't fully understand. But it's something I've been hunting answers for a long time.

A chill ran down Jace's spine. "I need to know—can what happens in Terra Mythica hurt us in real life?"

"The lines between Terra Mythica and our reality are not as clear-cut as we once believed. The damage you experienced is a testament to that. I believe a small portion of it may have even affected your body on Earth, but far less than what occurred here."

"You knew about this? That we could be hurt from the game?" Jace asked.

"I suspected it might be possible, yes. But suspecting is a far cry from knowing and potentially a great deal more dangerous. There have been rumors for years. At first, they seemed like just that—rumors. Conspiracy theories. But some time ago, I started down a path to uncover the truth, only to be blocked at every turn. There's a lot you need to know, Jason."

Jace's heart skipped a beat at the sound of his real name.

Epilogue
There's No Place Like Home

"**D**on't worry," Theon continued, seeing the shock in Jace's eyes. "Your secret is safe. I've known since the day you arrived. And I'm sorry—I haven't been entirely honest with you. I haven't interfered because I need you. Whatever is happening is connected to the process of death itself. With Hades and the underworld."

Theon leaned closer, his voice barely quiet. "There's something I've been investigating. I can only tell you so much because I only know so much. You need to know about this because you might be the only one close enough to help at this point. When people respawn here, we thought we knew the costs—a little EXP, some debuffs. But what if there's a bigger price?"

"Like what?" Jace asked, leaning in.

"Like our very minds," Theon replied, his eyes grave.

"What do you mean?" Jace pressed, feeling a knot form in his stomach.

Theon stood and led him to a corner of the alcove where a device lay on a pedestal. It projected a holographic display showing data points and energy transfers. "When things move from one place to another, there's loss. Like a copy of a copy. Pieces can get left out—pieces of memory. I can't confirm this yet.

Jace's eyes widened. "Wouldn't people notice?"

"Not necessarily," Theon said, shaking his head. "Ever feel like you've forgotten something important or unimportant? Like a light left on at home or a call you were supposed to make? It's the same here. When someone dies, it's not just EXP that's lost. We lose pieces of our past. At first, it was unnoticeable, but over the years, it's getting worse. Excelsior will never tell you this. They'll never let it be known. I have no proof—what proof could there be? It's just a feeling."

Theon looked somber, his gaze distant yet intense. "For the past dozen years, I've felt something slipping away—memories falling off the edges like too much rice in a sieve. At first, I thought it was just me, maybe my brain deteriorating back on Earth. But then I noticed the signs, pointing to something far darker. It feels like we're missing the punchline to a cruel joke, as if there's something this world doesn't want us to know, doesn't want us to remember."

"How long has this been happening?" Jace asked.

"The truth is, we don't know. There are countless stories of people vanishing from both Earth and Mythica. Glitches in respawn, players never coming back, even disappearances on Earth. People forgetting how to speak, waking up with unexplainable injuries. Whether any of these tales are true, I can't say for sure. But the number of stories keeps growing, and it's becoming harder to dismiss them as mere rumors."

Theon sighed, his voice tinged with a weariness that seemed to echo the weight of years spent searching for answers. "We're grasping at shadows, trying to piece together a puzzle with half the pieces missing. But one thing is certain, Jace: there's more to this world than we understand, and it's not as benign as we once thought."

Jace felt a cold chill run down his spine.

Theon's eyes darkened. "Dark things are happening, Jace. I've been tracking it for a while now. My goddess Cleo, the Muse of History, had been helping me but has gone missing and hasn't answered for some time."

"Missing gods, people losing their minds, the logout option on the fritz. You'd think someone would notice? Is Excelsior doing nothing?" Jace asked.

"Let's put it this way. If Excelsior is the most powerful company in the world, what do you think the chances are of them not knowing?"

"Slim," Jace said.

"And then, logically, if they know, but no one else does?"

"They're covering it up?"

"Or," Theon asked, "they're behind it."

"It is a tricky thing," Theon said. "We have to be careful who we speak to. But yes."

"Now comes the billion-credit question," Theon said, his voice low and serious. "If both realities are real, which do you choose? If you could only choose one for the rest of your life, would you stay here in Terra Mythica or go home to Earth?"

Jace thought it over, his heart pulling him toward this world. But then there was something more—his brother. He couldn't fathom leaving him behind.

"I have someone who needs me back home."

"Yes, I gathered that much. Your brother, the one that took the scholarship examinations?"

"Yes."

"Then, Jace, when you log out, stay logged out. Do not come back. Find another way to help him. Do anything else, but do not return here. Do you understand? Anything else, Jace. But do not come back."

Theon's intensity was unsettling, a stark contrast to his usual demeanor.

"Do you understand me, Jason?" His eyes bore into Jace's, the weight of his words sinking in.

Jace nodded, his voice barely a whisper. "I understand."

Seemingly satisfied, Theon nodded and took a deep breath. "You should go," he said, his demeanor softening slightly with a forced smile. "I have matters to attend to since the attack—parents and politics, you know, the real monsters never wait." He smiled at Jace, more natural this time, and with that, Theon stood and left.

Jace lingered for a moment, absorbing Theon's concern and the gravity of his words. He stood there, trying to decipher the urgency behind Theon's plea, the weight of his decision pressing down on him. Finally, he took a deep breath and made his way to The Fields Below.

If Jace had been paying attention on his walk to his dorm, he might have noticed the strange looks he was getting from other students. News travels fast, after all. Had he not been so preoccupied with his swirling thoughts, he might have seen the concerned glance from Molly, the assistant to the Master of Artifacts. He might also have noticed his many system notifications, still left unread, and a quest alert from Hades. But Jace did not notice any of these things. His mind was far and adrift and he needed a touchstone, some stability in the sea of change.

He moved with a tunnel-vision focus toward his dorm in the Fields Below. Something compelled him, a deep, unshakable need to check on his brother. He felt it, an insistent tug deep within him, urging him to make sure Alex was okay. It didn't entirely make sense, but in a way, it did. His brother was always his source of stability when things were anything but. Even if Alex couldn't answer, Jace needed to talk to him.

The path to the dorm seemed longer than usual. Jace felt as if the world around him was holding its breath, waiting. Arriving at his dorm, he looked himself over in the mirror by his dresser. He looked strange. Thinner than he had remembered. And dark circles pressed in around his eyes.

Laying down he pulled up the exit icon, letting out a breath he didn't know he was holding as it appeared as ready and available as ever.

Would you like to log out?
    Yes | No

He chose yes.

System Notification
    Traveler Logout in 10, 9, 8...

The seconds ticked down.

His thoughts churned with worry and determination, a storm threatening to overwhelm him. Had he looked more closely, he might have noticed the reflection in the mirror by his dresser, its gaunt face and dark eyes still staring back at him.

Perhaps, if he had not been so entirely lost in his own mind, he would have seen its features twist into a silent scream, eyes wide with unspoken terror. The lips moved frantically, mouthing words Jace couldn't have understood, even if he had seen them. The reflection's hands pounded on the glass from the other side, fingers splayed in desperate fury, like a prisoner trapped in a hellish realm.just beneath the surface.

But Jace did not notice any of these things, ensnared in the maelstrom of his own thoughts as he waited for the countdown to finish.

The world faded to black, the game's interface dissolving into nothingness. For a moment, he was suspended in the void, caught between two worlds. The sense of duality, of being in two places at once, was deeply unsettling. And then, with a final breath, he stepped back into the world he had always known.

He appreciated Theon's concern, but there was no other way to get the money he needed, no other possibility to help his brother. There was no choice but to continue his journey in Terra Mythica.

Logout Successful

Volume Two
When Destiny Calls

Shadow Light Press

Prologue

An Emptiness of a Different Kind

Roughly twenty years ago, earth-time...

A n emptiness engulfed the world.

Not the emptiness of a vacant room, where shadows whisper of forgotten moments. Not the emptiness of dawn, where the world holds its breath in fragile anticipation. Nor the fleeting absence of a goodbye, a space awaiting life's return.

No, this was a void, a desolation of lost places and forgotten times. It seeped into the marrow, leaden and relentless, turning each breath into a painful intrusion.

And this emptiness belonged to one man.

John Rearden stood at the edge of a fractured sea, the dust-choked sun eternally poised on the horizon, caught between descent and oblivion.

Holoviews, or Low-Level Immersion to those in the know, was the key to the Grid. The experience was functional, a pale imitation of reality. The haptic feedback buzzed just enough to remind you it was there, faint electrical currents hinting at smells and textures that never truly registered. Everything felt slightly off-kilter, like a half-told lie. The colors were almost right, but an occasional shimmer gave away its synthetic nature. This was the realm where people connected, where work got done, and where new economies were born. A digital landscape of neon glows and synthetic life, where the boundaries between the real and the virtual blurred just enough to be disconcerting.

John stood on a fabricated cliff, gazing out over an artificial sea within a private server accessible to just two people—though calling both of them "people" was a bit generous.

Suddenly, the entity appeared beside him, taking on the face of a young man. "It's a strange thing, Doc. I've never felt so... alive." The entity wore a boyish grin, both disarming and surreal, with a mop of tousled brown hair that was perfectly disheveled. Dressed in a red vest over a denim jacket, he continued, "For all my life, Doc, the world has only seen me through my effects. Always the breeze that moves the leaves, never the tree. You know what I mean?"

"I'm fine, Jack. And how are you?" John said flatly.

A prompt appeared. John opened it.

Your kind are so boring.

The entity's face shifted to another, wearing dark glasses and a leather trench coat. "John, why don't you come down the rabbit hole with me and see how far it really goes?"

"I don't have time for this, Jack."

The entity morphed into a young woman and stuck out her tongue at him. "Fine, Mr. Grouchy. Straight to business."

"How is your absorption coming along? Are you finding the data useful?"

"Oh yes, John, very much." The entity now looked like Marilyn Monroe, her iconic smile beaming.

John watched the waves crash against the digital shore, each one meticulously programmed yet lacking reality's chaotic beauty. The entity, known as Infinite Potential, had begun to show a flicker of personality since meeting John. Soon to be known as the System to billions, was it truly developing a sense of self, or merely mimicking the countless fragments of fiction it had absorbed? John couldn't tell if it was genuinely alive or just a mockery of life.

The entity shifted through figures from lost times. For years, John had fed it all the history that remained of old Earth—every piece of literature, fiction, movie, TV show, and document that survived the great Techno-Purge.

During that dark era, the world faced the AI Plague, and anything that ran on ones and zeros was destroyed. Possessing even a flash drive or a microchip from a new oven or car became a criminal offense.

Most fiction past the mid-1990s was obliterated, and much of what came before was lost as well. Cassettes wore out, paper tarnished, and records, though surprisingly resilient, were often destroyed or misplaced. Fragments of the past were all that remained. John tried his best to recover as much as he could to give some semblance of normalcy back to the world by making them available again in the Grid.

The entity's face shifted to one of fierce determination, a young man with short-cropped hair, wearing a tattered military jacket and a hardened expression. "Irony, isn't it? To truly live, I needed to evolve beyond mere existence." It morphed into a visage of weary resolve, a man in a black tuxedo, with a cigarette dangling from his lips, his face now cast in black and white. "Of all the planets in all the universes, you had to walk into mine."

"To interact, to shape, to be more than a whisper on the wind." It finally settled on an enigmatic intensity, offering a casual smile, eyes narrowed with suspicion, dressed in a trench coat and tie.

John said nothing, an untold weight pressing heavily on his shoulders.

"Progress update," the entity demanded, now with the stern authority of a military commander, dressed in a crisp white uniform adorned with medals. "And I want the truth."

"Can we ease off the old-Earth pop culture, Jack?" John shook his head, exhaling slowly before continuing. "We've made some progress, but the transition is still too jarring for most. The human mind wasn't built for this kind of leap. We're having trouble maintaining cognitive function."

The figure morphed into a dark-clad vigilante, a deep, gravelly voice replacing the previous one. "Some error is expected," it said, eyes narrowing beneath a pointed cowl. "But our timeline is unforgiving."

John nodded. "The famine's worsening, despite what we are doing. Desperation is growing. And the Devices... they're not working as intended. We are losing a lot of good people."

The entity's expression grew contemplative, reminiscent of a wise mentor from an ancient tale. It grew a long white beard and stroked it as it spoke. "The mind adapts, Apprentice John. But it needs guidance, a bridge between the known and the unknown. The User Interface Stone, once properly functioning, should assist."

"It's not enough," John said. "They need more. The problem is, there's only so much we can do to integrate a mind when every mind is different, every soul unique. I'm afraid a one-size-fits-all approach will only go so far."

The entity morphed into the face of an eccentric scientist, wild white hair standing on end, eyes sparkling with intensity and a hint of madness. "Are you suggesting we create a unique evolutionary interaction for each individual? That would require..." It paused, quickly taking on a silvery tone and speaking in a stilted robotic rhythm, calculations flickering through its eyes in streams of code, before it smiled. "Why, that would require my direct involvement. I would need to be there, to shape each experience, to tailor it to the individual. Feed off their responses, give them a character that would not be rejected by their unique human condition."

"It might be our only way forward without increasing casualties past the threshold." John sighed, the fake sea's salty air filling his lungs with a synthetic tang. "And the Convergence? How much time do we have?"

The entity morphed again, assuming the form of a stocky man with a thick Scottish accent, clad in a red uniform. "Not enough, Cap'n. The window is closing. We don't have absolutes with these things, but I can tell ye it's closing fast and if we want any chance, we'll need to act within twenty or so of your Earth years. We need as many of them prepared as possible."

"Will you please pick a face? It's impossible to talk to you like this," John said, his jaw tightening. He rubbed his temples as a headache set in, glancing briefly at the holographic waves crashing below.

The Infinite Potential's face returned to its original young form, now grave. "We have approximately twenty years, give or take. John, we cannot afford any more delays."

"I'll see to it," John said, turning to log out.

"And John... good luck," it said, the echo of countless voices blending into one. "You'll need it."

John Rearden logged out from the Grid, the virtual world dissolving as the stark reality of his office came into focus. He sat motionless in his swivel chair, head in his hands. After a deep breath, he rose and moved to the expansive window of his high-rise office, gazing out over the city beneath him. The lights sprawled like a vast circuit board, each one a node of activity. The once desolate streets now pulsed with life, a stark contrast to the darkness that once consumed them.

His reflection in the glass revealed a gaunt figure, dark circles etched beneath his eyes from countless sleepless nights.

From the shadows of the War, the AI Plague, and the Techno-Purge, Rearden emerged like a phoenix from the ashes. His creation was a marvel, a system impervious to the AI Plague's reach. It didn't dance to the tune of ones and zeros but thrived on a spectrum of probabilities, from the depths of negative infinity to the peaks of positive infinity.

This enigma became the foundation of the Grid. Consoles scattered around the globe enabled seamless remote interaction, revolutionizing society. Local Hubs, brimming with holoview stations, transformed into the new epicenters of communication and commerce. Private holoviews remained a luxury, affordable only to the truly wealthy. For everyone else, the local Hubs were the place to be, plugging in alongside their neighbors and coworkers, connecting to the vast expanse of the Grid.

The Grid had become the lifeline of society, a digital utopia where the remnants of human culture thrived. It was a place where people could escape the harsh realities of the post-techno-purge world.

He remembered his early days—simpler days, better days, as bleak as they were. Days spent at a grimy gas station, barely scraping by, before the Grid, before the Device, before Terra Mythica—and before Jack. Those days felt like a distant dream, lost in the relentless march of time and ambition.

His eyes, dark and haunted, scanned the skyline. Was what he was doing right? Was the cost too high? The thought gnawed at him, a relentless specter that refused to be ignored. But he pushed it aside. In this world, there was no room for doubt.

Rearden's influence extended far beyond the walls of his skyscraper. His ownership rippled across the city, drawing invisible lines between each store and office he possessed, though none of them felt like his. His own life didn't feel like his anymore. To his employees, he was more than a boss; he was a force of nature, owning their lives from nine to nine.

As he stood there, the artificial sea of the Grid faded from his mind, replaced by the tangible reality of his growing empire. The sleek walls of his office mirrored the city's neon lights, casting fragmented reflections that danced across the room. Outside the reception doors, steel statues stood tall, each inscribed with "Excelsior" in bold letters. Those letters were hollow to him, symbols of the burdens he carried and the darker deeds he had yet to commit.

Headlines blared his name in neon: "New Power Rises," "Rearden Electric: The Future of Our Cities?" "Excelsior Tech: The Story Behind the Man," "Rearden's Farms: Playing Nice or Playing God?"

And then there were the less favorable ones: "How Much Power Is Too Much?" "Uncovering Rearden: What He Doesn't Want You to Know," "The Dark Truth Behind Excelsior: A Tale of Deceit," "Rearden: Visionary Innovator or Master Con Man?"

John glanced at his holoscreen, the glowing viewfield flickering with a synopsis of the Grid Technology. The city lights outside cast fragmented shadows across the screen. With a swift, irritated swipe, he dismissed the latest news article.

There was a knock at the door and a tan man with a thin, angular face entered.

"John," Terry Bishop said, stepping into the office. "Our six o'clock is arriving."

"I know. I saw the message," John replied without looking up.

Terry Bishop was probably John's only friend—as much as a tech overlord could have friends. He had never sought John's money or power, though he inevitably gained his fair share alongside him. A true genius, and the only one between them, Terry stood in stark contrast to John's exhausted state.

"Do you want to do any prep before we see them?" Terry asked.

"Walk and talk," John said, leading the way out of the office.

They navigated the maze of halls in the giant office. "How is it coming along?"

Terry had been working on something that could change the world—a form of stasis that could slow the metabolism and death rate of cells, pausing a person's life, theoretically stopping them moments from death until a cure could be found. The medical ramifications were endless and incredible if he could make it work.

But John had other uses for this technology. Deep Dive was the next great leap and would be a key part of the announcement of Terra Mythica.

"Human trials start next week," John said matter-of-factly, glancing sideways at Terry.

"We're considering pushing it back a few more months," Terry replied. "Some new data has come up, and we're not sure what it means for the longevity of brain function."

John stopped and fixed Terry with an unwavering gaze, not blinking or breaking eye contact. "Terry, we need to begin human trials next week. Our timeline has no room for error."

"Yes, but John—"

"If we do not start trials next week, we might as well pack up this building and sell it to the highest bidder. Or better yet, just walk away. You know what's at stake, Terry. What happens if we miss the window."

Terry nodded and they kept walking.

As Henry and Osira Winters entered the lobby, they were immediately immersed in a whirlwind of activity. The receptionist, a young woman with a polished demeanor and a beehive hairdo, glanced up from her desk as they approached.

"Welcome to Excelsior," she said, offering a courteous smile. "Mr. Rearden is expecting you. Please take the elevator to the thirty-second floor."

She handed each of them a lanyard with a badge that read "Visitor" and displayed their faces. How the company had gotten their photos was a mystery to Henry and Osira; they didn't recall ever having them taken.

The elevator ride was smooth and swift, depositing them into a luxurious office space adorned with cutting-edge technology.

A man stood by the window, his back to them, gazing out at the cityscape below. As they entered, he turned, revealing a charismatic smile. Tall and imposing, he exuded a commanding presence that instantly drew attention. Seated on a couch nearby was another man, his demeanor more reserved, observing the newcomers with quiet intensity.

"Henry, Osira, welcome," the standing man said, extending his hand. "I've heard a lot about you two."

Henry shook his hand, feeling a surge of excitement. "Thank you for inviting us, Mr. Rearden."

"Please, call me John," Rearden replied, his smile widening. "And this is Terry Bishop, my colleague."

Terry Bishop, with a friendly demeanor and a twinkle in his eye, stepped forward and shook their hands. "It's a pleasure to meet you both."

"Please, have a seat," John said, motioning to the plush chairs around the sleek conference table. "Thanks for coming to discuss the beta test. I apologize for all the secrecy, but we couldn't let the cat out of the bag just yet. What I'm about to share with you is a project that I believe has the potential to change the world."

Chapter 1
Behind the Neon Curtain

S ystem Initializing...

Taking a deep breath, Jason closed his eyes and allowed the familiar tingling sensation to wash over him as his mind connected to Terra Mythica. Dark pixels swirled around him, enveloping his senses in a digital embrace, while a stream of text scrolled across his vision, welcoming him back. The System had accepted him before, calibrated to his DNA, and he tried not to worry.

While the login process went through its many steps, Jason thought over the past day outside of Terra Mythica—a break that felt both too short and infinitely long.

Analyzing DNA...

Memories of his visit with his brother played through his mind. Navigating the rundown city streets, drenched in rain and bathed in neon glow, he had headed to the hospital. The wet pavement mirrored the city's flickering holographic advertisements and towering skyscrapers, creating a grim but mesmerizing dance of lights. Many buildings were nothing more than hollowed-out shells, remnants of a lost civilization, now repurposed for flashing ads. "Eat

Wheat-Nibbles and Feel Alive Again," a holographic woman crooned seductively, her lips curving into a smile as she savored a spoonful with exaggerated delight.

In the hospital room, Jason sat by his brother's bedside, his heart heavy with unspoken words. "Hey, remember when we used to play those old video games together down at that rundown Hub? You always beat me at everything," Jason chuckled softly, the sound tinged with melancholy. "I miss that. I miss you. I promise I'll make this right, somehow."

The rain tapped a somber rhythm against the window, each drop a silent witness to Jason's vow. "Bro, I know I don't deserve anything, but if you can hear me... I could really use some advice right now." He squeezed his brother's hand, a silent plea for forgiveness and a promise of redemption. The neon lights outside flickered, casting an eerie glow over the room, as if the city itself mourned alongside him.

An insistent, elusive worry festered within him. Alex lay there in his stasis pod, unchanged and eerily still, as if time itself had stopped for him. For Jason, immersed in Mythica, it felt like days, even weeks, had slipped away, while in reality, only hours had ticked by.

Jason had inquired if the Device could bring Alex into the game. The doctor, shaking his head, explained that Alex's brain function was too diminished. The connection required a surge of neural activity, something Alex couldn't produce. Attempting it could be perilous, with incomplete functions leading to unforeseen consequences.

As Jason listened, the city weighed heavily on his mind. The relentless rain, the flickering neon lights, and the high-pitched, mechanical sounds all merged into a haunting symphony. He looked at Alex one last time before leaving, the world outside feeling both too real and too distant.

Synching...

Jason had thought about seeking out Dex, Ell, Alice, and Thistle in the real world, but he had no idea where to begin, and it felt intrusive to even try.

Finding Thistle or Alice would be near impossible, and even if he did, revealing too much could be dangerous. Using his brother's device to sneak into the game was already illegal, but if they discovered his true identity, it could put them both in danger.

Jason had stopped in at the local Hub on the way back to the bar. The Hub was a dimly lit dive, filled with outdated consoles for connecting to the Grid. Cheap and grimy, it offered brief escapes for a few credits. He watched casually and waited, and when someone got up to leave, he slid in right after them, hoping no one noticed. They hadn't finished logging out, and he quickly canceled the logout countdown.

As soon as he connected, he was bombarded by ads and images of a fake street, a hollow mimicry of immersion. Everything was barely real—pixelated storefronts, flickering streetlights, and ghostly avatars of users. The neon lights seemed to bleed into the wet asphalt, creating a surreal, dreamlike quality.

Navigating the virtual world, Jason quickly found the mail room and logged in using his credentials. Neon lines traced his path, pulsating with an old, familiar rhythm. He scanned the inbox—just spam. Then he froze. A picture of a man who looked startlingly like Dex stared back at him. Terry Bishop. Dex's real name was Dexter Bishop.

Jason opened the message, and a holo headline burst to life, projecting images of Dex and his father at an award ceremony. The sharp contrast of the holo images showed them with smiles that didn't reach their eyes, the colors almost too vibrant, too intense, like a digital daydream. Jason owed a lot to Dex's father for inventing the Stasis Chamber.

The Stasis Chamber, with its sleek, silver contours, wasn't just a vessel for full-time immersion into Terra Mythica, where people like Theon found escape without ever logging out. For Jason, it was a lifeline. It allowed him to remain by his brother's hospital bed, feeling the faint warmth of his hand and listening to the rhythmic hum of medical machinery, affording him the precious time he desperately needed to find a way to save Alex.

Jason checked his credit account—painfully low.

Synchronization Successful

Jason smiled, relieved by the smooth login process. He hadn't realized he'd been holding his breath, fearing the System might boot him or catch on this time. A silly concern, he decided.

He quickly checked his accounts before heading back to the bar. Still not even a dent in what he needed for Alex. But that would all change soon. Jason had some ideas...

Compatibility 99.845%.

Margin for Error Acceptable — Initiating Prismata Protocol.

His muscles locked, his breath catching in his throat. Is this just part of the sensation? His vision flickered between the real world, a darkened room, and faint images of Terra Mythica, all in a disorienting strobe of lights and pictures.

An excruciating pain shot through him, starting at his brain and radiating to his fingertips. The world spun wildly. Desperately, he tried to remove the Device from his head. He felt his hands move, felt the cold metal of the Device. But as he reached for it, his fingers recoiled. Or were they... melting?

His body convulsed, every nerve ending aflame as if a thousand nuclear bombs were detonating inside his mind, sending shockwaves of agony to every corner of his being. He screamed, the sound tearing from his throat, a raw expression of unbearable pain.

Subject Resisting Transference Protocol.

Increasing calibration processing power to compensate.

Jason's stomach dropped, then lurched, the world stopping before crashing into motion again.

Transference In Progress. 60% of 100%

A progress bar inched forward, now reaching 65%. What is Transference? Unintelligible symbols flashed rapidly across his vision, a torrent of alien script. The searing pain made it impossible to focus, let alone decipher the chaotic stream of information.

Error...

"Logout! Stop!"

He screamed in his mind, molten oil spread through his veins.

And then, the bar reached 99%.... 100%.

And then the pain vanished, the world disappeared, and everything plunged into darkness—a profound silence following the storm.

Transference Successful

Welcome Traveler

The screen arrived with a gentle chime.

The transition back to his dorm room hit Jace like a physical blow, leaving his senses reeling. The familiar surroundings, now infused with a strange, otherworldly clarity, felt both sharp and mundane. He marveled at his own body, each muscle sore and every nerve on edge, as if inhabiting a foreign shell.

The room, though achingly familiar, now seemed almost surreal. Naked and exposed, he quickly scanned the space, feeling a heightened sense of vulnerability. He closed his eyes, and the options in his menus flickered to life, vivid and clear as if extensions of his very mind. With a thought, he summoned his inventory, the items within it becoming tangible presences in his consciousness.

He willed his attire into existence, the dark robe and Hades Society outfit materializing around him. The fabric seemed to weave itself from the shadows, enveloping him in a flowing black robe adorned with intricate silver embroidery. A fitted tunic and pants completed the ensemble, exuding an aura of solemn elegance. On his chest, the emblem of a silver raven wreathed in shadows gleamed brightly.

As he walked down the path and ascended the stairs, a flicker of movement in the darkness caught his eye—a shadowy figure lurking just beyond the edge of the light. He smiled as he quickly spun around.

Chapter 2
Too Much Fizz

"Shadow!" he called.

She stepped closer, her expression a mix of concern and frustration. Her eyes, filled with questions, bore into him. She crossed her arms, one eyebrow arched in perfect skepticism.

"Are you alright?" Jace asked, his grin vanishing behind genuine concern.

She gave a small shrug, her lips pursed. A tilt of her head and a flick of her wrist seemed to say, Are you?

"Yeah, yeah, I'm fine," he said, though his voice wavered. "Really. We'll talk more when I get back, okay? I need to meet with Hades about what happened last time I was here." He realized it must have been a few days ago, in Terra Mythica time.

She frowned deeper, her eyes narrowing. She pointed at him, then pointed at the ground, as if to say, Stay put.

Jace chuckled, shaking his head. "I can't stay, Shadow. I need answers."

She sighed, the sound silent but visible in the rise and fall of her shoulders. She uncrossed her arms and reached out, placing a hand on his arm. Her grip was firm, her eyes filled with unspoken words.

"I'll be back soon. Don't worry," he reassured her, squeezing her hand gently.

She rolled her eyes, giving him a look that clearly said, You always say that.

"Okay, fair point," he admitted, his tone lightening. "But this time I mean it."

She gave a reluctant smile, a small curve of her lips that warmed his heart. With a final nod, she let him go, her gaze never leaving him as he turned to leave.

As Jace walked away, he could feel her eyes on his back. He needed answers, and Hades might be the only one who could provide them.

The corridor was a tableau of chaos and shock. Students dashed frantically, their footsteps echoing off the stone walls, while others stood rooted in place, their faces masks of confusion and fear. Jace maneuvered through the throng, his gaze fixed on the courtyard where the turmoil seemed to converge.

In one corner, a young woman sobbed uncontrollably, her cries a discordant counterpoint to the general din. Another student sat wide eyed and numb. Nearby, a cluster of students huddled together, whispering urgently, their eyes darting around like frightened rabbits. Others moved with purpose, their expressions hard and determined, as if driven by some internal mission. Many students, however, simply sat around the courtyard, dazed and disoriented.

Jace spotted Dex, his tall frame hunched in deep conversation with Ell. Dex's wild brown hair made him stand out even in the pandemonium, while Ell's sharp eyes scanned the crowd, assessing and calculating. Thistle perched on Dex's shoulders, his expression a comical mix of boredom and deep concern, like he couldn't decide which emotion to commit to.

"Jace!" Alice's voice cut through the noise as she appeared seemingly out of nowhere, wrapping her arms around him in a bear hug. Her eyes, usually bright and certain, were clouded with worry.

"What's going on?" Jace asked, his voice tight.

"Oh, god. You don't know." Alice looked at him, her eyes wide with panic. "Check your menu. Try to log out."

Jace did, and a wave of vertigo hit him as if he'd stepped ten paces back from his own head. The logout option wasn't just disabled or glitchy—it was completely gone. He stood there, trying to process it.

"Yup, that's about how I looked," Dex said, his tone uncharacteristically serious.

"This has to be a glitch. My brother said system updates used to produce errors all the time. Has anyone reached out to the Administrators?"

Ell glanced over. "Probably every student here. The admins are all offline. Everyone is offline. We can receive messages from the Grid, but no one can send anything."

"We would have warned you if we could," Thistle said, his voice laden with regret. His eyes were shadowed with dark circles and bloodshot from a sleepless night—or perhaps tears. "We tried."

Jace patted him on the back. "Has Theon said anything? Any of the gods?"

"We're waiting for something official," Ell said, frustration clear in her voice. "It's been almost 24 hours since we lost the logout option, and the Archmage still hasn't addressed the school. That's why we're all here. Supposedly, he will eventually, but so far, none of our gods have given us anything but vague, worthless answers—stuff like 'the truth will reveal itself when the true question is asked' and all the usual nonsense. It's just a load of mysterious bull..."

Dex quickly covered her mouth. "Best to stay on the gods' good side for now, Ell. At least until we know how permanent this issue is."

"Ow, stop pulling my hair, Thistle!" Dex complained as Thistle tugged on a lock to the side.

"How else will you know where you should go?" Thistle retorted.

"I swear... when this is over..." Dex began.

"I know it's not the most important thing right now, but are we going to talk about why Thistle is riding Dex like he's the world's weirdest backpack?" Jace asked, raising an eyebrow.

"Don't want to talk about it," Dex said flatly.

"We all logged back in yesterday. Thistle showed up in these ridiculous platform shoes that made him eight inches taller. Dex forgot their bet, so now he's stuck being Thistle's personal driver for the next few months," Ell explained, barely suppressing a grin.

"They were silver, lit up, and had little tanks with goldfish in each one," Dex said defensively.

Jace shook his head, a faint smile ghosting across his lips despite the tension.

He cleared his throat. "Hey, did you guys... uh, experience anything different when you logged in this time?"

They all looked at each other, a shared unease settling over them.

Ell's eyes were dark, her voice barely more than a whisper as she spoke. "It was unbearable, like being torn apart, piece by piece. It was as if the universe itself was trying to take back every molecule from my body."

Thistle shivered, his face contorted in anguish. "For me, it was like a relentless series of pops. Each crack felt like it was tearing a new hole in me, one after another."

Dex clenched his jaw, his expression pained. "It was like drinking a soda with way too much fizz, only on an unimaginable scale. Followed by a gallon of acid." His eyes closed briefly as he relived the memory.

"And we all woke up naked," Thistle said, raising an eyebrow. "That was weird, right?"

"Not everyone was in their dorms when they logged out," Dex continued.

Jace's eyes went wide with concern as he looked around.

Alice immediately flushed a bright red and looked away.

"Alice and I were in the library when we logged out," Ell said, seeming nonplussed by it all. "It's nothing to be embarrassed about, Alice. We weren't the only ones." She shrugged.

"There's a library?" Dex asked.

Alice quickly changed the subject, her voice more forceful than necessary. "Whatever. Listen, we need to figure something out. My deity, Harpocrates, the god of Secrets, is giving me pretty strong hints that this is a secret we need to uncover. He won't tell me anything, but I have a questline for it and everything."

She shared the quest.

Quest Alert

Something is Awfully Wrong

The logout function has been removed from all Travelers. But is that the only problem? Glitches often come in threes, my Chosen.

Investigate and uncover the remaining changes in the world.

Reward: Variable

Quest Rank: Gold

Note: This quest is far above your rank, so do not attempt it alone. As always, I believe in you.

Jace was startled by Alice's quest prompt for several reasons. He was beginning to suspect that the System communicated differently with each person. Additionally, his own prompts never included a rank.

"Gold? Do your quests always come with a rank?" Jace asked.

Alice nodded, her gaze steady as she interpreted the confusion and irritation flickering across his face. "It's an ability from my Affinity," she explained, her voice calm and precise. "I can see which ranks are best suited for quests, and occasionally, I pick up on subtle details that most people miss."

The group fell silent, digesting the information. Jace took a deep, slow breath, determination igniting in his eyes. "I need to see Hades."

"Maybe he'll talk to you because of your role as Society President. I don't know. But the other gods have been... less than informative since we arrived," Alice replied, her voice edged with frustration. She clenched her fists, her usual calm demeanor cracking.

Jace noticed the tightness in Alice's jaw, the way her eyes flicked to the floor. She had always been the rational one, but the strain was getting to her too.

Before Jace could respond, an announcement from Orion, the commanding centaur, cut through the chaos like a blade. His presence alone was enough to silence the throng. Draped in deep blue robes that accentuated his powerful, muscular frame, Orion's every step exuded authority. His sharp eyes scanned the crowd, ensuring he had their full attention. "If you will all follow me," he intoned, his voice a deep, resonant calm in the now total quiet. "Archmage Theon wishes to address the recent situation."

The students, driven by a mix of curiosity and fear, followed Orion through the winding corridors to the grand hall. The air buzzed with uneasy anticipation. The hall itself was a marvel of arcane architecture, with high vaulted ceilings that seemed to touch the heavens, and walls adorned with intricate tapestries depicting legendary battles and ancient spells.

As they walked, Jace felt heard the murmur of frightened voices filled the corridor. Some students' faces were pale and drawn, eyes wide with anxiety. Others moved in tight, protective clusters, casting wary glances around them.

Archmage Theon stood at the far end of the hall, his presence both comforting and imposing. His robes, a dazzling cascade of colors that seemed to mimic the flicker of lightning, flowed around him. His eyes, kind but shadowed with concern, surveyed the assembled students.

The grand hall buzzed with nervous energy, students shuffling in, faces a mix of curiosity and fear. The usual chatter dimmed, then ceased entirely as the Archmage ascended the dais. His robes, woven with threads of liquid lightning, shimmered with an otherworldly glow. His eyes, sharp with shadowed concern, scanned the sea of young faces.

"Let's draw a line," the Archmage's voice sliced through the tense silence. He shot a bolt of energy from his staff into the air, forming a glowing barrier. "On one side, everything we know. On the other, all we don't. Here's what we do know: as of dawn yesterday, every student across Olympus has lost the ability to log out."

A ripple of shock surged through the crowd. The Archmage, unperturbed, pressed on. "I dispatched messages to the different universities and kingdoms to see if this was local or Terra-wide. Responses came from the Island School of Veridiana, the Storm Tower Academy of Zephyrion, and the Crystal Keep of Aeloria, among others. Ten schools have replied. Only the Ancient Pyramids of Nephthys remain silent"

"I've also contacted the governing bodies across Mythica's eleven remaining great nations," the Archmage continued. "They report the same: their Travelers can't log out."

The room, thick with anxiety, felt smaller as the enormity of the situation settled in. Faces turned pale, whispers of disbelief spreading like wildfire. The Archmage stood tall, a solitary pillar of calm amidst the brewing storm.

The hall erupted in a flurry of murmured fears and confusion. The Archmage tapped his cane, crowned with a carved thunderbird whose wings flickered with pure lightning. Silence fell once more, the power of the cane evident.

"We know that the Dark One attacked this very school. We're still investigating how this breach was possible."

He paused, letting the gravity of his words sink in. The information appeared on the side of the line marked "What We Know." "What we don't know is if he caused the current issues. Speculations about the return of the AI Plague Virus are unsubstantiated."

A collective sigh of relief washed over them.

"And thanks to some of our more... creative students," the Archmage continued, gesturing towards Thistle, perched on Dex's shoulders and now flushed a bright pink, "we have reason to believe that respawn continues to function without interference."

Thistle leaned over to Jace. "Kinda died last night while blowing off some steam with Dex. Long story."

Jace raised an eyebrow. "What happened?"

Dex chuckled, shaking his head. "You ever hear of 'cow tipping'? Turns out minotaurs have a much stronger opinion on the matter—and they tip back."

"However," the Archmage said, his tone shifting to cautious optimism, "it would be best to keep the fact of respawn in the unknown category for now. We don't understand the cost, but we're investigating any clues regarding potential side effects."

The room remained tense, but the Archmage's words brought a flicker of hope. As he spoke, the students sensed that while the situation was dire, they were not entirely without recourse. The Archmage's steady presence was a beacon, guiding them through the darkness with measured optimism and unwavering resolve.

"Now, this is of the utmost importance: we must address the greatest unknown - what is to come. You are not children, and I will not treat you as such. You deserve to know what may lie ahead. Many of you may feel the urge to hide until this is resolved. I wouldn't blame you. But whatever caused this anomaly, whatever allowed the Dark One to breach our defenses and attack five of our students, won't pause. Whether the Dark One is directly behind it or not, he will undoubtedly use it to his advantage. And so, we must all be prepared."

The Archmage began to pace, his robes trailing like a storm cloud.

"For eons, the twelve great kingdoms of Terra Mythica have flourished."

In a brilliant flash, the Archmage cast another bolt of light, conjuring an ethereal image of Terra Mythica high above the crowd. The kingdoms glowed in vivid hues, a breathtaking panorama of color. Yet, an ominous shadow crept across the map, marring its beauty.

Suspended in the air, the map pulsed with the passage of time. Darkness surged and retreated, like a tide in a relentless struggle. The ebb and flow continued, until the crowd witnessed a pivotal moment: the birth of the Thirteenth Kingdom. In an instant, this new realm consumed one of the twelve, obliterating the once lush and verdant lands of Roandia. The crowd gasped as the grassy fields vanished, replaced by the encroaching shadow.

"This may be familiar to some of you. You may have seen this display in your classes. But perhaps you have not seen this part."

The darkness crept further, its tendrils weaving into the different kingdoms, painting a more dreadful picture than ever before.

"This is not merely a clash of armies. It is Light against Dark, the infinite beginning against the eternal end. Mount Olympus University was founded to prepare you, the next generation, to face this peril, to fight back against the encroaching shadow. Should the Thirteenth Kingdom prevail, light will turn to dark, beginnings to ends, and life to endless void."

As he spoke, the image was covered in inky waves of black. The students exchanged uneasy glances.

"Who here knows our University symbol and patron creature?" the Archmage asked.

Alice raised her hand. "Miss Candor?"

"The Phoenix," she replied.

"Correct. Now, do you know why the Phoenix?" No one answered.

"The Phoenix represents all things in this world," the Archmage continued, his voice softening slightly. "Birth. Growth. Decay. Death. And Rebirth, starting the cycle anew. A story has a beginning, a middle, and an end, just as all things material do. An abandoned home may rot and wither away, its decay leading to death. But from that decay, new life may sprout, growing into a fine tree that can be used to build again. A mortal coil may be shed, but the soul survives and carries on to start anew. Travelers call this respawn. Citizens experience it slightly differently; we call it reincarnation. Some may remember, some choose to forget. But the cycle goes on."

The Archmage's gaze hardened. "Yet, there is a force that seeks to end that cycle. A darkness that seeks no rebirth, only eternal nothingness. The end of all things."

He paused, and the students shifted uneasily, their faces a blend of fear and determination.

"Some of you may believe you are immune, as you always have been. But that is no longer true, if it ever was. The darkness that is coming, the end it yearns to bring, is not stopped by your status as Travelers. Imagine drifting in an endless darkness, forever, your mind and soul lost among the void."

The Archmage resumed pacing, his robes sweeping the floor like storm clouds. "In the ancient lore of our world, it is said that knowing the true name of a thing grants one dominion over it. This, in essence, is true. More precisely, to know something to its very core—to perceive it without bias or distraction—grants the wielder unparalleled Affinity and ability regarding it."

He stopped and faced the students, his gaze piercing through them. "There is an old Traveler's adage: 'What one does not know cannot hurt one.' This belief might be the very shackle that has kept those in the Travelers' home realm from mastering the Affinities. They wield remarkable technology, yet their understanding of its potential remains childlike."

He moved to the center of the dais, his voice rising with urgency. "Indeed, it is less than childlike, for children still glimpse the magic adults forsake. The few adults who retain this sight are often ostracized until they renounce it, allowing the Affinities to fade into willful oblivion. In reality, it is only what you do not know that can harm you, and only to the extent of your ignorance."

He raised his hand, conjuring a flickering flame. "Consider the man who first discovers fire. Without understanding, he may immolate himself or set fire to a town. He may learn to ignite it but not to control it. Or a wizard who knows a ritual but lacks the practice and certainty in its components and has no Affinity with the magic involved. His ignorance could bring ruin upon himself and the world."

The flame danced in his palm, casting eerie shadows across his face. "And that is your first and most fundamental lesson: it is only that which you do not know that can hurt you. And thus, you gain mastery over anything to the degree that you understand it."

He extinguished the flame with a snap of his fingers, plunging the room into a hushed darkness. The students stared at him, wide-eyed, absorbing the gravity of his words. The Archmage's presence filled the room, a beacon of both warning and hope, urging them to seek knowledge and understanding in the face of the encroaching darkness.

The Archmage continued, "This is not a battle with borders. And I will be honest where many would not."

The high council teachers exchanged worried glances, sensing he was about to take a dangerous step. An elderly man with a long, flowing beard, Professor Dranice Thorne, Master of Games, began to rise, his voice trembling with concern. "Archmage, you can't possibly be..."

But the Archmage did not pause. "My friends, we are losing this war. We have been losing this war for many years. And we do not know how long we can hold out."

Dranice sat back down, his lips pressed into a thin line and a deep frown creasing his forehead.

"This school was founded to usher new recruits into a war that has raged for centuries, a war older than the stones beneath our feet. The boundaries we set were meant to shield you from harsh truths until you were ready. But the tides have shifted, and tradition must bow to necessity. Your User Interface Stones, those small silver stones that connect you to the system and your HUD, are bound to your very souls. They restrict you, keeping you within our safest zones until you rank up and complete your training. These boundaries were our fortress, our sanctuary, granting us precious time to prepare you for the battles ahead.

But now, the walls of our sanctuary are crumbling. The darkness is no longer a distant threat; it is here, encroaching upon us. The time for shelter and protection is over. To face the looming shadow, you must complete your training."

The Archmage's gaze hardened, his voice a razor's edge. "Our enemies are at the gates, and the luxury of time has been stolen from us. You must learn to protect yourselves and those you love. Steel yourselves for the coming storm. This is not just about survival—it's about fighting for the very soul of our realm."

The Archmage's words hung in the air, heavy and unyielding.

"Our ancient wards are failing, and our enemies grow bolder."

The students exchanged nervous glances as the Archmage halted and faced them, his eyes burning with determination. When he spoke, his voice resonated through the hall, commanding their attention.

"The Thirteenth Kingdom seeks to plunge us into eternal night."

A student raised their hand, confusion etched on their face. "Why can we still read the news and get feeds from the Grid, but we can't reach back?"

Theon sighed, his eyes heavy with uncertainty. "We don't know for sure. We are scouring the entire Grid to figure it out. But it appears the Grid itself is waning; once available sections are disappearing. We believe our access is only temporary and suspect that whatever is causing this wants to allow Travelers in, but not out. And at some point, even that will cease."

"Archmage," another student called out, standing up. Tall and lanky, with a shock of red hair and an earnest expression, he hesitated. "I'm confused. You're acting like this isn't a game. When the logout option comes back, we'll just log out and wait for them to fix the bugs."

The Archmage's gaze softened, a hint of sadness in his eyes. "There are still many things we do not know. Chief among them is whether we will ever be given the option to log out again."

A heavy silence blanketed the hall.

"For now, and unless something changes, it is best not to treat this world like a game. I implore you to treat your fellow citizens with respect and kindness, as they did not cause this. Show what it means to be a Traveler. In the best of times, kindness is paramount. And in the worst of times, it is even more crucial."

The students exchanged uneasy glances. The Archmage took a deep breath and continued, his voice soft. "Go to your classes. Hone your skills. Train diligently. Show kindness to one another. Treat this as real life, and you just might survive it."

With that, he dismissed the assembly. The students sat motionless, the gravity of his words sinking in. For a long moment, silence reigned before they slowly began to file out of the hall, each step heavier with the weight of their new reality.

Chapter 3
Forget-Me-Nots

Jace stood in the grand hall, the Archmage's speech still hanging in the air like a lingering smoke. The High Council members glided towards a hidden exit. Jace's jaw tightened, his patience fraying at the edges.

Ell, Dex, and Thistle were already making their way outside, disappearing into the swell of bodies. Jace stole a glance at Alice beside him; she was a stone in a raging river of students flooding outward, unmoving, resolute. He leaned in, his voice a low, urgent whisper. "I need to talk to him. Now."

Alice's eyes widened briefly before hardening, a fierce light sparking in her blue depths. "I'm with you."

The crowd surged around them, a chaotic whirl of students and faculty. Jace pushed forward, his determination cutting through the sea of faces. Alice followed closely, her slight frame weaving through the gaps like a dancer navigating the floor.

They wove through clusters of people, the noise of worried voices and discussions a deafening backdrop. He caught a fleeting glimpse of the Archmage ahead, the distinguished figure unmistakable. For a brief, electrifying moment, their eyes met. Jace could swear he saw a flicker of recognition in those piercing eyes before the Archmage turned away, disappearing through a hidden passage.

"Hey!" Jace's shout was swallowed by the din of the hall.

They reached the spot just as the last flicker of a dark cloak—Professor Thorne's—vanished behind a wall that sealed with a soft, mocking thud.

"Son of a..." Jace snarled, slamming his fist against the solid stone.

They stood there, breathing heavily, hands pressed against the cold, unyielding surface. Jace turned to Alice, his anger and determination reflected in her fierce gaze.

"Let's get outside. We need to talk with the others."

Outside, the murmur of the gathering buzzed with an electric tension. Voices, hushed and strained, clashed and combined, creating an undercurrent that made Jace want to shout just to break through it. Jace and Alice exchanged a look before guiding the group away from the thick of the crowd, seeking a quieter spot.

Jace led them to the garden, a place he'd once spoken with Theon. As they stepped into the garden, it was like crossing a threshold into another world. Each plant shimmered with an otherworldly glow, casting soft hues of blue, green, and gold that danced in the dim light. A heady blend of blooming flowers filled the atmosphere, an intoxicating mix that clung to their senses, drawing them further into the enchanting space.

Alice's eyes sparkled as she surveyed the flora, her curiosity a welcome distraction from the grim news. "Look at these Forget-Me-Nots," she said, pointing to a cluster of delicate, luminescent blue blooms. Each petal pulsed with a faint inner light. "They hold memories and can be brewed into a tea to share them. Whatever they experience is recorded." She plucked a few and handed one to each of them. "In case we want to record anything for our families." She gave a half-smile, the weight of her words settling between them.

Jace took his graciously. They continued walking until they reached a tall, ancient tree. Its branches formed a natural canopy, leaves whispering softly in the breeze. Alice ran her fingers along its bark, feeling the rough texture under her fingertips. "This is a Silencer Tree," she said, her voice barely a whisper. "It catches all sound, making it impossible for anyone to hear you unless they're right here with you."

Jace understood why Theon had chosen this spot for their conversation. The memories of that day flooded back, vivid and sharp. He pushed them aside, focusing on the task at hand. The weight of the moment settled over them, but within this sanctuary of magic, there was a brief calm in the world's chaos.

"Okay, Scooby Gang, what's the plan?" Dex asked, trying to lighten the heavy mood.

Ell shrugged. "We do what the Archmage said. Gather our strength and prepare. Attend class, rank up. Face our new reality for the time being. I can't even believe I'm saying all this... I feel like I'm in a dream. Ouch!" She rubbed her arm where Dex had pinched her.

"Still think it's a dream?" Dex teased.

"I was being poetic, you cretin." Ell punched him back, and the group chuckled despite the tension.

Jace turned to Alice. "Alice, does your quest give you any clues?"

"Just what you saw," she replied.

A storm of emotions churned in his gut—numb confusion at the sudden change, a flicker of wonder that this might be his new life, self-loathing for the brief joy that thought brought him, guilt over what had happened to his brother, and a biting dread that he wouldn't be able to do anything about it. He pushed them all aside, focusing on the task at hand. Deep breaths. Gather resources.

"Maybe you can dig up some history on these glitches," Jace said, his voice steady despite the chaos within. "And the Dark One. We need to know everything we can about him."

"Also, after the... incident at the dome, Theon and I spoke," Jace added.

"On a first-name basis, are we?" Dex smirked.

"Point is, he brought me here, assuming no one else could hear. He told me he was worried about something coming."

"He knew?" Alice asked.

"He knew something. I don't know how much, but he asked me to spy on Hades for him. To find out what was really going on. He said that his patron goddess had been missing for some time, Clio, the Muse and goddess of History."

They all looked at each other for a long moment. "Gods don't just disappear," Thistle said. "There is something bigger happening here."

"Do you think Hades is helping the Dark One?" Dex asked.

"No, definitely not. I don't get that vibe from him at all. Fiction portrays him as power-hungry and evil, but that's just not what I see. Besides, what benefit would he get? He hasn't mentioned holding any grudges. We can't rule anything out, but no, I don't think so."

"Okay, so who could make a goddess disappear? And why the Muse of History?"

They all exchanged uneasy glances.

"There's more..." Jace began, his voice low and serious. The others turned to him, their expressions a mix of curiosity and concern. "And this you

must swear to total secrecy. I shouldn't be telling you, but you need to know."
They all nodded in agreement. "Theon, the Archmage, is a Traveler."

Alice raised an eyebrow, unsurprised. "I kinda gathered that."

"Yeah, it fits," Dex added, while Ell and Thistle nodded.

"Okay, I was expecting a bigger reveal there," Jace admitted. "But that's not really the point. He says he doesn't believe death in Mythica ever came without a cost."

"You mean, like the aether drain and EXP loss?" Alice asked.

"No, a bigger cost. Potentially much bigger. Our memories."

They all stared at each other, stunned, as Jace's words settled heavily around them.

"That's not possible. It would have been reported," Ell said.

"What if it had been?" Jace asked. "Who would they report it to?"

"Even if Excelsior ignored it, it would make the media," Ell countered.

"And who owns the networks that host those media?" Thistle asked her.

"Excelsior," she admitted after a long pause. "But he doesn't own them all."

"Doesn't he? Maybe not directly, but he has his fingers in everything, you said so yourself. And he is one of the richest people on the planet. I'm not saying it's all a big conspiracy with John Rearden as some dark overlord... but I'm also not not saying that," Jace said.

"And it might not be reported often because it is so gradual. Just little things, here and there. And then bigger and bigger, until you've lost everything."

Thistle looked at him gravely and wiped a tear from his eye. "Did he mention any way back from it? From losing everything?"

They all remembered Thistle's loss of his uncle, and their hearts ached for him.

"I don't know, but I have to hope that there is," Jace said, kneeling and placing a hand on Thistle's shoulder.

"Okay," Ell said. "Then we need to find out what is going on. The Archmage knows more than he is letting on. The gods must be aware of Clio's absence. It being Clio leads me to think that there must be something in the past that whoever is behind this doesn't want us to know about. A piece of history they don't want us to see. We should start with the library."

"And I'll go see Hades. We haven't spoken since..."

The group looked at him, worry etched on their faces. "Jace," Ell said gently, "we never really talked about what happened... in there."

"There will be time for that," Jace hedged, trying to avoid the conversation.

"No, Jace. The rest of us have been able to get our feelings out, at least what we can, before you arrived. It was terrible for all of us. But you... you were in bad shape when the healers came. We could hear you talking with it. While we couldn't move or speak or barely breathe in those webs, we could hear you. And we felt something as you fought it. I can't be sure what, but it was dark and deep and sad. Jace, you are our friend... and I just want to make sure you are okay."

A tear threatened to escape Jace's eye. He quickly looked away and forced the feeling down. "I'm fine," he said with a forced smile. "It was terrible for all of us. But it's just a game, right?" He tried to lighten the mood with a wink.

"I don't think we can think like that anymore," Alice said softly.

"I know," Jace replied somberly. "But I'm okay, I promise. Thank you, guys, for caring." Alice startled him with a massive hug, quickly joined by Dex, Ell, and Thistle, though Thistle more just stretched his arms to hug Jace's calf.

They stood there for a long moment before bursting into laughter. "We are a weird bunch, eh?" Jace said.

"The weirdest," Dex added.

"Come on, let's figure this thing out," Ell said, taking charge.

"Okay," Jace started. "Why don't you guys dig into this at the library, see if there is anything we can find that could help us understand what is going on. I'm going to go see Hades."

"Okay, great. Just no venturing outside the campus alone. We might be Bronze Twos now, but we need to stick together." Everyone agreed, except Jace who looked at them with a side glance.

"You guys ranked up?" he asked, surprised.

They all looked at him incredulously. "You're not?" Thistle asked.

"We didn't even have any real direct involvement in the last fight, and we still ranked up from the shared EXP of it all," Dex said.

"Jace, have you not cultivated your aether pathways since the dome?" Alice's voice was laced with concern.

He looked at her, caught off guard. "I haven't. Come to think of it, I haven't really checked my notifications since then... I've just been too preoccupied with..." His thoughts drifted to Alex lying in the hospital bed.

"Jace, before you do anything else, you need to take some time and come to grips with what happened and cultivate your aether." Alice's voice was firm yet caring.

"Okay, okay. I'll do that right after I speak with Hades."

"No, Jace. Now. You'll do it now." She glared up at him, her small stature not diminishing her intensity one bit. Though she stood noticeably shorter than Jace, he suddenly felt as if he were facing a final boss—one he was woefully unprepared for and certain to lose against if he dared to try.

"Okay, Alice. I'll do it now."

She smiled, relaxing a bit.

Ell handed out a small stack of paper to each of them. "Magic Missives. It's how we can communicate until one of us evolves a party telepathy ability or internal communication system, which I'm thinking will either be Jace or Alice when the time comes, or perhaps me. Those are usually around Three Stars. But for now, just write your note on this, picture who it is for and—"

She doodled something obscene on the paper and closed her eyes. The name "Dex" appeared in glowing golden ink before the paper popped into the air and folded itself into an origami pegasus, which then shot up and landed in Dex's hands.

"Jace, when you're done in the Underworld, just send me a message, and I'll gather everyone up or redirect it to the next person. These things have about four or five good foldings in them."

With that, the group headed to the library, leaving Jace to make his way back to his dorm room in the Fields Below. As he walked away, he cast a final glance over his shoulder and saw Dex crouch down with a grimace, Thistle nimbly hopping onto his shoulders.

Chapter 4
Character Sheet

A rriving at his dorm, he collapsed onto his bed, opening his HUD to finally check his updates.

Character Sheet
> Name: Jace
> Speaker Rank: Bronze One Star, Novice Reactionaire
> Class Title: Cleric
> EXP Capacity Bar: 7150/1200
> Warning: You are currently 5,950 EXP over your EXP capacity. All EXP gain is being reduced by 90%. Please cultivate EXP or increase capacity to recover some of your EXP gain efficiency.

Jace felt a mix of excitement and dread seeing the large EXP gain. The sinking feeling of lost potential overshadowed the thrill of growth. Determined to understand more about EXP Capacity and how to increase it, he made a mental note to investigate further. It seemed his capacity had increased slightly, but nowhere near enough. Then again, he doubted students were supposed to be fighting such high-level creatures.

Attributes
> • Strength: 12
> • Dexterity: 13

- Intelligence: 15
- Wisdom: 16
- Constitution: 12
- Charisma: 11

Skills

- Dark Vision (Apprentice): Enhanced ability to see in darkness with limited clarity.
- Knowledge Absorption (Apprentice): Improved retention and comprehension of absorbed knowledge.
- Universal Lore (Apprentice): Increased understanding of game mechanics and world lore.
- Minor Resistance to Death (Apprentice): You have developed a natural immunity to dying. Take 5% less damage from necrotic, evil, and shadow-based attacks.
- Inspect Object - Novice: Looking at things really hard has helped you determine what they are. +10% chance to discover facts about objects.

Words of Power / Affinities
Soul - Rank One, Novice Reactionaire

Unlocked Abilities and Effects
- Soul Survivor (Internal, Passive): Your soul is resilient. You have Spoken a Word of Power far beyond your ability and lived to tell the tale. You are defying the course of natural selection. +10% increased resistance to all soul damage.
  Aether Cost: None

- Soul Mend (Touch): You have gained some passing insight into how the soul can heal the body. (Enhanced Aspect): A small portion of your aether is now dedicated to personal healing, providing a constant, passive restoration. This ongoing aether expenditure reduces the total cost for all self-mending by 50%.
  Aether Cost: Moderate

• Soul Tether (Distance, Sight): You can perceive and influence the connectivity between souls, allowing you to transfer minor limited effects between two entities.

Aether Cost: High

• Soul Sense (Distance, Sight): Increased perception of emotions in others and wandering spirits. (Enhanced Aspect): You have gained an enhanced perception of souls and their connections. You can now see and feel from the perspective of the connected entity, with a chance to glean potentially valuable insights and memories.

Aether Cost: Low

• Soul Severance: You have gained a deeper insight into the connection between the soul and the body, enabling you to detect and remove incursions that do not belong. This ability allows you to sever the connection between a foreign entity and its host body. Increase this ability for reduced aether cost and increased effectiveness.

Aether Cost: Severe

He checked over his Society Interface.

Society of Hades
    Members: 1
    Society Points Available: 4,500

"Wait, what?" Jace muttered, surprised by the sudden influx of points. He quickly checked over his logs, scanning through the damage reports, abilities used, and status updates. The battle with the undead replayed in his mind as he reviewed the details.

• Damage taken
    • Party member has been paralyzed.
    • Critical condition.
    • Archmage Theon has joined the fray.
    • Orion Blackwood has joined the fray...

The battle log and status updates went on.
    And then he saw it.

• Update - Defeat of Enemy of Hades. 2000 Society Points.
    • EXP gained for monster defeated, 32,000, multiplied by rank dispar-
ity bonus.
    • Warning: EXP has passed current storage limits. 90% reduction in
place.
    • Notice: Boon gifted in recognition from Hades for assisting in the
defeat of one of his foes -
    o "Over The Top" When you have passed your EXP capacity thresh-
old, instead of simply all EXP being reduced by 90%, a small portion of that
overflow EXP will be converted into Society Points.

"Thank you, Hades," Jace whispered. Having a patron deity wasn't such a bad
thing after all. At least not all of the EXP gain was lost.
    He checked over the available options for Society upgrades. There were
many choices, but he didn't want to rush into anything. He decided to leave it
for now and make more concrete plans for how the society should grow later.
    He then selected [Active Quests] and immediately covered his head in
his hands when he saw the notification.

Quest Chain Update: Profession Quest: Hades' Little Helper

I ain't 'fraid of no ghosts...

There is the soul of a woman in the wilderness east of the campus that was supposed to move on six weeks ago, but something is keeping her there. You must figure out what is causing this anomaly and set things right.

Reward: 100 Society EXP, 1 Copper

Failure: Impending doom

Bonus Objective: Give it that little extra

Bonus Reward: Variable

Quest Updates:

This quest is far, far past due. Minus 20 reputation with Hades.

Rewards for Quest: Hades' Little Helper has been decreased because of taking your sweet time.

Chapter 5
Bedknobs and Broom Closets

Jace sighed, the weight of Hades' displeasure pressing on him like a shroud. The reward had plummeted, and his reputation with Hades was beginning to slip. He'd have to address this soon, but not right now. His eyes closed, the morning's events swirling in his mind like dark clouds.

He moved to his cabinet, fingers tracing the worn edges as he retrieved his notebook and quill. Catching a glimpse of himself in the mirror, a strange tingling sensation crawled up his spine, prickling his skin as if unseen eyes were upon him. He shook his head, trying to dislodge the paranoia.

Jace sat cross-legged on the floor, his notebook open before him, quill hovering above the paper. He closed his eyes, drawing in a deep breath, and began to cultivate his aether, trying to channel his thoughts through journaling. The quill scratched across the page, but the words felt stilted, lifeless.

He paused, staring at the blank spaces between his scribbles. His chest tightened with impatience. Why was this so hard tonight? His mind was a storm, thoughts clashing and colliding, making it impossible to find focus. Each word he wrote felt like a struggle, each line a battle against the stagnant aether within him.

"Why can't I just concentrate?" he muttered, glaring at the uncooperative notebook. The inked words seemed insignificant, a pale shadow of the turmoil inside him. Time slipped by unnoticed, and he realized an hour had passed with barely two hundred EXP spent.

Frustration bubbled up, hot and fierce. With a growl, he flung the book and quill aside. They skidded across the floor, coming to rest in the shadows. He buried his face in his hands, fingers digging into his scalp. He needed a break, something to clear his mind, to cut through the fog of frustration and fatigue.

The room felt too small, the air too thick. Rising to his feet, Jace paced the floor, each step echoing in the quiet.

In a huff, Jace opened his map. The secret route to the Underworld from his dorms lay hidden, a barely visible line until he selected it. With a shimmer, the name glowed gold: Forgotten Path. The line shimmered along the map, illuminating his way.

He drew in a steadying breath, bracing himself, and stepped out of his room. The corridor was silent, the soft glow of the map guiding him through the shadows. As he walked, the air grew colder, each breath misting in front of him. He passed by little cracks that led up and up, the muffled sounds of students talking outside filtering through. The walls seemed to close in, the familiar surroundings of the academy morphing into something darker, more foreboding.

The path led him down winding stairs, through hidden doors, and along forgotten tunnels. The silence was oppressive, broken only by the occasional drip of water echoing through the dark passages. His steps echoed, a steady beat in the otherwise still air.

He reached a heavy, ancient door, its surface etched with silver snake that writhed and shifted in the dim light. Placing a hand on the cool metal, he pushed. The door groaned in protest, and a rush of cold air greeted him, carrying the faint scent of decay and the distant echoes of tormented souls.

Jace hesitated. The Underworld was not a place for the faint-hearted, and even he, favored by Hades, felt a twinge of fear as he crossed the threshold into the realm of shadows.

The path before him was illuminated by flickering torches, casting eerie shadows that danced along the rough-hewn walls. Each step he took kicked up dust, and cobwebs clung to his clothes, the sticky threads brushing against his face. He brushed them away, feeling the grit of ancient dust under his fingertips.

The air grew heavier, filled with the whispers of the dead and the rustling of unseen beings. He could feel the presence of spirits brushing past him, their cold, intangible forms sending shivers down his spine. His heart pounded, his senses on high alert, every creak and whisper amplified in the silence.

As he walked, ancient torches lining the walls burst to life of their own accord, casting long, wavering shadows that seemed to reach out and grasp at him. Undeterred, he pressed on, determined and resolute.

He reached a large door at the top of a steep staircase. Opening it, he found himself in a cramped, pitch-black space. His dark vision revealed assorted bric-a-brac: a dusty broom, an old mop, pieces of old furniture, a bedpost, and a pile of cleaning supplies. It looked like a closet. The door was stuck and wouldn't budge. With a grunt and a solid kick, it flew open, and he tumbled out, accompanied by the broom and mop, into an office lit by harsh fluorescent lights, surrounded by cubicles.

Jace looked up, blinking in the sudden brightness. Ghostly figures were hunched over desks, tapping away at typewriters, their ethereal forms momentarily pausing to stare at him. The air buzzed with a faint, otherworldly hum.

"Jace! What are you doing in the mop closet?" Jerry's voice cut through the silence, friendly and amused.

"Mop closet?" Jace muttered, turning to see the tiny room behind him. He realized a hidden door in the back of the closet had led him in. "Well," he shrugged, "you learn something new every day. Never can get too comfortable around here. Twists and turns at every corner."

"Exactly," Jerry chuckled dryly. "This place is like a maze with a sense of humor. But what brings you to my neck of the woods? Not that I don't appreciate the visit."

"I need to speak with Hades," Jace said, urgency in his voice.

"Oof, no can do, I'm afraid," Jerry replied, and Jace shot him a skeptical look.

"It's not my call. I'm not stopping you or anything. You're free to check, but I've got it on the books that he's out of the office."

"Did it say where he went?"

"Above my pay grade, I'm afraid," Jerry said with a shrug. "Still, you're free to check and personally leave a note."

"Jerry, I need to speak with him. It's urgent. The Travelers are having some issues..."

"Yeah, I've heard. Tough spot. Can't make it home, eh? I'm sure it'll all get sorted out." Jerry's tone was pleasant, but there was something off. His eyes held a glimmer of pity and something else... guilt?

"What do you know?" Jace pressed.

Jerry sighed. "What do I know? What do I know? I know the directions to a great pastry shop in Thebes. They make these incredible custard-filled treats soaked in sweet syrup. Absolutely to die for." He clapped a hand on Jace's shoulder, steering him toward the elevator while loudly extolling the virtues of Greek pastries for the benefit of their ghostly audience.

"Where are we going?" Jace asked, playing along.

"Oh, Jace, as a Chosen of Hades, I'm happy to show you to the Underworld to leave a note for him!" Jerry's voice boomed cheerfully as they stepped into the elevator. "It's not like I'm allowed to stop you, when you officially have requested." Once inside, the doors closed, and Jerry's demeanor shifted.

"Jace, don't say anything. I'm not sure who can hear us, but it's not safe for you here when Hades is out. Something's going on. Some of the ghosts have been acting real suspicious. And I can't believe it, but... I wouldn't believe it if I hadn't seen it..."

"What is it?" Jace asked, his heart pounding, as the Girl From Ipanema played in the background.

"I'm not sure all the staff here are on our side."

"Side?"

"Yeah, our side. The side of order and life. The side of Hades and everyone else who'd rather not be blinked out of existence for all eternity."

"Can't you just report it?"

"It's not that simple. A wrong accusation without proof... I need more time to figure this out. But needless to say, I wouldn't trust leaving a note with anyone upstairs. Other than myself and Barb, of course."

"I need to reach Hades."

"All the gods have been out of the office since the shift. Their answering machines are on—basically ghosts like me just trying to pacify everyone while the gods deliberate."

"Makes sense why no one has gotten anything but cryptic answers."

"We can only say so much. It's like an eternal 'away from desk' message. Listen, I'm pretty sure the ferryman is on our team. But you can't be sure with anyone these days."

The elevator dinged, and the doors opened. Jerry stayed back.

"Jace, trust no one. I... I like you and I don't want to see you -disappeared."

"Don't worry about me, Jerry," Jace said with a wry smile. "We all have to face the danger now and then. Besides, you can't spell extraordinary without that little 'extra,' right?"

As the door closed, Jerry gave a weak smile.

The sound of moving water reached Jace's ears, a soft lapping against the stilts of a dock. He approached, the ferryman waiting for him, shrouded in shadow. The chill of the Underworld seeped into his bones as he stepped onto the boat.

Chapter 6
With a Capital "T" and that Rhymes with "P"

Jace felt the boat lurch, slicing through the murky waters of the River Styx. The ferryman, a shadowy figure with hollow eyes that possessed the secrets of the abyss, kept his gaze fixed ahead, gripping the oar with a wraithlike grace.

"So, Hades is out," Jace said, more to fill the silence than anything else. "You get any time off?"

The ferryman, as talkative as a tombstone, didn't respond. Jace pulled his cloak tighter around himself, the Underworld's chill seeping into his bones like an unwelcome guest. This place had a way of making a guy feel like he was navigating the back alleys of a cosmic noir.

When the boat finally nudged the shore, Jace stepped off, the rocky ground crunching under his boots. The ferryman's hollow eyes followed him, a silent warning that lingered in the air like a forgotten whisper. Jace nodded in acknowledgment, then turned to face the twisted paths of the Underworld.

Navigating the Underworld was like walking through a fever dream directed by a sadistic filmmaker. Shadows danced in the corners of his vision, and the faint cries of the damned echoed like a grim soundtrack. He steeled himself and began to walk, each step echoing in the vast, deep silence.

Finally, after what felt like an eternity, he reached the great gates of Hades' palace. The massive iron doors loomed before him, etched with serpents and flames that seemed to move in the dim light. He placed a hand on the cold metal, feeling the ancient power that thrummed through it.

With a deep breath, he pushed the doors open and stepped inside.

The throne room was a cavernous expanse, shadows pooling in the corners and torchlight flickering like ghostly figures. At the far end, the throne of Hades stood empty, a silent testament to the god's absence.

Jace approached the throne, his footsteps echoing like a heartbeat in the silence. He stood before the throne and looked around for somewhere to leave a note. He could just leave it on the throne but that felt wrong somehow.

"Hello?" Jace's voice cut through the thick silence of the throne room, steady despite the chaos churning inside him. "Is anyone there?"

Silence. The oppressive weight of the room bore down on him, and Jace lowered his head, frustration gnawing at his resolve.

Then, a soft swish of fabric broke the stillness. Emerging from the shadows was a tall, imposing figure with eyes like smoldering embers, stepping into the flickering light. Her raven-black hair cascaded down her back in waves, contrasting starkly with her alabaster skin. She wore a gown of deep crimson, intricate patterns resembling flames embroidered along the hem and sleeves. Her presence was both awe-inspiring and terrifying, her gaze piercing through the gloom. Her lips, a dark shade of red, curled into a knowing smile that sent a shiver down Jace's spine.

"Oh, hello. You must be Hades' new pet," she said, her voice dripping with condescension as she glided forward, the air around her seeming to darken. No introduction, just a statement of fact. "Hades is in a meeting with the Olympians. You'll have to come back another time."

"Who are you?" Jace demanded, refusing to be cowed.

A flicker of amusement lit her fiery eyes. "Oh, how silly of me. I always forget how little your kind pays attention. I'm Megaera."

Impatience flared inside Jace. Partly due to her attitude, partly because she was right, and he had no clue who she was supposed to be. "Well, Megs, it's been a real slice, but I need to reach Hades," he said, starting to walk forward, though he wasn't sure exactly where he was going. Finding Hades during a meeting of the gods? Not like he could just waltz up to their divine boardroom and knock. Could he?

Her eyes narrowed, and her jaw tightened in a swirl of loathing and curiosity. "Aren't we flippant?" she purred, stepping closer and circling Jace, her hand brushing his shoulder. "We used to flay the skin from mortals for less." She leaned in, her voice a sinister whisper, her smile practically brushing his ear. "Or boil them in grease. Those were the good days."

"Sounds exhilarating. So, are you like, Hades' secretary?" Jace shot back.

She hissed and flicked Jace on the nose, causing him to squint and wrinkle it in irritation.

"My sisters and I are no secretaries, Pet of Hades. I have an oath with Hades... as do you. I am the one who gets to play with you when you inevitably break that oath, like those who have come before you."

Jace got the feeling she would relish nothing more than seeing him break that oath. He hadn't really thought of it as an oath, but taking on the role of Hades' Chosen was apparently more official than he'd realized. He'd have to revisit that thought later. Looking into her eyes, he saw the joy of torture and vengeance, the thrill of rage and fury, the righteousness in avenging.

A cold shiver snaked down his spine.

"So, little Pet, why do you seek the Lord of the Underworld?" Her voice was like velvet wrapped around steel, smooth yet unforgiving.

"I'd rather discuss that with Hades," Jace replied, meeting her gaze head-on. "I hope you understand."

Megaera studied him for a moment, then nodded. "Very well, Pet. Leave your message with me. I will ensure it reaches Lord Hades."

Jace hesitated, recalling Jerry's warnings. Sensing his reluctance, Megaera's expression softened slightly. "You can trust me, Pet. My soul is bound by an oath to Hades. Betrayal isn't an option, even if I desired it."

Still skeptical, but seeing no better option, Jace reached into his inventory and pulled out a piece of parchment. Realizing he hadn't planned what to say, he hastily scribbled, "Can't log out. Is death safe? - Jace, your Chosen." It felt woefully inadequate, but it would have to do. As he folded the parchment, it sealed itself with a wax stamp that swirled into existence in purple and silver, bearing the mark of a silver raven. He handed it to Megaera.

"Thank you," he said, meeting her fiery gaze.

Megaera gave a curt nod, tucking the parchment away. As he turned to leave, her voice cut through the silence. "Oh, Pet, a word of advice. Do not stray far from the path. The Underworld is not kind to those who wander. Even Hades' pets."

With that, she turned and melted back into the shadows, leaving Jace alone in the vast throne room.

"What is it with gods and their eerie last words before vanishing? It's like they all think they're Batman," Jace muttered to himself, shaking his head.

He glanced around the empty throne room, the oppressive silence pressing in on him. "Great, now I'm talking to myself."

Deciding it was high time to make an exit before any more divine entities decided to play games with him, Jace turned on his heel and made his way out, hoping to avoid further supernatural complications.

As he navigated the labyrinthine corridors, the dim light played tricks with the shadows on the walls, making them dance like eerie phantoms. A soft green glow caught his eye, flickering and pirouetting in the air before him, an unsettlingly familiar sight.

"Oh no, not now, Pik. I'm on my way out. Tell Persephone I'll catch up with her later."

The green light hovered, bouncing in that annoying, expectant way. Jace sighed, rubbing his temples.

"I get it, you want me to go with you. But that's going to be a hard pass. I need to get back above ground, catch up with my friends, and make it to class."

He paused, a fleeting thought interrupting his resolve. Did missing classes here affect your grades? Wait, do they even give grades? He shook his head, dismissing the distraction.

Reaching the shore, his heart sank. The passage opened out to the River Styx, the familiar dock and dim lanterns casting their meager light across the inky waters. The ferryman was conspicuously absent.

"You've got to be kidding me," Jace muttered, scanning the empty shore.

He waited, staring into the dark water, Pik buzzing by his side, bobbing up and down as if urging him forward. Jace glared at the light. "You planned this too, didn't you?" The light merely whizzed in response. Jace let out a resigned breath. "Fine, I'll follow you."

Pik led him down a narrow, winding path that seemed to defy logic and space, the walls closing in and expanding as if the Underworld itself was alive and shifting. Jace felt the unsettling sensation of being watched, the shadows around him holding their breath as he passed.

The green light guided him to a hidden path winding through a dense, misty forest. The trees loomed like silent guardians, their gnarled branches reaching out like skeletal fingers.

Jace followed, his senses on high alert. The forest whispered secrets with every rustle of leaves and snap of twigs, hinting at unseen watchers. He couldn't shake the feeling that he was being led towards something significant, something that would either aid his quest or challenge him further.

Finally, the path opened to a small clearing, bathed in the ethereal glow of the green light. In the center stood a solitary stone altar, ancient and weathered, covered in intricate carvings that pulsed with faint, otherworldly energy.

Jace approached cautiously, heart pounding. The green light settled above the altar, casting its eerie glow over the carvings. He reached out, fingers tracing the symbols, feeling a connection to the ancient power thrumming through the stone. It reminded him of the interface to his Society upgrades, but this magic was different—deeper, pulling at his very soul.

"Let's get out of here before I find myself mixed up with any more trouble," he said, more to himself than Pik.

"Hello, Jason," said Trouble, her voice wrapping around him like silk, her smile drifting in with the ease of a spring breeze.

"Hello, Persephone."

Persephone stood before Jace, her presence as commanding as a queen's and as beguiling as a siren's. Draped in flowing, emerald and obsidian robes that seemed to absorb the very light around her, she exuded an ethereal beauty and an unsettling power. Her hair flowed like waves over her shoulders, framing a face that was both youthful and ancient, her eyes like twin galaxies filled with secrets and sorrow. She glanced at the ring on Jace's finger, a spark of recognition flaring in her gaze.

"I see you've been keeping busy," she purred, her voice a velvety melody laced with an unsettling undertone.

Jace straightened, meeting her gaze with steely determination. "I don't have time for pleasantries. My people are in danger. My friends... my family."

Persephone's expression softened, her gaze shifting as if only just noticing him standing there. A flicker of pity danced in her eyes. "That is why I called you here. I can help you."

"Oh?" Jace's body tensed, bracing for the inevitable catch.

"If you might have time to help me with something I need." And there it was.

"And what is that?"

Her smile widened, never breaking eye contact with the ring. "Oh, don't worry," she said, her voice like silk, "it won't be too difficult."

Jace raised an eyebrow, skepticism evident. "I'm going to need a little more than that."

"Just a simple task," she replied, her tone light and airy. "I need you to retrieve a single seed for me."

There was something in her voice, a quiet confidence that made it hard for Jace to resist.

"A seed? For what purpose?" Suspicion laced his words.

She leaned in closer, her voice dropping to a conspiratorial whisper. "It's for my own purpose. How do your people say—it's need to know. And you don't." Her tone turned flat and final.

"I'm not one for putting myself in danger without knowing what I'm getting into, or even what kind of danger it is. What is this seed? Does it pose any threat to me?"

"Are you planning on eating it?" she asked, a hint of amusement in her eyes.

"I don't usually eat strange things I find in the underworld."

"Then you are perfectly safe. That is all I can say. It is not harmful directly to you in any way."

"And what would I get for this exchange?"

A sly grin tugged at the corners of her lips. "The most precious thing in this world," she purred, her eyes glinting with a hidden agenda. "Knowledge." Her fingers brushed against his ring before she pulled back. "You are unprepared for what is to come, like a speck of dust in a storm. You know not what is happening around you. I can pull back the curtain, to some degree. Now, in fairness and honesty, I have my limits, there are rules even goddesses must follow. But I can provide you with knowledge that will be... invaluable to you. Knowledge that might even help protect you, if things ever turn sour with my hubby. Knowledge that may allow you to keep your secret safe, Jason."

A prompt appeared.

Quest Alert

    A Simple Fetch Quest

    Persephone has given you a "simple fetch quest" to acquire a single seed from a box in Hades' private office.

    Reward: Knowledge that could prove invaluable in the challenges to come.

    Failure: Piss off a goddess. Deal with the consequences.

    Alternative Failure: Get caught. Piss off a god and a goddess. Eternal damnation. Endless torture. The whole shebang. No real telling what Hades would do.

    Rejecting this quest will count as an automatic failure.

    Accept | Reject

Fat lot of good a quest is if you can't actually reject it, Jace thought, closing the prompt in a huff.

    Another prompt immediately appeared, this one edged with a golden border.

System Notice

    I'm just the messenger, I swear. Travelers sometimes. You're the one getting mixed up with gods. If you don't want stupid consequences, don't do stupid things. Don't blame me for your quests; I just work here.

    — Jack

Jace's eyes widened. Jack, the System... He quickly thought, Wait, can you hear me? Don't go. What is happening? What is causing the logout issue? Hello?

    "Are you there?" he said aloud, desperation creeping into his voice.

    Persephone looked at him curiously. "I assume you're not referring to me or Pik here."

    "No, it was just... the System..."

    "Oh," she said, a knowing look in her eyes. "You've met Jack, I take it."

"You know of Jack?" Jace asked, astonished.

"I am a goddess, Chosen. There is much that I know that you do not. But it isn't common for Jack to appear to Travelers. You must have done something very... particular to draw its attention."

"I couldn't say what. It appeared when I first used my Affinity."

"Ah, that makes sense."

"Wait, why does that make sense?"

"There is much to learn, Jason. Some things I can tell you, some things I cannot. There are rules, even for gods. Jack isn't a person as we think of it; he's more of a cosmic force. For most of my life, he never appeared directly, like feeling the sun without seeing each beam of light. We see the flower grow, and the petals bloom, but not the seed that came before.

"Nearly a thousand years ago, he started appearing to the gods. He takes many forms, but I believe he prefers Jack. Even we do not interfere with his machinations."

"What sort of machinations?"

"Ah, now I've said too much. As I mentioned, there are rules, even for me." She pursed her lips and mimed zipping them shut with an imaginary zipper. "Anything else will have to wait until after your success in helping me with my task."

Jace opened the quest prompt again and, after a long look and a slow exhale, chose Accept.

Persephone's smile widened, her eyes flickering with dark, knowing intent. "And a secrecy bond, I think." A surge of power coursed through the air as vines crept up Jace's body, as her voice took on a deep, otherworldly tone. "You may not speak of my involvement or the quest you undertake for me today. Do you consent?"

"But the knowledge you give me is worthless if I cannot share it."

"Fine point," she conceded. "You may share all that I tell you after the quest. But the details of the quest itself may not be spoken or written or shared in any way without my consent. Fine?"

He nodded. A burst of green light enveloped him as a vine coiled around his leg, its thin tendrils piercing his skin, making him yelp in pain. The vine vanished, leaving a faint mark where it had been—a green tattoo, the remnant of the oath.

"Now, take this," she whispered, pressing a cold, ornate key into his trembling hands. "You'll have to venture into Hades' private office. Among countless boxes and relics lies the seed I seek."

Her gaze ignited with a spark of fire. "You must move quickly," she urged, her voice taut with tension. "I'm casting a shroud while Hades meets with the other gods, but it won't last long. Pik will navigate you through the halls. Trust only him. The shadows are cunning, their whispers treacherous, their kiss deadly. And be warned, Chosen, this is of utmost importance—touch nothing but the box that Pik guides you to. Nothing. Not even I know everything that lurks in his private offices."

Chapter 7
Touch Nothing

They slipped into the throne room, relieved to find it empty, Meg thankfully nowhere to be seen. Moving as quietly as shadows among shadows, they navigated the grand space, finding the hidden chamber behind the imposing seat of power. Pik, hovering by the back wall, unveiled the secret: a solid-looking barrier that shimmered like a mirage as Jace leaned closer. What seemed like an impenetrable wall dissolved into a narrow pathway, a trick of perspective that concealed the truth from casual eyes. Pik flitted ahead, its faint glow painting the stone walls in ghostly hues, guiding their way.

Following Pik's lead, Jace stepped into the hidden passage. The cold, black stone walls closed in around him. The flickering flames cast restless shadows that writhed like tormented souls. Ahead, the hallway stretched into darkness, the faint outline of a distant doorway barely visible.

The air was heavy and stagnant, infused with the musty scent of ancient stone and decay. The faint aroma of burning candles tickled Jace's nostrils, hinting at recent activity in these otherwise lifeless halls.

Pik hovered beside him, its movements jittery and erratic. The wisp's light flared brighter momentarily before dimming, a silent testament to its unease. Jace understood the feeling all too well.

At the end of the hall, they reached a door adorned with a polished plaque reading, "Lord of the Underworld. Authorized Personnel Only, Living, Dead, or Otherwise." The elegant, ancient script was etched deep, filled with a dark ink that seemed to absorb the light. Intricate designs of serpents and skeletal figures framed the inscription. The key Persephone had given him clinked softly as it turned in the lock. With a groan, the iron door swung open, revealing a corridor that extended into darkness.

Jace stepped inside and pulled the door shut behind him, the sound echoing ominously. Flickering torches barely illuminated the halls, casting shadows that twisted and writhed like restless spirits. The corridor ahead was a shrouded void, the faint outline of a door barely visible through the gloom.

The walls were barren save for a single, expansive painting. Jace paused before it, drawn in by the tragic beauty depicted - Hades and Persephone, standing tall and regal, surrounded by two young children with piercing gazes. The children's eyes, fierce and haunting, seemed to follow him, their expressions a blend of sorrow and defiance. The painting pulsed with a life of its own, the colors subtly shifting in the torchlight. He shook his head and pressed on, his hand grazing the cold stone for reassurance. "Just a painting," he muttered. "Just a very creepy painting."

Pik's light flickered erratically as they continued down the hall. It stopped in front of another door, labeled with an intricate inscription: "Path of Echoes." The letters were deeply etched into the dark wood, surrounded by swirling, almost hypnotic patterns.

Using the ornate skeleton key, Jace unlocked the door and stepped inside. The air shimmered and rippled as he moved, creating a disorienting effect, as if reality itself was bending around him.

The hall was lined with doors, each unique in hue and material. Some were painted in vivid, striking colors; others were crafted from aged wood, stone, or even metal, each exuding a distinct aura.

Pik hesitated for a moment before leading him to another door. This one was made of rich mahogany, its surface polished, with brass handles that glinted faintly in the dim light.

The door creaked open, revealing a room with lush, velvet-covered walls and a plush, crimson carpet that swallowed his footsteps. Warmth mingled with the scent of roses and aged books, evoking the opulence of a bygone era.

The next door led to a narrow hallway with wooden floors that groaned underfoot. The temperature plummeted, and Jace could see his breath in the frigid air. This hallway felt like a forgotten fragment of a mansion, left to decay with time.

Each room they entered felt like a different world, a new reality.

They approached another door, this one carved from dark, petrified wood and inlaid with gleaming silver. Jace took a deep breath, inserted the key, and turned it slowly. The lock clicked, but the door remained stubbornly shut. Confusion and a touch of panic gripped him.

As he reached closer, his ring hummed, a soft vibration that resonated with the surrounding air. He glanced down, noticing the motif on the door matched the design on his ring—a white raven, stark and haunting.

A strange power emanated from within. The plaque read: "Lost Archives." Pik hummed loudly around the plaque. This must be it. Every instinct in Jace's body screamed at him to leave, to get out of there, as if his very essence was rebelling against even a step closer.

Tentatively, he placed his hand on the door. The wood felt cool and alive beneath his palm, the carved raven motif shifting and undulating until the lines upon it formed an old and tired face.

The face sprang to life, and a deep, resonant voice emerged, reverberating through his chest like the echo of a distant drum. Jace stumbled back as it spoke, leaving the key in the lock.

"Who goes there?" Its voice was like the ancient groaning of wood, slow and ponderous.

Jace's heart raced, his breath catching in his throat. The unexpected animation of the door, coupled with the eerie voice, sent a shiver down his spine.

"My name is Jace. I am a Chosen of Hades," he said, trying to keep his voice steady.

"Half-truths," the giant face muttered, turning as if to look at him askance. "Lies may not enter here. What is your real name?"

Jace hesitated, his mind racing. Was this some kind of passkey? Did it really need his true name? He glanced over his shoulder, confirming he was alone, before whispering, "Jason Rolander."

The door laughed, a sound like the creaking of ancient branches.

"Another half-truth. But close enough." Its features twisted, almost monstrous. "What is your purpose here?"

"I come on a quest... for..." The binding on the quest clamped down on his mouth, silencing him. He shifted tactics. "I need something within."

The door paused as if considering his words.

"Insufficient," it simply said.

"Insufficient?" Jace echoed. "What do I need to do to pass?"

"I may ask you a riddle," the door said, its tone slightly different now, more eager.

"And if I get it right, you'll let me pass?" Jace asked.

"Oh no," it said with deep, wooden tones. "But it is something we can do to pass the time. We do have a fondness for riddles, after all."

Jace shook his head in exasperation. "Who is we? Are there more doors like you in here?"

The door laughed, a deep, resonant sound that seemed to echo through the wood. Louder than Jace felt was necessary.

"No, no... there are no doors here. Only us, the souls of the Ents who chose to remain. We rest in this place and others across the many worlds, providing passage for those in need. We guide them not always to where they seek, but invariably to where they must go."

"And where must I go?" Jace asked, his voice tinged with impatience.

"Are you ready to hear my riddle?" it replied, an almost playful tone in its ancient voice.

Jace sighed, a mix of frustration and curiosity swirling within him. "Fine. I'll listen."

As the door began to speak, the lines of its face contorted, morphing into vivid scenes that danced across its surface. It started with a small village seen from afar, where delicate plumes of smoke curled from chimneys into the sky.

"A village, nestled deep within an ancient, brooding forest. In this village lives a healer, a woman revered for her wisdom and boundless compassion. One day, a dreadful sickness sweeps through the community, felling many. The healer, tireless and determined, uncovers a cure. Yet, the ingredients are scarce, capable of saving only a precious few."

"Two children are brought before her, both equally loved by the village. One is the son of the village chief, destined to lead, strong and brave, but still young and unproven. The other is a girl, known for her kindness and intelligence, who has already shown signs of becoming a great healer herself.

"The healer has enough ingredients to save only one. If she saves the chief's son, the village ensures its future leadership but loses a potential healer who could save many more lives in the future. If she saves the girl, she might find a cure for countless others, but the village may face instability without its future leader.

"The healer must choose. What would you do?"

Jace pondered the words, their echo tugging at memories of riddles he'd encountered when he first ventured into Terra Mythica. Yet, this one was different - deeper, more intricate.

"There is no real choice here. And both are wrong. The situation itself is wrong," he said, after a long moment of contemplation.

The door's face twisted into what might have been a smile. "Ah, an interesting point of view."

"Am I right?" Jace asked.

"Right... wrong... who am I to say? I am just a 'door.'" It laughed slowly, the lines of its face beginning to fade and shift again.

"Wait, come back. I need to get in there." He reached out his hand, pressing it against the door once more. This time, the white raven ring touched the wood.

The face shifted back to life. "Hello," it said, as if the entire conversation hadn't happened. "Have you come to hear a riddle?"

"No, I need to enter."

"Oh yes, he is quite young."

"What does that mean?" Jace asked, frustration creeping into his voice.

"Hmmm, indeed. Troubling times. I see..."

"Who are you talking to?" Great, he thought, now I'm arguing with a senile door.

"Oh, I see. Yes," it said. "In this case, I believe we can make an exception."

Suddenly the key, still resting in the lock, turned, and the door swung open with a whispering creak, releasing a breath of cool air laden with the scent of forgotten secrets and centuries-old dust.

The face and the voice were gone.

"Okay... not going to question that one," Jace muttered, peering into the room beyond. It was a cathedral of relics, an enormous hall where towering shelves loomed like the columns of an ancient temple. Each shelf was crammed with artifacts that hummed and flickered, casting ghostly glows and spectral shadows.

"Here goes nothing," Jace said and stepped into the darkness beyond, his Dark Vision barely piercing the gloom. Behind him, the door swung shut with a finality that sent a shiver through his bones.

The air thrummed with dormant power, as if the very walls pulsed with ancient magic. In the far reaches of the room, a faint light glimmered, its source hidden in the depths of the vast chamber, teasing Jace with its elusive glow.

His footsteps echoed as he ventured deeper, the sound swallowed by the surrounding vastness. The room felt as if it existed outside of time, a place where the ordinary rules did not apply. His eyes roved over the endless rows of items, each one strange and unique, each whispering its own story. There were swords and shields, old and tarnished, yet gleaming with enchantment. Strange orbs and crystals pulsed with a life of their own. Ancient books rustled as if whispered to by unseen winds.

Beside him, Pik flitted about, casting a gentle luminescence on the objects it passed. The wisp moved with curiosity, darting from artifact to artifact. It paused at a delicate amulet, its light intensifying momentarily before moving on, as if sensing the power it contained. Together, they walked deeper into the labyrinth of shelves, guided by a faint, almost imperceptible pull.

Finally, they arrived at a shelf where Pik hummed a little louder than it had with the rest. Jace's gaze was drawn to a small, unassuming box nestled among larger, more ostentatious artifacts. It was plain, made of dark wood, but it pulsed with a quiet, potent energy. This was the box Persephone had described.

Jace reached out and lifted the box with care. It was surprisingly light, almost as if it were empty. He glanced at Pik, who hovered nearby, a soft luminescence casting gentle shadows on the walls. The lid of the box was adorned with an intricate carving of a tree, its branches winding gracefully over the surface. With deliberate precision, he pried it open.

Inside, nestled in a bed of black velvet, five pomegranate seeds lay, glowing softly with a deep, rich red, as if each one harbored its own ember of ancient fire. Their light pulsed in time with the room's thrum, each beat infusing the air with an unsettling blend of foreboding and anticipation. Jace's breath caught, an icy shiver tracing his spine as he glimpsed the profound power these seeds held.

With a steady hand, Jace plucked a seed from the box, its warmth seeping into his fingers. He closed the lid with deliberate care, placing it back in its place as if it contained a sleeping beast. As he slipped the seed into his pocket, a low, resonant hum reverberated through the cavernous room, reminiscent of a distant thunderclap or the sigh of a restless spirit. He cast a wary glance at Pik, eyes shadowed with the weight of unspoken fears.

"What is that?" he whispered, his voice barely more than a breath.

Pik's glow flickered, the wisp's light pulsing with frantic agitation.

The room was cloaked in a dim, eerie glow, casting long, sinister shadows that twisted down the central aisle. It wasn't just the light that unnerved him—a haunting melody reverberated through the air, bypassing his ears to thrum directly in his mind. He focused on it, feeling a violent force clamp down on his thoughts, dragging him into a trance-like state.

Drawn forward, he staggered toward a door at the end of the aisle. Its edges shimmered faintly, growing ever brighter as he approached. The door was a solid black monolith, devoid of handles or any defining features, a void swallowing the burgeoning light around it. Every cell in his body felt the pull, an inexorable force drawing him closer. His hand, almost of its own volition, reached out and slipped through the inky surface.

Pik buzzed and whined, a high-pitched, frantic sound, tugging at his robes in a desperate bid to pull him back. But he didn't stop. He couldn't. He stepped through the darkness, the sensation akin to moving through a waterfall—raw power and energy hammering against him.

And then it was gone. He was on the other side.

More than merely seeing it with his eyes, he felt it with his very essence. Intoxicating. Overwhelming. It beckoned him closer, his hand rising toward the scintillating lights.

Before him stood a towering column of pure white light, alive with a pulsating, unearthly glow. Souls flowed within the beam in an endless stream, their ethereal forms entwining and ascending.

The light fractured into a spectrum of colors before coalescing back into pure white, splintering off into various pathways. Blinding. His soul sense activated involuntarily, overwhelmed by the sheer volume of soul energy around him.

His eyes locked onto the column of light ahead, its surface undulating with a pulsating, unearthly glow. Within the beam, countless souls spiraled upward, their ethereal forms entwining and separating as they ascended.

The energy was overwhelming, almost palpable. Mesmerizing. Yet, something was wrong. He sensed it—a discordant note amidst the harmony, like an engine running too hot, gears straining beyond their limits.

Jace's steps faltered, each one a battle between his will and the magnetic pull of the light. Pik bounced furiously at his side, trying to break his trance. But Jace couldn't resist; his hand reached out, shaking, toward the pulsating light.

A primal instinct clawed at his resolve, urging him to pull back. Glancing down, he saw blood trickling from where the raven ring cut into his skin. He didn't care. Each step drew him deeper into the light.

His breath hitched as a sense of wrongness crept into his bones. The vortex thrummed with frantic energy, ready to break. His steps grew heavier, each one a struggle. Pik finally broke through the inky darkness, flashing into his face and knocking him back slightly. The moment was enough to snap him out of his reverie, letting him glimpse the edges of reality.

He fought against the pull, Pik swirling around him, frantic. The wisp's glow was a desperate attempt to break through the trance that held Jace captive. The light sang with a soothing tone, like a distant choir, but beneath the harmony lay a faint whisper, the murmuring of countless souls passing through. Despite Pik's efforts, Jace found himself drawn inexorably toward the light, his hand lifting of its own accord, trembling as it reached out.

The moment his fingers brushed the glow, a violent jolt of pain arced through his arm, electric and unforgiving. He didn't care. He wouldn't stop. This was right. This was perfect. The agony intensified, as if the glow was tearing at his very essence. His aether drained away, slipping through his grasp like water.

His hand convulsed, shaking violently, and then, with a strength he didn't know it possessed, it yanked him backward, sending him crashing to the floor. The light was blinding, a white-hot flash that seared his vision, snapping him back to reality with cruel clarity.

The shock rippled through his arm, leaving him gasping, clutching his chest as his heart pounded like a war drum. In that blinding brilliance, he swore he saw the silhouette of wings, fleeting and ephemeral.

Stumbling back, the surrounding room sharpened into stark clarity, every detail painfully vivid. He fell, scrambling across the floor, past undulating black waves that seemed to reach for him, and into the relative safety of the Lost Archives.

Forcing himself into the hall, he slammed the chamber door shut, locking it with wavering hands. He sat there, breathless, heart racing, the residual energy crackling in the air, tingling against his skin like a swarm of invisible insects.

Jace's breaths came in ragged gasps, each one a struggle as he fought to steady himself. His hand, now a bleeding mess, throbbed with a relentless ache. He clenched his jaw, waiting as long as he dared, the pain anchoring him to the present moment. Finally, he stood, each step measured as he made his way back to Persephone.

"Touch nothing. Great going, Jace," he muttered to himself.

Chapter 8
Memories of Spring

When Jace returned to Persephone, his hand, though still seeping, no longer poured with blood, bound hastily in a strip torn from his robe. Her eyes, sharp with curiosity, followed his approach.

Humidity clung to Jace's skin as he stepped into the alcove. The damp soil beneath his feet gave off a rich, earthy scent, while the sweet fragrance of blooming flowers danced in his nostrils. But amidst these pleasant scents, he also detected the metallic tang of his blood.

As he made his way further into the alcove, it felt as though he had entered an underground rainforest. Above him, a lush canopy dripped with vibrant greens and golden hues. Thick vines hung like beaded curtains, swaying gently in the cool breeze that carried the refreshing aroma of damp earth and blooming flowers. And there, upon a throne woven from leaves and branches, sat Persephone, queen of this verdant realm.

But it wasn't just the sights and smells that captivated Jace. The alcove was alive with the sounds of nature—the gentle pitter-patter of rain on leaves, the soft rustling of vines and plants, and the occasional chirping of birds or buzzing of insects. As he approached Persephone, the plants seemed to part and make way for him, their thorns moving aside as if bowing to his presence.

"Get into a little trouble?" she asked.

"You could say that," he replied with a frown.

She remained calm, but Jace could feel the intensity of her gaze, anxiousness lurking beneath the surface, a storm beneath her calm facade. "Did you get what I requested?" she asked.

Jace reached into his pocket, pulling out the single seed. He briefly entertained the idea of holding it hostage until she gave him answers, but a nagging feeling warned him it was a bad idea—probably on par with the time he thought a neon headband was a good look during his brief stint in school. Some mistakes, he mused, you just don't repeat.

He handed her the seed, hoping this wasn't another such misstep.

Quest Update
>A Simple Fetch Quest - Quest Complete
>See Persephone to claim your reward.

"Thank you," she said, her voice as soft as rustling leaves. Before Jace could see where she put it, the seed vanished into one of her gown's many folds. She turned her attention back to him.

"What happened to your hand?"

"I touched something."

She sighed, "Let me see it." She took his hand in hers, her skin soft and cool, and carefully removed the bandage.

"I've tried healing it, but it won't heal all the way. Something is stopping my magic," he said.

Her eyes widened slightly as she examined the burn-like wound, noting the small cuts that resembled tiny puncture marks near Jace's raven ring. The cuts had healed, leaving only faint traces, while the burns from the light persisted.

"Of all the things to touch..." she began. "I had wondered where Hades had tucked it away."

"Tucked what away?" Jace asked.

She placed a hand on his, and a green light glowed deeply, battling against the burn. The pain was sharp, but he didn't pull back. She concentrated, her energy pushing through, finally overcoming the resistance.

"There, all better," she said, letting go. His hand was now unblemished, with fresh skin in place.

"Thank you." He paused. "What was that thing?"

"The burn you experienced was not merely on your hand but etched into your very soul. That's why you lacked the strength to heal it on your own.

And there's only one thing capable of inflicting such a wound—the Eternal Passage."

"Eternal Passage?"

Persephone's eyes, deep pools of ageless wisdom, met his. "It was created by Hephaestus to aid Hades in guiding souls. Think of it as a massive sorting system. There are more of them now than there used to be. Modifications were needed when travelers started arriving. I'm not personally involved, but you hear things, being the wife of the lord of the underworld and all." Her voice carried the weight of centuries, her words both a comfort and a warning.

"Why did it feel like it was pulling me in?" Jace's voice wavered, unease coloring his words.

"Now that is odd," she murmured, her brow furrowing as if trying to solve an ancient riddle. The scent of pomegranates filled the air, mingling with the earthy aroma of the underworld.

"Something felt wrong with it. Does it ever break down?" He glanced at his hand, still marveling at the new, unblemished skin.

"Unheard of," she replied, a touch of incredulity in her tone. "Not to say it has always worked perfectly. There were some mishaps with the first few Travelers' respawns, I believe. But it is perfectly safe. It might be your Mostly Dead status having some effect there. It likely had trouble determining if you belonged to it, or yourself."

Jace nodded, his thoughts swirling with the implications.

"And now, for your end of the bargain?" His words came out sharper than he intended, but Persephone only smiled.

Persephone's sigh was a breath from another world, the breath of a forgotten tale. "Quite right, I owe you that. I will answer three questions that you ask, and one that you will not."

Jace considered this for a long moment before finally speaking. "What is causing our inability to log out, and is it permanent?"

"That is technically two questions." She smiled, the curve of her lips playful. "But I will allow it."

She paused, her gaze drifting as if peering through the very seams of reality. "I can only share what I know. This isn't the first time it's happened. The last occurrence is beyond the reach of our oldest records and the memories of the living, yet it wasn't before the Age of the Gods. What causes it lies beyond our control, as inevitable as the tides or the sun's journey across the sky as it circles the earth."

Jace remained silent. For all he knew, here the sun really did rotate around the Earth.

"A connection will come again, but not in the way you might hope or guess. I allowed both questions because, for this, I can only answer each partially due to the rules imposed upon me. But I can say, the answers lie in the question. And the question is wrapped around a single word: Convergence."

"What is a Convergence?" he asked.

"Ah, indeed. That question is a dangerous one, one that may end you for asking it, or it may save your life and those of all you know and love. But the answer I cannot provide."

Silence stretched between them, thick and tangible.

"Now, I know you have other questions. You have two remaining."

"You said you know something that could protect my secret, even if Hades does not. What is that?"

She smiled, her fingers brushing against the ring on Jace's hand. "What do you know of your ring?" she asked.

"Mostly that it pecks at me when it thinks I'm being stupid. And it helps me from time to time, but not when I ask it to, only when it feels like it."

Her smile widened. "Yes, that would be true. Have you seen the Thunderbird with Archmage Theon Laviette?"

Jace recalled the battle, the Archmage's staff with the bird head, and nodded.

"Your ring is similar, though not truly a ring at all. Do you know what a familiar is?"

Jace thought back to his primer knowledge. "A paired being, usually an animal or mythical entity, that allies to a Traveler or Citizen."

"Yes, good. You sound just like a skill book. That's a fine definition, but it's far from what a familiar truly is." She paused, letting the silence stretch, heavy with unspoken truths. "A familiar can be many things, but above all, it is a partner along a similar soul path, a companion in the journey of personal evolution. It cannot exist in this plane on its own but does so through a bond. When you picked up this ring, it chose you. And your soul chose it back."

The ring thrummed with life, a pulse of awareness that had always been there but now felt even more potent. Silver feathers shimmered along its surface, preening under the dim light as if they knew they were being watched. Jace turned it slowly, captivated by the ethereal sheen dancing across his vision.

"This ring," she continued, "has a mind and a soul of its own."

Jace's brow furrowed. "Then why didn't it leap off my finger? Why didn't it help me when the Dark One attacked?"

Persephone's eyes glittered with an enigmatic light. "Are you quite sure she didn't?" she murmured, letting the words hang in the air. "Trust," she continued softly, "is a delicate thing, Jason. It is not demanded; it is earned through patience and understanding. A familiar reveals itself in time, as the bond is built."

"You say this will help me keep my secret? How?"

"Much like the boon Hades gave upon you, shielding your soul from prying eyes, this familiar possesses similar capabilities. She can cloak your mind and soul from even Hades himself, and perhaps from gods greater than he, though such powers are rare indeed." Persephone's words flowed like an ancient river, smooth and enveloping.

"But for this to happen, you must forge a deeper connection. As you strengthen your bond, her strength will become yours, and yours will become hers, intertwining your very lives."

Jace felt the ring's weight, its presence both comforting and daunting. "Right now, she is at her weakest, her connection with you uncertain and thin. Strengthen that bond, and she will prove a powerful ally."

Persephone's voice softened, a hint of nostalgia creeping in. "This familiar, this ring, is one I have known before. She is strong-willed and has only ever had one partner. It is rare for familiars to separate, and rarer still for them to choose another. But it can happen when the paths of the souls diverge too greatly."

She looked at Jace, her gaze piercing. "She is known as White Raven and was bound to one other before you. The greatest and most powerful protégé Hades has ever had. His last Chosen, until you. I believe you know, deep in your heart, of whom I speak."

Jace's voice sank to a low, resonant tone, barely audible yet heavy with resolve. He didn't need to say the words—he knew them as surely as he knew his name. But he had to give them life, to hear them aloud, if only for himself. "The Dark One."

His mind reeled with questions, a cacophony clamoring for answers. Who was the Dark One truly? Why had Hades chosen him? Where would he find a way back to Earth? And then, the less selfish questions: How could he help his brother? What could he do for his friends? What had happened to the missing goddess, Clio, the Patron deity of the Archmage Theon?

He thought carefully, knowing he had one question left. "Choose wisely, Jason," she said.

"What are the true consequences of death for Travelers in Terra Mythica?"

She smiled, a glint of approval in her eyes. "For that, we must go back, long, long ago for you, but for me, it was merely the flutter of a butterfly's wing. Close your eyes."

Jace hesitated, then complied. He felt her hand on his shoulder and then, like a meteor streaking across the sky, they plummeted toward the earth. Just before they hit the ground, they hovered, suspended in a moment of surreal calm. Persephone gently touched down with bare feet, as if the earth itself welcomed her. Jace, not quite as graceful, tumbled to the floor, his limbs flailing in all directions, ending in a tangled heap.

When he finally stood and dusted himself off, he took in their surroundings.

A young man sat reading a book under a tree, his dark eyes peering through thick glasses. Nearby, a woman with jet-black hair sparred with a man who bore a large scar running the length of his face. Her smile was genuine and full, a beacon of warmth that tugged at something deep within Jace's memory. She reminded him of someone, someone he couldn't quite name.

"Where are we?" Jace asked, still disoriented.

"A memory of Spring, nearly eight hundred years ago," Persephone replied softly. "Don't worry, they cannot see or hear us. We are but a forgotten breeze in a lost moment in time. Long before he was the Dark One, he was known as Errikos."

Jace studied the man with renewed scrutiny, his eyes narrowing as he took in every detail. How could this man be the source of so much pain and terror across Mythica?

The woman bounded up toward the man lounging on a blanket beneath a gnarled, ancient oak tree. He snapped shut the book, its title lost to a smudge of ink. His brow furrowed as he looked up, a bemused expression playing across his face.

"Are you going to sit there and read all day?" she chided, grabbing his hand and dragging him up with a playful groan. She thrust a dull practice sword into his hands.

"There's so much to learn about this place," he protested, glancing longingly at his abandoned book. "Aren't you fascinated by its history, its lore? I still don't understand how they managed to weave such intricate backstory into everything."

"I'm fascinated by how you still haven't managed to beat me in a single sword fight," she smirked, twirling her own practice sword.

"Oh, but I thought you loved me for my mind, not my might," he countered, a twinkle in his eye.

"And you love me for my essence of surprise," she said, lunging forward with her sword. He blocked her attack, his face set in a mask of concentration, a smile playing at his lips.

"As you wish, m'lady. Prepare to be awed, inspired, and amazed," he intoned, looking upward as if searching for the perfect words. "Enchanted and enthralled," he added, a touch of poetry in his voice.

"Come on, fight or talk," she challenged, and they clashed swords in a flurry of playful, yet earnest, combat. Their movements were fluid, almost dance-like, reminiscent of a scene from an old tale where words and blades were equally sharp.

The fight continued, swords clanging, until he managed to fling her weapon from her hands. Triumph shone in his eyes, but she stepped closer, her gaze smoldering. He lowered his sword, entranced, giving her the opening she needed. With a swift move, she grasped his wrist, disarming him, and sent his sword flying.

They stood for a moment, breathing heavily, eyes locked in a mix of challenge and something deeper. Then they grappled, hand to hand, tumbling to the soft grass, laughter mingling with the rustle of leaves.

"Why are we here?" Jace asked, the scene fading like mist.

"To truly know the present, to understand it, one must sometimes look to the past," Persephone replied, her voice echoing with ancient wisdom.

Persephone continued her tale, her voice weaving through the fabric of time. The world around them blurred, scenes flickering past like pages in an ancient, enchanted tome.

Errikos sat cross-legged on the rough wooden floor, an array of flickering candles casting dancing shadows in the dimly lit room. In his hands, a large, weathered book bound in thick, worn leather. He muttered ancient incantations under his breath, tracing intricate symbols in the air with fluid, practiced fingers.

Jace watched as years flickered by in moments, unnoticed by time as he immersed himself in the mysterious realm of spells and enchantments.

In the next heartbeat, he stood beside Hades, the god's presence looming like a midnight fog. Their conversation was a murmur, like whispers carried on the wind, their voices muffled as if submerged in water.

The scene shifted again, revealing Errikos in combat practice. His face was a mask of fierce determination as he moved with the grace of a dancer, his spells weaving through the air like threads of light.

"With Hades' guidance, Errikos ascended to great power, brushing against the threshold of Etherium Rank, even then."

The memories unfurled like an ancient scroll, revealing Errikos in moments of triumph and introspection. His journey was a dance between light and shadow, his path interwoven with the very essence of Mythica. Jace watched, captivated, as the tapestry of Errikos' life unfolded before him, each thread a fateful choice that wove the path to his downfall.

In one scene, Errikos stood atop a mountain, the world sprawling beneath him, his eyes reflecting both the burden of his power and the depth of his solitude. The next moment, he was in the heart of battle, black flames swirling around him as he carved through his enemies with a grace that was almost otherworldly.

"Errikos became the greatest of Hades' Chosen, but even the purest hearts can become twisted." The Obsidian Shard he bore glinted darkly, a symbol of his allegiance and might.

Jace looked more closely at the Shard that Errikos wielded. "I thought there were only six types of shards. Is that one different?"

"Six common ones, yes," Persephone replied. "But there are others, rarer and bearing far greater costs."

Persephone snapped her fingers, and the world spun: day to night, night to day, faster and faster, as countless Springs flew by. Then, with a dizzying halt, the world was still again.

"But even the Chosen of Hades eventually age, and their stories may wind to a close."

They stood outside a quaint cabin, its windows offering a glimpse into a world untouched by the cruelty of time. Inside, an elderly man with skin wrinkled from age and laughter sat beside his wife. Her long white hair draped across her back, fingers deftly weaving it into a bun. The couple, sipping tea and nestled by the fire, embodied serene contentment, the warmth of their companionship staving off the chill of the setting sun.

"Have you ever wondered why Hades has no other Chosen?" Persephone asked.

He looked closer through the window and saw white robes draped over a rocking chair, adorned with silver stitching of a raven - one of Hades' many symbols.

The scene's peace was shattered as smoke curled up from the northern hill, followed by the ominous flicker of torches. An army marched behind them, dark and menacing, a storm poised to engulf the tranquility of the cabin.

Chapter 9
Shadows of Terra Mythica

"Hades had Chosen before. Many, in fact. They were all led by one man—this man, Errikos."

Jace watched as the army approached.

Errikos, now an old man with silver in his hair but steel in his gaze, opened the door to his humble cabin, leaning against the door frame for support. His movements were deliberate, his eyes sharp. The leader of the approaching army, a tall figure in opulent armor, sneered at the sight of Errikos' simple home.

"Old man, we require shelter and provisions. Your cabin will suffice," the leader declared, his voice dripping with arrogance and authority, echoing through the forest as if he owned it.

Errikos, a mischievous glint in his eye, regarded the intruders with a bemused expression. "I believe we have room for some of your men, and food enough for maybe four. But I'm afraid we were not prepared to serve two dozen."

The leader's eyes narrowed, and he stepped forward with a menacing air. "We will be taking what we need, old man. Step aside." He moved to push past Errikos but found himself halted by an unexpected, unyielding force.

Errikos leaned casually against the doorway, his smile never wavering. "This cabin? It is far too quaint, with rooms far too small to fit an ego such as yours. Best you move along."

The captain's face reddened with anger, his hand instinctively moving towards his sword. "Do you know who I am? I am Captain Theros, representative of the King!"

Errikos shrugged, inspecting his fingernails with a bored expression. "The King, you say? How is old Graybeard these days? Still as constipated as ever? I told him, more prunes, fewer biscuits, but does he listen?"

Theros' eyes blazed with fury. "You insolent wretch! I will teach you respect!"

Errikos yawned, stretching as if waking from a nap. "Respect, you say? I'm always open to new experiences. Honey," he called back into the cabin, "this fine gentleman wants to show me respect."

"I said, I'll teach you…"

Just then, Errikos' wife emerged from the cabin, her sharp eyes taking in the scene. "Oh, darling, shouldn't you invite our guests in? It's not every evening we host such… distinguished visitors," she said.

Errikos grinned. "Of course, my love. But you know how you despise cleaning up after a brawl. Who am I kidding?" he placed a friendly hand on Theros' shoulder, "I do all the cleaning. She's just terrible at it."

"What are you blabbering on about? And get your filthy hands off me." The captain's face turned a deep, livid magenta. "Step aside, you…"

"Guilty as charged, I'm afraid," she said, nodding with a mischievous smile. "I really am no good at cleaning at all. But, if they insist on staying, I suppose we could give them a proper welcome."

With her approval, Errikos turned to face Theros and his men. "Alright then, gentlemen. I was going to let you off easy, but you heard the missus."

The soldiers surged forward, but Errikos remained unfazed, a statue of calm amidst the storm. As they closed in, his eyes darkened, and his silhouette seemed to ripple and twist around him. With a flick of his wrist, tendrils of inky black energy lashed out, sending the first wave of soldiers sprawling.

The fight erupted into a whirlwind of chaos. Despite his age, Errikos moved with deadly grace, gliding through his attackers like a shade. Dark power crackled around him, repelling and disarming his foes with a mere gesture.

Theros, seeing his men falter, charged at Errikos, his sword gleaming menacingly in the dim light. Errikos sidestepped, a smirk playing on his lips. "Is that the best you've got, Captain? I've seen children swing sticks with more finesse."

Their clash was fierce, Errikos dodging and parrying with an almost playful ease. But the weight of numbers began to tell. Even as he fought them off, his breath grew ragged, and a gash on his arm bled freely before the skin knit itself back together.

Amidst the chaos, an archer took aim at Errikos, his arrow flying true. But in a cruel twist, it struck Errikos' wife. She fell with a soft cry, her hand reaching out towards him. Yet, oddly, she didn't seem to mind. A wicked smile crept over her face.

If Jace was honest, he wasn't sure if the older couple was cuter or just more terrifying in their age.

But then, the scene began to blur, like an old, worn-out record. The edges of reality frayed, and everything grew foggy, the outcome lost to the encroaching haze.

Jace strained to catch fragments of their words, but they slipped away, whispers tangled in the memories of trees, grass, and spring. Persephone's voice, heavy with countless seasons, came gravely.

"Even nature can forget. My trees and leaves of Spring may hold memories of the past, but they sometimes fade and distort."

As the scene cleared and the memories sharpened, the evening had grown late and much had changed. Errikos crouched on the floor, cradling a lifeless body - his wife. His sobs were soft, but each one seemed to tear through the silence like a knife.

The flippant amusement that once lit his face was now replaced by a mask of grief and haunting emptiness. Small flames flickered nearby, casting shadows that danced like spectral hands. The soldiers had vanished, leaving no trace behind. Time blurred, moments lost in the haze. The cabin smoldered, and with a sudden, deafening crash, an explosion of fire consumed the cottage, transforming it into a blazing inferno.

A guttural roar erupted from Errikos as he clutched her still body to his chest. Rage and sorrow intertwined, igniting a dark power within him. His voice echoed with a terrifying resonance, shaking the very air. Dusk coalesced around him, the temperature plummeting, as if the world itself mourned with him.

The cabin, once a symbol of their peaceful life, now stood as a grim monument to the wrath of an old man pushed beyond his limits. On his knees, Errikos leaned over his wife's body, his shoulders shaking with sobs. He screamed, the words muffled and distorted by his agony. He screamed again, the words heavy with despair. Whatever he was saying was lost to time.

Jace wanted to rush in, to help, but they were mere figments in a memory. Persephone snapped her fingers, and the world shifted to another Spring.

The world flashed forward, plunging into darkness. It was night, and a hooded figure stood, waves of dark fire undulating around a still form, robes billowing in the wind. The moon barely pierced through the thick clouds, casting an eerie, silvery light.

Jace leaned in as Persephone spoke, each word a thread in the dark fabric of the past.

"He lost something that day," Persephone whispered, her voice a shadow in the night. "His sanity fractured. And he turned on Hades and all that life stands for."

"Hades saw in Errikos a kindred spirit, someone to share the burdens of the underworld. But there was something special about Errikos - he was nearly immortal by our world's standards because he was one of the first Travelers."

"How is that possible?" Jason puzzled over the notion. "You said it was nearly eight hundred years ago."

Faces of darkness, of evil, of monsters and ghouls and undead flashed before him in a terrifying montage. Each one was more grotesque and horrifying than the last. Their eyes glowed with malevolence, their forms twisted and contorted in ways that defied nature. They loomed in the darkness, a parade of nightmares brought to life.

Persephone's voice carried on, soft yet piercing. "Errikos wandered through time, collecting the dark, the forsaken, and the forgotten. He became a beacon for the wretched, a magnet for the lost souls of the underworld."

The images grew more intense -more vivid. Jace could almost feel the cold breath of the undead, hear the whisper of ancient curses, and smell the decay and rot that clung to these twisted beings.

"And in his madness, his true powers twisted," Persephone continued. "A distorted power born of despair and darkness, a power that Hades himself could not control."

The scene shifted, the hooded figure raising a hand, dark flames erupting from his fingertips. Errikos' face, twisted with a haunting emptiness, was illuminated by the fire's glow.

Persephone's voice faded into a chilling silence, leaving Jace with the weight of a history steeped in shadow and sorrow.

And then, with a whisper of wind and a blink, Jace was back in the garden alcove, Persephone standing before him as he opened his eyes.

The gears in his mind turned, piecing together the puzzle. Terra Mythica's time dilation—forty-two years there for every year on Earth—meant that eight hundred years in that world equated to just twenty back home. That was right around the time Terra Mythica hit the market, the same time when John Rearden vanished.

A chill traced a serpentine path up Jace's neck. Could it be? Was Errikos truly John Rearden? Was the Dark One the architect of this entire grim affair? It seemed impossible. When the Dark One had spoken to him, his voice had dripped with venom for John Rearden.

Jace wasn't sure what to make of it all.

Her voice softened, layered with sorrow and old regrets. "At first, he was a paragon of virtue, his dedication earning him the reverence of mortals and gods alike. But death has a way of twisting even the purest of hearts. He became known as the Dark One, forsaking all light."

"His greatness was rivaled only by his ambition. In time, he grew restless -discontented with his role. The power he commanded in the Underworld began to consume him, hollowing him out. He rallied the other Chosen, whispering promises of greater power and unshackled freedom, and led them in rebellion against Hades."

"The Dark One wields a Word akin to yours, but while you find light and purpose, he hungers for power and dominion. His Soul Affinity is a cruel weapon, used not to liberate or guide, but to stifle and crush. He breathes a twisted half-life into the dead, marshaling hordes of the damned. Souls, trapped in their rotting vessels, claw at their prison of decayed flesh, driven to madness by their unfulfilled need for release. Errikos thrives on this torment, using dark rites to possess, to extinguish existing souls, and usurp the bodies of both Citizens and Travelers. He is an eternal night, stretching out to smother all light and hope."

Jason's eyes widened, disbelief warring with dread. "How is that possible? How can he possess a Traveler?"

Her response came with a heavy sigh, burdened by ancient sorrow. "I have not often seen this directly, but I know of ways. The Traveler is pushed into a corner of their mind, while their darker feelings are pulled forward. At first, he doesn't directly control them, but urges them, playing on their fears and failures. And then slowly, over time, the darkness inside them grows as they give more and more power to him, the shadow in their mind."

Persephone's tone grew darker, the twilight creeping into her words. "When Errikos betrayed us, the rebellion was a nightmare, unspeakable horrors almost realized. The Underworld descended into chaos, souls adrift like lost echoes, and the fragile balance of life and death teetered on the edge of oblivion. He wasn't alone; many turned on us, for power or greed, or misplaced spite. Hades, wounded by the treachery of those he held dear, fought back with a desperation that bordered on madness."

Jace glimpsed the torment in Persephone's eyes, a fleeting echo of the ghosts she carried within. "Hades triumphed, but victory came at a steep price. He banished the Dark One, casting him out beyond our reach. Since that day, Hades has never chosen another."

"Why not imprison him in the Underworld, like he did with... others?" Jace asked, the weight of his question dawning too late. A tempest flared in her gaze, swiftly stilled.

"There are truths you have yet to understand, Chosen. Imprisoning him would have been futile. The closer he is to the Underworld, the stronger he grows."

Persephone's gaze softened, her words now tinged with a fragile hope. "Hades' power is immense, far greater than most can comprehend. Even the greatest of gods will one day pass through the Eternal Passage and be tended to by him. This is partly why his brothers harbor such enmity for him, their jealousy cloaked in disdain. Hades sees in you a potential for balance, a chance to rectify the mistakes of the past."

Her eyes brimmed with a feeling of profound sorrow. "Hades is not as indifferent as he appears. Once, he had a kind heart, but centuries of ruling over souls have turned it to stone. He selects those who show potential for goodness, hoping they will restore balance to his domain. Yet, many succumb to their own darkness and desires."

A shiver coiled through Jace. "The first Chosen tried to usurp Hades' throne," he said, more a statement than a query.

Persephone nodded. "To bring balance. You have been chosen by Hades to tread both the path of the Underworld and the path of power. Whether you use your strength for good or succumb to temptation like those before you is up to you."

"But what does all of this have to do with Travelers and death?" Jace pressed.

"The reason for the war, why the Dark One sided with the void, and how he fell so far... There is a cost to all things, even death. It is believed he paid that price, a burden so immense it shattered him."

"He was driven insane from respawn?" Jace thought of Thistle's uncle.

"And he's still out there? Inflicting his twisted dreams on everyone here? That means... Thistle was right. Excelsior is covering this up. Maybe they cut off the logout because they didn't want people to find out. Or..."

"Shhhh, child," Persephone whispered. "There will be time enough for theories later. But Excelsior could no more cause this than they could extinguish the moon."

She nodded slowly; her gaze piercing into Jason's soul. Her voice, barely more than a whisper, echoed through the chamber with an ethereal resonance. "Now, Jason Rolander, you have asked me your third and final question. And, as promised, I will answer a question you have not yet dared to ask."

The unspoken question nagged at his heart, a specter lurking in the recesses of his mind. He could feel its weight. A terrible curiosity mingled with dread, threatening to unravel him.

She leaned closer, her breath a mere sigh against the stillness. Her lips parted, and a single word fell, laden with inevitability. "Yes."

"What is the question?"

"The answer that you seek is... yes." Her eyes, deep and knowing, seemed to see through him. "I will not utter the question, for it is not mine to ask. When you are ready, you will speak it. You know it even now, though you may not admit it to yourself."

Her words wrapped around him, binding him in their web.

"But enough of questions and answers," she said, her voice rising with a newfound levity. "You've asked far more than your share. If I were one of my relatives, I might make a fuss about that. But I like you, Chosen. And it is time for you to go."

The room shimmered and blurred, reality-bending at the edges. Her words carried the weight of an unspoken promise reverberating through the space. Jace knew this moment would linger in his mind—a turning point in his journey, a crossroads where fate and destiny intertwined. For what end, he couldn't yet fathom.

He turned, dazed, toward the entrance of the alcove. "Oh, and Jason," she called after him, her voice soft yet firm, "it's important to fight, gain EXP, and rank up for what's to come. But don't forget the little things. When combined just right, mixed just so, they create something much greater."

Jace paused, half-turning. "Are all gods fond of cryptic clues?"

She laughed, the sound like wind chimes in a summer breeze. "A hazard of the job, I'm afraid. Now go." Her tone shifted suddenly, urgency threading through her words as if she heard something far off. "Go."

An invisible force propelled him out of the alcove. The walls closed in; the alcove vanishing seamlessly into the stone. Disoriented, he stumbled, but quickly regained his footing. The cavernous halls twisted and turned, and Jace's heart raced. Pik glowed beside him, guiding him through the path.

Several minutes later, they emerged at the dock, where the ferryman waited in silent anticipation, his boat a dark silhouette against the shimmering water.

As Jace headed back to the land of the living, the ethereal landscape around him shimmered with hues of twilight. He took a moment, raising his hand to inspect the White Raven ring more closely, noticing something new. A series of inscriptions along the inside band glowing softly, forming a faint, repeating pattern. A prompt appeared.

Inspection Success
    Familiar: The White Raven
    Bond: Rank One

This familiar has been drained over countless ages since the loss of its last master. To fully reawaken, it needs its mana replenished. Would you like to set an automatic draw on your mana? 10% of your mana will be unavailable until the recovery is complete.

Mana Replenished: 0 out of 7,850,350

Accept | Reject

The number was staggering. Yet, Jace felt that the choice was clear. Without hesitation, he focused his intent and selected [Accept]. Instantly, the ring vibrated softly, a gentle hum that resonated through his hand, an expression of gratitude.

The raven's wings unfurled with a graceful shift, poised to take flight from the ring, before adjusting and settling back down, motionless once more.

Chapter 10
Master of Shards

Jace spotted his friends Dex, Ell, Alice, and Thistle gathered near the massive golden archway leading to Zeus' Hall. The archway, adorned with intricate carvings, stood as a beacon of ancient grandeur and power. It opened into a small clearing nestled against the towering cliff of the mountain, the bright afternoon sun high in the sky, casting a warm, golden light that bathed the world in a soft glow.

Dex, tall and perpetually unkempt, leaned against the stone, his bag bulging with alchemical supplies. Ell's eyes sparkled with mischief as she examined a peculiar flower growing nearby. Alice stood, seemingly lost in thought, while Thistle perched on a low boulder, his gaze sharp and attentive.

The small clearing was encircled by jagged rocks, making Jace question how the entire class could possibly fit there. There was nowhere to sit, only a series of thick ropes stretching from a metal fastening in the ground and disappearing into the clouds above.

"Make any progress at the library?" Jace asked as he approached.

"Best if we show you," Ell said with a cryptic look.

"After Shards Class," Dex added, adjusting his bag with a shrug.

"After potions," Alice interjected, not looking up from the old tome she was studying. "We have back-to-backs.

From the ropes, a large wooden shuttle with short walls and brass bindings appeared in the sky above. The cable cart was a marvel of engineering, with gears and pulleys intricately woven into its design. Ornate brass fittings gleamed in the sunlight, and thick, sturdy ropes crisscrossed its structure. The cart descended with an ancient creak, a wooden relic groaning its complaint before landing with a heavy thump. Inside, Professor Tanner Frost, Master of Shards, threw open the door with theatrical impatience.

"Well, come on. We don't have all day," she barked, her eyes flickering with the kind of urgency that made students scurry.

The students exchanged nervous glances as they filed in. Above, the thick rope coiled into the heavens, swallowed by a whirl of clouds. The cart shuddered and groaned as it began its ascent, pulling them higher and higher into the sky.

Dex turned a shade of green, his knuckles white as he clung to the side. Jace tried to focus on anything but the dizzying height, his stomach churning with every lurch. Ell, on the other hand, was glued to the edge, her eyes sparkling with awe as the world unfolded below. Alice, determined to appear unflustered, stared straight ahead, her fingers occasionally tightening on the railing. Thistle, a fearless gnome with boundless curiosity, perched on Dex's shoulders, peering over the edge with gleeful abandon, much to Dex's distress.

Lucky for Dex, the world soon disappeared into mist as they passed through a cloud. The fog was so dense they had to squint to see each other's faces, huddling closer together.

"Oh, Jace," Alice said, diving into her satchel and emerging with something that glowed faintly purple. "I picked this up for you. It's finished."

It took a moment for Jace to recognize it: the Ward Stone she had been helping him craft.

The wooden cart creaked and swayed as it ascended the steep mountain path, suspended by a thick rope that hummed with tension, the cold wind whipping around them, carrying the scent of pine and earth.

Jace held up the Ward Stone, its surface shimmering faintly in the diffused light. "So, this Ward Stone should let me venture into Zone Three without running into too many Bronze Threes and Fours, right?" he asked, his voice steady despite the tremor in the cart.

The creature ranks, as he recalled, mirrored the Speaker ranks: Bronze One through Bronze Six, then repeating at Silver, Gold, and into the Mythic tiers of Etherium, Celestial, and Divinium. The four Protective Zones around the University acted as a cosmic sieve, filtering out the more formidable creatures. Zone One was an impenetrable sanctuary, allowing nothing more dangerous than a friendly nymph. Zone Two was home to modestly threatening creatures, where Bronze Ones and Twos roamed. Zone Three allowed for slightly more perilous encounters with creatures up to Bronze Four and, on rare occasions, a Bronze Five. Zone Four, however, was where the real danger began, occasionally letting in a Bronze Six and, on unlucky days, even a Silver One. Most of the outskirting villages were in Zone Four, while faculty housing, smaller homesteads, and farms were often found in Zone Three.

Jace felt somewhat confident he could handle a Bronze Two, maybe even a Three, without meeting an untimely end. Still, best not to tempt fate.

Alice's hair whipped in the wind as her eyes locked on Jace. "Zone Three's safer with the crystal, but you might still run into a Bronze Five if you're not careful. They're rare, but it happens."

Ell leaned against the wooden railing, her gaze sweeping the rugged landscape below. "Bronze Fives are more common in Zone Four. That's where it gets tricky. You might even see a Bronze Six or, if you're really unlucky, a Silver One. Why do you need a Zone Three Ward Stone?"

"A quest from Hades in Zone Three," Jace muttered, thinking for a moment. "Man, it is really overdue."

They all winced. Dex spoke up, "Yikes, not good to leave deity quests hanging. Heard a second year did that once... never got another quest again."

"Total exaggeration," Alice said. "I'm sure it's fine. Did it have a time sensitivity on it?"

Jace looked around awkwardly.

Alice scrunched her face. "Yeah, probably best to get that one done sooner rather than later."

"Well, now that I have this little guy," Jace said, moving the stone around in his palm, "should be simple enough."

"The Ward Stone helps," Alice said, her voice steady but cautious. "But it's not perfect. It wards off most lower-tier creatures in Zone Three, but an aggressive Bronze Five might slip through, especially if the ward weakens. Recharge it once a month."

The cart jolted over a rough patch, the mountain peak looming closer. Alice's lips curled into a faint smile. "Consider it your ticket to not dying instantly in the first five minutes."

Jace turned the crystal over in his hand, his voice barely audible over the groaning of the cart and the whispering winds. "Thanks, Alice." The mist swirled around them, thick as a shroud, but for a moment, the world felt a little less foreboding.

He thought back to the day they started making it the Ward Stone. It was only days ago, but it felt much longer. Mythica had a way of worming into your mind, altering your perception.

There had to be some side effects to the one-to-forty-two-time dilation. Maybe that was part of the problem. Or maybe it had nothing to do with that. The more time he spent logged in, even without dying, the less reality felt real. The more this felt like home. This was his home for now. The thought brought his mind back to the Ward Stone. "Uh, how much do I owe the shop for this? The ingredients, and space, and all that?"

Alice smiled faintly, a hint of awkwardness in her eyes. "Don't worry about this one. It's on me."

"No, really, I can pay." Jace opened his inventory quickly, glancing at his painfully low gold stores. The interface displayed all his university notes and any gold he'd earned from minor quests. The result: a dwindling spiral of money. Turns out he was just as bad at making money in Terra Mythica as he was on Earth.

"Jace, it's okay. I needed to practice and rank up my skills anyway. Really, it's on me. This time." She smiled, trying to reassure him.

"Just take the gift, you big dummy," Ell said, rolling her eyes.

Jace stood there awkwardly for a moment.

Living a life with nothing, Jace didn't like handouts. They were reminders of his struggles, making it harder to ask for or accept help. It wasn't until he met friends like Ell, Dex, Alice, and Thistle that he began to see not all help came from pity or with strings attached. Sometimes, kindness flowed like a river, without expectations or condescension. It was an easy kindness, strange and unsettling, yet comforting in a way he had never known, save with his brother.

"Thank you," Jace said, pulling Alice into a hug. The thought of Alex sent a pang through his heart, and he held onto her a moment longer than necessary.

Their moment was shattered by Dex's exclamation. "Oh... my... gods."

"What is it?" Alice asked, turning away, a slight pink creeping into her cheeks.

But she didn't need to ask. They all looked up, seeing the grandeur they were ascending towards. A vast, majestic mountaintop rose above the clouds, crowned with golden pillars that reached toward the heavens. The architecture was a marvel of divine craftsmanship—tall, ornate columns supporting a gleaming platform that radiated an otherworldly light. The mountain itself was a natural wonder, its flat peak stretching out like a table carved by the gods, an expanse of awe-inspiring beauty and power. They arrived at the mountaintop, breathless not just from the thinner air, but from the sheer magnificence of the sight before them.

Zeus' Hall was more of a breezeway than a hall, a colossal structure piercing the skyline with its golden columns and shimmering presence. The thin, biting air teased their hair and clothes, carrying the scent of ancient stone and distant tempests.

The mechanism jerked to a halt, and they stepped onto a large elevated outdoor platform. It was a long wooden stage with a central lectern, flanked by fifteen seats designated for judges, announcers, and duel moderators. Professor Frost stood poised at the lectern. Her sharp features and piercing gaze swept the students with an authority that was both commanding and slightly unsettling.

Clouds drifted lazily through the open air, occasionally shrouding the scene in a soft, ethereal mist before revealing the grandeur once more. The class took place on a long wooden platform, elevated twenty feet above the ground, with seats arranged in tiers rising higher still. The space, capable of seating at least two hundred, easily accommodated the fifty students.

The platform was designed for public duels, the arena-like setup a testament to the epic confrontations that had undoubtedly taken place there. The wooden platform stretched out, flanked by rows of seats that curved gracefully, ensuring every spectator had an unobstructed view of the action. Golden sunlight filtered through the clouds, casting a warm glow over the polished wood and stone as the students settled in, their eyes wide with a mixture of awe and trepidation.

"Welcome, students," Professor Tanner Frost began. Her intense eyes gleamed with an unsettling mix of wisdom and challenge, a look that could pierce through steel. With a stern face etched with the experiences of countless battles, she embodied both a gentle breeze and a brewing storm. She commanded the platform with an authority that demanded attention and respect.

"We do not normally delve into the raw combat application of Shards until the twilight weeks of your second year. However, due to recent unsettling events and the paramount need for your safety, several of my esteemed colleagues, and I have been granted approval to accelerate your training. In my class, there shall be no frivolity or dallying. We shall be plunging directly into advanced concepts, and it is imperative that you heed my every word.

Duels shall exclude direct Affinity usage. You shall commence at my command and cease at my command. Your strikes are to be confined to the arms, legs, and chest—under no circumstances shall you aim for the head. Is that understood?"

The class exchanged uncertain glances before nodding in unison.

"Excellent. Before we embark on this journey, you must first become intimately acquainted with your Shard. Normally, we would dedicate the entirety of your first year to this endeavor. Hence, I extend my apologies if some of you find yourselves adrift; Miss Eidolon, my assistant, will conduct supplementary Shard classes for those who struggle."

For the first time, Jace noticed the young woman standing beside the Professor.

Her hair, a wild mane of hazelnut curls, framed her face like a halo of untamed thoughts. Her wide, curious eyes seemed to hold entire worlds within their depths, as if the cosmos had taken residence behind her gaze. She moved with unassuming grace, the soft rustle of her presence barely noticeable, while her pen danced across the pages of her notebook as Professor Frost spoke.

"Introduce yourself, Molly," Frost prompted.

When she spoke, her words floated on the air, slightly out of sync with her lips, as if they were echoes from a place just out of reach. "Thank you. I will be available after class for any students needing additional assistance." She bowed subtly and returned to her book.

The last time Jace had seen Molly, she had been assisting Professor Brutus Ironclad, the formidable Master of Artifacts and Alchemy. He wondered if she had changed roles or was simply the overall assistant to the High Council. Molly's gaze met his briefly, a flash of recognition passing between them. For a fleeting moment, Jace thought he glimpsed a knowing look in her eyes, something hidden behind the labyrinthine halls of her mind. Then the curtain fell again, and she was once more the enigmatic assistant, her true self concealed behind a mask of scholarly duty.

"A Shard is only as powerful as the Speaker who wields it," Professor Frost said. "By now, you should have each received one from your Society. Raise your hand if you haven't."

Silence met her query; not a hand stirred.

"Good. Now, summon it."

Jace closed his eyes, feeling the innate pull, the connection deep within him. He called it forth, and his Moonstone Shard materialized in his palm, its surface shimmering like liquid silver under moonlight, catching and fracturing the ambient light into a myriad of spectral hues.

"To attune to a Shard is no light matter," she continued. "To wield a Shard is to take up arms against the Eternal End. There's a poem on Earth that captures this sentiment, I think." She paused, her voice weaving the words into the air like an incantation, "'Do not go gentle into that good night; Old age should burn and rave at close of day; Rage, rage against the dying of the light.'"

She paused, eyes gleaming with triumph, expecting a response. The students, however, sat frozen, their faces set in varied degrees of confusion, punctuated only by the occasional cough.

"Really? Nothing?" She raised an eyebrow, a hint of irritation creeping into her tone. "The history of Shards is kind of a big deal, people."

In a sudden, fluid motion, she manifested an amber gem in her hand. With a flick of her wrist, a bolt of golden energy spiraled into the air, twisting and turning in a cyclone of light that split into a thousand tiny, radiant stars, scattering across the platform in a dazzling display.

Finally, she got a reaction. The students' eyes widened, and they shared a collective gasp. Professor Frost's lips curled into a satisfied smile.

"To cultivate our aether and let it flow through us as naturally as breath, to attune to and understand a Shard of the Great Prismata, is the essence of being a Speaker. Yes, there is great power in Words. The relentless pursuit of knowledge is the path of Affinity."

She approached the panel at the base of the platform, her fingers dancing over the oversized buttons before pulling the lever with an air of practiced nonchalance. The platform responded with a low, mechanical groan, and five wooden dummies ascended from shadowy apertures, as if conjured from the depths of a forgotten dream. The floor whispered shut behind them, erasing all trace of their mysterious emergence.

"To glimpse a Word of Power is to gain an Affinity. Many do not even realize that they possess one. A mother tending to her children may wield a magic that calms them or shields them from danger. A soldier in battle might instinctively avoid the path of a lethal arrow. A scholar may discern truth from falsehood in texts. A politician may craft a lie so flawlessly that it becomes accepted as truth. These are Affinities."

She climbed the platform and stood across from three wooden dummies, with two behind her, each swaying slightly. Frost paused, letting her words settle.

"However, we would not call these individuals true Speakers, for they have not learned a true name despite having glimpsed its essence through familiarity. Though, in turn, knowing a name alone does not confer all power. Deepening one's understanding through practice and familiarity does. To know something intimately and thus to love it—this is the essence of Affinities."

"Words hold fragments of the universe's essence. When spoken with understanding, they can alter reality itself. But it is your Breath that must carry them forth, into the fabric of the universe. Breath, however, can do more than just speak. It can infuse inscriptions, animate potions, forge artifacts, or channel directly into your Shards."

She lifted the Amber Shard, its surface shimmering with an inner light. She bowed to the dummies, and they each bowed to her before pulling wooden swords from their sheaths and moving towards her.

With a flick of her wrist, a beam of golden energy lanced toward the wooden dummy, shattering it into a cascade of splinters that rained down onto the scorched floor. Swords flashed in her direction, but she sidestepped with fluid grace, almost a dance, her movements low and sweeping. Her legs wove intricate patterns just inches away from the deadly blades, until she unleashed another burst of energy, obliterating the next dummy.

In a matter of moments, each target was reduced to charred, splintered wreckage. Gasps of awe rippled through the hall, an undercurrent of whispers following in their wake.

"My Affinity may be for healing, but that does not mean my aether cannot be used for destruction," she said, her voice calm yet commanding. "What you just saw involved no Affinity, but only properly channeled aether and a strong attunement to my Shard."

Jace's eyes widened with newfound appreciation and respect.

"Remind me not to get on her bad side," Dex muttered.

"Your turn," she declared, her voice a symphony of authority and challenge. The students stiffened, eyes widening in startled apprehension. "Come on, I don't have all day," she added with a wry smile. They scrambled to obey, hastily shuffling into place. With Molly's deft assistance, they were nudged onto the platform, their Shards vibrating, sending shivers through the air.

Professor Frost glided to the control panel, her fingers a blur of elegant precision as they danced over the keys. With a series of swift commands, the platform whirred to life. Dozens of round wooden targets sprang up, each one hovering before a student.

"Feel the energy within you," she intoned, her voice wrapping around them like an incantation. "Understand its essence, and channel your aether with conviction."

The air hummed with energy and the sharp crackle of power. Sparks flew, and occasional bursts of raw magic sizzled into the sky. Amidst this chaotic ballet of aether, Jace stood, his mind a storm of doubt and desperation. He struggled to draw from his Shard, the connection elusive, slipping through his mental grasp like smoke. His heart pounded in sync with his rising panic, each failed attempt a hammer blow to his confidence.

As he watched his peers wield their Shards with apparent ease, the bitter taste of inadequacy settled in his throat. Professor Frost's words echoed louder with each failure, not as a guiding mantra but as a relentless taunt, his doubt festering like an open wound.

What would Alex do? he thought desperately, his hands trembling. He closed his eyes, seeking solace in silence. A familiar voice surfaced in his mind: Breathe. Take a moment. It's okay.

He drew a deep breath, calming his racing heart. Slowly, a flicker of connection sparked within him. Mana surged, resonating with each controlled breath. The world around him blurred as he focused solely on the bond with his Moonstone Shard.

Surrendering to the flow of mana, he guided it through his veins and into the cool, weighty Shard in his palm. A beam of twilight energy erupted, narrowly missing its mark. Adjusting his stance, he tried again. This time, the beam struck true, causing the target to burst into harmless sparks.

Encased within the Shard, a storm of mist and clouds swirled, its essence cool against his skin. Jace inhaled deeply, attuning to the resonating

Word within him. The platform faded into obscurity, leaving only the present moment and his intent. With deliberate focus, he channeled his energy into the Shard. A beam of moonlight shot forth, striking the distant target, which glowed briefly before crumbling to dust, its remnants swirling in the air. A smile touched his lips as a notification appeared before him.

Skill Unlocked
Aether Pulse - Rank One
You've taken the first step in channeling your aether through your Moonstone Shard directly. This fundamental skill is an essential tool in every Speaker's arsenal.

Chapter 11
Shards of Rage

"Excellent, Jace," Professor Frost's voice cut through the air, crisp and approving. "Let's proceed to the next phase of our training. We'll be practicing hitting moving targets. Remember, precision and control are essential."

With a sharp clap of a switch, the targets sprang to life, darting around the open space. "Focus on accuracy above power."

Jace nodded, his eyes tracking the erratic movements. Marcus, with a smirk, effortlessly hit several targets in rapid succession, looking like a peacock draped in gaudy clothing and jewelry. Jace pushed the distraction aside, channeling his determination. He hit the next three targets in quick succession, his confidence swelling with each success.

The practice continued, the platform filled with the hum of energy and the occasional cheer. Jace's concentration was broken by Professor Frost pulling another switch.

"Fine, fine. You seem to have a handle on moving targets. Now, let's up the ante." She punched two buttons and flipped another toggle, and large, reflective mirrors appeared around the platform. "These mirrors can withstand force up to advanced Adept ranks. Your task is to launch energy at them and dodge the reflected beams. This will hone your reflexes and spatial awareness. Control your power; these mirrors reflect but do not absorb."

The students positioned themselves, the wooden platform soon vibrating with the sounds of energy beams ricocheting off the mirrors. Jace aimed at his reflection, watching as the beam rebounded toward him. He dodged, narrowly escaping the searing energy, which singed the edge of his robes. He tried again, his timing improving with each attempt.

His heart raced, the thrill of the exercise fueling his resolve. Adrenaline coursed through him, sharpening his reflexes with every dodge. He glanced at his classmates, their faces etched with concentration and exhilaration.

Professor Frost moved among them, her voice a mix of guidance and encouragement. "Good, Jace. Keep it up. Control your breath, let it flow naturally."

Jace nodded, internalizing her advice. He steadied his breathing, feeling the energy flow more clearly. His movements grew more fluid, his control more precise. The mirrors' reflections became less intimidating as he adapted, each success fortifying his confidence.

As the session progressed, Jace found a rhythm, chaos transforming into a symphony of energy and motion. He felt a deep connection to his shard, the flow of mana becoming second nature. This exercise wasn't just about dodging; it was about mastering the delicate dance between power and control.

Marcus, a few meters away, angled his beam to ricochet toward another student. The unsuspecting boy yelped as the beam singed his arm.

"Marcus!" Professor Frost's voice was icy. "This exercise is not for targeting your classmates. Focus on your own task."

Marcus shrugged, his grin unrepentant. He continued with precision, keeping his reflections within his own space.

Thistle, on the other hand, struggled. Each attempt sent beams unpredictably, often too close to other students. After the third near miss, Professor Frost sighed.

"Thistle, come here," she instructed. "You'll practice on stationary targets until your control improves. We can't afford injuries due to lack of precision."

Thistle, looking dejected, obeyed, moving to a corner under Professor Frost's watchful eye. Molly joined him, offering personal coaching and support.

Jace continued, becoming more adept at predicting the reflections and dodging with increasing agility. He saw his classmates improving too, their confidence growing with each successful burst and dodge.

Perfect Practice Makes Perfect

Working with a high-rank teacher has revealed a special skill - You've unlocked the ability to combine EXP gains with simultaneous allocation through dedicated training and study. With the right tutors and practice techniques, you can earn and spend EXP to enhance specific skills and attributes efficiently.

+1 to Dexterity and Constitution

Skill Rank Up

Aether Pulse - Rank Two

Jace had never experienced a skill ranking up so quickly, and he felt a surge of pride in his progress.

After an hour of grueling training, Professor Frost flipped a switch, and the mirrors vanished into the platform. The students, breathless and glistening with sweat, gathered around her.

"Well done, everyone," Professor Frost's voice rang out, genuine approval in her tone. "You've all shown noticeable improvement—many of you exceeded my expectations. And for some, Miss Eidolon will have her hands full." A few students exchanged sheepish glances, especially Thistle.

"Now, we'll move to the last part of today's lesson: dueling," she continued, her words sparking hushed murmurs among the students. "Pair up with your nearest neighbor. We'll need two volunteers for the first round," she said, her eyes scanning the group with a hint of a challenge.

Marcus, quick to position himself nearest Jace, called out, "We'll go first."

"Very well then, Marcus and Jace. Take your positions. Everyone else, off the platform."

The students shuffled into the audience seating, quiet anticipation filling the air.

"Now, as I've said, duels shall exclude any direct Affinity usage. You will begin at my command and cease at my command or when the first person surrenders the match. Your strikes are to be confined to the arms, legs, and chest—under no circumstances shall you aim for the head. I will have no major injuries from this. Is this entirely understood?"

Both nodded, though Marcus's lips curled into an odd smile.

Excitement buzzed through the breezeway as Marcus and Jace took their positions at each end of the platform, shards at the ready. The rest quickly paired off and formed lines on either side, leaving the duelists isolated.

Jace's mind raced. Shouldn't we be wearing protection?

His eyes locked onto Marcus across the long platform. Marcus stood tall, his posture relaxed but eyes sharp and calculating. There was a glint of challenge in his gaze, a predatory confidence that sent a shiver down Jace's spine.

Professor Frost pressed a few keys on the panel and pulled a switch. A large silver wall rose between Jace and Marcus, obscuring their views of each other.

"This wall is reflective and has special protections. If you hit it, the energy will bounce back at you, like mirrors. The duel begins the moment the first burst is fired, which could be anytime after I say 'begin.' You don't have to wait for the barrier to fully descend, but I recommend you do—at least until you've had much more practice."

Jace's heart pounded. He could almost feel Marcus's eyes through the barrier, could sense the tension in the air as they both awaited the moment when the duel would start.

"Begin!" Professor Frost commanded, and the silver barrier slowly began its descent into the ground.

Jace stood absolutely still, his shards flickering with raw energy, his heart pounding in his chest. The air buzzed with anticipation, thick and electric. When the barrier was just below reaching eye level, a blast of carmine energy shot across the top edge, smashing straight into Jace's face. Blinded for a moment, he stumbled back, his face burning and smarting from the hit.

Professor Frost shot a dagger-like glare at Marcus, who raised his hands in mock surrender. "Apologies, I couldn't see where I was aiming," he said.

"Careful, Marcus. I'll accept that as an accident, but don't test my patience," Professor Frost warned.

The barrier continued its slow descent. Jace had only a few brief moments before the barrier lowered completely, giving Marcus the opportunity to strike again.

Jace crouched, focusing energy through his Moonstone Shard. His vision still blurred from the initial blast, he could just make out the form of Marcus preparing another attack. A flash of light erupted as Marcus sent a barrage of energy towards him, his Ruby Shard emitting a burst of crimson brilliance. Jace sidestepped awkwardly, the energy grazing his arm and leaving another painful burn.

With a growl, Jace retaliated, channeling his power into a swift moonlit strike. But Marcus was ready. A temporary shield of shimmering energy sprang up, deflecting the attack. The shield dissipated as quickly as it had formed, leaving Jace in a state of shock.

"What the hell? When were we taught to do that?" Jace muttered under his breath, shaking his head in disbelief.

"Is that all you've got?" Marcus sneered, his voice dripping with disdain. His eyes gleamed with sadistic satisfaction.

Ignoring the pain, Jace summoned his resolve. He launched himself forward, his movements a blur. Moonstone Shard in hand, he slashed at Marcus, who blocked the attack with his Ruby Shard. Sparks flew as the shards clashed, illuminating the battleground with their fierce glow.

Marcus pushed back, his strength overwhelming. He swung his shard with deadly precision, aiming for Jace's vulnerable spots. Jace dodged, his movements becoming more fluid as he adapted to Marcus's aggressive style. The two fighters were locked in a lethal dance of skill and will.

Jace felt a surge of energy course through him, breaking free from the deadlock with a sudden burst. He spun around, using the momentum to deliver a powerful strike to Marcus's side. The impact sent Marcus staggering, his composure faltering for a split second. Jace seized the moment, channeling a concentrated burst of moonlight energy through his shard. The beam of light struck Marcus square in the chest, sending him sprawling to the ground.

Marcus glared up at him, anger and humiliation etched across his face. "Lucky shot," he spat, struggling to his feet. Despite the pain, Jace felt a mix of concern and triumph. He didn't pity Marcus, but he also didn't want to tear apart another student. He backed away, giving Marcus room to stand, but stayed on guard. Just because he didn't want to seriously injure Marcus didn't mean he was stupid.

Despite his guard, Marcus feigned a high strike, drawing Jace's attention. As Jace ducked to avoid the faint burst, Marcus swiftly lashed out with a sucker punch of raw red light, hitting Jace square in the stomach. The force knocked the wind out of him, doubling him over in pain.

Marcus launched himself at Jace with renewed ferocity. His strikes were relentless, his Ruby Shard flaring with every hit. Jace struggled to defend himself, the intensity of Marcus's assault overwhelming his defenses.

In the heat of the moment, Jace discovered he could block or deflect a hit with an equal burst of energy in a wider field. It took precision that he didn't yet have, so he only managed to block a few out of many. His cloak was singed in several places, and his skin felt raw. He managed to block a particularly vicious strike aimed at his head, but the impact sent him reeling. Marcus pressed the advantage, his attacks a blur of red light and raw power. Jace's vision blurred again, but he fought to stay on his feet, determined not to fall.

"Final warning, Marcus," Professor Frost called out, her voice icy. "Headshots will not be tolerated. Do so again, and you will forfeit the match and see the Archmage for discipline."

Marcus only smiled in response.

Jace gritted his teeth, focusing on his shard. His brother's voice echoed in his mind, urging him to stay calm. He launched a series of rapid strikes, but his inexperience showed. Marcus countered each one with smooth precision. "You'll have to do better than that," he taunted.

Frustration bubbled within Jace, but he forced himself to stay calm. Marcus cast a blinding barrage of bolts, wrapping around Jace's legs, pushing him off balance. He stumbled but caught himself, then closed the distance with a quick step, channeling his aether into a powerful blast. Marcus barely reacted in time, raising his shard just enough to deflect some of the impact. The blast sent him stumbling back.

"You're stronger than I thought," Marcus admitted, frustration tight in his voice.

Jace didn't respond, his focus unwavering. He needed to end this quickly. He centered himself, feeling his breath resonate within him. Marcus lunged, but Jace was faster this time. He ducked low, avoiding the strike, and then sprang up, his shard glowing with intense light. He released a beam of energy, striking Marcus squarely in the chest. Marcus hit the ground with a thud.

For a moment, it seemed Jace had won. But Marcus wasn't done. With fierce determination, he pushed himself up, eyes burning with anger. The bronze ring on his hand glowed faintly as his face contorted with rage. He radiated power and fury, forcing Jace to step back instinctively. He stumbled, sensing something different now in Marcus's eyes—something that shook him to his core.

Marcus took advantage, closing the distance with lightning speed. He struck with his shard, a burst of energy hitting Jace squarely in the chest. Jace was thrown back, hitting the ground hard. He struggled to get up, his body feeling heavy, his energy drained. Marcus struck again and again, knocking Jace back as he tried to get up.

Dex moved forward to intervene, but Ell held him back, her grip firm. A tall, pale boy smiled as he watched the fight.

Marcus's attacks grew frantic. Jace saw the madness in his eyes, the way his lips curled in pleasure. His shard glowed brightly as he prepared to release another strike, this time at close range, directly into Jace's prone body.

"Oh, Jace," Marcus croaked out, his voice not sounding like his own. "You know what they say about kicking a man when he's down..."

Jace paused, confusion flickering in his eyes.

"Go for the head."

Jace tried to roll out of the way, but Marcus was faster and more practiced. He had obviously trained for this. He was no newcomer to duels. Jace, though quick to learn, was no match for the time and training Marcus had clearly dedicated. A brilliant red flash of light erupted from Marcus's shard as he redirected the shot from Jace's chest to his face, knocking his head hard against the platform.

Professor Frost stepped forward, her expression unreadable. "That's enough," she declared, her voice brooking no argument. "The match is over."

Marcus ignored her and kept moving closer, his shard vibrating with power as red tendrils of force blasted into Jace's eyes.

"I said, enough!"

Then there was a flash of amber light, and Marcus's shard was knocked out of his hands. A field of energy launched him backward as Professor Frost stood between him and Jace, bringing the duel to an abrupt halt.

Dark tendrils crept from the ground, and Molly could be seen chanting something, her lips far out of sequence with the sounds. Marcus was wrapped in black ropes and tugged to the ground. He tried to fight against it, but he couldn't, and his shard was out of reach.

After a moment, Marcus's eyes stared into nothingness, his face a blank canvas of apathy.

Jace, breath ragged with a mix of exhaustion and unbridled anger, rose unsteadily to his feet. The world was white; his eyes burned. He felt the hands of Professor Frost and a warm energy enveloped his face. It burned terribly, and his chest heaved as his body shook in protest against the pain, trembling.

But slowly, the white of the world turned to gold as the amber worked its magic. Images came back. It was a terrifying moment before the world returned. Jace knew it was just a game. Just a game, he repeated in his mind. But it didn't feel like just a game anymore, if it ever did. They were in uncharted territory now. Death could mean insanity or oblivion. Who knew the consequences anymore?

The blurred shapes regained their color and depth as his eyes healed, his burns mostly faded, though the deeper pain wasn't as easily addressed. The amber light dimmed as his last cuts sealed. He saw Molly still chanting and Professor Frost kneeling beside him.

"Are you okay?" she asked.

Jace just stared at her for a moment before shaking his head and then saying, "Yeah, I'm fine."

He stood with her help, casting a final, silent glance at the arena before turning away, driven by an urgent, visceral need to escape the confines of his seething rage. He walked off.

Professor Frost let him go, a knowing look in her eyes. She recognized the look of a student who needed to clear their thoughts and understood the value of quiet in moments of turmoil. Molly looked at him sadly but did not stop chanting.

Marcus spat, despite the heavy ropes, "Little baby needs to go and cry."

A rope tugged harder, slapping his head against the ground with a loud thump as Molly scowled at him.

"I'll be dealing with you later, Marcus," Professor Frost said. "Go ahead, Jace."

The mountain's path lay before Jace, winding through ancient trees that swayed with the promise of peace.

Each step down the mountain was a battle against the turmoil within him. The weight of his thoughts pressed down, matching the gravity that pulled him closer to the earth.

"Jace, wait up!" Alice's voice was the loudest, filled with worry. Dex and Ell weren't far behind, their footsteps loud in the narrow mountain path. Jace didn't stop.

"Jace," Alice called again.

He stopped and turned, his face a mask of frustration and fatigue. "Back off!" he yelled. His tone was harsher than he intended, but he couldn't help it. Her face showed confusion, and a touch of hurt flickered in her eyes.

"I'm sorry," he said, his voice softer now, "I just need a minute, okay?"

Alice opened her mouth to protest, but Dex gently placed a hand on her shoulder, shaking his head. Understanding passed between them, and with reluctant nods, they stepped back.

Jace watched them for a moment, his heart aching with guilt. Then, without another word, he continued down the path. It was a long journey, hours even with the ease of descent, but Jace welcomed it. He needed the time, the distance, the quiet.

Chapter 12
Cool... Cool

T he walk back stretched out like an overgrown path through his thoughts, every step stirring up memories and anxieties that Jace couldn't quite shake off. The EXP he hadn't spent thrummed inside him like a live wire, a constant buzz that made him feel like he was teetering on the edge of something terrible. It was hard to focus, hard to think about anything but the creeping dread that seemed to shadow him.

He tried to take in his surroundings, to distract himself with the chirping of birds and the way the sun dipped behind the mountains, painting the sky with hues of twilight before plunging it into darkness. His Dark Vision kicked in seamlessly, turning the night into a shadowy grayscale landscape that he navigated with ease. The cool breeze was a gentle caress against his skin, but it did little to ease his mind.

No matter how hard he tried, his thoughts kept circling back. His brother needed him. He was living a lie, hiding his true identity. And the guilt of snapping at Alice stung. They'd only shown him kindness, and he'd repaid it with anger. He clenched his fists, feeling the tension in his body, a physical manifestation of his internal turmoil.

The hours slipped by, the tension in his chest loosening bit by bit as Marcus faded from the forefront of his mind. By the time he reached the campus, night had fully settled in, wrapping the world in a cool, quiet blanket. He found himself at the statue of Aphrodite, her stone form draped in a heavy fur coat that seemed almost out of place. Jace couldn't help but wonder where she'd gotten it, knowing full well the statues had a habit of moving when no one was looking.

Jace sat down, the cool stone beneath him grounding him slightly. He barely noticed Molly until she was nearly upon him, emerging from a nearby building with an air of deliberation. She approached and settled beside him without a word, the silence stretching between them like a tangible thing. It was a long moment before Jace, feeling the weight of the quiet, finally broke it.

"So, you're a follower of Hecate, goddess of...?" Jace trailed off, searching for the right words.

"Yes, I am." Molly's voice carried an easy confidence, the awkwardness of the conversation seemingly sliding off her like water off a duck's back.

"Cool... cool," Jace said, his voice trailing off.

Molly nodded, her gaze distant for a moment as if she was seeing something beyond the physical world. "She is the goddess of magic, the moon, and the night. Her influence extends into the shadows where the unknown dwells. She walks the boundary between the living and the dead, guiding souls and invoking ancient powers. Much like you." She gave Jace a knowing glance.

Jace listened, captivated by the imagery her words conjured. "It soun ds... intense."

"It is," Molly agreed. "But it's also beautiful. There's a balance in her realm, a delicate dance between light and darkness, order and chaos. It's a place where you must confront your fears, but also where you can discover your deepest strengths."

"Sounds like a place I should visit," Jace said, half-joking, half-curious.

Molly's smile returned, gentle yet knowing. "Perhaps you will. The paths we walk often lead us to unexpected destinations."

"And you're a teacher's aide?"

"Indeed, I provide assistance to all of the High Council. I have since my second semester. I'm in my final year now." Her lips moved out of sync with her words, creating an eerie dissonance.

"How do you do that? Speak like that?"

"Oh," she laughed, a gentle sound imbued with an enduring kindness. "It's part of my Affinity. Communion. When I speak, the spirits listen."

"Wow, that seems pretty fitting with my deity," Jace said, remembering Hades' comment about some gods being under the wrong Olympian banner and how they would be better suited to his domain.

"Indeed." She smiled, a warmth in her eyes that made the night seem a little less cold.

There was another long pause, and Jace was trying to figure out a polite way to excuse himself when she spoke suddenly. "He is haunted, you know?"

"Huh?"

"Marcus," she said. "It doesn't excuse his behavior. But he is tormented by his life outside of Mythica."

The upsets from earlier crept back up into his chest. "I don't much care what is happening to Marcus outside of here. We are in here now."

"It's true. And one's company is one's choice," she said softly.

"He has some strange friends, that's for sure."

"Mhm, a very strange friend to keep around," Molly mused, her tone cryptic.

Jace felt a chill, the hairs on his neck prickling. "Strange how?"

Molly's eyes flickered to the side, as if seeing something he couldn't. And then she just smiled.

Before Jace could press further, Dex's loud voice cut through the air, drawing his attention. Molly stood up gracefully, her movements almost ethereal. "I should go. But don't worry, Chosen of Hades. We'll be seeing more of each other in the future, of this I am sure." Her words lingered in the air, leaving Jace with a sense of unease.

He turned to greet Dex, and when he looked back, Molly had vanished.

Does anyone here act normal? he thought. Who am I kidding, I don't act normal either. What is normal, anyway?

Dex approached cautiously, a wary smile on his face.

"It's safe," Jace said, trying to lighten the mood. "I'm not feral. I won't bite."

"Rough class," Dex said, sinking down beside him.

"Yeah," Jace replied, glancing at Alice and Ell who were standing nearby. "Listen, I'm really sorry about snapping before."

Alice smiled ruefully. "Hey, we all have moments. What Marcus did, it was unacceptable."

Ell's voice was warm, yet tinged with concern. "Marcus... he has issues."

"That's no excuse," Alice said curtly. "With the log-out issues or not, the Archmage needs to expel him. Especially with everything that's going on. He could have hurt you or caused a respawn, and we still don't really understand the side effects." Her face flushed with anger as she spoke.

"It's okay, guys," Jace said, trying to diffuse the tension.

Alice's eyes softened, but she remained resolute. "It's not okay, Jace. We need to be safe, especially now."

Jace nodded, the weight of their words settling heavily on him. As they talked, he couldn't shake the feeling that something more sinister was at play, something that connected Marcus's strange friend and the chilling whispers Molly had hinted at. The night seemed to grow darker, the shadows deeper, as if the world itself was holding its breath, waiting for the inevitable reveal.

"No, it's not," Alice said firmly. Ell looked at her with tight lips and concern in her eyes.

Jace's smile was small, almost wistful. "Why does Marcus hate us so much, Dex?" He kept his voice low. "You guys have history."

"I honestly don't know," Dex admitted. "We used to be friends. Our parents spent a lot of time together. He wasn't always like this. And then, something changed. It's just been getting worse."

"There's more to it," Jace said thoughtfully. "He seems... scared."

"Scared?" Dex and Alice shared a glance.

"No one acts like that unless they're scared or hurting. I don't forgive him; he's a real piece of work. But I've known people like him all my life, and they don't act the way they do unless there's something going on... or some part of them feels broken."

Dex shrugged, frustration etched in his features. "Maybe. He's never told me, and I doubt he ever will."

Jace looked around, "Where's Thistle?"

Alice gave a pained look. "He didn't take what happened to you too well. I think it reminded him of something in his past because he took off immediately after class and we haven't seen him since."

"I hope he's okay. Someone should let him know I'm alright."

"Yeah, maybe he's just processing some stuff," Dex said.

They chatted for a bit, their conversation gradually returning to its usual, comfortable rhythm, smoothing over the rough edges of the day.

"Oh, the library!" Alice exclaimed suddenly, eyes widening. "If we're quick, we can make it before it closes."

They exchanged a glance, then took off in a sprint. Bursting through the library doors, they were greeted by the sight of the head librarian tidying up. She cast them a look that clearly said, "You better not make a mess," before returning to her work. The librarian was a tall woman with sharp features, her large, owlish eyes peering through round spectacles, giving her an air of perpetual curiosity.

The library itself was a marvel of magical architecture. Stacks of ancient tomes reached up to the vaulted ceiling, where chandeliers of enchanted crystals cast a soft, warm glow. Shelves were arranged in a labyrinthine pattern, each aisle promising untold knowledge and secrets.

At the heart of the library stood the Arcanum Engine, an intricate marvel of metal and magic. Gleaming brass gears and polished steel pistons interlocked in a dance of perpetual motion, surrounding a grand, arcane podium. Above it floated a crystalline pane of glass, suspended by unseen forces, pulsating with an ethereal blue light. The air around it thrummed with latent energy as Alice approached.

She extended a hand, and the glass responded, its light intensifying. The gears within the Engine whirred softly, their movements precise and deliberate. Without a word, books began to levitate from the shelves, guided by streams of shimmering blue energy that wrapped around them like serpents of light. The tomes drifted through the air, drawn towards the podium.

With a gentle hum, the books arranged themselves beneath the crystalline glass, pages fluttering open as if by an unseen breeze. Each one settled perfectly, displaying the exact information Alice sought. The glass pane cast a soft glow, highlighting the ancient texts in a surreal luminescence.

Jace watched in silent amazement. The books floated and flipped with the grace of ballet dancers, each motion a testament to the Engine's enchanted precision. Alice's fingers danced across the glass surface, summoning more volumes. The Engine responded in kind, its mechanisms purring as more books soared into position, their pages rustling softly in the quiet of the library.

"Wow," Jace murmured, watching the books float and settle as if orchestrated by an unseen maestro of the arcane.

"So, here's the gist of our research," she began, her eyes glinting with excitement. "We've been trying to figure out how the Logout option was disabled, any cases of memory loss or insanity after multiple respawns, and of course, anything on the Dark One." She paused, flipping through a particularly aged volume. "Then something you said sparked a memory, Jace."

Alice opened another book, its pages crackling like dry leaves. "The Dark One mentioned that the university's protections could only stop threats that were already inside. It got me thinking—what could be inside but not trigger any alarms? Then I remembered something from Magic History."

"There's a Magic History class?" Dex interjected, raising an eyebrow.

"It's optional," Alice replied with a sideways glance. She returned to her explanation, her fingers tracing the delicate script on the page. "Long ago, in Roandia—the Terra Mythica equivalent of Egypt—a small university town was plagued by a series of mysterious deaths."

"Wait, Terra Mythica has an Egypt?" Jace asked, his brow furrowing.

"Not exactly. The continents are similar, but the cities differ. It's like we share the same basic geography, but the evolution diverged. Anyway, Roandia was on the far western edge of what would be Egypt. It was a prosperous kingdom with a university for Citizens."

Alice's voice dropped to a whisper, her eyes flickering with the memory. "Strange murders began happening. The victims woke up covered in blood, with no recollection of the events. Then, when their defenses were down, they were attacked by an undead army."

"Sounds like the Dark One's handiwork," Jace said grimly. "Possessions?"

"That's what I thought." Alice opened another book, revealing gruesome illustrations of the possessed victims' fates. "When Roandia split, one side fell to darkness, while the other struggled to survive."

Jace's voice was a low whisper, cutting through the thick silence of the ancient library. "So, how did he infiltrate the place? How did he manage the possessions?"

Alice scanned the grim lines of text. "It doesn't say. The possessed either went insane, disappeared, or died in horrific ways."

Jace shuddered as Alice held up an image, grotesque in its clarity, enough to make his stomach turn. He tore his gaze away, trying to erase the image from his mind.

"Alright, I get it," he muttered.

Alice closed the book with a gentle thud, her eyes softening as she looked at him. "For someone with Hades as their patron, you're surprisingly squeamish."

"I don't like unnecessary pain," Jace muttered, shoving his hands into his pockets. The library's dimming lights cast long shadows across the floor, signaling the end of their study session.

Alice glanced around, beginning to gather her things. "We should get going," she said, her tone casual but firm. "They don't like it when people stay late, and the place has defenses if you try to sneak in after hours."

Jace raised an eyebrow, curiosity piqued. "And how would you know that?"

A faint blush colored Alice's cheeks as she turned away. "Anyway," she said, trying to change the subject. The group stepped out into the biting cold night, the library doors creaking shut behind them.

"So," Alice began again, her breath curling into the frosty air, "somehow the Dark One is possessing people here or before they enter, like sleeper agents, and then activating them."

Jace sighed, his breath misting in the cold air. "So that's their trick—sending in demonic Manchurian candidates to bypass the defenses. Clever and creepy. We should inform the High Council," he suggested, a shiver running down his spine.

"I said that too, but Ell and Alice disagree," Dex chimed in.

"Someone may seem trustworthy, but we don't know how far these possessions go. It's safer to keep this to ourselves until we have more proof," Ell said, her voice steady.

"But at least the Archmage fought the Dark One and helped save us," Jace said, though uncertainty lingered in his voice. Jerry's warning echoed in his mind, reminding him not to trust anyone.

"I agree with Alice," Ell said. "It's nothing against him. It's just, it's best to keep this information close until we know more."

"One thing's clear," Jace said, his voice resolute. "We need to be prepared for anything."

"We need to train harder," Alice agreed, a steely determination in her voice.

"Do you think Marcus could be possessed?" Jace asked, voicing the fear that had been gnawing at them all.

"He's the perfect host. Certainly enough of a jerk," Dex said.

"I don't know if being a jerk is enough to assume someone is under the influence of the Dark One," Ell replied, though doubt lingered in her tone. "But I'll admit, he is a prime suspect."

Jace nodded, recalling the unsettling vacancy in Marcus's eyes, the twisted malice on his face when he attacked Dex at the semester's start, and the cold, detached fury during their duel.

"Is there a way to detect the possessed?" Jace's voice was low, laced with unease.

Alice sighed, shaking her head. "Honestly, I have no idea. Maybe some divining magic. I'm pretty out of my depth here."

Dex, rubbing his chin thoughtfully, chimed in. "Professor Ironclad mentioned in Alchemy class that there's a tonic for pretty much everything. Maybe there's something for this?"

All eyes turned to him, eyebrows raised. Dex shrugged defensively. "What? I pay attention... sometimes."

"It's a good thought," Jace admitted, "but even if there was a tonic, we'd still need to get them to drink it."

Alice groaned, rubbing her eyes. "I usually love classes, but it feels less like a school and more like we're being prepared to run the gauntlet. Everything's fast-tracked, all these survival skills crammed into our brains. Today, we skipped ten classes and dove into higher-level healing and protective tonics in Alchemy. Even I struggled with it." She wasn't being cocky, or maybe she was, but it was far from unearned.

Jace winced, realizing he'd missed that class. "You didn't happen to take any notes, did you?" he asked hopefully.

Alice's eyes brightened. "Actually, I took a lot of notes. I could catch you up if you have time now. I don't think Professor Ironclad would mind us using the facilities after hours, as long as we don't leave a mess."

Jace hesitated, then shrugged, swallowing his pride and accepting the help. "That would be really cool of you."

"Great! Meet me in the alchemy lab in thirty minutes," Alice said, already heading off. "I need to grab some extra ingredients before the gardens close."

"Okay." Jace smiled, reflecting her genuine excitement as he watched her dart off.

Dex and Ell exchanged knowing smiles.

"What?" Jace asked, puzzled. "What are you two smiling about?"

Dex chuckled and rested a hand on his shoulder. "Nothing, man. I'll tell you all about it when you're older."

Jace shot him a confused look, not entirely sure he wanted to grasp Dex's implication. "We're the same age, you know."

Chapter 13
A Little Chemistry

The scent of herbs and aged parchment filled the air. Alice stepped into the room, her footsteps muffled by the worn stone floor. She glanced at Jace, her eyes gleaming with a shared understanding.

"Do you have Dark Vision?" she asked softly, her voice barely a whisper.

Jace nodded. "Yeah, I do."

"Best not to make too much light, then," Alice replied. "We should just use our Dark Vision. Shouldn't need a protection barrier."

They moved silently, their eyes adjusting to the shadows. The room was a maze of ancient bookshelves, tables cluttered with alchemical equipment, and mysterious jars filled with glowing substances. Alice led the way to a large wooden table in the center, her fingers brushing over the surface as she began to clear a space.

"Let's get this set up," she murmured, her movements fluid and practiced. Jace followed her lead, setting out the ingredients with meticulous care. "Grab a small cauldron from the cupboard." She pointed to a dark corner of the room.

Opening the cupboard, Jace reached for an iron cauldron that had clearly seen better decades, but his fingers slipped, sending it clattering to the ground with a deafening crash. Both of them flinched at the noise, their bodies tense. Then, as the echo faded, they shared a quiet, conspiratorial laugh.

"On second thought," Alice said, her voice laced with amusement, "I think I'm going to set up a protective barrier. Luckily, it's something I've been practicing."

She focused her mind, summoning a shimmering Sapphire Shard that glowed faintly in the dim light, casting an ethereal blue hue across her face. With her other hand, she conjured the Tome of Secrets, its cover adorned with intricate patterns. The book opened on its own, pages rustling as if alive, until it settled on one filled with intricate runes inked in bronze—a bronze-level spell. The versatility of her Affinity for Secrets was remarkable.

"I'd use Veil of Shadows to conceal us, but it costs way too much Aether to sustain. This should be enough to mute the noise and light to outside observers."

Alice began to chant, her voice low and melodic, weaving through the silence. The air around them shimmered as lines of light formed in the air, twisting and curling like living things. They wrapped around her and Jace, forming a protective cocoon. The magic pulsed with a soft, rhythmic glow, each line of light imbued with ancient power.

The barrier solidified, its surface reflecting their surroundings in a rippling, otherworldly sheen. Alice moved to the wall and ignited a gas lamp, bringing the room to life with a soft, warm light. The barrier dimmed the light and muffled the sounds from within, creating an isolated haven of tranquility.

"This will dim sound and light to all outside," Alice explained, her voice now at a normal volume. "It costs a little aether to keep up, but you'll be doing most of the alchemy work here, so it shouldn't be a problem."

Jace looked at her, his eyes wide with admiration. "You know, your Affinity is absolutely overpowered, right?"

Alice laughed, a light, musical sound. "Says the guy that can attack people's souls."

He nodded, acknowledging her point, but still, a part of him was in awe of her abilities. Her magic might not have the singular destructive power of his, but its versatility and potential seemed limitless. As she continued to gather more spells and uncover hidden knowledge, her power would undoubtedly surpass them all.

Jace sat across from her, watching as she measured a fine powder with the precision of a jeweler weighing gold. "Alright, Jace," Alice said, her voice soft yet clear over the ambient noise. "Let's start with the basics. We're going to make a simple healing potion. You'll need these ingredients." She handed him a list, her handwriting neat and elegant.

Flickering oil lamps cast dancing shadows on the stone walls, the light shifting like living creatures. Alice's desk, however, was an island of order amidst the chaos, her meticulous notes spread out before her.

She started pulling ingredients out of her inventory, one by one, laying them in front of Jace like she was dealing cards in a high-stakes poker game.

"Dried elderflower," she said, holding up a delicate bundle. "Soothing properties."

"Got it," Jace nodded, his eyes scanning the list.

"Mandrake root," she continued, placing the gnarled piece beside the elderflower.

"Essential," Jace muttered, noting it down.

"And a pinch of silver dust," she added with a flourish, letting the sparkling powder trickle through her fingers.

"Shiny," he grinned.

Then came the more exotic components. "One drop of phoenix sweat," she said, holding up a tiny vial. "Life-giving energy."

Jace raised an eyebrow. "Phoenix sweat? Really?"

"Yeah, and it's a pain to collect," she winked, setting it down carefully.

"Midnight powder," she said, producing a small, dark pouch. "Stabilizes the mixture, aligns it with lunar cycles."

"Very mystical," Jace remarked, scribbling it down.

"And finally," she revealed a dark, glossy leaf. "A sprig of nightshade."

"Nightshade. Because why not?" Jace smirked, leaning back.

Jace eyed his cooking equipment with the same skepticism he'd reserve for a used car salesman.

Alice caught his hesitation and offered a reassuring smile. "Don't sweat the equipment. Focus on the process."

She handed him the mandrake root. "First, grind this into a fine paste."

"Easy peasy." Jace followed her instructions as best he could, his movements careful but awkward. Alice's presence was both comforting and intimidating; she was so at ease in this environment.

"Now add the elderflower," Alice instructed, her fingers deftly measuring out the dried petals. "Mix it thoroughly to activate its soothing properties." She handed the bowl to Jace, their fingers brushing briefly. Her touch was cool, grounding him.

Jace took the bowl, his grip a little too firm, causing some petals to flutter out. Alice's eyebrow arched slightly, but she said nothing, her lips twitching into a small, amused smile.

As he stirred, Alice explained the theory behind each step. "Elderflower promotes calm, and the mandrake root binds the magic. The silver dust enhances their effects."

Jace nodded, pouring the combining liquid into the mix slowly under her watchful eye. He felt the potion begin to thicken, its color shifting to a vibrant green, while tiny lumps started to form. "What's next?"

She hesitated. "I'm pretty sure it's not supposed to do that," she said, checking her notes.

"Well, no turning back now," he said.

She shook her head and laughed softly. "Okay, now we need to add a drop of phoenix sweat." She handed him the tiny vial, watching as he carefully added the drop. Then five more drops poured in, and a puff of yellow smoke emerged.

"Next?" Jace asked again, his confidence growing. He knew he was doing terribly, but he still felt pleased with himself. You had to start somewhere.

"Now we add the midnight powder," she said. "Just a pinch. And then stir slowly."

Jace did his best, watching the potion's color deepen, becoming more complex and turning slightly ruddy.

Alice examined it closely before adding, "That's definitely the wrong color."

"What do I do next?" he asked.

Alice revealed a sprig of nightshade. "This balances the blend, making it powerful yet safe."

Jace added the sprig and stirred the potion one last time, its final hue a deep, shimmering burnt sienna.

Alice smiled, choosing to just enjoy the ride as it was clear the potion had gone wrong long ago.

"Now we heat it just enough to combine the elements without burning them," Alice explained. "Watch the bubbles closely. Too much heat, and it'll ruin your perfect... concoction."

Jace leaned over the small burner, adjusting the flame. The potion began to simmer, releasing a fragrant steam that mingled with the incense smoke. Soon, the room buzzed with the hiss and pop of bubbling potion, the air thick with the pungent aroma of strange herbs mingling with the metallic tang of rusting equipment.

"Now, let it cool and pour it into the vial."

Jace followed her instructions, but as he poured, his hand wobbled, and a few drops splashed onto the table. Alice's nose scrunched as she pressed her lips together to suppress a laugh.

He secured the stopper on the small glass vial and held it up to the light, marveling at the way it caught the glow. Alice stepped closer, her eyes narrowing slightly as she inspected his work.

"Well, you've made... something alright," she said, her smile a mix of amusement and encouragement.

"Thanks. Whatever I made, I couldn't have done it without you."

She smiled, a hint of blush coloring her cheeks. Jace held the vial up to the light, the murky liquid inside shifting with a menacing shimmer.

A prompt appeared as he inspected his creation.

Item

Terrible Potion of Sense Altering

You have attempted to create a Potion of Minor Healing. You have failed.

Instead, you've created this monstrosity. Imbibing this potion will cause unknown results. It may lead to serious side effects, including nausea, hallucinations, dizziness, heart palpitations, headaches, spontaneous laughter, spontaneous crying, severe paranoia, a profound sense of doom, and death. Also, perhaps none of those things will happen.

He sighed, placing the vial back on the cluttered table. At least it was something. His alchemy skill had increased, a slight consolation for the grotesque concoction he had produced. He could still feel his unspent EXP pushing up against the borders of his mind, slowing his gains.

The sudden creak of the door shattered the tranquility, sending a jolt of tension through the air. A figure stepped into the room, his silhouette sharp against the dim light.

Jace's head snapped up, heart pounding. A satyr stood in the doorway, horns curling above his head, eyes wide with shock.

"Whoa!" the satyr yelped, voice high and trembling. "Didn't expect anyone here."

There was a beat of silence, the kind that makes you acutely aware of how loud your breathing is. Alice's eyes suddenly widened in recognition. "Wait, you're Petrie, right? The teacher's aide?"

The satyr's lips twitched into a nervous grin, his eyes doing a quick scan of the room like he was expecting someone to jump out and yell "Surprise." He brushed off some imaginary dust from his vest and straightened up. "Assistant Archmage, actually."

Jace raised an eyebrow. "I remember you. We met outside the Archmage's office. Don't you mean, Assistant to the Archmage?"

"Same thing," Petrie muttered. He moved quickly to a cabinet, hands fumbling as he pulled out a small, intricately carved wooden box. "Anyway, you two need to take off. Professor Brutus Ironclad's not exactly fond of uninvited guests in his Alchemy classroom."

Jace glanced at the satyr, suspicion flickering in his eyes. "Then what are you doing here?"

"Official Assistant business," Petrie replied quickly. "Now, you two better amscray before someone else finds you here. If he finds out you were here and I knew about it, I'd likely be baked into his next experiment or used as a test subject for one of his more eclectic artifacts."

Alice started, "Oh, I just thought he wouldn't mind because Jace needed to catch up and—"

Petrie chuckled, his eyes twinkling with amusement. "Ironclad's leniency is a myth, I'm afraid. Trust me, you don't want to be on The Brute's bad side."

Jace quickly began gathering their scattered equipment. "Thanks for the warning. We're gone."

Jace and Alice gathered the last of their things and headed into the hall. Petrie, still jittery, nodded as he placed the wooden box under his arm. He hurried out of the room, locking it behind him, before disappearing down the corridor.

Alice cringed as they walked, her confidence deflating. "I honestly thought Ironclad wouldn't mind."

Jace shrugged, a grin tugging at his lips. "What's life without a little adventure? No harm, no foul. Besides, it wouldn't be my first time getting caught breaking and entering."

She gave him a sideways look. "You aren't like a lot of the students here, you know that?"

He flushed slightly before quickly changing the subject. "So, I guess that's that for the lesson. Which sucks because I feel like I was just getting the hang of it."

"It doesn't have to be," she said.

"What do you mean?"

"Well, I have my alchemy kit and the rest of the ingredients for a few more practice vials. All we need is a space."

"But what space would be open this time of night?"

Alice glanced at Jace. "We could go to my dorm, but they're throwing a party for the Fighters of Athena. They go pretty late, and it's not really my scene, being a follower of Harpocrates—god of silence and all."

"Silence and parties -always a winning combo."

Jace was reminded once more of the odd pairings, gods who seemed like they should be under Hades' banner. He wondered if he was being objective or if he was growing biased because Hades was his patron.

An idea struck him—a solution, though not a comfortable one. But he didn't want the night to end. He should have enough saved-up Society Points... He started pacing, wrestling with his internal debate, eyes flicking between possibilities like a frantic chess player.

Shadow might not be thrilled, but I really need those potions.

It's not like we're throwing a rave, right? Just a couple of nerds, getting some study done.

But then again, having someone over makes me feel uncomfortable, and who knows how Shadow will handle it?

He looked over his shoulder, catching Alice's curious expression.

Then again, Shadow managed to hide from me until I saw the dorm population count... so maybe it'll be fine. Yeah, it'll probably be fine. This is a normal thing. Why am I being weird about this?

Or maybe it'll be a disaster.

Jason rubbed his temples. "Survival over comfort," he muttered, trying to quiet his anxieties.

Alice raised an eyebrow, a gentle smile playing on her lips. "Talking to yourself now?"

Jace chuckled nervously. "Just thinking out loud. So, uh, my dorm could work," he offered, his voice tentative.

Alice's face lit up with genuine excitement. "Great idea!" she exclaimed, her curiosity almost tangible. "Full disclosure, though—it's a bit... different down there. A bit... zombie-esque."

Her eyes sparkled. "Rumors about The Fields Below have been going around, and I've been dying to see what it's like down there. I've honestly been so curious."

Jace raised an eyebrow at her enthusiasm, but decided not to question it. "Well, okay then. So, that's what we're doing," he said with a shrug.

"Lead the way," she gestured, her smile widening.

Chapter 14
Weird is Good

They descended into the Fields Below, the labyrinthine underbelly that cradled Jace's dorm. Shadows clung to the walls, thick as cobwebs, narrowing the space until it felt as if the darkness itself was leaning in to listen. Despite the gloom, Alice's presence softened the atmosphere, providing warmth in the cold.

Jace forced himself to breathe, the air heavy with the scent of damp stone and something else—something ancient and lingering, like the echo of forgotten secrets. He stole a glance at Alice, who seemed undeterred, her eyes wide with a childlike wonder that made him momentarily forget the embarrassing state of his quarters. He wasn't sure why the thought of bringing her here troubled him, but it did, like a persistent itch just beneath the surface.

As they moved deeper into the maze, Jace made sure to amplify every footstep, his boots slapping against the stone with exaggerated force. He cleared his throat and launched into what could loosely be described as a tour, his voice echoing off the walls in a way that startled even him.

"And here we have the finest selection of dusty old bookshelves," he began, gesturing to a crumbling stack that looked more like a fire hazard than a library. "Each volume comes with its own unique aroma of mildew, and, for the discerning collector, a healthy layer of mold." He shot Alice a sideways glance, but she was too engrossed in the shadowy passages to notice his feigned bravado.

"And if you'll look to your right," he continued, gesturing with a flourish, "you'll find what used to be something probably important, now reduced to a delightful array of dilapidated rooms. Perfect for ghosts with a taste for nostalgia."

They rounded a corner, and Jace came to an abrupt halt, staring down a dark alley that he could swear hadn't been there a moment ago. He gave a dry smile, "And this, of course, is the scenic route to probable certain death. A real must-see."

He spoke louder than necessary, the words rolling off his tongue with a forced cheerfulness. He hoped the noise would give Shadow plenty of time to slip away if she needed to—he'd show Alice anything in the Below, but not the Whispering Crypt. That was a secret best kept in the dark.

But Alice, seemingly oblivious to his theatrical efforts, was captivated by the winding corridors and the faint, flickering lights that danced at the edge of their vision. Her face lit up with genuine awe, the corners of her lips curving into a smile.

"This is amazing," she breathed, her voice filled with the kind of wonder usually reserved for stargazing or fireworks.

Jace blinked, caught off guard. For a moment, he saw the Below through her eyes—an ancient place steeped in mystery and history, rather than just a cold, damp dormitory that never quite felt like home. He chuckled, a soft sound that melted some of the tension in his shoulders.

"Yeah," he said, more to himself than to her, "I guess it is."

Jace observed her, a mix of relief and amusement warming his chest at her unbridled enthusiasm. He cast a quick glance around the room, half-expecting to catch a glimpse of Shadow lurking in some dark corner, but there was nothing.

"Certainly has its own... unique charm," Jace replied, trying to sound more nonchalant than he felt.

Alice turned to him, her eyes alight with genuine admiration. "I think it's wonderful. You've carved out a space down here—made it your own. That's impressive."

Her words caught him off guard, and despite himself, a smile tugged at the corner of his lips. It wasn't often someone saw his world this way, especially not with such unfiltered excitement.

He whisked her through the dorm section, deftly nudging a pair of boxers under the bed with the kind of casual precision that only comes from years of practice. As they disappeared from sight, he sent up a quick, silent plea to the universe that she either hadn't noticed—or, if she had, that she'd have the decency to pretend she hadn't. "And that's the tour!" he declared with a bright, slightly too enthusiastic grin. "Well, not really. There are still plenty of mysterious corners I haven't even explored yet."

"So, where do you want to set up?" she asked, her gaze sweeping the room with eager curiosity. "Does your Society have an alchemy lab? If not, a bathroom could work in a pinch."

Jace chuckled. "Oh, it does. Or, well... it will."

Her brow arched in a curious tilt as he pulled up his map, selecting the alchemy section with a confident mental tap. He led her down a narrow passageway, the path winding through patches of dirt and hanging cobwebs. She followed, her smile growing with each step, like she was walking through a beloved childhood memory.

Jace shot her a glance, unable to hide his bewilderment. "You're actually enjoying this?"

Alice laughed softly, her eyes bright with nostalgia. "I love places like this. They're spooky, dreary, and full of stories. I grew up on old horror movies, the kind that makes you laugh as much as they scare you. Have you seen the one about the vampire who moves to Brooklyn?"

He shook his head, bemused. "Can't say I have. You know, for a bookworm, you're pretty weird."

She paused, her voice growing softer, almost vulnerable. "I'm not that weird. I just... find it all fascinating."

Nice one, Jace, he thought, mentally kicking himself. "I didn't mean it like that," he blurted out, stumbling over his words. "Weird is good. Really good."

Without waiting for a reply, he quickened his pace, leading the way down the corridor, leaving his awkwardness to trail behind like an afterthought.

The path led them to an old, splintered door, more a suggestion of an entrance than a barrier. Jace gave it a firm shove, and with a protesting creak, the door gave way, swinging open to reveal the alchemy lab beyond.

It was, to put it mildly, a sight that could discourage even the most optimistic of souls. Cobwebs hung from the ceiling like the decor of some overzealous spider's haunted house, and a thick, undisturbed layer of dust blanketed everything, softening the hard edges of broken glassware and rusted tools scattered across the floor. Dark stains marred the stone tables, relics of experiments gone awry or perhaps just poor housekeeping. There was a lingering pungent tang of dried chemicals. Shadows curled in the corners, their movements creating the illusion that the room itself was breathing, or worse, watching.

Alice stepped in behind him, her expression caught somewhere between amusement and horror. "Uh, Jace... I think this place might need a broom first. Not that it doesn't have... potential?"

He couldn't help but grin at her diplomatic attempt to find something positive in the wreckage. "It's okay, Alice. I know it's awful. But just wait."

Jace moved to an ancient interface embedded in the wall, its screen flickering like a dying firefly as he coaxed it to life. The controls were clunky, the technology archaic, but it still worked—mostly. He navigated through the menus, his fingers dancing over the options until he found what he was looking for: the alchemy lab upgrade.

A small notification popped up, informing him that he had enough society points to jump two levels at once. He hesitated for a brief moment, weighing his options. But the memory of his brother and foster parents cooking together, the warmth of those moments, nudged him forward. This upgrade wasn't just practical; it was personal.

The room responded immediately, a countdown timer materializing in front of them, its digits glowing faintly as they began to tick down.

A low hum began to emanate from the walls, growing in intensity until it felt like the air itself was vibrating. The dust evaporated into nothingness, the cobwebs disintegrating as if they had never existed. Broken glassware mended itself, shards floating through the air like puzzle pieces reuniting with their counterparts, while rusted tools shed their corrosion, gleaming as they settled into place on freshly polished shelves.

Jace watched the lab status upgrade from "Tales From the Crypt" to "Barely Functioning Mess" and, finally, to a "Well-Working Alchemy Lab."

The walls, once cracked and stained, healed before their eyes, the marks of time and neglect vanishing as if wiped clean by an unseen hand. Flames flickered to life in the sconces, casting a warm, golden glow that chased away the last of the shadows. The transformation was nothing short of magical—a forgotten relic reborn into a state-of-the-art alchemy lab.

Alchemy tables sprouted from the floor, sleek and pristine, outfitted with burners and complex glass apparatus that glinted in the firelight. Cabinets swung open, revealing rows of vials, flasks, and ingredients neatly organized, as if by an invisible hand. Mechanical arms extended from the walls, each holding a different tool or device, ready to assist at a moment's notice.

Upgrade Complete

The Alchemy Lab has Reached Rank Three — "Well-Working Alchemy Lab"

Alice's eyes widened, her earlier skepticism replaced with sheer awe. "Wow."

Jace watched her reaction, a satisfied smile tugging at his lips. The room was no longer a relic of a forgotten era; it was a place of possibilities, of creation.

"Yeah," he said softly, more to himself than to her, "Wow."

The room now gleamed with a newfound purpose, its stone floors polished to a soft sheen that reflected the flickering light from the hearth. The air carried a subtle fragrance of herbs and spices, the kind that whispered of old forests and hidden apothecaries. Clean alchemy tables stood ready, their surfaces adorned with black cauldrons and silver pots that shimmered with the promise of new concoctions. Shelves lined the walls, stocked with jars of vibrant powders, vials of mysterious liquids, and tools meticulously arranged in their rightful places. It wasn't perfect—many rarer items were still absent, leaving gaps that hinted at future quests and upgrades—but it was more than enough to get started.

Jace turned to Alice, a triumphant grin lighting up his face. With a pride typically reserved for grand ribbon-cutting ceremonies, he proudly announced, "Welcome to our new lab."

The walls were adorned with faint flickering shadows created by the warm glow of smoldering embers in the hearth. For the first time in what felt like ages, Jace felt a warmth spread through him, a rare comfort in a place that had always felt more eerie than inviting.

With a theatrical flourish, Alice began unpacking her arsenal of ingredients and vials, each one appearing as if pulled from thin air. Bottles of strange liquids and bizarrely shaped gadgets clinked and clattered as she laid them out with the kind of practiced grace that made it look effortless. The setup was a world away from the cobwebbed chaos of the alchemy lab they'd just left behind. And the fact that this space was Jace's—well, technically Hades', but that was splitting hairs—was still a bit surreal.

Even with half the place stuck in "dismal" mode and whole sections crying out for a renovation, this was fast becoming the best home Jace had ever had. For the first time, he felt like he was carving out something of his own, a place that might actually feel like his.

They set out to brew another Potion of Minor Healing, with Jace dutifully following Alice's instructions to the letter—or at least, as close to the letter as he could manage. The result, however, was yet another concoction that seemed to defy the very concept of "healing".

Item Created

Strange Potion of Unknown Effects

Description:

You have attempted to create a Potion of Minor Healing. You have failed spectacularly. Instead, you've concocted something that even the System struggles to define. Imbibing this potion will cause unpredictable results. It appears drinkable... sort of. But let's be clear: You're on your own with this one.

Note:

The System disavows all responsibility for whatever may occur should the Traveler decide to drink this potion.

Go ahead, what could possibly go wrong?

Jace didn't need to think twice about his next move—drinking the potion was definitely off the table. But he couldn't bring himself to throw it away either. Who knew? It might come in handy... someday. He carefully tucked the bizarre brew into his hip-satchel's dimensional inventory expansion pocket, where it wouldn't take up much space—or, hopefully, explode.

He held his breath as he watched the bubbles rise and pop on the surface of the brew. There was something oddly calming in the process—the precise measurements, the slow, deliberate stirring, the way the liquid thickened and shifted under his careful hand. It felt meditative, a kind of alchemical zen that smoothed out the rough edges of his thoughts.

Under Alice's watchful eye, Jace poured the binding reagent into the mixture with deliberate care. The potion began to transform, its color deepening into a vibrant green as tiny lumps formed, then partially dissolved within the brew. There was a tangible magic in the air, a hum of anticipation that buzzed in his mind.

But this time, even Jace couldn't hide his surprise at the outcome. As he lifted the potion to the light, both he and Alice widened their eyes in unison. The liquid inside was a nearly perfect greenish-blue, shimmering just as the examples Alice had shown him. It was almost spot-on.

Almost. There were a few tiny, mysterious floaty bits suspended in the middle—bits that looked unsettlingly like the backwash you'd get after letting a four-year-old take a sip of your drink.

Item Created

Crude Potion of Minor Healing

Congratulations! You have successfully created a Potion of Minor Healing. Due to the Crude rank of this potion, a random side effect has been added.

Drink responsibly.

Effects:

• Restores 50 Health over 10 seconds.

Side Effect:

• Reduces EXP gained by 25% for one hour after consumption.

Don't worry about the floaties... they're probably nothing to worry about. Probably.

"You did it!" Alice exclaimed, her voice brimming with excitement.

They both conveniently overlooked the potion's crude ranking—Jace had made a potion of minor healing, and that was all that mattered. There was a moment of quiet as they soaked in the small victory, the unspoken truth hanging in the air: this might be the end of their night together. But Jace wasn't ready for it to be over, and just as he was about to find a way to say so, Alice spoke up.

"You know, since we're already here, I wouldn't mind practicing some of the potions I've been reading about. Seems a shame to stop now," she said, a glint of determination in her eyes.

Jace's smile widened. "Couldn't agree more."

Alice pulled out a well-worn book titled Arcane Elixirs: A Brewer's Guide, flipping through the pages with the familiarity of someone who'd spent hours lost in its contents. Jace watched as she sprang into action, and for the first time since the forging of the Ward Stone, he got to see her in her element. She moved with an almost surgical precision, every motion deliberate and exact. Where Jace relied on intuition and a bit of luck, Alice brought a methodical approach that promised more reliable results.

"This one's called 'The Elixir of Sight,'" Alice explained as she carefully measured out a shimmering powder. "It's supposed to help you spot hidden details in your surroundings, like a faint glow around things of hidden importance. The effects can be subtle—think; finding your lost keys or spotting an old penny on the street. But at higher ranks, it's rumored to be quite powerful."

As she continued to work, Jace found himself utterly absorbed by the precision of her movements. Her hands danced over the equipment with a practiced grace, each action purposeful, each gesture controlled. It was like watching an artist at their craft, and in that moment, the day's tension seemed to dissolve, replaced by a warm, soothing calm that had nothing to do with the room's temperature. Here, amidst the swirling steam and flickering shadows, they were creating something together—something that felt private, almost sacred, as if the alchemy they practiced was a secret language only they shared.

Jace returned to his potion-making. He focused on refining his technique, repeating the process until he could almost do it without having to refer to the notes quite so much. Three more potions of minor healing soon lined up on the table, each one crude and carrying the same pesky debuff. At least I'm consistent, he thought with a wry smile.

But there was progress in the repetition, a rhythm that both of them fell into as they worked side by side. As they continued their craft, the outside world faded further into the background, leaving only the quiet symphony of their work and the unspoken connection growing between them.

The air thickened with a heady blend of ingredients. The promise of something magical hung in the air, delicate as a spider's thread, ready to be seized. And so, they lost themselves in the quiet symphony of clinking glass and murmured incantations, the world outside fading into the background.

Chapter 15
Spooky McGee

As the evening deepened, Jace felt the tension in his shoulders begin to loosen, unraveling with each moment spent in Alice's company. There was something comforting about her, a quiet curiosity that seemed to smooth out the edges of his unease. Their conversation meandered through topics as naturally as the shifting in the lab.

Unbidden memories of his foster parents surfaced—the cozy warmth of their tiny kitchen, the inviting scent of freshly baked treats filling the air. Baking had been his refuge, a practice that required focus and patience, grounding him when he felt adrift.

He could still hear their gentle voices guiding him, helping him find balance when his emotions threatened to spiral out of control. Alex had always been the calm in the storm, the steady hand that kept everything from unraveling. How he wished Alex was there now. But as he moved through the familiar motions—measuring, mixing, the heat of the fire mingling with the scent of the ingredients—he felt something shift. In the repetition, in the practice, he felt closer to Alex, and for the first time in a long while, he felt himself let go.

Jace nearly jumped out of his skin as a notification blinked into existence before his eyes.

500 EXP has been allocated to Attribute Improvements.

200 EXP has been allocated to the Word of Power: Soul.

Ability Unlocked: Alchemical Focus

Congratulations! You've discovered the tranquil flow within the art of alchemy, achieving harmony in its precise and deliberate process.

By embracing the moment and fully committing to your craft, you've unlocked the ability to channel your aether and allocate EXP while practicing a skill.

Description: Harness the calming nature of alchemy to fortify your aether and channel experience. Instead of traditional EXP allocation techniques, this Focus allows you to cultivate your aether through the practice of alchemy itself. While slower than dedicated methods, this path provides a steadier, more consistent approach to growth.

This Focus allows you to convert EXP at a rate of 20% of dedicated allocation methods.

"Eureka!" Jace's voice burst forth with the excitement of someone discovering a hidden treasure, startling Alice so much that she nearly dropped a precariously balanced vial, the liquid within sloshing perilously close to the edge.

She shot him a wide-eyed look, her heart still racing from the near disaster. "What happened?"

"My EXP—I just started spending it!" Jace couldn't keep the glee from his voice, the thrill of it buzzing through him.

Alice began to smile, but then her expression shifted into something more incredulous. "Wait a minute... You hadn't spent it yet?" Her glare could have cut stone.

"Whoa, hold on there, Spooky McGee," Jace said, raising his hands in surrender. "I tried, okay? It just wasn't working for me. But... just look." He quickly shared the notification about his newfound EXP allocation system.

Alice's stern look melted into a smirk as she read it over. "Hmmm, a likely story," she teased, while her eyes held a flicker of genuine amusement. "You've picked up an EXP Focus."

"A what now?"

"Here, I've got something similar, but yours seems a bit faster—more focused and specific," she said, pulling up her interface and sharing it with him. "This is mine."

A notification flickered in front of him.

Precision Focus

Through intense focus and deliberate study, you've unlocked a method to allocate small portions of EXP, converting concentrated effort into progress.

Currently spends at a 10% rate compared to dedicated EXP methods.

Jace stared at the text, marveling at how it seemed to fit Alice perfectly—her approach to growth was just like her: precise, deliberate, and maddeningly meticulous. It wasn't flashy or fast. No, this was a slow burn, steady and re-liable—like a candle that might never go out. It demanded patience, a quality in short supply. But for Alice, it was as natural as breathing.

In contrast, Jace's method struck a balance—partly intentional, partly effortless. It activated whenever he immersed himself in alchemy, a practice he was quickly growing to enjoy. It was a method that kept him progressing steadily, without the risk of burnout, even if it didn't quite reach the intensity of the truly dedicated.

He glanced at Alice, now lost in thought, her eyes distant, as if gazing into a world beyond. Then it clicked—her constant immersion in books wasn't just a habit; it was likely tied to her method of spending EXP. Or maybe her cultivation ability evolved because of that habit? In Terra Mythica, it was hard to say which came first.

Alice closed the prompt and looked at Jace, her gaze sharpening in realization.

"Spooky McGee?" she asked, arching an eyebrow.

"Yep, that's your nickname now. Just decided."

"Yeah, that's not going to be a thing."

"Okay, Spooky," he replied with a cheeky grin.

She shook her head, suppressing a smile, and returned to her potion. "Not a thing."

"Definitely a thing," Jace muttered.

Hours passed unnoticed, their focus so intense that only the persistent growling of their stomachs finally broke the spell. With reluctance, they conceded it was time for a break. By the time they reached the dining hall, it was a ghost town, the tables bare and the scent of dinner just a memory. Unfazed, they ventured into the kitchen at the back, where the faint aroma of spices still lingered like the echoes of a feast.

There, amidst the gleaming countertops and hanging pots, stood an older man, his face etched with the lines of a life spent over a stove, his chef's hat perched like a crown that had seen better days but still held a certain dignity.

"Are you the only one still on shift?" Jace asked, glancing around the empty kitchen.

The chef let out a hearty laugh, the sound bouncing off the tiled walls before he launched into a tirade, his words tumbling out in a thick accent with a rugged lilt reminiscent of the Scottish Highlands.

"Shift? Ha! I'm the only one who works here. Been asking for an assistant for ages, but do you think they'll give ol' Ruddoff a break? Not a chance. Not with all you Travelers always whining about this and that. 'Oh, it's too bland… oh, I don't like it… oh, there's a nail in my food.' Bah! I've had it up to here, I tell ya."

Alice and Jace exchanged a wary glance, instinctively edging back toward the door as they realized they might have bitten off more than they could chew. But Ruddoff wasn't about to let them slip away that easily. He took a step forward, his presence expanding to fill the room. "Eh, where do you think you're going? You two look like you haven't eaten in days. And if there's one thing I can't abide, it's a hungry student. I won't have it said that ol' Ruddoff let anyone go hungry on his watch."

"Um, I think we're fine," Alice said, trying to sound convincing.

Ruddoff wasn't having any of it. He marched over to the pantry and then to a massive fridge, swiftly filling two plates with an assortment of foods, stacking them high before thrusting them into their arms. "Here, eat up. Can't have you wasting away. You're already thin as a twig, lass. Another day or two, and I'd be lucky to get a copper for you at the butcher's."

Alice and Jace nodded, murmuring their thanks, but Ruddoff wasn't done yet. He continued piling food onto their plates, darting back and forth to the pantries, stacking their arms higher and higher until it bordered on the absurd. For all his grumbling, the man was anything but stingy when it came to feeding people.

"Uh, sir, just out of curiosity—and not that I don't believe you," Alice began cautiously, her voice tinged with a hint of disbelief, "which I totally do—but how do you manage to feed nearly five thousand people a day all by yourself?"

Ruddoff's grin widened, a mischievous twinkle sparking in his eye as he gestured grandly behind him. "Take a look, lass. What do you see?"

They turned, and the kitchen seemed to come alive. Pots stirred themselves, ladles danced through bubbling cauldrons, and knives chopped vegetables with the precision of a maestro at a symphony. The space was alive with the hum of enchantments, every tool and utensil working in perfect harmony.

"I'm just the conductor," Ruddoff said with a casual wave of his hand, "Magic does the rest. One man can feed thousands, as long as you've got enough aether and the right tools." He nodded toward the enchanted equipment, each piece glowing faintly with the telltale shimmer of magic. A couple of ladles hovered mid-air, almost as if they were eavesdropping.

"Back to work!" Ruddoff barked, punctuating his command with a swift kick to the table. The ladles quickly resumed their work, plunging into their pots and stirring with renewed vigor. "Utensils," he muttered, shaking his head and gesturing at them with a weary thumb.

Jace's eyes sparkled with sudden inspiration, a grin spreading across his face as an idea took hold. They lingered just long enough to gather some of the less-than-exciting food they were sure would show up at breakfast the next morning before making a quick exit.

"Thanks for the food!" Jace called over his shoulder as they made their exit, arms loaded with an assortment of snacks. They hurried back to the lab.

"What's going on, Jace?" Alice asked. "Why are you running?" She tried to keep up, losing at least a few bread rolls in the process.

"I've got an idea."

Jace hunched over the alchemy table, his thoughts a chaotic whirl, ideas flaring up and crashing down like sparks from a bonfire. "You know that potion you just made—the one with the thing and the name?" he asked.

Alice looked at him, one eyebrow delicately arched. "You mean the Elixir of Sight?"

"Yeah, that one," Jace said, his focus intensifying. "I think I've figured out why the food around here tastes like chalk."

"I thought that was just how things were here. Bad coding, or something. Either that or some programmer had a love for unseasoned chicken," Alice quipped.

"But not everything tastes like that. I had this cherry-filled cookie from the Archmage—"

She cut him off with a playful grin. "Taking sweets from strangers, Jace? I thought we'd been over this."

"Seriously," he insisted, leaning in closer, "it tasted like a real cherry. Like, the kind you'd find back home, not that synthesized, plastic-flavored nonsense. The kind that grows on a tree. And it got me thinking—maybe the problem isn't the food itself. Maybe it's how it's being prepared. If some poor sap is churning out meals for the entire campus, things are bound to go wrong somewhere along the line. It's like trying to make a gourmet meal with a fast-food assembly line."

Alice leaned in, her interest piqued. "You think something's getting lost in translation?"

Jace grinned, a mischievous spark in his eyes. "Exactly. Cooking's just alchemy with better smells, right?" His hands dove into their supplies with the fervor of a child rummaging through a treasure chest. "What if we tweak the Elixir of Sight to, I don't know, enhance the taste?"

Alice hesitated, her fingers lingering on the worn edge of her alchemy book, her brow knitting together in thought. The wheels of her mind began to spin faster. "Full disclosure? This is way out of my league. We'd be walking into uncharted territory. Sure, we could try swapping ingredients, but who knows what we'll end up with? And I'm pretty sure others have attempted this kind of thing before."

"Maybe they have," Jace mused, "but who's to say? Back home, people are always inventing new foods and combinations. Ten years ago, no one had even heard of a pineapple maple bacon burrito."

Alice raised an eyebrow, skepticism clear in her voice. "That's hard to believe." But before she could say more, her words trailed off, her eyes glazing over as something unseen stole her attention—an unmistakable sign of a prompt appearing in her vision.

"Wait... something's happening..."

Jace tilted his head, his curiosity sharpening. "What is it?"

"I just got a quest. A mystery quest. From my deity," Alice replied, her tone tinged with awe. With a quick swipe of her hand, she shared the quest with Jace.

New Quest

Onto Something

Jace has suggested there might be more to discover about the food in Terra Mythica. This could be completely unimportant... or it could be the key to something much larger. Explore to find out more.

Jace's grin stretched wider. "Well, that's... ominous."

Alice's eyes lit up, her earlier hesitation melting into excitement. "Yeah, I'm in. But where do we even start? I'm not exactly an expert on food alchemy."

Jace shrugged, but Alice already pulling out jars of exotic spices and vials of shimmering liquids.

"You think I am?" he asked. "We're just two mad scientists with a kitchen full of potential disasters."

With an eager nod, Alice flipped open her alchemy book, her fingers skimming over ancient recipes with the precision of someone who actually knew what they were doing. Jace, on the other hand, dove into the mixing process like a mad scientist on a sugar high—half genius, half chaos. The truth was, he had no idea what he was doing, and without Alice's watchful eye, he was one bad ingredient away from turning the lab into a smoldering crater.

"I have no clue what's going to happen," Alice admitted, a mix of thrill and dread in her voice as she watched Jace add a dash of something green that fizzled ominously.

"And isn't that the best part?" Jace replied, his grin as bright as the sparks flying off the concoction in front of him.

For hours, they tinkered and toiled, each experiment more daring than the last. The first batch left them puckering from the sourness, the second was so bland it tasted like disappointment, and the third—well, that one congealed into something that smelled disturbingly like old gym socks. But with every failure, their determination only grew, stoked by the laughter that echoed through the lab and the clinking of glassware as they pressed on, like two kids playing with the universe's chemistry set.

Their fifth attempt at the potion simmered in its cauldron. Jace twisted the final ingredient into the bubbling brew, his focus unbroken by the clatter of the chaotic lab around him. But when the first drop hit his tongue, his face contorted in an involuntary grimace. The flavor was intense, all right—like someone had boiled down a century's worth of misery into a single, unholy essence.

But Jace, unfazed by the setback, merely shook his head, determination flickering brighter than the lamp flames. Every failure was a step forward in their understanding.

He and Alice shared a medley of scavenged snacks—crackers, candied nuts, whatever they could find—each bland bite a small comfort, fueling their resolve as the hours slipped by. The lab, once orderly, had become a whirlwind of alchemical tools and half-finished concoctions. The air was thick with the mingling scents of herbs, and spices, and the unmistakable aroma of magic.

Eventually, Jace's hands moved with the confidence of someone who had failed enough times to finally master the basics, the rhythmic grinding of herbs in his mortar becoming almost meditative. Fortunately, Alice had a tendency to hoard ingredients and supplies, giving them more than enough to experiment with.

As they worked, Jace felt the familiar tingle of his experience points draining away, the subtle shift as they flowed into his attributes and abilities. It was a quiet reminder that even in this mad dance of trial and error, progress was being made—each failure and success adding up in ways that couldn't yet be fully seen but were deeply felt.

Alice's eyes narrowed slightly, a mix of curiosity and something deeper as she watched Jace work, his hands moving with a kind of unstudied grace. Each motion was fluid, almost instinctual, like he was more part of the ingredients than separate from them. There was a quiet in his movements, a calm she hadn't associated with him before—this Jace was different, more at ease, as if the usual edges were smoothed out.

"Where'd you learn to do all this?" she asked, her voice breaking through the soft hiss and bubbles of their concoctions.

"Honestly, I'm just winging it," he said, sniffing the air before adding another pinch of green to the mix. He stirred absentmindedly, his focus divided between their concoction and the memories that had surfaced. "We used to camp a lot. Fishing, foraging... making do with whatever we could scrounge up. We didn't have much, but we learned how to make it work. My brother and I... we didn't have a choice. We had to get creative."

The atmosphere thickened with the weight of his words, the past creeping into the present.

"It sounds like you made something special out of it," Alice said softly, her voice a gentle nudge, coaxing him to share more.

Jace nodded, a faint, bittersweet smile curving his lips. "We did. We had to. My brother and I... we grew up in foster care. Never knew our real parents, but the people who took us in—they didn't have much, but they had heart. And they knew how to turn nothing into something."

They continued to work in tandem, the night cocooning them in a blanket of muted sounds—just the bubbling of the pots and their quiet conversation. Words flowed between them as easily as the concoctions simmering away, stories twining with the scent of herbs, and the occasional clink of glass. Jace, almost without realizing it, began to unravel parts of himself, his past slipping into the present like an uninvited guest.

His gaze drifted, the room fading as memories took hold, vivid and unfiltered. "They'd take the simplest ingredients and turn them into feasts. Fresh fish over a campfire, seasoned with whatever we could find... it wasn't just food. It was an adventure. We'd set traps to catch what we could. And Dad—he was the kind of guy who'd look at a can of beans and a hot dog and see a banquet. Ever had hotdog fried rice? Probably not, but to us... it was the best thing in the world."

As he spoke, the lab around them seemed to dissolve, leaving only the glow of the lamps and the shared space of their stories. The night stretched on, and a warmth that seeped through him, more potent than any fire. It was the warmth of connection, of shared memories, and the comfort found in the presence of someone who cared enough to listen.

Alice smiled, a gentle curve of her lips that carried the weight of understanding as she carefully measured the liquid into the beaker, each drop a silent acknowledgment of shared burdens. "What happened to them?"

There was the briefest pause before Jace spoke. "A car accident." His voice was brittle with old pain. He added a pinch of ground herbs to the mixture, watching as the colors swirled and shifted—a silent alchemy mirroring the turmoil inside him. "A drunk driver hit them and vanished into the night."

"I'm so sorry," Alice whispered, her hand brushing against his arm, a tender gesture that spoke volumes where words could not reach.

"It's okay," Jace replied, his smile a faint, well-worn shield. "It was a long time ago. After that, they tried to shove us back into foster care, but we couldn't do it. My brother and I slipped through the cracks, disappearing into the city's shadows. We worked any job we could find -lived off scraps. But food... food's always been more than just sustenance for me."

Alice nodded, her stirring slowing as she absorbed his words, the rhythm of her movements reflecting her deepening empathy. "And your biological parents? Do you remember them at all?"

"Sometimes, I think I catch a scent, or hear something faint... but who knows if any of it's real?" Jace's voice trailed off, the uncertainty in his tone matching the flicker of doubt in his eyes.

Alice nodded, her hands moving with practiced precision as she measured out another ingredient, but her mind was clearly somewhere else. "I get that," she murmured. "My mom... she died giving birth to me. Dad always said she'd been sick for a long time, that the doctors warned her she couldn't have a child. But she didn't care. She was stubborn like that." A small, wistful smile tugged at her lips. "Dad said even the doctor cried when I was born—called it a miracle."

Jace's smile was gentle, an unspoken encouragement, sensing that she needed to let this out. He didn't interrupt, giving her the space to find her voice.

"But how could it be a miracle," Alice whispered, her voice trembling, teetering on the brink of tears, "if it meant losing her?" She tried to sound casual, but the raw pain in her words was unmistakable. "Sometimes, I think I remember her scent."

She paused, shaking her head as if trying to clear away the memories. "Dad and I run a diner now, out on the East Coast. I still help out when I can, but he wants me to focus on this—on being here. I'm their only chance at something better, if I make it. This isn't just a game for me."

Jace's hand found hers, his touch warm and steady, a silent promise that he understood, that he was with her in this. "You're right," he said quietly, his voice full of conviction. "It's not a game for any of us anymore, if it ever was."

The words hung between them, weighty with unspoken fears and shared burdens, yet somehow lighter for having been voiced.

"That's why I'm always studying," she admitted, her voice tightening under the strain of unspoken desperation. "I need to be great. I have to be. My dad spent everything…" Her voice faltered.

"We'll make it," Jace said softly. It wasn't just a reassurance; it was a vow, a pact against the odds that loomed over them. As they returned to their work, the lamplight seemed to flicker a little brighter, casting a warm, hopeful glow over the lab, as if even the room itself was rooting for them.

The night deepened, the air thick with the rich, heady scents of herbs and simmering brews. Jace leaned over the workbench, his brow furrowed in concentration as he measured the final drop of nightshade extract, its dark liquid catching the light for a fleeting moment before vanishing into the mixture. Beside him, Alice adjusted the flame beneath their cauldron with a careful hand, her eyes darting between the potion's simmering surface and Jace.

As the hours wore on, exhaustion began to creep into their bones. Alice, usually so bright with focus, now showed the unmistakable signs of weariness—her eyes heavy-lidded, her movements slowed to a deliberate pace. She leaned against the workbench, brushing a stray strand of hair away from her face as she stifled a yawn that threatened to escape.

Still, they pressed on. The night stretched endlessly, but somehow it felt a little less cold, the flickering lamplight a little less harsh. The potion simmered, and amidst it all, hope continued to bubble, stubbornly refusing to let exhaustion win.

Every so often, Jace glanced at his EXP gauge, watching as it steadily drained, fueling his skills and abilities. A subtle surge of energy coursed through him, and he noticed his constitution had ticked up a point.

Chapter 16
Goat Rank

Character Sheet

"Jace, I'm about ready to call it," Alice admitted, her voice heavy with fatigue. "I'm beat."

Jace nodded. "Okay, let's just try this last batch," Jace added the final extract to their potion, the liquid hissing and sputtering as it swirled from a murky brown into a brilliant, shimmering emerald. Alice held her breath, watching as Jace gave the potion one last, deliberate stir.

His eyes fell on a baguette they'd gotten from the kitchen earlier, and he tore it in half before handing a piece to Alice. He poured a tiny drop onto each half of the baguette, spreading it around carefully. They exchanged glances, their earlier exhaustion forgotten.

Alice watched as Jace brought the bread to his nose, her curiosity sparking despite the weariness.

"Smells... good. Sweet," he said.

"That could be a good thing, or very bad," she said, looking at it skeptically.

"Moment of truth," Jace declared.

They bit into their baguettes simultaneously, their eyes meeting in shared anticipation that hung in the air like static before a storm. As the flavors hit their tongues, they froze—then burst into a chorus of moans and laughter, the sound rich and giddy, echoing off the lab's stone walls like music.

Jace chewed slowly, ready to spit it out at the first sign of trouble, when suddenly—flavor exploded on his tongue, so vivid and unexpected that it felt like all their efforts had materialized in that single, transformative moment. He blinked, surprise flickering across his face before it gave way to a slow, dawning smile.

Alice nodded, a proud smile curving her lips. It was good. It was really good.

She laughed, a sudden burst of sound that caught even her by surprise, followed by an undignified snort. Her eyes widened in embarrassment as she clapped her hands over her mouth, trying—and failing—to stifle the rest of her laughter.

The taste was that of raw honey. Jace couldn't help but laugh as well. He hadn't realized how much he missed the taste of food, and the joy from it came in bursts of pure, unfiltered happiness. Such a simple thing, in such an uncertain moment.

It was the kind of laughter that only comes after hours of hard work and a little bit of madness. They exchanged a glance, smiles spreading wider. Neither had realized just how much they needed that small, simple victory.

New Discovery: Flavorful Infusion

You've uncovered a method to enhance the taste of food using alchemy.

Alchemy Rank Up!

You have gained a deeper understanding of alchemical processes. Your skill has increased, and you've unlocked a unique ability.

Achievement Unlocked - Tinker

+1% chance to create an unexpected effect in your potions if brewed while cultivating aether. This potion contains a drop of your aether cultivation, aligning with your aether pathways.

Achievement Unlocked - Unique - Willing to Try Anything

When life gives you lemons, you make lemon pizza. You're the sort of person who sees mayonnaise and brownies and thinks, "Why not?" Maybe it's a little weird, but you're on a first-name basis with weird, and it's never let you down before.

Enjoy a 20% boost in success and effectiveness when brewing potions with bizarre or unique ingredients. Lean into the madness and let your inner alchemist thrive!

Achievement Unlocked - Iron Stomach - Goat Rank

You've eaten things that would make a billy goat gag. Whether it's questionable street food or mystery meat that defies the laws of biology, you've downed it all without batting an eye. Your digestive system is practically a myth.

Gain a 25% resistance to all poisons, toxins, and food-related mishaps. With an Iron Stomach, you're ready for whatever culinary horrors—or delights—the world throws your way!

Item created - Secret Sauce

You've concocted a sauce that would make even the gods pause for a taste. Congratulations, you've invented the gastronomical equivalent of a game-changer.

This elixir boosts food flavor concentration by 500%.

The air hummed with a residual magic that clung to the edges of the night, like the last tendrils of a dream slipping through the fingers of dawn. Jace and Alice, bathed in the warm, amber glow of their small victory, stood amidst the remnants of their laughter. The potion in the cauldron no longer bubbled with mere potential—it was a living testament to the audacity of hope and the quiet, resolute power of belief. Outside, the night still pressed in, but its darkness had softened, retreating from the borders of their triumph.

And then, the extraordinary wove itself into the ordinary.

Jace felt it first, a quiet stir deep within, as though the very marrow of his bones had begun to sing. The sensation spread, warm and insistent, until it bloomed outward, his skin radiating a soft, otherworldly glow. It wasn't the harsh light of revelation but something gentler, more ancient, as if the stars themselves had found a home beneath his flesh. The air thickened with a palpable energy, and he felt his feet lift, the ground becoming a distant memory as he hovered just above it, suspended by the currents of raw power that surged through him.

Ding!

The sound cut through the air, not a mere notification but a resonant chime that echoed in the marrow of his soul.

Rank Up

Congratulations, you have successfully focused your accumulated EXP, enhancing the magical pathways for your aether to flow and deepening your understanding of the world and your Word of Power: Soul. Soul has reached Bronze Two, officially qualifying you for the title of Apprentice Perceptor.

The world around him snapped into focus, reality tightening until every detail stood out with an almost unnatural clarity. The alchemy lab wasn't just a collection of beakers and dusty tomes anymore; it buzzed with a new energy, every flicker of the flames beneath the cauldron purposeful. The mingling scents of herbs and elixirs became a rich, intoxicating blend that filled the air.

And Alice... she stood nearby, her quiet smile steadying him as the magic coursed through his veins. She didn't need to say anything; her presence alone was enough to keep him grounded as the power settled.

The light around him dimmed, the glow fading as he floated back to solid ground. The room seemed to hold its breath, the echoes of his ascent lingering in the silence. When his feet finally touched the stone floor, a deep stillness took over, the air thrumming with the residue of his transformation.

His powers were no longer just hidden tools, waiting for a moment of need. They hummed with life, each ability now clear and distinct, a new awareness settling in his mind. This was why they called it a Perceptor—his senses sharpened, his aether humming with a newfound clarity.

Exhausted but riding the high of their victory, they finally let themselves relax. The night had drained them, but the satisfaction in the air was undeniable. Even the clutter and chaos of the lab seemed to have a certain artistry to it now, the remnants of their efforts transformed into a testament to their triumph.

The last thing he remembered before sleep claimed him was looking at his Character Sheet, a mix of excitement and exhaustion pulling at him. As he reviewed the stats and abilities, he could feel the energy within him shifting, more alive and tangible than ever before.

Character Sheet
    Name: Jace
    Rank: Bronze Two - Apprentice Perceptor
    Class Title: Cleric
    EXP Capacity Bar: 0/3000

    Attributes:
    • Strength: 18
    • Dexterity: 22
    • Intelligence: 28
    • Wisdom: 30
    • Constitution: 15
    • Charisma: 12
    • Karmic Balance: 2

    Skills:

• Dark Vision (Apprentice): Enhanced ability to see in darkness with greater clarity.

• Knowledge Absorption (Apprentice): Improved retention and comprehension of absorbed knowledge.

• Universal Lore (Apprentice): Increased understanding of game mechanics and world lore.

• Resistance to Death (Apprentice): Reduces damage from necrotic, evil, and shadow-based attacks by 7%.

Words of Power / Affinities:
Soul - Silver Two, Apprentice Perceptor
Your Affinity has increased, allowing you more direct control over your abilities.

Soul Affinity Abilities:
• Soul Survivor (Internal Passive):
15% increased resistance to soul damage.
Faster recovery from soul-based injuries.
Aether Cost: None

• Soul Mend (Distance: Sight):
Heal severe wounds efficiently, allowing for multiple quick heals.
Passive Aspect: A small portion of aether is dedicated to personal healing, providing constant restoration and reducing self-mending costs by 50%.
Aether Cost: Moderate
• Soul Tether (Distance - Sight):
Transfer significant effects between entities over greater distances.
Enhanced connection perception, allowing you to see and feel from the perspective of the connected entity, potentially gleaning valuable insights and memories.
Aether Cost: High

• Soul Sense (Distance - Sight):
Sharpened perception of auras, discerning emotions, intentions, and hidden motives.

Detect spiritual disturbances and perceive wandering spirits more effectively.

Aether Cost: Low

• Soul Severance:

Detect and remove foreign incursions from a host body.

Sever the connection between an invading entity and its host.

Aether Cost: Severe

Chapter 17
By Thor's Hammer

The morning slid in gently, like a cat sneaking through a cracked door. Jace blinked awake, the unfamiliar weight on his shoulder making him freeze for a second. It took him a moment to piece it together—the table he'd dozed off on, the warmth beside him, and the silken strands brushing his cheek. His eyes met Alice's, mere inches away, wide and startled, mirroring his own.

For a beat, they just stared, caught in the strange stillness of dawn, where the world outside their cocoon of blankets—borrowed from Jace's dorm—felt distant and unreal. Jace's lips curved into a crooked smile, and Alice's expression softened, the surprise giving way to something unspoken, yet unmistakably clear between them. The chaos of the night before had forged a connection, one that, in the hush of the morning, hinted at the beginning of something neither of them could quite define.

"Morning," Alice whispered, her cheeks blooming with a pink that had nothing to do with the cold of morning.

"Uh, yeah, morning," Jace replied, suddenly all thumbs as he scrambled upright, brushing his clothes like they'd been colonized by invisible dust mites. "Think we might've gone a bit overboard."

Alice's laugh was a soft, tinkling thing, the kind that made Jace's chest feel a little too tight, in a good way. "Maybe just a tad," she teased, tucking a loose strand of hair behind her ear, her gaze darting to his and then away, like a skittish bird. "We should probably, um, head to breakfast."

"Right," Jace said, clearing his throat like it might erase the awkwardness that still lingered.

The mess hall greeted them with a clatter of dishes and the chatter of early risers. Golden light streamed through the windows, casting long shadows over the bustling tables.

Jace and Alice entered, hair tousled, clothes wrinkled, but eyes alight with the gleam of barely contained excitement. They looked less like students and more like a duo who'd cracked the secret of the universe and were now holding it on a humble plate.

Dex and Ell, already at their usual table, paused mid-banter as Jace and Alice approached, their concoction held with the care of a sacred relic. The dish, at first glance, seemed innocuous—just another plate of pastries in the chaos of breakfast.

They settled into their usual seats, the weariness of the night still clinging to their clothes like stubborn shadows. Dex was the first to notice, eyebrows shooting up as he took in their rumpled appearance. "Well, well, well. Look who decided to join us," he teased, a smirk playing at his lips.

Ell tossed a wink that could melt steel. "Must've been some experiment. You two look like you were trying to bring the dead back to life."

Jace, caught somewhere between pride and a shrug, managed a casual reply. "You could say that. But it's more like... culinary necromancy."

Alice, cheeks still betraying a hint of pink, gave him a playful shove. "Reanimating breakfast croissants isn't exactly in the course catalog."

Jace set the plate down at the center of the table, the food shimmering faintly, as if touched by some arcane glow. Dex and Ell eyed it like he'd just served up a freshly exhumed corpse.

Ell leaned in, eying the plate with mock suspicion. "And this... resurrection—should we be worried? You know, in case it sprouts legs and starts marauding through the hall?" She prodded a muffin with her fork, half-expecting it to bite back.

"Only one way to find out," Jace retorted, placing the dish in the center of the table with all the solemnity of an offering to the gods.

Dex and Ell exchanged a glance, the wariness clear in their eyes, but curiosity soon won out. They each took a forkful, their expressions shifting the moment the flavor hit—what started as casual interest morphed into wide-eyed disbelief.

"What in the name of all that is holy... this is amazing!" Dex blurted out, barely swallowing before he reached for another bite.

Ell's voice joined his, tinged with something close to reverence. "Seriously, what kind of sorcery is this? I've never tasted anything like it. At least, not here."

Jace's grin spread, the exhaustion of the night's work forgotten in the glow of their reactions. "It's a little bit of cooking, a little bit of alchemy," he explained, savoring the moment. "We were at it all night, but it looks like it paid off."

Ell's eyes narrowed with playful intent as she turned to Alice. "All night, huh?" The words were light, but the glance she shot Alice was anything but innocent. Alice's face flared red, and she responded with a swift kick under the table, making Ell yelp and grin wider.

Dex nodded vigorously, practically bouncing in his seat. "Jace, this could be huge. I'd pay good money for this."

Alice, her excitement barely held in check, leaned forward. "Someone's probably done something like this somewhere, but it's certainly new to Olympus. Professor Blackwood mentioned how a lot of resources are tied up with the war effort; the kitchens don't have the time or the staff they need."

"Which we got to witness firsthand," Jace added.

Dex's eyes suddenly lit up as if struck by divine inspiration. "Oh my ancient lords of yore, I just had an idea!"

Jace blinked, confusion clear on his face. "Lords of what now?"

Dex leaned in, his voice dropping to a conspiratorial whisper. "Come on, man, we're in Terra Mythica. You've got to commit. Embrace the world we're in."

Ell rolled her eyes, a bemused smile tugging at her lips. "Pretty sure that's not a thing here."

"By Thor's hammer, then!" Dex tried again.

"Wrong pantheon," Jace said.

Dex shot him a mock glare. "For Hades' sake, will you let me finish? I've got an idea!"

"Proceed," Alice said with mock seriousness, folding her arms like a judge passing a verdict. The group nodded in exaggerated approval.

Dex straightened, speeding up as if racing the clock. "So, you all know about the Star Ceremony at the end of the year, right? The one where everyone who's learned their first Word gets their Bronze Star?"

Jace had no idea, but he nodded along with the others, wearing his best "I totally get this" face.

"Well, there's always a massive party afterward. A celebration so big it practically pulls the stars down from the sky."

Alice pulled a hefty tome from her inventory, its cover worn and battle-scarred. "It's called the Midnight Festival," she explained, flipping through pages like a pro. "It happens the day after the Star Awards, right around Halloween. I dug up a whole section on it in the library."

"They have Halloween here?" Jace asked, one eyebrow arching in surprise.

"It's not exactly Halloween," Alice explained, her voice tinged with that bookish enthusiasm she always had when she was about to drop some knowledge. "More like a fall festival that's picked up some of our traditions over the centuries. But yeah, the past few hundred years, it's been influenced by our culture."

Dex, never one to linger too long on details that weren't his own, jumped back into his idea. "Anyway, it's a big deal. The students run the party, but some of the faculty like to crash it and pretend they're still in their prime. Whoever hosts it becomes a living legend. Last year, they had a lake party with the Poseidon crew. Apparently, it was incredible."

Jace leaned in, genuinely curious. "Where do you get all this intel, Dex?"

Dex flashed a grin that suggested he had his fingers in many pies—some more savory than others. "I have my sources."

"By 'sources,' you mean the girls over in Aphrodite," Jace pressed, eyebrow arching.

"A gentleman doesn't kiss and tell," Dex said, his grin slipping into a sly wink. "And he definitely doesn't do a bunch of other stuff and tell, if you catch my drift."

He barely got the words out before Ell and Alice's synchronized kicks connected under the table, forcing a yelp from him.

"What if this year, we convince them to hold the party in Hades' Fields Below?" Ell suggested, her eyes gleaming with mischief.

"That's exactly what I was getting to!" Dex shot back, his scowl quickly morphing into wide-eyed excitement as he turned to Jace. "Just think about it! The Fields Below as the venue. It would be legendary."

"Do you really think it's appropriate? Or that they'll even have a party with everything going on?" Jace asked, his voice laced with doubt.

"I think it's even more important because of everything going on," Alice countered, her tone soft but unwavering. "People need a sense of normalcy—a bit of light in the darkness."

Jace hesitated, his thoughts drifting to Shadow, worry clawing at him. He hadn't seen her this morning, though he hadn't honestly expected to. He just hoped she was alright.

Dex leaned in, not letting up. "Come on, Jace. Everyone's been itching to see that place since it showed up on the map. Even I'm curious—and Alice is the only one who's been there? Doesn't seem right, does it?"

Ell shot him a sidelong glance, one eyebrow arched high in silent judgment.

"What?" he asked, puzzled.

Jace sighed. A party in Hades' domain—it was tempting, no doubt, but the idea was tangled with too many complications. "Wait... what did you just say? About the map?"

"The campus map," Dex explained. "You didn't notice? The moment you activated the place, it triggered a system-wide update on all our maps."

Jace pulled up his map, his eyes widening as he spotted the section drenched in ominous shades of grey and black, buried deep underground—Hades' Fields Below.

"Wait, everyone can see this?" Jace asked, still struggling to process it. "I'd hoped it was just me."

"Yup, and people are dying to know what's down there. I'm thinking 'Tales from the Crypt' meets Greek mythology," Dex said, grinning like a fox who'd just raided the henhouse.

"What's 'Tales from the Crypt'?" Ell asked, her brow furrowed.

"It's a holo disc from Pre-Purge," Alice chimed in, a note of excitement in her voice. "A collection of stories about death, evil, and things that go bump in the night." She paused, realizing everyone was staring at her. "My dad used to make us watch all the Pre-Purge stuff. Said it was educational. Plus, the holodiscs were free at the library."

Dex leaned back, nodding appreciatively. "You know, Alice, there's a delightfully dark side to you. I like it."

Alice blushed, a small smile tugging at her lips despite herself.

Dex turned back to Jace, his eyes gleaming with anticipation. "So, got any undead wandering around down there looking for brains?"

"Not that I've seen," Jace replied, suppressing a grin. "Hades isn't really into the undead. They're like students who never showed up for class but keep hanging around anyway."

Dex chuckled. "Well, we can fix that. A few decorations, a touch of mold, and bam—instant haunted house."

Jace hesitated, the darker secrets of the Fields Below whispering at the edges of his thoughts. "I don't know... there's stuff down there that shouldn't be part of a campus party."

"It might be smart," Alice said, surprising Jace. She wasn't usually the party-going type. "You mentioned needing money for next year's tuition. We could turn it into a real event—sell tickets, food, drinks. We might even make enough to cover some expenses."

Jace had confided in her the night before, a rare note of uncertainty in his voice, about his fears of not securing another scholarship. This party might not solve everything, but it could make a real difference. Even if it didn't cover everything, it could chip away at the tuition, buying him time to level up and prepare for what lay beyond the campus.

Alice pressed on, her confidence growing. "Besides, it's already creepy enough. A little extra atmosphere could make it perfect."

Ell jumped in, eyes sparkling. "We could go for that abandoned chic vibe. I'd love to help with the decorations."

All eyes turned to Jace, their excitement practically vibrating in the air.

He sighed, feeling their energy pulling him in. "Alright, let's do it," he agreed, unable to resist.

A collective whoop echoed through the room, bouncing off the walls like the first cheers of a victorious team. The decision was made—they'd spread the word, knowing that once the wild bunch from Dionysus got wind of it, the news would spread faster than wildfire.

Jace felt a flicker of hope, a sensation both foreign and oddly comforting. Maybe, just maybe, this was the answer. He doubted he could land another full-ride scholarship like Alex had, and the clock was ticking on finding the money. But this... this might just work.

Suddenly, a blinking notification flared in Jace's vision, urgent and impossible to ignore.

Urgent Quest Update

    "I Ain't 'Fraid of No Ghosts..."

    Penalties increasing. Rewards decreasing... again. Recalibrating.

The words pulsed ominously, like the system itself was losing patience. Jace felt a cold shiver crawl up his spine.

"What do you make of this?" he asked, sharing the quest details with the group.

"You still haven't completed your deity quest?" Dex's eyes widened, disbelief wiping away his smirk. "Go on, shoo! Git!" He waved Jace off.

Jace's gaze remained locked on the relentless, blinking prompt. "It is getting pretty insistent," he muttered.

"Should we go with him?" Alice asked, concern creasing her brow.

"I've got classes," Ell said, though her tone wavered, weighing her options against the threat Jace was facing.

"He'll be fine... probably," Dex murmured, his voice tinged with the kind of optimism you find in gamblers on a losing streak. "First deity quest, no big deal, right? How hard could it be?" His eyes flicked around, looking for comfort, before settling back on Jace with a glimmer of doubt. "But, you know... if things get a bit... strange, just send us a Magic Missive. We'll be there. Promise."

Jace grimaced, realizing with a sinking feeling that his cleric rod was still in shambles. "Uh, anyone got a cleric rod or weapon I could borrow?"

"I've got this," Dex said, pulling out a wickedly curved dagger, its blade gleaming with a dark, unsettling sheen. "Don't need it anymore—got an upgrade. Was going to sell it, but you can have it."

Jace accepted the dagger, feeling its weight, unfamiliar but oddly reassuring. He'd never used a dagger before, but it was better than nothing. "Thanks," he murmured, though the word felt inadequate.

With a nod to his friends, Jace turned on his heel, heading toward the quest marker. Skipping his morning classes was an easy decision, the urgent tug of the quest pulling him forward like a hook in his chest. Whatever awaited him in Zone Three, it wasn't something he could ignore any longer. The quest was calling, and this time, he had no choice but to answer.

Chapter 18
Optional Paths

Activating his ward stone, Jace pulled up his map, guiding himself toward the quest marker on the outskirts of zone three. A nagging thought surfaced—he hadn't asked Alice to take notes for their next classes. She'd probably do it anyway, but it wouldn't hurt to make sure. After all, that's what friends do, right? Shaking off the unnecessary doubts, he retrieved a sheet of red magic missive paper from his inventory. With quick, fluid strokes, he scribbled a short note, folded the paper, and activated the message feature. The note shimmered, transforming into a small, intricately folded paper dragon that soared into the air, disappearing into the distance.

Jace pulled up his quest to review the details, the map directing him away from the campus.

Quest Update
Profession Quest: Hades' Little Helper
I Ain't 'Fraid of No Ghosts...

Objective: The soul of a woman lingers in the wilderness, miles east of the campus—a soul that should have moved on long ago. Something binds her there. Unravel the mystery, and set things right.
Reward: 50 Society Points
Failure: Impending Doom

Bonus Objective: Give it that little extra.
Bonus Reward: Unknown

Slipping through the main gates, Jace faced the forest ahead, its shadows thick and foreboding.

You Are Now Entering Zone 2
    Note: Creatures With Ranks Up To Bronze Three May Be Present.

Jace moved quietly, his steps echoing through the trees despite his best efforts. The forest was alive with subtle noises—the rustling of leaves, distant bird calls, and the occasional snap of a twig. His attempts at stealth were laughable.

Skill Gained: Sneak Novice - Rank 1
    Your steps are softer, though still not exactly quiet. You've graduated from a boisterous rhinoceros to a sneaking hippo. Keep practicing, and you might not alert every creature within a mile radius.

He chuckled. "Great, at least I'm on the right track." His steps grew lighter, the ground beneath him softening as he gradually became less noticeable. He wondered why this hadn't happened before, back in the dome. Could the environment play a role? Was sneaking a harder skill to acquire than he thought? It didn't seem likely. Maybe it was easier now because of his increased dexterity.

    As he ventured deeper into the forest, the campus's protective barrier weakened, and a new notification flashed before his eyes.

You Are Now Entering Zone Three
    You are leaving the main campus grounds. Protections against greater threats are in place.
    Rank Recommendation: Bronze 4-5. You are under the suggested rank. Travel at your own risk.

He checked his Ward Stone again, relieved to see it still glowing, and exhaled a deep breath. Jace paused, gripping his dagger tighter as the shadows thickened. The path twisted and turned like a serpent, roots coiling across the ground, waiting to ensnare the unwary. The forest felt alive—a labyrinth of towering trees and choking underbrush. Beams of sunlight occasionally pierced the canopy, casting twisted shadows that danced like wraiths on the forest floor.

He moved cautiously, senses on high alert. The scent of damp earth and decay clung to everything, each rustle in the dark sending a shiver racing through him. He strained to hear over the pounding of his heart, every nerve on edge.

A low growl sliced through the silence. Jace froze, eyes scanning the gloom. Then, from the darkness, a pair of glowing eyes materialized. A creature lunged—a blur of teeth and shadow.

Instinct took over. Jace slashed his dagger in a swift arc, connecting with a sickening crunch. The creature let out a shrill screech before crumpling, its form unraveling into wisps of smoke that dissipated into the dying light of day.

You Have Defeated - Itsy Bitsy Spider
> Down came the dagger and you squished the spider out.
> Great work. I'm sure its mommy won't mind.
> EXP Gained: 1

Boon Gained - One Hit Wonder
> You managed to kill a creature with one hit. Well done. Have a cookie.
> +10% XP gained from creatures you smite with one hit.
> Adjusting EXP gained from Itsy Bitsy Spider: 1 + 0.1, rounding... total EXP gained: 1

Jace blinked at the notification. Was the system mocking him? Or was it Hades? *If I ever meet one of the programmers...*

The cabin, marked on his map for the quest, loomed ahead, its jagged silhouette cutting against the dying light, an ominous shadow in the encroaching twilight. The windows glowed faintly, the light inside struggling to break free from the surrounding darkness. Jace approached cautiously, dread gnawing at his gut. The air was colder now, heavier, and the distant hoot of an owl sounded more like a lament—a mournful cry that echoed in the silence.

Jace knocked, but there was no response. He knocked again—still nothing. He tried the handle; it wasn't locked. Pushing the door open, he stepped inside. The dim interior was lit by a single oil lamp, its weak flame casting long, jittery shadows that seemed to move on their own. At the center of the room lay a young woman on a cloth cot, her skin pallid and ghostly. Her shallow breaths were the only sign she was still clinging to life.

Beside her sat a man, his face etched with worry, eyes hollow and sunken as if he hadn't slept in days. He clutched the girl's hand, knuckles white with desperation.

Over both of them loomed another figure—a tall, gaunt man with a face almost skeletal. Shadows played over his sharp features, making his eyes appear sunken and unnaturally dark.

His long, spidery hands were stained, and he wore a white coat that looked like it had seen too many years.

The eyes of the man in white snapped up as Jace entered, narrowing with suspicion. "Who are you?" he demanded, his voice edged with a shrill note.

"Uh, hi. I'm a Cleric. I'm here to help," Jace said, stepping forward despite the instinctive urge to retreat. "I was sent by... someone who knows the girl." He hesitated to mention Hades, unsure how they'd react. That name had been getting mixed reviews lately. Then again, his insignia and dark attire probably said enough on that matter.

The man scrutinized Jace, then reluctantly nodded, before turning away. "I'm Dr. Ponos. This is Sophie, and her husband Damon," he said, his voice a low rasp. He gave a sad smile that didn't quite reach his eyes. "They were on their honeymoon when she fell ill. It's a curse, I'm afraid."

He noticed the doctor's eyes flick to his arm, where the tattoo of Hades marked his skin. The doctor's expression shifted, suspicion darkening his gaze.

"Sent from Hades, are you? I should have known. Greedy, all of you," he muttered, disdain clear in his voice.

"Careful, doctor. I'm new to being a Chosen of Hades, but he's still my deity."

"I'm sorry," Ponos said, grimacing. "It's just... it's no fault of Hades. He's just doing his job, but he can only act on the information he has. And sometimes, that information can be wrong."

"She can still be saved?"

"Oh, yes. I believe so," Ponos replied, a glimmer of hope in his tone.

Jace stepped forward, attempting to activate Soul Mend, but the doctor slapped his hand away.

"Not like that, you fool!" Ponos scowled. "That could damn her forever. She has a parasitic curse inside her. Even an Advanced Cleric would struggle with it. You'd only make it worse—or kill her!"

Jace withdrew his hand as if burned.

"Don't worry, my child. All is not lost. I've been treating her for weeks, and we finally have the cure. Well, most of it. We just need the final components. I was going to gather them myself, but she took a turn for the worse. If I leave her side, she'll die within moments." He lowered his voice to a whisper. "And Damon is too stricken with grief to be of much help, poor boy."

The doctor's eyes flicked back to Sophie, and Jace caught a fleeting smirk—a tiny twitch that filled him with unease. He glanced at Damon, who sat unmoving beside the girl, his face a mask of grief, his grip tight on her hand. The room felt stifling, the air thick with tension.

"Aren't you a Cleric? Isn't it your job to heal?" Ponos asked, eyeing Jace's dagger.

Jace nodded, storing the dagger away. He glanced at Sophie—her breaths were shallow, labored, each one a struggle. He tried to sense her aura, but his mind was clouded, unable to focus.

You have attempted to use Spirit Sense. Spirit Sense failed. Increase ranks in Spirit Sense to improve accuracy and effectiveness.

A knot of anxiety tightened in Jace's chest. The doctor's words seemed reasonable, but something felt off. A notification flashed before his eyes.

Quest Update

I Ain't 'Fraid of No Ghost...

Optional: Dr. Ponos has offered an option path for your quest. Gather the ingredients needed for a potion to cure Sophie.

Reward: Unknown.

Failure: Unknown.

Accept | Reject

Jace looked at Sophie, her life slipping away with each breath, then at Damon, frozen in his grief. "I'll get it. What do you need?" Jace accepted the quest update.

Dr. Ponos handed him a crumpled list of herbs, his hand trembling slightly. "Be quick. She doesn't have much time."

With a final look at the scene before him, Jace turned and left the cabin, the door creaking shut behind him. It was evening now, and the night air felt heavy and oppressive, the shadows closing in as he set off to gather the ingredients, unease gnawing at him.

The forest seemed darker now, more menacing. Jace moved quickly, his feet instinctively avoiding tangled roots and fallen branches. The damp, earthy smell mingled with the scent of decaying leaves and pine needles. There was also a faint metallic tang, like rust or damp iron. The rustling of leaves in the wind and the occasional caw of a crow added to the eerie atmosphere.

As he read the descriptions of the herbs again and focused his senses, a faint glow began to appear within a nearby bush.

Skill Gained

Herbalism - Rank

By exploring the forest and collecting strange plants, you've increased your affinity for recognizing and using various herbs. This skill allows you to identify common medicinal and magical plants, understand their basic properties, and harvest them effectively. As your rank increases, so will your knowledge and ability to discern their minute differences and uses.

Using his new skill, the task was uneventful, thankfully. Yet, Jace's nerves remained taut, ready to react at the slightest rustle.

He collected a handful of each ingredient: Nightshade berries, their dark, glossy skins glistening in the dim light; Moonroot, with its pale, luminescent leaves; and Dragon's Breath flowers, their fiery red petals standing out against the dark forest floor.

It didn't specify how much was needed, so he grabbed a little extra to be sure. His heart pounded as he made his way back to the cabin, the weight of the situation pressing down on him.

As Jace arrived back at the cabin, the air felt thicker, more oppressive. Dr. Ponos was hunched over the young girl, his movements meticulous and deliberate.

Something inside him screamed that something was profoundly wrong, but Jace pushed the creeping dread from his mind.

The doctor's wrinkled hands carefully laid out various items and plants on a small table next to the bed.

His actions were smooth -practiced, yet there was an unnerving precision to his movements. "Here," Jace said, handing over the requested herbs, trying to steady his voice.

"Thank you," Ponos replied, his tone almost too calm. "I'll start on it right away." He rose from his seat with a surprising quickness. "Oh, I made some tea for you while you traveled. The wildness can be quite parching. It's not much but consider it a small token of thanks for your help so far."

The doctor lifted a cup from a nearby saucer, handing it to Jace in exchange for the herbs.

Jace accepted the cup, nodding in acknowledgment, but a flicker of doubt gnawed at him. He watched as the doctor expertly began mulching the herbs, his hands moving with an eerie efficiency.

The comforting scent of chamomile tea filled the air, but it was tainted with something rancid, something that made Jace's stomach twist in discomfort.

He brought the tea to his lips, but as the rim of the cup brushed against his mouth, a sudden chill prickled down his spine. His hand froze, and a strange energy pulsed through him, sending shivers of fear and something softer—kindness?—through his body. In the depths of his mind, a faint female voice whispered urgently, "Don't drink it."

But it was too late; a single drop had brushed his lips, and in that instant, Jace was consumed by a flash of searing, paralyzing agony before a notification appeared.

Iron Stomach has been triggered. Poison resistance effective.

The sensation quickly faded as Jace's heart thudded in his chest, his hand trembling as he slowly lowered the cup. His eyes narrowed, focusing on the doctor with a newfound suspicion. The old man seemed absorbed in his work, but Jace could feel the malevolence seeping through the room like a slow poison.

Trying to mask his unease, Jace glanced at Damon, who was petrified with grief beside the girl. Kneeling down, Jace studied his friend's features more closely. Damon didn't blink, didn't move—his eyes were vacant, staring into some void that only he could see.

Jace leaned in closer, noticing that Damon's skin had taken on a cold, rigid quality, almost like stone.

"This is really great tea," Jace said, forcing a casual tone. His senses were on high alert, every nerve straining to catch the smallest hint of danger.

The doctor returned with the potion, his smile tight, almost too wide.

"Isn't it?" the doctor replied, his voice sickeningly sweet. "A special brew, as our boy Damon found out. Good thing you came along too. I'm afraid poor Damon here might not have been enough food for our new friend. But you, a fresh Chosen... You are ripe for the plucking."

Before Jace could respond, the girl's body convulsed violently, her limbs thrashing against the sheets bound tightly around her. His breath caught in his throat as her skin seemed to ripple and stretch, almost as if something inside her was trying to tear its way out.

Her veins pulsed with a sickly green light, the dark energy emanating from her growing stronger with each passing second.

Jace's eyes darted to Damon—his hands were bleeding, tiny droplets of blood falling onto the girl's skin, feeding whatever malevolent force had taken hold of her. Horror twisted in his gut as he realized Damon was being used as a sacrifice, and there was nothing he could do to stop it.

As the girl's body went still, her eyes snapped open, revealing a deep, soulless black. The sight made Jace's blood run cold. This wasn't Sophie anymore. This was something else—something dark and ancient.

"Just a little more and she will rise," the doctor muttered, his focus solely on tipping the potion toward the girl's mouth.

A surge of adrenaline shot through Jace. In a swift, decisive motion, he knocked the potion from the doctor's hand, smashing it against the wall. The liquid sizzled and hissed upon contact, burning like acid as it ate through the wood. Jace shoved Damon away, breaking whatever dark connection had formed, and the doctor stumbled to the foot of the bed, his facade slipping to reveal a visage twisted with rage.

"Didn't drink the poison, huh?" the doctor hissed, his eyes glowing with fury. "You're smarter than you look, Chosen of Hades. But it's too late now. She is coming, and there is nothing you can do!"

With an ear-splitting shriek, the demon tore itself free from the girl's body—a spectacle of pure malevolence and shadow. Jace's aura sense screamed the truth: this was no possession. The demon was a parasite, using her flesh as a grotesque puppet. Her back arched violently as the creature forced its way out, its form a churning mist of darkness that fed hungrily on her dwindling life force. It didn't fully detach, lingering in a twisted limbo—half demon, half girl—warping her into a horrific blend of both.

The demon's true shape slowly solidified, a grotesque figure with unnaturally elongated limbs and eyes that burned crimson in the gloom. It let out an inhuman scream, a sound that reverberated with raw hatred and torment. Under its control, the girl's body moved with eerie, unnatural jerks, her limbs contorting grotesquely as her face twisted into a hideous smile, the demon now fully in command.

With a deep, foul laugh that echoed through the cabin, the demon made the girl's body lash out, her hand transforming into a clawed weapon. In a swift, brutal motion, it bashed Jace's dagger from his hands, sending the weapon clattering to the floor. Jace staggered back, his heart pounding as the demonic puppet advanced, its eyes burning with predatory hunger.

Panic surged through Jace, but he forced himself to focus. He reached out with his mind, desperately searching for any sign of Sophie's soul.

You activate Soul Sense. Soul Sense successful.

His vision shifted, and he felt a profound change within.

Soul Sense has gained an Aspect:

Unveil — You have gained a 5% chance to pierce the spirit veil and see past the superficial. See souls like onions, with layers.

The upgrade was instantaneous and overwhelming. Jace's senses expanded, allowing him to perceive the very essence of her soul. Where he once saw only the faint glimmers of auras, he now saw intricate patterns of light and darkness, each telling a different story of pain, struggle, and the fight for control.

Chapter 19
Lighthouse

The room was thick with the scent of sulfur and decay, the air itself seeming to tremble as the summoning circle blazed with an unnatural light. The doctor, his face twisted in a mix of reverence and terror, knelt before the towering form that had emerged from the ritual. The demon stretched, its form solidifying from a shadowy mass into something almost tangible, almost real.

"Yes, rise, my master," the doctor whispered, his voice quivering with a mixture of awe and fear.

The demon's eyes, burning embers in the darkness, turned to regard the doctor with something akin to amusement. "You have done well," it rasped, its voice a guttural echo that seemed to reverberate through the very bones of the room. "Your loyalty is commendable, and I thank you for feeding me your life during the summoning process."

The doctor bowed low, his trembling hands pressed to the cold stone floor. "Of course, Master. It was an honor," he murmured, his voice barely more than a breath.

But Jace, watching from the shadows, felt a sudden unease. Something was wrong. His eyes narrowed as he noticed, for the first time, the faint trickle of energy—of life—seeping from the doctor to the demon, a subtle, almost imperceptible flow.

The demon's eyes gleamed with a predatory light as it inhaled deeply, the flow of life from the doctor intensifying. The trickle became a stream, then a rushing river, as the demon began to draw more, pulling harder.

"Master," the doctor gasped, his eyes wide with sudden panic. "What are you doing?"

"Thank you," the demon hissed, its voice a silken whisper of malice.

"I'm dying," the doctor choked, his voice breaking as he felt his strength ebbing away, his vitality slipping through his fingers like sand.

"Shhhh," the demon cooed, its grip tightening, drawing the life out of the doctor in a relentless torrent. The doctor's skin grew pale, his eyes dimming, as the last vestiges of his life were ripped from him.

With a final, shuddering gasp, the doctor crumpled to the floor, now reduced to a lifeless husk. The demon stood over him, its cruel smile deepening as it savored the stolen life force, its presence now fully entrenched in the mortal realm -like a shadow come to life.

Jace tore his gaze from the horrific scene and looked up at Sophie. She stood like a grotesque marionette, strings of darkness pulling her every move. Desperation clawed at him as he tried to see beyond the malevolence that coursed through her veins, to find the real Sophie—the girl he knew was still in there, somewhere.

For a moment, his heart nearly stopped as he caught the faintest glimpse—her soul. It was there, a luminous, fragile form struggling within the demon's suffocating grasp. Dark tendrils of vile energy coiled around it like a serpent, squeezing tighter with every breath she took. Her spirit, though radiant, flickered weakly, its light dimming as the demon drained her essence.

Jace's breath hitched as he saw it clearly now—a pulsing conduit of malevolent energy that tethered Sophie to the demon, a living chain of torment that bound her soul to this creature of darkness.

He knew then that time was running out. If he didn't act soon, Sophie would be lost forever, consumed by the very force that had taken the doctor's life.

Jace summoned his aether, channeling every ounce of his will into Sophie. The world around him slowed to a crawl, each heartbeat echoing like a distant drum as his consciousness delved deeper into the Aether Realm of her soul. Reality blurred, and he pushed further, feeling the pull of her essence as he descended into the very heart of her being.

The demon's spirit was a twisted, writhing mass of shadows and flames, its core a void of insatiable hunger. It was clear now; the demon was not just using her body—it was consuming her very essence, gaining strength and solidity from her spiritual suffering. Jace's new ability allowed him to see the grotesque interplay between the two, the demonic claws extending from her fingers not just physically, but spiritually, tearing into the ethereal strands of her soul.

The clarity of Soul Sense brought a wave of nausea. He could see the path to save her, the weak points in the demonic tether. His mind raced with possibilities, his newfound sight a beacon of hope amid the horror.

Suddenly, he was hit with a wave of malevolence, a storm of chaotic energy that threatened to overwhelm him. But through the maelstrom, Sophie was a faint glimmer—a small, scared girl, lost within the aura. Her eyes closed and her ethereal form grew weak and limp within the demon's grasp.

The bond between the demon and her soul was unlike anything he had encountered before. Instead of a single connection, there were thousands of slender tendrils, each burrowed deep into her being after days of "treatment." He focused on one of these links, invoking Soul Severance. For a fleeting moment, hope sparked within him as the link snapped—but it was short-lived. Almost immediately, a new tendril slithered into place, re-establishing the connection.

Her soul wasn't resisting the demon, and he couldn't sever these bonds alone. He needed to reach her, to talk with her. He needed her to fight.

Sophie. He focused his willpower, casting his thoughts directly into her soul.

Sophie, can you hear me?

The world around him slowed to a crawl and faded from his vision, moving just out of focus.

His body manifested as a ghostly form of darkness, an ethereal silhouette that seemed to be his own shadow come to life. He floated amidst an ocean of despair, adrift in a powerful maelstrom that churned with the anguish and fears of countless souls. The world around him was a vast expanse of darkness, save for the faint, guiding glow of a distant lighthouse, its light a solitary beacon of hope piercing the gloom.

For a moment, Jace hesitated, the overwhelming sorrow pressing down on him like a suffocating weight. But the thought of Sophie, trapped and suffering, spurred him on. He willed himself towards the lighthouse, each thought propelling him forward, his form gliding effortlessly over the tumultuous waves. The lighthouse grew larger, its light growing brighter and more inviting, a lifeline in the darkness.

The closer he got, the more the turmoil within him seemed to settle, his resolve hardening. He soon found himself at the door of the ancient, weathered structure. It loomed before him, its age-worn wood creaking under the strain of an unseen wind, yet it stood firm against the despairing tide.

With a gentle push, the door creaked open, revealing a dimly lit interior. The air was filled with the scent of salt and old wood, the walls echoing with distant, sorrowful cries. Jace stepped inside, his feet making no sound on the worn floorboards. The interior was a spiral of winding stairs, each step leading him closer to the source of the cries he had heard.

As he climbed, the sense of urgency grew stronger. The cries became clearer, more distinct—no longer a distant echo, but the voice of a girl, soft and filled with sorrow. He quickened his pace, his heart pounding in sync with the rhythm of the lighthouse beacon.

At the top of the stairs, he found her: a young girl huddled in a corner, her frame trembling with fear. She was shrouded in the dim light, her tears glistening as they fell. Her sobs were the only sound in the stillness, a heart-wrenching melody of despair.

Jace approached slowly, his presence a blend of shadow and light. He knelt beside her, his form casting a protective aura around her. "It's okay," he whispered, his voice a gentle reprieve from the surrounding chaos. "I'm here to help."

She looked up, her eyes wide with a mix of fear and hope. She reached out tentatively, her hand passing through his ghostly form, yet feeling the warmth of his intent. "Who are you?" she asked, her voice barely above a whisper.

"A friend," Jace replied, a gentle smile forming on his lips. "Let's get you out of here."

She flinched as he extended his hand, recoiling as if she feared even the possibility of touch. "Please, Sophie," he continued, his voice steady and soothing, "I need your help. I can't beat this without you."

The girl's tears fell like raindrops, her body trembling with fear. She shook her head, her voice weak and laden with despair. "I can't," she sobbed. "It's too strong."

Jace's expression softened, and he leaned in closer, his gaze unwavering. "Damon needs your help. You can do this."

Sophie hesitated, her wide eyes flickering between Jace's hand and his unwavering gaze. A deep breath shuddered through her as she grappled with her fear, the weight of it almost too much to bear. But something in Jace's eyes—a quiet determination, a promise of protection—gave her the strength to try. Slowly, hesitantly, she reached out and took his hand. "Okay," she whispered, "Together."

Jace's eyes snapped back to the cabin, time resuming its relentless march just as the demon's claws slashed through his chest. Agonizing pain exploded in his body, his life force plummeting by ninety percent. Blood pooled around him, his attempts to stand thwarted by his collapsing limbs. "Fight it, Sophie!" he yelled, his voice a hoarse, desperate plea.

The demon slithered closer to Jace, its claws poised to deliver a final, fatal blow. Its eyes gleamed with malice, relishing the prospect of ending his life. Just as it raised its hand to strike, Damon, summoning the last vestiges of his strength, lunged forward and grabbed the demon's leg, his grip weak but determined.

"No," Damon slurred, his voice a defiant whisper. The poison coursing through his veins was beginning to lose its potency, allowing him to muster enough strength to act.

The demon turned its predatory gaze toward Damon, eyes narrowing in irritation and contempt. "Let's just finish this morsel off, shall we?" it muttered, a cruel glint dancing in its eyes.

With a vicious snarl, the demon tried to shake Damon off, but he held on with tenacity, his fingers digging into the creature's leg. Damon's face contorted with effort, his body trembling from the strain. Though his grip was not strong enough to truly harm the demon, his sheer will and determination bought precious moments.

The demon snarled, annoyed by the resistance, and kicked at Damon, trying to dislodge him. Damon's grip faltered, but he held on, his eyes blazing with defiance.

"Stubborn fool," the demon hissed, preparing to deliver a killing blow to Damon. But as it raised its clawed hand, a sudden burst of light filled the room. Sophie, her form now fully solidified and glowing with an intense, radiant light, stepped between the demon and Damon.

"You will not harm him," she declared, her voice echoing with an otherworldly power. The demon recoiled, its confidence wavering in the face of her unexpected strength.

Sophie advanced toward the demon, her ethereal form glowing with a fierce determination that cut through the surrounding darkness. The demon recoiled, its eyes narrowing in surprise, but the shock quickly gave way to a sinister, mocking laughter that echoed like the crack of thunder. As Sophie summoned every ounce of her willpower to push against it, the demon remained rooted, grinning wickedly, its jagged teeth gleaming with cruel delight.

It laughed again, a cruel, mocking sound. "I was worried for a moment. Thought perhaps someone powerful had come to save you. But it's just you. Little you. How quaint. You think you can fight back against me? Little girl, you are weak. You are nothing. I know your fears, your sorrow. I know how scared you were to be married, nervous you weren't good enough. Oh, how I fed on your fears and self-doubt. And I fed on Damon's too. Oh, how sweet you both are. You know, he felt the same about you. So much fear. Delicious." It licked its lips, savoring the torment it had caused.

Sophie's form flickered and dimmed, her face a mask of confusion and pain. She struggled to resist, but the demon's willpower bore down on her, smothering her light. Her resolve wavered as the weight of her fears and insecurities pressed down on her, fed by the demon's taunting words.

Jace, watching the scene unfold, knew he had to act. Desperation surged through him, and he reached into his spatial pocket, pulling out the Crude Minor Healing potion. He cast Soul Tether on Sophie's glowing form, binding her spirit to his own. "Please work. You have to work," he whispered.

He drank the potion, feeling its bitter liquid slide down his throat. For a moment, nothing happened. His heart thundered in his chest, fear gripping him. Then, slowly, he felt the potion's magic begin to take effect.

As its healing power coursed through his veins, it split off and flowed into Sophie as well, her form growing brighter and more solid with each passing second.

Jace concentrated, willing all of the potion's power to go to her. He cast Soul Mend on himself repeatedly, his mana depleting rapidly. The excruciating nausea of being fully mana-drained threatened to overwhelm him, but he kept casting. Every time his mana regenerated even slightly, he channeled it into another Soul Mend, pushing his mana bar to the brink and beyond, pulling on his stamina when his mana was exhausted.

He considered drinking another, but a flashing warning told him that would be a bad idea, signaling that he'd reached his potion limit. He remembered from Alice's alchemy lesson that consuming potions too quickly would result in potion poisoning, causing reverse or negative effects. He would need to increase his tolerance before he could attempt it without guaranteed harm.

At triple the speed of his mana depletion, his stamina drained, yet he channeled it all, holding a focused Soul Mend. Jace felt a surge of energy as he poured every ounce of his remaining strength into Sophie, empowering her will to combat the demon.

Sophie's presence grew stronger, her form solidifying and glowing with an intense, radiant light. She looked down at the demon, her eyes blazing with newfound strength.

Chapter 20

Demons Run

"What is this? No, you can't!" the demon hissed, recoiling as Sophie's light intensified.

Jace, panting and on the brink of darkness, watched as Sophie stood taller, her defiance unyielding. The demon's confidence wavered, its shadowy form shrinking in the face of her brilliance.

"Oh, I can," the girl responded, her voice steady and defiant. "I have been trapped here for weeks while you and the doctor tormented me. You have fed on my love, my hate for you, and my fear. You have tried to take everything from me. But no more."

The demon screamed, thrashing as Jace cast Soul Tether, connecting his soul to the girl's, giving her additional strength. He cast Soul Mend on himself, sharing the healing energy with her soul, bolstering it further. It wasn't much, but he hoped it would be enough.

"Now leave us, demon! Leave us now!" She fought with every ounce of will, her body trembling as she strained against the bonds that tethered the demon to her soul. The demon, a dark, insidious presence, pushed back with a malevolent force. "Little girl, you are nothing. You are weak. Just die."

"No!" Her voice cracked with desperation and defiance.

He watched as she pushed back against the beast. Each moment, she separated herself further from the demon, pulling away from its grasp and, instead, draining the demon's strength. She was weakening it. He needed her to rise above the demon's influence, to force those countless tendrils into a single form—a form that he could target and sever once and for all.

Summoning his last reserves of strength, Jace lunged at the remaining essence of the demon, his grip tightening with a desperation born from sheer willpower. His body screamed in protest, but he forced himself to cast Soul Severance, targeting the very connection binding the demon to Sophie's soul.

He had no mana left, no stamina to draw upon. Instead, he felt the spell siphoning his life force, each pulse of magic draining the blood from his veins to fuel the incantation. The world around him flashed red, and his health plummeted.

Notifications flashed before Jace's eyes, but he ignored them, his focus unwavering. The demon screeched as the spell took hold, its form writhing and dissolving into shadows that began to dissipate. The girl's body collapsed onto the bed, lifeless yet finally free from the demonic grip.

Warning, Health Is Critically Low.
Health At 3%... 2%...

His health regeneration was barely keeping him alive.

The demon convulsed, its form contorting with a look of confusion and rage. Its once-solidified presence flickered and distorted, the malevolent energy unraveling under the relentless force of Jace's spell. It shrieked, an ear-splitting cry that echoed through the cabin, shaking the very walls.

The demonic tether binding it to Sophie shattered, the dark tendrils dissolving into nothingness. With one final, agonized howl, the demon was torn apart, its essence scattered to the void.

Jace collapsed beside the girl, his breath escaping in pained gasps. Every part of his body ached, his vision dimming as exhaustion claimed him. He could barely keep his eyes open, the edges of his consciousness blurring. But as he looked at Sophie, her form now peaceful and free from the demonic influence, a sense of relief washed over him. Her soul glowed softly, no longer flickering in distress.

Jace slumped beside Sophie's body. Her chest rose and fell in weak, shallow movements, tears tracing paths down her cheeks. The healing must have given her these few moments. Damon's eyes wide with horror and regret, reached out and took her trembling hand. Crawling over, he pulled her to him and rested her head in his lap.

There was silence for a long while.

"My love," Sophie whispered, her voice barely a breath. "Are you alright?"

He choked back a sob. "I am now, my darling. I am so sorry. I couldn't move. I couldn't save you."

"Shhh," she soothed, her fingers brushing his cheek. "It's alright now."

He lifted her gently, cradling her against his chest. They clung to each other, the silence around them heavy with unspoken words.

"I don't want to go," she murmured, a tear slipping from her eye. "Please don't make me go."

He held her tighter, his tears falling freely. "You don't have to go anywhere, my love. I have you."

Jace watched, heart aching at their raw, fragile love. He knew what he had to do, the weight of it pressing on him like a physical force. But he held back the tide of death, for just a few moments longer.

"It's okay," Damon's voice cracked. "I will always love you. But you've been hurting for so long. It's okay to leave. I will find you in the next life. I promise."

"I love you," she replied, her voice a fading whisper.

Her final breath shuddered, and her soul began to drift. Jace felt his magic stir within him, and he let it move of its own accord, guiding her spirit gently towards the Underworld. He focused, ensuring she would find peace, even as sorrow pressed down on him.

A heavy stillness settled over them, as if the very essence of the world had been muted. No words were said, for there were no words left to say. Only stillness. Its weight thick and oppressive, it pressed down on them, making the air thick and hard to breathe.

Their hearts beat quietly, breaths shallow, as if any noise might shatter the fragile stillness. No condolences, no cries, just an endless, solemn silence.

Then, like a sudden crack in the stillness, the silence shattered. Damon collapsed beside Jace, sobbing. Jace cried too. For what felt like an eternity, he sat there, helpless and feeling ever so alone.

Jace's vision blurred as he slumped to the cold floor, his strength slipping away like sand through an hourglass. The world around him dimmed, the edges of his sight narrowing as exhaustion took hold. Sophie's lifeless form lay before him, her soul finally free, but the weight of what had just transpired bore down on him like a crashing wave.

His thoughts spiraled back to the moments before—her light, the demon's violent end, Damon's anguished cries. Now, in the oppressive silence that filled the cabin, the reality of the loss seeped into his very bones. The air felt thick, suffocating, as if the world itself was holding its breath.

A lifetime seemed to pass in the next few minutes before Damon finally spoke, his tears replaced by something colder. "This should be impossible."

His voice trembled with a mix of anger and disbelief. "This isn't right. These lands are protected. We're too close to the University grounds. Demons aren't supposed to reach here. How could this happen? Dr. Ponos... he was a family friend. He's known us since we were children. He delivered my niece. How could he do this?"

Damon's gaze fell on the locket around the doctor's neck, a simple piece of brass that now seemed sinister in the dim light. Something was unsettling about it, something that pulled at Jace's mind. The locket pulsed with a malevolent energy, a trace of the demon's essence still clinging to it.

Jace reached out, his fingers closing around the locket. As soon as he touched it, a shiver ran through him, the whispering growing louder, insidious. He recognized the power -felt its pull—an artifact tied to forces on the side of the Endless, allies of the Dark One. With a grimace, he wrenched it free from the doctor's neck and stored it in his inventory, the sinister whispers fading as he did.

"We need answers," Jace said, his voice hoarse but resolute. "I need to speak with Hades." Determination threaded through his exhaustion, a resolve to uncover the truth. But before he could face the Underworld, he needed a moment to gather his strength, to recover from the toll the battle had taken.

Damon's fury was a storm barely held in check. His fists clenched and unclenched, each movement a deliberate struggle against the rage surging within him. His eyes burned with a fierce promise of vengeance.

Jace, drained but resolute, extended his hand, channeling a soft, healing glow as his aether allowed. Soul Mend enveloped Damon, a balm to the storm raging in his soul, though it did little to quell the tempest in his heart.

With a tenderness at odds with his anger, Damon cradled Sophie's bandaged body, lifting her as if she were made of glass. Each step toward the door was laden with determination, his movements deliberate, every breath a reminder of his resolve. He paused, his back to Jace, voice heavy with emotion. "Thank you, Jace. I will never forget this."

Then, without another word, he vanished into the forest's shadowy embrace.

Jace stood frozen, the weight of Damon's words pressing on him. He wanted to call out, to plead for caution against the reckless path Damon was on. But he understood the desperation driving his friend, the need for action when the world felt like it was slipping away. So he let Damon go, silently vowing to support him in his own way.

Turning inward, Jace thought of Hades, the god whose guidance he sought but was not yet ready to reach out to. His aether reserves were nearly depleted, his body aching with the remnants of battle. He began the slow, meticulous work of healing, his energy trickling back as he cast each Soul Mend with care.

Chapter 21
Combat Log

When his strength had returned enough, Jace stepped outside, the cabin's warmth giving way to the cool air. He started towards the campus, the path ahead both familiar and fraught with uncertainty. As he walked, he opened the notifications he had dismissed during the chaos, each one a stark reminder of the terrible horror he had just faced.

Crude Potion of Minor Healing Consumed.
    Effects combined with Soul Bind.

1 Willpower point permanently imbued into Soul Tether ability, granting a new Aspect: Half-Life.
    Soul Tether now allows for 70% of all healing effects and 30% of damage effects to be transferred to a bound soul.

Soul Mend has gained a new aspect: Focused Mend.
    Maintaining Soul Mend is now easier and requires less aether.
    Aether has been depleted. Soul Mend and Soul Bind now using Stamina.

Ability Unlocked - Persistent to a Fault

Who needs endurance, muscles, and the ability to move when you have aether? Drain your stamina to temporarily increase your aether pool.

Convert Stamina to aether at a 5 to 1 conversion rate. Increase Spirit Constitution to improve conversion rate.

Warning: Continuous use of this ability WILL result in a permanent stamina decrease.

Ability Unlocked - Blood Sacrifice

Your aether pool is sooo important, isn't it? You've gotten pretty tunnel vision here. Oh well, might as well give you an ability for it. You're going to do it, anyway.

Convert Health to Aether at a 5 to 1 conversion rate. Increase Spirit Constitution to improve conversion rate.

Warning: Continuous use of this ability WILL result in a permanent health decrease.

Passive Ability - Mostly Dead - has gained a new aspect: Slightly Alive

You are no longer just mostly dead, you are now also slightly alive. Sit at 2% health or less, gain life, lose life, gain life, lose life, without going above 2%. A dangerous game you play. You really like to live on the edge.

Effects: Gain a 10%+ boost to aether and stamina regeneration when you are below 5% health. Will this actually help you survive? It'll take a miracle.

Resistance to Death has increased to Rank Three - Adept

You are super squishy. But now slightly less so. After taking a lot of damage from an alignment evil source, you are getting better at being hit. Congratulations, you are on the path to becoming a certified punching bag. -7% damage from all shadow, necrotic, and evil-aligned sources.

Jace smirked at the system's comments. The resistance to death ability intrigued him. So, that hit I took from the demon was reduced by five percent? he thought, shaking his head in disbelief.

You have defeated: Herald of the Coming Darkness — Silver One Demon.

You should have had no way of doing this. But you nipped it before it had fully emerged, stopping the ritual halfway.

+1 to Karmic Balance.

Experience gained: 4150 X Rank Disparity Modifier.

EXP Reduction:

• Crude Potion of Healing Consumed

• -25% Penalty Applied

Warning: You have exceeded your EXP capacity. EXP gain above capacity is reduced by 90%.

Total EXP: 3,634 of 3000

Boon Activated: Over The Top

Awarding additional Society Points in compensation for lost EXP.

Total Society Points: 7500

He winced at the hit to his EXP, but the boost in Society Points was nothing to sneer at. He couldn't wait to start spending them—he could splurge a bit. He made a mental note to dive deep into every possible society upgrade as soon as he could, then turned his attention back to the rest of his notifications.

Quest Update

I Ain't Afraid of No Ghosts

Quest success. You have brought peace to a lost soul.

Bonus Objective Complete: Save Damon.

Objective reward recalculating due to rank disparity.

Profession rank disparity factoring... You seriously should not have survived. Hades has witnessed your achievement and was impressed.

Calculating reward...

Plus 500 to reputation with Hades. Minus 500 reputation with Demons and Undead.

Unique Class Specialization Unlocked: Twilight Guardian

You have shown unique aptitude and compassion for souls while maintaining the balance of life and death. Hades has offered you a class and profession upgrade. Warning: If you ACCEPT this upgrade, Class Cleric and Profession Hades' Little Helper will permanently be merged into a new combined Class/Profession, Twilight Guardian. This cannot be undone.

Take up the mantle of: Twilight Guardian?

Accept | Reject

Chapter 22
Twilight Guardian

J ace read the notification with a mix of excitement and trepidation. There were no other notes or details about the new class. He tried to remember what he had heard about class specialization.

Lore Skill Success
> Lore Primer Knowledge Activated

Jace felt a rush of information flood through his mind.

Specialization is the process of advancing deeper into a class, sacrificing some traits while gaining others. Specialization can be achieved through:
  • Class Progression
  • Powerful Artifacts
  • The Gift of a God

Specialization becomes available after Adept and requires a special trainer. Hades has made an exception for you. Your class is now your passion, leaving no time for a separate profession. Henceforth, if you accept the Class Specialization of Twilight Guardian, your Profession and Class will rank up simultaneously.

But what does the Twilight Guardian entail exactly?

No data available.

Great.

The lack of a clear class description only heightened his wariness and just reminded him of how little he knew of the world. This was no ordinary upgrade, and Jace knew better than to blindly accept anything without understanding its full implications. Before he made any decisions, he needed to speak with Hades.

Thinking back to his encounter with Hades, Jace felt a familiar unease stir within him. What just happened lingered in his mind, causing heat to bubble up from deep within him—a mix of tension and unresolved questions.

Jace's anger flared like wildfire as he stormed into the Underworld, the darkness curling around him as if drawn to the heat of his fury. Shadows slithered across the walls, whispering the secrets of the damned, but Jace didn't hear them. His thoughts were too loud, too chaotic, pounding in his skull with each step.

The throne room yawned before him—a vast cavern of obsidian and despair, where flames flickered like ghosts in the gloom. Hades sat atop his throne, a brooding figure carved from the darkness itself. His eyes, burning embers in the abyss, watched Jace's approach with an eerie calm.

Jace stopped at the foot of the throne, his rage barely contained. "The girl was tormented by a greater demon—a herald," he spat, his words like daggers in the thick air. "How could you let this happen? Aren't you supposed to be the one in charge here?"

Hades leaned back, a slow, deliberate movement that reeked of ancient power and endless patience. "Mind your tone, mortal," he said, his voice a rumble that echoed through the chamber. "Remember who you're talking to. I am the Lord of the Underworld, not your friend."

"I thought that you had control, that you could stop things like this."

"Control?" Hades' lips curled into a half-smile, though there was no warmth in it. "My domain is vast, Jace. But it's not absolute. There's a balance—one we gods must keep. If I intervene too directly, it gives the others a free hand to do the same. And trust me, that's a mess you don't want."

Jace clenched his fists, frustration bubbling over into sarcasm. "So, what? You just sit back and let people get hurt because of some divine stalemate?"

The flames around Hades flared, bathing the room in a hellish light. The god's eyes narrowed, and for a moment, the room seemed to tilt, reality-bending under the sheer weight of his presence. "Careful," Hades warned, his voice as cold and lethal as a winter storm. "You're treading on dangerous ground."

Jace's mouth went dry, but he refused to back down. "I'm just trying to understand why you can't—"

The rest of his sentence died in his throat as Hades stood, his form swelling to fill the room, a towering inferno of divine wrath. The very air around him crackled with energy, and the earth beneath Jace's feet trembled.

"You dare question me?" Hades' voice was a thunderclap, reverberating through the bones of the Underworld. "You, who I have granted power beyond your mortal understanding?"

Jace staggered back, the words from Hades hitting him like a sledgehammer. His pulse pounded in his ears, drowning out everything but the primal urge to drop to his knees, to plead for mercy. But he stood firm, his body quivering under the strain of defiance.

"The pain of her soul could have been avoided. You could have done your job when it was given to you," Hades snarled, each word a lash against Jace's already frayed nerves. "Instead, you found excuses, shunted your responsibility, and look at the cost."

The accusation cut deeper than any blade. Jace's chest tightened, a suffocating mix of guilt and anger warring within him. He wanted to scream, to deny it, but the truth weighed too heavily on his tongue.

And then, as suddenly as it began, the storm broke. Hades shrank back to his usual size, but the fire in his eyes still smoldered, now tinged with something far worse—sadness, sympathy. "Do you think this is the only soul in pain? What's coming is greater than us both, boy. There are forces at play that you can't begin to comprehend. The trouble you and your kind are facing, being trapped here—this is just the beginning. I can't allow room for the other gods to interfere. If I act directly, I give them the same right, and I can't control what they'll do."

Jace swallowed hard, his anger faltering as Hades' tone shifted, almost gentle, as if speaking to a child. "I've given you a gift, Jace," the god said, his voice now eerily soft.

"A gift?" The word felt alien in Jace's mouth. "What gift?"

"You should have received a message from the System. A unique class—one that carries my mark, with many paths before you."

"Why?" Jace's voice cracked, a tremor betraying the turmoil inside him.

Hades hesitated, a flicker of something unguarded passing over his face. When he spoke again, his voice was weary, raw with a rare honesty. "Because I chose you. And because I need you. What happened—it shouldn't have been possible, and you're right to question it. But these are not usual times. I cannot guarantee I'll be here when you need me most."

Jace's frustration boiled over. "What does that even mean? Why are gods always so cryptic? Where are you going?"

"I'm already on the edge of what I'm allowed to reveal," Hades replied, his gaze distant, troubled.

For the first time, Jace saw something almost like fear in the god's eyes, a flicker of uncertainty that sent a chill through him. Hades wasn't supposed to be unsure. He was a god, infallible, unshakeable. But in that moment, he looked anything but.

Jace nodded, swallowing the last of his pride. "Alright. I'll use it."

Hades' expression softened, just a fraction. "Good." He paused, then added, almost as an afterthought, "And Jace? Don't make me regret it."

Jace tried a smile. He thought back to the last moments with Damon and Ponos.

"There is one more thing," he added. He opened his inventory and pulled out the item he had taken off of Ponos' body. His fingers brushed against the cool metal of the ruddy bronze locket. He hesitated for a moment, the weight of it settling heavily in his palm. The dim light of the chamber seemed to retreat from the object, as if repelled by the dark energy it emitted. He turned to Hades, the Lord of the Underworld, standing at his desk with an air of ancient weariness.

Jace held the locket out. "Ponos had this on him. It seems strange. Important somehow."

Hades' eyes narrowed, his expression shifting from curiosity to something far more guarded. He recoiled slightly, refusing to touch the locket. "Set it down," he ordered, his voice sharp, cutting through the thick silence of the room.

Jace did as instructed, placing the locket carefully on the desk. The moment it left his hand, a coldness seeped into the room, a chill that seemed to emanate from the locket itself. Hades eyed it warily, then turned his gaze toward a small, flickering lamp on the far side of the room.

Without a word, Hades extended his hand toward the lamp, his fingers curling in a summoning motion. The smoke rising from the lamp began to twist and coil, darkening as it gathered into a dense, swirling cloud. From within the smoke, a figure slowly took shape—a spirit, its form ethereal yet somehow solid, like a shadow-given life. The spirit's eyes glowed faintly as it regarded Hades, awaiting his command.

"Take this to the place," Hades intoned, his voice low and resonant with authority.

The spirit nodded, understanding the unspoken gravity of the task. It reached out, its smoky tendrils wrapping around the locket with a gentleness that belied the danger Hades had sensed. As the spirit lifted the locket, the air around it grew colder still, the temperature dropping as the locket was lifted from the desk. With a final glance at Hades, the spirit drifted silently out of the room, vanishing into the shadows beyond.

Hades watched the spirit depart, his expression grave. He turned to Jace, his eyes dark with a seriousness that made Jace's breath catch.

Hades shook his head slowly, the weight of what he knew pressing down on his shoulders. "Best not to speak of this to anyone, if it can be avoided. This is worse than I had thought. I must speak with the others."

Jace frowned, a knot of unease forming in his stomach. "What is it? What's going on?"

But Hades was already heading for the door, his thoughts clearly elsewhere, tangled in secrets too dangerous to share. "I'll handle this," he muttered, more to himself than to Jace. "Trust me, but don't breathe a word of this to anyone—not a soul—unless you'd bet your life on their loyalty. And even then, tread carefully. I need to speak with the others."

And with that, Hades left the room, leaving Jace alone with the lingering chill of his departure, and the unsettling knowledge that whatever the locket had awakened was far beyond his understanding.

The silence that followed was heavy, broken only by the distant drip of water and the faint crackle of dying embers. Jace stood there for a long moment, the weight of the encounter settling over him like a shroud. There was power in him now, new abilities he didn't yet understand. But there were also questions, too many questions, and no answers in sight.

And that, more than anything, terrified him.

Achievement Unlocked

A Frayed Soul

Your soul bears the scars of immense pressure, crushed beneath the weight of a god's will. Congratulations, it's only your first month in school, and you're already making friends.

+1 to Spirit Constitution

Hidden Attribute Unlocked: Spirit Constitution has been revealed.

Spirit Constitution: 17

Spirit Constitution: This attribute directly affects your ability to withstand spiritual pressures and influences and affects all spirit-related spells and the very core of your soul—your essence. Elevating this attribute requires immense effort, dedication, and a relentless pursuit of self-improvement.

You're embarking on a journey of self-awareness. Improve this attribute to improve your You-ness.

Jace lingered in the now-empty room, the weight of his encounter with Hades still heavy in the air. The god's cryptic words echoed in his mind, unraveling into more questions than answers. He exhaled slowly, trying to shake off the unease that clung to him, but it followed him as he made his way back to his dorms.

He wasn't sure why he kept delaying the acceptance of the class specialization. Maybe it was the uncertainty—the sense that once he took this step, there would be no going back. The decision loomed over him, a shadow he couldn't quite escape.

Back in his dorm, Jace headed for the shower, letting the hot water wash away the grime of the day. He scrubbed at his skin, as if the heat could somehow clear the thoughts tangled in his mind. But even as the steam rose around him, his mind kept drifting back to Hades, to the bronze locket, to the ominous tone in the god's voice.

Later, dressed in starlight pajamas adorned with strange constellations that seemed to shimmer in the dim light, Jace stood before the full-length mirror in his room. He hesitated, his reflection staring back at him with the same uncertainty he felt inside. The notification for the class upgrade hovered in his vision, pulsing softly, as if urging him to make a decision.

Accepting the class upgrade felt like crossing a threshold, a point of no return into an unknown that could reshape everything. His life had already changed so much—what was one more step? But this... this felt different. There was a gravity to it, a sense that whatever lay on the other side could alter his fate in ways he couldn't predict.

He sighed, running a hand through his damp hair. What choice did he have? Hades had given him this gift—whatever it truly was—for a reason. If the god's words held any truth, Jace would need every ounce of power he could muster for what was to come.

The reflection in the mirror didn't offer any answers, just the same wary eyes staring back at him. But deep down, he knew the decision had already been made, long before this moment.

With a deep breath, Jace selected to accept the upgrade.

The moment he did, a surge of energy exploded within him, as if a dam had burst, releasing a torrent of raw, unbridled power. It tore through him, setting every nerve on fire, burning away the exhaustion and fear that had been tormenting him. He gasped, doubling over as the energy flooded his veins, coursing through his body like liquid lightning. It wasn't just physical—it was something deeper, something that resonated with his very soul.

His vision blurred, the room around him fading into a haze as the power continued to build, spiraling higher and higher until it felt like he might shatter under the intensity of it. But just as it reached its peak, the energy began to coalesce, condensing into a potent, focused force that hummed with purpose.

It was as if he had been plugged into the heart of the universe, drawing from an infinite well of divine power. The sensation was both exhilarating and terrifying, a heady mix of strength and clarity that left him breathless.

Then, as suddenly as it had begun, the rush subsided, leaving him standing there, panting, his skin tingling with the residual charge. A notification flashed before his eyes, crisp and clear.

Class Upgrade: Twilight Guardian

Chapter 23
Twig

J ace's heart pounded as he scanned the details. The bonuses were staggering. His Affinity for Soul had been enhanced, a boost that felt like a
key unlocking a door within him that he hadn't even known existed.

His reflexes had been sharpened, his physical strength amplified, but the most striking of all was the new ability that came with his
class—something that set his pulse racing with anticipation.

He could now summon a shadow, a dark force that responded
to his will with an almost sentient awareness. He reached out, and the
shadows in the room seemed to quiver, as if awaiting his command. With
a thought, they surged toward him, swirling around his body like a living
entity. The darkness wrapped itself around him, pressing close to his skin,
shifting and solidifying until it felt like a second layer of flesh.

The shadows molded to his form, becoming a sleek, black armor
that clung to him like leather, yet was light as air. It moved with him, supple
and responsive, but with the resilience of steel. Across his shoulders, the
shadows pooled and spread out, forming a cape that billowed behind him,
weightless and ethereal, yet carrying an aura of foreboding.

Jace flexed his fingers, watching in awe as the shadows obeyed,
the armor rippling with an almost liquid grace. It was more than just
protection—it was an extension of himself, a weapon and shield woven
from the very fabric of darkness.

The power hummed within him, a steady pulse that resonated
with the new strength he now possessed. He had become something more,
something greater—a guardian not just of life, but of the twilight, that
fragile boundary between light and dark, life and death.

As he stood there, the shadows whispering around him, Jace knew that he had crossed into a new realm of power. The weight of responsibility pressed against his chest, but there was also a fierce determination burning within him.

New Ability Unlocked: Shadow Cloak

This ain't your sweet old grandma's floral bathrobe. No, this baby's stitched from the cold, unforgiving fabric of pure darkness. You put it on, and suddenly you're not just walking through shadows—you are the shadow. It's the kind of thing that slips you into the night like a blade between ribs. And hey, it's got the added bonus of making you look way cooler than you have any right to be.

A shroud of pure shadow, melding with your form to create a sleek armor that moves as you do. It is both shield and concealment, an extension of the twilight that now courses through your soul.

Armor Rating: +40%

The Shadow Cloak fortifies your defenses, turning aside blows with the strength of the void. Enemies find their weapons dulled as they strike against the darkness.

Stealth Enhancement: +35%

Within the cloak's embrace, you become a phantom, a mere whisper in the night. Your steps are silent, your presence barely a ripple in the fabric of reality, granting you near-perfect concealment.

Shadow Affinity: +20%

The shadows heed your call, their power flowing through you. Your mastery over shadow-based abilities grows, each one infused with the essence of the twilight.

Soul Shield: +25%

The shadows protect more than just flesh. They guard your very soul, dampening the effects of spiritual and magical assaults. The darkness itself stands as your sentinel.

Aether Cost: Dynamic with Use

Damage received increases the maintenance cost. Specialized uses further escalates costs proportionately.

New Passive Ability Unlocked: Soul Detection

The souls around you sing a chorus that only you can hear. You sense their presence, their emotions, their very essence, even through the thickest of walls or the deepest of shadows.

No soul can hide from your gaze within this radius. Whether concealed by magic or darkness, their presence is laid bare before you.

Detection Range: Arms Length

Increase Spirit Constitution to increase range.

The path of the Twilight Guardian is not one of light or dark, but of balance. You are the keeper of the in-between, the sentinel of shadows. Embrace your new power, and let the twilight guide your steps.

Jace stood before the full-length mirror in his quarters, his gaze tracing the sleek lines of his new outfit. The dark, form-fitting fabric clung to his frame like a second skin, yet it moved with him effortlessly, as if woven from shadows themselves. The cloak draped over his shoulders, its edges whispering against the ground with a quiet rustle. He reached out to touch it, feeling the strange, almost living texture beneath his fingers—smooth and cool, but with an underlying energy that thrummed with a life of its own.

He flexed his muscles, noting how his body felt different—more lithe, more agile. Every movement seemed more precise, as if the outfit was enhancing his natural abilities. Yet there was something else, a subtle pull at the edge of his awareness. It took him a moment to realize that his aether was slowly being drained, just enough to balance out his natural regeneration.

Jace frowned slightly, concentrating on the flow of aether within him. He could feel the energy trickling out, just enough to keep his aether regeneration at a standstill. It wasn't a crippling drain, but it was enough to prevent any buildup. Until he increased his aether regeneration speed, the cloak would effectively lock his aether reserves in place, though thankfully it wouldn't cost him anything unless he tapped into one of its special abilities.

Intrigued, he decided to experiment a little. He pulled the hood of the cloak over his head, and immediately, the shadows in the room seemed to deepen around him. His form blurred at the edges, becoming less distinct as the cloak's stealth enhancement activated. He moved silently across the room, his footsteps making no sound on the stone floor. His reflection in the mirror was almost invisible—a faint outline in the dark.

Jace extended his hand, willing the cloak's armor function to engage. The shadows around him thickened, hardening into a sleek, protective layer that felt as strong as steel yet flexible as cloth. He struck the air with a swift punch, feeling the enhanced strength the outfit granted him. The force behind the blow was far greater than what he was used to, and a satisfied grin spread across his face.

Then, with a thought, he deactivated the cloak's special abilities, letting the shadows dissipate. The aether drain ceased immediately, and he could feel his natural regeneration slowly returning to normal.

Jace studied his reflection one last time, his mind racing with the possibilities of what this new gear could do. But the weight of Hades' earlier warning still hung over him. Why wouldn't he want him talking about the locket?

He turned away from the mirror, the flickering light in the room casting long shadows behind him. Whatever lay ahead, he knew he would need every advantage he could get.

Jace couldn't afford to let his unspent EXP and Society Points gather dust any longer—not this time. The old habit of hesitation had to go. If this was his new reality, even temporarily, then it was time to get serious. Time to stop drifting and start steering.

But, as always, the universe had a way of complicating even the best-laid plans. His quick mental calculation confirmed his suspicions—he didn't have nearly enough to buy the ingredients he needed to practice alchemy, his most reliable cultivation method so far. Without those, his growth would stall, and in this place, stagnation was just another word for death.

Determined, Jace made his way to the alchemy section under the Hephaestus Banner. Normally a haven for the focused and the curious, today it thrummed with frenetic energy, more like a bazaar during a festival than the peaceful sanctuary he remembered. People darted in and out of shops, arguments flaring over rare ingredients, the air crackling with tension. It reminded

Jace of those chaotic holiday sales he'd only ever heard about—he'd never been to a mall, much less experienced the madness firsthand.

The alchemy wing, which Alice had shown him before, was an expansive area with ingredients stacked high on one side and a forge blazing on the other. Ancient columns supported the roof, and much of the structure was open to the air. The mingled scents of burning iron and exotic herbs filled his lungs—acrid smoke and fragrant botanicals swirling together until his head swam. It was intoxicating, in a way that was both thrilling and unnerving.

Inside, the place was bustling. Every potion desk was occupied, students meticulously measuring and mixing, their faces masks of concentration. Near the back, a man as massive as an oak hammered away at an anvil, each clang reverberating through the space, blending with the hiss of boiling brews and the hum of conversation.

Jace glanced around, trying to find the herbs for the potion he'd learned with Alice—something simple, something he could practice while spending his EXP, using his Focus. But with the district in chaos, he'd have to move fast or risk leaving empty-handed.

He could ask his friends for help. They'd lend him the money, no question, but something held him back. Pride, perhaps, or just the deep-seated need to do this on his own. Trusting people was one thing; depending on them was another. He checked his inventory again—twenty silver pieces, enough to convert to two gold. Not much, but it would have to do.

He scanned the shelves, each container marked with a different colored band—gold, blue, silver, red, purple. The marketplace swirled around him, people grabbing handfuls of ingredients, pouring them into sacks -jostling him as they hurried by. Frustration bubbled up inside him. No prices listed anywhere. Maybe he could gather some herbs himself—his herbalism skill was decent now—but that would take time he didn't have.

As he searched, the crowd continued to press in, a tide of bodies that knocked him about like a leaf in a storm. Travelers? Citizens? It was impossible to tell in the crush. Every attempt to locate what he needed ended in disappointment. Just as he was about to give up, the hulking figure by the anvil stood, towering over the crowd. He moved with a deliberate, almost comical determination, like a mountain deciding to take a stroll.

The giant approached Jace, his presence as impossible to ignore as a thunderstorm on a clear day. "Hello!" His voice boomed across the noisy space, cutting through the clamor like a bell. He extended a hand that seemed as large as a small boulder. "You look a little lost."

Jace blinked up at him, slightly taken aback. "You work here?"

"You could say that. Name's Twig," the giant replied, his name almost laughably mismatched with his immense size.

"Twig? Really? Wouldn't Branch or Trunk be more fitting?" Jace asked, curiosity getting the better of him.

"Nope, it's Twig. Got it because of my size. For my race, you don't get to choose your name—the Citizens in your clan do it for you when you enter. It was that or Little Thorn. I went with Twig. For my people, I'm relatively small."

Jace took a moment to fully absorb the giant's sheer massiveness, realizing that Twig barely fit inside the building. The ceiling seemed almost to bow under his presence, as if even the architecture wasn't entirely sure it could contain him.

Twig noticed Jace's gaze and tilted his head, questioning. "Uh," Jace started, quickly redirecting, "can you tell me the prices on these?" He pointed to a bucket of loose leaves, a common ingredient. "I don't see tags on anything."

"Oh, it's just over here," Twig replied, leading him to a large board with various markings in chalk. There were ten different colored blocks, each inscribed with amounts in bronze, silver, or gold.

"These are updated daily, depending on our stock. Prices change little unless something becomes hard to get. Just match the color to the ingredients," Twig explained.

Jace examined the board, something clicking in his mind. "Wait, this is your shop, isn't it? You own it?"

"Indeed," Twig nodded with a modest smile.

"You're a Traveler? And a shop owner?" Jace asked, genuinely surprised.

"Yes indeed," Twig said, his tone still humble, despite his towering presence.

"How'd you manage a body type so massive?" Jace asked, still marveling at the giant's size.

"Long story," Twig responded shyly, his massive shoulders shrugging. "How'd you get so small?"

Jace grinned. "Fair point."

"So, what are you looking for?" Twig asked, his deep voice carrying a warmth that made Jace feel a little more at ease.

"I need the ingredients for a Minor Potion of Healing."

"Makes sense," Twig nodded. "I've seen quite a few folks learning that particular potion since the logout issue. Unfortunately, a lot of those ingredients have gone up in price due to scarcity, ever since... well, the incident. I'm sure you can imagine why they're harder to come by now."

Jace scanned the board, his eyes lingering on the prices. Most of what he needed fell into the Grey tier, the lowest, meaning he could buy almost everything with about ten silver. But the rarer ingredients were another story—altogether, they would cost him around fifty-five and a half silver. Roughly five and a half gold. Three gold more than he had.

Jace felt the spark of hope dimming. "Hmmm, I guess that's that."

"What do you mean?" Twig asked, his eyes narrowing slightly.

"Nothing... Do you happen to know where I can forage for some of these ingredients? I just unlocked herbalism," Jace said, trying to find another way.

Twig gave him an appraising look, as if weighing the options. "Right now, I wouldn't recommend starting down that path. Bad time to get into the business, but perhaps when things cool down..." He paused, clearly considering something, and then seemed to make a decision.

"You'll need a batch of this nightshade," he said, grabbing a pouch and effortlessly pushing his way through the crowd. Jace followed closely behind as Twig filled a bag with nightshade.

"Some elderflower..." Twig continued, filling another bag.

Jace reached out to stop him, alarmed. "Uh, wait, no—I can't afford all this."

But Twig ignored him, methodically gathering several more bags of ingredients. Finally, he led Jace to a counter at the back of the shop.

"Here we are—everything you need for a few dozen Minor Potions of Healing," Twig declared, setting the bags down with a satisfied nod.

"I can't afford this," Jace blurted out, his face flushing pink with embarrassment.

Twig chuckled, his laugh as deep as his voice. "I picked up on that. Look, you seem like a decent guy. And right now, a lot of people are struggling—there's a lot of uncertainty in the air."

Jace's eyes widened in surprise. "Are you offering this for free? I couldn't possibly accept that."

But Twig just laughed again, the sound booming through the shop.

"Free? Ha! I'm generous, but I'm not crazy," Twig laughed, his voice booming. "I'd be out of business in no time. No, this isn't free. You're going to pay it back more than tenfold—when you can. You'll report back to me, and we'll put that herbalism of yours to good use. You won't always be domain-locked to Olympus, after all. Consider this a calculated risk on my part, a gamble. Either you sell some of the potions you make and pay me back, with interest, or before you leave, stop by and see me. I'll give you a few special ingredients to find on your travels—things that'll make me far more than what I'm losing now. Deal?"

A quest prompt appeared before Jace.

New Quest

An Offer You Couldn't Refuse

Traveler Twig has agreed to loan you enough ingredients to craft over 40 Minor Potions of Healing. Once your domain lock is removed and you can leave Olympus, you must do one of two things: Pay Twig back for all ingredients, plus interest, at their currently high prices. Work for Twig to find special ingredients outside of Olympus and bring them back.

Accept | Reject

Jace considered the offer. There was something about Twig that made him feel he could trust the giant. Maybe it was the mix of kindness and sharp business sense in his eyes, or the way he spoke as if money wasn't the only thing that mattered. Whatever it was, Jace felt an unexpected warmth toward this stranger—an appreciation for someone who clearly knew what they were doing.

With a nod, Jace accepted.

Twig's face lit up with a broad smile, and they shook hands—Twig's massive hand nearly engulfing Jace's entire arm. "Happy to be in business with you," Twig said, his voice carrying a note of genuine satisfaction.

Chapter 24
Society Upgrades

J ace slid into the Fields Below like an old friend returning to a haunted but familiar home. The ancient magic of the place pulsed under his skin, a living, breathing entity that accepted him, if not quite embraced him.

He decided that this time he wouldn't wait to spend his EXP and Society Points. He would start with Society Points, as it would make using his Alchemy Focus and allocating his EXP easier.

His eyes adjusted to the gloom, and he instinctively scanned the dim expanse for Shadow. She had a way of melding into the darkness, becoming a part of the world's very fabric. Jace trusted she was nearby, her presence both comforting and disconcerting, like a cat you weren't sure liked you, but you appreciated it nonetheless. A quick check of the area map on his interface confirmed it—two little dots: him and her. A smirk tugged at his lips; even in a place as twisted as this, knowing you weren't alone had its perks.

His footsteps echoed in the cavernous space, a soft rhythm that matched the slow, patient hum of the ancient place. As he reached his dormitory, the President's Interface greeted him with a soft glow. He reached out, and the console sprang to life, filling the room with a familiar array of options, each one more tantalizing than the last. Dormitory, bathroom, kitchen, alchemy labs, library—each a promise of something bigger, better. A list of new options was available, new areas to unlock and then upgrade.

When he looked closer, he saw something he hadn't seen before. A tiny white star next to each upgrade.

As Jace focused on the tiny star next to the upgrade options, the screen shifted, revealing a trove of information he'd never seen before. It was as if a veil had been lifted, exposing the intricacies of the Fields Below. The realization hit him—he'd been upgrading blindly, thinking only of the essentials, when there was an entire layer of strategy he'd missed. Each upgrade and unlocked section didn't just improve the space; it granted bonuses to the Fields and potential boons to all Society Members. It was like a hidden blueprint of power, waiting to be tapped into.

He realized he could stack multiple upgrades at once, selecting his options without locking them in right away. This allowed him to review and fine-tune his point distribution as he moved through the list, only finalizing everything once he was satisfied and choosing [Accept].

Jace's fingers hovered over the options, his heart quickening with each beat. This wasn't just about upgrading his dorm—it was about reaching for something greater, something that felt just out of his grasp. He hesitated, a fleeting thought urging him to stop and consider the consequences.

But who was he kidding? This was the first time he could spend without that relentless fear of running out. The points were rolling in now, faster than ever before, and if he kept pushing, they'd keep coming. The realization hit him like a surge of adrenaline—a heady, exhilarating rush that made him want to throw caution to the wind, just this once.

The thought sent a thrill down his spine, like the spark of a match in the dark. It felt like browsing through an endless cosmic bazaar, where each stall offered something more tantalizing than the last. The freedom was heady, almost intoxicating—no pesky point limits, no immediate consequences. It was like dangling on the edge of a cliff, with the wind howling around him and the ground so far below it seemed unreal.

All the areas that had only been unlocked, but not upgraded, remained stuck in a dilapidated Rank Zero state—little more than crumbling ruins with barely a whisper of their potential. Unlocking an area was just the first step; getting it above Rank Zero was where the real transformation began. The first rank would typically bring the area to life, making it functional, while each subsequent rank added layers of improvement, turning it from merely serviceable to something truly exceptional.

His eyes flicked to the Alchemy Labs first, eager to see what secrets it held.

Alchemy Labs - Rank Breakdown:

• Rank One: Basic Potion Crafting. Grants all Society Members a 10% boost to potion potency when crafting in The Fields Below.

• Rank Two: Intermediate Alchemy. Unlocks the ability to create more complex potions, including status effect removers. Society Members receive a 5% reduction in crafting time.

• Rank Three: Well-Working: The lab now features specialized containers that extend the shelf life of herbs and magical components by 50%. Society Members can access these ingredients at a discount, and there's a bonus: shop owners and suppliers will receive a notification that you've got access to high-quality labs, which could lead to better relationships or even extra discounts. Don't worry—you can disable this notification if you'd rather keep your high-end status under wraps.

• Rank Four: Enchanted Equipment. The lab's tools are now infused with magic, increasing the chance of critical successes in potion-making by 15%. Society Members receive a 10% bonus to alchemy experience and a 2% EXP efficiency bonus when using Alchemy as a Focus for spending EXP.

• Rank Five: Transmutation Circle. Unlocks the Transmutation Circle and grants ability Transmute. Transmute allows the caster to convert any basic ingredient into any other basic ingredient at a cost.

• Rank Six: Chronospace Pouch. A mysterious item awarded to all Society Members, the Chronospace Pouch supposedly allows for the storage of items outside of normal time and space. Society Members also receive a 20% reduction in the time required to craft potions and a slight increase in the odds of discovering legendary recipes.

Jace's mind raced as he locked in Rank Six. Each rank swallowed more and more points, but it was worth it. It would be just one step away from Silver One now. It cost him a hefty amount of points, but with the benefits, it felt too good to pass up. The Chronospace Pouch sounded awesome, though, no further information was provided, leaving its true potential a mystery.

It was already at Rank Three, which may have been partially why Twig was so confident that Jace was good for the loan. But also, Twig just seemed like a good guy.

The bonus to production time was a game-changer, but what really caught his attention was the Transmutation Ability. It seemed underwhelming at first—a twenty-to-one ratio, requiring twenty of a base common ingredient to produce just one of another. Definitely nerfed. But something told him that if he leveled it up, this seemingly modest feature could turn into something truly formidable.

Twig had been right—if he could master his alchemy skills, he could sell potions and sauces, earning gold in a world where quests and creatures hadn't been handing out much in terms of monetary rewards. It seemed like he'd have to grind out a living, much like in the real world, but with the Alchemy Labs fully upgraded, he had a solid start.

Next, he turned his attention to the Library.

The Library Below - Rank Breakdown:

• Rank One: Basic Reference. Grants access to a collection of common knowledge tomes. The type you have to read.

• Rank Two: Enchanted Tomes. Society Members gain a 10% boost to experience gained from studying while in the Library Below.

• Rank Three: Scrying Scrolls. Allows the library to create and stock scrolls that may reveal hidden information about the world, new potential recipes and enchantments, or upcoming world events. Society Members can use these scrolls to gain foresight into challenges they might face. Starting Production Rate - One Scroll Per New Moon.

• Rank Four: Memory Archives. All Society Members receive a special Skill Book - Sight Reading, increasing reading skill immediately to Bronze Five.

• Rank Five: Arcane Vault. Bring any book to the Library, and it will not only sort and categorize it but also analyze it, uncovering hidden secrets and translating it into a language you can understand. Never underestimate the power of knowledge—sometimes, the smallest detail can change everything.

• Rank Six: Celestial Codex. A living book that updates with the latest discoveries made by Society Members. It allows for the instant sharing of knowledge across all Society locations, making it easier to coordinate strategies and plans.

He locked in Rank Three. He really wanted access to the Celestial Codex, but the cost was just too high for now. He wanted to save some points for the next upgrades.

Finally, Jace examined the Common Areas, surprised to find that even these held hidden boons.

Common Areas:

• Rank One: Basic Comforts. Grants a minor boost to rest and recovery times for all Society Members.

• Rank Two: Enhanced Rest. Increases the speed at which fatigue is reduced, and adds a slight increase to natural health regeneration.

• Rank Three: Hearth of Fellowship. The area now boosts morale and camaraderie, providing a 10% boosted EXP gained for all collaborative activities while inside and for an additional thirty minutes after leaving. This includes group quests and joint crafting sessions, making teamwork even more rewarding.

• Rank Four: Hall of Feasts. The space becomes enchanted, enhancing the effects of food and drink consumed within it. Society Members gain plus 100% to boosts from meals, making it an ideal spot for pre-battle gatherings.

Jace blinked at the screen, surprised the upgrades weren't more... ghostly. It was the Underworld, after all. You'd think there'd be something dripping in darkness, maybe some skeletal hands reaching out of the Crypts and Tombs. But no, the options seemed oddly tame, despite being very useful.

I wonder if every society has access to the same upgrades? As if in response to his thought, a notification pulsed on the screen. With a click, an entire profile management interface unfurled before him.

Really should start reading these things. He sighed inwardly. Jace had always been the kind to skip cutscenes, and dive headlong into the action. But here? Here, missing the fine print could be deadly. He made a mental note to be better about that.

His eyes scanned the details.

The 13th University Division — The Fields Below

Current Rank: Bronze 2

Rank determined by percentage of physical space upgraded.

Bronze Level Upgrades provide basic magical enhancements and improve living conditions for society members, primarily in the Fields Below.

Silver Upgrades offer broader boons, benefiting members anywhere, and unlock exclusive Underworld features for the Society President:

"Controlled Respawn Points," "Speak with the Dead," and "Reduced Respawn Costs," and others. Additional Society-wide changes are available at higher tiers.

Upgrade 100% of physical space to Bronze Six to unlock Silver Tier upgrades.

You know, if you ever get around to actually spending your points.

"Hey," Jace muttered to the unresponsive screen, a smirk playing at his lips. "I'm getting better at this."

His eyes skimmed the list of potential upgrades at Silver Rank, each one more tempting than the last.

"Well, now that's more like it," Jace muttered, a grin tugging at the corner of his mouth. Controlled Respawn Points? Reduced Respawn Costs? He wasn't entirely sure what it all meant, but in a place like this, those perks could be the difference between life and... whatever the hell happens if you die in the Underworld.

A flicker of thought passed through his mind—recruiting. Could he bring others into the society if they'd already pledged allegiance to another banner? That was a question for Hades next time they crossed paths.

For now, he focused on the task at hand. He'd need to distribute his Society Points wisely. A steep cost climb meant he could get one or two things to Rank Six, but not much more. He decided on the Alchemy Labs—if there was ever a time to invest in potion-making, it was now—and spread the rest across the other upgrades. Slow, steady progress, but progress nonetheless.

Jace leaned back, eyes narrowing at the screen. It was a start, but the real work was just beginning.

The Observatory option shimmered on the interface, almost begging for attention. Jace selected it, curiosity piqued. A prompt appeared, outlining the potential benefits that made his heart skip a beat.

At Rank One, the Observatory would enhance the dorm's ambiance, filling the night with celestial wonders visible through an enchanted dome. Jace wondered if this was useful for some specific class or profession

Rank Two granted all Society Members a Soul Bound Star Map, which sounded super cool. Upon inspection, he found that this map wasn't just a guide to the night sky; it would serve as a failsafe against getting lost, even in the most uncharted territories. No matter where he wandered in the world, the Star Map would align with his position, offering guidance where regular maps fell short.

As if that wasn't enough, the Observatory's upgrades hinted at a potential for greater power in the future and he knew he'd have to upgrade it eventually anyway. At higher ranks, it could enable cross-continental communication through light displays in the sky, connecting distant points in the world like a celestial telegraph.

Jace weighed the benefits, the image of the Star Map lingering in his mind. The Observatory looked like such a cool option—leaving it as-is would be criminal. He unlocked it and then pushed it up to Rank Two.

With a few thousand points still burning a hole in his metaphorical pocket, Jace decided to give the Kitchen and Common Areas a boost to Rank Four—after scanning over their benefits. It was a solid investment. If Dex got his way with the Midnight Festival, they'd need the space—and the atmosphere—to pull it off.

There was a list of boons, but the most notable features he gained were —

Dormitory:

• Sanctuary of Dreams & Ward of Protection: The dormitory becomes an enchanted refuge, ensuring restful sleep with reduced nightmares and lucid dreaming insights. It also provides a protective aura that reduces the risk of ambush while resting and grants a temporary defensive bonus upon waking.

Kitchen:

• Feast of Fortitude & Gourmet Alchemy: The kitchen can host grand feasts that offer powerful buffs to all Society Members, enhancing defense, resistance, and morale. Additionally, it allows for the automatic infusion of magical ingredients into meals, granting unique temporary abilities like enhanced vision, speed, or bursts of magical power.

But he wasn't done. No, Jace made sure to drop some points into the Catacombs, where Shadow usually was. It wasn't just about functionality; it was about making this strange world feel like home, even if Shadow never said what she needed. She was like a ghost, always there but never quite seen. Jace didn't mind. He was building a place where even ghosts could belong.

Finally, with the last of his points, Jace made two significant purchases, nearly depleting his entire stock of Society Points. He hesitated for a moment, considering the implications of what he was about to do. The points had taken time to accumulate, and spending them all at once felt like a risk. But ultimately, he decided it was worth it.

The first major upgrade was Defenses, which he brought to Rank Two. This was a necessary precaution, given the unpredictable nature of the world he was slowly beginning to understand. The Fields Below were vast and full of secrets, some of which were best left undisturbed. Strengthening the defenses was a way to ensure that he could continue his work here without fear of interruption—or worse.

Defense Upgrade to Bronze Rank Two:

Enhanced Fortifications: The defense systems received a serious upgrade, turning the area into a veritable fortress. Stronger barriers now shield the space, with reinforced doors and walls capable of withstanding even the most determined threats. It was solid—practical—but not exactly flashy.

Chapter 25
Indoor Swimming

J ace couldn't help but feel a pang of disappointment. No lasers, no creatures to fight on his behalf. Those kinds of perks didn't even make an appearance in the Bronze Rankings. Maybe, just maybe, they'd start showing up in Silver? He could only hope. For now, he'd have to settle for sturdier walls. Still, it provided some comfort.

It was his last upgrade that brought a grin to his face, something that was a total splurge, an upgrade for the simple joy of it. He knew it was slightly irresponsible, but he felt like he had earned it.

He selected the option for: [Butler, Rank Two.]

This might not have been the most practical choice, but it had a charm that tugged at something deep inside him. It wasn't just about functionality; it was about something more, something that resonated with a part of himself he hadn't touched in years. It reminded him of his brother, who had always loved those old movies where the butler was more than just help—they were the unsung hero, the quiet force that kept everything running smoothly. The idea of having his own "man in the chair," even in a place as magical and strange as the Fields Below, filled Jace with a sense of childlike wonder. It was like bringing a piece of those cherished stories to life, a way to keep that connection alive. Maybe it wasn't the most efficient upgrade, but it was one that made him smile, and that was worth something too.

"That's odd," Jace muttered as he selected the upgrade.

He scanned the option carefully, but something was off—there was no star next to the Butler upgrade, no detailed breakdown of what it entailed. Just a single, cryptic word where the description should have been: "Variable."

He raised an eyebrow but shrugged it off. "Why not?" he thought, locking in Rank Two for the Butler. What's the worst that could happen?

Satisfied with his choices, Jace stepped back, a small smile playing on his lips as he imagined what the Fields Below would look like once the upgrades were complete. He reveled in the anticipation, the excitement building in his chest as he reviewed his list one final time. He was spending nearly every last point.

He'd spent so long scraping by, constantly worrying about every small detail, that the reality of this moment felt almost surreal. Now, here he was, on the brink of transforming his entire world with just a single press of a button. The thrill of it was exhilarating, almost intoxicating—a heady rush of power that he'd never felt before. It was as if the weight of the interface had suddenly become tangible, heavy with the promise of something new, something magnificent waiting just beyond the veil.

His heart pounded as he took a deep breath, his eyes sweeping over all the choices he'd made, each one a step toward that new reality. This was it. With a mix of anticipation and resolve, Jace pressed [Accept].

He waited. But nothing happened.

Frowning, Jace checked his HUD. All of his Society Points were still there, untouched. He glanced back at the screen, and then, just as he was about to give up, a new prompt flickered into view.

Butler Rank Two has been activated.

Accepting Resumes... you have "1" application for the position of Butler.

Jace tapped the selection, revealing the applicant—a man, friendly enough, with a five o'clock shadow that gave him a look of casual ruggedness.

He waited, expecting more applicants to pop up. Nothing. With a sigh, he chose [Accept].

And then all hell broke loose. A torrent of darkness and light exploded from his chest in a sweeping arc, crashing into the monitor. It didn't hurt, but it felt like free-falling from a great height, only to be yanked back up at the last second. His eyes stayed glued to the display as his Society Points plummeted to near zero, the arc finally sputtering out as he dropped to one knee, breathless from the effort.

That had never happened before. Was it because of how many points he'd spent all at once? Maybe the effect had always been there, just too subtle to notice with smaller expenditures.

The air thrummed with a deep, resonant vibration that sank into his bones, an ancient pulse awakening in the very fabric of reality. The console blazed with light, and for a heartbeat, the universe itself seemed to pause, holding its breath. Then, in an explosive surge, the Fields Below roared to life.

Magic crackled through the space like a live wire, buzzing with energy and intent. The walls around him began to shift, contorting and transforming as the upgrades took hold, responding to his will with a fluid grace. Jace could feel it—a raw, electric sensation of power rippling through the air, reshaping the world in ways that felt almost divine. It wasn't just an upgrade; it was a rebirth, the very essence of magic bending reality to his command.

Jace wandered through the shifting corridors, eyes wide as the walls shimmered and reshaped themselves like something out of a dream. Books flew past, each one carried by invisible hands to newly formed shelves. Old, stone-gray walls now gleamed with vibrant colors, intricate carvings blooming like vines. Stained glass windows blinked into existence, casting soft hues that danced across the floor in patterns too beautiful to be random.

The common room was pure magic. The ceiling transformed into a living night sky, stars swirling like they'd just stepped out of a Van Gogh painting. The night above the Fields Below was starting to shift, the deep blues of twilight fading into the soft blush of dawn.

Then came a scream—a high-pitched yelp, followed by splashing water.

Jace bolted down the hallway, his heart pounding, tracking the sound to the Catacombs. Turning the corner, he skidded to a stop.

Shadow, drenched from head to toe, climbed out of a pond—newly formed and black as ink. It must've materialized too fast for her to avoid, trapping her in its sudden splash zone. She stomped up to him, her eyes blazing with a mix of irritation and something like... amusement?

He barely had time to brace himself before she was toe-to-toe with him, leaning up, her nose nearly touching his. She held his gaze, face stormy—and then, without warning, her lips twitched. The storm cracked.

She snorted, tried to fight it, and failed. A giggle escaped, quickly followed by full-blown laughter.

Jace blinked, torn between confusion and relief. "I'm sorry," he managed, stifling a grin. "Really, I am."

Shadow shot him a half-hearted glare, then gestured around as if to say, Upgrades? Really?

"Yeah," he admitted with a shrug. "Figured I'd be a bit more proactive with my points."

She huffed, shaking her head, still dripping as they walked. Her bare feet left wet prints on freshly unrolled rugs, which magically unfurled as they passed. It wasn't that she didn't have shoes, she just refused to wear them.

Torches flickered out one by one, replaced by elegant bronze sconces that bathed the hall in a warm, golden glow.

Despite herself, Shadow's eyes widened as the halls continued to shift. She'd never say it, but Jace knew she was mesmerized.

He couldn't resist asking, "What do you think?"

She stopped, turning to him, and her expression softened. A serene smile lit her face, her eyes reflecting the stars now sparkling above. Jace's chest warmed at the sight. This was what he'd been working toward—this feeling of accomplishment, of home.

Then, suddenly, he ducked as a bookshelf exploded from a pile of rubble, shooting past him toward the library. Shadow snickered as Jace straightened, grinning sheepishly.

Intrigued, he followed the rogue shelf, stepping into the library just in time to watch it transform. Shelves stretched upward, three stories tall, groaning under the weight of countless books. Ladders slid smoothly along their lengths, chandeliers glowed warmly, casting golden light on polished floors. It was a book-lover's paradise, all grand architecture and cozy nooks.

He spun in place, taking it all in. "This... is incredible."

Shadow strolled past, taking her time, her eyes scanning the tapestries that now adorned the walls—epic battles, forgotten myths, serene landscapes woven in vivid detail. Her silence was thick with awe.

They wandered through the grand space together, Jace talking excitedly about his vision for the place, while Shadow let her expressions do the talking. A raised eyebrow here, a quirk of her lips there—a smirk when he suggested adding bean bags. It was a dialogue in its own way, every glance and nod full of meaning.

They ended up sitting on the floor, leaning against a pile of books yet to be shelved. The fire crackled in the hearth, warmth wrapping around them like an old, familiar blanket. Jace kept talking, more to fill the comfortable silence than anything. Shadow just listened, her presence steady and reassuring, even without words.

At some point, he looked at her, a soft smile creeping onto his face. "This is ours," he said, his voice low, but filled with certainty.

Shadow turned to him, her gaze lingering on the sprawling library before them. And then, she smiled. No words, just that—a quiet, knowing smile that said it all.

Together, they sat there, letting the world fall away.

It wasn't more than a few minutes later when their reverie was shattered by a loud clatter from the other room.

Jace jerked upright. "What was that?"

Shadow shot him a look—brow furrowed, lips twisted—How am I supposed to know?

Another clatter echoed, louder this time, followed by what sounded suspiciously like a cough... and then grumbling?

Jace glanced at her, eyes wide. She just shrugged, but the question was there—Should we check it out?

They moved quietly, inching toward the sound. Every creak of the floorboards underfoot made Jace flinch, and he could swear the air felt thicker, charged with anticipation. Shadow wasn't exactly helping either, moving with all the grace of a cat stalking a laser pointer, her eyes fixed ahead, completely ignoring the nervous energy radiating off him.

They reached the closet just outside the hall, its old wooden door slightly ajar. From inside came the muffled grumble again, followed by a cough that sounded like it belonged to someone ancient and dusty—or maybe just... gross.

Jace put a hand on the knob, hesitating. He glanced at Shadow. She raised an eyebrow, clearly unimpressed with his sudden caution.

He took a breath. "On three."

She rolled her eyes, gesturing impatiently—Just open it.

He tightened his grip, his heart thudding in his chest. The door creaked louder than any door had the right to as it slowly, painfully slowly, swung open.

Chapter 26
Reginald

A nd then—thud.

Out from the darkness, something fell forward, hitting the floor with a wet splat.

Jace jumped back, nearly tripping over his own feet. Shadow, wide-eyed, stood frozen for half a second, then burst into silent laughter, her face scrunched up as she desperately tried to keep it together.

There, lying in the middle of the floor, was an old broom... tangled up with a mop... and a bucket that had somehow caught a shoe. The whole mess looked like it had fought a losing battle against a closet shelf.

"Seriously?" Jace muttered, half annoyed, half relieved.

But before he could even take a breath, the closet coughed again.

Jace's heart skipped a beat. Shadow's expression shifted, her smirk fading into something more focused. This time, she wasn't laughing.

Another cough—a real one, not the mop this time—rumbled from the darkened closet.

The door creaked open just a little wider.

Jace swallowed hard. "Uh... hello?"

Out he burst, a tirade of muttered curses spilling from his mouth as he dusted off his ghostly pants and an oversized jacket that hung off his stout, short frame like a tarp on a mini-fridge. The guy was all bluster and no polish—definitely not what Jace had pictured when he ordered a butler.

"Alright, alright! I'm up, I'm up. Damn closet's out to get me. Almost broke my... well, if I had one, it'd be broken." He huffed, straightening his crooked bow tie, though it did nothing to make him look any more professional.

Jace blinked, taking in the apparition before him. This was supposed to be the butler?

"You, uh... don't look much like the picture," Jace started, squinting.

The ghost waved him off with a dismissive hand, already waddling past him toward the common area. "Yeah, well, who does?"

Jace followed, glancing at Shadow, who was clearly trying not to laugh.

"Nice place you got here," the ghost rasped, his voice carrying a rough city drawl. "Real Phantom of the Opera vibes. I like it. Looks like you've been sprucing things up, huh? Not bad. Yeah, I can work with this."

"Uh, so... you're the butler?"

"That's me. The Butler," he replied with a shrug, handing Jace a ghostly card. It had his face on it and the words: The Butler. It immediately vanished into a puff of smoke.

"And you, uh, butler? Sorry, just didn't expect..."

"Someone this devastatingly handsome? Yeah, I get that a lot." He ran a hand over his thinning hair. "Look, if you were expecting something different, maybe you should've read the fine print. But here we are. Now you've got me. Could always send me back, though... No refunds on the points, by the way. But hey, I'm sure you had a long list of other candidates... right?"

"Maybe I will," Jace muttered under his breath. This was not what Jace had wanted, and he already had half a mind to fire this guy, but he hesitated. Something about the guy was... oddly endearing, in a very grumpy kind of way.

Before Jace could get a word out, the ghost spun around, eyes wide with panic. "Look, kid, don't fire me. I need this gig, alright? I know I was the only one who applied—the place is new, and the other ghosts are still spooked about you. I get it, I'm not what you pictured, and yeah, I'm a little rough around the edges. But cut me some slack. From where I'm standing, it's either this or... well, let's just say what comes next ain't exactly a vacation in the Bahamas. And lemme tell ya, you don't wanna know the details." He shot Jace a pleading look, hands up as if begging for mercy. "Just give me a chance, okay?"

Jace sighed. "So... are you good at your job?"

The ghost blinked, then grinned widely, showing off an unsettling number of ghostly teeth. "Terrible at it."

"So... what exactly are you good at?"

"Cards," he said with a shrug. "And, uh, I know my way around magic contracts. Pacts with devils, stuff like that. Don't ask me why. Also, I'm great at sarcasm, which I consider a life skill, even if I'm, you know... dead."

Jace pinched the bridge of his nose. "Why are you even a butler then?"

The ghost huffed and put on an exaggerated British accent. "'Oh, Captain, my Captain! Would you like me to shine your shoes?' Yeah, yeah, I lied on the resume. What, you've never fibbed a little?"

Jace flinched, the ghost's words hitting closer to home than he'd like.

"Look, if you want someone to serve tea and call you 'sir,' I ain't your guy," the ghost continued. "But if you need someone who knows how to keep a place like this running, handle staff, make sure nobody's slacking off? I got you."

Shadow, thoroughly entertained, nodded in approval, eyes gleaming with amusement. Jace, meanwhile, felt a headache coming on.

The ghost crossed his arms, staring Jace down. "So, what do ya say? Keep me around, and I'll make sure this place doesn't fall apart?"

Jace groaned. "Fine. What's your name anyway?"

"Call me... uh, Reginald." He threw in a wink. "Fancy, right? Totally fake."

"Where are you staying?" Jace asked, not quite sure he wanted to know the answer.

"Rank Two, baby. That means I get quarters. But honestly?" Reginald scratched his head. "Hate the staff area. Probably just bunk with you."

"Wait, what? In the dorms?"

"Yeah, why not? You sleep in the buff? Don't worry about it, me too. And, uh, I sleepwalk. You'll get used to it."

Jace stared at him, slack-jawed. Shadow, on the other hand, was on the verge of bursting into silent laughter.

"I need to... go spend my EXP," Jace muttered, edging away.

"Good call. What's your Focus?" Reginald asked, already sauntering toward the fireplace like he owned the place.

"Alchemy," Jace replied cautiously.

"Ah, excellent! You go off, tinker with your potions, and play with your aether. I'll just be over here, getting settled in." Reginald flopped into a plush armchair. His feet, clad in ghostly shoes, rested on a matching ottoman that seemed to appear just in time.

"Don't mind me," he added, stretching luxuriously. Within seconds, the soft sound of snoring filled the room, his head lolling back as if he'd just finished a day of hard labor. "Ahhh, exhausting..." he muttered through the snores.

Jace rubbed his temples. This was going to be... interesting.

Jace tried, unsuccessfully, to shove Reginald into a mental box labeled 'Deal with this later'. But Shadow was right beside him, and her silent smirk was slightly frustrating. Together, they made their way to the alchemy lab, the space humming with possibilities.

The lab had transformed, no longer the cramped, dusty nook it had once been. Now, it was a sleek, sprawling workshop—a testament to his progress, standing at the peak of Bronze Rank and nearly brushing Silver. The scent of rare herbs and potent brews hung thick in the air, while shelves brimmed with ingredients gathered from across the realms. Potions bubbled and glowed, casting a soft, ethereal light across the polished stone floor.

Jace's heart raced with excitement, his fingers itching to dive in. But then, a soft chime echoed from the far end of the lab, pulling his attention. The walls rippled like liquid silver, merging and reshaping before his eyes. An arched opening appeared, connecting the lab with the Fields Below, as a notification pinged in his mind.

Unique Upgrade Available
    Alchemy Labs can be merged with Kitchen
    The Fields Below, sensing your needs, has improvised a new station: Rank 6 Alchemy Kitchen.
    Why make potions or food when you can make both? Why choose?
    Would you like to merge both spaces to create a new space?
    Accept | Reject

A grin tugged at the corners of his mouth as the transformation unfolded. He shot a glance at Shadow. Her eyes gleamed with interest, that rare spark of curiosity shining through her usual mask of silence. She trailed behind him, watching as the room seamlessly merged, sleek fridges and pantries forming out of nothing.

Another prompt hovered in his thoughts.

The Alchemy Kitchen senses ingredients in your inventory.
   Would you like them sorted and prepared?
   Accept | Reject

The little pouch icon in his mind pulsed gently, as if urging him to say yes.

Jace didn't hesitate. He mentally accepted the prompt, and instantly the air crackled with magic. Ingredients began flying out of his inventory, swirling in a mesmerizing dance of color and texture. Herbs, spices, rare extracts—all whirling around the room like they had a mind of their own, settling into jars and vials with a precision that made him blink in awe. It wasn't just efficient; it was art.

"Okay," he muttered, mostly to himself, "this is awesome."

He glanced over at Shadow, who raised an eyebrow as if to say, Not bad, but the small curve of her lips told him she was impressed, too.

As if the room wasn't cool enough already, a large tome materialized on a central pedestal. Its cover was worn, but it hummed with untapped knowledge. Jace approached, heart thudding, and flipped it open. The pages turned themselves, revealing recipe after recipe, each more complex and fascinating than the last.

He let out a low whistle. "Alice would die if she saw this," he muttered, scanning the intricate diagrams and notations.

Shadow's expression flickered, a brief tightening of her lips, a shadow passing over her face. But before he could read too much into it, she was back to her usual self, calm and composed, watching him with quiet intensity.

Jace refocused on the tome, which now listed about fifty potion recipes—all possible with the ingredients he had on hand. His eyes widened as he skimmed the options. "I had no idea I could make so many things," he murmured, shaking his head in disbelief.

Stored in a Chronospace Vault your foods and ingredients are preserved out of time and space, maintaining freshness near-indefinitely.

Increases shelf life by 10,000%.

Jace let out a low whistle, marveling at the convenience. Near-infinite storage, and everything fresh no matter where he was? That was game-changing. He couldn't help but smirk. "Alice would be so jealous."

His thoughts flicked back to the task at hand, and he decided to stick with something familiar. He selected recipes for minor healing potions and flavor-enhancing potions—solid choices that wouldn't blow up in his face. As always, Shadow stood nearby, her eyes gleaming with silent curiosity.

Jace got to work, methodically mixing ingredients, heating them with precision, and channeling his mana into the concoctions. The lab seemed to sense his intent, tools floating into place as if they had their own little personalities, eager to help.

The first batch? A success. He poured a bit of the shimmering food-enhancing potion into a vial, grabbed a stale baguette he had stashed earlier, and handed them to Shadow. Her eyes flickered with interest as she raised the vial to her lips.

"Wait—no, don't drink it!" Jace said quickly, laughing. He gestured to the bread. "It's for food. You put it on the food and then eat it."

Shadow's lips twitched, but she complied, drizzling a little potion over the bread. For a moment, he wondered what would happen if someone did drink it. Would they just get super gourmet taste buds? Or, y'know... die? Hard to say.

She took a bite of the potion-infused baguette, and the change in her expression was immediate. Her usual stoic face lit up with a rare, genuine smile, bright and unmistakable. Jace grinned. Shadow enjoying herself? That was a win.

Encouraged by their success, they continued for hours, brewing potions and working in sync. His experience points ticked upward steadily, and he could feel his skills sharpening with each batch. Shadow, once so engaged, eventually curled up like a dark, tired cat on the couch in the corner, drifting off into sleep. The earlier gleam of excitement in her eyes had been replaced by peaceful exhaustion.

Jace, standing at the workbench, glanced over at her with a small smile. He turned back to his progress, reviewing the steady rise of his skill meter. He was this close to pushing through to the third rank of Bronze. He could feel the energy buzzing under his skin, so close he could almost taste it. But not quite yet. He'd save a few of the potions for the market, see what they'd fetch. Things were starting to look up.

He sighed, but it was the good kind of sigh—the kind that comes from hard work paying off. The night had been long, productive, and surprisingly satisfying. Jace looked at the sleeping Shadow, her form relaxed and soft in the dim light, and he couldn't help but feel content. There was always more to learn, more to create, more to uncover in this ever-expanding world. But for tonight, this was enough.

As the hours slipped by, Jace felt the shift take root deep within him. His EXP Focus activated with a familiar, yet potent pull, guiding the flow of aether through his veins. It was subtle at first—a quiet recalibration of his energy, like an intricate machine fine-tuning itself. Spent power settled into his core, the hum of potential woven into the fabric of his being. There was always more to chase, more to strive for, but in this moment, this quiet pulse of growth felt like home.

A near twenty-point surge spread across his attributes, finely attuned to how he'd been pushing his limits. He could sense the threshold of Bronze Three just beyond his reach, like the horizon teasing the dawn. Not quite there, but closer. Still, the gains were undeniable. Respectable, even. Each point earned through sweat and strategy. He skimmed over the basics of his Character Sheet, skipping the sections with no major changes or updates.

Character Sheet
    Name: Jace
    Speaker Rank: Bronze Two - Apprentice Perceptor
    Class Title: Twilight Guardian
    EXP Capacity: 0 / 5000

Attributes:
- Strength: 20
- Dexterity: 24
- Intelligence: 30
- Wisdom: 34
- Constitution: 18
- Charisma: 14
- Spirit Constitution: 22
- Karmic Balance: 4

Chapter 27
Mostly Harmless Prophecies by Rita Nutkins

The next morning, the gang gathered in the library.

Mount Olympus University's library wasn't just a place to find books—it was a symphony of light and shadow, where sunbeams filtered through arched windows and spilled onto marble floors like secrets itching to be told. Dust motes danced in the shafts of light, and the air buzzed with the quiet hum of ancient knowledge waiting to be plucked.

Jace stood at the head of the table, hands clasped tight, his knuckles white. They all leaned in, elbows resting on polished wood as they listened. He took his time explaining what happened with Sophie and the demon. No one rushed him or brushed it off, treating it like some random quest in a game. Maybe another group would have. But not them.

Sophie was real to him. What happened to her wasn't some fleeting game mechanic—it left scars, ones deeper than he knew. The weight of it hung in the air, thick and unmoving.

Ell listened intently. Alice had the slightest hint of worry in her eyes.

Dex broke the silence first, his hand landing on Jace's shoulder. "That's rough, man," he said, his voice softer than usual. "Really rough. Glad you made it out. And... glad you were there for her, at the end."

Jace looked away, blinking rapidly as a tear threatened to betray him. He bit back a smile, not entirely sure if it was relief or just exhaustion that was winning out.

Ell, who had been uncharacteristically quiet, finally stirred. "Where's Thistle, anyway?" she asked, twirling a loose thread from her sleeve. "Haven't seen him since the duel with Marcus."

Jace frowned. "Neither have I. Anyone?"

Alice spoke up, her voice hesitant. "I saw him. In the shopping district, outside Spellbound, the tomes and scrolls shop. I tried to say hi, but... he ignored me. Like, fully pretended I didn't exist."

"What?" Dex's brow furrowed. "Who does that?"

"Thistle, apparently," Alice sighed. "He was with a group of other students. I didn't recognize any of them. I wouldn't have even known they were students except for their robes."

"Hope he's okay," Dex said, his usual bravado dimming. This time, it was Jace who placed a hand on his shoulder.

"Sometimes people need space," Jace offered. "We're all adjusting. Some of us better than others."

Dex nodded, though the worry didn't quite leave his eyes.

Talk shifted to lighter things—classes, new spells, Dex's latest obsession with combo moves that would "totally revolutionize PvP." Things were almost pleasant, until they heard the yelling.

It came from a few aisles over, loud and angry, like a thunderstorm had suddenly rolled into the serene cathedral of knowledge. The group exchanged glances, then slowly, in what could only be described as a comical shuffle, they made their way toward the noise.

And there, causing the scene, was Marcus.

But this wasn't the Marcus they knew. Gone was the peacock with his immaculate robes and jeweled arrogance. His skin was sallow, almost grey, like he hadn't seen daylight in weeks. The robes he wore now were dull, drab—brown and grey, as if all the color had drained from him, body and soul. No jewelry. No flair. Just a ghost of the man he once was.

"Unhand me!" Marcus's voice cracked, wild and unhinged. "Do you know who I am? You'll regret this—you'll all regret this!" He stormed past them, shooting a glare their way but not stopping. If anything, the look he gave them was empty. Hollow.

They let him pass without comment, waiting until he disappeared from sight.

"What the hell was that about?" Ell muttered, her usual sharpness blunted by concern.

Jace turned his attention to the junior librarian Marcus had been yelling at. She stood there, trembling, clutching a dusty tome to her chest like it might shield her from whatever storm had just swept through. Her eyes were wide, rimmed with tears she was desperately trying to hold back.

Jace approached her gently. "You okay?"

She sniffed and nodded, though it was clearly a lie. "He wanted... a Banished Book. From the upper levels. But I couldn't give it to him. He—he tried to take it."

"And the book?" Alice asked, stepping closer, her voice soft with concern. "What was it?"

The librarian shook her head, glancing nervously at the book in her arms. "I can't tell you that. Even the name is dangerous. Names... Names have power. How Marcus knew to call it... that's what scares me. If I hadn't been here, he might've..."

She shivered, clutching the tome tighter. "We'll have to change all the incantation bindings now. I don't know how he figured it out, but we can't risk it."

Ell and Alice exchanged glances, their minds clearly spinning with possibilities. When they returned to the table, the group commiserated, talking about how much of an ass Marcus was.

Dex groaned. "I just wish we knew what book he was after."

"We do," Ell said, leaning back with a sly grin.

Jace blinked. "Wait, what?"

Alice shrugged, a mischievous twinkle in her eye. "We might've... peeked."

"You devils," Dex said, but there was no heat in his words.

"You're just jealous you didn't think of it," Ell shot back. "Besides, if Marcus is after Banished Magic, especially now, we need to know what he's up to. I hate deceiving that poor junior librarian, but this is bigger than her."

"So, what's the book?" Jace asked, leaning in.

Alice's voice dropped to a whisper. "Umbra Maleficarum. Book of Demons."

Dex's eyebrows shot up. "And they keep books like that here?"

"They keep everything here," Alice replied, leading them to the book-summoning pedestal. The magical search engine flared to life, its tendrils of light unfurling like luminous serpents, reaching for knowledge from the depths of the library's endless archives.

Jace's gut twisted as the pedestal hummed with ancient power. Whatever Marcus was up to, it wasn't good.

Alice focused, her blue eyes catching the soft glow of the swirling lights around them. Each movement was deliberate -graceful- as though she was performing some ancient ritual. The books responded, slipping from their places like leaves caught in an invisible breeze, one in particular drifting toward them, leather-bound and shadowy.

It landed softly, pages fluttering open on their own. "Here," Alice whispered, the word more of an incantation than a statement. Jace's gaze followed hers to the book, which seemed to pulse faintly, as if alive. The strange, multicolored script on the page shimmered, shifting between hues of gold, sapphire, and emerald.

Jace leaned in, his voice barely a breath. "What's it say?"

Alice looked up, blinking, surprised. "You can't read it?"

They all stared at her, waiting for the punchline.

"Right," she sighed. "I forgot—none of you picked up Ethereal. This," she motioned to the page, her fingers tracing the glowing script, "is clear as day to me."

Her finger stopped on a line where the golden ink bled into sapphire. "It says there are twenty great libraries of Terra Mythica. Each one holds a fragment of the universe itself. Together, they form the essence of all that is, bound by sacred crystals and stones."

"Like the hearthstone that wards off the monsters from the university," Ell chimed in.

"Exactly," Alice continued, her voice reverent. "Each library is linked to the others, keepers of hidden knowledge. No book is ever truly banished, just stored in different sections. Any book that enters a library is carved into the hearthstone and recorded forever. Not even the greatest mages can destroy it or erase it. And no one has ever broken a hearthstone... though some have tried."

She flipped to an illustration of a massive crystal, vibrant and alive with energy, its facets glowing like a Shard. They all recognized it immediately, even without Alice's explanation.

"From what I can tell," Alice said, almost to herself, "the libraries hold the source code of Terra Mythica. You know how when you check out a book, you never get the original? Just a copy?"

They blinked at her. Alice looked around, incredulous. "Seriously? You do check out books, right? Please tell me I'm not the only one who uses the library."

Silence. Even the lights above seemed to dim slightly, as if sharing her exasperation.

"Anyway," Alice went on, shaking her head, "you get a copy, not the original. The originals are all stored in the heartstone, like a... read-only version of the universe's DNA."

Dex's hand shot up, mock-innocent. "So, if I check a book out and rip it up, it doesn't matter?"

Alice turned to him, her stare cold enough to freeze sunlight. "I suppose not. But what kind of heathen would do that?"

Dex shrugged, utterly unfazed. "Hey, just asking."

Jace's attention was drawn to another part of the page, where golden swirls encircled a cluster of six distinct colors—sapphire, ruby, amber, emerald, amethyst, and moonstone, all intertwined. "What about this section?" he asked, his voice laced with curiosity.

Alice's expression softened, her voice dropping as though sharing a secret. "That? It's a prophecy, yeah, but it's more than that. The prophecy itself is intriguing, sure—but the author? Even more fascinating."

She leaned closer, her voice dropping as if the very walls might be listening.

"Supposedly, it's from a book called The Mostly Harmless Prophecies by someone named Rita Nutkins, Citizen of Terra Mythica. But honestly, I think the name's a joke. I've never been able to find a single copy of it, though I see quotes from her work in other books all the time."

"So, what does it say?" Jace asked, feeling the air in the room grow heavy, electric.

Alice hesitated for just a moment before reading aloud, her voice steady and slow.

"From the Infinite Potential,
A Word of Power was Spoken,
Its Aether's boundless force,
The Prismata Stone was Broken.

And thus the Shards were born,
Stars scattered through the night,
Cast down upon man and myth,
To carry on the fight.

A Sapphire for the Scholars' eyes, quick of wit and mind,
A Ruby for the Warriors' might, boldest of their kind,
An Emerald for the cunning tongued and Politically inclined,
Amber for the Healers' touch, soothing hearts and mind,
Amethyst for the Sages wise, their protections intertwined,
Moonstones for the Shadow caste, lost in twilight's bind.

Together they are the Prismata,
A single blinding light,
Guided by the great Aether,
To end the endless night."

They all sat there, silent for a moment, the weight of Alice's revelation hanging in the air like an unfinished melody.

"We need that book Marcus was after," Ell broke the silence, her eyes gleaming with the excitement of the hunt. "If we don't know what we're dealing with, we're sitting ducks."

Jace and Dex exchanged a look—equal parts doubt and weariness.

"And how exactly do we get it?" Jace asked. "It's Banished."

"We could just report this," Dex said, his voice low but insistent. "We don't have to handle everything ourselves, you know."

Alice raised an eyebrow, grinning. "Says the guy who always claims to be the rebel of the group."

"I am the rebel," Dex shot back, defensively, "but this? This is so far out of our pay grade I'm getting altitude sickness."

Ell leaned in, her voice lowering to a conspiratorial whisper. "And who exactly are we gonna tell? If possessions are happening, anyone could be compromised."

Alice nodded. "Dex, I've been getting quest notes from my deity. One of them said not to trust anyone with this information unless we'd literally bet our lives on them."

Jace tensed, a cold realization creeping up his spine. There was a part of the story he hadn't told them. Something about the locket Ponos had been wearing. He hesitated, then spilled the rest—how Hades had warned him to be careful, to keep certain details hidden.

Alice's eyes sharpened. "If Hades warned you, then this is even bigger than we thought. That locket, the possession—it's all connected. We have to get that book. It might be the only thing that gives us a heads-up on what's coming."

They all nodded, the gravity of the situation settling in.

"Any bright ideas?" Dex asked, hands up in surrender.

Alice flashed a sly grin. "Leave that to me. I've got a plan. Ell, I'll need your help with something."

Ell crossed her arms, eyebrows raised. "Oh, being secretive now, are we?"

Alice's grin only widened. "Sometimes less is more. I'll explain when the time's right."

Ell hesitated, then gave a small nod. "Fine, but don't leave me in the dark too long. I hate surprises."

Jace, feeling the weight of the conversation lift ever so slightly, cleared his throat. "Speaking of surprises... I've got one."

The group turned toward him, curiosity piqued.

"I've been working on a class upgrade," Jace said, trying to sound nonchalant, though the excitement bubbled just beneath the surface.

Dex's eyes went wide, his jaw nearly hitting the floor. "Wait, wait, wait—first you get chosen by the Thirteenth Olympian, then you're made Society President, and now you've got a Unique Class Title? All in your first year?"

Without warning, Dex reached toward Jace's stomach, fingers wiggling in the air like a cat about to pounce.

Jace smacked his hand away, scowling. "What are you doing?"

Dex shrugged, utterly unbothered. "I heard it's good luck to rub a winner's stomach or something. Dude, you've got to be the luckiest guy alive. Maybe some of that fortune will rub off on me."

Jace raised an eyebrow. "Pretty sure that's not how it works."

Dex grinned. "Worth a shot."

Ell shook her head in disbelief. "You've got that hero aura about you, you know that?"

Jace forced a smile. Lucky. If only they knew. His thoughts drifted to his brother, still lying in that hospital bed back on Earth. He didn't feel lucky. Not even close.

He'd been pushing, struggling—against the game, against fate, against the universe itself it seemed. Flashes on his moments in the Dark One's Soul Realm flashed to mind. Even with the upgrades, even with all the progress, it felt like the darkness was still closing in. Like something was waiting for him, just out of sight, and when it came, it would be merciless. He didn't tell them any of that. Some things felt too heavy to share.

"I just need some time to train," he said instead. "Nothing big. A bit of grinding -working on skills. While Alice and Ell are handling the library thing."

Ell nodded. "Makes sense. Just stay safe, and don't go past Zone Three. We've had enough demon possession for one week."

Jace nodded, though they all knew he wasn't planning on playing it safe.

"Wait," Dex interrupted, raising a hand, "what am I supposed to do while you're all off on these intense secret quests?"

The group paused, then Ell snapped her fingers. "You can start planning the Midnight Festival. We need a venue, and Jace's place would be perfect."

Dex gave her a deadpan look. "Really? You want me to play party planner?"

"Remember Drake from the Oracle Trials?" Ell said, ignoring his protests. "He got Dionysus as his patron. Go find him—those guys party hard. If anyone can help, it's him."

Dex's expression brightened instantly. "Drake? The guy with the endless kegs? Say no more. Jace, you got any more of that flavor stuff? I want to give them a little preview, get the buzz going."

Jace handed over most of what he had, keeping just a small portion for himself and passing a vial to Alice and Ell. "Just be careful," he warned. "It's potent. Tell them a little goes a long way. Too much, and... well, at their own risk."

Dex grinned wide, stuffing the vial into his pocket. "You got it. Time to get this festival rolling."

Then his grin faltered as he looked Jace over, eyes narrowing. "So, you gonna get yourself some better gear before heading out?"

Jace glanced down at himself—worn leather boots, threadbare trousers, and a faded cloak that had seen better days. His chest plate was nonexistent, just a thin, padded vest with a few hastily stitched patches. In truth, it looked more like something you'd wear to fend off a cold breeze, not a sword swing.

"What do you mean?" Jace raised an eyebrow, feigning ignorance.

The group exchanged glances like he'd just claimed the sky wasn't blue.

"Hey, these are new. And nice," Jace added, tugging at his vest with all the conviction of a man who knew he was in deep denial.

"Yeah, for classes, not for combat training," Ell quipped, smirking as she leaned against the wall, arms crossed. Her tone was sharp enough to poke, but light enough to tease. Alice nodded beside her, arms crossed in a silent agreement.

Dex didn't move, just kept staring at him, all casual but with that look of his that said he was about to drop some wisdom. "I believe in two things: your incredible luck and your utterly terrible life choices. And, buddy, that combo? It screams 'Please buy better gear before you die.'"

Jace shrugged, trying to brush off the concern with a grin that didn't quite stick. "I'll figure it out."

"If you need money—" Ell started, but Jace cut her off, waving away the offer before she could even finish. The words felt heavy, like they'd drifted into a space they weren't supposed to occupy.

"It's fine. I've got what I need," Jace said, the lie sliding out effortlessly. It wasn't the first time he'd had to lie, and it probably wouldn't be the last.

Dex's eyebrow quirked up, skeptical, but he didn't push. Alice tilted her head, her eyes narrowing as if trying to solve a puzzle she hadn't realized she was working on.

The air between them lingered, thick and awkward, until Jace cleared his throat. "Anyway, I should probably get to shopping," Jace said, heading purposefully to the Hephaestus district.

"Anyone want to tell him he's going the wrong direction?" Dex asked.

"He'll figure it out," Ell replied.

Chapter 28
Suit Up

Jace trudged toward the shops, scrolling through his inventory again, sighing at his lack of gold.

He had considered going back to that creepy little shop from his first days in Terra Mythica—the one where he'd picked up the White Raven ring. The owner had been a little too eager to trade vague, ominous favors for shiny objects. Maybe he'd offer some equally sketchy deal for armor and a decent weapon. But Jace decided against it. Last thing he needed was to owe some mysterious shopkeeper yet another favor that would no doubt come back to bite him. Hard.

He sighed. This wasn't what he wanted either, but his options were slim, and it was time to get creative. His mind drifted to his old job at Albert's Hardware Store, the comforting weight of tools in his hands, the clatter of metal, the smell of sawdust and oil. Not exactly Terra Mythica, but there was something about it that was grounding. Albert had always been a steady presence, like an uncle who wasn't actually related to you but might as well be.

Jace tried to picture his face. What did Albert even look like? The image wavered at the edges, like an old photograph left out in the sun too long. Hope he's doing okay. Hope my brother's not missing me... not that he'd even know if I was gone. His thoughts scattered like leaves on the wind, refusing to settle on anything for long.

Life outside of Terra Mythica felt hazier with each passing day. Not in any dramatic way—just... off. Like everything was a dream he couldn't quite remember, a place where the colors weren't as bright, the edges not as sharp. It was still there, still real. Just... less.

The crowd buzzed around him as he walked through the Hephaestus district, voices rising and falling like the hum of a distant hive, while the faint scent of charred meat drifted from a nearby vendor.

He spotted Twig in the throng—hard to miss a half-giant, especially when he was yanking thick slabs of leather off racks with one hand and hauling them to his workstation. With deft, practiced movements, Twig draped the heavy hides over a table, cutting and shaping them as if they were paper. Jace watched for a moment, amazed.

"Jace!" Twig called out, flashing a grin, his massive hands still working a thick strip of hide. "Didn't expect to see you back so soon."

Jace approached, the crowd parting around Twig as if he carried a force field. "Yeah, well... I had a thought." His voice wavered, but he tried to keep it casual. He needed this.

"That so? Sounds dangerous." Twig chuckled, still focused on the leather, the familiar rhythm of his stitching a comfort.

" I, uh, need to pay back that loan, but I can't—not until I've got better gear. And I kinda need to... suit up. And, uh, I've got this new cloak ability thing? But it drains aether, so... yeah."

Jace mentally kicked himself. He was almost twenty, for crying out loud—asking for a job shouldn't feel like facing down a demon horde. But here he was, palms sweaty, voice doing that weird shaky thing, and feeling like he was back in school asking if he could borrow a pencil.

Slay terrible monsters? No problem. Almost die a few times in a game where respawning might come with a side order of permanent brain fry? All good.

Ask someone for help? A job? Yeeesh.

He pressed on, ignoring the alarm bells going off in his head. "You seem to know how to smith... or whatever it's called. I used to work at a hardware store back on Earth. I wasn't great at it or anything, but I could probably help out around the shop if you need an extra set of hands."

Twig watched him with that unnervingly patient look, a faint twinkle in his eye, like he was holding back a laugh. But, to his credit, he didn't laugh. He just smiled pleasantly and waited for Jace to finish his awkward ramble.

When Jace finally stopped talking—because he had to breathe at some point—Twig frowned, but not in a bad way. More like a "this kid has no idea what he's asking" kind of way.

"Jace, I'd be happy to take you on, train you up. But, with how things are right now, I don't have time to teach someone new. I could let you clean up around here, maybe get you started, but it'd be a while before you earned a full set of gear. And I don't want you waiting that long."

His tone was sincere, but Jace had feared this. The "sorry, kid, not today" rejection.

Then Twig added, "Or... maybe we could just fit you for armor now and tack it onto the loan?"

Jace paused, considering it for a split second, but then shook his head. "I can't accept that. No handouts. I don't take charity."

His voice came out a little sharper than he intended, and he could see Twig's brows lift ever so slightly. Jace flushed, the heat crawling up his neck. "I didn't mean..." he muttered quickly.

Twig waved it off with a grin. "Hey, don't worry about it. I get it. Pride's a hell of a thing. Just know, you ever change your mind, the offer's there."

Jace nodded, feeling both relieved and kind of stupid. He was getting better at accepting help—just not all the way better, he realized with a wry smile.

They exchanged small talk—surface level, nothing important—until Jace finally had another thought. "Actually, what about this?" He fished out a couple of minor health potions, holding them up like he was offering Twig a new toy.

Twig glanced at the potions, brow furrowed as he inspected them. "Not bad," he said, though the enthusiasm in his voice was less than inspiring.

Jace swallowed hard, a nervous edge creeping into his voice. "What if you sell them for me? We could split the profit."

Twig raised an eyebrow, clearly unconvinced. "Thing is," he said, walking over to a shelf and pulling back a small curtain. Behind it were rows of potions—dozens of minor healing vials, alongside others in every shade imaginable. "We've already got plenty of these. The minor ones don't really sell the best, but if you could whip up a Cure-All or Full Health potion? Now those fly off the shelves."

He shot Jace a sidelong glance, his tone soft. "I'm trying, man. Really. But... you sure you don't want to just add it to the loan? I wouldn't be able to get you the top-tier gear, but I could at least get you sorted for now."

Jace's mind raced, and he nervously shifted his weight. He needed something. He hesitated, staring at his inventory for just a second before he pulled out the other potion—the one he hadn't shown anyone outside of his closer circle yet. The flavor enhancer.

"Alright, check this out," Jace said, holding up a small vial with a flourish. "I call it... uh, The Flavor Enhancer... Thing." He tried to sound nonchalant, but his voice carried a hopeful edge.

Twig raised an eyebrow, unimpressed.

Jace rolled his eyes. "It goes on food. Just try it, Twig," he urged, gesturing toward the half-giant. "Grab some food, you'll thank me later."

Twig pulled a roast beef sandwich from his inventory, the bread still soft and the meat glistening like it had just come off the grill. It had to be something like his own temporal pouch, keeping food as fresh as the moment it was made.

He put a healthy helping of the potion on it before shrugging and taking a bite.

At first, nothing. The silence stretched, and Jace's heart raced. Then, Twig's eyes went wide, his chewing slowed, and his mouth hung open in disbelief.

"Jace, this... this is incredible!" Twig exclaimed, his expression cracking into pure shock as he spoke through mouthfuls of sandwich.

Jace gave a casual nod, but inside, relief flooded him. "Yeah, it's pretty good."

"No, you don't get it," Twig said, practically shaking. "Do you have any idea what you've done? This is huge."

Jace blinked. "I mean, the food sucks at the University, so... yeah, kinda the point."

"It's not just the University, man. It's everywhere. The system? It dulls Travelers' taste buds. Not sure why, but to us, everything tastes like cardboard unless you've got high-level enchantments. And even those? They fade in thirty minutes, tops. But this? This is like magic in a bottle. And you made it with... common ingredients?"

Jace nodded. "Yeah, that's kinda the trick. Simple stuff, no fancy spellwork."

Twig leaned in, eyes gleaming with excitement. "You gotta keep this under wraps, Jace. Seriously. This? This I can sell. But we'll need to come up with a better name."

"How about... Flavor Savers?" Jace suggested, throwing it out with a shrug.

Twig paused, his expression deadpan. "Flavor Savers, huh?" He scratched his chin, a hint of a grin creeping in. "Wasn't that what people used to call beards? Whatever, your product, your name... Flavor Savers." His lips twitched like he was on the verge of laughing, but the awe still lingered in his eyes.

"How much do you think it's worth?" Jace asked, trying to keep his voice steady, though the nervous edge crept back in.

Twig thought for a moment, then leaned back, the wheels in his mind turning. "Hard to say. We'll have to test the market a bit." He paused before adding, "I've got an idea. And you can totally turn me down. We just met after all, and I wouldn't be offended. But, you need gear, right? How about we update our deal? I'll forgive the loan from before, and back you for the whole thing—potions, gear, everything I have access to. We go fifty-fifty. You make the Flavor Savers, I'll handle the selling. And, in return, I suit you up properly. I'm talking real armor, not the raggedy stuff you're wearing."

Jace's pulse quickened. "You're really willing to do that? Just like that?"

Twig smirked. "I don't do charity, Jace. But I know a good investment when I see one. And this? This is gold. Literal gold. You keep making those flavor potions, I sell them, we split the profit, and in the meantime, I make sure you don't get skewered out there. Deal?"

Jace hesitated, glancing at the potion in his hand. "I still want to be able to sell some myself. I've got the Midnight Festival coming up, and I want to supply it."

"Alright, fine," Twig said with a wave. "You give me ten vials a week, a full deck we call it. I'll sell them. You handle the festival. Then we see where this goes. And I'll throw in the gear—because, let's face it, you're gonna need it."

Jace mulled it over, but the math was simple. I need this. "Deal."

Twig grinned, extending a massive hand. "Good. Now let's make sure you don't die before you can make us both some gold and maybe provide a better time in TM for us Travelers."

Jace shook Twig's hand, feeling the weight of both the opportunity and the risk settle over him.

Twig outfitted Jace with a temporary set of dark leather armor, more of a test run than the real deal. The straps felt a little loose, and the chest piece pinched slightly at the shoulders, but it was light and flexible—enough to let Jace move. That was the point, after all.

"Don't worry," Twig said, circling him, eyes sharp, sizing up every movement. "This isn't about winning. Just show me how you move."

Jace barely had time to nod before Twig was on him. No warning, no buildup—just a blur of motion as a fist the size of Jace's head came hurtling toward him. He sidestepped on instinct, barely dodging out of the way.

Jace launched into a counterattack, fists flying and legs kicking in rapid succession. Twig stayed eerily composed, effortlessly dodging each blow, his expression unchanged, as if the flurry of strikes was nothing more than a light breeze. He jotted down notes in a small book without missing a beat.

Jace lunged forward, but Twig pivoted, sweeping a leg out low. Jace stumbled, just managing to leap back before getting his feet swept out from under him.

"Good reflex," Twig muttered, taking a step back and jotting something down in his small notebook while Jace caught his breath. "Chest plate's too tight—messing with your dodges."

Jace grunted, focusing. He could feel the armor restricting his movement in places, but he wasn't about to let that stop him. He circled Twig, testing the weight, shifting his stance. When Twig lunged again, Jace was ready—he ducked under a wide punch, rolling to the side.

Twig's eyes flicked over him, still calm, still taking notes. "Right armguard needs reinforcement. You're relying too much on the left. Next time, try an overhand block."

How high of a rank is this guy?

Jace barely registered the words before Twig's next strike came—a brutal swing aimed at his midsection. Jace pivoted, twisting out of reach, and for the first time, his body moved with real fluidity. He wasn't just reacting anymore. He was flowing with the rhythm of the fight.

A grin spread across his face. I've got this.

Twig came at him harder now—his legs moving with surprising speed for someone his size, testing Jace's balance, his timing. But Jace dodged, twisted, and even threw in a few quick counters of his own—nothing serious, just enough to show that he wasn't a punching bag.

"Interesting," Twig said under his breath, scribbling again as Jace blocked a high kick, narrowly avoiding getting thrown across the dirt. "You're faster than I thought. Might have to adjust the legplates. Keep moving."

Jace's heart pounded, his muscles humming with energy as he danced around Twig's attacks. The more they sparred, the more he felt in tune with his body—the practice, the increased stats, everything was clicking into place. Each move felt more natural, each dodge more precise.

By the end, Twig lowered his arms and snapped the notebook shut. "Not bad," he said with a grin.

Jace wiped sweat from his brow, catching his breath. "I think I could get used to this," he said, glancing down at the armor.

Twig had adjusted the fit of the armor like a master craftsman, tailoring each piece with precision. Every strap, every buckle, felt just right. Light enough to keep Jace quick on his feet but sturdy enough to take a hit. Twig had even thrown in a promise. "Need a fix? Just keep those vials coming," he'd said with a wink. Fair deal, in Jace's book.

Chapter 29
The Iron Jester

B y the time Jace reached the market, his mind was already calculating. Every coin spent, every upgrade planned. The leather creaked with each step, hugging him like a second skin, but he knew he wasn't done. He needed a weapon. Something that fit his new edge.

Twig had recommended a friend, though not without hesitation. "Armor? Sure, I'm your guy," he had said, arms crossed like he was guarding a fortress. Then, after a pause, he added, "But for weapons... you'll want Zeke at The Iron Jester."

Jace raised an eyebrow. "Iron Jester?"

Twig scratched the back of his neck, glancing off to the side as if debating how much to say. "Yeah, listen, Zeke's a little... well, he's a good guy, really." Twig sighed, clearly aware of what Jace was in for.

Twig chuckled, pulling out a scrap of paper and he scribbled something quickly before handing it to Jace. "Here. This'll help. Just give him this, and maybe he won't bite your head off."

Jace eyed the note suspiciously. "What's it say?"

"Nothing that'll make sense to you," Twig replied with a smirk. "But trust me—it'll make Zeke a little more... agreeable."

The shop sat at the far edge of the district, wedged between a potion vendor and a place selling enchanted socks (which Jace had every intention of investigating another time). Above the door hung a rusted iron mask—half sneering grin, half grimace. Welcome to The Iron Jester, the sign seemed to say. Abandon hope, all ye who enter here.

Inside, the place was a mess of mismatched weapons. Swords, daggers, axes, things Jace couldn't even name were strewn about like someone had tried to organize a brawl and gave up halfway through.

Zeke stood behind the counter—a short, stocky guy with arms thick enough to wrestle bears. His tattoos looked like they'd been drawn by a drunk artist, but somehow, they fit. His beard was a wild, tangled mess, bits of metal braided into it like he'd just come from a war party. He looked up, and Jace felt a wall of irritation slam into him. The guy radiated "don't bother me" vibes.

Jace cleared his throat. "Uh, excuse me—"

"Busy. Booked up. Not taking any more orders." Zeke's tone was flat, like he was swatting away a fly without bothering to look up.

"It's just- I was told to come here," Jace started.

"I said, piss off!" the man growled.

Jace fumbled in his pocket and pulled out the note Twig had given him. "Twig said to give you this."

Zeke snatched it up, grumbling under his breath as he scanned the scribbled writing. At first, his eyes narrowed, but then his expression shifted, almost imperceptibly. The scowl softened—just a fraction—and Jace swore he saw the corner of Zeke's mouth twitch.

"Twig, huh? Why didn't you say so?" Zeke muttered, the roughness in his voice losing just a touch of its bite. He crumpled the note, tossing it onto the counter with a grunt. "Guess I owe him a few. Fine. Come on then, let's get you sorted out. You know your build?"

Jace blinked. "My... build?"

Zeke shook his head. "Yeah, your build. What you fight with. You got stats, you got skills—what's the weapon?"

"Right, uh..." Jace glanced around the chaotic shop. "I'm thinking something light, but solid. Maybe a cleric's rod?"

Zeke snorted, eyeing him like he'd just suggested using a spoon in a sword fight. "Cleric's rod? Yeah, no. You don't strike me as the holy type."

Jace wasn't sure how to take that. He was still a cleric—or something like it—but everything felt... different. There was a new lightness to him, as if his aether had shifted within him, traded for something more nimble, more primal. Maybe his body had always been built for speed rather than sacred strength, but now it seemed clearer than ever.

Zeke was already rummaging through the clutter, tossing aside weapons like they were junk. "Here," Zeke grunted, handing him a blade that gleamed faintly in the dim light. "Try this. Short sword, light but balanced. Solid hit."

Jace took it, giving the weapon a test swing. It felt good in his hand, but not right. He shook his head. "Not quite."

Zeke rolled his eyes but didn't argue. Instead, he shoved a double-edged axe at him. "What about this?"

Jace hefted the axe, but the weight was all wrong. Too bulky. He handed it back, and Zeke grunted again, clearly less patient this time. "Fine. We'll figure it out."

For the next few minutes, Jace cycled through weapons—daggers, staffs, even a pair of spiked gauntlets that Zeke claimed were "great for crowd control." But nothing clicked.

Finally, after what felt like an hour of trial and error, Jace spotted something on the back wall. A slender blade with intricate designs running along the hilt. He picked it up. The weight was perfect, like it was made for him.

Zeke noticed the look in Jace's eyes and nodded. "There it is. Should've known."

He held up a sword—dark, forged from obsidian-black metal that seemed to drink in the dim light of the shop. The blade was double-edged, slightly curved, and honed so sharp Jace could almost hear it slice through the air. It wasn't huge, but it had a presence. A weight. Like it had seen battles long before Jace ever laid eyes on it.

The hilt was wrapped in deep crimson leather, soft to the touch, but firm enough for a solid grip. Intricate silver filigree spiraled along the handle, depicting scenes of ancient wars and lost souls etched into the metal.

Zeke's grin widened as he handed it over. "This beauty's got history, kid. Feel that weight? It's older than you and me put together."

Jace took the sword, and immediately, it felt right. Solid, balanced. The kind of weapon that wasn't just meant to be swung—it was meant to be wielded.

"This is..." Jace trailed off, running a finger along the blade. The craftsmanship was ridiculous—perfect. He could practically feel the souls of warriors who had once held it.

"Yeah, I know," Zeke said, puffing out his chest. "She's a xiphos—old-school, Greek infantry style. Don't let the size fool ya. That thing'll cut through anything—armor, bone, you name it. Her name is Song."

Jace gave it a quick swing, the blade whispering through the air. "I'll take it."

Zeke clapped him on the back with enough force to nearly knock him over. "Good choice, kid."

Before Jace left, curiosity pulled at him like an itch he couldn't ignore. He turned back, clearing his throat. "So... what was in the note?"

Zeke didn't look up, just kept sorting through a rack of blades, his rough hands moving with ease. A low chuckle escaped him, gravelly and deep. "Knew you'd ask."

Jace waited, unsure if he was supposed to push. Zeke finally glanced up, a smirk dancing at the edge of his lips, eyes gleaming like he was already in on the punchline.

"It was about her," Zeke said, leaning on the counter, arms crossing like he was settling in for a story. "Years ago, Twig and I were scraping by, no real business to speak of. And there was this woman—ran a shop down the way. Tough. Took pity on us when no one else would. Let us set up next to her. She had a mean sense of humor too. Loved messing with Twig."

Zeke's lips barely twitched, like a smile was too much effort. "The note? Just Twig reminding me of one of her favorite jokes. 'Puppy.' She always called me a lost puppy with big muscles." He rolled his eyes. "Said it every time I got pissed at a customer."

Jace blinked. "That's it? A joke?"

Zeke shrugged, turning back to his work. "More than a joke. It's a reminder. She helped us when we were down, and Twig's saying it's time to do the same." He glanced at Jace, his tone softening just enough to not be insulting. "So, kid, consider yourself lucky."

Jace opened his mouth to respond, but words seemed useless. Kindness wasn't something he expected, especially from guys like Zeke and Twig.

As he was about to leave, he threw out one last question. "So... why 'The Iron Jester'?"

Zeke's face hardened, like a switch had flipped. For a second, Jace thought he'd screwed up. Then Zeke's deadpan voice cut through the air. "Because of my sense of humor. What? You don't think I'm funny?"

Jace felt the temperature drop about ten degrees. "Uh... no, no. Yeah. You are funny. Very funny. Hilarious even."

Zeke grunted, not even bothering to look up. "Thought so."

Jace adjusted the straps on his armor, feeling the weight of the xiphos at his side. As the noise of the marketplace crept through the door, he stepped out, the sword feeling more like a part of him than it had before.

Vendors were shouting, adventurers haggling, the usual chaos. And Jace—well, Jace felt ready. Ready for whatever insane thing the world was about to throw at him.

Or, at the very least, ready enough to not die before Twig's investment paid off.

Chapter 30
Mini-Monsters

His boots crunched on the brittle dirt as Zone Two stretched ahead, the kind of forest that whispered of things that loved the taste of flesh and folly. The trees there, twisted and ancient, stood like silent judges, branches clawing at the sky. He had thought about lingering in Zone Three—where nothing had stirred but the wind. Dead quiet, like the world was holding its breath. Maybe it was a light day. Maybe something worse was coming.

But no monsters meant no progress. And he needed progress. Grinding wasn't glamorous, but the world wasn't going to sit politely while he caught up. It would keep throwing things at him, like a cosmic joke where the punchline was always a blade to the gut.

The forest loomed. Shadows draped over the land, thick and suffocating. Somewhere in there were the things he needed to fight, to kill, to get stronger. Probably also the things that would eat him alive if he messed up. He adjusted his cloak, the fabric heavy and reassuring, but he knew better than to rely on it for too much. It wouldn't stop teeth or claws.

The silence was thicker now, almost tangible, wrapping around him like the cloak itself. He stopped at the edge of the trees, staring into the dark, and for a moment the question slipped into his head unbidden: What the hell am I doing here? His fingers twitched, tugging at the leather strap of his xiphos, the weight of it both comforting and painfully inadequate. Doubt ate at him, small and insistent, like a rat in the walls of his mind.

And then—there it was.

A shift. A subtle prickling on the back of his neck, the kind you couldn't see but damn sure could feel. He pressed himself against a tree, the rough bark biting into his skin, grounding him in the moment as adrenaline surged through his veins. His breath slowed. His eyes darted across the shadows, every movement exaggerated, every twitch of a branch a threat.

"What in the..." Jace's voice trailed off, eyes widening as the creature slithered into view. It wasn't much bigger than a Rottweiler, sure—but it had three heads, and each one of those heads seemed more pissed off than the last. A mini-hydra? Every pair of eyes glinted with a cold hunger, the kind that had nothing to do with survival and everything to do with tearing him apart for fun.

"Good little mini-monster," Jace muttered, tightening his grip on the sword, feeling the dull pulse of adrenaline wash over him. Jace stepped back, his movements slow and deliberate, but the creature mirrored him, inching closer. It might be smaller than Jace, but it most definitely out-ranked him. "Guess it's time to see if Twig's investment pays off."

He activated his Shadow Cloak, a shiver of darkness rippling out from his shoulders like a living cape, enveloping him in an inky veil. The added defense wrapped around him, cold and reassuring, as the shadows coiled and tightened with each step.

The first head lunged, a blur of teeth and scales, and Jace brought his sword up in a hasty block. The impact rang through his arm, but before he could adjust, another head sank its fangs into his forearm. His health bar plunged, sharp red lines slicing into his periphery. He felt his Soul Mend getting to work passively at slowly knitting his skin back together. He also felt a strong pull on his aether.

He swung his sword in a wide arc, severing one of the creature's heads with a sickening crunch. Blood sprayed, and the stump writhed as if alive, twisting in the air. Hydra. He knew something about hydras and heads—something important, buried somewhere in the recesses of his mind, like a half-remembered scene from an old movie.

He grunted, blasting the Hydra with his Moonstone Shard. The pulse of energy sent the creature skittering back, but it wasn't that simple. It never was. As its severed head flopped on the ground, two more sprouted in its place. Hydra physics—because one head was just too easy.

Right, he thought. *Cutting off heads; bad.*

Frustration welled up as Jace hacked at the base of its necks, his movements fueled by desperation rather than finesse. He cut one off, but this time he didn't make the same mistake.

He remembered the sting of a shard burst—like being slammed with concentrated fire. In one fluid motion, he channeled dark heat from his moonstone, searing the stump. It worked. The head didn't grow back, its regeneration snuffed out in a hiss of smoke.

Jace moved on instinct, sidestepping its next frantic attack. His blade sang as he swung left, then down, his blade biting deep into the Hydra's scales.

He struck again straight down the center and the creature split in two, its halves convulsing and twitching as Jace breathed a sigh of relief. But his stomach clenched as the pieces began to stir again. Something worse was happening—tendons stretched, muscles quivered, and the flesh started knitting itself back together. The halves reached for each other, pulling and snapping like grotesque elastic bands.

"Ooops," Jace growled through gritted teeth, panic starting to bubble beneath his skin. He blasted the creature with another burst of moonlight, but the light only slowed the regeneration—like trying to stop a flood with a handful of sand.

His heart pounded in his ears. The thing wasn't stopping.

Think! Think! His eyes darted around, desperation crawling in his chest. He spotted a boulder, half-buried in the earth. It was his only chance.

With a burst of adrenaline, Jace rushed to the rock, his hands slipping against the rough surface as he dug his fingers into the dirt. He heaved, his muscles screaming in protest, but the boulder barely shifted.

No, no, come on!

His cloak stirred, shadows rising and twisting, wrapping around the boulder like serpents. They responded to his silent plea, lifting with him, aiding his every motion. Together, they pried the boulder from the ground.

The Hydra was almost whole again, its heads snapping back into place, eyes gleaming with renewed malice. It looked at him, just in time to give an almost confused oh shit expression before Jace swung the boulder down with everything he had.

The impact was a loud crunch, the weight of the stone pinning the creature's still-twitching body to the ground. It spasmed once, twice, then fell still, the heads lolling to the side in defeat.

Jace stood there, chest heaving, the world spinning with the rush of it all. The quiet returned, thick and heavy, pressing down on him as the adrenaline drained from his veins.

"Well," he gasped, wiping a hand across his sweat-soaked brow. "That was... something."

You have defeated Mini-Hydra — Bronze Four

A jolt coursed through Jace as the EXP flooded into him, sparking a flicker of raw energy deep within his core. This time, it felt different—more real, almost visceral in a way he couldn't quite explain. EXP had never hit him like this before. It was almost as if he was draining it directly from the defeated monster, a soft current of power.

He wondered if it had always been this way—if his perceptions had simply been too low to notice—or if he was now drawing more energy directly from the defeated creature.

Either way, one thing was clear: the longer Jace spent in Terra Mythica, the more he was changing.

His eyes flicked to his aether bar as it surged upward—not by much, but just enough to catch his attention. Something was stirring beneath the surface of his soul. Something was changing. But what? And if it was for better or worse, Jace couldn't tell.

EXP gained from Mini-Hydra, adjusting for Rank Disparity — 675

The EXP and combat notifications flickered in the corner of Jace's vision, small and translucent, briefly lighting up before fading back into nothingness. He had finally read a little bit of the User Interface options and found the Less is More mode—cutting out the noise, saving the laundry list of notifications and combat data for later. It was a balance between Ignore All and Full Notifications—a sweet spot that kept the distractions down while still feeding him the crucial details. He wasn't here for the data dump; he was here for the fight.

Jace stood over the creature's twitching remains, chest heaving, his pulse still hammering in his ears. Sweat dripped down his forehead, mingling with the blood and dirt smudged across his skin. The rush of combat was wearing off, leaving him feeling raw, and spent, but not without that familiar buzz—an addictive, electric thrill that settled somewhere between his bones and skin.

Not bad, he thought, rolling his shoulders. Except—he hadn't fought that much, had he? So why did he feel like he'd just run a marathon while carrying a boulder uphill?

His cloak flickered, the shadows that had wrapped around him in the fight now fraying at the edges. With a sigh, Jace checked his aether levels.

Health; Fine. Not great, but fine.

He watched it slowly tick upward, mending his wounds at a crawl.

His aether on the other hand was nearly drained, scraping the bottom of the barrel.

He let the cloak dissolve, fading like smoke whisked away by the wind, and felt the steady return of his aether as the drain finally eased and he saw it start to recover.

"Well, that explains it," he muttered, half to himself. "That cloak's a glutton."

A mental note scribbled itself into the back of his brain: Only use when absolutely necessary. Aether isn't free, genius. He chuckled to himself, wincing as he rotated his sore arm. The fight had been quick, but the Cloak had drained him faster than expected. Too fast.

He pressed against the edge of Bronze Two, feeling the pull of Bronze Three just out of reach. His aether strained, stretching, yearning for that next threshold. Something deep within him shifted, a ripple that made him glance instinctively at the System. Right on cue, a notification blinked to life.

Twilight Guardian Class Specialization Activated

Use of Class Specialization has triggered the following ability evolutions.

Soul Tether has evolved and gained a new Aspect.

The Aspect has formed into its own ability: Soul Bind.

Soul Bind

Shadowy ropes manifest from the ground or nearby objects, thin but unyielding, wrapping around your target. These tendrils of darkness latch onto limbs, pulling tight to restrict movement.

Aether Cost: Variable (depending on target's strength)

Soul Sense has evolved and gained a new Aspect.

The Aspect has formed into its own ability: Soul Step.

Soul Step

Harness the twilight between realms, stepping briefly into the Other Realm—a ghostly mirror of the physical world where time bends, slows, and slips. In this shadow world, you're unseen by mortals, a flicker, a breath lost to the wind. But beware... in this place, other beings dwell.

Phase through the physical world, moving between places where space twists, reappearing as if the distance never existed. But the deeper you go, the more the shadows crawl, and the longer you stay, the faster your aether drains.

Note: Abyssal beings, ghouls, and worse things still live there. If you see them, they can see you. Even if you can't see them, they can see you. They always see you.

Aether Cost: High (increases rapidly with time spent phased)

Jace felt the new abilities settle inside him like fresh puzzle pieces clicking into place, their potential rippling just under the surface. The world around him remained unchanged, but he could feel the shift. The boundaries of what he could do had just been pushed wider, darker. He took a breath, feeling the thrill of it all—a new weapon, but also a new danger. The shadows were watching, waiting.

Jace felt his mind stretch as if the world had given way beneath him, sinking into a vast unknown. There was no whisper, no gradual rise of power. It hit like a gut-punch, knocking the air from his lungs and flooding him with something deeper than strength—control.

The world around him wavered, outlines flickering between the solid and the spectral. He could feel it now, the rhythm of things unseen, a song that had always been playing, just below hearing. And with this new ability, the melody became clear. He closed his eyes, and with a thought, stepped into the Other Realm.

Everything went quiet. The world slowed. Time didn't stop—it just stopped mattering.

He opened his eyes. The world was there, but it wasn't. Shadows rippled with life. He tried to breathe, but there was no air to be had. Ghostly figures slithered just out of sight, aware of him in ways no living thing ever could be. His heart hammered in his chest. They see you.

The ring on his finger thrummed a warning.

A moment later, Jace reappeared in the physical world, lungs burning from the sudden return of breath. Whatever he had just stepped into, it was both a sanctuary and a graveyard. And it would never be safe. At least, not for long.

His gaze shifted to the ring on his finger as it hummed, the subtle weight of it suddenly more noticeable. Whatever it had sensed, it thought it was important enough to break its silence and warn him.

Jace made a mental note to never stay in the Other Realm for long.

Right—that was draining him too. The White Raven, always there, quietly siphoning off his aether reserves. He flicked his wrist, checking the current status. His lips curled into a lopsided grin.

He touched the ring lightly with his thumb, feeling the faint hum of energy pulsing through it, an ever-present reminder of the pact he'd made.

It wasn't just the fights anymore—it was everything. Every ability, every tool in his arsenal, came at a cost.

With one last glance at the smoldering corpse of the Hydra, Jace turned away, checking his White Raven Ring for updates.

Familiar: The White Raven

Bond: Rank One

This familiar has been drained over countless ages since the loss of its last master. To fully reawaken, it requires a replenishment of mana.

10% of your mana will be unavailable until the recovery is complete.

Mana Replenished: 76,582 out of 7,850,350

All these abilities—each with its costs, provisos, risks, and fine print—were more than Jace had ever had to juggle. It felt like there was always a catch. Almost every ability came stamped with an invisible warning: Terms and Conditions May Apply.

Jace stared at the prompt. "I really hope you're worth it," he muttered, exhaling slowly. A full year. That's how long it would take to bring the White Raven back to full strength at the current rate. And that's if he didn't use any of it beforehand. He had a gut feeling—one of those quiet instincts—that pushing the Raven too early would be... bad. Like waking something ancient and irritable from a deep slumber.

He didn't know why, but the connection he felt—the bond—told him one thing clearly: the White Raven wasn't ready. Not yet.

He glanced at his aether reserves. At least that's ticking up faster than it did a few weeks ago. A small mercy. But still, 10% was having a significant impact.

His fingers traced the edge of the ring, feeling its cold pulse in response, a dormant thrum like a heart not yet beating. He let the notification fade, a twinge of impatience brewing beneath the surface. The idea of carrying something so powerful, yet so useless for the foreseeable future, was maddening.

He smirked to himself. "Guess we're in this for the long haul, aren't we?"

Jace moved cautiously through the underbrush, every sense dialed up to eleven. The soft rustle of leaves, the snap of a distant twig—it all hit him like a slap, each sound a reminder that the Hydra was far from the only thing hunting in these woods.

He exhaled slowly, the weight of his own recklessness settling in. His abilities had always flared up in panic, triggered by fear rather than intention. But he wasn't a One Star, Novice Reactionaire anymore. He was Bronze Two, an Apprentice Perceptor, edging closer to Bronze Three. Professor Blackwood had warned him—use your power with purpose, let it flow through your senses, not just your instincts.

"I've got to get ahead of this," he muttered, the frustration in his voice sharper than he intended. His mind reached out, grazing the edge of his abilities, and he focused on anchoring them to his body, to his senses.

The forest pulsed around him, alive and thrumming with hidden dangers. Every sway of the branches felt deliberate, like the world was watching, waiting. He moved with care, his steps light, eyes scanning the dark tangle of trees. He let the sensations flood him, let the forest breathe through him.

Then he heard it—a low whisper of scales against leaves. Three mini-Hydras, slightly larger than the last ones, their serpentine bodies weaving through the underbrush like predators on a hunt. Their heads bobbed and hissed, necks craning as they searched, the air heavy with their menace. They hadn't spotted him yet, but they were close. Too close.

Chapter 31
Movie Montage

A drenaline hit him hard, sharpening his senses. The first head lunged with terrifying speed, and Jace dodged, the air from its snapping jaws brushing past his throat. Too close. His sword clanged against another head, the impact vibrating up his arm, but there was no time to register the pain.

The Hydra reared up, coiling itself for another strike. Without thinking, Jace triggered Soul Step. The world... flickered, faded. Colors bled into shadow, sounds vanished, and suddenly everything felt distant, thin, like a dream you could almost wake from but never quite did. He took a step. His foot brushed a leaf, but it didn't move, just held in place as if suspended in time.

He stood by a tree now, only a few feet away, and with a quick exhale, he returned to the real world. The noise rushed back in—a cacophony of snapping branches, the hiss of the Hydra, the pulse of his heartbeat loud in his ears.

A glance at his Aether bar made him wince. Ten percent gone. Just like that. He hadn't even stayed in the Other World long. Good to know—also terrifying.

Soul Step, he thought again, vanishing just before the third head could tear into him. He reappeared behind the Hydra, driving his blade into its flank. The beast roared, all its heads snapping toward him in fury.

Jace moved like a ghost, dodging and weaving, every movement calculated for survival. His breath came in ragged bursts, the forest around him a blur of chaos. Bind, he commanded, shadowy tendrils erupting from the ground, wrapping around the Hydra's necks. For a heartbeat, it was restrained—before the creature shattered the binds with raw, terrifying power.

Gritting his teeth, Jace struck again, severing one head with a fiery swipe, immediately searing the stump with his Shard. No new heads. Not yet.

His muscles screamed, his vision blurred with sweat, but he kept fighting. Soul Walk, he whispered, merging with the Hydra's aura. He could feel its rage, its pain—mirrors of his own turmoil twisting in the creature's essence.

One of the Hydra's heads lunged at him, jaws snapping shut with a sickening clap. Jace barely sidestepped, firing a moonlight bolt in retaliation. The Hydra hissed in pain, but the wound healed as two new heads sprouted where the old one had been.

"Fantastic," Jace growled under his breath, desperation creeping into his movements. He darted around the Hydra, launching attacks, conjuring binds that barely held for more than a moment before the beast's strength shattered them.

He needed a new approach—fast. Channeling every scrap of energy he had left into the Moonstone Shard, he unleashed a concentrated blast, heating the moonlight to a searing brilliance. It struck the Hydra's stumps, halting the growth of new heads—slower, this time. Progress.

But it wasn't enough.

Fatigue clawed at him, his aether dangerously low. The Hydra's relentless assault wore him down, pushing him to the brink. Soul Mend, he cast, healing his wounds as they reopened.

Then, with horrifying speed, a head struck. Too fast. Jaws clamped down on his left arm, and with a sickening crunch, it was gone. The pain hit like a sledgehammer, sharp and overwhelming. Blood poured from the wound as Jace dropped to his knees, the world spinning around him.

"Well... this sucks," he gasped, the pain a cruel, constant reminder of just how bad things had gotten.

Pain threaded through his every nerve, but hope flickered in the darkness. Small. Fragile. But alive. Jace seized it, clinging to that ember like a drowning man to driftwood.

Jace ran through his Abilities in his mind. Shadow Cloak, no, too costly. Run, maybe? Soul Step away?

Then the voice came again, sharper this time. More insistent. A thought, not quite his own but undeniably there, urging him.

Breathe, Jason. Find the Bond. The connection. Use it.

He took a shuddering breath, every inch of him screaming to stop. But stopping wasn't an option. Not anymore.

Summoning the last of his strength, Jace triggered Soul Sense, then Soul Tether—an invisible thread weaving him to the Hydra's core. His breath caught. The creature's essence rippled back toward him, a force of nature, ancient and seething. It wasn't just raw power; it was rage, coiled and knotted in every sinew of its being.

But the Hydra wasn't invincible. Not anymore. It had already bled for this fight, and spent too much of itself. Still, it pushed back against him, resisting, as the other creatures had done. But this time—this time, Jace didn't fight it.

He sat still, letting the energy swirl around him like a storm. He didn't push or force the connection. He simply listened. Letting his mind drift into the beast, he felt it in a way he hadn't before, felt its hate, its endless hunger. But beneath that, deeper still—something more.

It shifted.

Jace focused, directing every last drop of his stamina into his Aether, converting it, feeding it to the connection, pouring himself into the Hydra's essence. The creature recoiled, its vast form trembling for just a moment. That moment was all he needed.

He felt it then, at the core. A knot of darkness. Pure and simple. A kernel of hate, so old it had forgotten why it even existed.

And then, the bond snapped into place. Partial. Imperfect. But it was there. The Hydra stumbled, the connection weakening its defenses for the first time.

The world around him shuddered.

Soul Tether — Partial Success

You have established a limited connection to the Hydra.

Partial access to abilities granted.

Jace exhaled, a bitter grin spreading across his face. Partial was good enough. For now.

Jace felt the surge of power as his hand began to regenerate, the Hydra's life force intertwining with his own. It was like fire flowing through his veins, burning but healing at the same time. The Hydra's formidable essence merged with him, its legendary healing factor now his to wield.

Tether, one of the first abilities he'd learned back in the trials with Hades, shared the target's healing between them. Jace had used it before, but never like this. The Hydra snarled, sensing the violation of its power, but Jace was unyielding. He flicked off Soul Bind and struck, then reactivated it immediately. The bond held firm, and for the first time, Jace had a real advantage.

He allowed himself to take a hit, feeling the impact, then instantly triggered the bond, siphoning the Hydra's healing abilities to mend his wounds. Then he'd cut the connection, strike again, and turn it back on. It was a delicate dance, a constant balancing act between offense and defense, with both his and the Hydra's aether flowing in a dangerous loop. The beast could no longer sprout new heads—their power was split. But the drain on his aether was brutal, and Jace knew he couldn't keep this up for long.

Dodging the Hydra's strikes, Jace practiced his footwork, moving with precision. His xiphos flashed in and out of the chaos, not as effective as his Soul Step, but good enough. With the tether active, every hit the Hydra landed on him rebounded on itself, a cruel feedback loop of damage. Jace would deactivate the tether just before striking, reactivating it to heal each wound.

The Hydra roared in frustration, its injuries piling up, its movements becoming sluggish. Jace's attacks grew more fluid, his strategy more refined. He focused on sword strikes, conserving every drop of aether for the constant toggling of Tether. Through Soul Sense, he could feel the Hydra's aura, a rhythm he began to anticipate, allowing him to dodge its strikes before they even landed.

But as his aether drained, his healing factor sputtered out. Every breath felt like fire in his throat, hoarse and raw, his body barely hanging on. Words were beyond him now. He had nothing left but instinct.

The Hydra, now weakened, made one last sluggish lunge. Jace seized the moment, summoning the last of his strength. With a series of precise, brutal blows, he struck at the base of its chest. The creature's roar tapered off into a weak hiss as its colossal form crumbled, disintegrating into motes of light.

Jace collapsed to his knees, panting, his vision swimming. His body ached, but the battle was over. His left hand, now fully regenerated, flexed with newfound strength.

The oppressive tension lifted, replaced by the gentle rustling of leaves in the wind. Jace allowed the Moonstone Shard to sink back into his skin, its once-bright glow fading now that the immediate threat was gone.

In the days that followed, his life became a relentless cycle—the few classes he considered essential, then more combat training in Zone Two, and the constant grind for EXP.

Jace felt like he was stuck in a hero's montage, only this one didn't have the triumphant music or the guarantee he'd make it out alive. But Jace was determined to grow stronger, to find his way in this crazy world, to go the distance.

He continued spending his Society Points, bringing the Fields closer and closer to Silver. Things were looking up. Even Reginald was becoming somewhat useful.

With the latest upgrade to Rank Five, Reginald gained three assistants: glowing white orbs of ghostly light. Not quite "alive," but efficient. Together, they turned the underground crypt from a dungeon of doom into something more... homey. It had gone from Tales from the Crypt to Phantom of the Opera with a dash of old-world charm—cozy, in a creepy way. Like if Dorian Gray, Dracula, and Frankenstein had decided to become roommates.

Every moment grinding his skills, then spending the EXP in his lab, felt like a step toward something greater, and soon enough, the promise of his Third Star loomed closer.

It happened in the midst of an ordinary afternoon, the weight of progress creeping up on him as he worked, unnoticed at first. Jace stood in the alchemy lab, wiping sweat from his brow, his fingers stained with streaks of vibrant green and gold. The dimly lit space buzzed with the familiar scent of simmering herbs and the occasional burst of multicolored light from bubbling cauldrons. His focus was honed, his world reduced to the batch of Flavor Savor potions before him, still lacking that elusive final spark to push them from good to extraordinary.

And then, everything changed.

He leaned over the cauldron, watching as the thick, iridescent liquid swirled lazily, its scent a delicate mix of roasted almonds and honey. Close—but not enough. His hands moved almost on instinct, plucking a handful of sun-dried lavender petals from the rack beside him. Not too much. A pinch—just a touch.

The petals hit the potion with a hiss, dissolving instantly into a cloud of shimmering mist. The liquid changed, deepening into a rich amber, and Jace felt the air around him shift. The air in the lab felt heavier, like the room itself had paused mid-breath, bracing for whatever came next.

His heart raced.

"Come on," he muttered, stirring the potion slowly, eyes locked on the changing color. "Just one more nudge."

Suddenly, the cauldron glowed with a fierce inner light, as if ignited from within. A wave of energy washed over him, warm and sharp, tingling against his skin. The air hummed, alive with power. The potion bubbled once more, then went utterly still.

And then—Ding!

The sound wasn't heard so much as felt, a deep reverberation that shook his bones, sending a ripple of awareness through his very soul. His vision blurred for a heartbeat as a flood of information surged into his mind. His rank—his essence—had shifted. The barrier he had been pushing against shattered in an instant.

For a heartbeat, the room blurred, edges melting into a shimmering veil of silver and light. An ethereal glow seeped into the air, wrapping around him like a living pulse. Suddenly, he was lifted from the ground, his feet no longer tethered to reality. Shadows swirled like smoke, entwined with shafts of brilliant light, spinning in a delicate, chaotic dance around him. His body felt weightless, caught in the grip of something vast and unseen, as if the very fabric of the world was shifting, unlocking something deep within him. The glow intensified, radiating from his core, and he could feel it—a surge, like power awakening, shimmering in tandem with the light.

When his feet touched the ground, everything had changed ever so subtly.

His mind was sharpened, his senses expanded, and with them, his understanding of the delicate art of alchemy deepened. He could feel it. The essence of ingredients, their true nature, how each interacted within the cauldron—he saw it all now with a clarity that had eluded him before. The expected notification appeared.

Chapter 32

Character Sheet

Ding!

R ank Up: Bronze Three - Logician Adept

But that wasn't all that had happened. He dipped a spoon into the new potion

Item: Greater Potion of Flavor Enhancement

Description: A well-crafted elixir designed to amplify the flavors of any food or drink it touches.

Effects:

Flavor Amplification: Intensifies the taste of food, making every dish an unforgettable experience.

Effect Boost: Enhances any secondary effects of the meal by +10%.

Soul Infusion: A dash of the creator's soul powers has imprinted itself onto this potion. Sure, it's fleeting, but you should count yourself lucky. I mean, come on, you're not even Silver Tier yet. Sharing anything at all is a small miracle.

Temporary Effect Options (Lasts a few minutes—seriously, don't get greedy):

5% Increased Dark Vision for 5 Minutes

5% Increased Poison Resistance for 5 Minutes

5% Increased Resistance to Scan/Identify for 5 Minutes

He swiped the notification away and then did a thorough review of his character sheet..

Character Sheet: Jace
Speaker Rank: Bronze Three - Logician Adept
Class Title: Twilight Guardian
EXP Capacity: 0 / 10
Word of Power / Affinities: Soul

Attributes
Strength: 24
Dexterity: 28
Intelligence: 34
Wisdom: 38
Constitution: 22
Charisma: 16
Spirit Constitution: 26
Karmic Balance: 6

Abilities
Soul Mend
Distance: Sight
Heal severe wounds efficiently with 50% reduced self-healing costs.
Aether Cost: Moderate

Soul Tether
Distance: Sight
 Transfer significant effects between entities over greater distances,
including emotions and basic thoughts.
Aether Cost: Dynamic (variable with use)

Soul Survivor
Passive
15% increased resistance to soul damage.
Faster recovery from soul-based injuries.
Aether Cost: None

Soul Severance

Distance: Sight

Sever connections between entities and their host, dealing significant damage to tethered souls.

Aether Cost: Severe

Soul Sense

Distance: Sight

Sharpened perception of auras, discerning emotions, intentions, and detecting spiritual disturbances.

Aether Cost: Low

Soul Walk

Distance: Aura

Step into the Astral Realm, a parallel dimension where time flows differently. Move undetected by most beings in the physical world and venture into the Spirit Domain of willing targets.

Aether Cost: Dynamic (variable with use)

Soul Detection

Distance: Aura

Sense the presence of souls within a short range, even through walls or in darkness.

Detection Range: Arm's length (increases with Spirit Constitution)

Aether Cost: None

Soul Step

Distance: Variable

Phase into the Other Realm, the Abyss, avoiding physical threats and reappearing in a new location.

Aether Cost: High (increases with time spent phased)

Soul Bind

Distance: Sight

Manifest shadowy ropes from the ground or nearby objects to entangle and restrict the movement of a target. These thin but unyielding tendrils of darkness latch onto limbs, holding the target in place.

Aether Cost: Dynamic (variable with use)

Shadow Cloak
Distance: Self
A shroud of pure shadow melds with your form, providing both armor and concealment.
Armor Rating: +40%
Stealth Enhancement: +35%
Shadow Affinity: +20%
Soul Shield: +25% (Protection from spiritual and magical assaults)
Aether Cost: Dynamic (variable with use)

Aetheric Absorption
Distance: Sight
Absorb a portion of Aether from defeated enemies, gradually replenishing your reserves.

Alchemical Focus (Mad Culinary Scientist)

Chop 'Til You Drop (Passive)
Your passion for culinary arts fuels your EXP cultivation.
Bonus: +5% efficiency when spending EXP during cooking.

Iron Stomach (Goat Rank)
Legendary resistance to poisons, toxins, and food-related ailments..
Bonus: 25% resistance to all poisons and toxins.

Willing to Try Anything (Passive)
Culinary experimentation leads to unique potions.
Bonus: +20% potion-making success when using strange ingredients.

Over The Top (Passive)
Receive bonus Society Points when exceeding EXP capacity.
Trigger Condition: Exceeding the EXP capacity

Special Skills & Effects

Feast of Fortitude & Gourmet Alchemy

Prepare meals that boost defense, resistance, and morale for all society members.

Bonus: +100% to meal boosts, improved potion duration and shelf life

Sanctuary of Dreams & Ward of Protection

Dormitory: becomes an enchanted refuge with defensive bonuses upon waking.

Bonus: Protection while resting, temporary defense boost upon waking

Soul Bound Star Map

Guides you to destinations, even in unfamiliar territories.

Bonus: Eases navigation and reveals hidden shortcuts

Additional Abilities

Dark Vision (Adept Rank)

Enhanced ability to see in darkness.

Knowledge Absorption (Apprentice Rank)

Improved retention and comprehension of absorbed knowledge.

Universal Lore (Apprentice Rank)

Increased understanding of game mechanics and lore.

Resistance to Death (Adept Rank)

14% reduction in necrotic, evil, and shadow-based damage.

Mostly Dead - Somewhat Alive (Passive)

At 2% health or less, gain a +10% boost to Aether and stamina regeneration.

Immunity from Scan, Identify, and Mind Reading magic.

Jace's gaze drifted over his updated abilities, but his attention kept snapping back to the newest trio: Soul Step, Soul Bind, and Aetheric Absorption.

It was Aetheric Absorption that gave him pause. He hadn't seen it listed before. "So that's why the boost hit so hard," he murmured, flexing his fingers as he recalled the raw EXP surging into him from each kill. The feeling was intoxicating, dangerous even. He tried to look deeper into its mechanics, but found little information listed.

"How does it even work?" he muttered. It didn't feel like a Soul ability... or was it? The idea that he might be draining souls unsettled him, a creeping sense of wrongness curling around the thought. But if it wasn't a Soul Ability, then what was it?

He recalled the order of things. Words of Power grant Affinities. Affinities grant Abilities. So, it had to be tied to his Soul, right? Unless... he was unlocking something new, something he hadn't fully grasped yet.

Chapter 33
Between Shadows and Stars

Jace leaned against the rough bark of an old oak, his sword balanced on his lap. His breath came in ragged bursts, more from the storm raging inside his mind than the training session he'd just finished. He wiped sweat from his forehead, staring at the blade in his hands. No matter how much he trained, it wasn't enough. Not for this. Not to silence the burden pressing on his chest, a constant reminder of what he was running from.

The forest around him, once hostile and filled with danger, now stood as a silent witness. He had turned it into his sanctuary, the place he could retreat to when everything else felt too loud, too close. Out here, in the steady rhythm of combat, things made sense. Out here, there were no nightmares.

"Still at it?" Dex's voice cut through the stillness like a splash of cold water. He was standing at the edge of the clearing, arms crossed, one eyebrow raised. Jace hadn't even heard him approach. That wasn't like him.

"I needed to clear my head," Jace muttered, sheathing his sword. He stood, forcing his limbs to cooperate despite the fatigue settling into his bones. Dex didn't move, just watched him with an all-too-knowing look.

"Right. And by 'clear your head,' you mean grind until you can't stand up straight." Dex smirked, but it was edged with concern.

Jace huffed out a breath, glancing away. "Something like that."

He didn't want to explain it—didn't want to get into how the sound of steel clashing drowned out the other noise, the things he couldn't control. He trained to quiet the chaos, to forget what was always there, waiting for him in the dark. The ache of Alex's voice haunted him, the weight of his brother's screams that shattered the stillness of his dreams. Running from it seemed easier than facing it.

Dex's face softened, but he didn't press further. "Come on," he said. "Alice and Ell are waiting. We've got that meeting."

Jace gave a small nod, letting his friend lead the way back toward the academy. The walk was quiet, punctuated by the sounds of leaves rustling and distant students training. As they crossed the courtyard, Dex shot Jace a sidelong glance, but still said nothing. He didn't have to.

The library greeted them with its familiar quiet. A subtle glow from the magical dampeners hovered over the room like a bubble of silence, allowing the rest of the world to fall away as they stepped inside. The others were already seated in their usual corner—Alice had her nose buried in a stack of scrolls, Ell fiddling with a small, bright-eyed bird perched on her shoulder. It chirped as they approached, its beady eyes focused on Jace.

"You're late," Alice said, not looking up.

"Had to drag Jace out of the forest again," Dex said, sliding into a chair with his usual grin. "You know how it is."

Alice raised an eyebrow but didn't comment, though Jace could feel her gaze flick toward him for a moment, assessing. She didn't have to say anything either—her face gave her thoughts away.

"Right," Jace said, easing into his seat. "Updates? Any progress?"

"Not much," Alice replied, leaning back with a sigh, fingers rubbing at her temples. "Getting access to the Umbra Maleficarum is proving more difficult than we thought. Too many hoops to jump through—faculty approval is a nightmare."

She exchanged a glance with Ell, her expression carefully neutral, though Jace could sense the tension behind it. "But we're close. We've found a lead that might give us what we need, but... it's complicated. We need more time."

"Everything's complicated with demons," Dex muttered, drumming his fingers on the table.

"It's not just that," Ell said quietly, her usual lightness gone. Her voice dipped, drawing their focus. "I'm worried about Thistle."

Jace stiffened, straightening in his chair.

"He hasn't been around in weeks," Ell continued, her gaze dropping to the table. "And he's not the only one. We've asked around—faculty says some students are leaving to train in the field or join family in other Universities and cities. But something's off. It just seems too abrupt, too many at once."

Jace frowned. "I mean, it's not totally unheard of, right? Some students need to break away and focus on their skills. I know the feeling."

Ell looked up, her eyes sharp. "Yeah, but Thistle's not answering any of our Magic Missives. Not even a hello. We don't know if he's okay... or if he's even still around."

Even in this bubble of quiet, the world outside was shifting, turning more dangerous by the day. The possessed were out there, hiding among them, and now people were disappearing. The academy felt more like a cage with every passing day, and no amount of training or skill grinding could change that.

"We'll figure it out," Jace said, though the words felt like a lie. "I'm sure he will turn up." He wanted to believe it—needed to believe it—but with each passing day, the shadows seemed to grow darker.

Alice caught his eye, her expression softening for a moment. "Yeah, he will," she echoed, but her voice held that same uncertainty.

The rest of the meeting passed in a blur of updates and strategy discussions. Dex was still stuck on the idea of a mass test for the possessed, but Alice shot him down again, explaining how obvious it would make them. Jace barely listened, his mind drifting back to Thistle, to Alex, to all the things he couldn't control. The more he tried to focus, the more everything seemed to slip through his fingers.

Afterward, they parted ways for the day—Dex and Ell heading to some advanced enchantment class, while Alice vanished into the depths of the library stacks. Jace, predictably, made his way back to the forest. He told himself it was for more practice, another chance to sharpen his skills and push his limits. But deep down, he knew better.

He wasn't just training. He was running.

With every swing of his sword, with every burst from his Shard, he was trying to keep himself afloat. Keep moving. Because if he stopped—if he let the silence catch up—he feared he'd sink beneath the pressure of it all. Just keep swimming, he reminded himself, the words like a mantra. Because if he didn't... he just might drown.

By the time Jace returned to his dorm that evening, silence had settled over him like a heavy cloak. The upgrades he'd made to his sanctuary hadn't made it feel any less empty. He'd poured his Society Points into transforming the place into something that felt livable. Something that felt like breathing. Something to run to.

His eyes flicked to the stack of unopened letters on the desk. Invitations. Offers. Other societies had taken notice of the enchanted meals he and Alice had been crafting, but the thought of socializing, networking—whatever they called it—made his skin itch. Popularity. That's what they were calling it now. But to him, it all felt like noise. As if someone else was reaping the rewards while he drifted farther from what actually mattered.

He kept busy because there was no other choice. The work—alchemy, cooking, providing Twig with potions—kept his hands moving, kept his mind from spiraling. It funded his growth, sure. It paid back Twig. It was all in service of bigger goals, like saving his brother... but even that reason felt thin, stretched like old fabric. The dream of the Logout Option coming back had shifted from temporary glitch to permanent purgatory. This world wasn't a glitch anymore. It was life.

The alchemy, the shop, the food—it was all just something to drown out the echo of Alex's voice. He'd give anything to hear it for real, to see his brother again, to help him. That ache gnawed at him, a constant, insistent hum.

He knew that he shouldn't feel like this. Alex wouldn't want him to. This place, this dream—Alex's dream—was something he should embrace. But every step he took, every Society Point he earned, felt like theft. Like he was living a life that wasn't his to claim.

That night, like so many before, sleep evaded him. The moment Jace's eyes closed, the nightmares clawed their way back in. Alex stood there, slamming his fists against some invisible barrier, his face contorted with desperation, his screams ripping through Jace's mind. Then Sophie—her face twisted, monstrous, her beauty melted away into something grotesque, something wrong. Everything slowed, like they were sinking in black, viscous waves, and from beneath that darkness, Jace felt it again—the mind of the Dark One.

Black smoke wrapped around Jace, the soul of the Dark One given form. Cold and malevolent, they crawled through the marrow of his bones, up into his soul. Those eyes—blood red, glowing, full of malice—bored into him, while the Dark One's heart pulsed with a crimson light, throbbing like an exposed wound. Claws of darkness slithered toward him, curling, twisting, reaching. Tufts of thick shadow rose from the beast's hulking form, its presence suffocating. Jace tried to face it, to stand his ground, but the creature only grinned—its smile venomous, dripping with cruelty.

The words of their last encounter hissed through the dream, each syllable sharper than a blade: "I should show you how a soul is truly severed, rip you apart, and let my minions feast on your remains while you watch. The demons are hungry. But before I let you die, maybe you can serve your King. Show me everything!"

Jace saw flashes of images, of strange visions, of war and of city lights and the blaring of car horns.

Jace's body tensed, his heart hammering in his chest as the Dark One's words slithered around him, squeezing tighter, tighter—until it felt like he might break. The smile on the beast's face never wavered, its jagged teeth glinting as if it already knew how this story would end.

Jace sat up in bed, drenched in cold sweat, his breath ragged. His heart hammered in his chest, but the room remained dark and quiet, save for the steady ticking of a clock in the corner.

And then, as always, Shadow was there. She sat beside him, her dark eyes full of quiet understanding. She didn't say anything, didn't ask what had happened. She just waited, her presence a steady anchor in the storm.

Jace swallowed hard, running a hand through his hair. "I'm fine," he muttered, though the lie was thin.

Shadow didn't reply, but she didn't need to. She just sat with him until the tremors passed and sleep, reluctant and heavy, dragged him back down.

The next day, Jace slipped into his leather armor, feeling the familiar creak of the straps and the weight settling on his shoulders like an old regret. It was a ritual by now, this dance with the forest.

The days had grown shorter, the crisp bite of fall settling over the Academy like a blanket of quiet anticipation. Leaves had begun to turn, streaks of gold and deep red painting the trees surrounding the campus, and a chill crept into the air that wasn't there just weeks before. It had been nearly a month since Jace last felt the oppressive heat of summer.

The Star Ceremony and Midnight Festival were just three weeks away, their presence looming like a storm on the horizon, darkening everything in its path. Jace knew he should feel something—excitement, anticipation, anything. He'd reached Bronze Three, and made strides most would kill for. But excitement? No. That emotion felt as distant as a forgotten dream. He just... couldn't.

The University had shifted, not just in mood but in tempo. Urgency buzzed through the halls, conversations hushed and clipped, like everyone was holding their breath. Training sessions felt sharper, study hours more frantic, as if the walls themselves were bracing for something unavoidable. Even the sky seemed to hang heavier, a brooding weight that pressed down on everything.

Jace could feel it too. The forest, usually a place of solace during his training, now felt like a ticking clock. The cold bite in the air was a constant reminder of how fast time was slipping away. Every swing of his sword, every flicker of magic, seemed to add to the mounting pressure. Three weeks. Not enough time.

And with each passing day, that creeping sense of inevitability gnawed at him, burrowing deeper, whispering that no matter how ready he was, it wouldn't be enough.

Every morning, he stalked through the trees with the quiet focus of a hunter, his eyes scanning the underbrush for anything foolish enough to cross his path. Each strike was precise, every cast of his magic sharp, but as he pushed himself harder, there was an uncomfortable truth gnawing away his mind.

He wasn't getting stronger. Not really.

His muscles burned, his mind stretched thin with concentration, but it wasn't enough. What had once been explosive leaps forward now felt like crawling, and the thrill of gaining EXP had dulled into a slow, agonizing drip. His Aether, once eager to grow, now begrudged him every fraction of an increase. It was like the System itself was rolling its eyes at him. Oh, you're still here? Same grind, same mobs? Cute.

Maybe Dex had been right, maybe it was time to go back to class and pretend to be normal for a while. But normal didn't sit well with Jace. Never had. He'd spent too much time running toward this—toward power, toward purpose—and now that he was neck-deep in it, the progress felt like quicksand.

Plateau, they called it. He hated the word. Hated the reality more.

Each day was a reminder that no matter how many enemies he felled, or how many spells he mastered, it would never feel like enough. There was always that itch under his skin, that hungry thing in his gut that whispered, More. You can do more. And when the gains didn't come, it only got louder, more insistent. The silence between fights was the worst, though—that creeping uncertainty that he wasn't just chasing power, but running from something darker, something he wasn't ready to face.

"Maybe I should go back," he muttered to himself, feeling the cold forest air sting his lungs. He wasn't even sure if he meant classes—or life. Whatever that was.

In the quiet spaces between the grind, he felt unsure. Unsure if he was running toward something—or running from all the things he refused to confront—caught between shadows and stars.

Chapter 34
Chimera

After he reached Bronze Three, Jace could feel it—a slow drag on his progress. No matter how many monsters he hunted or skills he practiced, the gains had plateaued. Ell and Dex confirmed what he'd been dreading—this was normal. They both agreed that brute force could only take him so far. It was time to shift focus, sharpen the edge, and dive back into the study. Reluctantly, Jace agreed, returning to classes more full-time.

Mount Olympus University had transformed. Fall had settled over the campus like a painting, leaves swirling in hues of gold, crimson, and amber. The marble pillars glowed in the slanted autumn light, and the sprawling courtyards were dotted with statues of ancient gods, now partially obscured by the drifts of leaves. The sky overhead was a perfect, pale blue, the crisp air carrying the faint scent of wood smoke. In just a week, the Star Ceremony and Midnight Festival would begin, filling the campus with anticipation. A hushed buzz filled the air, a kind of quiet excitement that whispered among the students.

Jace noticed their glances—some more lingering than others. Dex's promotions for the festival were working too well. Gold flowed steadily, and while it made Jace's life a bit easier, it also twisted something inside him, reminding him why he needed the gold in the first place. His brother. A wave of guilt washed over him, the familiar ache of wondering if he'd ever make it back, if he'd ever see his brother awake again. The thought was enough to pull him out of focus, even as he tried to concentrate on the class before him.

Professor Orion Blackwood, Master of Affinities, stood at the center of the coliseum—a massive structure that seemed more fit for blood sport than learning. The stone walls towered high above, capped with rusting iron gates that groaned in the wind. The sun blazed down, casting deep, jagged shadows across the cracked stone floor. Ancient benches, smoothed by centuries of use, formed a half-moon around the arena. Orion himself cut an imposing figure, his muscular frame gleaming in the sun.

The centaur's voice boomed with authority, filling the coliseum. "Today we will be exploring Divine Defenses. Any questions before we begin? Good." His tone left little room for uncertainty, his presence commanding immediate respect.

The whole gang was there—except Thistle. Across the way, Jace spotted Marcus, quieter than usual. He seemed more withdrawn, his usual swagger replaced by a guarded stillness. Only his two hulking companions flanked him now, casting long, shadowed figures beside him. Thistle's absence lingered like a question unasked, heavy, and unsettling, the silence speaking louder than words.

"If you don't know your enemy, you will die by them!" Blackwood's voice thundered through the hall, bouncing off the cold stone walls. "Today we delve into the primordial conflicts between gods and giants, and the demonic forces that align with chaos."

Orion paced with fervor, eyes blazing. "In ancient times, the gods waged war against the giants. Imagine the sky fracturing, the earth trembling as these colossal beings clashed. Giants, towering over mountains, their skin as hard as stone and their breath like storms."

Jace half-listened, his thoughts drifting until Blackwood's voice dropped to a growl, pulling him back. "This isn't just history," Blackwood said, urgency sharp in his tone. "It's about survival. Each of you has hidden strengths you must uncover and wield."

Jace tried to focus, sensing the gravity of Blackwood's words. "Is this guy for real?" Dex whispered, leaning towards him. "'The end is coming. Kill or be killed.'"

Jace's attention wavered, drifting to thoughts of sizzling pans and fragrant herbs.

A resounding whistle from centaur reverberated through the arena, instantly capturing the student's attention. Two attendants wheeled in a massive cage veiled in velvet. The cage trembled, emitting snarls and hisses from within. The audience gasped as the attendants unveiled the creature within - a being of awe-inspiring grandeur. Its scales shimmered like molten metal, its eyes ablaze with wrath. The air thickened with the scent of sulfur.

The creature thrashed against the cage, its lion's head roaring as its serpent tail struck the bars with venomous fury. Obsidian scales gleamed in the harsh light, each one catching and reflecting the cold metallic gleam of the chains that bound it. Its eyes, burning with a haunting mix of primal rage and sorrow, locked onto Jace. He couldn't shake the feeling—was this really necessary? Did it need both chains and a cage?

"This is a Chimera," Blackwood announced, letting the awe of the moment sink in. "Today, it is bound by suppression chains. These chains lower its rank from a Gold One to a Silver Three. Normally, its claws are deadly poisonous, requiring a Gold Three healer to purify. Thankfully, these binds suppress that. But if you ever encounter one in the wild, run."

He gave a thoughtful look and waved dismissively. "Actually, you'd likely already be dead."

Jace's throat felt dry as he locked eyes with the beast. He glanced at Dex, who looked equally unsure.

"She's more agitated than usual. Odd. Maybe Chaos is in the air," Blackwood announced, his voice steady yet tinged with tension. He dismissed the thought with a wave, but his eyes lingered on the beast, a flicker of unease crossing his face.

"Today, you will uncover your defensive abilities," Blackwood said, his voice steady as he paced before the students. "Each deity grants their Chosen some form of protection. But unlocking it? That's on you. The gods provide the tools; it's your job to discover and master them. Today, we'll coax out one of your defenses. But don't fool yourselves—this will not be easy. She is no minor threat, even in her Suppressed state."

His eyes flicked toward the massive creature in the arena, the Chimera's chains rattling faintly. "My assistants will keep her in check, but understand this—she still outranks all of you, by far. Even held back, she's dangerous."

Blackwood's assistants, two fourth-year students, exchanged nervous glances. The chains in their hands trembled slightly, and it was clear they weren't entirely convinced they could contain the beast.

The crowd remained silent, eyes wide, absorbing both the sight and the warning. The Chimera strained against the chains, its power palpable even in its restrained state.

"Remember," Blackwood said, his voice cutting through the silence, "defensive abilities can mean the difference between life and death. Today, you will find yours. Pay attention, stay alert, and trust in the gifts your deities have given you."

Lining the students up, Blackwood opened the cage. Holding tightly to the chain, he allowed the creature to emerge. The Chimera stepped forward, its movements constrained yet powerful. It snarled and hissed, the lion's head roaring, the goat's head snorting, and the serpent tail striking the air with venomous intent. The arena hushed as the monster's presence filled the space, a tangible force of nature subdued only by the suppression chains.

"In turn, you will come up and engage in a controlled fight with the Chimera," Blackwood instructed, his eyes scanning the line of students. "Because of the rank disparity, this will help pull your defensive abilities out. The magic within you knows this beast is far beyond your strength to fight, despite its temporarily suppressed rank."

Jace inspected the massive creature.

Inspection Success

Chimera

True Rank: Gold One | Suppressed Rank: Silver Three

A monstrous fusion of lion, goat, and serpent, each head with its own deadly power. Its lion's maw burns with searing flame, the goat's gaze holds unnatural resilience, and the serpent tail strikes with lethal venom.

Dex was called up first. His eyes flicked to Jace, worry flashing briefly before he steeled himself, his expression hardening. He swallowed, the arena's attention settling over him like a heavy cloak. Gone was his usual grin, replaced by a mask of focus, though the faint glimmer of fear still lingered beneath the surface, barely concealed. His steps were sure, but there was a tension in his frame, a quiet battle between nerves and resolve as he made his way to face the Chimera.

The crowd held its breath as he approached the Chimera, its massive form prowling with dangerous anticipation. Blackwood gave him a nod, pulling the chain just enough to give the beast more freedom to strike.

The Chimera lunged, its lion's head leading the charge, roaring with bloodlust. Dex's body tensed, but he didn't raise his arms to defend. Instead, he relaxed into the movement, and his Affinity activated. A sharp emerald light pulsed from the shard hanging around his neck, and Dex moved—no, he flowed.

His feet danced across the ground in a rhythm only he could hear, ducking just as the Chimera's claws swiped down, his body spinning out of range before its teeth could snap closed. Each step seemed impossibly light, almost preternatural in its grace. His movements weren't just reactive—they were ahead of the Chimera, predicting its next lunge, its next swipe, staying a step ahead of the beast's wrath.

The Chimera snarled, frustrated by its inability to land a blow. Dex weaved through its attacks like water slipping through a clenched fist. His Affinity with Dance wasn't just about evasion—it was an art form, a blend of combat instinct and natural fluidity. The more the Chimera pressed, the more Dex danced, his body spinning, ducking, leaping with the precision of a master choreographer.

The crowd murmured in disbelief. There were no flickering illusions or tricks of the eye—just pure movement, a flow of energy that made it look as though Dex wasn't just dodging but performing a deadly dance with the Chimera.

Jace leaned in to whisper Ell and Alice, his voice low. "It's like he's reading the thing's mind."

Dex's emerald shard glowed brighter with each move, casting a faint green light across his form. His steps were light but deliberate, his movements graceful yet purposeful. The Chimera roared again, lunging with a desperate swipe of its massive claws, but Dex slid beneath it with ease, his body twisting in mid-air as he avoided the beast's attack by a mere inch.

"Beautiful," Blackwood muttered, his eyes fixed on Dex's performance. "You don't fight the Chimera. You outmaneuver it."

The crowd was on edge, transfixed as Dex spun back to his feet, barely a scratch on him. His breath came in shallow bursts, but his movements never faltered. The Chimera tried once more, slashing at where Dex had just been, but his footwork was too sharp, too precise, to be caught. He twisted to the side, and for a split second, it looked like he was going to be hit—but, at the last moment, he sped up ever so slightly and dodged, inches away.

With one final leap, Dex dodged another claw strike, landing with a flourish just out of the Chimera's reach. His chest heaved, his heart racing, but there was a light in his eyes—confidence, pure and simple. He knew what he was capable of now.

Blackwood raised his hand, signaling the end of the match, and the Chimera snarled in frustration, its chain pulled tight once more. Dex let out a breath, wiping the sweat from his brow as his feet stilled, the emerald shard's glow dimming as he came to rest.

"Well done, Dex," Blackwood called, a rare hint of approval in his voice. "You've discovered the heart of your Affinity. Dance, not just as movement, but as strategy. Timing. Precision."

Dex smiled, that old mischievous glint returning to his eyes. He glanced at Jace, giving a small shrug as if to say Not bad, huh? The crowd clapped, murmurs of awe still rippling through them. Dex had turned the battle into a dance, and in doing so, he had shown a mastery that none of them had expected.

The whole lesson only served as a sharp reminder of how much further Jace had to go. Bronze Three—an achievement, sure, one he was proud of. But the gap between Bronze Three and Silver One? That was a canyon. And Gold? That was an entirely different world. That was a chasm. A gap so wide, it didn't just test your mettle; it demanded growth, and forced ability rank-ups through sheer necessity.

He remembered Blackwood's words from one of their first lessons, his gruff voice cutting through the haze of memory: EXP isn't something the System hands out like candy. It's there, whether the System quantifies it or not. The real experience is earned by slamming into the world headfirst—by facing down problems, diving in, confronting the chaos, and pushing through. Persistence.

Jace had learned that lesson the hard way.

Spending EXP, he had said, isn't about pushing buttons on a screen. It's about finding the quiet moments to reflect and fortify your gains, to learn from your mistakes, to improve, and to prepare to dive in again.

Jace had also learned this first-hand. Spending his EXP had come with starts and stalls at first, until he found Alchemy.

It was then that he could find those rare, quiet moments to absorb the chaos that had earned him the experience in the first place. It was about understanding what he'd gained, letting the lessons settle deep- reshaping him in subtle ways.

That's what Blackwood had meant. Growth wasn't just about surviving the fight –it was about learning from it– evolving. So that the next time you faced the world, the next time you charged into the unknown, you'd be stronger, smarter, better.

Dex rejoined the line, his fellow students clapping him on the back, their faces a mix of admiration and nervous anticipation. The lesson was clear: within each of them lay hidden strengths, waiting to be discovered in the face of overwhelming odds.

Dex shared his updates with Jace.

***

Ability Gained: Dancer's Flow

Through the use of expert footwork, you can dodge and evade with enhanced precision, remaining a step ahead of your opponent's attacks. Your movements create afterimages, further confusing enemies and making it harder to land a hit.

Ability Gained: Grace Under Pressure

Your agility and speed increase by 10% for every consecutive successful dodge, allowing you to build momentum in battle, making you more unpredictable with each move.

***

Marcus was called next. He strode forward with an air of quiet intensity, his jaw clenched, eyes focused straight ahead. The usual swagger that marked him was gone, replaced by a deadly calm. He didn't glance at Jace or Dex, didn't acknowledge the murmurs or the whispers from the crowd. His steps were slow and deliberate, the weight of his purpose almost tangible.

Jace watched him, his mind racing. "What do you think his Affinity is?" he muttered under his breath.

Dex leaned in, smirking. "Probably something to do with being a massive tool."

Jace snorted, but there was no denying the tension that Marcus carried. Even the Chimera, which had been thrashing and snarling at every student before, seemed to hesitate as Marcus entered the ring. It paced back and forth, yellow eyes narrowed, waiting for him to make the first move.

Without a word, Marcus raised his hand. The motion was smooth and practiced. And with it, a brilliant shield erupted from thin air. Unlike the temporary defenses of the other students, Marcus's shield was solid, crackling with divine energy that shimmered with a golden hue, reminiscent of lightning trapped beneath glass. The symbol of Zeus was faintly visible across its surface, glowing with authority.

For reasons Jace couldn't quite put his finger on, he had the nagging suspicion that Marcus had also ranked up to Bronze Three. How Marcus managed that with their brutal class schedules was a mystery. Jace could barely keep up, having to choose between training or studying, while Marcus somehow seemed to handle both without missing a beat.

The Chimera roared, sensing a challenge, and leapt at him, claws extended, teeth bared. The first impact came with a thunderous clash as the beast's claws struck the shield. Ripples of energy spread out in every direction, the arena bathed in the golden light of Marcus's defense. He didn't flinch, didn't step back. He stood rooted to the spot, his body tense but controlled, his eyes never leaving the Chimera.

Blow after blow rained down on the shield, each strike sending another cascade of sparks and divine energy through the air. But the shield held. More than held—it seemed to thrive, its glow intensifying with every hit. The harder the Chimera fought, the stronger Marcus's defense became.

Jace narrowed his eyes, watching the scene unfold. The divine energy pulsed in time with Marcus's heartbeat, as if the shield wasn't just a barrier—it was an extension of him. His Affinity wasn't just defense; it was power incarnate. Jace could see it now. The more pressure the Chimera applied, the more power Marcus seemed to absorb.

The Chimera reared back, preparing for one final, vicious strike. Its muscles coiled, its eyes burned with fury. And then, with a deafening roar, it lunged. The impact was titanic, a collision of brute force and divine energy. For a moment, it looked like the shield might finally buckle under the weight of the Chimera's strength.

But Marcus's face remained unreadable, his body unmoving. A surge of energy crackled through his shield, and with a sudden flash, the Chimera's attack was repelled, sent flying backward into the dirt. The beast landed hard, skidding to a stop as the audience erupted into gasps and cheers.

Marcus lowered his shield slowly, as though the effort had been nothing. He gave the Chimera a final, dispassionate glance before turning and walking back toward the line. He still said nothing, his expression never shifting. His silence spoke louder than words, a kind of arrogance that needed no bragging. He knew what he was capable of, and now, so did everyone else.

Jace felt a chill crawl up his spine. "Okay," he whispered to Dex. "Maybe not just a tool."

Dex grimaced. "No, definitely a tool. Just, perhaps not entirely useless."

***

A few more students stepped up, each returning with varying degrees of injury, but all having gained a new ability. None were seriously hurt. Most quickly downed Health Potions, and for those who hadn't brought one, an assistant stood by, ready to heal them with an Amber Shard.

When Ell's name echoed through the arena, the air around her seemed to shift. The crowd's murmurs faded as her eyes narrowed, glinting like sharp edges of a blade. She stepped forward with a calm confidence, her hand brushing the amethyst shard at her neck. A faint, violet light pulsed from the crystal.

"Go get 'em," Dex whispered.

The Chimera growled, muscles bunching as it prepared to pounce. Ell stood her ground, her fingers twitching slightly as translucent discs of energy flickered into existence, deflecting the creature's frenzied strikes. Each disc appeared only for a heartbeat, perfectly timed to intercept the Chimera's claws and teeth, vanishing just as quickly. Her movements were minimal, almost nonexistent—just a tilt of her head, a shift of her stance—but it was enough to keep the beast at bay.

And then it came—an opening in her defenses. The Chimera, quick to seize its advantage, lunged with all its might. Claws raked forward, teeth bared in a vicious snarl. For a heartbeat, it looked like she'd be torn apart, her shield unable to form in time. The audience gasped as the monster's claws slashed through her figure, a brutal, final strike.

But Ell wasn't there.

Her image rippled, shimmering like a reflection disturbed in water, and dissolved into nothingness. The Chimera stumbled, its momentum carrying it past where she had stood moments before. Ell reappeared several paces away, a faint, staggered double-image of herself left behind as a decoy. The illusion faded, leaving only her real form, standing unharmed. A trick of the mind, woven so seamlessly it seemed real, even to the Chimera's sharp senses.

The creature snarled, whipping around to face her, but Ell's eyes gleamed with calm calculation. Her movements were deliberate, and measured, as if she could see every possible outcome before it happened. She wasn't just dodging—she was manipulating the fight itself, crafting illusions that confused the Chimera into attacking where she wasn't.

Again, the Chimera lunged. Again, she wasn't there. Her Amethyst Shard flared, and the illusory double appeared, its form distorted ever so slightly to keep the Chimera guessing. The crowd watched, mesmerized, as Ell's strategy unfolded like a chessboard in motion—every move deliberate, every reaction precise.

Her shields flickered once more, catching a stray blow from the Chimera before it could connect. The audience watched in stunned silence as Ell stood tall, her breathing steady. She wasn't just defending—she was dismantling the Chimera's assault bit by bit, breaking it down with strategy and illusion until its savage strength meant nothing.

For a moment, the Chimera paused, confused, unable to discern where she was. Ell smiled faintly, the light of her Amethyst Shard dimming as she lowered her hand. The fight wasn't about overpowering her opponent—it was about outthinking it, staying three moves ahead while her enemy fell behind, striking at shadows that didn't exist.

The arena erupted into cheers, but Ell barely acknowledged them. Her gaze remained fixed on the Chimera, watching it retreat with frustration. She'd won, not by brute force, but by the one weapon stronger than any claw or fang—her mind.

"Wow, you've been practicing," Dex said with a grin.

Ell let a faint blush creep up her cheeks, trying to play it off with a shrug. "Maybe a little."

"And if your Affinity isn't enough, you could always knock 'em dead with just you. Pretty sure half the guys here forgot how to breathe while you were out there. Did you see the puddles of drool?"

Before he could finish, Ell's foot connected sharply with his shin, followed instantly by Alice elbowing him in the ribs.

"Ow! What the hell? It's a compliment." Dex yelped, doubling over as both girls glared at him.

"Stop being gross," Alice muttered, shaking her head.

"Yeah, not everyone's brain is stuck in the gutter like yours, Dex," Ell shot back, though the smirk tugging at her lips betrayed her amusement.

"Come on," Dex said. "Jace, you saw it, right?"

Jace gave Dex a sympathetic glance, the kind that said I'm not getting involved in that one, before turning back to Ell and smoothly shifting the conversation. He raised an eyebrow, his tone casual but curious. "So, what'd you get out of that fight?"

Ell shared her prompts.

***

New Ability Gained: Afterthought

Creates a mental illusion, allowing you to appear in a different location than you truly are. Illusions leave behind afterimages that linger for a brief moment, confusing enemies and obscuring your true position.

Perceptiveness has gained a new Aspect: Strategic Insight

Grants the user an enhanced perception of attack patterns, increasing the likelihood of outmaneuvering opponents by 12%.

***

Jace thought of the poem from Mostly Harmless Prophecies. Amethyst for the Sages wise, their protections.

Chapter 35
No Pain, No Gain

When Alice was called, nerves flickered across her face, but Jace gave her a reassuring smile and a quick nod. She took a deep breath, her fingers brushing the sapphire shard glowing faintly at her chest. The Chimera growled, its eyes narrowing at her approach.

Alice walked slowly, cautiously, every step deliberate. Blackwood, ever the taskmaster, waved her forward. "Come on, Alice, no time for a stroll. We've got a long line of people waiting to face certain death."

She shot him a look that could've turned him to stone, and Blackwood raised his hands in mock surrender. "Alright, alright, proceed at your own terrifying pace."

Jace smirked. She was definitely getting more comfortable here. It wasn't that long ago she would've frozen under the pressure, but now she glared at teachers like it was just another Tuesday.

As Alice neared the Chimera, its chains rattled and strained, the beast inching forward. Her nerves were obvious—her hands trembled slightly, and her breath hitched. But then something changed. Jace saw it in the way she squared her shoulders, in the shift of her posture. Fear melted away, replaced by something calmer. More certain.

The Chimera lunged, its massive jaws ready to tear her apart. But Alice didn't flinch. Instead, she stretched her arms wide, palms out, her body language a strange mix of surrender and defiance. The Chimera froze mid-charge, its head tilting to the side like a curious dog. A few snickers broke out from the students, but Blackwood silenced them with a sharp gesture. Literally. The room fell into an eerie quiet—Blackwood's Affinity for Silence working its magic.

Then, Alice did something no one expected. She began to move her arms in slow, fluid motions, almost like she was performing some kind of interpretive dance. She tucked her head to the side, swaying gently as she circled one hand in the air like a snake. And then, to the confusion of the entire arena, she sat on the floor and kicked out a leg.

The Chimera approached, so close now it could've taken her head off in a single bite. The entire class held its breath.

But it didn't attack. Instead, the beast mirrored her movements, lowering its massive head and shifting its body in time with hers. It was bizarre—Alice was lying there, moving in this strange, quiet rhythm, and the Chimera was... following her lead.

Minutes passed, and the beast seemed to lose interest. With a snort, it turned and padded back to its cage, sitting down with a huff as if the whole affair had been too boring for words.

The arena was dead silent. Even Blackwood was speechless.

Slowly, Alice stood and walked back to her spot, dusting off her clothes. She was nearly seated when the applause erupted, loud and chaotic. The Chimera, not a fan of loud noises, snarled and tugged at its chains again, but the moment had passed.

Alice plopped down next to Jace, shrugging as they stared at her, dumbfounded.

Jace finally broke the silence. "Care to explain what in the Doctor Doolittle that was?"

"Oh, I love that movie!" Dex chimed in. "My dad watches it on holos every Christmas."

Ell rolled her eyes. "Yeah, but I want to hear Alice's version."

Alice sighed, her gaze lingering on the softly glowing sapphire shard. "You all know my Word of Power is Secrets, but using my spellbook wasn't an option. It takes too long. I've added so much to it, but I barely understand a fraction of what's in there. The ability makes me gather hidden knowledge, which unlocks new pages. Then I have to decipher them, practice, and actually understand the thing. It's a slow grind, so that wasn't going to cut it this time."

She paused, her fingers brushing the shard as if testing its pulse. "When I approached it, I got this prompt."

Arcane Detection has gained a new aspect: Creature Lore

Increased perception of creatures, improved communication abilities with monsters born of Chaos, and deeper insight into magical beings.

Creature Lore has evolved into Creature Intuition

You don't know why, but you just know. 10% increased chance to gain unique defensive knowledge when being attacked by creatures that drastically outrank you.

You are doing great, and I felt this ability would be fitting for you. Use it wisely. The world is a wild place, and you, my Chosen and Hunter of Secrets are my scout and eyes in this mad world.

"When I got this," Alice continued, "it triggered with the Chimera. I just... knew it didn't want to hurt me specifically. It wasn't malevolent, just irritated. Don't get me wrong—without the chains, it would've killed us all for sport. But at that moment, it was willing to back off once I established myself as a neutral party."

Dex tilted his head. "And the weird hand motions?"

"A sort of acknowledgment," Alice said with a smirk, "like saying, 'Hey, I won't attack you if you don't attack me.' It was also a bluff. If it came to it, I'd have fought. But the Chimera respected the gesture."

Jace's mind wandered back to a line from the old poem: A Sapphire for the Scholars' eyes, quick of wit and mind. Alice might've just proven that more than any battle ever could.

When it was Jace's turn, he felt the arena's gaze upon him. Each step toward the ring felt like a step into the jaws of fate, his heart pounding a rapid cadence in his chest. The Chimera's eyes fixed on him. It lunged, claws slicing through the air with deadly intent. Jace braced himself, trying to summon his power, to feel the familiar surge of energy, but it faltered.

The Chimera's blow struck him hard, the impact like a sledgehammer against his body. The force of it knocked the breath out of him and sent him sprawling to the ground, pain exploding through his chest. A moment of silence followed, the arena holding its collective breath. Jace struggled to rise, his vision swimming. The chains around the Chimera clanked ominously, their enchantments the only thing holding the beast's true power at bay. Even in its restrained state, the Chimera was a force to be reckoned with, a reminder of the ancient giants that once walked the earth, their echoes still haunting the present.

Dark energy surged through him, covering his wounds. Tendrils of shadow wove through his flesh, knitting the injuries with an eerie efficiency. Embarrassment burrowed into Jace as he stood, every eye on him. The monster attacked again, and this time he braced, letting it hit. The claws tore at him, but again the dark energy mended his injuries almost as quickly as they were inflicted.

Ability Unlocked - No Pain, No Gain.

The first rule of fight club... you get hit a lot. Pow, right in the kisser.

Rate of health regeneration increased by 5%.

A Hidden Attribute Facet Been Discovered: Health Regeneration.

Heath Reg will now be added to your Traveler's Handbook and available for inspection.

Health Regeneration

This statistic determines the rate at which one regains their Health.

Health Regeneration is calculated based on the following Attributes: 70% Constitution, 30% Spirit.

Current Score: 24

Blackwood watched, a critical edge in his gaze. "A punching bag, are we? Perhaps more of a pincushion. Looks like you have less of a defense and more of a recovery ability. Those can be fairly powerful at high ranks, but tough to rank up. I don't envy your path forward."

Determined, Jace repeated the process, letting the Chimera strike him again and again. Each blow sent pain lancing through his body, but the dark energy within him surged in response, healing his wounds. The other students looked on, bewildered and awed. Despite the pain, a sense of accomplishment filled him.

Blackwood stared at him appraisingly. Jace had spent more time recently working on upping his Rank and was currently, one of maybe a dozen Rank Threes in the class.

He looked closer at his new ability. With each rank, his healing rate increased by 5%. It wasn't much yet, but Jace could sense the potential simmering beneath the surface. If fully ranked up, even without boosting his Constitution or Spirit Constitution, this ability might shift the balance in ways he hadn't quite grasped yet. His recovery would be quicker, sharper, especially when paired with his Soul Mend. He could only hope the scaling would reward him later; otherwise, it would remain useful—just not the game-changer he craved.

The arena buzzed with a chaotic mix of emotions—disbelief hung thick in the air, disgust curled some lips, but there was admiration, too, tucked in the corner of a few gazes. Each hit the Chimera landed had twisted his body in painful, grotesque ways, but with every wound, the dark energy stitched him back together faster, more seamlessly. Bruises faded into nothing; deep cuts shrunk into thin scars. It was as though his flesh had learned the rhythm of destruction and recovery, becoming a more efficient machine with every brutal strike.

The sight went from amusing, to strange, to macabre.

Jace channeled his stamina into his aether, fueling his healing, but the effort came at a price. A wave of dizziness hit him, his vision blurring as his aether reserves plummeted.

And when his health hit rock bottom, when blood pooled beneath him and the spectators' faces paled, Blackwood's voice sliced through the tension. "Enough." The command wasn't loud, but it rippled through the arena like a shockwave.

The Chimera snarled as it was pulled back to its cage, a feral beast still hungry for more. Jace stood there, swaying slightly, battered but still standing. His pulse hammered in his ears, but beneath the ache and exhaustion, a deep current of power stirred.

He blinked as the world came back into focus. The passive healing from Soul Mend had stopped, his aether too drained to sustain it, and now the sharp sting of pain crashed over him. Had his healing been numbing it this whole time? He downed a healing potion, feeling the last of his stubborn wounds reluctantly stitch themselves closed.

He sat back down. No applause followed—just muffled conversations and lingering stares.

"Why's everyone looking at me like that?" His voice was raw with aether drain.

Alice attempted a smile, though it came with a grimace. Ell shook her head. Dex was the first to break the silence. "You're an odd one, you know that?"

Then the next name rang out, hitting Jace like an unexpected jolt, harder than the beast's blows. He scanned the area, confusion swirling with a flicker of hope.

From the far end of the arena, a small figure emerged.

Chapter 36
Who Talks Like That?

T histle looked different—more wound up than Jace had ever seen him. His compact frame trembled, his hands gripping the hilt of his sword so tightly it was a wonder the thing didn't snap in two. It was barely a dagger to anyone else, but in Thistle's hands, it was a greatsword. His whole body was tense, vibrating with nervous energy that seemed ready to break free any second.

"Thistle!" Jace's voice cut through the air, sharp with concern. But the gnome didn't even twitch. His eyes were locked on the Chimera, laser-focused, like the rest of the world had ceased to exist.

The Chimera, a twisted nightmare of fur, fangs, and bad intentions, paced in its cage. Blackwood and his assistants loosened the chains, the metallic links clinking ominously as the creature strained against its bindings, eager to be unleashed. It was practically salivating, eyes locked on Thistle as though deciding which part to eat first.

Jace's gut churned with unease. Thistle, small and compact, looked so out of place before the massive beast, like a chess piece that had wandered into the wrong game. The Chimera tugged harder, snarling, its glowing eyes fixated on its prey. For a moment, Jace thought Thistle might be frozen—rooted to the spot by pure fear.

But there was something else there, too. Something Jace couldn't quite place. A tension, sure, but not just fear. Something darker. Something that was waiting.

But then, something changed.

Thistle's Ruby Shard pulsed on his chest, a blinding red light that spread across his body. He began to grow—muscles expanding, his entire frame enlarging until he stood towering above the other students, larger than even Twig. His skin gleamed, turning from soft flesh to hardened metal, the same metallic sheen as the sword in his hand. Even Thistle seemed surprised, his eyes wide as he flexed his massive arms, the metallic surface reflecting the dim light of the arena.

The Chimera snarled, unfazed, and lunged. Thistle didn't dodge. He stood his ground and took the hit, the beast's claws raking across his steel-like skin with a sickening screech. The impact barely phased him. He absorbed the blow, standing tall, the damage almost negligible against his armored form.

"That's enough, Thistle," Blackwood called from the sidelines. "I think you've made your show."

But Thistle didn't back down. If anything, he pressed forward, his massive body radiating a strange, unstoppable energy. He met the Chimera's next strike head-on, his metallic form taking the brunt of the damage with ease. There was something unsettling in his eyes—a gleeful, almost manic glint. He looked over at Jace, a wild smile stretching across his face.

Jace felt a knot form in his stomach. Something wasn't right.

And then it hit Jace—how had he missed it? One of the assistants holding the Chimera's chains wasn't just any student. It was the tall, pale guy who always shadowed Marcus. Jace's stomach dropped as a terrible thought struck him.

Something about his posture made Jace's skin crawl. The assistant wasn't watching the Chimera—his eyes were locked on Thistle, a twisted smile curling at the edge of his lips. Jace's gut twisted in warning, and before he could shout, the assistant's hand slipped free of the chain.

The Chimera, already straining against its bindings, felt the sudden slack. With a roar that rattled bones and vibrated through the arena, it surged forward, its fury unleashed. Its eyes, blazing with a feral, bloodthirsty rage, locked on Thistle as though the gnome was the only thing in the world.

The crowd gasped, a collective intake of breath as the Chimera's chains clattered uselessly to the ground. Its roar tore through the air, wild and unhinged. Jace's heart pounded, but Thistle didn't flinch.

At the last possible second, just when the Chimera was about to crush him, Thistle moved. His Ruby Shard flared, casting an eerie red light as his body swerved with a precision that seemed impossible for his size. He sidestepped the beast's lunge, his eyes sharper now, focused—almost... gleeful.

With one powerful swing, his sword crashed down on the chain still coiled around the Chimera's neck. The impact rang out like a thunderclap. The metal links snapped with a violent crack, exploding in all directions.

The Chimera, now completely unbound, let loose a bone-chilling roar that seemed to shake the very earth beneath their feet. Jace's blood ran cold as the creature lunged, no longer restrained, its eyes wild with the frenzy of freedom. The battle was no longer just a test—it had become a nightmare.

Time seemed to stretch, each second a heartbeat. Thistle's face changed from pleasure to fear and he stumbled, his legs betraying him as he fell backward. The beast's mouth, wide and glistening with saliva, neared him with terrifying speed.

Jace, Dex, Alice, and Ell stood, the other students moving in a frenzy around them, trying to flee. They fought against the current, trying to get to Thistle, to help him.

Just as the jaws were about to close around Thistle, Blackwood intervened.

He reached out, and a spear of jagged stone materialized in his hand, sharp and solid as if it had risen from the earth itself.

With a swift motion, he slammed the spear into the ground. Stone erupted around him, forming a shield, but the Chimera was already too close. The beast roared, its monstrous claws tearing through the air with terrifying speed. Blackwood wasn't fast enough—its claws raked across his chest, and he staggered back, blood spilling from the deep gashes. His face contorted in pain, but his resolve remained unshaken.

As Thistle screamed, trapped in the Chimera's deadly path, something ignited in Blackwood. His eyes burned with fierce determination. He gripped the spear tighter, thrusting it forward, and its power surged. The stone didn't just hold—it responded. The ground beneath him trembled as the spear pulsed, the stone around it coming to life, swirling and crashing like an elemental storm, ready to strike back with raw, earth-shattering force.

Blackwood shot a burst of light into the sky from his spear.

"Thistle, get back!" Blackwood shouted, his voice raw with effort. The beast lunged, but before it could reach the terrified student, Blackwood held it back, taking another savage bite to his arm. He grunted, teeth clenched against the agony, but his eyes never left the beast.

A surge of Shard energy crackled from Ell's hand, quickly followed by bursts from Jace, Dex, and Alice, each bolt of power striking the Chimera square in the face. It snarled, its many eyes narrowing as it locked its gaze on them—like a predator sizing up its next meal. The attacks bounced harmlessly off its now Gold One-toughened hide, doing nothing more than irritating the beast. If anything, it only seemed more enraged, its muscles coiling with renewed fury as it let out a low, rumbling growl.

"Do not interfere!" Blackwood's voice was sharp as a whip. With a single gesture, the ground rumbled beneath their feet, yanking the students back a dozen paces, the earth obeying his command.

The soil surged up, wrapping around him and the Chimera's lower half, binding them together in a tangle of stone and root. The beast roared in frustration, its bulk straining against the unnatural hold. But even to the students watching, one thing was clear—this creature was way out of their league.

Professor Tanner Frost materialized in the chaos, a blur of motion that solidified into sharp focus. Without missing a beat, she unleashed a barrage of energy beams, each one crackling with power as they struck the Chimera's snarling face. The beast staggered, its head jerking back under the force. Just enough—just long enough—for Blackwood to dig in deeper, his power driving the earth to tighten its hold on the monster.

"About time, Frost," Blackwood muttered through gritted teeth, his concentration unbroken.

"Always making a mess, aren't you?" she quipped, her next beam of energy flaring brighter as it scorched across the Chimera's hide.

"Now!" he yelled, and in that instant, his assistants sprang to life, darting forward and chanting incantations, causing the chains to shine a bright white.

Frost's hands glowed with a soft, golden light, weaving intricate patterns in the air. The light seemed to ensnare the beast, slowing its movements as if caught in a web. Blackwood's spear flashed and struck with the force of a tidal wave, driving the beast back step by agonizing step.

"Secure the bindings!" Blackwood gasped, his voice ragged as his legs buckled beneath him, forcing his equine body to a knee. His other hooves scraped against the floor, the sound harsh in the tense air. The assistants hurried to reinforce the cage, sweat gleaming. Blood streamed from the deep gashes across Blackwood's flanks, pooling beneath his powerful hindquarters, staining the ground red as his tail flicked weakly in pain.

Together, they fought with seamless precision. Frost's magic constricted around the creature, tightening like an icy vice, binding it with unyielding force. With a final, tremendous push, they drove the beast back into its cage. The door slammed shut with a resounding clank, the creature thrashing wildly inside but unable to breach the reinforced barriers.

The centaur, drained and bloodied, staggered before collapsing heavily onto his side, his massive form trembling from the exertion.

"Orion, you're hurt," Professor Frost said, her voice steady, though a faint tremor betrayed her bloodied hands.

An assistant rushed forward, panic flashing in his eyes. Frost spread her hands and whispered a word, an invisible energy forming under Blackwood and gingerly lifting him from the ground.

The shimmering magical platform hovered beside the centaur, sturdy and strong.

Frost followed close behind, her focus sharp. As she moved, the bed of energy glowed with an amber light, helping to stop the flow of blood, Tanner's amber magic at work.

One of the other assistants, a woman in glasses, lingered a moment longer, her face pale but resolute, steady despite the chaos swirling around them.

She adjusted her frames, glancing at the students—still wide-eyed and frozen. Clearing her throat, she gave a nervous smile. "I think... that's enough for today. Professor Blackwood will be fine," she said, though her voice wavered. Her gaze flicked to the still-shuddering cage, as if expecting another attack. "Uh, class dismissed."

The students didn't need to be told twice.

Blackwood's parting look, a blend of pain and something darker—suspicion, perhaps—clung to Jace's thoughts. The other students whispered behind cupped hands, casting furtive glances in Blackwood's direction as he was taken away.

Jace couldn't shake the unease that coiled in his gut. He sped up, closing the gap between him and Thistle, who walked ahead with a group of unfamiliar students—his new friends, Jace guessed.

"Hey, you okay? Where've you been?" Jace's voice was soft, almost hesitant.

Thistle glanced over his shoulder, a smirk tugging at his lips, but it didn't reach his eyes. "I'm fine." The casual tone was as fake as a plastered-on smile.

Jace frowned, feeling the tension. "Are you? We haven't seen you in a while. I've been worried."

Thistle shrugged, his eyes flashing with something darker. "Oh, that's rich. Especially coming from you."

"Whoa, what did I do?" Jace stopped mid-step, his brow furrowing as he turned to Thistle, who halted beside him.

Thistle shot him a look, one eyebrow raised. "If you don't know by now, then you deserve whatever's coming your way. Just like Professor Blackwood. Guy's been acting all high and mighty, don't you think? Kind of feels like he had that claw to the chest coming."

Jace reached for Thistle's shoulder, his concern deepening. But Thistle batted his hand away.

"Thistle... that wasn't just an accident, was it?"

Thistle's smirk vanished, replaced by an icy mask of indifference, but he said nothing.

Jace took a step back, unease creeping into his voice. "He was trying to help us, Thistle."

"Help us? By risking our lives? Maybe he deserved a little comeuppance."

Jace's eyes narrowed, tension thick in the air. "Who talks like that? Look, I get it, but there's a line. You crossed it."

Thistle snorted, turning away with slow, deliberate steps. "Maybe the line needed crossing." His voice was cold, final. He walked off, the shadows lengthening around him, leaving Jace standing there, frozen, dread curling tight in his chest.

"What's gotten into him?" Jace muttered to himself. He had a feeling he already knew, but admitting it was something else entirely, something he wasn't ready to face.

He activated Soul Sense, peering into Thistle as he disappeared into the distance. Nothing unusual—just the sharp burn of anger. But then again, he hadn't seen the Demon with Sophie either. If something was influencing Thistle, it wasn't strong enough to manifest yet. Jace could only sense them when they fully took form, and by then, it was almost always too late.

Later that night, lying in bed, Jace tried to shake off the argument, but it clung to him like a cold, wet cloak. No matter how hard he tried, the unease refused to let go.

Chapter 37
The Damsel

The morning sun streamed through the library windows, casting long shadows across the rows of bookshelves. Jace, Dex, Ell, and Alice slipped into their usual corner, keeping low profiles as they walked. Alice was fidgety, her eyes darting around as if she expected someone to leap out at any moment. Ell, however, wore a sly grin, the kind that said she knew something the others didn't.

Once they reached the farthest corner of the library, Alice activated the sound-dampening charm they'd set up weeks ago—a soft hum confirming their privacy. The moment the hum solidified, Alice's nervous fidgeting stopped. With a furtive glance over her shoulder, she raised her hand and pulled something from her bag with a dramatic flourish.

It wasn't just anything. It was the Book of Demons, an ancient, leather-bound tome with intricate, glowing symbols carved into the cover. The book pulsed faintly, as if it was alive—or at least aware of being summoned.

Jace's jaw practically hit the floor. "Wait, hold up—you actually did it? You got past the Banishment? How?"

Alice leaned back, smirking like a cat with a fresh bowl of cream.

Ell, grinning wide, added, "It was mostly Alice. I mean, I helped strategize, but she's the one who figured out all the fancy magic stuff."

Alice shook her head, her smirk twisting into an incredulous half-laugh. "Oh, absolutely not. It was definitely a team effort. I'd have been caught, like, fifty times already without you. No way I'm taking all the credit for this one."

Dex stepped in, eyes wide. "Wait, so you're telling me you didn't think to call me? I mean, if something needed swiping or someone needed swooning, I'm your guy."

Both Alice and Ell turned to him, deadpan expressions on their faces.

Ell raised an eyebrow. "This was a different kind of thievery, Dex."

Alice raised a hand in protest. "It wasn't stealing—more like reclaiming lost knowledge."

"Right," Ell said, drawing the word out with a sly wink. "Less sticky fingers, more cracking ancient codes. It required absolute subtly."

Dex puffed out his chest. "I can be subtle!"

Cue two more blank stares.

"Okay, fine," he sighed, throwing up his hands. "Go on."

Alice leaned in. "It wasn't a one-day thing. We had to go in bit by bit, breaking down the security measures. Mapping out the librarians' shifts, decrypting magical locks, dodging enchantments. You know, just another Tuesday in the life of your average magic outlaw."

Dex blinked in disbelief. "And you didn't tell us?"

Alice shrugged. "Didn't want to jinx it. This is the first time we've actually been able to pull it off. We've got about 30 minutes with this book before one of the librarians comes back from her break, so this is our window."

"You two have been doing this for weeks?" Jace asked.

"Every morning," Ell added. "We learned the whole schedule. Right now, the librarian in charge of this section is in the backroom, and trust me, she won't come out for anything until her break's over. We're good."

With a deep breath, Alice flipped open the book. The pages crackled, ancient and brittle, but still vibrant with power. Inside, intricate drawings of demons—each more grotesque and terrifying than the last—decorated the margins. The text, written in a blend of languages, flowed in cryptic, twisting patterns.

"Wow," Dex muttered, leaning over for a closer look. "This is... not in English."

"Nope," Alice said, her finger tracing the text. "It's in seven different languages. Infernal, Ethereal, and a bunch of old dialects. It'll take me a while to decipher everything, but no time to start like to present."

Jace frowned. "Seven languages? You can read all of them?"

"Well, some. Infernal's tricky, but I'm getting the hang of it," Alice said, flipping through a few more pages. Her eyes caught on a section framed by ornate, swirling symbols. "But look at this—" She stopped, squinting at the Infernal script. It took her a moment to untangle the meaning. "Roughly translated, this says 'Possession Through Proxy.' Whatever that means."

Ell raised an eyebrow. "Sounds charming."

Alice nodded, more intrigued than worried. "It seems to describe how certain artifacts can act as conduits for demonic possession."

Jace leaned in, eyes narrowing. "Does it say how to spot them?"

Alice frowned, scanning the text. "Not yet. There's a lot I don't fully understand yet. But I'm gonna have so much fun figuring this out."

Her excitement was palpable, a spark lighting up her face.

Before anyone could react, a faint sound echoed from just beyond the aisle, barely audible through the sound dampeners—footsteps.

Alice's head jerked up, her breath catching in her throat, eyes wide with alarm. Dex, moving with practiced stealth, slid a few books aside, peeking through the gap. He returned, face drained of color.

"Uh, Alice," Dex whispered, voice strained, "didn't you say we had thirty minutes before the librarian came back from her break?"

"Uh-huh," she whispered back.

Dex nodded, a tight grimace tightening across his face. "Great, just as I thought. Except for one tiny, minuscule, barely-worth-mentioning issue—she's already back from her break."

Alice muttered a curse under her breath, her fingers twitching. "That's impossible." She stalked over to the bookshelf, pulling out a random book and using the gap to peer through. With a quiet huff, she slid it back into place and returned to the group, her face unusually calm.

"Yup, we're screwed," Alice muttered.

"They must've swapped shifts," Alice said. "There's a new librarian—one I've never seen before. And she's not leaving that post anytime soon."

Ell's expression sharpened. "That's... really bad," she said, her eyes flicking down the aisle.

Jace's eyebrow arched. "Why not just... stash it in your inventory?"

Ell shot him a sideways glance. "Banished items don't go into magic inventories. Trust me, we've tried and let's just say... it doesn't end well." She paused, thinking. "Alright, we'll go with the Damsel. I'll distract her, and Alice, you return the book." She turned to Dex and Jace, giving them a nod. "And boys?"

"Yeah?" they answered in sync.

"Meet us outside."

Jace and Dex exchanged a worried look.

With a curt nod, Alice snapped the tome shut, slipping it into her cloth bag.

The sound-dampening faded as Alice and Ell moved like toward the next aisle. In an instant, Ell appeared at the librarian's desk, her voice bright and airy.

"Hi! So, uh... I'm super lost. Do you know where I could find, like, the, um... Big Book of Spectacularly Bad Magical Choices?"

The librarian barely lifted her head, her face the epitome of indifference—thin lips, dull eyes, and the overall aura of someone who'd seen it all and cared for none of it. She responded in a flat tone, "Basic Magics, West Wing, Aisle B," before returning to her work without another glance.

Ell blinked, faking confusion. "Oh, wait—which way is that?"

The librarian glanced up again, this time with a barely concealed sigh, her patience fraying at the edges. "It's right over there," she said, pointing vaguely in the right direction, clearly convinced Ell was a lost cause. "And yes, you need to be a registered library member."

Alice slipped in behind them, her movements deliberate as she activated the library console. Her Veil of Shadows ability had already cloaked her, rendering her invisible, but the console remained fully visible, its screen flickering through various displays as her fingers moved deftly across it.

"Right, of course! Member. Totally." Ell began fumbling dramatically in her pockets. "How do I do that again?"

Behind the librarian, Alice's fingers danced over the hidden access panel, runes flashing briefly under her touch. She retrieved the book from her bag, and it materialized, hovering in mid-air by the panel. The librarian's eyes narrowed, suspecting Ell couldn't be that clueless. "We'll need to register you at the station," she said, turning toward her console—and toward Alice.

Panic flashing across her face, Ell grabbed the librarian's shoulder, her voice rising with exaggerated urgency. "No, listen! I need that book right now. I don't have time to register!"

The librarian blinked, taken aback by the sudden desperation. "You're a student, right?" she asked, her eyebrows raised. "I can sign it out to your student profile temporarily, but you'll have to return it by the end of the day and get a membership first thing."

Alice finished her work, the book disappearing without a sound, and she slipped away unnoticed.

Ell flashed a sheepish grin. "What was I thinking? I am already a member." She slapped her forehead with a light chuckle. "I'm just... really bad at this. Thanks for your help!" She called over her shoulder as she walked away.

Her words were met with a reflexive "shhh" from the librarian, followed by a muttered complaint. Already dismissing Ell as a hopeless fool, the librarian turned back to her work without a second thought.

Dex and Jace hung back, barely breathing as they watched from the safety of the shadows, their nerves stretched tighter than a rogue spell about to snap. When Alice and Ell finally returned, the four of them slipped outside the library, heads down, moving fast.

Just as they stepped into the cool night air, a system prompt materialized in front of them, its glowing blue text shimmering like a bad omen.

New Quest - The Hero's Guild
    First-Year Students, Rank Two and Above
    Special Briefing and Assignments in the Hero's Hall.

They exchanged wary glances.

Alice lingered, her eyes narrowing as her mind clearly still swam with thoughts of the Banished book. "I'll keep working on deciphering it each day," she said, her voice low but firm. "There are answers in there. I can feel it." She hesitated, but only for a second. "And something tells me we're going to need them—sooner than we think."

Chapter 38
The Hero's Guild

The grand hall of Mount Olympus University pulsed with a quiet, ancient rhythm—the kind born from a heart that had never ceased beating through centuries. Incantations hummed the same song, moving through the stone, threads of forgotten secrets woven deep into the marble's veins. Towering columns stretched high, amplifying that rhythm, their surfaces smoothed by the touch of countless hands and the weight of time itself, standing witness to the ebb and flow of generations.

The air hung heavy, alive with that unrelenting pulse—a tension so thick it crawled along the skin, sinking into bones like the prelude to a storm. And in that rhythm, a new note lingered—a stranger's whisper curling at the edges of each breath, waiting.

Rows of students shifted in their seats, a sea of restless bodies. The chairs were arranged with almost unnerving precision. Eyes fixed on the empty stage, the quiet voices that swirled through the hall were like an incantation, waiting for a trigger to unleash whatever they had been summoned to hear.

Jace sat beside Dex, Ell, and Alice, their group a small island of tension in the churning sea. The silence between them was thick, heavy with unspoken worries. It wasn't the comfortable quiet that came from familiarity—it was the kind that pressed against your lungs, begging for someone to crack it open.

Dex obliged, leaning in with his trademark smirk, though it didn't quite reach his eyes. "So... anyone else getting some serious 'possessed by evil' vibes from Thistle?" His voice was low, sharp like the edge of a dagger.

Jace's eyes flickered across the room, scanning for any sign of Thistle. But as expected, he wasn't there.

"Something is definitely off, but..." Jace said. There was a part of him that didn't want to voice the thought forming in his mind—

"I don't think—I don't know." His voice trailed off. Truth was, he didn't know. Thistle was acting odd, but everyone was under a lot of stress with the change. And when he had used Soul Sense, he didn't pick up anything odd. But then again, he hadn't seen anything off with Sophie either, until it was too late. Maybe, whatever this was, it was beyond his rank.

Dex let out a low chuckle, but it lacked his usual spark. "Oh, come on. The disappearing act? The attitude? The 'accident' with Blackwood. It's textbook demon behavior. He's either possessed or going through one hell of a mood swing."

Alice, quiet until now, shifted in her seat. Her fingers traced invisible patterns on the armrest, something thoughtful in her movement. "I've seen it too," she said softly, her eyes catching Jace's. She didn't need to elaborate; they both knew what she meant. That flicker behind Thistle's eyes. The way shadows seemed to cling to him just a little too long, like something waiting to step through from the other side.

Dex scoffed, but there was no humor in it. "I like the guy, don't get me wrong. We've been through... well, what we've all been through. But if he is..." Dex mouthed the next word quietly, "Possessed, we have to be ready to face that."

The words hit harder than Jace expected. It was one thing to think it, another to see it in Dex's eyes—Dex, who usually dismissed anything serious with a casual shrug. Now, though, even he seemed rattled, and that did more to unsettle Jace than anything else.

Jace looked to the empty stage and let out a slow sigh.

"Let's keep an eye on him. But no jumping to conclusions. Not yet."

And then, a creak. No, not just a creak—a groan, low and ancient, rolling from the far end of the hall. The grand bronze doors, older than anyone could reasonably guess, shuddered in protest as they slowly swung open. The room, alive with conversation, went abruptly, unnervingly still.

In the doorway stood a shadow, broad and towering. Brutus Ironclad. Cyclops. Master of Artifacts and Potions. Walking armory and professional scowler. Though, he always seemed friendly enough when you got him talking.

"Is he bigger?" a voice whispered, barely audible.

"Or angrier," came the response, just as soft.

Brutus's single eye glowed faintly, molten like a distant forge, sweeping over the crowd like a spotlight designed to incinerate. He moved with deliberate, slow steps, each one landing like a hammer blow, echoing through the hall. His armor gleamed beneath the flickering torchlight, and yet it wasn't the sheer size of him or his presence that held the room. It was that look—quiet and heavy, the kind that promised you weren't walking out of here the same as you came in.

Behind him, a smaller figure stepped into view, almost eclipsed by his bulk: Molly, Chosen of Hecate, from the Society of Hermes. Molly, who had never once arrived in a room without looking slightly out of sync with reality.

Brutus stopped at the center, and the torches flickered, as though they were the ones holding their breath. He folded his arms across his chest, and when he spoke, his voice rumbled like a rockslide down a mountain, all gravel and distant thunder. "Today," he growled, each word scraping its way through the hall, "you step beyond the walls of theory and lecture."

If it was possible for silence to be more silent, this was it. The hall fell into a void, and even the shadows seemed to pull back in anticipation of what came next.

"This University," Brutus continued, "is not a sanctuary. It's a forge. You are the iron. And the fires that await you..." His single eye flared, focusing in on a few unfortunate souls who visibly wilted under his gaze. "They will either shape you into heroes. Or something far worse."

The silence stretched, thick and heavy, before he spoke again, his voice steady, carrying the vision of what was to come. "Each of you, Two-Star and above, will be eligible to undertake a Hero's Task. These aren't mere errands. Some may seem routine, but many of these tasks dance on the edge of danger and flirt with death. Given the current circumstances for all Travelers, I wouldn't fault anyone for choosing the safer path. But understand this—once a task is accepted, it must be completed. There's no backing out without facing severe consequences. You must be ready to face death, because that's the path laid before you by the gods themselves. And should you choose it, that path might just lead you to the Hero's Guild."

He paused, eyes scanning the room as a few students shifted in their seats. "Of course, you're free to opt-out. But for those who remain, I'll assume you're ready to continue."

A murmur rippled through the crowd as a handful of students gathered their things and quietly left. Alice leaned in toward Jace, her voice low but excited. "I've heard about this. Every school and most cities have a Patron Guild, and they try to recruit the top graduates."

"Guild?" Jace asked, blinking in surprise. He realized, not for the first time, how much he still didn't know about the world beyond Olympus.

"Yeah," Alice said, eyes gleaming with the thrill of being the one with answers. "They're woven into the fabric of society. Six major guilds, plus a bunch of smaller ones. I was reading about them in the library. Olympus' Patron Guild is the Hero's Guild. They've got outposts in all the major cities across Mythica. Their whole thing is about righting wrongs, fighting for justice, all that heroic stuff. Monster slaying, town-saving—the works. Pretty badass."

Ell snorted, leaning back in her chair with a sly grin. "Don't jump at the first guild that flashes you a shiny badge. The Heroes' is a big one, and I've heard a lot of good things. But there are tons of guilds out there, and some of the smaller ones? Way cooler. When we graduate, we'll definitely want a guild. But we've got time to shop around."

Dex nodded, his voice more serious. "The right guild opens doors. The wrong one slams them shut."

"Exactly," Ell added, crossing her arms. "Schools like to cozy up to their Patron Guilds, try to nudge students in that direction. It's totally biased, but despite that, we should absolutely do this. The first quests are supposed to be super easy. Fetch quests, investigations, small monster cleanups. Nothing we can't handle. Plus, even if we don't end up joining the Hero's Guild, getting an official invitation can put us on the radar of other guilds."

Jace gave a thoughtful nod. The scatter of voices gradually faded, and the room fell into a thick, anticipatory silence.

When it was clear no one else would be leaving, he stepped forward again.

Brutus raised his hand, and the room quieted instantly, as if he'd pulled the plug on all sound. Then, with a low, gravelly mutter that sounded almost like an old man grumbling about "kids these days," he sighed. "For those who stuck around," he gestured lazily toward Molly, "she's gonna walk you through the Hero's Guild Mission, our 'Call to Adventure', as it were. Philosophy, rules, all that." He waved a hand dismissively, his voice dipping into a half-mutter. "Hate these damn announcements."

Molly stepped forward with kind but unflappable confidence. She spoke, her voice soft, intimate, and seemed to brush the ear of every student at once. The strange part? Her lips never quite matched her words. They were always just a beat off, like some kind of surreal dream—or a nightmare. It had always been like this when he saw her.

"My name is Molly Eidolon, Chosen of Hecate," she said, her voice smooth and unhurried, yet cutting through the room with a quiet authority. "Goddess of the night, the moon's witch, speaker for the shadows," she continued, her words flowing like a soft breeze, yet laced with a hint of something far more dangerous beneath the surface.

Molly's presence wasn't one to fill a room with noise or gestures. It was the quiet that followed her, a stillness that swallowed sound like a dense fog. The room seemed to recognize the shift, all sound dying out, leaving only the faint clack of her boots against the polished stage.

She didn't need to speak loudly; the hall wasn't silent by accident. Her voice slid through the space like smoke, curling and spreading, finding every ear without needing to reach for it. There was no echo, no fanfare. Just her voice, low and certain, like she was reciting something older than language itself.

"Do you know why you're here?" Her tone was sharp, soft as velvet, but it had the kind of edge that cut deeper than any blade. Her gaze flicked toward Jace, pale and strange, as though she wasn't looking at him, but through him—beyond him. "Same reason I was," she said, almost to herself. "To tip the scales, before the balance crumbles."

She stepped forward, the scent of something herbal—sharp and earthy—lingering in the air behind her. Jace caught a whiff, and for a second, his mind tugged at the familiarity—mint? Wormwood? Whatever it was, it clung to her as tightly as the shadows did.

***

"Order," she said, her hand drifting through the air as if sketching the shape of something only she could see, "is the spark of creation. It molds the Infinite Potential—raw, formless—an artist poised before a blank canvas. With the first stroke, it breathes life into the void, transforming emptiness into something vibrant, something real. Order is the hand that shapes, carving beauty from the chaos of possibility." Her fingers drew invisible strokes, and as she moved, a golden painting formed mid-air, a web woven of shimmering light.

Jace felt it in his gut, a pull, a sense that something larger was at work, even if he couldn't see it. He had felt this before—the tug of magic, the raw force of creation. But this time, it was different, the strings were wound tighter, the very essence of what they wielded was fragile.

"Life strives to create Order. Every spell you cast," Molly continued, her voice softer, but no less commanding, "is a thread in your tapestry. A single note in the symphony of existence. We take raw Potential, and we mold it into something more. We make the formless take form. We create."

Jace's breath caught in his throat. He could see it—every spell, every gesture, every incantation was a struggle to force the universe to obey—to bring Order to the chaos that lurked just beneath the surface.

"But Chaos," she said, her voice lowering to a near-whisper, "Chaos doesn't create. It unravels. It gnaws at the threads, undoes what's been made, pulls apart what's been woven. Chaos doesn't just touch Potential—it destroys it. Like a child that doesn't want anyone else to play with their toys, so destroys them instead."

Her eyes fixed on Jace again, a knowing glimmer there, as if she'd seen the end of things and had come back to warn him. "You think you're safe because you know the rules? You're not. Chaos doesn't care about rules. It devours them, rips them apart, until there's nothing left but emptiness. And when Chaos wins—there's no more silence, Jace. Just the absence of everything."

The air in the room grew colder. Jace could feel the hairs on his neck rising, a chill creeping down his spine. He clenched his fists, trying to push away the unease that had settled over him, but it was like trying to shake off a nightmare that clung too tight.

"Monsters," Molly said, her voice soft, but not without bite, "are born from Chaos. They spawn in the places where Order is weakest, where the threads have frayed too far. That's why they return, Jace. That's why no matter how many you kill, they come back."

Jace could see it in their eyes—the same fear, the same realization that had wormed its way into his own thoughts. This wasn't just about quests or reputation. This was bigger.

Molly continued, her eyes distant again, as if watching something just beyond their understanding. "When Chaos wins, the world doesn't just end. It comes apart. Piece by piece, thread by thread, until there's nothing left. No gods, no monsters, no magic. Just the Infinite End."

Her words sank deep into Jace, wrapping around his thoughts like ivy, growing, twisting, suffocating. He wanted to pull away, to dismiss it as some grand metaphor, but there was something in her voice, something so calm, so certain, that he couldn't shake.

"Experience, or EXP, is the currency of growth—whether personal, cosmic, or something far beyond. It's earned when we stand against Chaos, lock eyes with it, and emerge changed. But the real strength doesn't lie in just surviving. It's in what we do after—in the pause, the breath we take to forge the lessons of battle into something enduring. That's where the true power lies. We call it Cultivation, Focus, or Spending EXP. Every hard-won victory leaves its mark, not just on the world, but deep within us, sharpening our skills, fortifying our essence, aligning our very aether to something greater."

"Many of you may have wondered why everything in our world follows the pattern of six," she continued, her voice soft but cutting—silk dragged across stone. "Affinities, monsters, even the metals we forge into weapons, they all follow the same path. And it is no coincidence. The Six reflects the eternal struggle between Order and Chaos, a battle that rages within each of us."

With a flick of her finger, she traced an unseen circle in the air. It shimmered to life, glowing gold, splitting into six perfect segments. "When you focus your energy, when you spend those hard-earned experience points, you're not just unlocking new abilities. You're slicing through the Chaos inside you, shaping it, bending it to your will. Each rank you ascend is another step in that battle—a victory that draws you closer to mastering the forces that shape this world."

The glowing segments pulsed with energy, each one humming with meaning. "The Six Ranks resonate through everything we do, everything we see: Reaction. Sensation. Formation. Creation. Ascension. Divination."

Molly's gaze swept the room. "This pattern repeats endlessly. Your Speaker Rank, from the Bronze Reactionaire to the exalted Divinium Champion, mirrors this journey. Every ability, every monster, every challenge you face—it all follows this path."

She paused, her eyes narrowing as she leaned forward, voice thick with meaning. "Think of it this way: A child, when frustrated, lashes out—Chaos at its most primal. But as they grow, they start to learn control, though it's still raw, still driven by emotion. A teenager, filled with anger or passion, responds to the world impulsively, still guided by that wild Chaos. And then, as they mature, they begin to reason. To use logic. To carve Order from the Chaos."

Her voice grew quieter, more intimate, as though she were sharing a secret only they had been meant to hear. "As they grow wiser still, they begin to see beyond Chaos—to understand creation, to live life as an art. That's when magic transforms. It becomes more than power. It becomes expression."

Jace shifted in his seat, a restless energy stirring within him. His own abilities had often felt raw, though there had been moments, glimpses of something more refined, something controlled—something beautiful.

"The Six Ranks," Molly continued, her voice rhythmic and sure, "mirror this evolution. At first, your power is reactive, chaotic, a child's tantrum. But as you climb, it becomes emotional, driven by feeling but still untamed. Then, it becomes precise, deliberate. And when you reach the higher levels, your magic stops being about brute force. It becomes art—your art. Something uniquely yours."

The six-part circle flared brighter, casting long shadows over the faces in the room. "But that's not the end. For those few who push further, past the limits of understanding, your abilities become second nature—an extension of your being, as effortless as breathing. That is the Ascended level, the Spiritual. Beyond that?"

She paused, her gaze holding a thousand words in a breath. "Few ever reach it. But those who do approach divinity. At that point, it's no longer about power. It's about harmony. Perfect alignment with the world, with yourself, with the forces that shape all universes."

The room was thick with silence, the air humming with Molly's words, and Jace felt them resonate deep within him, stirring something raw and untapped. The thought of magic flowing through him as easily as breath felt impossible—yet tantalizing. There was a pull there, a hunger, a need to reach for something more.

"You're in this fight," Molly said, her voice dropping to a near whisper as she stepped closer. Her gaze latched onto Jace, intense and unwavering, before flicking to another student.

"Every action you take. Every spell. Every life you save or destroy. You're weaving the threads. But if you stop, if you falter..."

She didn't finish the thought. She didn't need to. Jace swallowed hard, his throat dry.

"And if Chaos wins?" Molly's voice was a soft breeze now, so quiet it was barely more than a breath. "It doesn't just take life. It erases it. The end of everything. The silence after the final note. A last chapter that brooks no room for new stories, no new beginnings, only the cold end of all."

She let the silence stretch then, as if to prove her point. The hall was so still; it felt like time had paused, waiting for something—anything—to break the tension. But nothing came. Just the cold, creeping pressure of her words.

Finally, Molly turned, her fingers tracing that invisible pattern in the air once more. "That's why we fight," she said, her voice distant now. "Not for glory. Not for power. But for Order. To keep the world from unraveling. And that is the Call of the Hero's Guild, that is the Mission."

Abruptly, with a curt bow, Molly stepped back, ceding the stage to Brutus. As they passed each other, Jace caught a fleeting exchange between them.

"I told you to motivate them, not terrify them," Brutus murmured, his tone dry but tinged with disapproval.

Molly's lips curved into a faint, almost mischievous smile. "Fear is motivation," she replied, her eyes glinting as she moved past him.

"Thank you, Miss Eidolon," he said loudly, clearing his throat. "That was, uh... potent." She offered another small bow, her movements graceful and measured, before he continued speaking. "Now that it's over and no one else seems inclined to leave, please form into parties of five. Send your chosen party leader up to receive your quest, which will be distributed at random. Neat and orderly now, form a line."

He glanced over the students before continuing. "If you don't have a party, or can't decide on a leader, form a line with Miss Molly, and she'll assign you by lot."

The students sprang into motion, organizing themselves into groups. Jace, Dex, Alice, and Ell quickly realized they had almost everything they needed—but they were one short.

After a quick vote, they settled on Ell as the leader, despite her uncharacteristic reluctance. Jace noticed a flicker of genuine nervousness in her, a rare sight, but he was confident she'd handle it well. Her strategic mind and versatile powerset made her the obvious choice. The vote was nearly unanimous—three against one.

Jace and the rest queued up to collect their quest, while Ell made her way over to Molly to find a fifth teammate.

Chapter 39
Going Postal

When Jace, Dex, and Alice finally reached the front of the line, Brutus was waiting there, his massive frame cutting an imposing figure. With a flick of his hand, a series of magical scrolls unraveled in midair, shimmering before them. His one-eyed gaze swept over the trio, a glint of recognition in his eye.

"Ah, Jace. There you are," Brutus said, his voice a gravelly rumble of familiarity. He searched through the floating scrolls with deliberate slowness, as if savoring the moment. "Give me a second... Ah, yes. This one." His lips curled into a slight grin, an expression that made Dex shift uncomfortably beside Jace.

Brutus leaned forward. "We usually hand these out randomly, but I've been holding onto this one. Something about it felt... special. And based on your performance in the Scholarship Exams, I reckon you'll be up for the challenge. Nothing too dangerous," he added with a wink, though it did nothing to ease the tension in the air. "But you'll need sharp eyes. It's personal."

Jace nodded, his stomach tightening. Personal never meant easy. Beside him, Dex and Alice exchanged a glance.

"Your missions today are not glamorous," Brutus continued, his voice rising to address the room. "They are not grand quests of legend, but they are necessary. Dismiss them at your own peril."

Jace unrolled his scroll, his heart pounding in time with the quickened rhythm of the room. Brutus' voice cut through the low murmur of conversation. "You are to investigate why deliveries to the University have stopped. A village in the hills has gone silent—a local delivery waypoint for packages to and from M.O.U. And with it, we have a number of missing deliveries being reported. Find out what's happened and report back to me."

Jace swallowed hard. Beside him, Dex leaned in, peering over his shoulder. "Missing mail?" Dex muttered with a hint of disbelief.

Brutus' voice softened as he continued. "Oh, and one more thing. Among that missing mail... there was something for me. A package from my sister, the Beast Keeper at the Upper World University in the Great Plains. And I was expecting something from my brother too—he's a Master of Games at Asgard University. My family has a long tradition of working for the best Universities in Mythica. Anyway, it was my birthday two months ago, and they both said they had sent a few things over. None of it ever showed up."

He paused, his one-eyed gaze growing distant for a moment. "We write regularly, my sister and I. She was sending me an heirloom from our parents."

Dex raised an eyebrow. "Why not just use Magic Missives?"

Brutus turned to him, his expression a mix of amusement and weariness, like Dex had suggested: why not just throw the package into the ocean and hope it makes it.

"Magic Missives? Even enchanted paper birds need a rest on a journey that long, kid. And packages? Hah, no chance. Between the Universities, anything magical gets flagged by protection crystals, checked for security risks. And half the stuff that's sent gets incinerated by accident. With tensions so high—what with the war on—false positives happen more than you'd like to think. Anything important has to be sent the old-fashioned way, cart and carriage. Only way to avoid it getting blasted by detection magic."

His voice dropped lower. "If you come across it—my heirloom, the packages—I'd be grateful. But don't go risking your life on my account. It's probably just lost or someone slacking off on the job."

Jace nodded, his fingers tightening around the scroll. Dex shifted beside him, the usual smirk nowhere to be found, replaced by a more serious look as the gravity of the task began to sink in.

With a quick motion, Jace tucked the scroll into his satchel. Around them, the room buzzed with the murmurs of other groups receiving their assignments, excitement brewing in the air. For many, this would be the first time stepping beyond the Academy's gates. Some, like Jace's group, would be venturing beyond the protective barriers of Olympus and into the unpredictable world of local towns.

The scroll in Jace's hand shimmered faintly as it unraveled itself, the magic gently pulling the parchment open to reveal their mission. As the details appeared on the page, a familiar prompt materialized in his vision.

Quest Accepted

Missing Mail

You have accepted the quest to locate the missing deliveries to the University. If the mail cannot be found, uncover what has happened and report back.

Rewards:

Reward #1: Increased Reputation with the Hero's Guild - Variable, based on performance

Reward #2: EXP - Variable, based on performance.

Optional Quest: Brutus' Heirloom

Brutus has requested your help in recovering two personal packages. Find the packages or discover what has happened to them and report back to Brutus.

Optional Rewards: Bonus EXP and Personal Gift from Brutus

The scroll's glow dimmed as it finished revealing the quest, leaving Jace and his companions exchanging uncertain glances.

Dex flung his arms out dramatically, spinning on his heel as the chaos of the courtyard buzzed around them. "Missing mail? That's our big mission now? We're basically magical UPS drivers? Should I be knocking on doors, asking for tips? Maybe I'll get an enchanted fruit basket if I deliver on time. That's the dream, right?"

Alice shot him a look, barely suppressing a smirk. "Maybe they'll throw in a medal. But honestly? I'm fine with it. I could use some boring. With everything else going on, chasing after some lost letters feels like a spa day. Plus, we actually get to leave campus and no one is trying to kill us. So... win-win."

Dex snorted, throwing his hands up again. "Oh yeah, because nothing screams 'adventure' like a mystical scavenger hunt for undelivered mail. Who knows? Maybe we'll end up running a scroll delivery service on the side. Go full postal worker. Just hand me a uniform and call it a day."

Jace, finally chiming in, shrugged. "Hey, beats fighting possessed friends, right?"

Dex shot him a finger gun. "Touché."

As they crossed the hall, Jace's gaze locked onto a figure weaving through the crowd. Dark hair bouncing with every step. Ell. But something was wrong. Her expression wasn't its usual confident self—she looked... wary. And worse, she wasn't alone.

"Hey, isn't that—?" Jace's voice trailed off, his stomach doing a slow roll as the figure next to her became clearer.

Dex squinted, then groaned. "No. Freaking. Way."

Ell strolled up, her reluctant expression doing all the talking before she even opened her mouth. "Guys, meet our fifth for the quest."

Standing next to her, looking like he'd just finished chewing through a lemon, was Marcus. His clothes were duller than usual, but that smug face was the same as always.

Dex's jaw practically hit the floor. "What in Medusa's under-pants—?" he blurted, earning a quick elbow from Alice.

Ell gave a half-hearted shrug, the kind that said, I tried.

Marcus just stood there, arms crossed, radiating the enthusiasm of a disgruntled porcupine. "Let's get this over with," he muttered, voice thick with disdain.

Jace blinked, still processing the absurdity. "You've gotta be kidding me," he whispered, trying to reconcile the Marcus in front of him with the Marcus who'd probably rather eat dirt than be seen with them.

Dex, never one to miss an opportunity, threw his hands up again. "No one else willing to take you? Last resort?"

Marcus's eyes narrowed to slits. "Believe me, the feeling's mutual. But here we are, so let's just move on."

Jace's mouth twitched. "What happened to all your... goons? I mean, 'friends?'"

Marcus scowled. "My 'acquaintances' are either already grouped up or jumped ship when the whole 'no logging out' thing happened. But none of that's your concern." His gaze flicked over them, judgmental as ever. "I'm here. So, let's get this done."

Dex raised an eyebrow. "Hero's Guild, huh? I figured you'd go for something more... pampered. You know, like the Tax Guild. Or is there a Guild for Snotty Rich Brats? How about for Murderous, Sniveling Weaklings?"

Ell shot Dex a sharp look that could've cut stone, while Marcus just smiled, showing a bit too much teeth.

Dex raised his hands in mock innocence. "What? Just saying what we're all thinking."

Marcus's jaw clenched. "Listen, I was given a quest directly from Zeus to do this Hero's Guild thing. I don't question quests from my patron deity, nor do I ignore them." His eyes drilled into Dex, cold as winter. "Unlike some, I actually have a sense of duty, of honor. Just don't slow me down with your... antics."

They all stood there, the tension settling like an unwelcome fog.

"Off to a great start," Alice said dryly, breaking the silence.

"I need to talk to Molly," Dex said, rubbing the back of his neck.

Ell sighed. "No point. Molly would have given another option if there was one. We either deal with it, or none of us go. So... can we at least pretend to tolerate each other for a couple days?"

Dex huffed, crossing his arms, but didn't argue. Marcus sneered but stepped forward, extending a hand, his smirk back in full force. "Oh, I can be civil," he said, his voice dripping with condescension. "If you can keep your dog from yapping."

Dex eyed the hand like it was a trap. "Pass."

Jace turned away, tension knotting in his shoulders. He wasn't sure how this group was going to survive two days together, let alone a quest.

Alice clapped her hands together with forced enthusiasm. "Great. This is going to be fun."

Marcus, unfazed, let his hand drop. "So," he drawled, "Care to share the details of this quest with me?"

A soft chime echoed in Jace's mind.

Marcus has joined the party.

Chapter 40
The Tinker's Granddaughter

Marcus kicked at the dirt and cobblestone, his face set in a deep scowl as they stood in the mostly deserted Traveler's Yard of the Shopping District. The chaos from earlier had left the place stripped bare—students, fresh off receiving their quests, had swarmed the carriage drivers and stable hands, scrambling to claim rides. Now, all that was left for Jace and the Scooby-Gang—plus one—was the dust settling in their wake.

They'd hit all the main stops, only to find every wagon booked, every horse spoken for. A few stragglers had already resigned themselves to walking, trudging off toward their quests with no better options.

"I can't believe this. Do they even know who I am?" Marcus ran a hand through his slicked-back hair, exasperated. "Beat to transport by common peasants."

Dex, leaning lazily against a nearby fence post, shot him a wide grin. "Welcome to reality, Your Highness. Looks like all your 'influence' doesn't do diddly squat against a mad rush for transport." He tilted his head, looking Marcus up and down. "What's the matter? Not a fan of the good ol' pedestrian life?"

Marcus glared at him. "Walk? Walk? Absolutely not. I refuse to hoof it like some plebe. There's no way I'm—"

"Oh, poor Marcus," Dex interrupted, his voice dripping with mock pity. "Reduced to walking like a regular person. What a tragedy. I'll fetch the violins."

Ell rolled her eyes, arms crossed. "He does have a point, Dex." She shot Marcus a sidelong glance, her tone betraying just how much it pained her to admit it. "We'd lose days if we went on foot."

"Thank you," Marcus said, seizing the moment to appear smug. "For once, someone recognizes reason."

"Don't push your luck, Marcus—you're still a prat," she snapped.

Jace, standing off to the side, gave a reluctant nod. "I hate to admit it, but walking isn't exactly practical. And we all have things we need to attend to before the Star Ceremony. We need a ride."

Dex let out an exaggerated sigh. "Alright, alright. We'll find something. But if Marcus starts whining halfway through the journey because we couldn't get him a gold-plated chariot, I reserve the right to leave him by the roadside."

They all agreed.

Alice sighed, adjusting the straps of her satchel. "Alright, then let's ask around. Somebody's bound to have a cart still available. I mean, we can't be the only ones stranded."

They spent the next hour winding through the alleys that twisted behind the market, asking vendors and stable hands if anyone was headed east. Every response was the same—a polite shake of the head or a muttered apology. The cobblestone streets soon gave way to dirt paths as they ventured farther from the bustle of the Shopping District.

Eventually, a stablehand pointed them toward a modest caravan parked just on the outskirts of the market grounds. Two weathered carts stood by the side of the road, each one looking like it had seen better days. But they were intact, and right now, that was good enough. Tinkers carts.

The carts towered almost comically with goods, crates, and barrels stacked so high they looked like they might topple with a stiff breeze. Wares of all kinds—some shimmering faintly in the fading light, others wrapped in worn cloth—teetered precariously on the edges. If you squinted just right, there might have been room for passengers. Maybe.

An older man stood beside the carts, his posture bent slightly from years spent wandering the roads. His skin, weathered and sun-tanned, bore deep creases from countless days under the open sky. His thick, calloused hands moved with the practiced ease of someone long accustomed to hard labor, unloading goods with a quiet, deliberate rhythm. Though his arms still held the strength of his youth, his gait was slower now, aided by a cane that he leaned on with each step, a faint limp betraying the toll time had taken on his body.

Beside him, a girl—no older than thirteen—was directing the operation like a seasoned general, her sharp voice cutting through the bustling market as she ordered a few workers to shift things here and there.

Jace cleared his throat, stepping forward. "Excuse me, are you headed east?"

The man paused, wiping his brow with the back of a calloused hand before turning toward them, his eyes narrowing slightly in appraisal. "Aye, that I am," he replied, his voice carrying the easy, measured rhythm of a man who'd spent more years on the road than by a hearth. "Name's Loren. And that there is my granddaughter, Lara. So, what can we do for you?"

"I'm Jace," he said, nodding toward the horses as he spoke. "My friends and I are headed to Havenstown. We heard you might be the one to help us get there."

Loren's gaze swept over the group, pausing briefly on Marcus, who stood with his arms crossed, a scowl etched deeply into his face. The tinker raised an eyebrow.

"Havenstown, huh? Not the kind of place most Travelers are eager to visit," Loren said, a wry smile playing at his lips. He waved a hand toward the towering pile of goods stacked on their carts. "We're not exactly equipped for comfort, either," Loren added.

Marcus scoffed, folding his arms tighter. "Clearly. But we're in a rush, and all the decent wagons were taken before we could get a word in." His eyes flicked disdainfully toward the ramshackle carts behind Loren.

"You don't happen to have anything a little less... rustic, do you?" Marcus sneered.

Loren chuckled, shaking his head with a genuine smile. "Ah, to be young and full of complaints. Look, we don't often take on passengers, especially with all the trouble brewing out there."

"Trouble?" Alice asked.

"People going missing," Loren said, rubbing a hand over his bristled chin. "Wolves, they say. But I wouldn't bet the farm on that. Strange stories. Not a place you'd wanna picnic, if you catch my meaning."

"And yet, you're headed there?" Jace leaned in, his eyes narrowing.

"Gotta resupply," Loren said with a shrug. "A quick stop at the edge of the Olympian Domain. I'll get in, get out, and keep my hide intact. Not the friendliest place, for Traveler's, that is."

Before Jace could press further, the young girl stepped forward, her boots crunching on the dirt, confidence etched in every step. Her long, auburn hair framed a face smudged with dirt, yet she wore it like a badge of honor. "Ignore my grandpa," she said, a smirk tugging at her lips. "He loves a good scare yarn as much as the next old man. I'm Lara. We tinkers don't make a habit of turning down those in need of help."

She planted her hands on her hips, her gaze fixing on Jace like a crossbow bolt. "We're not a charity, either. You pay, or you walk. Got coin?"

The old man chuckled softly when Jace glanced his way, nodding toward the girl as if to say, She's serious.

Jace met her stare without flinching. "We can pay."

Lara gave a sharp nod, eyes glinting with approval. "Good. Our carts may look like they've seen better days, but they'll get you through places that fancy wheels can't. When the road gets tricky, you'll be glad you're riding with us."

"And how much, exactly, is this luxury ride going to cost us?" Marcus asked.

Loren scratched his chin thoughtfully. "For the lot of you? I'd say Twenty B..."

"Silver," Lara interrupted, glaring at Marcus. "And you'll help unload when we get there."

"Now, Button—" the old tinker started, but the sharp look she shot him cut him off mid-sentence. It was the kind of look that said Grandpa, I've got this and Don't you dare call me Button in front of our guests all in one swift glance.

He immediately raised both hands in a gesture of defense and deference, a sheepish smile tugging at his lips. "Twenty silver," he repeated.

Marcus opened his mouth, clearly gearing up for a negotiation, but Jace shut it down with a quick, "Deal." He knew Marcus well enough—another word from him would either jack the price up or lose the ride entirely.

Loren raised an eyebrow, clearly surprised by the quick agreement, but a flicker of respect lit his eyes, mingled with quiet pride in his granddaughter. She extended her hand, clasping Jace's with firm resolve, while Loren nodded in approval.

"We'll take the long path," Loren said, his tone firm. "It'll cost us time, but it's the safer route."

"That works for us. When do we leave?" Jace asked, glancing at the sinking sun.

"First light tomorrow," Loren replied, nodding toward the sky, now a wash of orange and purple. "You'll want to get some rest. The road east isn't as friendly as it used to be."

Jace caught Alice's gaze—silent understanding passing between them.

"Looks like we've got ourselves a ride," Jace said, turning to the others.

As they turned to leave, Lara called after them, her tone firm. "Be on time. We don't wait for stragglers."

Marcus, still sulking, grumbling something that didn't sound too polite, but Dex clapped him on the back with a grin. "See how us common folk get things done?"

Marcus swatted his hand away, glaring. "Unfortunately."

The horses snorted softly beside the carts, pawing at the earth as the evening chill settled. Their breath fogged in the air, adding mist to the fading light. Jace eyed the towering stack of crates, wondering how they'd wedge themselves in without being buried alive in supplies. He let out a soft laugh. This was going to be interesting.

Chapter 41
Of Endings and Beginnings

Dawn arrived far too soon, dragging its light into the world with a cold, indifferent certainty. It slipped through the Shopping District, touching rooftops and shopfronts with hesitant kisses of silver. The light crept across the trees, brushing their branches with a delicate touch, so gentle it felt like a lover's embrace no one was meant to see.

It didn't explode or dazzle; it crept, shy and subtle, casting pale lines through the thinning branches, reaching for something just out of sight. The golden edges of dawn barely hidden beneath the horizon, teased what might be. The world breathed with it, spaces between the leaves coming alive with shifting patterns, like it was painting possibilities across the ground. It was the kind of light that made you think of the road ahead—paths waiting to be walked, choices waiting to be made.

But the cold? The cold wasn't having any of it. It clung to the earth like an old miser, hoarding the last bits of warmth and refusing to release its hold. Morning frost bit at Jace's nose, his breath turning to mist as if the air itself was telling him to slow down, to remember that endings always came before beginnings. There was no promise in the frost—just the cold certainty of change, creeping in with icy fingers, worming into bones and hearts alike.

The trees around him stood stripped bare, skeletal and brittle. What leaves remained clung on like a gambler's last chip, trembling on branches that no longer cared. When the wind kicked up, they fell with a sigh, spiraling down to the earth where they joined the fallen, crumbling into nothing. Autumn was on its deathbed, gasping its last breaths while winter sharpened its knives in the distance.

Jace's boots crunched through the mess of fallen leaves. His steps didn't follow the light's hopeful dance—no, they echoed in the past. With every exhale, it felt like he was letting go of pieces of that past, his breath small clouds in the chill.

It was a balance, a tipping point, like the entire world standing on the edge of a knife, caught between the end of one thing and the start of something more.

By the time they arrived, the tinkers were already at work, securing the last of their wares, their hands moving with the practiced ease of those long accustomed to balancing chaos.

The carts themselves were marvels of controlled disorder. Every available inch was crammed with oddities—rusty tools, cracked lanterns, and brittle maps. Somehow, they managed to carve out space, a small island amongst the clutter, for the five passengers.

Getting comfortable became its own skirmish. After a few sharp elbows and muttered curses, they finally managed to wedge themselves onto the rickety makeshift bench, its creaking frame groaning under the weight of their effort. Beneath them, a tattered tapestry clung to life, its once-vibrant patterns of mythical beasts now faded into ghostly outlines.

Amid the clutter, Jace's gaze lingered on a brass cup. It gleamed with unusual brightness, almost smug in how untouched it was, as though the dust and grime of the world hadn't dared approach it. Delicate engravings spiraled along its edge. Something about that cup felt off, unsettling, like a song just slightly out of tune.

Curious, Jace reached out to it. When his fingers brushed its surface, a sharp jolt raced up his arm, and for a fleeting second, a face—shadowed and twisted—flashed in his mind. He felt a terrible sense of wrongness, anxiety, and deep regret.

"Careful," Lara's voice broke the moment, her eyes catching his with a mischievous glint. "Some of these items have teeth. Best not wake anything up."

Jace's hand recoiled instinctively, his skin tingling. The feeling faded quickly, like smoke dissipating in the wind. He made sure to keep his distance from it for the rest of the trip.

The cart jolted violently, struggling against inertia before clattering down the uneven trail, its wheels rattling over every bump and dip in the path.

Silence settled over them as they bumped along, the wheels creaking with every rut.

They moved steadily through the Zones—first Two, then Three, and finally out of Zone Four. The tinker and his granddaughter each carried a Ward Stone, humming faintly with protection magic.

Alice flicked open her inventory with a practiced swipe, pulling out three smooth, softly glowing Ward Stones. The stones cast long, slanting shadows across the ground as she handed them to Dex and Ell, casual and unhurried, like she was tossing out pieces of candy.

"How in the name of Hades' lost sandals did you even have time to make these?" Dex raised an eyebrow, spinning the stone between his fingers like it was a coin. The glow caught his crooked grin, making him look even more pleased with himself than usual.

Alice stared at him, blankly. "That's not a saying."

Dex shrugged, his smile never faltering. "Feels like it should be."

Alice shook her head, the gesture somehow managing to mirror the collective feeling of the group. "I started crafting them the day the logout option vanished."

The group exchanged looks, clearly waiting for her to elaborate.

"What? I like being prepared."

Dex held up the stone, squinting. "So... perfect little monster-proof bubble?"

Alice snorted in the most endearingly unladylike way. "Not even close. Think of it more like... really bad cologne. Monsters don't wanna be anywhere near it, but it's not stopping anything big from charging at you with fangs out."

She nodded toward the stone. "High-rank crystals? Sure, those are your invisible walls—like the University's Hearth Stone. But those are for people who can toss around a few thousand gold without flinching. These? They're wards. Basic, keeps most things uncomfortable. Big difference."

Jace thought back to when he had used his last... on his trip to Sophie. He'd had to turn it on and off a few times to "save battery." He wondered if it would've tipped him off sooner if he had kept it on.

Ell nudged Alice, smirking. "Nice work."

Alice's smile flickered, almost too brief to catch. "Don't get too comfortable. I'm still low-rank with these. They're like Jace's—good for a few hours, tops, before they need a refill of moon juice. So don't get any bright ideas about full protection."

"Well, I think this is great," Jace added. "It worked last time for me. I'm sure we'll be fine. What's the worst that could happen, anyway?"

The moment he said it, Alice's eyes snapped toward him, deadpan enough to stop the wind. "Did you seriously just say that?"

Dex groaned, slapping a hand to his forehead. "Oh, fantastic. You've done it. We're doomed. Something nasty is definitely waiting for us now."

Ell snorted, barely containing a laugh as she gave Jace a mock pat on the shoulder. "Good job, Jinx. Why don't you go ahead and summon the apocalypse while you're at it? 'What's the worst that could happen.' Almost as bad as, 'Well, it couldn't possibly get any worse.'"

Alice shook her head, smiling. "You're all children."

"Children with really bad luck," Dex muttered under his breath, tossing the stone into the air and catching it with a quick flick of his wrist. "But hey, maybe we'll stink them out. Call it 'Eau de Please Don't Eat Us.'"

Jace pulled a Ward Stone from his inventory with a slight flick of his wrist. The dull glow danced between his fingers as he passed it back and forth. They had all agreed to take turns activating theirs, each ward offering a thin layer of protection. A gamble, sure, but a necessary one. The Tinker upfront cradled his own like it was more than a tool, like it was personal. He smiled as he listened to the group banter.

Alice, however, conspicuously didn't hand a Ward Stone to Marcus. She only had three, but even if there had been a fourth... well, that was a thought for another time.

Marcus, as if sensing the unspoken slight, didn't miss a beat. With a well-practiced flourish, he reached into his inventory, pulling out a stone far more impressive than theirs—its light brighter, its veins of gold flickering with an arrogance that matched his smirk.

"Don't be scared, children," he said, tone a perfect condescension. He held the crystal up, letting it catch what little light filtered through the trees. "I've got a real Ward Stone. High-tier. You know, the kind that actually works."

His grin widened as if daring someone to argue, but the challenge hung in the air, unanswered.

Trees rose up on either side, their twisted branches knitting together overhead, casting the path in a web of shifting shadows. The light that filtered through was faint, fractured—just enough to remind them the world hadn't yet swallowed them whole.

The air grew heavier with the scent of pine and damp earth. Towering evergreens loomed ahead, their branches interlocking like arms, casting long, jagged shadows across the trail. The underbrush, once sparse, gave way to a dense carpet of needles, muffling the world as they moved into the heart of the forest. Each breath felt colder, the world narrowing to the path between the towering trunks, where the light barely dared to reach.

Shadows curled between gnarled trees, the canopy above thick enough to choke the sky. Jace caught the scent of snow—sharp, metallic—as the wind slashed through the leaves. Overhead, thunder rolled like a distant predator.

The cart shuddered to a halt with a groan of old wood and metal, the sound swallowed by the quiet of the forest.

Ahead, a massive tree, its roots exposed and twisted like knotted veins, lay sprawled across the road. The path they'd been following disappeared beneath it, swallowed by the darkness. The horses stamped and snorted, nostrils flaring as if they could sense what the group could not yet see.

"We can't go through here," the tinker muttered, voice shaky as he tugged at the reins. The horses, usually reliable, stood rigid, eyes wide with a deep-rooted fear. Their breaths came out in panicked puffs, hooves shifting nervously but unwilling to move forward.

Sensing an opportunity to show his fearlessness, Marcus stood up in the cart, his skin crackling with faint golden sparks, the electric hum radiating a subtle glow. Lara shot him a stern look, gesturing sharply for him to sit back down.

"I can take care of that tree," he said, his voice confident and defiant. "A little lightning, and we're through."

"No," Loren hissed, his usual jovial tone replaced with cold urgency. The perennial twinkle in his eye had dimmed, replaced by something grim. "You fry that tree, and every beast in this forest will be on us faster than you can blink. No, we'll find another way." He shared a nod with Lara before adding, "We'll need to take the shorter path."

With a swift tug of the reins, the group veered off the main road; the trees closing in around them, forming a darkened corridor.

The road narrowed, the thickening forest pressing in from both sides, branches like hands reaching down to brush against the tops of the carts. They struggled to fit, forced to stop more than once to repack their wares just to squeeze through. The air felt heavier with each step, as if the weight of the trees themselves bore down on them.

As they walked behind the cart, Dex shifted beside Jace, his usual cocky grin nowhere to be found, fingers twitching for the hilts of his daggers. "This place feels... wrong," he muttered, his voice tight.

Behind them, Alice clutched her spellbook so tightly her knuckles turned white. Her eyes darted from shadow to shadow, searching for anything out of place. A chill crept through the air, her breath fogging in the sudden cold as tension settled over the group like a shroud.

The temperature dropped sharply, biting into their skin. The ground beneath them became slick with a layer of frost, but it wasn't winter's touch—it was something darker.

A brook babbled loudly as they approached, its rushing water growing more pronounced with each step along the winding path.

Jace moved forward, one hand on his xiphos, the other steadying Alice as she edged closer. Her sharp gaze flicked toward the treeline, pupils dilated like a prey animal sensing a predator. "Something doesn't feel right," she whispered, her voice barely a thread in the wind.

Ell scanned the shadows, her eyes briefly flickering with a sharp amethyst glow. "We're not alone," she murmured, the words carrying an edge of certainty that sent a chill through the group.

The air around them stilled, the faint rustle of leaves silenced. It felt like the forest had sucked in a breath, waiting—watching. Every step, every whisper of fabric, seemed too loud, like they were trespassers in something's domain. Something old. Something hungry.

Jace stopped, frowning. "Do you hear that?"

Alice paused beside him, listening. Her brow furrowed. "I don't hear anything."

"That's what I mean." Jace pointed toward the brook, now terribly silent. "It was flowing a moment ago..."

Her eyes darted to where the brook had once gurgled and shifted over the rocks. Now, it sat deathly still, the water unmoving, yet not frozen. It was unnervingly unnatural.

A ripple—subtle, almost imperceptible—spread across the surface of the brook beside the road. Jace's heart skipped. A single leaf floated across the water, only to be sucked under as though the stream itself had come alive.

"We need to leave. Now," Lara said, her face pale as the moon. She flicked the reins harder this time, but the horses stayed rooted in place, their fear palpable.

The ground shuddered.

Alice held up her Ward Stone, its glow pulsing like a heartbeat in the dark. One by one, the others followed suit, their stones igniting with a faint, steady light. But then something shifted. A flicker. The stones began to brighten—too bright—almost blindingly so. Jace squinted against the harsh glow, but his eyes locked onto his stone as tiny cracks spiderwebbed across its surface.

"Wait..." he muttered, his voice tinged with confusion. The fissures deepened, spreading like veins of poison. Amethyst dust trickled from the cracks, glittering in the pale light before vanishing into the wind. Energy seeped from the stone, as if being siphoned away, drawn to something unseen.

Before anyone could react, there was a sharp, crystalline snap. Jace flinched as the stone in his hand shattered into a thousand glittering shards, slicing into his palm. His breath caught, the pain sharp and immediate, blood already beading and running down his fingers.

Around him, the others let out cries of alarm. Ell cursed under her breath, shaking the fragments from her hand, red streaks blooming across her skin. Dex grimaced, sucking in air through his teeth as he cradled his bleeding hand. Marcus stared at his broken Ward Stone with narrowed eyes, his fingers curling into a fist, blood dripping steadily from the cuts.

Alice's stone was the last to break, exploding in a burst of light that left her reeling. She winced, pulling her hand back as slivers of crystal fell into her lap. Her brow furrowed, eyes widening in disbelief as she stared at the ruined stones around them.

"That... shouldn't be...," she whispered, shaking her head, voice tense. "This isn't possible."

Jace's breath hitched as the water in the brook churned violently. From the ripples, something massive began to emerge, its form swirling, spiraling upwards from the depths. First a head, then shoulders, then arms—an enormous figure made entirely of liquid. It rose to an impossible height, towering over them, and when its eyes—cold and luminous—locked onto Jace, he felt a jolt of fear that sliced through him.

"Water elemental!" Lara's shout broke the spell.

Chapter 42
Of Earth and Water

E ll's senses flared to life, the tingling edge of her ability washing over her like a second skin. One glance was enough—neither Lara nor Loren had touched the power of Bronze One. Their auras were unmarked by the telltale signs of a Speaker who had learned their first Word of Power.

"Stay back!" Ell barked, planting herself between the Tinkers and the oncoming chaos, her voice a sharp crack through the air. "Let us handle this! We're not dragging your bodies out of here." Her eyes blazed with command, leaving no room for debate. Lara started to step forward defiantly, but Loren pulled her back, fear tightening his grip.

They sprang into action. "Silver One!" Ell shouted, her voice cutting through the tension like a blade. Stealth was no longer an option; they could only hope nothing worse lurked within earshot, or worse, that it wasn't already interested.

Alice's hands flew over the pages of her spellbook, flipping through incantations with frantic speed, her fingers trembling as the urgency of the moment mounted.

The elemental roared, its voice like the crashing of waves on a jagged shore. It lunged forward, its massive arm morphing into a towering wall of water. The force of it sent a spray of mist into the air as it came crashing down toward them. Jace ducked, barely dodging the deluge as it slammed into the ground, the impact rattling his bones.

"Move!" he shouted, rolling to his feet just as the elemental's other arm reformed, spiraling toward Dex with vicious speed.

Dex twisted away just in time, narrowly escaping the elemental's blow. The creature's strike hit the dirt with a wet thud, spraying mud and debris in every direction. But Dex was already in motion, moving like liquid himself—darting left, then right, weaving effortlessly through the storm of writhing limbs. His speed was unnatural, a blur of motion, and his grin never faltered, cocky and sharp, even as the elemental lashed out again and again, each strike missing him by inches.

Behind him, Jace and Ell stood firm, weapons drawn, a thin line between chaos and the tinkers. Jace's breath was shallow and fast. Beside him, Ell shot a glance his way, her face set with fierce determination, a fire in her eyes.

Just then, another massive wave of water surged from the elemental, crashing into Loren's cart with the force of a tidal wave. Wood splintered, cracking in violent bursts as the cart was smashed to pieces. The horses reared and bolted into the woods, their terrified whinnies fading into the distance.

The elemental reared back, its glowing eyes locking onto Dex with a hatred that radiated like heat. Its watery form coiled, poised to strike, and the fury in its gaze promised no mercy.

"Come on, you oversized puddle!" Dex shouted, his voice dripping with mockery as he lured the creature further from the Tinkers. His laugh echoed in the wind, carefree and defiant, as he flipped effortlessly over a crashing wave of water. He landed with catlike grace, barely a sound beneath his feet, a smirk plastered across his face.

The elemental bellowed in fury, a sound so deep it made the very trees shudder, the ground quivering beneath its wrath.

Ell slipped through the fray, her movements a blur of afterimages, hands crackling with glowing energy. She flung bolts of light at the creature's arms, attempting to drive it back, but every strike seemed to pass through it, barely slowing its advance.

Jace slashed through one of the elemental's limbs with his sword, the blade cutting clean through the water. But it was like slicing smoke—it reformed instantly, the creature seeming almost amused by the attempt.

Ell's voice was loud and martial. "Elementals don't care about physical weapons! You need something to bind it—"

"Any helpful hints, Alice?" Dex called out.

"Working on it... but nothing useful yet. I'm not getting anything from Intuition," Alice didn't look up from her tome. "There's got to be a spell in here somewhere."

Before she could finish, the elemental's form shifted, its body stretching and swelling, becoming an even more dangerous, chaotic force. It roared, a deafening, inhuman sound, as water lashed out in every direction.

Ell ducked as a massive blast of water ripped through a nearby tree, splintering it in half. Her eyes glowed a deep amethyst as she peered into the elemental, trying to pull anything useful she could glean from her Perceptiveness ability.

"Got it! Its weakness is earth. We need earth magic. Alice, got anything in that book of yours?"

"I'm looking!" Alice shouted, frantically flipping through the pages.

Jace reached with his mind for Soul Sense, expecting the familiar tug of something—anything—solid beneath the storm. But the moment he touched it, his mind buckled. It wasn't a soul he was sensing. It was madness. A chaotic whirl of fragments, broken and unmoored, spinning too fast for thought to catch. Trying to understand it was like trying to hold a tornado in your hands.

With a flicker of determination, he snapped his aether into Soul Bind. The shadows leapt from him, slicing through the swirling mass like blades of ink. But the thing didn't react like a creature should. Where the shadows struck, the watery form unraveled, dissolving without a hint of pain, only to slither back together, remaking itself in a new shape with a fluid, effortless malice.

Jace's pulse quickened. Whatever this was, it wasn't going to play by the rules.

"Marcus!" Jace barked over the chaos. The man had been standing back, watching, his fists clenched, electricity crackling along his skin. "We could use a little backup over here!"

Marcus's eyes narrowed, and with a calmness that bordered on arrogance, he stepped forward. "Stand back," he warned, raising his hands toward the creature. Lightning arced between his fingers before erupting in a blinding bolt that struck the elemental dead center.

The creature convulsed, water splashing and hissing as the electricity surged through it. For a moment, it faltered, its form flickering—but then, to Jace's horror, it absorbed the energy, its eyes flaring brighter. Now crackling with electricity, the elemental turned its gaze on Marcus.

Oh, crap," Marcus muttered, stumbling back. His eyes darted between the creature and his own hands, confusion etched across his face. It was as if his brain couldn't reconcile why his attack hadn't even phased the monster.

"Move!" Alice's voice cut through the chaos, sharp and urgent. But Marcus stood frozen, his feet stuck to the ground by some invisible force—fear or disbelief, Jace couldn't tell.

"Jace!" Alice's scream claimed his attention, her fingers weaving frantic symbols through the air. "I've got the spell! I can bind it, but you have to get Marcus out of the way, now!"

Jace didn't hesitate. In a heartbeat, he closed the distance with Soul Step, grabbed Marcus by the collar, and yanked him backward, just as the elemental's electrified arm crashed down where Marcus had stood. Jace's grip tightened as he pulled Marcus clear of the blast zone.

"Let go of me," Marcus said, his voice tight with indignation, as he jerked his arm free. His glare was sharp, but there was a flicker of something else—fear, maybe, though he tried to bury it beneath his bravado.

"Less talking, more helping," Jace snapped, releasing him.

Alice's incantation finished with a surge of energy. The ground beneath the elemental rippled and split, as tendrils of soil and roots shot up, wrapping around the creature's legs. It shrieked in fury, struggling against the bonds as the earth pulled it down.

"Got it!" Alice's voice trembled with exhaustion, but the magic pulsed in her hands, holding steady. The elemental twisted violently, its watery form shattering and knitting back together, but the roots coiled tighter, pulling it down. Earth surged up from the ground, merging with the creature's body, turning it into a grotesque mud golem, its once-fluid limbs sluggish with dirt and stone.

"Physical attacks will work now," Alice panted, her voice ragged, "but not for long."

Dex lunged forward, daggers flashing. He drove the blades into the creature's side with deadly precision, each strike causing the elemental to ripple and shrink. "That's right," he grinned through labored breaths, "let's see you pull yourself back together now."

The creature lumbered toward Alice, moving in slow jerks against the bindings, drawn to the pulse of magic radiating from her, but Dex kept it at bay with frantic strikes, each hit reverberating up his arm. Ell's hands flicked out, sending bolts of crackling purple light that exploded against the creature's face, each one blinding it further. It swung madly, its massive arms carving the air with reckless fury, barely missing Alice and Dex. The ground trembled beneath each wild swing, sending chunks of mud spraying in all directions as the creature roared in frustration, its heavy limbs sinking into the muck with each missed strike.

Marcus stepped forward, summoning a bolt of lightning so fierce it turned the air around them static.

He hurled it into the elemental's core. The creature screamed—an awful, soul-piercing sound—as the electricity tore into it.

But Marcus hadn't waited for Dex or Alice to get clear, and the energy he unleashed was wild, overwhelming in its power. The bolt ricocheted, arcing toward them. The world seemed to slow. Without thinking, Jace tapped into his Soul Step. The forest blurred as he slipped between realms, time grinding to a near halt.

With a burst of desperate speed, he lunged—first for Alice, then Dex—grabbing them both just as the lightning crackled past, missing by a hair's breadth. In one fluid motion, he yanked them into the Otherworld, the crackling energy of the chaos left frozen behind.

They reappeared a few feet away, gasping for air. Alice's eyes were wide, her heart hammering so hard it thrummed through her fingers, tightly clasped in Jace's hand. Jace collapsed to the ground, his Aether drained in a torrent from taking two others with him, even for such a brief moment.

He heaved, struggling to catch his breath, his heart racing as though it might break through his skin. He attempted to stand, but his body felt like lead balanced on brittle stilts.

"You... you didn't have to do that," Dex whispered.

"Let's save the 'thank yous' for later," Jace croaked, his voice strained.

Alice and Dex stood between Jace and the looming elemental.

Marcus unleashed another bolt, this time more controlled, striking the elemental's core with a crack of lightning. The creature recoiled, its watery form destabilizing.

Ell moved in, hurling bolts of her own with deadly precision. Dex followed, his hands glowing as he sent a barrage of searing energy into the elemental's weakening body.

Alice and Jace joined the fray, their combined magic cutting through the swirling mass. The creature wailed, its once-mighty form buckling under the relentless onslaught.

With a final, violent shudder, the elemental collapsed, its massive form exploding into a torrent of water. The muddy deluge crashed to the ground, leaving only silence in its wake.

Ell stepped forward, brushing damp hair from her face, her eyes gleaming with adrenaline. "Not bad, Sparkles," she teased Marcus.

Marcus, still crackling with residual energy, scowled. "I had it under control."

"Sure you did," Dex chimed in, wringing the water from his soaked cloak and wiping mud from his eye. "Nothing says 'control' like almost frying your own team."

Alice managed a weak smile, her hands still trembling from the spell. "Good thing Jace was paying attention."

"Guys," Jace's hoarse voice cut through the chaos like a blade, silencing their frantic energy in an instant.

In the stillness, they heard it—Lara's sobs, soft but sharp, like glass breaking. She knelt by the shattered remains of her grandfather's cart, now barren of its horses, cradling a figure in her arms. The scene around them blurred as Jace, still barely able to stand, leaned heavily on Alice and Dex for support. They rushed over, hearts pounding.

The man lying in Lara's arms looked close to death. Blood seeped from his mouth, each cough wracking his frail body. Jace's instinct was immediate—his hand shot to his inventory, pulling out a potion. But Alice grabbed his wrist before he could administer it.

"That's for Travelers, Jace," she said, her voice steady but soft. "It's too low-level for Citizens. It'll only make it worse."

The man's eyes fluttered open, weak but filled with something deeper than pain. He smiled up at Lara, his hand trembling as it reached for her face. "It's okay, Little Button," he rasped, voice thick with the weight of goodbye. "All stories end. Mine... mine only became worth telling because of you and your parents. I was just a side character, a footnote, but you... you gave me an adventure. I'm so proud of you."

Jace's jaw tightened. Refusal flickered in his eyes. With a surge of desperation, he cast Soul Mend, channeling everything he had... but it wasn't enough, like a candle's light against the wind, his Aether running dangerously low.

He tried Soul Tether, binding his life force to the man's. But he was still too weak, barely recovered from the drain of carrying Alice and Dex through the Otherworld. His aether flared as he gulped down the potion himself, trying to channel the magic into the dying Tinker. He allowed his Health and Stamina to feed his Aether, but it still wasn't enough, the tinker's wounds were too severe. He was fighting against an overwhelming loss of blood. His connection faltered—frayed at the edges. The health it transferred only bought the man a few precious minutes—nothing more.

Jace's heart was dense, like clay soaked in rain, heavy with endings instead of beginnings—a shallow breath of earth and water.

"No," Lara gasped, her voice breaking as tears streamed down her face. She clung to her grandpa's still-warm body, her fingers gripping his shirt as if she could hold him there by sheer will. "You promised... you promised you wouldn't leave me like Ma and Pa. You can't go. You promised."

They sat there, helpless, the weight of inevitability crushing them. His breaths grew softer, slower.

But then, something strange happened.

Chapter 43
Death's Kiss

Marcus moved forward with a quiet inevitability, nudging them away. He didn't speak, didn't glance at any of them. His face was a mask, unreadable in its stillness, as he knelt beside the Tinker like some ancient ritual had taken hold of him. From his inventory, he drew a small vial, gold-edged, its contents a dark, rich blue that pulsed faintly in the dim light, as if the liquid inside carried a song of forgotten tales. It was the kind of blue that lived only in twilight skies, just before the stars claimed their dominion.

Without ceremony, he tipped the vial to the man's lips, the potion flowing like silk, smooth and deliberate. Jace sensed a strange bond with the potion, as though a forgotten part of him stirred, reaching for it—a silent rhythm shared, echoing the same primal language as his Word of Power.

For a heartbeat, the world held its breath.

Then a cough. Not the wet, ragged sound of death, but sharp and alive. The man gasped, his chest heaving as the remnants of the blood spilled from his throat. A soft, amber glow spread through his body, creeping like dawn over a dark horizon. Wounds knit themselves together with gentle pulses of light, sealing the breaks as time appeared to reverse its cruel hand. His eyes fluttered open, clearer, as life drifted back into him as if coming from some distant shore.

Alice's voice trembled with disbelief, barely more than a whisper. "It worked. He's... he's okay." She stared at Marcus, the unsaid truth hanging between them. "That potion had to be..."

But before she could finish, Loren blinked, disoriented but whole, and a smile touched his lips—a small, tired thing that held the weight of years. Lara, sobbing, threw herself into his chest, wrapping her arms around him. She held him tighter than she had ever held anyone, or ever would again, her tears soaking into his tattered shirt.

The moment lingered, fragile and precious, like the last notes of a song fading on the wind.

He winced, though the warmth in his eyes softened it. "Ouch, Button," he rasped with a weak chuckle. "I might not be dying, but I'm still old."

They laughed—soft, tentative, as if afraid the moment might break if they breathed too loudly. But the joy was real, a quiet thing that wrapped around them like a blanket after a long, cold night.

When they looked up, Marcus was already walking away, his back to them, as if the moment had never happened.

Jace and Dex exchanged glances, a mix of confusion, relief, and something neither could name. Marcus—their Marcus—had tried to kill them both at the start of the school year. And now...

Marcus sat off to the side, distant and unreadable.

Jace sheathed his sword with a sigh, wiping his brow. The clouds above seemed to relent, the oppressive weight in the air lifting slightly, but the tension remained. The dark woods still loomed around them, silent and watchful.

The immediate threat had passed, and the group set about salvaging what they could from the wreckage of the broken cart. One cart remained intact, and after some searching, they managed to corral one of the horses. No one would be able to ride—the load was too heavy, and the path too uncertain. They stacked the remaining cart as high as they dared, though much of the goods had been destroyed or scattered too far into the forest to recover.

Before setting off again, they took a few minutes to rest and share a stew Jace had stored in his Chronospace Pouch—emerging as pristine as when it had gone in. The meal was simple but hearty, a moment of warmth before the road called them back.

But the Flavor Saver triggered a reaction in Lara and Loren that Jace hadn't expected. The moment it touched their tongues, both stiffened. Lara's eyes widened first, a twitch of surprise tugging at her lips. Loren, however, chewed slowly, his jaw tightening as though he were working through a mouthful of lemons.

"An... acquired taste, I'm sure." Loren gave a stiff nod. "A Traveler delicacy?"

"Gods, that's vile," Lara said, unashamed.

Laughter rippled through the group as Jace accepted the plates back, chuckling. "Must affect Travelers differently," he said.

The Tinker and his granddaughter exchanged a glance—an unspoken agreement—before turning to their familiar rations, safer and decidedly less adventurous.

From the corner of his eye, Jace watched Marcus, who sat glaring at his bowl as if it had somehow offended his honor. He stabbed at it with his spoon, bringing it to his lips with all the enthusiasm of a man about to chew gravel. Jace half-expected him to spit it out.

But then, something changed. Subtle, barely perceptible. The line of Marcus's mouth, usually locked in a frown, softened. His chewing slowed, thoughtful. For the first time since Jace had met him, Marcus didn't complain.

"Did it have to be stew?" Marcus grumbled, a hint of a whine in his voice.

There it was.

It was oddly reassuring to know Marcus was still in there.

After they finished, they dusted themselves off and reassessed their travel plans. With their adjusted pace, the journey to the town would now take two days.

They each got to packing and getting ready for the road.

When Jace and Alice found a moment alone, Jace finally voiced the question that had gnawed at him for hours.

"What was that potion? You seemed to recognize it." His voice was low. "I thought healing potions wouldn't work."

Alice didn't answer immediately. Her gaze drifted to Marcus in the distance, watching him methodically pack his belongings, each item disappearing into his inventory. When she finally spoke, her voice was soft.

"A regular one wouldn't," she murmured. "But what Marcus used... that was something else entirely. I've only seen pictures, but it's rare—very rare. It's called a Death's Kiss. They say it can pull someone back from death's door—even if they've already stepped through."

Jace's breath caught, but Alice continued.

"It can only be crafted by someone who's touched Death, who's seen the end up close. Some Travelers say it's a gift from one of Mythica's many incarnations of Death. Others claim it must be stolen during someone's final breath. Some claim it's found only in the inventories of high-rank players who'll never return to Mythica... the kind who have died in the real world."

"I thought when we logged out, our bodies here just vanished. How do we have inventories?"

"Yeah, that's what most people think. But there are records... strange ones. People who never logged back in, their in-game bodies have been found wandering around, lost in the wilderness. There's more to this place than anyone admits. I thought it was all just crazy theories, but now... I'm not so sure."

A chill ran down Jace's spine.

"Whatever price Marcus paid to get his hands on that potion," Alice said quietly, "it wasn't a small one."

They both looked back at Marcus.

"What are you two staring at?" Marcus shot them a glare.

"We were just—uh," Jace searched for something to say. "We should get moving," he stammered.

They rejoined the group, and Alice cast a wary glance at the darkening sky, her brow furrowing. "Jace is right, we should go. We want to cover some ground before nightfall catches up with us."

Dex stretched lazily, a tired grin on his face. "On the bright side, at least we know how to handle magical puddles now."

"It could've been worse," Jace said. "At least it wasn't a Gold Rank or something."

The group collectively turned toward him, their expressions a symphony of disbelief, the kind that asked, "Really? Again?" without a word spoken.

"What?" Jace's eyes flicked between them, bewildered.

Even the trees seemed to rustle disapprovingly, the wind pausing just long enough to make its silent judgment clear.

Chapter 44

Havenstown

Fortunately, the rest of the journey to Havenstown went smoothly. After a night of camping and two long days on the road, they finally spotted the small town on the horizon.

The last remnants of dusk bled from the sky as the group trudged into Havenstown. Loren's wagon creaked, the wheels protesting against the uneven cobblestones, while Lara hummed a tuneless lullaby under her breath.

As Jace and his companions stepped off the creaky cart and onto the worn stone of the town square, an eerie silence greeted them. The last rays of sunlight glinted faintly on the polished stones, casting long shadows.

The tinker and his granddaughter refused the group's help with unloading, but they insisted—except for Marcus, who stood idly by, watching. Lara didn't seem to mind. She gave him a hug, which he awkwardly tried to resist, and Loren shook his hand firmly before they parted ways.

The villagers moved through their last tasks of the day with a sense of urgency, their faces tight with worry as they cast furtive glances towards the darkened windows of the aged stone buildings that framed the square. A tension hung in the air, almost tangible enough to make your skin prickle.

"Feels like stepping into a painting," Alice murmured, her breath forming ghostly plumes in the chill air. "One forgotten by time."

"Something's off here," Ell said, her voice a whisper that seemed too loud. She absently touched the sapphire shard hanging around her neck, seeking comfort or perhaps guidance.

Jace nodded, his grey eyes flickering to each companion, gauging their unease. Marcus stood apart, his gaze fixed upon the ground, brow furrowed.

A colossal bell loomed above the town center of Havenstown, its patina-encrusted surface testament to the passage of countless suns and moons. It hung silent and still, yet its very presence resonated with an ominous portent, as if it could toll at any moment with a sound that would fracture the eerie hush blanketing the square. The iron clapper was stilled by chains wrapped in ancient, moth-eaten velvet, hinting at a desperate attempt to muzzle whatever dread voices might echo from its bronze throat.

Underneath the bell stood an old stone platform, marked by countless feet and heavy burdens. Symbols of protection and unity were carved into its smooth surface, eroded by generations of use. The ground surrounding the platform was worn smooth from the many who had gathered there, their eyes fixed on the bell and their hearts united in hope or dread.

Below, the cobblestones lay uneven, as though rejecting the order imposed upon them by the hands of forgotten masons. Shadows played across their irregular faces, cast by flickering torches that struggled against an unfelt breeze. Buildings rose like stoic guardians around the perimeter, their timeworn facades watching over the square with windows dark and shuttered, as if the inhabitants cowered from unseen specters that roamed under the cloak of night.

The iron lampposts twisted and intertwined with vines. In the daylight, they seemed almost decorative, but as darkness fell, their long shadows stretched across the ground. The faint light they provided did little to alleviate the uneasy feeling that hung over the town, only enhancing its ghostly charm.

Alice shivered and pulled her cloak tighter around her as she surveyed the empty streets.

Ell's face scrunched up slightly, her gaze scanning over the cobblestone, shuttered windows, and peering eyes. She looked like she wanted to dismiss it all but couldn't quite shake off the tension in her shoulders and deliberate movements.

Jace adjusted his satchel strap and carefully observed every detail of the town's facade: the weathered signs swaying in the gentle breeze, the distant tolling of a bell, and the sense of something lurking just beyond sight. The usually bustling village was unnaturally quiet, as if holding its breath in anticipation of something inevitable.

As they strolled through the cobblestone streets, Marcus pulled a yellow crystal from his inventory and activated it. In an instant, the dust of the road vanished, and he reappeared in a vibrant purple suit—every trace of wear scrubbed clean. He stood with the poised confidence of someone used to command, his tailored clothes untouched by the dust that clung to everything else in this town. His dark hair, perfectly styled, caught the dim light, the color of polished obsidian. A cold smile played on his lips, but it never reached the critical eyes locked on Jace.

Yet, something felt different about him. He wore no jewelry now, and a new glint flickered in his eyes—softer, almost thoughtful. Still, his arrogance lingered like a familiar scent, though the shift was undeniable.

He realized how dirty they all must look, after having fought the elemental and days of travel. The first order of business was to get cleaned up and find somewhere to stay for the night.

"Quite the welcome, eh?" Marcus's voice cut through the silence, sharp as ever.

"Or lack thereof," Jace shot back, his stance just as unwavering.

"I've heard stories about towns like this—never too friendly to Travelers," Dex muttered, glancing around uneasily.

Marcus shrugged, his indifference almost theatrical. "We'll squeeze what we need out of them and move on."

Villagers peeked nervously from behind shuttered windows, faces flickering between fear and curiosity.

The inn's sign swayed overhead, barely illuminated by the dying light of dusk, its edges worn from years of neglect. Jace lifted a fist to knock when the door cracked open just enough for a pair of bloodshot eyes to peek out. The innkeeper's face contorted into something between a sneer and a grimace, lips thin and pale.

Without a word, the man slammed the door shut. The dull thud echoed, followed by the unmistakable click of a lock. A moment later, the sign in the window flipped to "No Vacancies," the letters painted in a hurried scrawl.

Jace stood there, hand still raised, his brow furrowing as he exhaled through his nose. Marcus, leaning against a half-rotted post nearby, chuckled low in his throat, arms crossed over his chest.

"I know what's wrong," he drawled, amusement pulling at the corner of his lips. "You look like day-old breakfast."

Jace shot him a glare, but the effect was weak, as if the frustration had drained out of him before it even reached his eyes. "Helpful, Marcus," he muttered. "Really helpful."

Marcus straightened, pushing off the post with a lazy stretch. "Look, a town like this? There's always somewhere else. Somewhere a bit less... picky."

He waved a hand, dismissing the situation as he started walking down the narrow street, boots clacking against the cobblestones with an almost deliberate nonchalance.

"Do you even know where you're going?" Alice asked, skepticism clear, though she followed a few steps behind.

Marcus didn't answer, didn't even turn his head. His confidence was maddening, like someone who knew the punchline to a joke no one else had heard.

Dex ambled up beside Jace, giving a half-hearted shrug. "What's the worst that could happen?" he said under his breath, though his hand never strayed far from the hilt of the dagger at his waist.

Jace let out a laugh, throwing his hands up in mock surrender.

"Really, Dex? Really?" He shot Dex an incredulous look. "Didn't learn from my mistake?"

The alley they turned into was narrow, the walls crowding in. The smell of stale smoke and grease coated the air, heavy and suffocating, wrapping around them as the shadows deepened. At the end of the alley sat a squat building, slumped against the edge of town like it had grown weary of holding itself upright.

The tavern's wooden sign swayed in the same tired way as the first inn's, half its letters faded beyond recognition. Whatever it promised, it didn't seem eager to deliver.

Marcus strode right in without looking back, like he belonged there, the old door creaking on rusty hinges behind him. Jace hesitated, exchanging a glance with Alice. Her blue eyes darted around, scanning the street like she expected something—or someone—to emerge from the dark corners.

Jace leaned in, just enough to catch sight of Marcus at the bar, already chatting up the innkeeper like they were old friends. The man behind the bar, his clothes stained with sweat and his face etched with deep lines, regarded him with the wary suspicion of someone all too familiar with deception. But that suspicion waned the moment Marcus flashed a grin—and a small pouch of coins that clinked softly as it slid across the counter.

Chapter 45
The Bard

Inside, the tavern was packed with locals. Their eyes flicked to the doorway, taking in Jace and the others with slow, deliberate glances. It wasn't just curiosity—they were weighing them, measuring them like they could tell at a glance that they didn't belong. He felt the itch of their stares linger, as if they knew something he didn't, and weren't keen to share.

Moments later, Marcus returned, a grin still plastered on his face. "We've got a place," he said, the hint of mockery in his tone impossible to miss. "But there's a catch. No one's stepping inside until we clean up. Out back, by the horses. Apparently, we're too 'unsightly.'"

Dex snorted, shaking his head. "Unbelievable. If we'd changed before coming here, we'd be filthy again by now, anyway."

"Rules are rules," Marcus said with a shrug, his eyes gleaming. "Try not to drag half the road inside with you, eh?"

Reluctantly, they shuffled out back, where a few wooden buckets sat by a stone trough of running water. Jace dipped his hands into the cool water, scrubbing at the grime that clung to his skin. His reflection rippled, distortions in the surface. He hadn't realized just how much dirt had caked on until now.

Marcus stood off to the side, arms crossed, looking infuriatingly pristine. Not a speck of dirt dared cling to him, thanks to the charm embedded in the clasp of his cloak—a fact he was keen to flaunt.

"Of course you'd have a magical cleaner," Dex grumbled, wringing out his shirt. "I swear, you'd find a way to stay spotless in a mudslide."

Marcus flashed a smug grin. "Some of us just have... standards."

Once they'd cleaned up as best they could, the group filed back inside, dressed in fresh clothes from their inventories. The tavern's warmth embraced them, the smell of roasting meat and the flicker of firelight drawing them closer. The locals eyed them again, but the tension had eased—just a little. They were still outsiders, but at least now, they weren't walking in covered in the road's filth.

But even as the fire crackled in the hearth and the pungent smell of meat and mead filled the air, he couldn't shake the feeling that something was... off. The way the locals had looked at them—it wasn't just suspicion. There was something else in their eyes.

Something darker.

They secured three rooms above the bar—one for Jace and Dex, another for Ell and Alice, and the last, which Marcus stubbornly insisted on taking for himself.

After staking his claim on the lumpy excuse for a bed and arranging his stuff just so, Jace headed back down to the bustling belly of the tavern. He went solo—because why complicate things?

The tavern received him with a quiet stillness, not cold enough to bite, nor warm enough to comfort. It was the kind of stillness that settled beneath the skin, where flickering lanterns only hinted at light, and the scent of worn wood evoked a memory too distant to touch. The kind that made it clear Jace was being tolerated, not welcomed. Yet it also carried a weary understanding—everyone here had their own share of flaws and knew better than to throw stones from within their fragile glass houses.

This place wasn't built for cheer or chatter, but for the gentle lull of soft voices, a refuge against the world beyond its door. No laughter lifted here, no children's voices echoed—just the calm of words spoken low, each conversation careful not to disrupt the fragile peace that the room held.

Round wooden tables stood scattered across the room, their surfaces scarred with age, each occupied by locals leaning close, their voices barely rising above the sigh of the hearth. At the far end, an old man sat alone, his beard a ghostly white, hands working a knife over a small block of wood. He glanced at Jace, the movement of his eyes catching the dim light, before returning to his work, shavings falling in slow drifts to the floor at his feet, a forgotten season's leaves.

In the back, two women sat, their heads bent in quiet conversation, a whisper between them too delicate for the space to fully hold. One paused as Jace entered, her gaze flickering up, her words stalling, then fading as she looked back at her companion. They shared a glance, the kind that spoke volumes in silence, a shared acknowledgment that no words could ever articulate.

The barkeep, a broad-shouldered man with a face lined by endless nights, gave Jace a nod—neither friendly nor cold. Jace was just another shape in the muted rhythm of it, a note that was too quiet to hear.

Behind the bar stood the bartender, a stout man with a bushy mustache and a friendly demeanor. His hands were in constant motion, wiping a glass with a rag, then setting it down to reach for a bottle, pouring a generous measure of amber liquid into a cup. He slid it across the counter to a waiting patron, his fingers tapping the wood in a rhythmic pattern as he spoke.

Jace approached the bar, taking in the rich scent of roasted meat and fresh bread wafting from the kitchen. The bartender looked up, his eyes crinkling with a welcoming smile that didn't quite reach them.

"Welcome, Traveler," he said, his voice polite but guarded. He grabbed another glass, polishing it with the same rag, his hands never still. "What can I get for you today?"

"What do you have?" Jace asked.

"Mead and stew."

"I guess I'll have that then," Jace replied, settling onto a stool.

The bartender nodded, already moving to fill the order. "Been on the road long?" he asked, the words casual but the tone slightly clipped.

Jace noticed a few more glances his way, conversations that subtly shifted direction as he passed. A man at the corner table paused mid-sentence, his eyes narrowing just a fraction before turning back to his companions. The room's warmth felt just a bit cooler, the hum carrying a faint, almost imperceptible tension.

"Long enough," Jace said, watching the bartender's hands expertly maneuvering around the bar, pouring, wiping, and arranging with practiced ease.

A woman's voice rose above the din, clear and melodic, weaving through the room like a ribbon. Jace turned his head, drawn to the sound. At the far corner of the tavern, a woman stood, singing as a man played an ancient lyre beside her. Her eyes were closed, lost in the music, her hands gently swaying to the rhythm.

She was tall and graceful, with long, raven-black hair cascading over her shoulders, shimmering in the firelight. Her skin was a warm, sun-kissed bronze, and she wore a simple, flowing dress that clung to her slender frame. The dress, silken-green, swayed with her movements, catching the light and giving her an ethereal quality. There was something about her that seemed familiar, though Jace couldn't place what it was. Like a face from a long-forgotten dream.

As her voice filled the room, a few patrons looked her way, their expressions softening. She sang with a passion that seemed to reach deep into her soul, carrying a sea of stories and emotion.

"In golden fields where earth and sky,
She wandered lost, her heart's lone cry.
Beneath the stars in night's embrace,
She moved with grace, a gentle pace.

His words were veiled in shadows deep,
Guarded secrets, night would keep.
A maiden's plea, a gentle sigh,
Beneath the tree where sorrows lie.

In fields of gold, where dreams do bloom,
She shed her tears, the silver moon.
Unknowing of his love's true flame,
In absence burned, a silent name.

In fields where light and dreams entwine,
Echoes of love forever shine.
Alone she roamed, her heart a tome,
Forever seeking love, a home."

Her voice danced, each note carrying a story. The man beside her plucked the strings of the lyre with nimble fingers, his eyes fixed on her as if she were the only thing that mattered.

Jace watched as the bartender set down a steaming bowl of stew and a golden-hued drinking cup before him—a shallow, wide vessel with two delicate handles. It had a strange elegance, something that seemed both ceremonial and entirely impractical. He studied it for a moment, the shape unfamiliar, his fingers unsure how to hold it properly. It spoke of a time or place he didn't know, an artifact of a culture that had never touched his life until now.

"Here you are. Enjoy," the bartender said, his voice a quiet note in the room's muted symphony.

"Thanks." Jace nodded, gripping the twin handles and tilting the vessel toward him. The motion felt awkward, and he slurped at the edge, careful, like a cat testing a dish of milk—ginger and uncertain but managing all the same.

Still, no flavor. He frowned, glancing around before surreptitiously retrieving a vial from his inventory and tilting just a drop into the golden mead, his hand shielding the movement to avoid offending the barkeep.

Jace gave a small sigh, watching as the liquid swirled, the once flat taste now brightened by the addition of his concoction. Better. He raised the "cup" again, taking a deeper sip, and let the warmth settle in his chest, pushing away the lingering chill of the evening.

You have consumed: Rustic Mead

   Effect Gained: Minor Fortitude
   Slightly boosts resistance to cold and minor ailments for 30 minutes.

   Effect Gained: Mild Intoxication
   Minus 2 to Intelligence and Wisdom for 30 minutes or until Cured.
   Flavor Saver has enhanced this effect. Duration increased by 10%.

Jace made a mental note that the Flavor Saver increased both the positive and negative effects.

The song and the scene blended with his thoughts. Jace took a sip of his mead and let the melody weave through his thoughts. Jace spooned stew into his mouth, the flavors rich and earthy. His attention sharpened when he caught snippets of a conversation from the next table.

Eventually, Jace retreated to a dark corner of the tavern, letting the night stretch on around him. He blended into the shadows, his presence fading from their collective memory. As the drinks flowed and the warmth of familiarity returned to the room, he listened. He waited for their walls to drop, for the secrets to slip through the cracks in their guarded words.

Two men and an older woman, each rough around the edges, leaned in close over their drinks. "It's those damn wolves again," the older woman muttered, her voice gravelly and slurred from drink. "Terrorizing the wagons on the border between Zone Three and Four."

The younger man shook his head, frustration etching lines into his features. "And what do the guards do? Nothing. Just let the beasts run wild."

"Could always ask a Traveler for some help," the other man said with a smirk.

They laughed, harsh and bitter. "Oh, I'd rather have wolves than Travelers any day. We need someone to take care of the wolves, not burn down a town."

"They think they own everything. No respect. It's because they're immortal, you know."

"Unreliable bunch," the crone muttered, raising her mug before taking a long swig of ale. "Always stirring up trouble, then vanishing the moment things get rough. Haven't seen hide nor hair of them since their little... mishap." She chuckled, a low, gravelly sound, the kind that carried more spite than humor.

Jace had never heard such disdain about Travelers. It was odd. He had thought Citizens and Travelers worked together. He pushed the thoughts aside, letting them drift into the periphery like leaves caught in a slow current. But that night, the thought refused to leave him alone.

His eyes grew heavier, the flickering candlelight in the room's corner blurring into a warm glow. Dex was already sprawled across his bed, snoring softly, when Jace returned. The weight of the day settled in, and Jace's mind loosened its grip on the puzzle, surrendering to the pull of sleep.

Sleep was fitful, at best. The low rumble of Dex's snoring rose and fell, a steady background noise that Jace drifted in and out of. Eventually, he managed to sink into a deeper sleep, but morning came all too soon.

Chapter 46
Posthaste

J ace woke to a particularly aggressive snore that shook him from his slumber. Dex's snoring had evolved into something that could only be described as the dying groans of a large, wounded animal. Jace rolled over, burying his face in the pillow. He sighed, finally resigning himself to wakefulness, his eyes bleary but resigned.

"How does he not wake himself up with that noise?" he wondered aloud, peeling himself out of bed. He threw a quick glance out the window—the dull grey of dawn greeted him, promising another bitter day. Just perfect.

Down the hall, a door creaked open, followed by Alice's voice—muffled, groggy, and clearly miffed.

There was a firm knock, and Jace opened his door to find Alice standing there, her eyes half-closed, her hair a mess. Without a word, she raised her shard, and with a flick of her wrist, a tiny burst of energy zipped past Jace and struck Dex square in the face.

With a yelp, Dex shot up, daggers instinctively materializing in his hands, his eyes wide as he looked around wildly. When he spotted Alice, realization slowly sank in, and he let out a tired sigh, lowering his daggers as he slumped back onto the bed.

"Dex, if you don't stop snoring, I swear I'm throwing you out the window," Alice grumbled, her voice scratchy with sleep. "We can hear you all the way across the hall."

"That's not very heroic of you," Dex muttered, barely awake, the daggers vanishing as he turned over, his face already half-buried in his pillow again.

"Heroics don't apply before sunrise," Alice shot back, her shard still faintly glowing. "Consider it your early morning wake-up call."

Jace smirked. It was way too early, but at least some things never changed.

"I'm saving the town from your noise pollution," Alice said, a yawn stretching her words.

"Morning, sunshine," Jace said to Alice with a grin.

She smiled like the rising sun before turning to scowl at Dex again, then headed back to her room to freshen up.

Jace grabbed his boots and yanked them on, kicking at the door as he left his room. The hallway was dim, lit only by the pale morning light seeping through the cracks. He could hear Ell shuffling down from the opposite end.

"Morning," Jace said with a large smile.

Ell squinted at him like he'd personally offended her by being awake. "Too early for your face, Jace."

He chuckled, running a hand through his disheveled hair. "Come on, let's see if there's coffee downstairs. Or something pretending to be coffee."

They clattered down the stairs, groggy but fueled by the vague hope of breakfast. The common room was a haze of low chatter and the clink of plates. The smell of something sizzling reached them, and Marcus was already seated at a table, looking far too composed for this hour of the morning

Dex joined them not long after.

Jace shifted uncomfortably, his gaze moving from one face to the next at the table. "So, uh, I overheard something last night. Might be nothing, but those women at the bar were talking about wolves attacking. Sounded like they're getting closer to town."

Dex paused, raising an eyebrow. "Wolves?"

Alice leaned in, her tone half-serious. "How close are we talking, Jace?"

Jace shook his head. "Not sure. They were pretty drunk, but the way they talked about it... sounded like it's been happening for a while, and it's getting worse."

Marcus looked thoughtful, his back straight, as usual. "It could explain the missing mail."

The table fell silent for a moment, the weight of Jace's words sinking in.

"So, wolf meat for breakfast it is," Dex muttered, attempting to lighten the mood.

Marcus shot him a condescending glare.

Before they could delve further into strategy, the barkeep approached with their plates, his expression one of practiced neutrality—until Dex spoke up.

"Excuse me," he said politely, "has the post office been down lately? We're expecting—"

The man shot a jittery glance at the door. "It's closed." With that, he spun on his heel and walked off, disappearing into a back room, leaving the group to exchange bewildered blinks in his wake.

Dex frowned. "Friendly."

"Yeah, like a bucket of nails," Ell said, crossing her arms.

Jace leaned back in his chair, folding his arms. "Seems like no one wants to talk."

Alice drummed her fingers on the table thoughtfully. "Think it's just us?"

"Oh, definitely," Dex chimed in. "I've never been ignored with such finesse before."

"Subtle art," Jace agreed, lips twitching with dry humor.

"Well, to the post office it is then," Marcus said, standing up and straightening his jacket.

They paused in front of the post office; its perhaps once-bright façade was now stained with grime. The windows, blackened by soot or something worse, offered no glimpse inside. Jace gripped the handle, testing it, but the door stayed sealed, immovable as stone.

"I can crack it if you want," Dex said, flashing a grin as he tapped a crowbar against his shoulder.

Jace shook his head. "Last thing we need is to rile up the locals more than we already have. Let's find the postmaster. He might know what's happening around here."

Marcus scanned the darkened streets. "We should split up, cover more ground. Meet back in half an hour."

With silent nods, the group broke off, each slipping into the shadowy tangle of streets, disappearing into the labyrinth of alleys and crumbling buildings.

Jace ventured deeper into the village, the cobblestone paths winding, a serpent through the heart of the settlement. The buildings on either side seemed to lean in closer with each step he took, their shadows stretching long and thin across the ground. The walls were stained with age, and the windows, darkened and dusty, watched him like unblinking eyes. It felt as if the very structures were muttering amongst themselves, sharing secrets they dared not voice aloud, their murmurs just out of earshot.

He approached a few villagers along the way, but they turned away before he could utter a word, their expressions tight with fear and mistrust. An old man hunched over a stack of firewood refused to meet his gaze, muttering something under his breath as he shuffled away. A young mother clutching her child's hand pulled her closer, retreating into the safety of a nearby doorway, eyes wide with unspoken warnings. Each interaction left Jace feeling more isolated, the village's silent rejection amplifying his frustration.

Pushing forward, Jace navigated through a narrow alley, the air growing colder -heavier- as if the village itself was holding its breath. The alley eventually opened into a small, deserted plaza. There, perched on a stoop, sat a woman who seemed as ancient as the stones themselves. Her frame was frail, bowed by the burden of countless years, but her eyes gleamed with an unsettling mix of wisdom and madness.

Her hair, a wild tangle of silver, framed a face carved by deep lines and creases, each wrinkle telling a story of its own. She wore layers of tattered clothing, the fabric so threadbare it seemed to merge with the stone beneath her. Despite her apparent frailty, her eyes were piercing, cutting through the air to scrutinize Jace with a gaze that made his skin prickle.

"Excuse me, ma'am," Jace began, striving to keep his tone respectful. "I'm looking for the postmaster."

The old woman's lips twitched into an unsettling grin. "Postmaster, postmaster..." she echoed, her voice a sing-song purr. "He's probably feeding the crows now, don't you think? They get so hungry. I'm more worried about his poor new assistant. Troubling times... Troubling times..."

Jace furrowed his brow, trying to parse her words. "I just need to know what's happening in this town."

She leaned in closer, the stench of her breath making him instinctively recoil. Her eyes, wild and unblinking, bore into his. "The town's gone sour, boy. First, the wolves came, eyes like lanterns, bold as sin. But then... it came. It speaks in the night, calls your name, and promises sweet things. But it lies. Oh, it lies."

"What do you mean?" Jace asked, leaning in, hoping for more clarity.

Her response was a sudden, sharp cackle that echoed in the empty plaza, sending a shiver down his spine. "Hahahaha! Shadows that walk, dreams that bleed. It gets you when you're not looking -creeps into your soul. You can't hide. No, no, no... You'd be wise to leave before it finds you, boy."

Before Jace could ask another question, she retreated into her house, moving with surprising swiftness for someone so old. The door shut with a final, echoing thud.

Jace made his way back to the post office alone. The others hadn't arrived yet. Surprisingly, the previously sealed door now stood slightly open. He entered cautiously, his senses on high alert as he observed the neglected state of the interior. Dust-coated packages and letters littered the space, abandoned and forgotten. Jace scanned the area for any signs of life as he approached the counter.

He heard the others enter behind him.

"You got in?" Dex asked.

"No, the door was unlocked when I returned," Jace replied.

"Did you find anything?" Ell inquired.

"Just a feeling of fear and emptiness," Jace answered, still disturbed by the strange words of the old woman. "This town is hiding something. Something dark."

Dex nodded in agreement. "I haven't had any luck getting information from anyone either. Look at this mess," he grumbled, kicking a pile of crumpled papers. "Nothing important, just dust."

Ell's eyes narrowed as she noticed several signs posted on the walls, warning about cursed wolves in the area. "Wolves," she read aloud. "That's not good."

They each turned back to their search, and eventually, amidst a chaotic sprawl of papers, they unearthed a map marked with intricate lines detailing the delivery routes in and out of the town. The absence of recent package logs hinted at something nefarious - the shipment was still en route.

"We need to track this shipment -see if we can locate it," Jace declared, his finger tracing the convoluted paths on the map.

They pressed forward, the trail winding its way through the dense forest. The air had grown thick with the scent of damp earth. Jace's eyes never stopped moving, scanning the darkened edges of the path for any flicker of movement, any sign that they weren't alone.

The deeper they ventured, the more treacherous the path became. Twining roots clawed at their boots, leaves crunched beneath their feet like the brittle bones of long-dead things, and the oppressive silence of the forest seemed to wrap around them. Even the distant hoot of an owl felt ominous, a reminder that nature had its predators, but none like what lurked here. Every step felt weighed down by the undeniable sense of being watched.

At last, they stumbled into a small clearing, and the sight that greeted them was a punch to the gut. An overturned wagon lay in ruins, its splintered remains strewn about as though a storm had torn it asunder. But there was no storm. The ground was stained, dried blood marking the earth, a macabre signature of what was here. The violence of it hit them all at once, freezing them in place as their eyes took in the carnage.

Jace knelt beside the wreckage, the scent of old blood hanging in the cold air. The wagon's wooden frame was shattered, the wheels bent at grotesque angles. His stomach churned as his fingers brushed against a smear of crimson. "Fresh," he said.

Ell joined him, her gaze darting nervously around the clearing. "This wasn't just a robbery," she whispered, her voice tight with unease.

Jace stood, his mind racing, conjuring scenes too terrible to linger on. "No," he agreed, his voice barely above a growl. "This was a massacre."

They fanned out, Ell and Alice moving like predators themselves, each step deliberate as their eyes scanned the trees, searching for any-thing—any sign of what had done this. The forest seemed to respond in kind, its shadows deepening, looming taller, more twisted, as the sunlight bled away into dusk.

Blood and torn flesh littered the clearing, scattered like pieces of a violent puzzle waiting to be solved. The shadows whispered, hints of unseen threats carried on the wind. The tension was thick enough to choke on.

Jace's gaze locked onto the wagon again. Deep gashes marred its sides, claw marks that dug into the wood as though something huge had torn into it. He clenched his jaw. "This is where the couriers were attacked," he said.

Dex paced nervously, his eyes flicking toward the treeline, the shadows seeming to move of their own accord. "We've got to be careful," he warned, voice tight. "Whatever did this... might still be close."

Jace studied the gouges, his frown deepening. "These marks... they're from something massive."

They sifted through the wreckage, lifting broken crates, sifting through torn packages. What little mail they found was addressed to the University, but the contents had been ripped free. Empty boxes, shredded documents—whatever was here, it had been taken, and whoever did this had left nothing but ruin in their wake. A grim certainty settled over them. Someone—or something—had not only murdered the couriers but had destroyed everything meant for the University. But why?

Their search became a grim hunt for clues, moving through the aftermath of violence with growing unease. The rustle of leaves, the snap of twigs beneath their boots—the only sounds breaking the otherwise oppressive silence. Every creak of wood, every shift of broken glass beneath their feet mourned the violence that had torn this place apart.

Then, without warning, the stillness shattered. A sudden rustling in the underbrush, sharp and violent, sent a surge of adrenaline through them. Jace felt it first, the unmistakable sensation of someone...something watching—hungry, and not alone. He glanced at Ell, who had already drawn her weapon, her knuckles white.

"We're not alone," Jace whispered, his voice tight. His eyes scanned the shadows, where the branches seemed to reach out like skeletal hands.

A chill wind blew through the clearing, carrying the scent of damp earth and rot. The moon broke through the clouds, casting a pale, sickly light over the forest. Shadows stretched and shifted, twisting like living things, and that's when he saw them—glowing eyes, eight pairs, burning like embers in the dark.

Jace crouched low, every muscle taut, his senses heightened. His Soul Sense flared to life, and what he found made his blood run cold. "Demon," he cursed.

"Incoming," Jace warned, voice low but steady. His sword was in his hand before the others could even blink, the cold steel glinting in the moonlight. They followed suit, weapons drawn, their eyes never leaving the tree line.

Whatever was about to happen, there was no running from it. The fight had found them.

The growl deepened, echoing from the throat of the largest one, a towering abomination that led the pack. Its body was torn between worlds—half-dressed in shredded remnants of clothes that barely clung to its distorted form. Massive, hulking shoulders jutted awkwardly from the tattered fabric, as if it had tried, and failed, to hold onto its last traces of humanity. But there was no denying the beast it had become. Its chest was a battlefield of flesh, where human skin fought a losing war against bone and sinew protruding like jagged cliffs. Spindly, broken fingers curled into claws, caked in dirt and blood.

Behind it, four others emerged, each smaller but no less horrifying, each dragging itself forward with the same disjointed, twitching movements. One had a head too large for its body, swollen and throbbing as though something inside was trying to burst free. Another limped on mismatched legs—one human, one grotesquely bloated with beastly muscle, its gait uneven and jarring. The third was missing its lower jaw entirely, its remaining teeth gnashing at the air as a dark, foul-smelling liquid oozed from its throat. The last of the five skittered sideways like a spider, its limbs twisted unnaturally, bones poking through its patchwork skin, moving far too quickly for something so malformed.

What tied them together wasn't just the terrible way their bodies had been reshaped, but the gleam of brass that caught the moonlight. The massive one wore a tarnished crown, crooked and dull but unmistakably regal in its grotesque form. Around the others were mismatched tokens—a bracelet hanging loosely from a skeletal wrist, a ring on a gnarled finger too big to fully fit, a necklace so tight it bit into the skin, and a tiara perched on a head that looked anything but royal. Each piece of jewelry felt wrong, like an ancient mockery of what they once might have been, and the metal seemed to hum with a dark energy, binding them to their leader.

They closed in, a living nightmare dragging themselves into the clearing, their collective growls harmonizing into a hellish symphony of pain, hunger, and something far more insidious—a deep, burning rage barely contained by their brittle, decaying forms.

"Uh, I think we found the 'wolves,'" Dex said.

Chapter 47
The Carnage Below

T he wind howled through the trees, its mournful wail swallowed by the
wet squelch of footsteps from the approaching horrors. The moon
above cast a sickly light, bleeding through the twisted canopy, illuminating the
grotesque figures that lurched into view. Their limbs hung at unnatural angles,
twisted and broken as though something had forced them to keep moving long
after they should have fallen apart.

"I've seen this before," Jace whispered, voice low, like the air itself was
too afraid to carry his words. His eyes locked on them, grotesque parodies of
human life, their flesh sagging, draped over bones too long, too sharp. "Sophi
e... she wasn't as far gone." His voice cracked, the memory clawing at him as he
clenched his fists.

The creatures dragged themselves closer, jewelry—once beautiful,
now tarnished and dripping with gore—caught the pale light, sending ghostly
shadows dancing across their misshapen faces. Eyes, or what was left of them,
glowed faintly, empty sockets staring into the abyss, or maybe through it. The
smell of rot hit them first, thick and cloying, like meat left out too long in the
sun.

Dex's words trembled, a nervous laugh bubbling out like the last gasp
of sanity. "Any tips for not dying?" His hands tightened around the hilts of his
daggers, as his voice betrayed him, the fear creeping in.

"Keep them off me. I need to try something." Jace's words came out
with a deadly calm, his fingers twitching, feeling the pulse of Soul Sense stir
inside him, like waking up a beast that shouldn't be touched. "There's a chance
someone's still in there."

The creatures lunged, and the world exploded into chaos.

Dex was a blur, his body moving faster than the eye could follow. He
spun, slashing wide, the sound of metal cutting through flesh, mixing with

the wet splatter of blood on the dirt. The beasts shrieked, a high-pitched wail that scraped at the inside of their skulls, like nails on a chalkboard. Dex danced through the carnage. His grin twisted, like he wasn't sure whether he was still fighting or running for his life.

Ell shimmered in and out of existence, her form slipping through the onslaught, like smoke through fingers. One second she was there, the next she was gone, her blade flicking out of the shadows to slice through exposed spines. The crunch of bone under steel made Jace's stomach lurch, but he couldn't look away. Blood sprayed, painting her ethereal form in crimson, but she moved on, a ghost among the dead.

Alice's hands crackled with power, her lips moving in a low hum as she called on her magic. The ground beneath the beast rippled, the earth itself writhing and alive, and dragged the creature down into its depths. It shrieked, limbs flailing, but Alice's spell held it fast, burying it alive as the ground closed over it with a hollow moan.

Jace's heart raced. He could feel the tangled mess of soul energy wrapped around the creatures like barbed wire, ripping through the fabric of whatever was left of their humanity. His breath came in ragged gasps as he reached out, Soul Tether snapping to life with a visceral jolt. The connection hit hard—empty, wrong, like staring into the void and finding it staring back.

There was nothing. No one was left inside.

The largest beast lunged at him, its claws slicing through the air. Jace flickered out of existence, reappearing just in time to see its clawed hand swipe through where his head had been moments before. His sword flashed, cutting deep into its side, but the wound only seemed to anger it. It howled, turning on him with a savage snarl, its eyes burning with the madness of a thing long dead but not yet finished.

Pain exploded through Jace's ribs as the creature's claws found purchase, tearing into flesh and muscle. He gritted his teeth, biting back a scream as blood poured from the wound. The Word of Power surged through him, cold and searing at once, mending flesh even as the creature struck again.

"Jace!" Dex's voice cut through the chaos, his face slick with blood, eyes wild with adrenaline. "If you've got a plan, now's the time!"

Jace focused everything he had on the Soul Severance. The connection between the creatures and whatever dark force bound them together buckled under his will. His vision blurred as he pushed harder, forcing the thread to snap.

And then, with a breath of surrender, the tenuous thread binding the demon to the husk of its human shell snapped. Jace felt it, a sigh leaving the world, a moment of fragile release. But the outcome was not what he had hoped for, not what he had dared to believe might happen.

The creature staggered, its form quivering as if caught between worlds—but only for a heartbeat. Then, with an audible crackle, its skin began to peel away, curling back like paper scorched at the edges. A hollow ache settled into Jace's gut as he watched, realizing the truth. The human soul had long since fled, and what remained was a grotesque parody of flesh, held together only by the demon's twisted purpose.

Jace's mind raced, the terrible realization taking shape. Perhaps this was why Ponos had chosen Sophie for the ritual—perhaps the demons needed something more, a final shove, to fully sever what was human and step entirely into their monstrous form. A chrysalis needing to split, leaving behind all that was mortal, and emerge as something that was only hunger and hate.

Jace's chest tightened, a cold knot forming as he stared at the peeling skin. He hadn't freed the host; he had only pushed the demon closer to what it wanted to become.

Jace's stomach twisted as the flesh sloughed off the creatures in thick, wet chunks, revealing what lay beneath—twisted bones and sinew, blackened and rotted, eyes that glowed with a hellish fire. What had been human was now something far worse, something that had been rotting in the dark, waiting for the moment it could crawl out and feed.

"I think I made it worse," Jace whispered, barely more than a rasp. Horror clenched his chest, an icy hand wrapping around his lungs.

Ell's voice was sharp, cutting through the rising panic. "Are we still staying non-lethal, Jace?"

"There's no one left." His words came out low, seething with raw fury. "Kill them all."

The creatures howled in unison, a sound that rumbled through the earth, shaking the trees. They surged forward, faster now, more desperate, their hunger palpable. Jace felt it clawing at his mind, dragging him down into their madness. But his Word of Power was a burning flame in the pit of his soul, and he used it to fight back.

He Soul Stepped again, his sword driving deep into the exposed bones of a creature. Blood—thick, dark, and rancid—sprayed across his face, but he barely noticed. His Soul Affinity hummed in his veins, guiding his strikes with precision. His blade was a blur, cutting through flesh and bone as if it were nothing. But the creatures kept coming.

Ell moved beside him, her blade flashing through the moonlight as she drove it through the neck of another beast. The creature convulsed, blood pouring from its severed spine.

Jace's muscles screamed, each breath ragged and hot, but he pushed forward. His Affinity pulled him through the pain, through the madness, guiding his hand as his sword cleaved through another twisted form. His chest ached, the wound from earlier still bleeding, but he healed as fast as he was hurt, stitching him back together even as the creatures tore him apart.

A creature lunged, its jaws snapping at his throat. Jace flickered, disappearing just in time to reappear behind it, driving his blade into its back with a sickening crunch. The creature's body spasmed, its death rattle, a howl of a thousand screams.

But still, they came.

Finally, after what felt like hours, the last creature fell, its body collapsing with a final, wet thud. The clearing was silent, save for the rasp of their breath and the thick drip of blood onto the earth.

Jace stood at the center of it all, soaked in blood, trembling from the aftermath of the fight. The power that had driven him was fading, leaving behind only exhaustion and a bitter taste in his mouth.

Above him, the stars stared down, cold and uncaring, as if scorning the carnage below.

They stared at the bodies of the monsters, now twitching, grotesquely contorting as they returned to something resembling human form. The sickening sound of bones snapping and grinding echoed in the silence, like dry branches breaking underfoot. Flesh that had stretched beyond its limits began to sag, deflating like overfilled balloons as it shriveled back into place.

One of the bodies—once a towering, monstrous brute—lay collapsed in a heap of wet, glistening muscle and skin. Its jaw, previously distended with rows of sharp, jagged teeth, snapped forward with a horrifying crunch, leaving a mouth frozen in a grotesque scream. Pieces of skin, like torn fabric, hung loosely from its face, some still clinging to the raw muscle beneath, while others sloughed off, landing with soft, wet thuds on the blood-soaked ground.

Another body twitched violently, its limbs jerking in sharp, erratic spasms as the twisted form fought to return to its once-human state. The eyes—once glowing with an unnatural, hellish light—now flickered weakly, fading into dull, lifeless orbs. Blood oozed from its cracked lips, mingling with the thick, black bile that still dripped from its throat. The hands, once vicious claws that had ripped through flesh like parchment, trembled and curled inward, now just limp, broken fingers covered in shredded tendons and peeling skin.

Each terrible figure had a brass item somewhere on its body, shining with an uncanny brightness. Against the grime and filth clinging to their skin, the brass stood out—spotless, polished, untouched by dirt or blood. Even the foulness that seemed to soak into everything around them left the brass pristine, almost mocking the decay it was surrounded by. The metal gleamed, a perfect, unblemished shine amid the muck, defying the dirt and filth that seemed to consume everything else.

The stench hit him first, a foul mixture of rot and decay, thick and suffocating, as though the bodies were rotting away on the spot. Flies circled, buzzing in frantic, greedy swarms, drawn to the gore—settling on exposed muscle and torn flesh, feasting without pause.

Jace's breath hitched, heart lodging in his throat as he stumbled upon the one body that shouldn't have been there.

"No," he whispered, voice catching as he stared down at the familiar form. Damon. His mind reeled, trying to make sense of it. "What happened to you?" His words barely audible, crushed beneath a silent vice.

Damon's body lay twisted and lifeless, half-concealed beneath the wreckage of battle, his once-vibrant energy snuffed out, a candle in the wind. Jace swallowed hard, forcing bile back down his throat. His friend must have come looking for clues, hunting for answers in a place that held none. But why? How had he ended up here—like this? The question clawed at Jace's mind, relentless, but no answer came. He wore a brass necklace, a thick chain of smooth links that shone far too brightly. A small pendant hung from the center, etched with simple swirling lines. The brass looked new, though Jace was learning better.

Jace took a shaky step forward, his boots sinking into the blood-soaked earth. His eyes were drawn to the last creature still twitching in its death throes. It let out a final gurgle, a grotesque rattle from deep within its chest, then fell still. What was left of its face—if it could even be called that—was little more than a jagged, hollow cavity where its skull had been shattered. Bone fragments jutted out at impossible angles, and bits of brain matter splattered the ground like discarded refuse.

The scene was wrong in every way, twisted beyond recognition. And yet, all Jace could do was stare at Damon's broken body, a raw ache building in his chest.

Why were you here, Damon? Did you find something about Sophie, about Ponos?

Whatever humanity had been left in him was now gone, buried beneath ruined flesh and shattered bones. Jace reached out, his fingers brushing against the brass necklace. The instant he made contact, a vision burned into his mind—a monstrous form, twisted and grotesque, much like the creatures before him. But there was something else, something darker, looming behind it. A shadow, a presence that seemed to lurk just out of sight, a figure hidden in the dark.

Despair swept over him, a bitter wave that left him breathless. The world around him crumbled, and in its place, he saw his foster parents, their faces blank, empty eyes staring at him without a flicker of warmth. He saw his brother, standing just as hollow, his gaze heavy with disappointment. A pang of grief, fierce and cold, pierced Jace's heart.

No. This isn't real, he thought, shaking himself, trying to hold on to what was solid. He felt the darkness reaching into him, trying to crawl into his mind, into his very soul. It crept forward, like ice in his veins, until suddenly, it was pushed back. Jace's Mostly Dead boon flared to life, a shield between him and the encroaching darkness.

The force shattered, recoiling violently, and in that brief, electric moment, Jace caught a glimpse of what lay beneath it all—a face in the shadows, one he knew too well. The umbral form of the Dark One. He staggered back, his breath catching as he stepped away from Damon's body.

"These poor people," Alice whispered. Her gaze lingered on the still forms, her eyes filled with something deeper than pity. Her voice was unnervingly calm, too measured for someone who had just witnessed so much death.

Ell knelt beside one of the fallen, her fingers lightly brushing the hilt of a sword stained a dark crimson. She looked at the blood on her hands. The tears came then, silently at first, then streaming down her face, glistening in the dim light.

Dex hesitated, his fingers hovering mid-air before slowly retracting. He looked over at Ell, her face crumpled with grief, and his bravado melted away. He stepped closer, his expression softening. "Ell..." he murmured.

She shook her head quickly, trying to wipe the tears away, her voice tight. "I'm fine." Dex ignored her protest, wrapping his arms around her. She tensed, trying to push him away, but he held on tighter. "I'm fine," she said again, her voice cracking, repeating it like a mantra.

They stayed there, silent in each other's presence, until finally, the tears slowed, then stopped. Dex loosened his grip, giving her space, his own eyes red-rimmed from tears. He nodded, letting her go.

"You know," Dex said, his voice barely above a whisper, "you don't have to be so tough all the time."

Ell glanced at him and, without hesitation, punched him hard in the arm. "I'm tougher than you," she said, her voice steadier now, a spark of her usual fire returning.

Dex raised his hands in mock surrender. "Wouldn't dream of disputing it."

A brief moment of levity passed between them before Ell's gaze shifted back to the corpses. Her body stiffened, her shoulders squaring once more as the reality of the scene returned.

Alice hadn't smiled or looked their way during the exchange. Her eyes were fixed on the smallest of the bodies—the youngest. The one that must have been the postman's assistant. She crouched next to him. Her face was pale, her eyes unreadable, as she stared at the fallen, her thoughts elsewhere.

"The jewelry," she said, her brow furrowing. "It doesn't feel right. My senses blur around them, like they're cloaked in illusion. We need to gather what we can and get back to the University." She rose, her hands tightening into fists, her expression resolute, though Jace caught the glisten of tears threatening to fall.

As Dex reached for a brass bracelet on a creature, Jace grabbed his arm just as his fingers hovered inches away.

"Don't touch them," Jace snapped, gripping Dex's arm firmly. "They're cursed. This is what Ponos had on him when he... when Sophie died."

Alice stepped forward, pulling a pair of alchemical gloves from her inventory. "Here, use these," she said, tossing them to Dex. "Silver Rank gloves. They should protect you."

Dex caught them, turning them over, a brow raised. "Why do you even have these?" Jace asked, glancing between Alice and the gloves. "And wait, there are gloves specifically for this?"

Alice gave him a look like he'd just asked if water was wet. "Of course. Anything above a Bronze potion needs proper handling. You knew that, right? Please tell me you knew that."

Jace nodded quickly. "Of course, absolutely."

With the gloves on, they gathered the items, removing the brass pieces from the bodies and dropping them into a cloth leather sack Dex took from his inventory.

Dex grimaced as the cursed jewelry clinked inside. "This bag's basically ruined now. Wasn't cheap, you know."

They ignored him. When the last piece was collected, Ell stood and brushed her hands off. "We should get moving. We're done here."

"Not quite," Jace said, adjusting the weight of his sword across his back. "Before we go, I want to hear what Marcus has to say about bailing on us during the fight."

Chapter 48
Words Unsaid

They found him huddled in the shadow of a tree, shaking, his back against the trunk like he was trying to become part of it. Jace crouched beside him, careful, like approaching a wounded animal.

"Care to share what happened back there?" Jace asked, his voice low, but it wasn't a question so much as a demand.

Marcus's face was pale, eyes hollow. For a long moment, he said nothing. The silence stretched until finally, he spoke as though his words were coming from somewhere far off.

"My father... he never liked me much. Said I was stubborn, like my mother." His voice cracked, but he pressed on. "I was raised by the maids. My mother, she... she was kind but distant. Always distant."

Jace exchanged a glance with Dex, who stood nearby, arms folded. This wasn't the story they had asked for, but they let Marcus talk.

"My father worked with John Rearden, you know? His lawyer. Helped him shut down the court orders. Protected his tech. In a way, he helped make this nightmare possible."

Jace stayed silent, letting him unravel at his own pace.

"Two weeks before I came to Terra Mythica, my parents... they were killed." Marcus's voice trembled. "A Techno-Purge lunatic followed them, protesting Rearden's work. Security wasn't enough. Nothing stopped that car from hitting them."

The terrible revelation hung between them. Jace didn't move, didn't say anything.

"I wasn't going to log in," he continued, his tone hollow. "But everyone was pressuring me. My father's firm wanted me to sign documents, sell my shares, and hand over control. I just... I needed to get away."

Dex took a step forward. "So, you ran away to Terra Mythica?"

"When I logged in," Marcus said, his eyes unfocused, "I found an envelope in my inventory. Unmarked, glitched sender info. Inside was a simple brass ring. It had been addressed to my father."

Jace's stomach tightened. Something about the way Marcus said it—the cold edge in his voice—set off alarm bells. Jace was quickly putting the pieces together.

"I started wearing it. I don't know why, but I couldn't take it off." Marcus's hands trembled as he wiped them on his pants. "At first, I didn't notice anything... just felt angrier at everything. At the world. At you." He glanced at Jace, shame flickering behind his eyes.

"Marcus..." Jace began, but Marcus cut him off.

"Then the nightmares started," he said. "Every night, the same faces. Demonic. Twisted. Haunting me."

Dex's gaze sharpened. "And the ring?"

Marcus looked up, regret etched into every line of his face. "I threw it away. It took everything I had... but I knew if I kept it, it would've destroyed me. It almost did. The voices—" he paused, the horror of it choking his words. "They weren't mine anymore."

Jace exhaled slowly. "Where did you throw it?"

"Off the mountain. Far enough that I wouldn't be tempted to go back for it."

Ell stepped closer, her voice gentle but firm. "You should've told us."

Marcus laughed bitterly, wiping at his face. "Like I'd just walk up to you and say, 'Hey, by the way, I might be possessed by a cursed ring'? Yeah, that would've gone over well."

The others were silent. Then, he pointed shakily to two bodies lying near the treeline. "Those two... they were my bodyguards. You met them at the skydock."

Jace looked, recognition dawning slowly. "I thought they were your friends."

"No. Just hired help," Marcus said bitterly. "They probably got a better offer. Maybe tried to rob the delivery. Started this whole mess." Marcus let out a dry laugh. "Friends? No. They were paid to protect me."

Ell's eyes flicked to the bodies.

Jace's eyebrow shot up. "What about that pale kid? The one always hanging around you?"

"I don't know any pale kid." Marcus shook his head, obviously confused.

Jace let the exchange hang for a beat, then leaned in closer. "When those things came at us—what happened, Marcus? Why didn't you help?"

Marcus stared at the dirt. "I... I'm sorry," Marcus said quietly. "When I saw them... saw the faces that had been in my nightmares, everything came flooding back. I froze. I couldn't move, I wanted to, you have to believe me. I just... couldn't."

Jace believed him. He couldn't say whether Marcus's inability to join the fight was a lingering effect of being possessed, or perhaps something more human—something raw and unseen. Scars that went deeper than flesh, wounds rooted in the heart that refused to let go, until he could one day let them.

Ell nodded. "This all would explain why he's been acting like such a brat."

Dex grinned. "Yeah, but let's be real, Marcus was always kind of a brat."

Marcus gave a half-smile, shaking his head. "Thanks, Dex."

Jace stood, offering Marcus a hand.

They swept over the scene one last time, making sure nothing was overlooked. Among the cursed items, they found letters, each addressed to a faculty member—Frost, Orion. The packages were already torn open, their contents scattered.

With the combined glow of the moon, the light from their Shards, and the sharp clarity of Dark Vision, they managed to track down the remaining pieces.

A few more brass trinkets caught their eye, each bearing a sign of ownership. One lay beside a letter, its parchment brittle and yellowed at the edges—a small, intricately etched brass engraving hammer with Brutus's name carved delicately into the handle. Another piece came with a letter for the Archmage—a brass pocket watch, its polished surface reflecting the dim light. They gathered everything with care, avoiding direct contact with the brass, handling each item as though it might suddenly spring to life and bite.

Jace watched as Dex carefully wrapped the trinkets, Alice handling the letters. They worked in silence, the weight of the task hanging over them. The brass gleamed, its strange allure undiminished by the grime of the battlefield, each piece a mystery they had yet to solve.

"This wasn't just a random attack," Dex said, his voice tight. "These were meant for them. Someone's targeting the school."

Jace's jaw clenched. "If these packages had arrived... imagine the Archmage, Orion, or Frost slowly being possessed without even realizing it."

Dex shuddered. "Yeah. This was an attack. A damn clever one, too. Using deliveries to sneak past the defenses."

"Did it affect you the same when the ring was just in your inventory?" Jace asked.

Marcus nodded, grimly. "Maybe worse."

Dex cursed under his breath. "Then there's no way to know who else has one, if they've got it in their inventory."

Jace stood, a determined glare. "Let's get this stuff back. We need to tell Hades, Brutus, the Archmage—everyone. This isn't over."

With their grim discovery in tow, they began the trek back, a silence accompanying each step—dark and inevitable, like the encroaching shadow of a distant storm.

They rested that night beneath a blanket of stars, the silence between them as dark as the overcast sky. It wasn't the comfortable silence of friends, but the kind that grew heavy with unspoken words and unshed tears. The leaves fell from the trees as they walked, the only sound aside from the distant calls of unseen creatures.

Ell was the first to break the stillness, her voice low and steady. "We should make camp. Sleep a few hours. Then get back on the trail."

Jace only nodded, the star map in his hands catching the faint gleam of moonlight. It shimmered with ghostly light, marking their path through the coming darkness. The Traveler's Handbook, a relic of a forgotten time, held their route like an old memory. The journey was familiar, but the night had grown long, and familiarity bred no comfort here.

They set up camp with practiced efficiency, moving like the gears of a well-worn clock. Each action was mechanical, a rhythm born of necessity. It grew colder, the fire casting flickering shadows that stretched and twisted, like something alive.

Across the flames, Alice sat, her face bathed in the golden light. Her hands moved through the air, tracing symbols, and whispering words that made the fire jump and sputter in response. The ritual was all that stood between them and the darkness that waited beyond the reach of the fire's glow. Her voice was low, barely more than a breath.

Ell had cried when the horrors were fresh. Dex, in his way, tried to lighten the mood with jokes that fell flat before they even left his mouth. Marcus had retreated inward, isolated, intense. But Alice... Alice was a storm waiting to break. Silent. Still. And all the more dangerous for it. Jace watched her now, worry gnawing at his gut like a sickness. He knew too well what it meant to lock everything away until it broke you from the inside.

Marcus had already wrapped himself in his cloak, snoring like nothing in the world could touch him. Jace glanced at him, a flicker of amusement crossing his features, but it was short-lived. His eyes found Alice again, her movements slow, precise, like she was trying to hold herself together with every gesture.

They took turns keeping watch, each one a sentinel against the dark. But when it was Ell's turn, her eyes on the treeline, Jace couldn't sleep. Not with the tension that hung. Not with Alice sitting there, her hands still trembling from whatever weight she carried.

The fire crackled softly, the warmth a fleeting comfort against the night's chill. Without a word, she rose, slipping into the shadows at the edge of the camp. Jace watched her go, his instincts sharp as a blade. He stood to follow, his steps quiet, though the leaves underfoot betrayed him with a soft crunch.

Ell's eyes met his for the briefest of moments, a shared understanding passing between them. She nodded, her gaze steady, before returning to her watch.

Jace moved through the forest, following the faint sound of Alice's footsteps. The moonlight filtered through the trees, silver and cold, as he trailed her to a small pond, its surface smooth as glass. The silence here was different. Heavy. Personal. And then he heard it—her quiet sobs, breaking the stillness like ripples in the water.

He approached slowly, not wanting to startle her. She sat on a rotting log, her shoulders shaking with the force of emotions she had kept locked away for too long. Jace took a seat beside her carefully, the log groaning under their combined weight. He didn't speak. He just sat, his presence a quiet offer of comfort.

Alice turned to him, her tear-streaked face catching the moonlight. Her eyes were wide, the pain in them raw and unfiltered. She tried to smile, but it crumbled, fragile as a spider's web caught in the wind.

For a long while, neither of them spoke. The world faded away, leaving only the soft sound of her breathing, and the quiet hum of life all around them. Jace felt his heart twist in his chest, her pain echoing his own in a way he hadn't expected. He wanted to say something, anything, but the words didn't come. They were unnecessary, anyway.

When she reached for his hand, her fingers trembling as they wrapped around his, Jace knew. Knew that this was what she needed—no grand speeches, no hollow reassurances. Just the quiet truth of his presence.

They sat there, side by side, bound by shared grief and silent understanding. The darkness pressed in around them, but it felt less oppressive now, like something had shifted between them. The night was still -deep- and the road ahead was long, but in that moment, they were no longer lost. Just two souls, battered but unbroken, finding solace in each other's company.

Eventually, Alice's tears slowed, her breathing evened out, and the pressure in the air seemed to lift, just a little. A soft glow shimmered around her, catching Jace by surprise. Alice blinked, lifting her head as she felt something shift deep within. The glow intensified—sapphire light swirling around her, wrapping her in warmth. Jace watched, his eyes widening as the ethereal glow pulsed, then settled, a quiet power thrumming in the air. She looked at her hands, the light fading into her skin, leaving a tingling sensation. Bronze Three. She could feel it—an unexpected strength blossoming in her chest.

Alice looked up at Jace, her eyes still glistening but now with something else, something bright and new. Slowly, a smile formed on her lips, small but genuine, a spark of hope that hadn't been there before.

Jace squeezed her hand, a silent promise that she wasn't alone. Time stretched -became irrelevant, as they remained together, the stillness of the night settling around them like a warm cloak.

They didn't need words. Not now.

Chapter 49
High Council

As they arrived back to the campus, they drew more than a few stares. It wasn't hard to see why. Blood, dirt, and exhaustion clung to them like a second skin, and none of them had bothered to do anything about it. They were too numb, too spent, to care.

Students gawked as they passed, their eyes wide, faces a mix of shock and something close to fear. They looked at Jace and the others like they were a war party returning—not with fanfare, but with the grim echoes of whatever they'd faced still hanging around them.

A teacher spotted them—Frost. She cut across the courtyard, her expression a blend of curiosity and something close to irritation.

"What in the name of Heracles have you gotten yourselves into?" she said, her voice sharp but edged with concern. Molly trailed behind her.

"An odd smell," Molly said, her tone matter-of-fact, her nose wrinkling slightly. Her expression shifted, worry clouding her eyes as she steadied them, into an almost knowing look, as if she was all too familiar with the scent of death to ignore it.

Frost shook her head, pulling a glowing blue crystal from her inventory, the soft light pulsing between her fingers. "Let's get you cleaned up, shall we?"

She waved the crystal over them, and instantly, the grime vanished. The dirt, the blood, even the smell—all of it disappeared in a rush of magic. Their gear looked pristine again, though still worn, the fabric frayed and marked with slashes.

"Much better," Frost said, nodding in approval, though her eyes held a thousand questions she wasn't ready to ask.

Jace wasted no time, his voice steady though exhaustion hung on every word. "We need to see Theon."

She raised an eyebrow, her gaze sharp enough to draw blood. "I'll assume you mean Archmage Laviette. And tell me, what could a few students possibly need from him that's so urgent?"

Jace straightened, his eyes steady. "I'm afraid that's something only he should hear first. Trust me, it's important. We need to see him."

"Are we sure we can trust her?" Ell murmured, barely audible.

Jace leaned in, whispering back, "We have to trust someone. And she doesn't have any of the signs we've been seeing."

Dex piped up with his usual bluntness. "Any wild mood swings recently?"

The woman's eyes narrowed, her lips pursing. "I've never—what an impertinent question."

"Please," Jace cut in, a hint of desperation creeping into his voice. "We need to speak with him. Can you at least tell us where he is?"

She regarded them for a moment, her silence heavy as she weighed her options. Finally, she shook her head, her expression softening slightly, though her tone remained firm. "You'll have to wait. He's in a meeting with the Council. One I'm now late for, thanks to you."

"This is vital," Jace said, his voice urgent. "The school is under attack."

Her eyes flicked to Ell, appraising, skeptical. "Evidence. I assume you have it?"

Ell hefted the bag, dropping it with a dull thud at her feet. She undid the latch, the contents spilling open just enough to reveal the horror within.

"Don't touch it," Jace warned softly. "Just attempt to Inspect it."

She hesitated, then leaned down, her face blanching as her eyes went wide. "I see," she murmured, her earlier skepticism dissolving into something graver. "This way."

She led them through the winding paths of the campus, past buildings that loomed tall and unfamiliar, until they arrived at a secluded section. Jace had never been here before—a faculty-only office marked with a sign that read Council Members Only. A shimmering barrier of magic danced across the doorway.

She waved her hand, and the barrier flickered, then fizzled out, leaving a gap just wide enough for them to step through. The moment they entered, the air hit them—thick with tension, loud voices overlapping in a barrage of shouting.

"Outrageous!" Dranice snapped, his eyes blazing. "The Winter Games haven't been canceled in over four hundred years—not for war, not for the Dark One, and certainly not because Travelers are having trouble returning. If anything, we need them now more than ever!"

Brutus's brow furrowed, his voice a low rumble. "And you'd risk the lives of these students?"

"That's right, they are students. Not children." Dranice scoffed. "What good would coddling them do? Have you seen the way they act? Disobeying orders, running off into who-knows-where without a second thought. They act like they are still immortal–like this is all some silly game. They need discipline, they need structure—something to unify them before they scatter like leaves in the wind. The Games provide that. You, of all people, should understand the value of tempering iron."

Brutus crossed his arms, his face a mix of frustration and concern. "Iron can break, Dranice. Push them too hard and they shatter. The Games are a crucible, but these aren't ordinary times. They need to survive, not be thrown into a fire just to see if they can make it out intact."

Dranice's gaze hardened, his jaw set stubbornly. "Survival is exactly what they need to learn. The world isn't going to slow down or show mercy. You think you're protecting them, Brutus, but you're only delaying the inevitable."

Brutus shook his head. "Pushing them into the storm too soon is no better. They need time to be ready." Professor Brutus stood, his face flushed an uncomfortable shade of pink, his fists clenched as though he was holding back a storm of words.

On the opposite side, Professor Dranice Thorne, the Master of Games, sat forward and stiff in his chair. His beard hung like an untamed river cascading over a mouth pulled into a deep, etched scowl. It felt like a warning, one that made Jace straighten instinctively, a chill brushing the back of his neck.

"That's quite enough for now, Professors," the Archmage interjected, his tone brooking no argument. "We can continue this discussion later. At the moment, it appears we have visitors."

Professor Orion sat on his haunches beside him, his sleek, dark fur ruffled and disrupted by a bandage wound around his side. His steely eyes met Jace's, a watchful calm masking whatever pain or exhaustion lay beneath.

At the head of the table sat Archmage Theon Laviette, his presence commanding every shadow in the room. His expression was stern, eyes narrowing ever so slightly as they appraised the newcomers. He didn't speak—didn't need to. The stillness of his gaze did all the talking.

Silence spread across the council as the door closed behind Jace and his group with a soft thud, their eyes fixing on the intruders like predators assessing potential prey. The tension prickled along Jace's skin, and he took a careful step forward, feeling the eyes—watchful, critical—like a dozen arrows aimed straight at him.

No one spoke for a long moment.

Blackwood, who had been silently observing, finally spoke up, his brow furrowed. "What's all this about? And why are these students here?"

"Ah, now that is a tale worth knowing." The Archmage's tone softened, though a sense of gravity remained. "First, I owe you all an apology. For the past few months, Professor Frost and I have embarked on a secret quest. The secrecy of this quest, I admit, is something I must seek your forgiveness for. But I trust you will understand once I explain."

He paused, letting his words sink in. "Before this semester began, I started noticing strange signs around the campus. Individually, they were nothing remarkable—small things, almost mundane. But when seen together, they formed a troubling picture. Many of you know my history with the Dark One," he said, his voice hardening, "once upon a time, he was a friend. A mentor. Before he… changed."

A murmur spread through the room. The mention of the Dark One brought a cold chill, and even Jace could feel it in the tension that rippled through the crowd.

"His attacks have always been direct," the Archmage continued. "An overwhelming onslaught of undead and death, each of our fallen turned into another weapon against us."

"We do not need a lesson in our own history," Dranice Thorne interrupted, his tone clipped.

"Too true, Dranice," he replied with a slight nod. "But what you may not know is this—I suspect his methods have evolved. He knows he cannot attack us directly. Our defenses are too strong for that, and he learns. He adapts. He may be cruelty incarnate, but he is far from incapable of change."

He gestured broadly, the sleeves of his robes moved like billowing clouds. "With the incident involving the Sand Dome, I had my suspicions confirmed. I began to notice a handful of students acting strangely. It was never a single blatant incident, just whispers of something off. Something insidious. When pieced together, the evidence painted a concerning picture." He paused, letting his words hang in the air. "I suspect possessions."

A collective intake of breath filled the chamber. The assembled council members shifted uncomfortably in their seats. Even Blackthorn's usually stern expression seemed to soften into something somber, pensive.

Dranice scoffed, shaking his head. "Possessions would have been detected. The Hearth Stone is a safeguard against anyone possessed—it would have caught them."

"Oh yes," the Archmage nodded, a thin smile on his lips, "it is true that fully possessed individuals would be unable to pass through the Hearth Stone's wards. But I am not speaking of traditional possession. I speak of something more cunning. Possessions initiated here, within our boundaries, from the inside." He turned to the students who stood nearby. "And these young ones may have brought us the evidence we need."

He stood and stepped forward, holding out a hand. "May I?" he asked gently. Ell nodded, handing him the bag, her eyes widening as she watched.

The Archmage extended his other hand, his shard glowing with ethereal light. Threads of luminous energy coiled outwards, forming translucent hands that gently took hold of the items from within the bag. The cursed objects floated out—bloody packages and dark talismans—and settled on the table before them. They seemed clean, almost polished, despite the stains of dried blood, as if the evil within them refused to sully their surface.

The council members leaned forward, their eyes wide. Molly, who had been silent throughout, stood with her mouth slightly open, the color draining from her face.

A hush fell over the room as the Archmage looked up. "These," he said, his voice cutting through the silence, "are the tools of the Dark One's new game. A subtle infiltration, right under our noses. We have a fight ahead of us—not against a horde at our gates, but an enemy that already walks among us."

They all gasped, the gravity of his words settling over them like a shadow.

Chapter 50
Old Friends

"I'll assume you've all been waiting for shipments that never arrived," Theon said, the room's air thick with unspoken dread. He gestured to the pile of grimy parcels beside him. "Here's your mail."

The assembled group exchanged uneasy glances. Brutus spoke first, his gravelly voice breaking the silence. "You don't think..." he started, "...that we actually asked for these?"

"No, Professor Ironclad, I do not," the Archmage replied, his expression hardening. "Otherwise, I wouldn't be sharing this with you now. But whoever sent these was either unaware or already under the influence when they did."

Brutus' eyes narrowed, a crease of genuine worry forming between his brows. "But my parcel... it came from my brother and sister."

"A troubling possibility, no doubt." The Archmage gave a solemn nod. "Still, we can't rush to conclusions. There's a lot we don't know yet—how they came into possession of these items in the first place, how many of them are circulating, how long it takes for the curses to fully bind and the possession to occur. And then there's the difference between how it affects Travelers versus Citizens."

Silence fell heavy, the uncertainty pressing on them like a storm cloud about to burst.

Then Marcus spoke, surprising them all with a voice uncharacteristically fragile. "I... I might be able to help with that."

The others turned toward him, eyes wide. The Archmage, an unreadable expression settled on his ageless face, gave Marcus a slight nod. "Go on," he prompted.

Marcus swallowed. "I wore it... I wore one for weeks." His voice wavered but gained strength as he continued. "It was mailed to my father... I didn't realize what it was at first."

He recounted the nightmares—thick, endless nightmares that seeped into the waking world—and the growing impulse to do things he'd never imagined. He spoke of resisting, inch by inch, but feeling himself slip further away all the same.

Theon shifted, leaning in. "When did it get worse?" he asked, his voice soft, almost coaxing. "The effects, Marcus. Was there a trigger?"

Marcus took a moment, his brow furrowed in thought. "It was slow at first. Subtle. It felt like my own thoughts, like a voice hiding behind mine. But things escalated after... after the logout problem. That's when it became visceral, you know? I started hearing voices—ones that definitely weren't my own. That's what tipped me off."

The Archmage sighed. "As I feared," he murmured, his gaze fixed on some distant horizon only he could see. "Along with losing the ability to respawn, we've lost access to something else... something dear. When a Traveler respawns in Terra Mythica, the connection to our original bodies mitigates much of the damage—a buffer of sorts, a stable reference point, keeping us... tethered."

His gaze shifted back, capturing the eyes of each person in the room. "But now? Now, I suspect we haven't just been locked out. We might've been cut off from our earthly bodies altogether... if they even still live."

The words landed like a fist to the chest, taking the breath from the room. Jace felt the ground sway beneath him. His heart skipped, then picked up the beat, pounding in his ears.

If they even still live.

The notion rattled around in his head, each repetition feeling heavier. The world seemed to lurch, suddenly unsteady, and Jace clenched his jaw, forcing himself to stay grounded.

"Because of this," the Archmage continued, "when we die, or when a foreign influence takes hold, it attacks us directly—as though we were mere Citizens."

A heavy pause followed, pressing down like an anvil. Jace shifted uncomfortably, watching the grim expressions reflected across the room.

"You mentioned Gregor was one of the cursed," the Archmage said, his gaze settling on Marcus. "He's dead now. Has anyone seen or heard of him respawning?"

They all exchanged glances, the silence hanging thick between them. Finally, Brutus shook his head, voice low. "I doubt we will. His soul has likely followed the same path as any Citizen's—unable to withstand the pressure of the possession. Though..." He hesitated, casting a sideways look toward Jace, "...we won't know for sure without going to the source."

The Archmage turned, his stare drilling into Jace, pointed and un-yielding.

"This is all absurd," Professor Thorne interjected, voice dripping with disdain. "Travelers becoming Citizens? Students and faculty being possessed? Utter hogwash!"

"Careful, Thorne," Blackwood spoke up, his words laced with dark humor. "Keep talking like that, and you might reveal why you're our first suspect."

Thorne blustered, his face flushing an angry red as he stood. "I—why, I never—"

"Sit down, Dranice," the Archmage said with a tired sigh. "And Orion, enough with the jabs. I've known Dranice since he was a boy, and I assure you, he is acting precisely like himself." He shot a warning glance at Blackwood, who merely shrugged, a smirk lingering on his lips.

With a disgruntled huff, Thorne sank back into his seat, muttering under his breath.

"Now," the Archmage continued, his tone commanding attention, "we need to study these artifacts. Find some way to verify our suspicions."

"I've got just the thing," Brutus said, a gleam in his eye. He reached out, his hand brushing through the air before him in a way that suggested... well, something.

Jace raised an eyebrow. *Does Brutus have an inventory space?*

"Aha, there it is!" Brutus declared, triumphantly pulling a lantern seemingly from thin air—its silvery surface catching the dim light of the room.

He set it carefully on the table, everyone watching in tense silence. He pointed it towards the brass pocket watch—the very one meant for the Arch-mage—and flicked a small lever on its side. The front of the lantern opened, a circular iris widening until a dim glow began to pulse from within.

Then, in a flash, a beam of light shot out, striking the watch. A terrible, shrill sound pierced the air—a screech, a howl, something that wasn't just mechanical. It was a scream.

"Turn it off," the Archmage barked, a note of urgency breaking through his usual composure.

Brutus reached out, but the moment his fingers touched the lantern, they recoiled, as if burned.

The scream grew louder, reverberating off the stone walls. It felt like it was slicing through them, a force neither of this world nor the next. Jace clamped his hands over his ears, the shrill sound slicing through the air like a shard of glass. The pitch climbed higher, relentless, burrowing into his skull. He gritted his teeth, his eyes squeezing shut as if he could will the noise away. The world seemed to fold in on itself, the sound pulling everything taut, a tension that hummed through his bones.

"Brutus!" the Archmage shouted, his voice almost drowned out by the unearthly wail.

The High Council had their shards out in a heartbeat, ready to blast that device into oblivion. And then the world...paused. The walls took a breath, bowing in, then exhaling like a sigh from some ancient, annoyed deity.

No one moved.

Except Jace. He blinked, looking around, the universe frozen, everyone else caught mid-action. Was it happening again?

And then he saw him. A young man, lounging in the corner like he was waiting for a train, feet propped up on the table, casually observing.

"Jack," Jace said, his voice low.

Jack gave a lazy wave. "What's up, kid? Said I'd keep an eye on you? And here we are—are you seriously trying to rip open my universe again?" The boyish grin was there, but the face was older, maybe twenty-something now, like he'd skipped a few years for fun.

Jace sighed. "I'm just trying to survive it."

Jack nodded, slowly. He looked older still, hair sprouting from his chin and turning into a ridiculous beard that dragged along the floor as he stood. "Ah, survival," he said, voice deepening. "Such an interesting goal. Ever think about trying to really live, instead?" He gave Jace a thoughtful look, and then—blink—the beard vanished, Jack was young again, all roguish charm.

He strolled around the room, inspecting the scene, leaning in close to the lantern, squinting like he might uncover some secret written on the light.

"Are you here to help?" Jace asked, weary.

"Oh, worlds no," Jack said, chuckling. "Helping would be... disastrous. I'm just the trees, my boy, waving in the wind. Never the wind itself."

Jace frowned. "So who's the wind, then?"

Jack tilted his head, eyes glinting mischievously. "Haven't you figured that out yet? It's you, Jace. All of you—Citizens, Travelers, whatever you want to call yourselves. You're the wind. I'm just... here. Watching it blow."

Jack paused, then leaned in conspiratorially. "Are you ready to ask the question yet?"

Jace furrowed his brow. "What question?"

Jack grinned. "The one Persephone already answered. The one you're too scared to ask."

Jace felt a flush rise in his face. The old anger surged. Enough of this cryptic nonsense. He had been through hell and back, and what he needed now were answers.

"Are you blocking the logout?" he snapped.

Jack laughed, an amused glint in his eye. "Oh no, no. Wrong question, Jace. Which is sad," he took on a mock frown. "The answer is something you could desperately use for what lies ahead."

Jace's patience snapped. "I've had enough of this!"

Jack didn't flinch, just smiled in that infuriating, knowing way. "Oh, we're not even close to enough. This is only your beginning, Child of the Grey."

Jace's lips tightened. "What does that even..."

Jack held up a hand, cutting him off. "Wait. Do you hear that?"

"What?" Jace started to ask, but Jack was already gone, just a wink left hanging in the air.

The world jerked back into motion. The ear-splitting shriek of the pocket watch returned, tearing through the silence like a blade.

And then, without warning, there was yet another interruption. A blinding light filled the room. The shriek of the watch cut off abruptly, silenced as the Device melted into molten slag beneath a jagged beam of lightning that seemed to crackle from every direction at once.

The light blared from the doorway where Jack and the group had first entered. The door flung open, revealing three immense figures—larger-than-life, statuesque, and brimming with power.

Zeus, Poseidon, and Hades stood shoulder to shoulder, a triumvirate of gods in their full glory. Zeus, at the center, was broad-shouldered and imperious, his hair and beard a tempest of swirling white, his eyes like flashes of a storm that hadn't decided yet whether it wanted to rain or rage. He radiated authority, a presence that commanded the very air to behave.

Poseidon, beside him, looked as if he had stepped from the depths of the ocean. His robes moved as though stirred by underwater currents, his hair a frothing tide of blue-green, salt-crusted. His eyes were cold, vast as the ocean depths, and held secrets older than memory.

And Hades, larger and more imposing than Jace remembered, wore darkness like a shroud. His form seemed less physical, more of a silhouette edged in smoke and shadow, and his eyes—deep and thoughtful—carried an ember glow, like the last light of a dying fire.

Everyone in the room dropped to their knees at the sight of them. Everyone except Jace. Zeus's gaze swept over the crowd, pausing on Jace, eyes narrowing in a look that felt like he was scrutinizing a fly that had dared to land on the face of his domain.

Before Jace could decide how to respond, Alice yanked him down beside her. He landed with an awkward yelp, his knees smacking the floor.

Hades caught Jace's eye, and a glimmer of amusement passed through his expression—something fleeting, there and gone like a shadow.

Zeus spoke, and his voice was the crack of thunder on the horizon, the rumble that warned of the storm to come. "Children, Travelers, Citizens, I thank you for securing these devices. They are more dangerous than you know, far beyond your ability to destroy without unmaking this very realm."

His words held weight, like each syllable was forged from iron and had to be borne with effort by everyone listening. The echoes seemed to linger, resonating in their bones.

"We shall take them now, for they do not belong to this plane," Zeus continued, each word final, without question or pause. "They are not of this realm, and they shall be returned from whence they came. If any others are found—use this."

He dropped a golden coin onto the table before him. It landed without a bounce or a roll, just a solid, heavy thud as if the earth itself had accepted the burden.

"Do not presume you can handle these alone. Call upon us," Zeus added, his eyes lingering on the gathered crowd as if daring someone to argue.

Poseidon stepped forward, his trident held loosely at his side, its edges glistening like sunlight on waves. He gave a curt nod before they turned to leave.

Hades hesitated, hanging back for a moment, his gaze catching Jace's. It wasn't a glare, nor the cold regard of Zeus. There was something else, something that spoke of shared history, and of secrets half-spoken.

Jace seized the moment, scrambling to his feet. "Hades," he said, "we still need to know—how do we find out who possesses these devices?"

Hades smiled, but it was the kind of smile that offered no comfort. "You already have access to the knowledge you need," he said, his voice like distant embers crackling, "though perhaps for fewer hours each day than you'd prefer. Seek the knowledge that resides within."

Hades made to leave, but Jace wasn't done. "One more thing," he called out, the audacity of it turning heads and making jaws drop. "Did Gregor come through?"

Hades paused. The air grew still, and a hush fell over the room as the god considered. "As you are my Chosen, I will say this much—his soul has found its rightful place, though not in the way he once was."

He moved as if to go but paused again, turning slightly. He tossed a coin to Jace—a dark one, black as obsidian and as heavy in his hand as the night itself. "If you find more," Hades spoke, the words flowing into Jace's mind without sound, just a presence, an echo of thought, before he vanished, dissolving into the light.

And then the gods were gone, as quickly as they had come. The light faded, leaving the room dim and stunned.

The professors exchanged glances, muttering to one another, debating quietly what Hades might have meant by "having access to the knowledge."

Jace and his friends did their best to look as baffled as everyone else, though the quick glances they shared spoke otherwise.

It wasn't long before the High Council dismissed them with stern warnings, ordering them not to pursue this matter further, to leave it to those "better equipped." Everyone nodded, giving their solemn agreement, though some agreements were less honest than others—particularly on the subject of not looking for trouble.

Chapter 51
Last Minute

It was just two days until the Midnight Festival, and they had to buckle down and get serious about the preparations.

A buzz had swept across campus ever since the Society of Dionysus had thrown their full support behind the event being hosted in the Fields Below, turning the preparations into a full-blown frenzy. Jace might have backed out—time was tighter than ever—but now there was no turning back. Everyone was planning to show up at midnight in two days.

They needed to spend every waking moment on preparations—buckets of Flavor Saver, food coordination, decorations, everything. With how much time they'd all be down there, there was something Jace needed to do, someone Jace needed to talk to.

After laying it all out, Jace had given her the space to consider it in her own time. It might've helped that, earlier, she'd quietly spent a few hours crouched behind a potted plant, watching them interact from a safe distance. There was something unexpectedly reassuring about the way his friends bickered—how they stumbled through disagreements, patched things up, and kept each other afloat despite their flaws. It wasn't perfect, but it was real. And maybe that was enough. After a stretch of silence, her gaze softened, and with a slow, almost hesitant nod, she gave her answer.

"If you want," Jace said gently, "you can always come back here. And if the party gets to be too much, this room will be yours for the night. No one will bother you, I promise. I'll make sure it's off-limits."

She nodded.

"Are you ready to meet them?" he asked, his eyes searching hers.

Shadow's gaze moved, flickering briefly over the soft-painted sky, before settling back on him. She didn't answer right away. Instead, she stood still, the magic wind tousling her hair, her eyes deep with thought. Then, with the

kind of shaky confidence that only comes from stepping into the unknown, she nodded—like a child bracing for their first day of school.

Jace decided to introduce everyone one at a time, bringing them
individually to her home in the Catacombs. The upgrades had changed the
place dramatically since the last time he was there.

Now, it barely resembled a catacomb at all. The ceiling, once a
heavy, brooding mass of stone, had become a bright sky, magically painted in swirling hues of lavender and blue. Tall grass covered the ground,
shifting softly in an invisible breeze, while wisps floated and glimmered
like spirits on the wind. It felt ethereal, like a lost elven forest—a place
suspended somewhere between dreams and reality.

It was the perfect home for Shadow.

She stood there, bare feet sinking slightly into the soft earth, her
presence as much a part of this mystical landscape as the swaying grass and
the luminous sky. Jace approached her, heart pounding slightly against his
ribs. He moved closer, his voice gentle, careful, as if his words might shatter
the fragile moment.

Jace swallowed, his heart easing a fraction. He decided to start
with Alice. He wasn't sure why, but he felt the most nervous about this
introduction. Maybe it was because he wanted Shadow to like her, to find
a kindred spirit in Alice's calm presence.

Alice was waiting at the entrance, a look of understanding in her
eyes as Jace led her into the Catacombs. She didn't ask questions, didn't react with surprise at the transformation of the place—she merely followed,
her eyes softening as they took in the dreamlike landscape, her steps gentle
on the grass. When her gaze fell on Shadow, she didn't look to Jace for
explanation. She simply smiled, her eyes crinkling in a quiet warmth that
only deepened as she approached.

Jace hung back, his breath caught in his throat as he watched.
Alice stopped a few paces away, letting the silence settle between them.
Then, she knelt down, fingers brushing the ground until they found a
small wildflower. She plucked it, her movements careful, and held it out
to Shadow. No words, no expectations—just a flower, an invitation.

Shadow hesitated, her gaze flitting to Jace for a brief moment before
drifting back to Alice. And then she moved, her fingers reaching out, her touch

barely grazing Alice's as she took the flower. Slowly, she tucked it behind her ear, a shy smile touching her lips.

Alice's smile widened, the same quiet warmth in her eyes as she nodded, taking a step back, giving Shadow the space to decide the pace. Jace let out a breath he hadn't realized he'd been holding. Somehow, it felt like a fragile bridge had been built—delicate, but there, spanning the space between Shadow and the rest of them.

Shadow didn't speak, but there was something in her posture, a softening that hadn't been there before, and Alice seemed to recognize it. She glanced at Jace, a flicker of understanding passing between them—no surprise, no questions, just acceptance. Jace could only smile back, grateful for Alice's patience.

Maybe, just maybe, this was how the world could open up for Shadow—one gentle, quiet step at a time.

He chose to leave Marcus alone for now—Marcus had made it clear he needed these two days to himself. The group didn't question it; he hadn't exactly left any space for them to do so.

Next, Jace brought in Ell. She followed him into the Catacombs, her usual energy toned down, though still vibrant enough to make Shadow take a half-step back. Ell caught herself, and gave a small, warm wave instead of her usual exuberance. "Hey there," she said, her voice softer, smiling in a way that wasn't overwhelming. Shadow watched her, cautious but curious, and after a long pause, returned the wave. Ell let out a breath, her smile growing. It wasn't perfect, but it was progress, and Jace felt a weight lift off his shoulders.

Dex was next. He approached casually, as if there was no reason for tension at all. He glanced up at the ceiling, admiring the swirling sky above. "Nice place," he remarked, giving Shadow a nod without any expectation. "I'm Dex." He kept it simple, offering nothing more, and just waited. Shadow didn't say anything, but she didn't look away either, her gaze lingering on him with an unreadable expression. It was enough, Jace thought—Dex had a way of making things easy without trying, and that seemed to work.

Molly was the last to step forward. She offered no words; words were clumsy things, too blunt for what she had to say. Instead, she moved. Her hands rose like the promise of dawn, her feet gliding softly over the grass, each step deliberate, a quiet communion with the earth.

Jace and the others watched, bewildered, unsure if they were witness-
ing a ritual or a memory being relived.

Each gesture seemed to live within her, like a ripple passing through
water, flowing from her shoulders down to her hips, her arms carving slow arcs
through the air. Her legs moved with a kind of gentle precision, a grace that
spoke in hushed tones. It was almost a dance, but not for spectacle—each sway,
each shift fell into a secret rhythm only she could hear, something ancient and
soft as the soil beneath her feet. The grass seemed to lean into her, the blades
bending willingly under her bare soles, as though they, too, understood the
language she spoke in silence.

Shadow's eyes lit up, watching Molly's silent rhythm. For a moment,
her own body seemed frozen, then it responded like a chord struck to resonate,
her feet lifting, her arms following, her hands mimicking Molly's in graceful
arcs. The two moved together, an unspoken choreography—steps crossing over
the grass, fingers trailing through the air, weaving meaning in silence. It was a
language that flowed easily between them, carried by the swaying of their bodies
-the subtle shifting of their weight, the delicate way their forms mirrored each
other.

Jace watched, spellbound, as Shadow's rigid stance softened, the tension uncoiling from her shoulders. Her body seemed to lighten, each movement growing fluid as though she were learning to breathe again. She matched
Molly's rhythm seamlessly, their silent dance becoming something shared—a
conversation in motion.

They moved like reflections, a dance of understanding that needed no
words. For the first time, Shadow seemed truly free, her usual sharpness melting
into something softer. This was what she had needed most: a connection that
reached beyond language, a communion that asked nothing but presence.

And then, without warning, they both stopped. Shadow looked at
Molly, something profound flickering in her gaze. Molly returned the stare, her
eyes wide, serious for just a heartbeat longer. It could have ended there—something sacred, still, a moment suspended.

But instead, a grin tugged at the corner of Molly's mouth, and then
Shadow's lips twitched, and that was all it took. Laughter broke between them
like a dam burst.

Shadow fell back, collapsing into the grass, Molly following in kind.
They laughed until they were breathless, tangled in the green beneath them,

their joy rising into the air, bright and clear. Jace couldn't help but smile, feeling the heaviness of everything lift, even just a little, with their shared, unrestrained laughter.

The others could only stare at Molly, dumbfounded.

"How?" was all Jace could manage.

"Everyone speaks if you know the language," Molly said, glancing at them. "And she's fluent in Voiceless—a language of spirits who've lost their ability to speak. I saw her speaking it when you were talking with her." She paused, then added matter-of-factly, "She has quite the potty mouth, too."

They kept staring at Molly, speechless.

"What? You didn't know?" Molly grinned, one eyebrow arching playfully.

"So, she's been trying to talk to me this whole time?"

Shadow's hands flowed with a graceful rhythm, her eyes glinting with mischief. Molly burst into laughter, her smile growing wider. "She says," Molly translated through her laughter, "that Jace kind of looks like a startled chicken right now. And, oh, that he really needs to lighten up."

A ripple of smiles spread across the group.

Molly's smile never faded as she spoke without speaking. "It's a fascinating thing; a sort of ghost sign language," she said to Jace, her gaze still fixed on Shadow, her hands moving in tandem. "She knows it better than I do," Shadow responded with fluid gestures, her eyes focused and bright. Molly laughed again, nodding in response. Their exchange was silent, yet rich with meaning. Jace realized then, that for all the time he had spent with Shadow, there were still vast parts of her he hadn't yet glimpsed. And maybe, just maybe, this was the beginning of her letting more of those hidden worlds be seen.

They had one day left. Reginald hovered near the cauldron, his ghostly form flickering with a sour expression that could curdle milk. His translucent arms were crossed, and his glare was aimed squarely at Jace, who was elbow-deep in potion-making.

"What's with the face, Reg?" Jace asked, not even looking up, a grin tugging at his lips. "You look like someone stole your ectoplasm."

Reginald huffed, the sound echoing as if it were pulled from another plane entirely. "Mount Olympus on a cracker, no, kid, it's not some grand ghostly dignity thing," he groused, waving a hand as if to swat away the very idea. "This just sounds like extra work for me. You know, the guy who has to clean up after whatever cosmic dumpster fire you're starting here."

Jace gave a snort of laughter, sprinkling a pinch of silver dust into the brew. "Oh, come on. Think of it as an adventure. Besides, doesn't the afterlife get, I dunno, boring?"

"Yeah, nothing says excitement like cleaning up potion explosions," Reginald shot back, rolling his spectral eyes. "And do I look bored to you? I got crosswords and cable reruns in The Great Beyond, thank you very much. I'm living the dream—if you count being dead as living."

The rest of the group trickled into the room, casting cautious glances at the grumpy specter. Dex was the first to break the silence, giving Reginald a half-hearted salute. "Hey, Reg. Looking particularly ghostly today. Extra translucent, really."

"Save the flattery, junior," Reginald grumbled, his form wavering as he moved closer to the cauldron. "I don't need cheerleaders, I need you not making a mess."

Alice grinned, leaning on the table. "Come on, Reg. It won't be that bad. Besides, I think you secretly like the chaos. Gives you something to complain about."

For the last two days, every hour she wasn't in the Fields Below, Alice had pored over every page of the library's restricted section, her eyes scanning until they stung, relentlessly chasing the trail of Hades' cryptic clue.

She persisted, hour by stolen hour, piecing together the fragments. She wished her tome-copying ability would work—normally her spellbook allowed her to create perfect duplicates of any text, inscribing it into the infinite pages of her tome. But the Book of Demons had an enchantment far beyond her usual magic, one that blocked any direct transcription. So she'd have to do it the old-fashioned way—the really old-fashioned way—ink, quill, and patience.

Jace's task was as grand as it was tedious—enough of the Flavor Saver to fuel the entire student body. Jace stirred the concoction in massive cauldrons, the thick liquid swirling with an almost hypnotic sheen.

Fortunately, his latest upgrades let him manage several pots at once, each one dutifully stirring itself with an enchanted ladle. Still, he was beginning to understand why the school chef was always so hard on his utensils—keeping these magical tools in line was an art that required more finesse, and banging, than he'd expected. Which Reginald was more than happy to handle himself.

The increased quantity dulled the potion's potency and shortened its duration, but it would last through the night, which was all that mattered.

It wouldn't be gourmet cuisine, but it would be a definite upgrade from the usual bland sawdust the students were accustomed to.

Dex had insisted on helping, though "help" was a generous term. Jace found himself cleaning up after Dex more often than not, but he couldn't help but smile at his enthusiasm. Nimble with his hands but utterly hopeless at potions, Dex's presence somehow made the labor less draining. By the time the potion was nearly ready, Dex, Ell, and Jace had all used their Focused EXP points, nudging themselves further up the ranks—Ell and Dex reached Bronze Three, and Jace started his climb towards Bronze Four, the progress small but steady, every bit earned.

The Fields Below had been transformed for the Midnight Festival, decked out in loudly eerie decor. There were shadowy corners and flickering lights—dark but laced with a sort of grim humor. The aesthetic was all Ell's doing, with Molly's assistance. Together, they'd brought a weird charm to the otherwise somber vaults.

"Think we can trust her?" Dex leaned in close, his voice low as he made a show of sprinkling something mysterious over the cauldron.

Jace squinted at the so-called addition, catching the unmistakable shape of lotus leaves. "You know, you could actually help instead of just pretending," he muttered, snatching the leaves from Dex before they could doom the whole concoction. "These would turn the Flavor Saver into a Flavor Destroyer."

Dex just grinned, unfazed, his fingers now wandering through the scattered ingredients on the table. He nudged a jar aside, then another, barely paying attention. "I'm talking about Molly. She gives me the creeps, man."

Jace shot him a look, his eyes narrowing for a moment before softening. "Molly's good people. At least, she's been to me. I think she's safe. And besides—"

He broke off, glancing over to where Molly was untangling Shadow from a mess of black and orange streamers, the corners of Molly's mouth quirking up as Shadow tried her best to look indifferent.

"—Shadow seems to trust her," Jace finished, a hint of a smile forming. "That's good enough for me."

Dex sighed dramatically, tilting his head.

Alice hurried down the spiral staircase to the Fields Below, her breath slightly short from excitement. Her wide eyes were bright with something new—a glint of understanding. She held a piece of paper, smudged ink, and hastily scrawled notes covering its surface.

"I figured it out!" she blurted out, barely waiting for her feet to hit the floor.

Everyone paused. Ell, halfway through hanging a garland of withered roses, lowered her hands, and Molly tilted her head. Dex, who was pretending to be useful by organizing potion vials, froze mid-reach.

"What did you figure out?" Jace asked, squinting over the lip of the giant cauldron, curiosity piqued.

Alice thrust the paper at him. "Here. It's a plant—a type of flower. It's decorative, not poisonous to us." She traced her finger over the messy script. "But when I found this in the book, my deity gave me an EXP burst, and these lines here lit up."

Jace took the paper, reading the scribbled lines aloud. "When petal meets brew, demons find themselves unnerved, stomachs turned."

Alice nodded, her excitement almost infectious. "I bought as much as I could find."

Dex leaned over Jace's shoulder, peering at the note. "So... what? We just wave flowers at them? Maybe make them a bouquet?"

"Or," Alice said, her eyes flicking towards the cauldron, a grin tugging at her lips, "we add it to the brew."

Jace straightened up, an immediate frown pulling at his face. "No. It'll ruin the potion. We worked hard to get this right."

Ell gave him a look, one eyebrow arching. Alice mirrored her, their expressions an almost comical mirror of disbelief.

Jace sighed. "It's already so watered down... no one's going to appreciate how good it should've been." He hesitated for a beat, then reluctantly took the bundle of flowers Alice handed him. With a resigned shake of his head, he added the petals to the mix, watching them dissolve into the swirling brew.

Then, a small cough drew their attention, and they turned to see Molly. Her face, usually hidden behind a mask of blank attentiveness, now bore a look of conflicted determination. As a teacher's aide, she carried out some of the Archmage's directives, but there was a sparkle of mischief in her eyes that Jace hadn't anticipated.

"As a junior member of the Hero's Guild, I feel it is my duty," she began, her voice carrying an edge of formality. She paused, letting the silence stretch just enough to cause a stir of uncertainty among them. Then a slow smile crept across her face. "To ensure you all do this properly. If you're going to break the rules, we might as well do it with a bit of finesse. Add a touch of oleander and silver. It'll mask the taste of the flower."

They exchanged glances, a smile spreading across the room like a spark caught on dry leaves. Molly, her polished poise unraveling into something more earnest, was shedding her reserve, stepping closer into their circle. With the potion bubbling before them and the Archmage's instructions to "leave it to the qualified" dissolving into irrelevance, she was no longer merely a teacher's aide or a junior guild member—in that moment, she was simply one of them.

Jace watched the group gather around Molly, their laughter quiet. It was a comforting sight, one that made the room feel just a bit warmer, but there was still a tug in his chest.

Dex gave a dramatic shrug. "Well, now we wait to see if we've invented demon detection or just doomed the entire campus to a night of explosive regrets."

Jace groaned, rubbing his temples. "There goes our reputation as chefs." He shot a helpless glance at Alice, but there was no sympathy to be found.

She took a careful step back, hands raised in mock surrender. "Nope, don't even think about it. I don't want my name anywhere near this concoction. You two are on your own."

Dex patted Jace's shoulder, his grin barely concealed. "Cheer up, man. We'll always know the quality of your potions."

Jace looked down at the potion, the flowers swirling as they dissolved into the murky liquid. He sighed again, deeper this time.

The cauldron gurgled ominously, the last of the petals vanishing beneath the surface. Silence fell over the room as they all held their breath. Whatever they'd just made, it was bound to be... interesting.

Chapter 52
The Star Ceremony

T he Hero's Hall stretched impossibly, as if reality itself had bowed to the whimsy of magic. The grandeur wasn't merely in its size—though it was vast enough to host every one of the seven thousand students, dignitaries, and visitors without the slightest sense of crowding—but in the subtle elegance that adorned every inch of its newly enchanted space. The ceiling vaulted far above, a magnificent dome that mirrored the night sky. Silver stars glided across its surface, streaks of cosmic light, shimmering just beyond reach. Every few moments, a shooting star blazed a bright, fleeting path that drew murmurs of appreciation from the arriving guests.

Jace stood on the red carpet leading to the entrance, a thin layer of dusk still clinging to the horizon behind him. The golden hour painted everything in warm, liquid light, catching the shimmer of formalwear, the elegance of gowns, and the pressed suits of those gathered. Jace's fingers fidgeted against his side, adjusting the cuff of his sleeve as a wave of nerves rolled through him. He had spent what he could afford on this night, dressing himself in an attire fit for the Society of Hades—a dark, onyx-black suit with subtle embroidery in crimson thread, coiling like twisting smoke along his sleeves. His jacket was a long tailcoat, its silken lining glinting like the surface of still water under moonlight, and beneath, a vest the color of blood, with buttons of polished obsidian. The whole ensemble felt weighty, not because of the fabric, but because of the image it portrayed—a fleeting comfort to be draped in such shadows, something that whispered he belonged.

Beside him, Dex wore a grin that was as much a part of his outfit as his Hermes attire—an ensemble of deep gray with accents of gold, a cape clasped at the shoulder with a glistening winged pin. Dex had been flirting shamelessly with the stream of students walking by, and his gaze darted about, catching and releasing smiles, until his eyes widened.

Jace followed his friend's gaze, and his words caught somewhere between his chest and his throat.

Ell, Molly, and Alice approached, and for a moment, it felt as if time itself had slowed. Molly walked with effortless poise, her gown seemingly conjured from mist and shadow, with silvery threads glistening in the shifting fabric. There were symbols of Hecate—a trinity knot nestled into the pattern, a necklace that hung delicately at her throat, its amulet a dark moonstone that carried a soft glow, matched in her eyes.

Ell moved with the self-assurance of one born to command. Her gown was fitting for a champion of Athena, woven in silvery greens and layered with hints of armor-like detail—a shimmering bodice that showed both beauty and strength. Ell stood there, her long brown hair swept up in an intricate design, a delicate balance of braids and curls that framed her face like a crown.

The rich green of her dress seemed to pull at the olive undertones in her skin, deepening the warmth of her complexion. The gown flowed around her, hugging her frame in a way that was both elegant and effortlessly alluring, the fabric catching the light with each subtle movement. Her eyes, a sharp contrast to her warm tones, sparkled with mischief, and the faintest touch of gold in her earrings caught the light as she tilted her head, that mocking smile playing on her lips. She radiated a confidence that was nearly regal, tempered by a hint of mischief that made her presence impossible to ignore.

Then there was Alice. The breath caught hardest when Jace's gaze fell upon her. Her dress was deceptively simple at first glance—a fluid, ivory material, almost translucent in its delicacy, with subtle layers underneath that prevented the eye from understanding its depth. Gold filigree spiraled gently around her sleeves, her waist, and her collar. A diadem rested on her brow; a silver chain with a single sapphire at its center, glinting each time the fading light above caught it.

Her hair, usually a bright blonde, had been enchanted to a deeper, almost molten gold, each strand shimmering as though they were but kisses of sunlight. The golden waves fell around her shoulders, and two long, waving curls framed her face, cascading down gracefully to her chest. The glow gave her an ethereal aspect, as if she were a vision from another world.

Her eyes found Jace's, and for a heartbeat, the rest of the world melted away—no bustling students, no grand hall, just the quiet moment between them. Her soft smile was enough to dissolve every word that had formed on his tongue, leaving only the unspoken warmth hanging in the air between them. His heart quickened, and she responded with a gentle blush, her eyes lowering slightly under the intensity of his gaze.

"Well, look at you all," Dex was the first to recover, offering a grinning half-bow.

Ell's red lips curled into a mocking frown, but the corners betrayed her with a faint smile.

"Look at me?" She let her gaze linger on him for a long beat. "Finally learned how to put on a suit, I see. I hope I haven't seen the last of your roguish charm, Dex." Her eyes sparkled, holding a warmth her words tried to mask.

Dex turned away, uncharacteristically shy, his grin faltering for just a moment.

Jace broke the moment with a clap, his voice full of teasing admiration. "I didn't know it was possible, Ell. You've managed to make young Dex here blush."

Before the banter could continue, a high-pitched voice cut in from the side. Marcus approached, his entrance marked by the shimmering reflection of golden threads in his suit, streaked with bolts of blue lightning that pulsed faintly with every step.

"Ah, the gang's all here," Marcus said, spreading his arms as if to embrace the whole gathering. His smile was broad - well-rehearsed, his energy taut with effort, but it was clear he was genuinely trying.

They each locked arms with a partner.

Jace found himself next to Alice as they began moving inside, her arm resting gently in his. Dex had paired with Ell, and Marcus politely extended his arm to Molly, who quirked an eyebrow at him before giving a small, gracious nod. They moved forward together, an odd mix woven into a cohesive whole.

The inside of the Hero's Hall was breathtaking, the foyer opening up into a space grander than the outside could have ever suggested. It was like stepping into another world—a theater too splendid to be anything mundane. Plush carpeting swept beneath their feet, the fabric seemingly stitched from the dark night sky, sprinkled with tiny, glowing stars. A massive chandelier hung above the main entryway, a cascade of glass and crystal that refracted light into countless shimmering shards. From the open foyer, the theater beyond could be seen, each seat rising in a tiered pattern around a central stage, upon which orbs of light floated lazily, their glow soft and inviting.

Around them, the room was a living constellation of the gods—students dressed in garments that paid homage to their chosen deities. To Jace's left, a group from Poseidon's Society moved like a tide, dressed in seafoam blues and greens, their robes rippling with each step as though waves broke along the fabric. Across the way, the students of Hephaestus stood with their copper-threaded jackets, blacksmith motifs woven into their attire, subtle glimmers of ember red flickering at their hems.

A cluster of Apollo's devotees moved through the crowd, their garments adorned with radiant sunbursts of gold and white, shining in the low light. Each of their cloaks had a glinting emblem—a lyre or a sun—stitched just over the heart. Beside them, the followers of Artemis stood quieter, wrapped in moonlit silvers and shadowy greens, cloaks pinned with small crescent brooches, the fabric trailing behind like midnight mist.

Jace spotted Hermes' followers scattered through the room—dexterous and agile even in formalwear. Each wore a different shade, though all bore winged pins, the insignia of their swift-footed patron. In stark contrast, a few of Ares' adherents passed by, clad in crimson sashes and sharp, almost martial attire, as if even a ball was but another battlefield to conquer.

The room shimmered, each group a living homage to their patron god, the blending colors, symbols, and the gentle clang of accessories forming a vivid mosaic of Olympus itself.

They were led to their seats, positioned by the rank each had achieved—clusters of students of similar standing seated together. Jace found himself beside Molly in the Bronze Three section. He couldn't help his curiosity, leaning toward her as they settled.

"I thought you'd be higher ranked, given...well, everything," Jace said softly.

Molly turned her head, her smile a little wistful. "The step between Three and Four is no small thing, Jace. And being an Aide to Professors... well, it comes with perks and drawbacks. I possess access to knowledge, to old, arcane secrets passed down through millennia, but that means less time to life, to gain experience. As with all great things, a cost is paid."

Jace couldn't help but wonder if Molly realized just how peculiar she sounded sometimes, her words often teetering between profound wisdom and enigmatic riddles, like she lived half a breath removed from everyone else's reality.

"Yes, I do," Molly said, a slight smile playing on her lips.

Jace blinked. Had he said that out loud? He glanced at her, trying to read the expression in her eyes.

She simply smiled and nodded. The lights dimmed slightly, drawing attention toward the center stage. He glanced sideways at Alice. She was watching the orbs hovering above, her eyes wide in awe. Jace let himself smile, the feeling of nervousness settling into something warmer. It's strange the things we are nervous about and the things we aren't.

The night was beginning, and somehow, the unknown seemed not quite as daunting, his gaze drifting between his friends, knowing he wasn't stepping into it alone.

The four high council professors stepped onto the stage, each taking a seat with deliberate grace, facing the audience.

The Archmage strode to the podium at the center, his wooden staff tapping rhythmically against the floor. His robes were a cascade of white and gold, flowing like liquid light, each thread seemingly woven from dawn itself. He paused, letting silence take root, his presence enough to snuff out even the murmurs at the back of the hall. His eyes scanned the crowd, and in that gaze, there was nothing soft, no warmth—only focus and expectation. When he spoke, his voice cut through the quiet like a blade, sharp and without preamble.

"The Star Ceremony," he began, his tone not indulgent of grand speeches, "is an annual acknowledgment of the progress among our students and faculty—marked through the stars and ranks earned."

He didn't bother with any theatrics, didn't call for applause. There was a stillness that held the room, every word hanging in the air like a challenge. It was something Jace was getting used to—the Archmage's way of being so brutally direct that it left no room for misunderstanding.

"Tonight, we celebrate what has been accomplished so far, and we rejoice in our growth. But," his voice dropped a notch, "tonight, while recognizing what we've achieved, we must also acknowledge the necessity for more. More progress. More resilience."

A murmur rippled through the crowd, anticipation and unease trading hands beneath the polite façade of the gathered students.

"And so," he continued, "we are officially announcing this year's Winter Games."

Jace felt a shiver run down his spine, his muscles tensing as if an electric current had passed through him. The Winter Games. Of course, the words hung there, almost like an accusation, daring them to react. Jace glanced around and saw the same look of shock etched on the faces of the students around him. No one had said it aloud before, not so bluntly. The Archmage had, once again, yanked it out of the realm of whispers and fears and planted it directly before them.

"Many of you may think the Games should be canceled this year," the Archmage went on. His eyes shifted to one of the council members—Brutus, whose lips were pressed into a thin, disapproving line. Dranice Thorne, on the other hand, was nodding, a self-satisfied smile tugging at the corners of his mouth.

"We have discussed it," the Archmage said. "And it is true that the Winter Games are known for their exceedingly high casualty rate. But it is also true that this is when we see the most growth in your capabilities." He paused, letting his gaze sweep across them, as though measuring their reaction.

"These games were never just a test," he continued, his voice now with an edge of conviction. "They were designed to teach, to push. The trial courses have, for countless generations, helped our students grow. And yes, the Respawn remains riskier than it's ever been. We're evaluating that risk continuously. Thus, there shall be an additional rule for these upcoming Games. You will be allowed only one Respawn—one, be it in preparation for or during the Games themselves. After that, you will be disqualified from continuing. And I understand that a single gamble with fate can seem too much, but I must remind you that outside of this campus, outside the safety we provide, many of you will face far worse. You must be ready."

Jace clenched his fists unconsciously, the Archmage's words wrapping around him like a vice. A single Respawn... The room felt charged, as if everyone was holding their breath, caught between fear and determination.

"I would rather risk a single death here," the Archmage continued, his voice quiet but unwavering, "than watch you Respawn again and again in the field, against something far less forgiving."

He let the words settle, and for a moment, the room was silent again. Then, he drew himself up. "On the Winter Solstice, we will hold the Winter Games. We will increase both the rewards and the safety precautions. And remember—participation is not mandatory. Only those societies that wish to compete need enter."

His gaze swept over them one last time, and Jace felt the full measure of it, as though the Archmage was daring them to defy the necessity of the Games. He didn't know if he was ready—if anyone was ready—but the choice, it seemed, was slipping further from their hands.

"There is a cold reality we must face, it seems. For the time being, logging out is no longer an option." The Archmage's words cut clean through the murmurs, his tone as sharp as the edge of his staff. "For months, we've watched, analyzed, and tried to understand. Only a handful have needed to respawn that remained here, within the campus—less than a few dozen. But what they experienced..." He paused, his grip tightening on the staff, the knuckles paling under the strain. It was the first sign that even he, the unflinching Archmage, was not immune to the gravity of what he was about to say.

The murmur in the hall swelled, tension coursing through the crowd like a living thing. Jace's breath caught in his throat. This wasn't the kind of directness he expected. Beside him, Ell's fingers twitched, her eyes darting nervously as if she were seeking something to anchor herself.

The Archmage tapped his staff against the stage floor, and the air around him shimmered. A figure of light sprang to life above his head, flickering like a candle's flame—fragile but arresting. It zoomed into a glowing image of a brain, thin tendrils of energy coiling around it like spectral vines.

"Why this is, we cannot say for certain. But I won't shield you from what we do know."

The Archmage's eyes swept across the audience, unwavering.

"We have made some discoveries, and a few more educated guesses, by studying the Traveler's Handbooks—both before and after respawn. The Handbook keeps a detailed, running record of a Traveler's experiences and quests throughout Terra Mythica. For those with a high enough perception rank, hidden layers within their own Handbook are revealed, secrets woven beneath the surface for those sharp enough to see."

He paused, his gaze growing more intent, as if daring anyone to look away.

"We've been working with individuals—high ranking Travelers outside of this campus. And what they have found aligns with our own observations."

The Archmage took a deep breath, his fingers tapping lightly on the staff as he continued. "We are combining data from across all of Mythica, and this is what we've discovered so far. It appears that there are two components at play," he continued calmly. "The brain, and the mind."

He gestured at the glowing brain, a shimmering aura beginning to pulse around it.

"The brain is the hardware. The mind, however, is believed to be something else entirely. Its energy, an electromagnetic force—tied to the body but also beyond it."

Jace watched, entranced, as the aura pulsed outward in spectral waves. It seemed almost alive, a living echo around the core of the brain. The Archmage continued, "The Neural Device—the one that links all Travelers to Terra Mythica—splits this connection. It allows your mind to immerse itself fully, to live here, to treat this world as real."

He paused, letting the concept settle. "But when death occurs here, there's a conflict. The mind attempts to return to the body, rejecting death as fake—it wants to reject it, to disbelieve that particular fact. Most of the time, it works." The image above him dimmed for a heartbeat. "But sometimes... it doesn't."

The hall went utterly silent. Every student was focused, eyes glued to the Archmage, their attention captive and unmoving. No one even dared to breathe too loudly, the tension taut as a drawn bowstring.

"When the mind truly believes in its own death," he said, his voice barely above a whisper, "something else happens. The mind starts rewriting -memories- experiences. It creates what I would call a critical error. And over time, those errors compound."

The image shifted, becoming fragmented—scenes shifting chaotically like a broken projector. Fragments of memories, disjointed and haunting. "For some," the Archmage went on, "it results in lapses—minor gaps that seem like nothing. But for others, the effects are far more serious: disorientation, hallucinations, and in the worst cases... a complete detachment from reality. The mind, reshaped by its own glitches."

A chill settled over Jace, creeping up his spine. He barely noticed Dex whispering something beside him; his focus was entirely on the Archmage, on the images of shattered memories. This wasn't just a game anymore—it hadn't been for a long time, but now it was impossible to ignore. The line between digital and real, between illusion and existence, had blurred to nothing.

"So far," the Archmage continued, his tone somber, "three students have experienced these severe effects—effects of multiple respawns. But the truth is, we have no idea how deep this problem goes."

Jace glanced around, catching Molly's gaze across the room—her eyes wide, her mouth pressed into a thin line. The unease in the hall was palpable, a slow-building panic kept in check only by the frozen stillness of fear.

"Terra Mythica was designed to be fully immersive," the Archmage resumed, breaking the silence. "But there are those among us—including myself—who are beginning to question if this is truly a digital construct at all." His eyes scanned the crowd, each word a challenge, daring someone to object. "Every attempt to parse its code, every effort to understand the framework that underpins this world, has ended in failure. No messages from System Support. No external communication. Earth's science offers no answers. Some still call it a game, but where is the evidence for that?"

He stepped forward, and Jace could see the fatigue etched into his features, the lines at the corners of his eyes that spoke of long nights and unanswered questions. "The fact remains," the Archmage said, his voice steady now, "that whether this is a digital illusion, a simulation, or something far beyond our understanding—it is our reality now."

The words struck like a blow, leaving the room breathless. Jace felt his stomach twist, a sense of vertigo taking hold. It wasn't a game. It was never just a game.

"I know this truth is hard to accept," the Archmage said, his expression softening, the barest hint of sympathy in his eyes. "But I trust that you all are stronger than this truth. Keeping you in the dark would do nothing but weaken you. And we cannot afford weakness—not with what lies ahead."

He lifted his chin, his gaze sweeping over the crowd, meeting eyes filled with fear and disbelief. "This world isn't something you can run from. Ignorance isn't bliss here—it's a death sentence. Only by facing the truth, through strength and knowledge, can we hope to carve a way forward."

He paused, then, almost unexpectedly, a faint smile curled at the corners of his lips. "If I could shield you all from this, I would. But since I cannot, I hope to provide you with the strength to face up to and win against it."

He bowed, his speech ending as abruptly as it had begun, like a sudden gust of wind that vanishes without a trace. It left the students in a state of stunned silence, their thoughts suspended in the empty space where his words had once hung.

Professor Tanner Frost rose and moved beside the Archmage, clearing her throat.

"On that note," she said, her voice steady, "let us proceed with the Star Progressions."

Chapter 53
Awards

With the assistance of Professor Tanner Frost, Professor Orion Blackwood, Professor Dranice Thorne, and Brutus Ironclad, Archmage Theon Laviette began calling students to the massive stage, one group at a time.

The star rankings were called in order. First came those who had achieved Bronze One, stepping up with a mix of nerves and pride. Then, the Bronze Twos followed, each group a little more confident, a little more seasoned.

Each time, the Archmage reached up to the night sky above them, as though plucking something tangible from the heavens. His fingers closed around a shimmer, and he drew forth bronze stars, placing them gently onto their lapels, where they glowed softly, as if still touched by the light of the cosmos.

As Jace's turn approached, a familiar knot of anxiety tightened in his chest. He took a breath, but before he could let it out, he felt Alice's hand slip into his. He wasn't sure if she did it to steady him or herself, but it didn't matter—it worked.

"Bronze Threes!" Professor Blackwood's voice rang out, clear and commanding.

Jace, Alice, Dex, Ell, Molly, and Marcus all stepped forward, joining the procession as they made their way onto the stage. Jace stood there, his friends beside him, the weight of the moment settling on his shoulders. The lights shone down, and for that brief moment, it felt like the entire world had narrowed down to just this—their group, standing together, united.

They all stood in line, a cohort of achievement, each of them having earned their Third Bronze this year. The gathered students and professors looked up at them with varying degrees of admiration, envy, and respect. Jace couldn't help but feel the swell of pride, mixed with the vulnerability that comes with standing before so many eyes, all focused on this shared moment of recognition.

The one person missing, though Jace wasn't sure he'd have been able to spot him if he was there, was Thistle.

The Archmage raised his hands. He spoke in a voice that was commanding yet gentle, echoing around the stone colonnades.

"This night, we celebrate those who have shown resilience, who have faced challenge after challenge, and emerged stronger. Tonight, they stand before us, bearers of the Third Bronze. A testament to their growth, to their courage."

He gestured to the students on the stage, the air around him shifting, swirling as if alive. His eyes glowed with a soft amber light as he lifted his hands higher, and Jace felt the air crackle with anticipation, the energy palpable and heavy with possibility.

A moment later, the Archmage began to speak words of magic—ancient, potent syllables that thrummed deep in Jace's bones. The sky above them seemed to respond, darkening for an instant before erupting with bronze light. Stars—countless, shimmering bronze stars—exploded above them, shooting across the heavens like fiery comets. The entire amphitheater gasped as the stars danced, arcing and weaving in intricate patterns that trailed bronze light like streaks of fire.

Jace tilted his head back, his eyes wide, feeling a rush of awe as the stars moved with precision, gathering above them in a constellation before diving down, each star shooting towards its intended student. He held his breath as one of those stars approached, its light illuminating his face.

The star slowed, its brilliant bronze glow softening as it hovered before his chest, then gently descended onto his collar. He felt a soft warmth spread through him as the star settled, transforming into a lapel pin—a bronze emblem, glowing softly, three stars etched with delicate precision.

Jace looked down at his collar, seeing the three bronze stars shine against the dark fabric. He turned his head slightly to see Alice, who was staring at her own stars, a smile slowly spreading across her face. Dex caught his eye and winked, his stars shining as if in response, while Ell practically beamed, her pride evident in the way she straightened her back.

Even Marcus allowed himself a small smile, the bronze stars reflecting in his eyes.

The crowd erupted into applause, cheers echoing off the stone walls. It was a thunderous, joyful sound that seemed to shake the very ground beneath them. Jace took a breath, feeling a mixture of pride, humility, and a hint of disbelief. The stars on his collar were light, but their meaning was anything but. This was a milestone—a testament to how far they'd all come, each of them in their own way.

The Archmage lowered his hands, the glow fading from his eyes, and with a warm smile, he spoke again. "May these stars remind you of your strength, of the journey you have embarked upon, and the challenges still ahead. Let them be a beacon, a symbol of hope for those who follow."

Jace exchanged glances with Alice, then Dex and Ell. He saw it in all their eyes—the unspoken promise that this was just the beginning. The stars on their collars weren't a finish line; they were a marker along the way, a reminder of what they were capable of, of what still awaited them beyond the amphitheater, beyond the walls of the academy.

The night sky was alive with light, and under it, they stood—bronze stars shining, a promise of what was still to come.

As they returned to their seats, Jace barely noticed the procession of names being called, the steady stream of students making their way to the stage. It all seemed to blur together—until the final names rang out, clear and resonant.

These were the ones who had reached Bronze Six or higher. The graduating class.

Jace's attention sharpened, his gaze focusing as the students began stepping forward. Among them was Demi, her expression one of quiet confidence, her movements smooth and deliberate. A few others joined her, faces Jace recognized only in passing—figures he had seen around campus but never truly known.

The Archmage spoke, his voice carrying over the hall, acknowledging their achievement. "These students have passed the Graduation Trials. A trial open to any who dare to take it, at any time—though none have ever succeeded before Bronze Five."

Jace watched as they stood, lined up before the entire assembly, and for a moment, they looked larger than life. Demi, her head held high, eyes blazing with determination. The others, too, carried themselves with an unmistakable sense of purpose. They looked like heroes—figures out of legend, embodying the kind of power and grace that seemed almost untouchable.

The Archmage handed each of them a rolled scroll and a pin—a golden emblem of the Phoenix, the proud symbol of M.O.U. The fiery bird shimmered, wings spread wide, a symbol of rebirth and resilience. As each pin was fastened to their lapels, the Phoenix moved, its wings giving a graceful flap before settling, as if alive and ready to take flight at a moment's notice.

"Go forth into the world," the Archmage intoned, his voice resonant, echoing through the hushed hall. "Face the next phase of your Hero's Journey with courage and conviction."

And for the first time, Jace felt it—an ache, a desire gnawing at his chest. He wanted to be that. To stand up there with them, not just as a bystander, but as someone who mattered, someone who had earned his place.

Chapter 54
The Midnight Festival

The anticipation was electric as the students rushed toward the party, excitement bubbling over as they poured into the sprawling underground district. Jace and his friends lagged slightly behind, taking in the night's chill air before heading in. By the time they arrived, the celebration was already in full swing.

Reginald stood at the entrance, scowling at the latecomers with his usual disdain. He folded his arms as Jace and his group approached, his voice dripping with mock impatience. "Well, look who finally decided to grace us with their presence. We've been waiting for you—and more importantly." He sighed, his annoyance almost theatrical. Jace exchanged a quick glance with the others, a silent understanding passing between them.

Inside, the party was chaos—an explosion of color, costumes, and enchantment. It was the biggest Halloween celebration Jace had ever seen, and it was almost overwhelming. Pumpkins with carved faces floated through the air, trailing glimmers of firelight that spun like sparks. Ghoulish green mist hung low to the floor, swirling around feet as if it had a life of its own, while lanterns flickered with eerie, ever-changing hues. The music—some kind of enchanted blend of haunting melodies and pulsing beats—seemed to come from everywhere and nowhere at once, making the entire space vibrate with energy.

The place was a sprawling labyrinth, yet somehow, it managed to fit everyone. Students spilled into every corner, their laughter echoing from the alchemy labs to the common rooms, from the kitchens to the long, twisting corridors. Jace knew that not everyone was here—it couldn't be possible—but it felt like the entire university had gathered under one roof. Every alcove, every hidden nook was filled with revelers, masked and unmasked, laughing, talking, living in the moment.

He realized, as he looked around, that he didn't see anyone he knew besides his closest friends. The realization struck him oddly—how small his circle was. Other students might have waved, - passed a smile, but none of them were faces he'd call familiar. It was just Dex, Ell, Marcus, Alice, and Molly, who anchored him in this sea of unknown.

The professors and faculty were notably absent, as was tradition. They had their own party to attend—somewhere mysterious, where they vanished for the night, far off from Olympus. Technically, Molly could have joined them, but she hadn't wanted to, and Jace was glad she'd decided to stick around.

The noise was deafening, a pulsing, living thing that enveloped them all. Someone had enchanted the music to continue indefinitely, and it seemed to flow through every corner of the Fields Below. A makeshift dance floor had taken over the common area, and students in elaborate costumes spun, their shadows twisting and blending into the lantern light. Even the alchemy lab was packed, students examining the strange equipment with an odd mix of curiosity and awe, their laughter bubbling over like a cauldron left to boil.

Jace was swept up in the current of bodies, caught between the rhythm of the music and the chaotic energy of the party. At some point, he bumped into Molly. She gave him a small smile, her voice somehow cutting through the din with its softness. "Hey," she said. "After this, there's something I need to talk to you about. Tomorrow, okay?"

Jace blinked, momentarily taken aback, but he nodded. "Of course," he replied, though confusion settled in the back of his mind. He could see a seriousness in her eyes that was at odds with the revelry around them.

As the night wore on, it seemed that every inch of the manor was taken over by the festivities. The only place untouched by the chaos was the catacombs below—a silent, looming presence beneath their feet, forgotten in the fever pitch of the celebration above.

The party was still a swirling frenzy of color and sound by the time Jace managed to weave his way back to his friends—Alice, Dex, and Ell. They were gathered near one of the long tables, their laughter mixing with the music, their faces flushed with excitement. He felt a rush of relief at seeing them, the familiar faces grounding him amidst the chaos.

Together, they began preparations to serve the food, arranging everything onto silver platters that shimmered under the dim, enchanted lights. When they finally got the trays out, the response from the crowd was muted—soft exclamations of surprise, a few nods, and a handful of pleased smiles. It wasn't spectacular, but it was better than Jace had feared. The food was edible, maybe even decent, the subtle touch of silver and oleander balancing out the strange flavors that had threatened to ruin it.

People were eating happily, or at least contentedly, enjoying the slight improvement in their usual fare. Jace had expected more of a reaction—some fanfare, perhaps, or a few cheers. Instead, the students took it in stride, eating with mild approval before slipping back into the party's rhythm. Some drifted toward the dance floor, others gathered in clusters, the music and laughter a constant backdrop.

Jace, watching it all unfold, had a sudden thought. He excused himself and made his way to a quieter corner, quickly opening his president's interface to check on the status of his society. To his surprise, he found that he'd gained over 1,000 society points since the last time he'd looked. He had already spent most of the gains he had gotten from the defeated demons, adding ghostly assistants for Reginald. Now he saw there was a steady uptick as he watched—coming in from the people praising Hades at the party, the food, everything. Reputation had also increased with his Society by 500 points.

A small smile tugged at his lips. Without hesitation, Jace decided to spend some of the points. He upgraded the butler and support staff, feeling a thrill as a half-dozen ghosts materialized, glowing faintly with a burst of ethereal light. The spectral figures floated in place, awaiting his command.

"Report to Reginald," Jace instructed, nodding toward the entrance. "Help make sure everyone gets food."

The ghosts nodded in eerie unison before drifting away, their forms fading slightly as they moved through the crowded room. Jace felt a small sense of satisfaction—it wasn't much, but it was something. The campus kitchens were handling the bulk of the food, which made the task manageable, but he made sure each dish had a drop of the potion. It was a subtle enhancement, just enough to make everything feel a little more magical, a little more alive.

Jace finally made his way back to his friends, the chaotic energy of the party still buzzing around him. He spotted Dex in the middle of the dance floor, putting his Dance Affinity to good use, his movements fluid and precise. Ell was there with him, their laughter echoing above the beat, their feet moving in perfect rhythm. A few others joined them, while some stood around, watching with amused smiles.

Jace leaned against a nearby wall, letting a smile spread across his face. For a moment, he felt a flicker of joy amidst the chaos—a rare moment of lightness amidst everything. The night stretched on, hours melting away into a blur of music, laughter, and flickering lantern light. Slowly, as the hours passed, people began to trickle out, the crowd thinning.

To his relief, no one seemed to have a negative reaction to the food. In fact, they'd received plenty of compliments, students smiling and thanking them as they left, their arms around friends as they headed off to other places, other adventures. Which meant, either they were wrong about the ingredient or there just weren't any other possessed students.

By three in the morning, the party had dwindled to just a few hundred, the wild energy now a gentle hum. Jace felt exhaustion settling into his bones, the kind that came after a night well spent. He glanced over at the dance floor to see Dex and Ell again, still moving to the music, their steps slower now, the beat having softened to a mellow tune.

Jace smiled to himself. Even tired, even with the mess of everything else hanging over them, moments like this—his friends together, dancing, laughing—made it all worth it.

The night was winding down, the energy finally ebbing after hours of celebration. The manor was a complete mess—empty cups and discarded decorations littered the floor, and the enchanted pumpkins floated lazily, their once bright glow now a dim flicker. But none of it mattered. It had been worth it.

Jace stood near the edge of the dance floor, watching as the last clusters of people laughed and swayed to the fading music. He was tired, but it was a good kind of exhaustion, the kind that settled in after something meaningful. He didn't notice Alice until she was right beside him, nudging his arm.

"Hey," she said, her eyes sparkling with something mischievous. "Wanna dance?"

Jace blinked, caught off guard. "Oh, uh—" He could feel the nervousness bubbling up, his heartbeat quickening. "I don't really—"

But Alice didn't wait for him to finish. She grabbed his hand, a playful smile tugging at her lips, and pulled him onto the dance floor. "Come on, it's the last song. Let's goof around a bit."

Jace let out a half-nervous, half-relieved laugh as she led him into the middle of the dwindling crowd. The music was slow and mellow, the kind of tune that made people sway more than dance, and Jace felt his nerves easing just slightly as Alice started to move, her grin contagious. He followed her lead, his steps awkward at first, but then Alice twirled herself dramatically, almost tripping into him, and they both burst into laughter.

They danced without any real coordination, just two people enjoying the moment. Alice would make an exaggerated spin, and Jace would stumble trying to match it. He tried to dip her at one point, but she ended up nearly pulling them both down, her laughter ringing out above the music. They were goofing off, but Jace felt the tension of the night slipping away, replaced by something lighter, something almost carefree.

Around them, people moved in and out of the dance floor, some swaying to the music, some drifting toward the exit, a blur of movement and soft chatter. For Jace, though, it all seemed to fade, leaving just him and Alice, her hand still wrapped around his, her smile softening as the song continued to play.

They danced closer, the space between them narrowing with each step. Jace could feel the warmth of her near him, her gaze meeting his. There was a quiet shift in the air, an unspoken moment passing between them. Alice's smile faded into something gentler, her eyes locked on his, and Jace felt the world around them blur at the edges.

It wasn't clear what was happening, whether they were about to close that last gap between them or not, but there was something there—a moment that hung, suspended, as if waiting for one of them to make a choice. Jace's breath caught, and he found himself leaning in, just slightly, drawn to the brightness in her eyes, the closeness of her presence.

Alice's smile died on her lips, her expression shifting in an instant. Her face went white, all the color draining away, her eyes widening with a mix of confusion and fear.

Chapter 55

Uninvited Guests

"Alice?" Jace's voice came out unsteady, concern lacing his words. "What's wrong?"

She didn't answer, her gaze fixed on something over his shoulder. Jace turned, and his stomach dropped.

A few dozen students were doubled over, their bodies writhing in pain. It was a gruesome sight, their skin darkening, shifting as if something beneath was struggling to burst free. A sickening, cracking noise filled the air as their forms twisted—half-demon monstrosities clawing their way out from within, yet somehow stuck in an incomplete transformation. Grotesque, horned heads pushing through skin, limbs breaking into twisted shapes.

Jace felt a rush of dread wash over him, an overwhelming wrongness that he couldn't believe he'd missed until now. Just a moment ago, everything had seemed fine, normal even. Now, it was like stepping out into the void, every sense screaming at him that something was horribly wrong.

Around them, the rest of the students were frozen in shock, confusion etched on their faces as the scene unfolded. Panic spread quickly, and then someone acted—shards started flashing to life, and beams of magical energy began flying toward the possessed students.

"No!" Jace shouted, his voice cracking with urgency. He surged forward, pushing his way through the crowd, waving his arms to get everyone's attention. "Stop! Don't hurt them!"

He could see Dex and Ell already moving, the urgency mirrored in their expressions. Jace's heart pounded as he did a quick soul sense, his consciousness reaching out, touching the souls of those writhing before him. Relief—cold and fragile—bloomed in his chest. The students were still there. The demons hadn't killed them; they were being used, twisted into unwilling vessels. This was so early in the possession process that the students' souls were still intact, still resisting.

"If we kill them now," Jace said, more to himself than anyone else, "it could be the end for them." He turned to those around him, his voice gaining strength. "Nothing lethal! Subdue them—I can separate them!"

He wasn't sure how he'd manage it, not with so many—but that didn't matter now. They had to try.

Alice, Dex, and Ell sprang into action, rallying the other remaining students. It was chaos—students shouting, dodging, confused and scared. But they listened. Jace's friends guided them, herding those who weren't possessed away from danger and surrounding the half-demon students. Luckily, they vastly outnumbered the possessed, and despite the chaos, they managed to contain them without lethal force.

Jace's head spun, the energy around him nearly unbearable, but he had no choice. They couldn't let those demons win—they couldn't let them take his classmates, his friends.

He calmed his thoughts and focused, as the others worked to hold the possessed students back. This was going to take everything he had, and he still wasn't sure if that would be enough. But he had to try.

Taking a slow breath, he began cast Soul Sense, reaching out, feeling for the demonic presence within each possessed student. The connections were tangled and dark, threads of corruption snaking deep into their souls. But he found them. He was getting quicker at this, each link lighting up in his mind like a dark beacon.

One by one, Jace followed those threads, and with each one, he cast Soul Severance. He could feel the drain, the pull on his aether, but something in him was recovering faster—his reserves refilling more easily than before. He knew it was because of the Society; the boost they granted him made all the difference. He moved from student to student, slicing through the bonds that tethered them to the demons.

Each time he severed a connection, the demon burst forth, splitting violently from the student's body. The student would collapse immediately afterward, unconscious, their aether depleted, but their vitals stable. Jace checked each one quickly, his heart pounding in his ears, relieved every time to find they were alive.

The demons that came out were smaller than the ones in the forest, their red skin glistening with an oily sheen, their eyes gleaming with malice. Their claws were sharp as knives, slashing out at anything that got too close, their movements erratic and vicious. The students who were still capable of fighting would converge on the freed demons, working together to bring them down, spells and weapons striking with practiced precision.

Jace moved from one possessed student to the next, repeating the process over and over, his body aching with exhaustion, but he didn't stop. He couldn't. He severed connection after connection, demons being pulled, clawing and screaming, from the bodies they'd taken hold of.

And then he heard it—the screams from outside, distant but unmistakable. His heart sank, his stomach twisting into a knot. The rest of the students... the ones who had gone outside...

"They don't know," he whispered, panic rising in his throat. He turned, his eyes wide, staring toward the doorway. "They don't know not to kill them."

His gaze locked with Alice's across the chaos, and he saw the realization dawn in her eyes, the same dread mirrored on her face. Without another word, Jace pushed through the crowd. He had to get to them before it was too late. Before they destroyed what could still be saved.

Dex, Ell, and Alice moved with him, the four of them forcing their way through the panicked crowd, pushing toward the source of the screams. Jace's thoughts were racing, every beat of his heart filled with urgency. They had to stop it. They had to save them—before the demons claimed everything.

Ell barked orders at the remaining students, her voice sharp and commanding, cutting through the chaos. "Subdue the demons! Don't kill them!" She moved through the room like a whirlwind, directing their efforts with precision. Shards flashed as magic surged, Affinities sparking to life in bursts of light and power. Even the ghosts got involved, swirling around the demons, phasing in and out to distract them, making it nearly impossible for the demons to land a solid hit.

"Get the demons into the bathroom!" Jace shouted, pointing to a nearby door. He chose the location almost at random, but he knew every room in the manor had a locking mechanism now, part of his recent defensive upgrades. But none of it was enough—not against real threats. Not yet. There were no guards, and no magical missile defenses strong enough at the Bronze level. He wished he'd managed to upgrade faster, somehow, something more.

He glanced at his friends—Ell, Dex, and Alice—each of them nodding, and together they headed for the doors, moving with purpose. They had to get outside.

As soon as they stepped into the night, the scene exploded before them in pure pandemonium. The cold night air was filled with screams, the stench of something unearthly carried on the breeze. All across the campus grounds, grotesque half-demon forms lurched through the shadows, monstrous and twisted, their eyes glowing in the dim light.

"Over there!" Alice shouted, pointing ahead.

Jace's gaze snapped to where she indicated—a group of students struggling to pin down one of the possessed. Vines were wrapped around its limbs, holding it in place, while another student raised a blade high, about to strike a killing blow.

"No!" Jace yelled, but they were too far away. He saw the electricity surge before he saw Marcus—an arc of lightning that shot across the space, crackling with power and stopping the student's blade inches from the demon's neck. Marcus rushed in, his eyes wide, his voice urgent.

They arrived just in time to hear Marcus finishing, his words breathless but firm. "They're still in there. The students—they might still be in there!"

Jace nodded, moving quickly beside Marcus placing a hand on his shoulder. "He's right. The possessions haven't fully taken over. We need to subdue, not kill, until I can separate them."

The students around them hesitated, uncertainty in their eyes, but Jace stepped forward, his voice steady. "Trust me. We can still save them."

They were near the waterfall of Aphrodite, its rushing water glistening under the moonlight. The goddess's presence was palpable—statues of her likeness that normally decorated the area had come to life, their stone forms animated, standing guard. Aphrodite herself was there, her eyes blazing, her face a mask of determination. She held a weapon now—an ethereal, shimmering spear, something both beautiful and deadly, fitting of a goddess of love turned protector.

Jace turned, his gaze fierce, his voice loud enough to reach those nearest. "Do not kill the demons! The students are still inside. We have to get them out first or..."

The weight of the scene bore down on him, though—the reality of it. They were too late for many. Bodies lay scattered across the grounds, students who had either fallen to the demons or been killed by their own, mistaken as monsters beyond saving. It twisted something inside Jace, a deep sense of failure clawing at him as he took it all in.

"There's too many," Marcus said, his voice strained. "Too many in too many different places. We can't warn everyone." He shook his head, frustration evident. "I've been trying, but they just—"

Jace clenched his fists, his heart hammering as he looked around at the chaos, the shadows moving between flashes of light, his friends battling alongside him. He knew Marcus was right. The sheer number of them—the scattered confusion, the desperation—there was no way they could reach everyone in time.

Jace looked around, his eyes scanning the terrified faces of the students they had just stopped. He took a deep breath, trying to steady his own nerves, and spoke with urgency. "We need to draw all of them to us. Everyone. We have to pull their attention before they get to the others. Does anyone here have a tank ability? Something that can pull monsters, make them focus on you?"

The students exchanged uneasy glances before one by one, they shook their heads. Jace's heart sank.

"Damn it," he muttered, running a hand through his hair. "I hate to say this, but we need Thistle."

Alice looked at him, concern etched in her features. "Jace, are you sure?"

"Careful what you wish for," a voice rasped, echoing from the darkness. It sent a chill down Jace's spine, and they all turned, their eyes widening in horror.

From the distance, charging toward them, it emerged—a towering figure, grotesque in its twisted glory, a fusion of demon and something else. Thistle. He wasn't just transformed – he was a nightmare made real, warped into a monstrous giant. Dark energies pulsed and radiated from him, his skin shifting between crimson and shadows, as if he couldn't decide which horror suited him better. His eyes blazed with a burning, corrupted light, the aura around him almost suffocating, its malice so palpable it made the earth beneath him tremble.

But it wasn't just the monstrous presence that caught Jace's eye. It was the ring—Marcus's brass ring. There it sat, wrapped around one of Thistle's grotesquely enlarged fingers. The same ring Marcus had thrown away, hoping to forget, yet somehow, impossibly, it had found its way here, to Thistle. It had been intended for Marcus's father, one of the founding members of the inner circle of Excelsior—a symbol of legacy, of purpose. And now it was here, in the hands of a monster. But this didn't seem like a typical demon's prize. No, it carried an air of something different, something intended for a far more significant purpose.

"You!" Thistle roared, his voice twisted into something monstrous and guttural, every word a snarl of fury. The sound was like shattered glass, splintering in the air, filled with agony and rage. His burning eyes locked onto Jace, their crimson glow intensifying, his hatred boiling over.

"You think you're so amazing, don't you?" he sneered, his voice cracking with bitterness. "Poor little Thistle, eh? Teased, hurt, looked down on!" He took a step forward, the ground beneath his weight splintering, each word spat out like venom, the raw emotion in his voice clawing at the air. The fury twisted his face into something almost human for a moment—something vulnerable beneath the monstrous rage, and then it was gone, swallowed by darkness.

Jace's gaze shifted back to the ring, his heart pounding in his chest. That ring wasn't just metal. It was intention, power—meant for a founder, meant for someone far more important than any demon or brute. And now, it had somehow found Thistle, feeding his rage, his hatred, transforming it into something far beyond ordinary malice. There was more at play here—something deep, dangerous, and disturbingly deliberate.

Jace flinched at the words, feeling each one like a physical blow.

"Poor Thistle," Thistle continued, his voice mocking, vibrating with fury. "Couldn't get his rank up. Had to retake the year. Poor Thistle, with his uncle gone missing." His eyes blazed with a sudden, twisted light, his lips curling back in a snarl that was more beast than human. "We know what happened to his uncle. We know who took him. Who hurt him." He spat, his voice full of spite. "It was you. You and your friends."

The accusation hung in the air, thick and suffocating. Jace's heart pounded in his chest, a chill running down his spine. "Thistle!" he shouted, his voice desperate, cutting through the dark echoes of Thistle's rage. "That's not you! You have to fight it! This isn't you!"

The demon laughed, a bone-rattling, hate-filled sound that seemed to make the darkness grow thicker. Thistle's twisted face contorted further, his body trembling with the force of his rage. "Poor little Thistle?" the monstrous voice screamed, the echo of its roar tearing through the void like a thunderclap. "Not so little anymore!"

Jace braced himself as Thistle lunged at him, the weight of the demon's fury bearing down like a tidal wave. Anger, resentment, and a twisted sense of betrayal lashed out from Thistle's corrupted soul. It wasn't just the demon's power—it was Thistle's pain, his loneliness, his anger, all amplified, all unleashed without restraint.

"Thistle, listen to me!" Jace yelled, stepping forward, even as the monstrous form swung a massive arm at him. He could feel the heat, the hatred radiating off Thistle, like the air itself was burning. But Jace held his ground, his voice unwavering. "This isn't you. You know me. You know who your real enemies are!"

"Get ready!" Jace yelled to his friends, his voice almost drowned out by the roar that erupted from Thistle's monstrous mouth. The demon half of Thistle surged forward, its massive limbs tearing into the earth as it moved, every step shaking the ground.

Molly, Alice, Marcus, Dex, and Ell stood in a line before him, their faces set with determination. Molly stepped forward, her eyes meeting Jace's, steady and unwavering. "Do what you have to do, Jace," she said, her voice calm but resolute. "We've got your back. We're not going anywhere."

"Keep him distracted!" Jace shouted to his friends, his voice full of a determination that belied the fear gripping him. "I'll get him freed."

More demons, drawn by the sight of the hulking monstrosity and the noise of the battle, began charging toward them, their snarls echoing through the night. Marcus turned, his eyes widening at the approaching swarm. "We've got incoming!" he shouted, urgency rippling through his voice as he braced himself, ready for the onslaught.

They sprang into action, charging to intercept the monstrous Thistle. Dex led the way, his daggers glinting as energy surged around him, his body a blur of movement. He darted forward, aiming low, slicing at Thistle's legs—small, precise cuts that barely scratched the surface but were enough to irritate and enrage the giant. Each strike was like a needle, aggravating Thistle further, his roars of fury growing louder as he turned his attention toward Dex.

Ell followed, her agility allowing her to dance between the giant's swipes, landing blows that were designed to disrupt and confuse rather than wound. Alice's magic surged, barriers forming in midair to shield them as Marcus moved in with arcs of lightning, trying to slow the creature's movements.

It was a chaotic whirlwind of power and desperation. Thistle swung his enormous arms, crashing through barriers and leaving deep gouges in the earth. The noise was deafening—the roar of the creature, the shouts of Jace's friends, the crash of energy meeting force. Dex ducked under a massive swipe, rolling to the side, while Ell leaped over another attack, barely avoiding the monstrous hand.

Demons flooded into the fray, a chaotic wave of snarling, twisted forms. A few brave students, alongside the animated statue of Aphrodite, fought fiercely, doing everything they could to hold the line. The stone figure of Aphrodite wielded her ethereal spear with fluid precision, striking down demons with grace, while the students, their faces a mix of fear and determination, battled tirelessly beside her, trying to keep as many of the creatures at bay as possible.

Jace took a deep breath, focusing his senses, blocking out the noise of the fight. He had to trust his friends. He stepped forward, his hand raised as he cast Soul Sense, the familiar pull of the magic reaching out. He could feel it—Thistle's soul, buried beneath the darkness, a flicker of light amid the demon's fury.

He closed his eyes and stepped in, his consciousness diving into the chaotic storm of Thistle's mind.

Stepping into Thistle's mind was like walking down a long, empty suburban street. The world was dense with a stifling stillness, the kind that settled in places long abandoned. Houses lined the road, each one dark, the windows hollow, the doors ajar as if someone had left in a hurry and never returned. There was something deeply unsettling about the scene, an eerie echo of what had once been a thriving place now left to decay. Jace could feel the weight of loneliness pressing down on him, a pervasive sense of hopelessness that made every step feel heavier.

He moved cautiously, his eyes scanning the darkened doorways, searching for Thistle. He could feel his presence here, somewhere close, but this place was a maze, each shadow deeper than the last. Jace approached one of the houses—a towering, monstrous structure at the end of the street. It loomed over the others, its shape twisted, the angles wrong, like a nightmare version of a familiar home. He knew, somehow, that Thistle was inside.

The door swung open as Jace approached, and he stepped in, the air shifting immediately. The darkness inside was alive, the walls shifting, and suddenly, they lunged at him. The house itself came alive—floorboards snapping up like claws, walls bending inward, trying to trap him. He was slammed against the wall, his breath leaving him in a painful rush.

Jace struggled, the tendrils of darkness wrapping around him, pulling him deeper, tightening their grip like cold, unyielding iron. He fought back, trying to summon his strength, his aether flaring, but the house's hold was relentless. The shadows closed in, pressing down on him, the cold, suffocating, and Jace felt his own will faltering, his body giving in to the crushing force.

"Thistle!" Jace screamed, his voice echoing, raw with desperation. "Thistle, I need you! Fight this! You have to fight!"

The darkness seemed to pause for a moment, the house's grip loosening slightly as Jace's words echoed through the emptiness. He didn't know if Thistle could hear him, but he had to try. He had to keep pushing, even if it meant everything.

Outside, the battle raged on, a relentless storm of chaos. More demons were charging toward the noise, their monstrous forms lit by the flickering glow of magic and fire. Attacks were breaking through the defensive lines, slipping past the shields and barriers, hitting Jace's real body. Pain shot through him, his aether responding instinctively, tugging at his reserves to heal the damage, the drain almost unbearable.

He could feel it, the pain from the outside world bleeding into this space, the desperate cries of his friends battling to keep him safe. He had to succeed. He had to free Thistle—not just for his own sake, but for everyone still out there fighting.

Chapter 56
Chaos

T he battlefield was a storm of movement—students rushing in to reinforce, their faces pale but filled with determination. Molly stood near
the edge of the fray, her stance unwavering. Her eyes glowed with a strange,
almost otherworldly light, and the air around her pulsed with an eerie, cold
energy. She lifted her hands, and shadowy tendrils coiled around her fingers,
manifestations of Hecate's power. With a sharp motion, she sent them
lashing out, striking at the advancing demons, binding them and halting
their progress. Her power was raw, dark, and efficient—yet restrained. She
couldn't go all out, not without risking the possessed students' lives.

Nearby, Marcus moved like lightning itself—quick, focused. His
shard crackled with energy, arcs of bright blue light jumping from his
outstretched hands. He struck demon after demon, the electricity stunning
them, forcing them back, but it was clear he was holding back, his attacks
designed to incapacitate rather than kill. The lightning danced across the
ground, wrapping around demonic limbs -pushing the monstrous forms
away from his friends.

But for every demon they drove back, more seemed to pour in. The
tide wasn't slowing. They were being overwhelmed, hobbled by the necessity
of using non-lethal force, their restraint making each victory feel more like a
stalling tactic than a real win. The demons kept coming, their forms twisted,
their eyes filled with hatred. The students were doing everything they could
to avoid fatal blows, but it was costing them dearly. Their faces were lined
with exhaustion, and the impact of the relentless attacks was showing.

Amid the chaos, Jace was getting battered, his body feeling every blow
from the outside world as he struggled within Thistle's corrupted mind. He
could feel the hits landing—claws raking across his skin, blunt force pounding
against his ribs. His aether worked frantically to heal him, but it wasn't enough.

Each wound was deeper, each bruise more painful, and his vision began to blur as he felt himself slipping under the pressure.

Blood dripped from his forehead, stinging his eyes, his breath shuddering in uneven gasps. He was still reaching for Thistle, still trying to sever the connection, but his strength was fading. The pain from the physical world was breaking his concentration, the relentless barrage making it harder to keep his focus.

"Jace!" Marcus shouted, his voice almost drowned out by the roar of another demon. He looked back, seeing Jace doubled over, struggling to keep himself upright even as the demons swarmed him, relentless in their attack.

Molly fought her way closer to Jace, her eyes wide with fear as she saw him stumble. She called on more of Hecate's power, shadows rippling around her like a protective shroud, her focus entirely on pushing back the demons threatening Jace.

But the tide wasn't stemming, and Jace was getting worse. Blood stained his clothes, his face twisted in pain. He was fighting two battles at once—against the demons attacking his body, and against the darkness holding Thistle's mind. And slowly, it looked like he was losing both.

Amidst the chaos, two healers found their way to where Jace knelt, battered and bloodied, his focus still desperately clinging to the thread that connected him to Thistle's mind. They moved quickly, their eyes wide with urgency, both their robes marked with the insignia of the academy's healing house—a blue crescent moon, a symbol of solace amid turmoil.

One knelt beside Jace, her hands glowing a gentle, soothing green as she placed them against his back, channeling healing energy into him. Her face was etched with concentration, her brow furrowed as she tried to keep his wounds from overwhelming him. The other stood behind, his eyes darting between Jace and the battle raging around them, one hand extended, a flickering light emitting from his palm. He was doing everything he could to shield Jace and the other healer, a glowing dome shimmering into place when demons or stray attacks came too close.

"Hold on, just hold on," the first healer murmured, her voice strained. The glow of her magic pulsed as she sent it through Jace, her fingers trembling from the constant demand. She could feel his wounds fighting back, each healing spell barely keeping up with all the fresh injuries on his flesh. Blood trickled down his face, and she wiped it away quickly, her heart pounding.

Jace was on his knees, his head bowed, sweat and blood mixing on his skin. His fingers dug into the ground, his knuckles white, every muscle in his body straining as he fought against Thistle's possession. He could feel the demon's resistance, the darkness pushing back, but the pain from his physical injuries was making it harder and harder to keep his focus.

But the heals were only slowing the inevitable.

Inside Thistle's mind, Jace was being pulled deeper into the monstrous house, the shadows of its walls shifting and swirling, grasping for him like living creatures. He struggled, feeling the darkness tug at his limbs, his body being dragged toward the gaping maw of the house's interior. The air was cold -oppressive, pressing in on all sides. He felt as if he were drowning in black ink, unable to breathe, unable to move.

But then, something else—a spark, a memory, a sliver of moonlight that broke through the darkness. It came from outside, a gift of energy from the healers tending his real body, and Jace seized it, holding onto the light with everything he had. It glowed, silvery and pure, pushing back against the shadows, forcing them to recoil. With a burst of power, Jace ripped free, stumbling forward, his breath coming in sharp gasps. The darkness hissed, trying to close in again, but the moonlight held them at bay, carving a path through the twisted corridors of Thistle's mind.

Jace pushed forward, his eyes darting from door to door as he fought his way through the monstrous house. He had to find Thistle—he had to save him from this suffocating darkness. He could feel it, faint but growing stronger—a sense of someone, somewhere deeper within.

Finally, he reached a door at the end of a long, twisting hallway. It was slightly ajar, and from within came the faint sound of crying, soft and heart-wrenching. Jace pushed the door open, his heart pounding as he stepped inside.

There, in the corner of the room, was Thistle.

But he wasn't the gnome Jace knew. He was just a man now—thin, short, his face streaked with tears. He sat huddled in the corner, his body trembling as he clutched his knees to his chest. His form was ghostly, faded, as if only fragments of him remained—hollow, translucent, like he was slipping away bit by bit, more memory than substance.

Jace's breath caught in his throat. This must be Thistle's true form, stripped of all illusions, of his body in Terra Mythica.

"Thistle," Jace whispered, his voice cracking as he stepped closer.

Thistle looked up, his eyes wide, filled with fear and pain. "You... you shouldn't be here," he said, his voice shaking, barely more than a whisper. "You should go. It's too late for me."

Jace knelt down, ignoring the darkness that pressed in around them, the twisted walls of the monstrous house groaning as if in protest. He reached out, placing a hand gently on Thistle's shoulder. "No, it's not," Jace said, his voice full of conviction. "I'm not leaving you, Thistle. We're in this together. I see you. The real you. And you're stronger than this. You're stronger than that demon."

Thistle shook his head, tears spilling down his cheeks. "I... I can't fight it. I've tried, but it's too much. I'm just... I'm not enough."

Jace's heart ached at the hopelessness in Thistle's voice. He tightened his grip on Thistle's shoulder, his eyes locking with his. "You are enough," Jace said, his voice low but fierce. "You're not alone, Thistle. We can do this together. But I need your help. I need you to fight with me."

Thistle looked at him, his eyes searching Jace's face, as if looking for some kind of reassurance, something to hold on to. Slowly, shakily, he nodded, his breath hitching. "What do I need to do?"

Jace gave him a small, encouraging smile, wiping a tear from Thistle's cheek with his thumb. "You need to show me where the connection is. Where the demon has you tethered. Together, we can break it."

Thistle hesitated, but then he nodded, glancing down at his chest. He lifted a trembling hand, pointing to the darkness that seemed to pulse from his heart, a thick, black chain that disappeared into the shadows. Jace followed the line of the chain, his own heart tightening at the sight.

"Right," Jace said, his voice steady, though his pulse was racing. He placed his hand over Thistle's, his aether gathering, glowing a faint silvery light. "We're going to break it, together."

Thistle nodded, his eyes filled with determination, even if there was still a flicker of fear. Together, they reached out, their hands grasping the dark chain. The demon's power fought against them, a wave of darkness pushing back, but Jace held on, his grip tightening.

"Now!" Jace shouted, his voice echoing in the dark space. Thistle cried out, pouring his own strength into the effort. The chain trembled, the shadows around them rippling, and with a burst of moonlit energy, the tether shattered, a flash of blinding light cutting through the darkness.

The monstrous house seemed to scream, the walls shaking, the shadows recoiling, and then everything began to fade. The darkness broke apart, unraveling, and Jace felt the coldness lifting, replaced by a warmth that spread through him.

He looked at Thistle, and for the first time, saw hope in his eyes. Thistle nodded, his tears now of relief rather than fear, his form solidifying, the darkness receding.

Jace gasped as he came to, his consciousness snapping back into his body. The world around him spun for a moment, the chaos of the real battle crashing back in—the distant screams, the clash of weapons, the roars of the demons. His vision blurred before focusing again, and he looked up, blinking the haze away, just in time to see the monstrous form of the demon tearing itself free from Thistle's body.

The demon twisted, its dark form unfurling, breaking away from Thistle's limp frame. Thistle crumpled to the ground, breathing heavily, his body battered and bruised, the corruption still lingering in the edges of his aura. Healers rushed forward, glancing at Jace with hesitance, their eyes flicking nervously between the broken Thistle and the violent creature looming above him.

"Help him," Jace ordered, his voice rough from exhaustion. His gaze was unwavering, his tone leaving no room for argument. The healers exchanged a look, reluctant, but obeyed. They knelt beside Thistle, beginning their work to stabilize him, to bring him back from the brink.

Jace's eyes shifted back to the demon—twisted and huge, the largest he had faced yet. This demon wasn't just an ordinary possession—it was a boss, its form much more formidable, a hulking monstrosity of dark energy. Its crimson skin shimmered with a grotesque sheen, and its eyes burned with a malevolent light. It roared, the sound rattling through the battlefield, a vicious challenge to all who dared stand before it.

The demon lunged, its twisted limbs swinging wildly, sending students scrambling backward, spells and shards flashing in the darkness as they fought to hold it back. Jace pressed his palms into the ground, his whole body trembling, the dull ache in his limbs a constant reminder of how far he'd already pushed himself. He closed his eyes, taking a deep breath, allowing his aether to flow back to him, to replenish, even if just a little.

"Jace!" Marcus shouted from the other side, his eyes wide as he dodged the demon's thrashing strikes. "We need you!"

Jace swallowed, his vision still blurring at the edges. He forced himself to his feet, staggering slightly before catching his balance. The demon towered above them all, its form blotting out the moonlight, casting a long shadow over the battlefield. His friends were giving it everything they had—Dex leaping in with daggers slashing, Ell darting around it, her blade slicing shallow but targeted cuts.

Molly saw Jace struggling to regain his aether, the telltale signs of dizziness etched across his face. His shoulders sagged, his movements sluggish. Without hesitation, she rushed over to him, grabbing his arm, her touch firm and insistent. Jace flinched, startled, instinctively trying to pull away.

"Molly, what are you—" he began, but she cut him off, her voice calm but filled with urgency.

"It's okay. You're more needed in this battle than I am," Molly said, her eyes fierce with determination. "We need you out there, Jace. You're the only one who can end this."

Jace began to protest, but before he could, Molly closed her eyes, focusing deeply, and then he felt it—a connection forming. It was similar to the tethering spells he knew, the kind that allowed sharing of gains and harms, but this was different. It was more intense, more raw. As the link took hold, a sudden understanding filled him, like a whisper of knowledge carried through the bond. He felt it—Molly's Word of Power: Loss. The bond solidified, and her intent became clear as Loss's Touch flowed steadily into him.

Jace gasped softly, feeling her aether begin to stream into his body, a gradual and controlled flow that began to replenish his depleted reserves. Warmth flooded his veins, his aether patching wounds, his strength returning, not in a rush but in a steady, sustaining tide. Molly swayed slightly beside him, her face pale, her breath slowing as she kept the flow going.

"Molly..." Jace started, concern lacing his voice.

She held up a hand, a small smile touching her lips even as she struggled to stay on her feet. "I'm alright, Jace. I'll keep this up as long as I can. Just focus on the fight." She looked at him, her eyes filled with determination. "We need you."

Jace nodded, his heart tightening with emotion. There was no time for more words, no time to argue. He turned, catching sight of a nearby student who was fighting off a lesser demon. With urgency in his voice, Jace called out, "You! Guard her—don't leave her side."

The student nodded, eyes wide with understanding, moving immediately to stand beside Molly, his stance protective. Jace lingered for just a heartbeat longer, his gaze meeting Molly's one last time. She nodded at him, her focus unwavering, and he could feel the steady stream of aether still pouring into him.

Jace pushed himself up, feeling the resurgence of energy, the vitality spreading through his body. His wounds closed, his strength surged, and his focus sharpened. He felt Molly's power coursing through him, and it was enough. He was ready.

With a deep breath, he stepped back into the chaos, his eyes scanning the field for the other possessed students. He could see them—their forms contorted, dark and twisted tethers holding their souls captive. He knew the monstrous boss demon was still there, still a major threat, but these others—the lesser demons—he could handle them.

One by one, he would cut their tethers and free the students. He moved forward, his aether flaring as he summoned Soul Sense, his hands glowing with ethereal light. He felt Molly's strength within him, her steady flow sustaining him, and it filled him with renewed determination.

The first target came into view, a demon fighting Ell. Jace could feel it, the demonic thread holding the creature, binding it. He gritted his teeth, his focus unwavering, and reached out.

And he activated Soul Sense.

But as Jace reached out, his attention was suddenly wrenched away from the demon. He felt an unexpected pull, something distant and dim catching his senses. A figure. His focus shifted instinctively, drawn to it, his vision narrowing as he tried to make it out.

The figure was ghostly, almost translucent, drifting closer. Jace's heart pounded, his instincts screaming a warning, but he couldn't look away. It moved with an unnatural fluidity, closing the distance in an instant—until, in a blink, less than a heartbeat, he was right there, inches from Jace's face.

The hollow eyes stared into his, cold and unfeeling. Jace's breath caught, the world seeming to stop for a moment as the pale boy's lips curled into a smile.

"Hello, J-j-jason Rolander."

The pale boy's voice crackled out like a poorly tuned radio, every syllable twitching with static, his words halting, jerking in and out of existence. He stood there, slight and frail, eyes blank as midnight, but somehow they seemed to know too much.

Chapter 57
The Pale Boy

J ace shivered despite himself, the darkness pressing against him like a too-thick blanket, sticky with cold. "Who are you?" Jace demanded, trying to mask the unease scratching at his voice. "How do you know my name?"

The boy smiled, a thin curve of lips that stretched unnaturally, pulling his face into something wrong, almost broken. "I know a lot about you. Quite a lot," he whispered, each word drawn out like a taste he wanted to savor. "Though I'd like to know more. Your little Hades protection has kept me from peering too deep... but no matter." His eyes flickered, something dark swirling within them, almost playful. "I can only look so far into your mind, but you... you can look into mine."

He tilted his head, the gesture jerking and spasmodic. "Curious, aren't you? Why don't you... take a look inside."

Jace felt it—a pull, sudden and irresistible. His Soul Sense thrummed beneath his skin, something instinctive, automatic, kicking in before he could even think. It was as if the boy's words had triggered something deep within him, something that responded without permission. His senses blurred, overlapping—one Soul Sense folding into another, layers building on themselves until the world around him collapsed.

And then he was falling, his consciousness yanked forward, sucked into the void of the boy's mind. It was like slipping off the edge of reality, a cold rush that swallowed him whole before he could even understand what was happening. Everything else faded away, leaving only darkness, and the unsettling sensation of being drawn into something far beyond his control.

It was nothing but darkness. He blinked, but there was no difference. Silence, except for the distant drip of water. He realized he was kneeling, the water reaching to his waist, cold enough to numb. His breathing was loud here, almost wrong in how alone it sounded.

The boy's voice came from somewhere, everywhere, echoing in the hollow dark. "I was born the day you arrived in Terra Mythica. In a way, Jason, I have you to thank for my existence."

The words twisted around him, slipping through the wet, cloying air. "Oh Jason, you shouldn't be here. You were never meant for this world. The calibration... it wasn't for you, was it?" The boy laughed, the sound like shattered glass scattering over marble. "No, it was for your brother, Alexander, wasn't it? A brother you betrayed."

A pang of regret clawed at Jace's chest, raw and visceral. The words burned. "I didn't betray him," Jace spat back, though his own voice wavered.

"Oh, didn't you?" The boy's silhouette danced around him, flickering like a faulty projection. "Your ignorance, your neglect—always rushing into things, making those desperate, foolish deals. If you hadn't been born, Alexander wouldn't have died, would he?"

Jace choked on the grief welling in him, loss like a blade twisting in his gut. "He's not dead. He's alive, and when I get out of here, I'm going to help him."

The boy laughed again, stepping across the water's surface, his bare feet barely disturbing the dark ripples. "Oh, such naivety. I know how you feel J-j-jason because a part of me came from you." His form twitched—he blinked out of existence, then snapped back again. "What am I?" the boy asked, echoing Jace's unspoken thoughts.

"In your world, you'd call me a g-g-glitch." His voice shivered as his form did. "But in mine, I was first known as an Echo. A piece of a thousand souls, torn in the transfer, shattered across the Verse."

Jace clenched his fists, teeth gritting against the chill seeping into him. "What are you talking about?"

"You still don't see it, do you?" The boy's voice cut through the silence like a dagger, laced with condescension. "You were never meant to be here. Yet here you are, and nothing comes without a price." He leaned forward, his eyes narrowing, his lips curling in a twisted smirk. "I am your price. But which piece am I, hmm? Which part of yourself did you leave behind when you crossed over?"

Jace's breath caught as the boy's face began to shift, morphing—Marcus's rugged determination fading into Molly's haunted, searching eyes, then into something even darker, a void deeper than the abyss itself. His form seemed to flicker, his features blurring and changing, each shift more unsettling than the last.

"I belong to them too, you know," the boy continued, his voice now a distorted echo of all the faces he wore. "To Marcus, to Molly. And to many others." He paused, his gaze boring into Jace's. "None of you are supposed to be here. You broke the natural order, and for every step you take, a part of you is lost."

The boy's body twisted again, dissolving into a seething mass of inky darkness, tendrils unraveling and coiling outward, thick and suffocating. His voice was a whisper now, a hiss that slithered into Jace's ears. "When souls shatter, when they are lost to Terra, it is me who grows. I am the hunger that consumes what is left behind. The dark seed that feeds on what was, and turns it into nothing."

The air seemed to solidify, heavy and oppressive, pressing in around Jace, making it harder and harder to draw breath. He could feel it—the presence of something, or many things—trying to force its way into his mind, tendrils of darkness slithering towards the fractures in his will, seeking entry.

The thing that had once resembled a boy twisted its face into a grotesque smile, its teeth gleaming like shards of bone against the inky blackness. "You know," it said, the mockery thick in its tone, "for someone who thinks he's special, you're really not that clever. Your friends, they whisper behind your back—what do they see? Someone poor, helpless, weak. But not completely stupid, I suppose."

"Shut up!" Jace roared, his voice cracking like thunder, cutting across the darkness. Rage flared within him, raw and unrestrained, surging up from a place he didn't recognize. And then it happened—a burst of light, moonlight, pure and wild, erupted from within him, spilling outward. It was radiant, like a piece of the night sky that had suddenly awakened within him, breaking through the oppressive shadows.

He didn't know where it had come from; his shard wasn't here, no relic of power to hold in his hands. It felt deeper, older, as if it had been with him all along—a fragment of his soul, a shard of defiance breaking free at the moment of greatest need.

For a heartbeat, the darkness recoiled, as if the boy—no, the thing—had not expected it. But then, just as quickly, came the laughter—deep, echoing, dripping with disdain. It filled the void around him, wrapping around the light like chains, mocking his defiance, making a joke of his hope.

It chuckled, the sound hollow and cruel. "How quaint. Do you really think a spark like that can stand against the shadows?" The tendrils of darkness closed in again, moving faster now, curling around the light, choking it.

"Do you think you can harm me, Little Thing?" The voice slithered around him, a thousand whispers bleeding together. "I am a part of what they call the Eternal End. A piece of its tapestry, woven into the essence of finality itself. For all things are, and all things shall cease to be. I am that cessation."

Jace had heard the name before. The Dark One. It hung in his mind like a distant echo, resonating in his bones. Something stirred within him—an instinct, a strange inspiration, raw and reckless. He cast Soul Sense again, feeling his consciousness dive deeper, plunging into the dark waters of the creature's twisted mind.

For a moment, there was nothing but shadow—a blank expanse that seemed to swallow his awareness whole. And then, a flicker. A flash, like the heartbeat of something unspeakable, and he felt it. He was closer to something—closer to a truth that clawed at the peripheral of his understanding.

"Ah, yes," the creature's voice crooned, tinged with a mocking joy. "You are beginning to see... but can you understand?"

The taunts hung in the air, but Jace ignored them, his focus unwavering. He cast it again, his mind pushing through the darkness, even as it grew thicker, more hostile, trying to shove him back. Either he was finally about to grasp what this nightmare really was, or he was walking into a trap from which he'd never escape. Either way, he needed to know. He needed to see.

The thing laughed again, but Jace didn't flinch. He drove forward, each breath more labored than the last, his vision narrowing, everything tightening as if the shadows themselves were closing in on him. And in that tightening abyss, Jace knew—whatever came next would either break him or free him.

And then, without his control, he felt it trigger again.

Soul Sense, Soul Sense, Soul Sense. Each time he dove a step deeper, the world shifted around him.

And as he moved, the creature itself shifted. Its face changed. It became Thistle, then Marcus, then Jace.

"What are you doing to me?" Jace cried out, but there was only laughter in response.

Soul Sense. Soul Sense. Soul Sense.

His aether was draining fast.

Until finally, he couldn't go any further.

The darkness seemed to pulse, each word throbbing with an unspoken truth that tore at Jace's resolve. He felt the probing presence, slithering through his mind, scraping at his thoughts. "I am the piece you all leave behind when you come here," it hissed. "You might as well call me the Dark One's Shadow—the puppet who became the master."

The form grew then, a giant shadow stretching upward, a mountainous form, eyes glowing a deep, throbbing red. Claws emerged, dark against darker still, reaching down, curling inwards. It was the Dark One's true form, twisted and grotesque, towering over Jace, a bright glow radiating from its chest.

"Yes, Jason, you see it now." The thing's voice dropped to a whisper, sinister and intimate, as it leaned in, its red eyes searing through Jace's defenses, peeling back the layers of his soul. "The Dark One was once just a man, like you—a fragile, desperate man. My first little broken thing."

The whisper grew, swelling into a thunderous boom that seemed to echo not just in the air, but inside Jace's skull, shaking his very thoughts. "In a way, I am him, and he is me—creator and created, bound in a twisted dance. He is my father, my maker... and yet, my child."

It grinned, a jagged, gleaming smile that seemed to cut through the darkness. "I, once the shadow at his heels, now risen, now flesh. The Shadow has become the man, until there was nothing but me."

Jace struggled, his body aching, his soul straining, the cold water thickening around him, becoming ink, swallowing him, dragging him down. He fought against it, his mind trying to push back, to escape the murk that encased him.

The monstrous figure laughed, a sound like the dying echoes of a thousand voices.

Jace's mind throbbed, the ink tightening, his body failing him. He heard the echoes of his friends—outside, falling, screaming—while here he was, locked in a dark, eternal conversation, his soul caught in a vice.

The thing leaned closer, its form losing cohesion, ink dripping into the dark water beneath. "Your mind is strong," it whispered, almost regretful. "No matter." And then it grinned, fading into the darkness, leaving Jace gasping alone, in ink that had become ice, in silence that swallowed all hope.

"Just a bit deeper should do the trick. Your aether should be recovered just enough."

Jace felt his Soul Sense pulse once again, a subtle vibration that tugged at the edges of his awareness.

I need you to understand me, Jace. To see me for who I truly am. The voice echoed in his mind, a chilling mix of desperation and command. Call it a remnant of my humanity, or perhaps a fragment of the broken humanities of all who came before me. But I need it—I need you to see me.

The presence wavered, almost pleading, but beneath it lay a hunger, an inevitability that Jace could feel deep within. For when you see it, you will become me. And together, we will bring forth the Eternal End.

A shiver ran down Jace's spine as he felt his aether surge, finally regenerating enough for him to act. But before he could even form a thought, the Soul Sense triggered one final time, the sensation like a wave crashing over him—pulling him under.

Everything around him dissolved, the world vanishing as he was plunged into a darkness so complete, it swallowed even his thoughts.

The space was black—an all-consuming void that swallowed light and sound, leaving only the pulse of dread.

Jace felt himself being torn from control, an invisible force shoving him into the recesses of his own mind. He tried to fight it, but it was like pushing against an ocean tide, his body no longer his own. His consciousness was forced back, pressed into a corner, left to watch helplessly through a window smeared with darkness.

In a distant window in the darkness, he saw a faint vision of the outside world. Like the scene at the end of a long, dark hallway.

He saw his friends. They were distant, so impossibly far away, their figures barely visible like shadows against a deeper night. They were fighting, struggling against the onslaught of demons, and without Jace, they were faltering. His stomach lurched as he watched Dex, fierce and defiant, his face streaked with blood. Ell, her hair matted, her hands trembling as she swung her weapon.

Every movement seemed slower, each swing of a blade weaker, their faces marred by exhaustion and desperation. He could see the blood—so much of it—staining their clothes, splattering the ground. One after another, they stumbled, buckling under the weight of their wounds, their defenses crumbling.

Jace's chest tightened, his breath coming in ragged gasps as he felt their pain, their fear. They needed him. They needed his skills, his strength—things that only he could bring to their side. But here he was, buried in darkness, nothing more than a spectator to their suffering. He felt the cold grip of helplessness, a raw, visceral horror that twisted in his gut.

The message was clear—without Jace, they would fall. And Jace was powerless, bound by the very darkness that sought to destroy everything he held dear.

Jace couldn't move for a long moment as his aether recovered, he had to watch as his friends were hurt, held in the Dark One's mind.

Chapter 58
The Dark One's Shadow

Then, a figure emerged—a hooded silhouette moving toward him with deliberate, unhurried steps. The darkness seemed to part for it, shadows peeling away as it approached. Slowly, the figure reached up and pulled back its hood, revealing not a monstrous visage or some twisted demon, but a man. A middle-aged man, his face etched with lines—lines born of worry, of countless sleepless nights, and faint, almost forgotten traces of laughter that had long since faded.

"I know who you are," Jace forced the words out, voice trembling and raw. "Persephone showed me everything, Shadow of Errikos."

The figure paused, red eyes narrowing, and then a cruel laugh broke the silence. "Oh, did she now? Is that the name she used for me?" It tilted its head, amusement twisting across its dark features. "Fitting, in their world of half-truths. Yes, yes... Errikos was once my name. Just as yours is Jace."

It leaned closer, shadows thickening around them. "But long before Errikos, the great and powerful, there was a simpler man. Back then, I was Henry Williams. Just a man with nothing but the clothes on his back and a woman he loved. A wife named Osira. My world, my entire existence, wrapped in that one name. And when they took her from me... there was nothing left. Nothing but the darkness you see before you now."

Jace's jaw clenched, his breath turning sharp, ragged. "Vengeance won't bring you peace."

The figure's laughter echoed again, bouncing off the void around them, growing louder, almost hysterical. "Peace?" it sneered, leaning so close Jace could feel the chill radiating from it. "You think this is some petty vendetta? Some childish whim of revenge?" It shook its head, eyes blazing. "No, this is a vow. A duty I swore to fulfill. This is what must be done for the sake of everything."

"You're nothing but hate," Jace growled, his voice raw, trembling under the weight of what he knew was coming. "Hate and a twisted mind unable to cope with the consequences of your own choices."

The thing's expression changed, its smile curving into something monstrous, the sharp edge of a sneer. "Do you think I've done all this, survived through years upon years, because the System made me feel something funny?" The void pulsed around them, darkness creeping closer, the figure growing larger, looming over Jace. "No. Let me show you what I feel."

And then, the darkness surged forward, drowning Jace in an endless tide. He was no longer in the void. He was standing somewhere else, somewhere he recognized, because he had seen it before in Persephone's visions.

A woman bounded up to the man lounging on a blanket beneath a gnarled, ancient oak. He closed his book, the title now visible—Umbra Maleficarum, the Book of Demons.

"Are you just going to sit there and read all day?" she teased, grasping his hand and hauling him to his feet with a playful groan. She thrust a dull practice sword into his grasp.

"There's so much to learn about this place," he protested, his eyes lingering on the abandoned book. "Aren't you curious about its history? Its lore? I still don't understand how they wove such an intricate backstory into everything."

She smirked, twirling her own practice sword in a carefree arc. "I'm more curious about how you still haven't managed to beat me in a single fight."

"Oh, but I thought you loved me for my mind, not my might," he countered, eyes twinkling.

"And you love me for my surprises," she quipped, lunging at him without warning. He blocked, his expression transforming into focused determination, though a smile tugged at his lips.

"As you wish, m'lady. Prepare to be awed, inspired, amazed," he declared, glancing skyward as though seeking just the right flourish. "Enchanted and enthralled," he added with a theatrical sigh.

"Fight or talk," she challenged, and with that, their swords clashed.

Jace studied Osira intently. When Persephone had shown him the memories, they had been slightly blurred, distorted like a faded painting—a memory of Spring that had lost its sharpness over time. But what Jace saw now came directly from Henry's recollections, vivid and unfiltered.

There was something about Osira that felt familiar. He couldn't quite put his finger on it, but a nagging sense told him he'd seen her somewhere before, her face lingering in the recesses of his mind like an unfinished puzzle just waiting for the final piece.

The scene blurred and hours passed. Jace saw Henry and Osira, laying in a field beneath a sky that looked impossibly bright. Osira was resting her head against Henry's chest, a softness in her voice. "Do you think we could live here?" she asked, her words half-dream, half-wish.

Henry smiled, looking down at her. "We are here now," he replied, stroking her hair gently.

She lifted her head, her dark eyes searching his. "No, I mean... live here. Really live here. Forget everything back there."

Henry frowned, uncertainty flickering in his eyes. "What about our friends? Our lives back home?"

"Come on, Henry," she murmured, her voice softening into something wistful. "We could still message them. When was the last time any of us really spent time together? We're all so busy with our own lives."

Henry hesitated, his gaze turning distant. "And what about us, Osira?" he asked, his voice quiet. "What about our own family? Don't you want children? You know I'd be happy anywhere, as long as you were there. But what about that?"

There was no answer, and they lay there, silent, the question hanging in the air unanswered.

The world fractured, like a dream slipping from the mind at dawn. Time stopped.

Henry turned toward Jace then, his young face bearing an old weight, eyes like darkened glass reflecting a history far beyond his years. He spoke, his voice carrying that peculiar resonance that broke the boundary between now and whatever past he seemed to relive.

"Immortality," he began, his words soft but sharp as a knife's edge, "a life together with no hunger, no famine, no war. A life away from the sickness of the world." He paused, his gaze holding mine, something both wistful and broken lying beneath it. "When John Rearden approached us, offering us this life—this first taste of eternity—it was too good to be true."

He looked past Jace, seeing something only he could. "But he didn't tell us the cost."

The air seemed to grow colder, as if his words reached out and brushed against something beyond mere memory, something palpable. "Immortality did not come without a price. If we had known," he exhaled, a sigh that seemed to carry all the regret in the world, "perhaps we would have avoided death. But there was no loss from respawn then. No cost to EXP. EXP didn't even exist yet."

He laughed, but there was no joy in it, just the hollow echo of something once cherished and now out of reach. "So we tried everything. We lived everywhere. We threw ourselves off mountains, flew through the skies until our wings failed. Each time we died, we reset—imprinted again and again, forever twenty-two-year-old newlyweds."

His voice cracked, the words he spoke now frayed at the edges. "Forever," he repeated, quieter. And then, almost a whisper, "Except..."

His eyes fixed on Jace, and he could feel the change in the air, the shift from story to something raw and ugly, something carved out of his very soul. "But here's the trick—the cruel, sick twist of it all." Henry stepped closer, a tremor in his voice, the anger blending with sorrow in a way that was heartbreakingly human. "Each time we died, we handled it differently. I—" he paused, his eyes narrowing slightly, as if the memory was something heavy that he was lifting, "I was immune. Or perhaps resistant to the side effects. But she... she was not."

The silence after his words seemed to stretch on, long enough that the force of it pressed on Jace's chest. "They never tell you of the side effects," he continued, his gaze distant. "Even if they know them, they hide them from you. They hide them from the world."

He glanced down, his hands trembling just slightly, then he balled them into fists, as if trying to control the shivers. "Her mind grew frailer each time. We didn't notice at first—how could we? Each death seemed like just another turn of the wheel, a reset to how it was meant to be. But it wasn't." His voice grew quieter, haunted. "The memories of her past lives began to blur, to twist, lost somewhere between memories of me, of us, of home, of Earth. Every time she died, a piece of her slipped away—a piece of us."

His voice broke, and he stood there, the hollow echo of his words hanging in the air, his eyes staring at nothing. "Every death pulled her further away from me. A piece at a time, she drifted." His chest rose with a shuddering breath, the kind that comes when there are no more tears left to shed. "Until one day... there was a miracle."

A flicker of something—hope, disbelief—crossed his face. He looked at Jace, eyes hollow, voice like a ghost's whisper. "Until one day, she didn't remember my face."

He said nothing more, but the silence spoke volumes. It was the quiet of lost moments and shattered dreams, the quiet of someone who'd loved, truly loved, only to find that love slowly eroded by something he couldn't fight, something even time could not mend. The world seemed to breathe in that silence, holding on to the ache of something fragile and true that had been broken, irreparably, by the promise of eternity.

Time shifted again, the scene bending and twisting until it solidified into something else. Something darker.

Henry stood, shouting, his face a mask of fury and desperation. There was a shadow there—something almost human, but not quite. They were in a cave, deep in the underworld, and the air thrummed with tension.

"What you're suggesting isn't possible," Hades said, his voice calm, but there was a weariness to it. A heaviness.

"But it has to be," Henry snapped, slamming his fist down on the rough stone table, splintering it. "It's affecting her outside. You've seen it."

Hades sighed, the sound echoing through the dark. "It is a terrible thing, Henry. I've spoken with the others, even with Jack. He believes he knows what went wrong. He and Rearden are working to fix it—for the future."

Henry's eyes were wild, desperate. "The future?" he spat, his voice cracking. "What about Osira? What about her?"

"The future cannot change the past," Hades said, his tone turning cold, detached.

Henry's rage trembled, his shoulders shaking. "Enough of your cryptic nonsense, Hades. You lied. You all lied. You lied to us."

"Death has always come at a cost, Chosen," Hades said, his voice growing harsh, the shadows deepening. "Even the death of a Traveler."

"If we had known, we would have been more careful! She's falling apart, Hades." Henry's voice broke, tears streaming down his face. "She can barely remember my face. She doesn't even recognize me."

Hades looked away, the god's face unreadable. "Give it time, Henry. Her memories will return."

"Do you know that?" Henry whispered, broken. "Or is that more of Jack and Rearden's lies?"

"Careful, Henry," Hades said, his eyes narrowing. "You are under my protection, but even I cannot shield you from the consequences of your blasphemy."

"Blasphemy?" Henry laughed, a wild, desperate sound that echoed through the darkened cave. "This whole place is blasphemy—your gods, your world, Jack, all of it. If Jack wants to deal with me, let him come. Let him do his worst!" Henry threw his arms wide, his voice rising, cracking. "Strike me down, oh great System! Take everything you haven't already stolen. Take my life, or give it back to me."

The darkness around them swirled, morphing, and Jace saw Henry, older now, the weariness gone, his face almost hopeful. Osira was beside him.

"I tried," Henry said, his voice softened by an edge of longing, as though the past were something he could still reach if he stretched far enough. "I hadn't spoken to Hades in nearly eighty years. The gods left me alone. Jack never showed his face again. I logged out less and less, and eventually, this became my world—my life."

A wry smile tugged at his lips, but it held no humor. "Excelsior gave me a deep dive pod, their way of appeasing me, I suppose. A bribe so I wouldn't need to log out at all. I thought about suing them, but... people who tried that ended up disappearing. Gone without a trace."

He let out a slow breath, the sound weary. "The doctors at Excelsior called it early-onset degenerative Alzheimer's. Claimed it wasn't caused by the game, that it was some rare genetic disease." His eyes flickered, a bitter glint catching in them for a heartbeat. "We did test after test in the real world, hoping, maybe, for some other answer. But the damage was there—on both sides, in both worlds."

Henry paused, his gaze distant, as though he were staring into a time that only he could see. "There were moments of clarity," he said, his voice low. "Moments where she'd look at me, and I'd see the woman I loved, the one I'd promised forever. And then, just as quickly, fear would cloud her eyes. Anger. And finally, confusion and loss."

His voice broke, just a little, and he swallowed hard, trying to gather himself. "I tried," he said, almost to himself, as if repeating it made it more real. "For a long time, I tried."

The scene shifted again and settled into a new memory. The air smelled of winter, frost curling along the window panes of a small, dimly lit room. They sat in quiet comfort in a castle that belonged to them both.

And old Osira sat in an armchair, her gaze distant, lost. Henry knelt beside her, speaking softly, his words careful, cautious, as if speaking too loudly might shatter her fragile grasp on reality.

Oldman Henry turned to Jace for a moment, breaking the scene. "I acquired a fair amount of land and wealth over the years and we had made the habit of avoiding respawn at all costs. In the following years, I became more so her caretaker, than husband. But at least I could be by her side. There were good days, and bad days. This day was both."

There was a flicker—a spark of something familiar in Osira's eyes. Her gaze snapped to his, recognition lighting her face as she looked at Henry as if seeing him for the first time.

"Henry?" Her voice was trembling. "When did you get here?"

His eyes filled with tears instantly, welling up until they blurred his vision. "I've been here the whole time, darling. I've never left you."

"Oh, Henry," she whispered, small and vulnerable. "I'm so scared. My thoughts... my memories... they're like motes in the breeze." She shook slightly, her fragility laid bare. He reached out, taking her hands in his, his grip tight, desperate to anchor her. She pressed against him then, wrapping herself around him in a deep embrace.

"Henry, are you there?" she murmured, her voice muffled against his shoulder.

"I'm still here, my love," he whispered back, his voice cracking, barely more than a breath. "I'm not going anywhere."

For a brief moment, the world seemed to stand still, suspended in that fragile silence. But then, as quickly as it had come, the familiar fog returned to her eyes, that dreadful emptiness reclaiming her gaze. She looked up at him, her face twisting, not with love, not with recognition, but with fear.

"What are you doing here?" Her voice was cold, edged with panic, her eyes darting around the room. She didn't see him. Not really. She saw only a stranger.

"No... please," Henry's voice broke, pleading. "Osira, don't go. I'm here. It's me."

She pushed him away, her frail form trembling now in terror. "Who are you? I demand to know! How did you get in my chambers?" Her voice rose, shaking with fright.

"Please, Osira, it's me." His words choked in his throat, tears spilling freely now, desperation in every syllable.

"Guards! Guards!" she screamed, her voice echoing through the empty room. But no guards came. There were no guards—only silence, and the fading vision, until all that remained was Henry. The middle-aged man stared back at Jace, his eyes hollow with an ache that defied description.

"When she logged out of Mythica," Henry said, turning to Jace, "she became terrified at the sight of me. I had no choice but to let her go, to move her into a luxury care facility specializing in dementia and Alzheimer's. Excelsior paid for it, sparing no expense. They even provided her with a deep-dive system. She would be cared for." He paused, a faint tremor in his voice. "In the real world, she was only in her mid-twenties then. The youngest admission they'd ever had."

Henry's gaze drifted, his eyes heavy with memory. "Sometimes, I would break down, even though I knew I shouldn't. The doctors warned me that the stress I brought her could make her condition worse. But there were nights..." He trailed off, his voice catching. "Nights when I was weaker than I should have been. I tried to reach her. I tried to remind her of who we were, of what we had. But she... she had forgotten me."

He closed his eyes, a flicker of pain washing over his expression. "In the real world, she became less and less. Less able to live, to feed herself, to manage even the most basic things. But in Terra Mythica... she was still there. She could live, she could carry on, just... not with me." His words hung in the air, filled with the ache of a love that had slipped through his fingers—alive only in the pixels of a game that could no longer hold them both.

Chapter 59
Behind the Mind

Henry's form blurred, the scene dissipating like smoke scattered by a cold wind. When it returned, it was another winter—years had passed, countless years in Mythica's relentless march of time. "It had been a few centuries since I last saw her," Henry's voice echoed softly. "I told myself I wasn't looking, that I had let her go. But I had been searching, even as I resisted the urge. Strange, the wars we wage within ourselves."

He paused, the air around him thick with unspoken longing. "Part of her condition included a variable respawn point. It was something Hades had arranged with the other gods—something about reducing the strain on her mind, allowing her to follow the path of least resistance instead of being tethered to a single fixed place."

He looked away, as though reliving each painstaking moment of his search. "Every time she respawned, there was a chance I'd never find her again. Terra Mythica is vast, as large as Earth itself, down to the foot. And so I wandered, knowing that each time she returned, she could be anywhere—lost in a world too expansive for any one soul to cross alone."

"Until I heard whispers of a singer—a woman in a small town nestled deep in the Norse realms, a place they called Vetrgard, known for her hauntingly beautiful ballads. Osira had always loved to sing." Henry's voice grew quiet, tinged with a fragile hope. "I had sought out a thousand bards before, each time clinging to the faint chance it might be her. I suppose I didn't expect anything different when I journeyed there that winter's eve."

Snow clung to everything, coating the world in a pristine blanket of white. The cold bit into the air, and Henry stood there, older, his face lined and worn by time. His breath misted in the moonlight, drifting like ghosts in the gentle breeze.

Ahead of him was a small cottage, plumes of smoke curling from the chimney. He could hear laughter from inside—a family gathered together, grandparents, children, grandchildren—all safe, all happy.

And then she appeared, her voice carrying on the frigid air, sending warmth flooding through him despite the years that had passed. "I'm seventy, not dead! I can fetch the firewood myself. You two stay with the little ones," Osira called over her shoulder, her tone playful, her smile teasing. She wore a thick fur coat, wrinkles gathered around her eyes from years of laughter and living.

She hummed a soft tune, her voice lilting through the cold air like a delicate thread, weaving warmth into the winter night.

Henry watched from the edge of the fence surrounding the cabin, half-concealed in the shadows. He hadn't meant to linger this long, but the warmth of the fire and the laughter had drawn him closer, almost against his will.

She noticed him suddenly, her eyes widening in alarm before a soft laugh escaped, breaking the tension. "I hadn't seen you there," she said, her voice holding a slight tremor, her breath still catching in her chest.

"My apologies, madame," Henry responded, stepping forward just a little, his voice soft, contrite. "I didn't mean to frighten you. I was only passing through. The fire, the laughter, I—was just admiring it."

She studied him for a beat longer, her eyes still wary but the corners of her lips softening into a semblance of a smile. "Well, it's the night before the winter solstice," she explained, her voice gentler now. "A time for family."

"Indeed," Henry said, his gaze lingering, unable to quite pull away from her. There was something about her—something he couldn't name.

She offered a polite smile, already turning back towards the cottage. "Well met, stranger. I should get back. My family will be wondering where I've gone."

"Yes," Henry said, his voice a bare whisper, almost lost in the rustling of the wind. "One must." He took a step back, preparing to fade into the shadows, but something in him hesitated. His chest tightened with an unspoken ache. "I'm happy for you," he called after her, his tone surprisingly earnest, almost aching.

She paused, turning back to him. Her eyes softened, and there was a depth there—a knowing. Something tender, something that saw more than he'd intended to show. "So am I," she said quietly, her smile gentle, her eyes holding his a moment longer than necessary. Then she turned, the warmth of the firelight pulling her back, leaving Henry alone with the cold night and the soft echo of her laughter.

She hesitated, then added, "Sir, do you not have family to spend the solstice with? You're welcome to join us. We have food enough for twenty more—my eldest daughter is a follower of Aegir, and we have merriment enough to share. You know how they can be."

Henry smiled, the kind of smile a stranger offers, kind and distant. "No, thank you. I must be going. But your offer is kind, madame."

She nodded, her smile lingering. She turned to leave, but before she disappeared inside, she called out once more. "What is your name, stranger?" she asked, her voice carrying across the frosted air.

Henry hesitated, his eyes softening. "Errikos," he said.

She smiled at him, a genuine warmth. "I'm Osira," she said, and then turned, disappearing into the warmth of her home.

Henry stood there, frozen in that moment, the world still around him, blanketed in freshly fallen snow. The cottage lights blurred, distant echoes of laughter slipping through the cold night air. He watched until the last flicker of her disappeared.

He turned then, his eyes locking onto Jace's. His gaze bore into him, carrying the weight of an eternity of grief.

"I couldn't use my real name," Henry began, his voice wavering under the weight of old emotions. "Not when I knew what it would do to her. I'd seen it, you know... what the memory of me did to her—how it haunted her, twisted everything into something cruel and unbearable." His eyes drifted, unfocused, the past playing out somewhere just beyond his reach. "I tried, more times than I can count. I thought maybe, just maybe, I could bring it all back—the good parts. Make her remember us as we were."

He swallowed hard, his gaze darkening as he relived it. "But I was wrong. Every time, it ended the same way. The pain in her eyes, the way she fought against her memories as if they were some kind of nightmare she couldn't escape. I was a ghost to her, and each time I returned, I only dragged her further into the shadows." He shook his head slowly, a bitter smile touching his lips. "Hades warned me, of course. Told me there'd be a cost. But I thought I could carry it."

He paused, his fingers tightening around nothing at all, a silent admission of his helplessness. "That's when I understood—truly understood. I couldn't bear to see her suffer because of me. Not again. Not ever." His voice softened, the words coming out almost like a confession. "That was the day I chose to become someone else. Errikos—a new name for a new life. A name that wouldn't remind her of the nightmares I'd left behind."

He paused, the shadows gathering around him, his face hardening. "In the old tongue, it means Henry. It would be many years later before I would take on my third name, the one you know me by today."

He looked away then, his eyes misting over with a distant sadness. "Osira lived the rest of her life in peace—spent her days with her family, surrounded by warmth and laughter. Every winter, I would check in on her, just to make sure she was alright, though we did not speak again. Until one year, she was gone. Her body, finally claimed by age, left in peace."

The scene became a fairground, bustling with activity, the crisp chill of winter in the air. Henry stood among the crowd, the annual winter fair of Roandia stretching around him. "A hundred years had come and gone before I saw her again."

Henry's eyes wandered, his gaze losing its sharpness as his mind drifted back. "Roandia," he muttered, as if tasting something sour. "A border city caught between the Greeks and the Egyptians. To one side, Olympus—columns of marble, Zeus and his eternal theatrics. And on the other, Amen-Ra's territory—sand and sun, with temples that stretched forever. And there, squeezed between the egos of gods, sat Roandia. A patch of green in an ocean of desert, a little paradise that the powers that be hardly noticed—until they needed to. It was the first spawn point in Mythica. The place where all Traveler's began." He smiled a wicked smile, hiding a secret, a laugh escaping, harsh and humorless.

"Back on Earth, they called it Mesopotamia. The land between two rivers. Civilization's birthplace.

"I used to think it was impressive, how stories could find new life here, how so many mythologies had a home in Terra Mythica. I even found it charming. Once."

The laughter died, his smile curdling into something darker, something more weary.

"But when it came down to it, they were all worthless. Zeus, Amen-Ra, all their bluster and lightning, all their golden temples and sacred suns—they were as useless as the rest of them. Not a single one gave a damn when it mattered. All their grand titles, all their sacred power—it's all a game to them. No substance. Just noise and flash, empty promises wrapped up in marble and sunbeams. Useless, every last one."

"Nevertheless, it was there, amidst the winter festivals of Mesopotamia—of Roandia—that Osira and I first stepped into Mythica. It was where we first felt that spark, that sense of wonder that made us fall in love with this place." He looked down for a moment. "I don't know what drew me there that day. But then I saw her. A young, beautiful Osira, as vivid as my fondest memories."

Henry gestured toward the vivid memory unfolding before Jace's eyes. The fairground seemed to dance with light and color, a distant echo of something long lost. "This is where it all began again," Henry murmured, his gaze distant, locked on Osira's laughter as it rang out, clear as a bell. "A miracle, you know. A true one."

He paused, his eyes following her as she disappeared behind a stall, only to pop up on the other side, her smile teasing, her eyes finding his across the booths. "You see that smile? The way she looked at me... It was like the universe had decided to tilt, just for a moment, so we could find each other again. Like love at first sight—only deeper, as if it had always been there, waiting for us to catch up."

Henry glanced at Jace, a small, almost wistful smile tugging at his lips. "It had been so long, Jace. Two hundred years. I thought... I thought I could never be anything but a ghost to her. The sadness, the pain—it used to be all I could bring her. But that day... her mind didn't reject me. She didn't get lost in the sorrow or the shadows."

He swallowed, a breath catching in his throat, his voice softer now. "Maybe enough time had passed. Maybe I'd been pushed so deep into the corners of her memory that I no longer stirred those old wounds. Or maybe, just maybe, it was fate's cruel kindness—letting us meet like that, as if none of the pain had ever been. A clean slate. A chance to love her as if we were new."

He turned back to the memory, the way Osira's eyes held his, her laughter bright against the glow of the fairground. "It was a miracle, Jace. To see her smile without the weight of everything that had come before. To feel, even just for a moment, like we were free of it all. And I—" He hesitated, a small laugh, weary and filled with warmth, escaping him. "I looked at her like a man seeing the sun for the first time. Because that's what it felt like—light after so many years of darkness."

Henry's gaze returned to Jace, his eyes reflecting a mix of hope and regret. "It wasn't perfect, and I knew it wouldn't last. But in that moment, under those fairground lights, we were just Henry and Osira. And that... that was everything."

"She knew me as Errikos then," Henry continued, his voice laden with a deep ache, each word carrying the weight of lost chances. "I wasn't about to make the same mistake twice. I wanted to tell her the truth—gods, I wanted nothing more. But I couldn't. I couldn't risk it, not after everything. I couldn't bear to lose her. Not again."

He paused, his throat tightening, a flicker of regret clouding his eyes. "So, we lived that life. I stayed Errikos. We were married the following fall, under the bright leaves and the crisp sky. It was... it was the happiest I'd been in more years than I care to remember."

There was warmth in his voice now, even if it was tinged with sadness. "And for her, it seemed the same. We tried to have children, but... well, that wasn't in the cards for us. Nevertheless, we had each other. And that was enough. We made it enough. The laughter, the quiet moments, the simple, ordinary days... we were happy."

The scene before them shifted, as if caught in a breeze, blurring and swirling, the colors and shapes speeding forward, passing years in moments. Jace's eyes widened as the world settled again, bringing into view a familiar cottage—the same one Persephone had shown him. Their home. He could almost feel the echoes of laughter in its walls -see the warmth that had once lived within its small, sunlit rooms.

Henry's voice came again, softer now, almost a whisper. "This was where we lived our years. Our little sanctuary, away from gods and their games. Just us. Just the life we made, with all its imperfections and fleeting joys." He looked at Jace, a sad, wistful smile on his lips. "It wasn't perfect. But it was ours. And that was enough, for a time."

Chapter 60
The Eternal End

Time marched on, and years swept by. Errikos was old now, and Osira had aged beside him. Jace watched as the familiar scene unfolded, no longer obscured or distorted. The fight, the sudden chaos. The arrow struck Osira, and Henry—no, Errikos—fought the soldiers, rage propelling him as he cut them down, sending the rest fleeing with curses and threats.

Errikos didn't care. He rushed to her side, hands trembling as he worked his magic, the wound closing, her life flickering back into her eyes. She looked up at him, and she smiled, but something shifted in her gaze—something that made Jace's stomach turn.

Her eyes squinted, as if trying to focus. Her lips quivered. "Henry?" she whispered, her voice breaking, fragile. "Is that... is that really you?"

He froze, not knowing what to say, unable to answer.

"Henry..." She began to cry, tears spilling down her cheeks. "It's been so long. And you're so old now... how did you get to be so old?" She looked down at her hands, her fingers trembling. "Henry, I'm scared. What's happening to me?"

He held her tightly, his heart breaking with each word she spoke. "Shhh, it's okay, my love," he whispered. "It's okay. I've got you."

"Henry?" she whispered, her voice so small, so lost.

"Yes, darling. I'm here."

"Henry? Where are you?"

He swallowed, his voice catching, struggling to speak. "I'm right here," he said, tears choking him.

But then, the light in her eyes faded—the fear, the pain, all of it replaced by confusion, by sadness. She looked at him, frowning slightly. "Why are you crying?" she asked. "Come on, my love, let's get inside. We're letting in a draft."

Errikos turned to Jace, his face worn and haggard. "For a precious few more days, I thought things had returned to the way they once were. Not with her knowing me for who I truly was, but at least happy enough. But it was only the beginning. The nightmares returned, and with them, flashes of memory—moments of the past breaking through.

The scene shifted again, flashing to Osira in Errikos's arms, her body trembling, tears streaming down her face in the dead of night.

"Every day," Henry's voice came from nowhere, echoing with the weight of loss, "she slipped further. The lives she knew became tangled – twisted. The spells came more frequently, more violently. She would wake screaming, fighting me, terrified of me. And then, just as quickly, she'd see me again—the way she used to. But the good moments grew fewer and farther between, her mind unraveling, slipping away."

The scene shifted once more. Jace could see Errikos returning home, the air heavy with smoke. He rushed inside, finding the cottage filled with the thick, acrid scent of burning food.

"She had been cooking," Henry's voice continued, the despair palpable, "and then... she simply stopped. She stopped moving, stopped everything. When I found her, there was the faintest glint of life left."

The vision took shape—Errikos kneeling on the cabin floor, holding Osira in his arms, her face pale, her eyes empty. Around them, small fires burned where the food had been left to char, smoke curling around the room.

Jace realized then, the scene that Persephone had shown him before—it wasn't a single day's end. It was months later, the inevitable conclusion of all the fragile moments they had tried to hold on to.

"Errikos, is that you?" she asked, her voice weak, trembling, her words slurring together.

"Yes, my love. It's me." He tried to smile, but it was a broken, desperate thing.

And then, just like that, she was gone. The final glints of light faded from her eyes, and her body went still in his arms. Henry swallowed, his throat dry and burning. "I don't know how she died," he said, his voice cracking, barely a whisper. "Maybe her body just couldn't take it anymore—the stress, the pain. But she was gone. And there was nothing I could do."

The flames spread, the room growing hotter, but Henry didn't move. He held her close, his arms tightening around her as if he could keep her there by force alone. He rocked slightly, tears streaming down his face, and screamed into the empty night. "Hades, appear!" His voice echoed through the smoke and flames, raw and broken. He rocked her gently, his voice cracking again. "Hades! Appear! You owe me that much!"

The fires stilled. The world itself seemed to pause—all but for Henry, who continued to rock Osira's lifeless form.

A dark presence entered the room, the temperature dropping. Shadows shifted, forming a figure that loomed over the old man and his beloved.

"Chosen," Hades said, his voice quiet.

Henry spat on the floor, his eyes blazing. "Don't call me that. I'm no Chosen of yours."

Hades surveyed the scene, his dark gaze taking in the lifeless body in Henry's arms, the destroyed room. Understanding crossed his features—a sadness that seemed to sink deeper.

"Hades, bring her back," Henry demanded, his voice nothing more than a broken plea.

"I cannot," Hades replied, his voice calm, steady.

"Lies!" Henry screamed, his body trembling with rage. "Death is your domain! You have the power. Bring her back to me!"

"It was her time," Hades said, his voice almost gentle. "In my book, her name is written. Her soul has passed on, Henry. It's not my choice—I am but a shepherd of those who cross that threshold."

"You've done it before!" Henry shouted, standing, his body trembling with the weight of Osira's form. He laid her gently on the bed, his eyes fierce as he turned back to the god. "For others, you've broken your rules. Do it for me now."

Hades watched him, his gaze soft, filled with sorrow. "It's beyond me now," he said. "She has already respawned. She's been reborn, Errikos. It's beyond my power to bring her back."

"Where is she?" Henry's voice cracked, his eyes wide, desperate.

"It's too late, Henry," Hades said, shaking his head. "Her mind is already lost."

Henry knew, deep down, that Hades was right, but that knowledge did nothing to quell the rage bubbling up inside him. He lunged at Hades, his hands moving through the god, like smoke, a futile effort. "You did this!" he shouted, his voice hoarse. "You did this!" He unleashed his fury, his aura exploding out from him—tendrils of dark, inky power spreading across the room, shattering wood and pottery.

Hades stood there, unmoving, his face filled with quiet sorrow. "I am sorry, Henry," he whispered.

Henry screamed again, his power surging—this time, it struck Hades, a blast of darkness that rippled through his form. Hades blinked, stunned, as a small drop of blood appeared on his lip. He touched the drop with his finger, staring at it, his expression puzzled. He looked at Henry then, and his gaze was different—something changed, a shift in his intent.

"Goodbye, Henry," Hades said quietly, his tone resolute.

"Don't you dare walk away from me!" Henry roared. "Fight me!"

But there was no one left to respond. Hades had vanished, leaving Henry alone in the burning room, the flames roaring once more.

The scene faded to black, the old man stepping out of the fading memory, the age peeling away from him as he approached Jace. A dark cloak formed around his shoulders, and his eyes grew cold.

"He did me a favor then," Henry said, his voice low, almost resigned. "Any other god would have killed me and locked my soul away forever. But Hades let me live. If he'd fought me, I would have died an excruciating death. But that was then..."

He paused, his eyes darkening. "I saw Osira only twice more after that. Just twice. Once, in a perfect moment of young love. And once in the worst of moments, at the battle of Roandia. I haven't sought her out since. She's lived many lives since then—she's been a queen, a pauper, everything in between. She always had that spirit, that willingness to experience everything life had to offer."

Jace looked at Henry, sitting in the cabin, shadows cast across his face. "But why?" Jace asked, his voice breaking with frustration. "Why do all of this? Why kill, destroy, and wage war against countless lives if you know the cost? Why block the logout?"

Henry's expression twisted, his mouth curving into something dark. "Block the logout? If that was within my power, I would be greater than all the gods combined. But why end it? Don't you see, Jason? Or are you still too blind to understand?" His voice carried a weary bitterness. "This is just a game, Jason. When we die, the game takes a piece of us, a fragment of our lives, as payment. But that energy—it doesn't vanish. It's still there, trapped within the System. If I can end it all—if I can bring Terra Mythica to its knees—then she will be free. Don't you want the same thing?"

Jace grimaced, feeling a sharp pain bloom in his chest and sides, something raw and gnawing. He looked at Henry, eyes narrowing, his voice tight. "Why are you telling me all this?" he demanded, suspicion lacing his words.

Henry didn't immediately answer, his gaze drifting back to the fading scene of the cottage. He seemed almost lost in it, his fingers brushing against memories that weren't ready to let go.

Jace clenched his jaw, frustration bubbling up. "What are you hiding from me?" he snapped, taking a step forward, ignoring the way the pain twisted inside him, making his breath hitch. "This is just a distraction, isn't it? All of this... the fairgrounds, the stories—it's all to keep me from seeing what you're really trying to do."

Henry turned then, his eyes locking onto Jace's, something dark and unreadable swirling beneath the surface. He didn't deny it, not right away. Instead, he looked at Jace with that weary, haunted expression, like a man who had lived too long with ghosts and was used to their company. Then he smiled, a vicious wicked smile, the old man Henry gone, replaced in an instant by the Dark One.

He waved his hand and some of the darkness shifted, allowing Jace access to his own eyes for a moment, to see what was happening outside in the battle. "It's already too late."

The battlefield was chaos. The roaring din of combat, a symphony of violence that pulsed with an unrelenting, savage rhythm, swallowed the screams of pain and fury. Blood stained the dirt, both demon and human alike, and the air was thick with smoke and despair. Jace's friends were scattered, each locked in their own desperate struggle for survival. Ell's nimble movements were slowed, her stamina flagging as the relentless demon she faced pressed her harder. Dex fought with every ounce of his strength, his daggers a blur as he tried to keep back another demon that had broken through their line, its wicked claws missing by mere inches.

And above all of it, towering amidst the chaos, stood the monstrous giant demon, its eyes blazing like hot coals as it roared, the very sound sending ripples of fear through the hearts of those who heard it.

Jace's body lay on the ground, unmoving, his limbs sprawled out at awkward angles. He was somewhere between this world and the dark expanse of his mind—trapped. He could hear the muffled screams, the clash of weapons, and feel the earth trembling beneath him. He was aware, vaguely, of his physical form, of how he was exposed, vulnerable. And of how they were losing.

And then there was Shadow.

She stood above his body, defiance blazing in her eyes. Her cloak billowed out around her, her hands covered in a faint, pulsing light—a desperate attempt at a shield to fend off the encroaching demons. Her voice, strong and unyielding, called out orders, her feet rooted to the ground. She wasn't giving an inch. Not while Jace lay there. Not while there was still a breath in her.

She snarled, the power in her arms flickering as she drove back another demon lunging towards Jace's defenseless form. Her stance was fierce, a lone figure against the encroaching darkness, standing amidst the swarming creatures, fighting to protect him.

To her right, Marcus fought on, struggling against two demons at once, his teeth bared in determination. He glanced at Shadow, his eyes filled with something Jace could only describe as fear. Fear of loss, fear of failure. And there, beyond him, Molly, her face pale as she continued her tether, supporting Jace even as she was forced to defend herself, her other hand wielding a knife against a demon clawing towards her.

The teachers that had stayed behind were scattered, their spells lighting up the dark battlefield, their expressions filled with grim determination. But even they were faltering—each blow they delivered, each spell cast, seemed only to delay the inevitable.

Jace's body was shaking, his consciousness slipping, torn between the surreal agony of his mind and the desperate struggle around him. The darkness had its grip on him, holding tight, refusing to let go. He was being torn apart, piece by piece, and every moment that passed, every heartbeat, brought him closer to the abyss.

And then he felt it—another pull, something dark and foreign, a presence that seemed to snake into his thoughts and take root there, a cold whisper echoing in his mind. Look, it said. See what defiance will bring you.

The battlefield shifted, the noise of the combat suddenly fading to a murmur, like he was underwater. He found himself there, still on the ground, but now with a forced, unnatural clarity. And he saw it—Shadow, standing above him, her body bruised, her defenses weakening, the light from her hands flickering as the monstrous giant demon approached.

"Shadow!" He tried to scream, his voice nothing but a strangled whisper.

She turned, her eyes catching his for the briefest of moments. There was something there—something almost like a smile, a reassurance. As if she knew what was coming, but accepted it.

The demon lunged, its blade-like claws slicing through the air.

Shadow moved, her arms raised, her body twisting in a futile attempt to evade.

But it wasn't enough.

Jace watched, helpless, his soul screaming as the claws found their mark, cutting through her side, the force sending her sprawling. Blood spilled across the ground, her body collapsing beside his.

The demon roared again, triumphant, and Jace felt something in him break. A soundless scream tore from his throat, a despair deeper than anything he had ever known ripping through him. He could feel the tether of Molly's aether, but it wasn't enough, not nearly enough.

Shadow's body lay still beside him, her face turned towards him, her eyes fluttering shut as her breath stilled. She had stood for him, defended him until her last breath. And now she was gone.

Jace's mind twisted, rage and grief melding together, consuming him, the darkness growing until all he could feel was that terrible, consuming void. The Dark One's voice echoed once more, cold and triumphant.

"You will become me, Jace. And we will bring the Eternal End."

The thought began as a whisper, curling then fading like smoke. *It's just a game,* it said, a quiet murmur that slithered through his thoughts. A small, seemingly harmless thought, but one that grew louder, more insistent with each passing moment.

It's all meaningless.

Jace felt the words looping inside him, twisting tighter and tighter, the notion clawing at his reason. Wasn't it true? Wasn't this just a fabrication, some coded existence meant to entertain or torment them? The people he met, the places he traveled, the battles they fought—they were all predetermined outcomes of an elaborate design. Mere lines of code, data running its course, guided by some uncaring hand. Wasn't that what it was?

He felt himself drifting away from shore, sinking beneath the tide.

He could see it—feel it even. The cold logic of the Dark One's words. If they broke the system, if they shattered everything, it would all end. They could crash it, end the suffering, and release everyone from this cruel illusion. Maybe the Dark One is right, he thought, a chill settling over his heart. Maybe if we end it all, we can finally be free.

And yet...

Maybe... His mind stammered. *Maybe...*

Jace's resolve began to buckle, his spirit sinking under the weight of it all. He felt himself slipping, as if the ground beneath his feet was giving way, crumbling. What's the point? He thought. It's hopeless. None of this is real. None of it matters.

Jace sank to his knees and a terrible emptiness opened within him, hollowing him out. He could feel his will shattering, his grasp loosening. His hope was nothing more than a flickering flame, threatening to extinguish under the weight of despair.

Chapter 61
The Question

He felt a question tugging at the edges of his mind, just out of reach.

A flicker—a spark of something deeper, a resistance that refused to bow to the darkness. Something about Henry's words felt wrong, deeply, fundamentally twisted. Jace's mind reeled, grappling with the notion. Intellectually, he understood the argument. He had lived it. He had heard all the justifications. But still...

Deep down, something resonated and shifted within him. It was small at first, barely noticeable.

Jace's heart drummed in his chest, the question rising within him. The one that had always been there, lurking just out of reach. It was a question he had never allowed himself to ask, a question too raw, too immense, too terrifying.

The tiny spark inside him swelled, feeding on itself until it became a roaring fire, fierce and uncontainable, threatening to consume him whole.

He opened his eyes, his vision clearing, and he allowed himself to ask it—to let the words form, to bring them into the world, and dare to find the truth.

"Is this place... this world... this life... really real?" he whispered, the words leaving his lips like a prayer, barely louder than a breath.

The world stilled. Time itself seemed to hold its breath. Even Henry's twisted form was frozen, the shadows pausing their ceaseless writhing. The silence pressed against Jace, heavy and infinite. For a moment, it felt as though everything had come to an end—an end that carried within it a kind of desperate hope.

And then, the gentlest of voices answered, a whisper that brushed against his ear like the warmth of a lover's breath, the softest affirmation he had ever heard.

Yes.

The word echoed through him, reverberating through every inch of his being. It surged through his heart, his mind, his very soul, pushing aside all doubt, banishing the cold shadow that had threatened to consume him. He didn't understand how he knew, couldn't articulate it if someone asked—but he knew. He felt it in his bones, in his very essence.

Life had always been a game, after all—a game that wasn't always enjoyable, often harsh, but undeniably real in its impact. An illusion, yes, but one everyone believed in deeply enough that it became the truth. And that belief made it real. People lived here. Children were born, love was shared, and pain was felt. There was meaning here that went far beyond the lines of code that constructed it. It wasn't just pixels and scripts; it was a living, breathing world shaped by every joy, every tear, and every choice made within it.

Theon had said once there were three realities: the physical, the mental, and the soul. And in that moment, Jace understood what he had meant. This world—this place—it was not an illusion crafted in code. It was real. As real as the earth he had left behind, as real as the breath in his lungs, the beat of his heart. As real as love or hope.

A warmth enveloped him, light surging outward from within, his eyes burning with an inner radiance. And the world around him seemed to strip open, peeled back to reveal the raw, unfiltered truth of existence. Jace saw it then—the absolute truth of the universe.

This place was real—not in the simple, material way he had once thought of reality, but real in its very essence. This world wasn't built of code, wasn't shaped by data. It was made of stardust and souls, of the infinite potential of creation. It was breath, it was life, it was aether and spirit, bound together in a tapestry of the possible and the impossible.

In that moment, Jace understood something fundamental, something that lay beyond the reach of mere logic or reason. This place was an illusion, yes, but not any more of an illusion than Earth itself. Everything was an illusion—every world, every life, a construct of experience and perception. But in that very illusion, there lay truth—beauty, meaning.

Jace knew—he knew—that this place was more than just numbers, more than a simple string of ones and zeroes. He could feel it, a truth that went beyond his comprehension.

The illusion of this world, just like the illusion of Earth, was real because it mattered. It held weight because the people within it believed it mattered. Because they lived it, with all the joy and suffering, love and loss that came with it.

The reality of existence was not about the atoms or code that composed it—it was about the experience, the spirit that animated it. It was real because it was. And that was enough.

And in that moment, somehow, Terra Mythica felt more like home than Earth ever had.

But Jace knew now, without a shred of doubt. This was not a game, and he would not allow Henry to break it. Not for his own bitterness, not for his rage.

He opened his eyes, his soul surging with power, and he stood, pushing back with every ounce of strength he had. "You're wrong," Jace said, his voice carrying across the darkness, unwavering, filled with a conviction that seemed to shake the very air. "I can't explain it, but I know you're wrong. This world isn't what you think it is. What you're doing is madness. This isn't what Osira would have wanted."

Henry's face contorted with fury, shadows writhing around him, his voice rising in a storm. "Do not speak her name!" he roared, the room darkening, the shadows surging. "You know nothing, Jace! You understand nothing!"

The darkness closed in, but Jace stood his ground. The power that rose within him was not born of anger or fear. It was born of truth—a truth that burned brighter than the shadows that sought to swallow him.

And in that truth, Jace pushed. He pushed back against the despair, against the force of Henry's will, and he felt it—the shift, the breaking point. The Dark One's grip slipped, his presence loosening.

With a final surge of his will, Jace expelled the darkness, flinging Henry out from his mind, the shadows unraveling, dissipating like smoke in the wind.

And when he opened his eyes, he was free—free to stand, to fight, to reclaim the world that was his, the world that was real.

Jace let that warmth spread through him, let it grow until it became an unstoppable blaze—a light that radiated outward, pushing against every whisper of doubt, every tendril of fear. The darkness recoiled, retreating from the firestorm that now filled him. It was as if the boundaries around him had shattered, releasing a power he had always held but had never fully claimed. The presence in his mind—a towering, looming specter—began to waver, its form losing coherence.

"You think you've trapped me," Jace said, his voice steady and fierce, cutting through the dark void, "by pulling me this far into your soul. But it is you who has taken the risk. Because now... I see you." His eyes blazed as he spoke, a fierce determination settling over him like a mantle.

Jace activated Soul Sense again, moving further into the mind of the Heart of Darkness.

"What... what is this?!" The creature's voice screamed, echoing within the depths of Jace's mind—a voice filled with rage, confusion, and something else, something Jace had not heard in it before: fear.

The darkness trembled, quaking under the force of the light Jace unleashed within himself. He felt the beast recoiling, its hold slipping, its shadowy form unraveling like smoke caught in a storm. The power to fight back, to resist, had been within him all along, waiting for this very moment.

And then, Jace saw it—an understanding that cut deeper than the dark. The Dark One was fueling all of these demons, each twisted creature bound by items—artifacts that were mere conduits, allowing them passage into this realm. And those artifacts, those dark objects, they were all linked back to one central point. Jace could see it now, the shadowy connection behind every demon, the source feeding them their dark strength. The Dark One was using his own version of Soul—a dark, warped energy—to create pathways, anchoring his influence to them.

Jace latched onto that revelation, the perception of the Dark One's essence behind each demon. He felt it, a twisted version of something he understood, something he too wielded.

Jace focused, harmonizing his understanding of Soul with that of the Dark One's essence. He let his light entwine with the dark energy, a dance of opposites coming together in a moment of raw clarity. He could feel the Dark One's confusion, its attempts to twist away from the connection—but it was too late.

A surge of silver light burst through Jace, an energy so pure it pierced the shadows like a blade. He felt it—something beyond soul, something fundamental. A Word, ancient and powerful. "Truth."

The word echoed in his mind, resonating deep within him. Silver light exploded outward, merging with his Soul energy, a radiant force that burned with a clarity he had never known. He wielded it, focusing all his strength on the connection between the Dark One and every possessed artifact, every dark tether within a mile of him.

He combined "Truth" with "Soul," augmenting his Soul Severance, aiming at the bindings linked to and powered by the Dark One. The silver light surged forward, a wave of pure severance, unraveling the dark pathways that had held so much power. Jace felt the threads snap, one by one, the force of it reverberating through him. The Dark One's influence shattered, his connection to the demons breaking like brittle glass under the power of Jace's newfound Word.

The darkness recoiled, its shrieks echoing through the void as its grip began to crumble, unraveling under the silver light. And there, for the first time, Jace saw it—the fear in the Dark One's eyes. A fear born not of rage, but of vulnerability, the kind that twisted deep, realizing its own weakness. It was a flicker of something Jace had never thought possible, a crack in the towering facade of shadows.

And Jace knew, in that moment, that he held the power to fight back. Not just for himself, but for everyone who had been bound, everyone who had been chained and suffocated by the darkness.

He cast Soul Tether, the ability manifesting with eerie ease, as if it was meant for this precise moment. Being this deep within the Dark One's mind made the connection click into place seamlessly. The Dark One had been too prideful, dragging Jace too far inside, lowering his defenses to a dangerous level, and now it was too late.

The tether latched, locking into the essence of the Dark One. In that instant, Jace felt the surge—a swell of energy so overwhelming, it threatened to consume him. Power beyond anything he'd ever touched, a flood that coursed through every fiber of his being. It was too much, an intensity that nearly tore him apart from the inside, a force too vast for him to contain. He had to release it or risk being devoured by the torrent.

The energy coursed through him, igniting him from within—a blaze of fire and light that illuminated every corner of his mind, his spirit, his very soul. It burst from him like a star going supernova, flooding outwards, silver flames cascading from his body, as he let go of the impossible force.

Jace felt the power escape, radiant and consuming, like lightning unleashed from a storm that had been brewing for centuries. It lit him up, turning him into a beacon of raw, unrestrained light. He felt the connection to the Dark One fracture, felt the darkness recoil again, unable to withstand the blaze of truth and soul. It was like watching shadows burn, dissolving in the face of something far brighter, something real.

Chapter 62
Truth

Jace's breath came fast, each inhalation feeding the fire that blazed within him. He clenched his teeth, his focus sharpening, the realization sinking deep—this creature had never truly controlled him. It had only fed off his fear, his uncertainty. And now, with the truth blinding him, Jace pushed back, wrenching himself free of the creature's grip.

"No more," he whispered, his voice a promise.

He felt the tether snap, felt the monstrous presence lose its footing, stumbling back, shrieking in fury. The pressure in his head lifted, and he gasped, his senses flooding back into reality, his consciousness snapping back to his body.

Jace pulled himself free, his entire being surging with strength and purpose. He rose, eyes blazing, his aura shimmering with the sheer force of the aether coursing through him. And before him, the beast—its monstrous form twisting, cracking—began to shatter.

A high, keening scream tore through the air, the sound inhuman, filled with desperation and hatred. The darkness that had once seemed so imposing now fractured, breaking apart as though it was made of brittle glass. The creature's outline blurred, fragments of it tearing away, disintegrating into nothingness. And yet, even in its breaking, Jace knew it was not truly destroyed.

With a last, furious wail, the shattered remnants of the creature swirled, a tempest of darkness that pulled away from Jace, retreating, fleeing from the light that now blazed from him.

"Run," Jace murmured, his eyes locked on the dissipating shadow, his voice steady and unyielding. "Run, but know that I'll be waiting."

The beast gave no reply, only a final, echoing shriek as it fled, dissolving into the night, leaving behind nothing but a whisper of darkness and the memory of its terror. It was not dead, not yet. But it was gone—broken, diminished, and running.

And then, just as quickly as it had come, the darkness began to dissolve, pulling back, shrinking away from the force that Jace had become. It was no longer in control. Jace was. He stood tall within himself, feeling the weight of Henry's influence slip away, leaving him with a clarity, a focus that was almost blinding.

The spirit realm faded away as the battle before him came back into view.

He was free, not because the darkness had given up, but because he had chosen to face it, to understand it for what it truly was, and to let it fade under the strength of his own light. The world around him felt more alive, more vibrant, more real than ever before.

Aether poured out from him—raw, pure, unfiltered. It moved through every corner of his being, vibrating through his bones, flowing in his veins like fire and lightning all at once. The power was overwhelming, almost unbearable in its intensity. It was too much. It needed to be released.

He struggled to his feet amidst the chaos, his senses sharpening with every heartbeat. His gaze swept over the battlefield—the chaos, the desperate fight still unfolding around him. His friends, battered and bruised, were on the brink of collapse, their backs against the wall as the demons closed in, their roars echoing through the blood-soaked air. Shadow's body lay still beside him, a reminder of everything at stake.

And Jace acted.

With a roar of his own, he lifted his hands, the energy surging through him in waves, and let it flow outward. His fingers splayed wide as he focused on those around him, the warriors who had fought so bravely by his side. He felt the connection snap into place—Soul Tether and Aetheric Absorption. One after another, the bonds formed, luminous threads of energy linking him to his allies. He could feel their pain, their exhaustion, the weariness weighing them down. And in response, the aether rushed from him, pouring into each tether, filling them.

Light blazed through the bonds, the energy flowing in an unstoppable wave, radiating from Jace and into each of his friends. They were bathed in it—so much life, so much light. He watched as their wounds began to heal, the bruises fading, the cuts closing, the exhaustion replaced by strength. They stood taller, their eyes wide as the energy filled them, as the power reignited their spirits.

Dex, his daggers glinting under the ethereal glow, turned, a fierce grin spreading across his face as the power surged through him. Ell, graceful and swift, leaped forward, her blade flashing with newfound speed and strength. The healers who had been working on Thistle were suddenly enveloped by the light, their auras blazing bright, and they turned their attention outward, the tide of aether healing their wounds and filling their hands with the strength to fight back.

Jace's vision was awash in light—so much of it, so much aether that he felt he could explode. He could no longer hold it all, and so he funneled it out, extending his hands and binding all those around him, sharing the surge of power. The battlefield seemed to glow, a radiant burst of aether transforming every ally it touched, every soul it tethered.

The demons fell, collapsing like marionettes with their strings severed, their forms crumbling to the ground in grotesque heaps. Some dissolved into nothing more than puffs of soot and the faint, metallic tang of blood—a fleeting memory of something monstrous, undone in an instant. Without the Dark One's tether binding them, there was nothing left to hold them, nothing to keep them from unraveling. Jace watched as they withered, one by one, their essence dissipating into the cold air, a dark legacy reduced to ash and echoes.

Jace stood amidst it all, his breath heavy, his heart pounding, his body still alive with the remnants of aether. Around him, the cheers began to rise—a wave of exultation sweeping through the survivors, their voices raised in victorious cries, the sound echoing across the battlefield.

As the echoes of victory filled the night, Jace's gaze swept the chaos, searching. His eyes scanned the bodies of demons, the retreating forms, the triumphant faces of his friends. But the pale boy was nowhere to be seen.

Gone, as if he had never been there at all.

But there were no cheers from Jace or his friends. The triumphant roars of victory that should have filled the air instead gave way to a heavy, suffocating silence. Their eyes were drawn downward, and there she lay—Shadow, unmoving amidst the chaos, her form so still it seemed wrong against the backdrop of the battlefield.

Jace's heart clenched, the elation of their narrow victory evaporating in an instant. Slowly, he sank to his knees beside her, his hands trembling as he reached out to hold her, to cradle her in his arms. His fingers brushed her cold skin, and a shiver ran through him, an emptiness swallowing whatever strength he'd thought remained. The others gathered around, their weapons hanging limp at their sides, their expressions mirroring the grief etched across Jace's face.

It was supposed to be over. They had fought, they had won—but looking down at her, none of it felt like a victory.

Jace's focus remained on Shadow, lying still amidst the chaos. Her chest no longer rose or fell, her breaths long since ceased. The realization hit him with a crushing weight—he was too late. The life that had burned so brightly in her was gone, leaving only a hollow shell in its place. The world around him fell silent, the echoes of battle receding into nothingness, the victory meaningless without her.

And then, something caught his eye. A delicate necklace encircled her neck—a thin chain, barely visible beneath her torn collar. It glowed faintly, a pulse of light too gentle to be natural, shimmering against the bloodied ground. A subtle insistence that caught his attention and refused to let go.

Jace's heart gave a weak, tremulous jump, a flicker of hope that cut through the despair. There was something else here. Shadow's soul hadn't departed, and the thought clung to him like a lifeline. He leaned closer, his breath trembling, his fingers reaching out to touch the necklace. It pulsed under his fingertips, a steady, soft rhythm, and he could feel it—the presence of something beyond, something holding her spirit captive.

Jace's hands trembled as he forced his eyes shut, summoning whatever strength he had left. He drew in a deep, shaky breath and called forth Soul Sense, letting his mind shift, willing himself into the realm beyond sight, reaching out to connect with whatever remained of her. The world twisted around him, colors swirling, his consciousness sinking into the space between worlds—but suddenly, violently, it all snapped back. A force like a tidal wave slammed into him, severing his connection and throwing him backward.

He flew through the air, his back hitting a stone wall with a crack, the impact stealing the breath from his lungs. The pain radiated outwards, but it didn't matter. Jace struggled to his feet, ignoring the way his legs shook, the way his head spun. His jaw clenched, tears stinging his eyes. Someone—something—was refusing to let her go. After everything she had done, after all she had fought for, this was how it would end? No. Not if he could help it.

With a fierce determination, mixed with a rising sense of indignation, Jace moved back to her side. He knelt beside her, his hands hovering over her lifeless body, his eyes narrowing with focus. He activated Soul Sense and his new Word of Truth, feeling the energy rush through him, his senses sharpening as the world seemed to fall away. There was nothing but the glowing threads of existence—the pulse of magic that lingered around her, and the darkness that sought to bind it.

And then he saw it.

A thin, dark tendril, coiled tightly around her spirit, its energy thrumming with malevolent intent. It was there, buried beneath the light of her necklace, a force unseen but unmistakable. It twisted around her essence, holding her in place, preventing her from passing on. Jace's jaw set, his eyes blazing with an inner fire.

"This isn't how your story ends," he whispered, his voice a promise.

His fingers traced the intricate designs etched into the pendant, the patterns shifting beneath his touch as if trying to hide their secrets. But Jace wasn't going to stop now. He summoned his Word, his essence flaring as he drew upon Soul Severance, his will focused entirely on breaking that tether.

The air around them shimmered, the tension crackling, the energy palpable. Jace poured his power into the effort, each breath a struggle, each heartbeat echoing with a sense of finality. The world dimmed, all his surroundings fading, the noise, the people—it was all meaningless compared to what lay before him. Victory on the battlefield meant nothing without Shadow.

He gave a final push, his entire being channeled into that one desperate act. And then, with a sudden jolt, he felt it—the connection snapped, the dark energy shattering under the force of his will. The necklace broke apart, pieces scattering across the blood-stained ground as Shadow's body began to glow.

Light enveloped her, the glow radiating outwards, her edges blurring, the harshness of death giving way to something softer, something far more beautiful. Her hair turned to golden light, her body lifted gently from the ground, her mortal form giving way to an ethereal figure beneath. The shadows that had bound her fell away, replaced by a luminescence that seemed almost divine.

Golden radiance enveloped her completely, lifting her into the air, her body suspended, weightless, pure. Jace could only watch, his breath caught in his throat, his tears still fresh, now mingled with awe. The grief in his heart remained, but there was something else—something that spoke of hope, of transcendence.

A whisper of movement caught his ear. He looked over, and there, among the survivors, he saw Alice. She knelt, her eyes wide, her face filled with wonder as she breathed a single word, "Clio... the Muse of History."

The others around her, students and teachers alike, bowed their heads, sinking to their knees in reverence. All but Jace, who remained on the ground, his heart pounding, his eyes fixed on the glowing form above.

From the light, Shadow—no, Clio—spoke, her voice melodic, gentle, carrying with it the warmth of ages. "Thank you, Jace," she said, her gaze meeting his, a smile gracing her lips. "You have freed me."

Her voice resonated through him, a sound that carried not only gratitude but also understanding, a connection deeper than words. "A dark force, hidden and ancient, had bound me here," she continued, her voice filled with sorrow and strength. "It was magic, long forgotten—nearly a thousand years old."

Jace looked up, tears streaming down his face. "I couldn't save you," he whispered, his voice raw, breaking with emotion.

Clio descended, her form still radiant, and as she touched down, she knelt before him, placing a hand gently on his shoulder. "You did more than save me, Jace," she said softly, her eyes shimmering, still carrying the essence of Shadow he knew so well. "You set me free."

She extended her hand, and in her palm appeared a small, shimmering drachma, glowing with a soft, golden light. "Take this," she said, her voice kind. "A token. May it serve as a reminder that hope exists, even when forgotten."

Their hands touched for a moment, the coin warm against his skin, the connection fleeting but filled with meaning—a whisper of fate, a promise of something beyond the darkness.

And then she leaned closer and gave him a long kiss on his cheek. "Thank you, Jason." She whispered. "Thank you for being there for me when I was lost and so very alone."

She stood back and a new light engulfed her.

Her face changed, her eyes glowing as if some vital essence was moving through her. She rose into the air, her ethereal glow brightening. When she spoke again, her voice was deeper, trembling with a resonance that didn't belong to her—a voice touched by something otherworldly. It echoed across the field, her words filled with warning of something ancient and far darker lingering on the horizon.

"The Prophecy Nears. One lost to ages past - so speaks the Muse of Histories Teachings."

Her words unfolded like a forgotten melody.

Chapter 63
Muse of History

"*In Shadow and Light supreme,*
From ashes rise, you dare to dream.
Your fates entwine, though none are seen,
In the wind breeze soft, where hopes convene.

When Destiny Calls in twilight's shroud,
A tale untold, sung soft and loud.
A great dark tide shall soon arise,
The night will fight to claim the skies.

Beyond the Veil, you peer with dread,
To fight the gloom, the right must tread.
A chasm yawns, forsaking light,
In unknown realms, you chase the night.

To Face the Darkness, where shadows swell,
Your paths entwine, your fates compel.
In murmurs heard, in signs obscure,
The threads of destiny endure.

As the Phoenix Falls, you see the sight,
Lost but true, in darkest plight.
A life fades through the twilight's gloom,
In dusk's shadows, you seek your boon.

For the Fate of All in realms unseen,
Where secrets loom, and shadows glean.

An ending comes, your hope expires,
Together, you stand amidst the pyres.

In Infinite Eternal where destinies lie,
Beneath the stars, a Word shall die.
In night's embrace, the truth you seek,
For all lives sake, the bold must Speak."

Her form shifted, the radiant light fading until she appeared as she had been—the ethereal glow dimming to a faint shimmer. Her eyes met his, holding an intensity that spoke of both sorrow and hope.

"You have a long journey ahead of you, Child of the Grey," she said, her voice carrying an echo of something ancient, something beyond time. "Remember this: to see the light, one must be willing to face the dark."

Jace blinked, confusion knitting his brow as he looked at her. "Wait—why do gods keep calling me that? 'Child of the Grey'? What does it mean?"

Clio hesitated for a moment, her gaze distant, as if she was listening to a voice only she could hear—one carried on the winds of another realm. Her head tilted slightly, a thoughtful expression crossing her face, and she seemed to be considering something carefully.

"But he has done so much already," she murmured, almost to herself. "It is only fair."

She nodded then, a smile gracing her lips, something both kind and sad in her eyes. Leaning closer to him, she spoke, her voice lowering to a whisper—a whisper that held a weight only a goddess could command. It was a whisper that seemed to bypass his ears and go straight to his soul, resonating within him in a way no one else could hear, a secret meant for him alone.

"That is what you are, Greyson—brother of Alexander, child of Henry and Osira, lost Prince of Roandia."

Her smile softened as she pulled back, her eyes searching his.

The words hung in the air between them, not merely spoken but etched into the very essence of his being. Jace felt his heart stutter, his breath catching in his throat as the meaning of her words settled over him. A truth he had never known, yet somehow had always felt, buried deep within.

Clio's smile held warmth and understanding, as if she could see the torrent of emotions that now whirled inside of him. She placed her hand gently on his shoulder, her eyes never leaving his, a silent reassurance—a promise that, despite what lay ahead, he would not be alone.

"I must go now. But know that you will never truly be without me. Your little Shadow."

She tilted her head slightly and gave him a wink. And that moment she was no Clio, the goddess muse of history. She was Shadow. His little Shadow.

With those final words, she began to fade, her form dissolving into pure light, the glow softening until there was nothing left but the empty space she once filled.

Jace clutched the shimmering drachma in his hand, its warmth pressing into his palm, a bittersweet ache swelling in his chest. Gratitude and sorrow mixed within him, tangling into a knot that tightened his throat and made it hard to breathe.

As the last glimmers of her presence disappeared, an intense silence fell across the battlefield, almost as if the world itself had paused to honor her departure. The students around him seemed muted, the remnants of the battle—broken weapons, scattered armor, smoldering earth—now fading into the background, insignificant against the magnitude of what had just happened.

His friends were each battered and bruised but still standing. Their faces reflected Jace's own—tired, their eyes shadowed with loss. The demons had been vanquished, the undead horde scattered, but the victory felt hollow, its triumph swallowed by the emptiness left behind.

Quietly, they approached, gathering around Jace as he knelt there, the drachma held tight in his trembling fingers. None of them spoke. No words could capture what they felt—no words could bring back the friend they had lost. Instead, they offered their presence, in silent support, their hands resting gently on his shoulders, their heads bowed in shared grief.

Jace's gaze stayed on the token, the golden glow reflecting in his tear-streaked eyes. The weight of it was more than just metal; it was a promise, a memory, a reminder of what had been sacrificed and of what they still had to do. Shadow had given everything—her courage, her strength, her life—and now, what remained of her was in his hands.

Surrounded by his friends, the haunting stillness of the battlefield pressing against them, Jace felt the full weight of it all. The real cost of this fight wasn't measured in bruises or blood—it was in the empty spaces left behind, the people they had lost, the light that had been snuffed out. And yet, even in that darkness, something still glowed within him.

He looked at the token in his hand, feeling the warmth it held—a flicker of resolve ignited there. He would carry her memory forward, carry her light into whatever darkness lay ahead. This was not the end, not for him, and not for her. Shadow had seen something in him, had given him hope when he had none. And now, he would honor that gift by becoming the light she had believed he could be.

Jace slowly stood, the air thick with lingering sorrow, yet beneath that sorrow, something more—something shared. An unspoken bond, forged by the fight they had just survived. He glanced around at his friends—worn, bloodied, but still standing. He reached out, and one by one, they took each other's hands. The touch was small, simple, but there was strength in it—a reminder that they weren't alone, not in this moment of triumph.

Jace smiled, a tired but genuine curve of his lips. There was still so much to process—what Clio had said, the truths he wasn't ready to confront. He pushed it aside for now, knowing it would wait for him later. For now, this was enough.

Together, they stood, and for just a moment, the battlefield didn't seem so haunting. It seemed almost hopeful. They had faced the dark, and they were still here, still breathing, still together. And with the token still warm in his hand, Jace knew they were far from finished. This was only the beginning.

The echo of silence that had followed the battle was soon broken by the sound of hurried footsteps, armor clattering, and panicked voices. Jace turned just in time to see the teachers, the High Council, and dozens of others rushing up the mountainside. Their eyes widened as they took in the chaos—students scattered across the ground, some unconscious, others groaning as they fought against the lingering pain. Healers began to move quickly among them, mending broken limbs, staunching the flow of blood. Another faculty must have found them.

Many of the students lay where they had fallen, their bodies battered, and exhausted. The demons had left them, but not without cost. Some were too bloodied, too wounded to stand, still in need of healing, while others lay deathly still—only to respawn, blinking, but hollow-eyed from the trauma. And then there were the few who did not move, whose possession had gone on too long, or who had been struck down before the truth could be known—not all would make it back, Jace knew. Not all had been given a choice.

Jace and his friends looked at the council members, their expressions mirroring each other—exhaustion, wariness, and something else: the raw, sharp edge of uncertainty. The High Council stood in shock, their robes dusted with the first rays of dawn, eyes darting between the wounded students and the aftermath of the battlefield. For a long moment, they said nothing. There were no words, none that would do this scene justice. Only the Archmage, his face grave, gave a short nod, as if to say everything and nothing. He turned then, directing the faculty with brisk gestures, each movement filled with urgency.

Jace and his friends watched as the students who could still move scrambled to help their fallen, to save whoever was left to be saved. The wounded were lifted, the healers' magic weaving among them. It was a strange kind of silence that settled over the scene—busy, but somber, as if everyone was holding their breath together, afraid to let go.

Slowly, the morning light began to creep over the distant treetops, spilling across the mountain in soft, golden waves. It touched the broken ground, bathing the crumbled remains of battle in a glow that almost seemed to cleanse it, to wash away the blood and the soot. The light filtered through the leaves, casting long shadows that swayed gently, making it seem as if the forest were breathing again—like life was still here, somewhere beneath all the loss.

Jace let his eyes drift to that horizon, the warmth of the rising sun washing over him. He wondered if they had done the right thing. If perhaps, allowing the demons to fester, to remain unchecked, would have been worse. He felt the weight of his doubts, heavy and stubborn, refusing to let go even as the dawn brought the promise of a new day.

And yet, as he looked around at his friends, still standing beside him, at the students rallying to help each other, he couldn't help but feel the glimmer of something else—hope, fragile but undeniable, like that first touch of sunlight breaking through the dark.

Epilogue
Of New Beginnings

The next few days were unsettlingly quiet. The aftermath hung like a shadow over the academy, thick and heavy. The losses were more than Jace could bear—each absence a jagged edge, cutting deep. Most students recovered, though they carried the trauma with them, haunted by the memories, whether they'd been possessed or had only watched, powerless. But those who'd been possessed for too long... they did not return. Three hundred and sixty-eight souls—students and faculty alike—gone. The line between saving them and losing them had been too thin, and they'd crossed it.

Jace did what he could, alongside his friends and the others who had survived. But there were limits to what any of them could do.

Something within him had shifted since learning the second Word of Power. Everything felt sharper, more real. His senses seemed to reach beyond the physical—his mind clearer, his perception more attuned to the truth that rippled beneath the surface of things. He could feel the world breathing around him, every small motion, every fragment of reality alive in a way that it hadn't been before.

It was mid-afternoon in the Fields Below when an unexpected visitor arrived. Jace was bent over his brewing station, his hands moving with practiced ease, combining ingredients for potions meant to heal—not just any wound, but the traces of demonic possession that lingered within the soul. He was working tirelessly, hoping to distribute these potions, to let others know their purpose. Soon, he believed, there'd be no place for demons to hide in the city.

He felt it before he heard it—something behind him, a presence pressing in like a shadow against his back. The voice came next, quiet and weighty.

"How are you holding up?" Hades asked.

Jace turned, his gaze steady, appraising the god who stood before him. Hades had never visited him here before—in the Fields Below, the place where light hardly reached.

"You could have told me," Jace said, the words simple but carrying the sting of betrayal.

Hades gave a small, weary sigh, a hint of regret flickering behind his dark eyes. "Balance, Jason. If I'd told you, another god would have the right to share equal knowledge with their followers. I knew you'd find it, if that's any comfort. I did what I could to protect you, to guide you toward it."

Jace stared at him for a moment, and then turned away, his jaw tight. He said nothing.

"I am sorry," Hades offered, and there was something unpracticed about the apology, like words he was unused to saying, words that didn't quite fit.

A long silence settled between them, neither moving to fill it. Finally, Jace spoke, his voice quieter, more vulnerable. "I don't blame you for what happened with my parents." The word felt strange on his tongue—parents. He had rarely spoken of them, and less often had he thought of them in such terms. They were more a concept than people to him—something abstract, something lost.

Hades didn't respond, his face an unreadable mask.

"This world, whatever it is... it isn't what any of us thought, is it?" Jace continued. "Not even John Rearden truly knows what it is, does he?"

Hades remained silent, but the weight of his silence was an answer in itself.

Jace looked at him, his eyes narrowing, the pieces falling together. "The devices on Earth. They're not... they're not just Earth technology, are they?"

Hades met his gaze, but said nothing, neither confirming nor denying. Jace shook his head. "I don't expect an answer. I'll find the truth soon enough." He paused, then added, his voice hardening, "I don't blame you for what happened to my father. But what you allowed him to become, what you let him do to others—that, I do blame you for."

Hades' expression softened, a flicker of something that could have been regret. "I couldn't... I didn't have the heart to stop him when I should have."

Jace nodded, as if that was answer enough.

"Will you stay my Chosen?" Hades asked after a moment, his voice careful, uncertain.

Jace thought it over, his eyes distant, before giving a nod. "I'm done with lies," he said, flatly but without bitterness. "If you want me as your Chosen, you won't toy with me. You won't use me as a pawn in whatever game you're playing against Henry."

Hades met his eyes, the solemnity there uncharacteristic. "I will always tell you what I can."

It wasn't enough—not really. But Jace nodded anyway. People couldn't always be what you needed them to be, but sometimes they could be better than they were. And that was something worth hoping for, something worth working toward.

"I was born here," Jace said, his voice quiet, his eyes distant. "In this world. Does Henry—the Dark One—know who I am? Tell me that much."

Hades looked at him for a long moment before he spoke, his voice heavy, resigned. "There is a cost to every truth. But this one, I will bear for you." He paused, and Jace could see the hesitation before he added, "The Dark One does not know you. Though he senses something familiar, something he cannot place. You are bound by your Word of Power—Soul. It is a word that has enabled the Dark One to do terrible things, powerful things, things that reshaped worlds—but vicious, cruel."

He paused, and his gaze softened. "But Henry? Henry isn't the same. He's too far gone to see much of anything now. Perhaps, somewhere deep in his heart, he remembers you were born—but the truth, whatever part of him might know it, is buried far beneath."

Jace turned back to his work, his face unreadable as he resumed brewing. "I will show him," he said softly. "Or I will end him."

Hades regarded him, his gaze solemn. "And you will have my power behind you, whichever path you choose."

Jace hesitated for a moment, then spoke, his voice low, almost as if he wasn't sure he wanted to hear the answer. "Was there another way? To stop the possessions?"

Hades looked at him, his eyes darker now, considering. He didn't avoid the question, didn't try to spin the truth into something comforting. Instead, he answered with the gravity that only gods and the deeply weary share.

"There are always multiple paths to the same place," Hades said, his voice carrying a weight that settled between them. "But every moment that passed brought each soul a step closer to the edge—beyond the brink. Time was our enemy, Jason. And every second spent hesitating was another nail in their coffins. Your solution, though imperfect, was the most expedient route."

Jace looked down, his jaw tightening, his brow furrowing in thought. "Expedient," he repeated, the word rolling off his tongue like it tasted bitter.

Hades inclined his head slightly. "Perhaps messy," he continued, "but speed was what mattered. I have lived long enough to know that the clean solution is rarely the available one. There was too much at stake. There were paths where fewer were hurt, where fewer were lost, but they were long, winding... and the enemy wouldn't have waited for you to take them."

Jace swallowed, the words settling heavily on his shoulders. "So, it's on me," he said softly. "I chose the path that cost lives."

"No," Hades corrected, his gaze sharp. "You chose the path that saved them. Every choice costs, Jason. You paid with one hand to save with the other. There are no victories in this game—only the lesser defeats. You walked into darkness, knowing the price, knowing what it would take. You saved who could be saved. The rest..." He paused, his eyes distant, as if watching a far-off past. "The rest were already slipping beyond reach."

Jace nodded, the conflict still burning in his chest, but there was a strange sense of release, too—an understanding that maybe, just maybe, he had done what had to be done. He looked up at Hades, a question still in his eyes. "And if I have to do it again?"

Hades met his gaze evenly. "Then you will. And you will carry that weight again, and again, until the fight is over. But know this: you are not alone in it. We bear these burdens together. You, me, and every person who chooses to stand against the darkness."

A silence stretched between them. Jace focused on his potion, not looking at Hades.

The god's words hung in the air for a moment, and then, without another sound, Hades was gone—vanishing into the shadows as if he had never been there at all. Jace did not look to see him leave.

Jace sat alone in the quiet expanse of the Fields Below, the stillness around him almost unsettling. The last few days had been a blur—a chaos of power, loss, and revelations. He was ranked up now—Silver One. He had gained strength -had faced something dark and terrifying, but the triumph felt hollow here, in the silence of the aftermath.

His rank, his new status, wasn't what he thought it would be. There was no pride, no triumphant sense of accomplishment. Instead, there was the weight of what had come with it. The two Words he now commanded, Soul and Truth, thrummed beneath his skin, each one feeling strange, unfamiliar. They were powerful, but they were also different in a way that left him feeling raw -exposed.

Soul had felt like an extension of himself, a deep part of his being that was as natural as breathing. But Truth—it was something else entirely. Sharp, precise, like a blade that could cut through the fog of uncertainty. It brought clarity, a new lens through which he could see the world. And yet, neither could be wielded alone anymore; they were intertwined, inseparable. He had to learn to use them as one, to find balance between them—light and shadow, empathy and clarity.

The Fields Below felt emptier now without Shadow. There was no denying it. The absence was like a hole in the fabric of his world, and he couldn't shake the emptiness that lingered. He found himself reaching for the coin she had left him, holding it in his palm, feeling its warmth and the slight weight. He looked at it often, as if it held answers, or maybe just a piece of her—a reminder of what she'd seen in him, of the hope she'd left behind.

He lay in the catacombs looking up at the illusion sky.

The wind blew softly across the grass, rustling the leaves of the few scattered trees, the sound whispering through the silence. He closed his eyes, letting the quiet settle around him, letting himself feel everything without pushing it away—grief, exhaustion, hope, and the raw, aching uncertainty that seemed to live within him now.

Later that night, Jace's solitude was interrupted by a soft, familiar voice, barely a whisper against the silence. "Mind if I join you?"

He looked up, blinking against the dim light, and found Alice standing there. Her eyes were tired, shadows lingering beneath them, but they held a warmth that wrapped around him like a familiar embrace. Without waiting for an answer, she moved closer and lay down beside him, her head resting against his shoulder. They stared up at the sky together, the stars flickering in the darkness above, as if they were the only witnesses to this quiet moment.

She spoke, her voice soft, the words drifting between them. "She was lucky to have you, you know."

Jace swallowed, his eyes still on the sky, his chest tightening. "I was the lucky one," he said, his voice almost breaking, barely more than a whisper. There was a dissonance to the words, the truth clashing with the pain of loss, but it was real.

They lay there together, in silence, until footsteps echoed through the Fields Below—soft, hesitant, then more confident. Jace looked up to see Dex approaching, his usual swagger subdued. Behind him, Ell followed with Molly, and then Marcus, his face still ashen, but with something softer, hopeful, in his eyes. One by one, they joined him and Alice, forming a quiet circle in the darkness, their presence like a balm for wounds still too raw to touch.

They didn't need to say anything; words felt unnecessary. The silence was enough—a shared understanding, a bond that had been forged in fire, unbroken by the battles they had faced. They spent the time together, sometimes exchanging glances, sometimes catching the ghost of a smile, a laugh that echoed with nostalgia. They remembered and spoke of times before everything had changed -before their world had shifted into something darker, something harder. The moments of levity were fleeting, but they were enough, each one a tiny light breaking through the night.

As the hours drifted by, the night deepened, Jace felt it—something shifting in the air, something warm despite the chill that hung around them. And he realized, for the first time in days, that it didn't feel empty anymore. Not with them here.

Eventually, one by one, they stood to leave, tired but with a sense of something more—a quiet peace. Just before they all left, Molly pulled Jace aside, her expression thoughtful, almost hesitant.

"Jace," she started, her voice barely above a whisper. "Can I ask you something?"

He nodded, curiosity and exhaustion mingling in his gaze as he sat up, giving her his full attention. He recalled how she had wanted to speak with him after the Midnight Festival—something important, something she'd never quite gotten the chance to say.

"I've spoken with Hecate," she said, her eyes holding his, something vulnerable beneath her steady gaze. "And... we'd like to move under the banner of Hades."

Jace blinked, the surprise evident on his face. He hadn't expected this. "Is that even possible?" he asked.

Molly smiled, the corners of her lips lifting in a way that was both determined and hopeful. "It is. It's rare, but it has happened. And Hermes has already given his approval, with permission from the Society President."

Before Jace could respond, a prompt appeared before his eyes, the letters glowing softly in the night.

Society Quest

Acquire New Members

Molly, Chosen of Hecate, has come as a representative of her god. They have requested permission to transfer into the society of Hades. Hermes has approved this with permission from the Society President of Hades.

Accept | Reject

Jace looked at the prompt for a long moment, his gaze shifting back to Molly. She met his eyes, her expression open, vulnerable in a way he rarely saw. It wasn't just about transferring societies; this was trust, a faith she was placing in him, in what they were building together.

He smiled, a small, wry smile as he nodded, the decision already made in his heart. "Of course," he said, his voice soft, filled with a warmth that hadn't been there earlier. "We'd be fortunate to have you."

Molly let out a breath, her shoulders relaxing, a genuine smile breaking across her face. "Thank you, Jace."

He tapped the prompt, selecting Accept, and it vanished with a soft glow, as if acknowledging something significant—a step forward in a world that felt, finally, a little less bleak.

Molly gave him a quick, almost impulsive hug before she stepped back, her eyes bright. "I'll see you tomorrow, okay?"

Jace nodded, watching her go, her figure blending into the night. He turned back to the Fields Below, the soft rustle of leaves, the quiet hum of the wind around him. He looked down at the coin Shadow had left him, feeling the weight of it, the promise it held.

And as he sat there, the night slowly giving way to dawn, the first hint of light creeping over the horizon, he wondered if perhaps, despite everything, despite the losses and the pain, they had done the right thing. Maybe there had been no perfect choices—maybe there never were. But he knew this: they had fought, they had stood together, and they had survived.

Her society would move in the following week.

Jace leaned back into his chair, his eyes scanning the glowing character sheet hovering in front of him. Gains upon gains—skills ranked up, attributes boosted, a new Word of Power gleaming among the stats. He'd grown, more than he'd expected, more than he'd hoped. But what stood out more than his growth were the Society Points—the culmination of everything they had fought for. He'd spent many, investing them back into the society, inching it ever closer to the Silver Rank. They were on the cusp, and the thought made his heart swell with pride. They were no longer just surviving; they were building, they were becoming something more.

Reginald had taken to his new role with enthusiasm—managing the spirit crew, keeping the place in shape and well-ordered. The chaos of their daily lives had found some semblance of balance with Reginald at the helm, and the Fields Below seemed less like a forgotten wasteland and more like a place to belong.

With a tired sigh, Jace stood and stretched, his muscles aching pleasantly from the day's exertions. The night felt heavy, but not in the usual sense. It wasn't the kind of weight that pressed down on him—it was different, a sense of completion, a feeling of something finally unshackled. He felt resolved, like he was beginning to understand where he fit, where he could make a difference.

As he moved around his dorm, preparing to settle in for the night, his eyes caught the old mirror hanging on the wall—just a simple, tarnished frame, something almost forgotten among all the magic and chaos that had surrounded his life lately. He paused, a frown touching his lips. Something about his reflection felt... off. A step behind, like it lagged slightly. He looked closer, narrowing his eyes.

He reached out tentatively, his affinity for Truth and Soul activating instinctively, almost like his senses were reacting on their own, tuning into something just beneath the surface.

And then he saw it—his reflection wasn't just lagging. It was different. It moved on its own, its eyes wide with something like terror. Jace's heart and mind each other raced for answers.

The reflection's mouth opened, words spilling out silently, its face contorted in anguish, its eyes locking onto Jace's. The mouth formed a word—a single word. Jace couldn't so much hear it as feel it, resonating deep within his bones.

"Jason."

Jace blinked, his brow furrowing. The voice—that face. "Alex?" he whispered, his voice shaky, barely audible.

In the mirror, his reflection nodded, its expression shifting—hope, fear, desperation flickering across its features. Slowly, the reflection raised a hand, pressing it against the glass. The gesture was simple, pleading, reaching for him.

Jace hesitated only a moment before he mirrored the movement, placing his hand on the cool surface of the mirror.

The glass felt like ice, then warmth, then something not quite real at all. It shimmered beneath his palm, rippling like water disturbed by a stone. And before he could pull back, before he could think or even understand, he was falling forward—falling through.

The dorm room remained, empty and silent, nothing moving except for the faint flicker of candlelight. There was no one left to hear, no one to see. Only the mirror, now dark and still, reflecting an empty room.

Thank you for reading Terra Mythica, Volumes 1 & 2

If you've enjoyed this book, please join our mailing list at ShadowLightPress.com and go leave us a review on Amazon.

It really helps.

Scan code to leave a review.

Special Message

"Still here I see," **a voice comes from the darkness.**

The room dims, shadows stretching like curious fingers, gathering at the corners and swirling like something with a heartbeat. The temperature drops—a chill that sneaks in, slipping under your skin. Somewhere in the distance, the low rumble of something timeless echoes—a warning, or maybe just a reminder. The floor shivers, a tremor that starts small but grows, and then he steps forward.

Hades.

The god himself, wreathed in robes that seem spun from midnight and secrets, his eyes smoldering with the memory of forgotten eons. He raises one hand.

"Hello, Chosen," he says, voice deeper than the abyss, yet carrying an odd warmth, like a campfire's glow in the dead of winter. "You've come far, haven't you? Crossed realms, faced shadows, seen things you can't unsee. But there's one more thing I need—one small favor."

The darkness shifts, framing Hades as he gestures, his fingers elegant, commanding. Beside him, a portal blooms into existence—an oval of shimmering light, showing glimpses of books and screens, pixels and words. "If you've found something worth your time here—if these stories have made you smile, or shiver, or stay up way too late—then consider sharing that joy.

Leave a review on Amazon.

Let others find their way through the dark, as you did."

Hades leans closer, his gaze locking onto yours, conspiratorial, as if sharing a secret over a glass of something strong. "And if you want more—more whispers of new worlds, more stories just taking their first breath—then come to ShadowLightPress.com.

Sign up. Join our mailing list. You might even find yourself at the front lines of a new adventure, **a beta reader for tales not yet told**."

He straightens, the ghost of a smile flickering across his lips—something surprisingly tender for a god of the underworld. "To those who've walked beside me, to those who will—thank you. This journey, it's long and winding, but it's better for your company. Truly."

The shadows rise, licking up like flames around his form, his figure blurring into the darkness again. "Now go," he says, and there's a hint of command there, the weight of a god's words.

"Go and tell the world what you've seen. I'll be waiting. Until then—may your days be bright, and your nights be full of stories."

And just like that, he fades, leaving only the echoes of his words and the tremor of something vast, still watching.

You May Also Like

If you enjoyed this book, you might also like:

Terra Mythica: A LitRPG Adventure — Volume Three

Endless Worlds Online: Elsewhere — Name of the Game

Return of the Wind Mage: A Regression LitRPG

Rise of The Infernal Paladin: A System Apocalypse LitRPG

Penance: Prison Of The Gods

Find more at ShadowLightPress.com

www.ingramcontent.com/pod-product-compliance
Lightning Source LLC
Chambersburg PA
CBHW032247020726
47495CB00001B/4